The Cornish Novels

Also by Janie Bolitho

THE CORNISH NOVELS

JANIE BOLITHO

a&b

ALLISON & BUSBY, LONDON

This edition published in Great Britain in 2003 by
Allison & Busby Limited
Bon Marche Centre
241-251 Ferndale Road
London SW9 8BJ
http://www.allisonandbusby.com

A catalogue record for this book is available from
the British Library.

ISBN 0 7490 0612 9

Printed and bound by Liberduplex, sl.
Barcelona, Spain.

CONTENTS

SNAPPED IN CORNWALL

1

Life always seemed to catch Rose Trevelyan by surprise. She constantly told herself that now she had passed forty she might occasionally try to be a bit more organised: ever since her early twenties, when she wrongly considered herself to be a mature adult, nothing had gone to plan.

But no matter how prepared she had been, she could not have guessed at the consequences which arose out of a meeting later that day.

Another perfect day, she thought, as she gazed out of her window at the ever-changing view of which she could never tire. It was early but already the sun was rising higher in an unrelieved expanse of blue which held no traces of the thundery clouds which had rolled around the bay the day before. The much-needed rain had not come. The sea shimmered and already Rose could feel the heat building up.

She squeezed a grapefruit and drank the juice while she made coffee and one slice of toast which she took outside to the wrought-iron bench. The crumbs she gave to the house sparrows who had nested in a hole in the masonry in the side of her shed.

At nine thirty she loaded her equipment into the back of the Mini, a car small enough to negotiate the narrow and awkward angle of the drive, then headed down the hill.

Crossing Newlyn Bridge she slowed at the bus stop to offer a neighbour a lift. She received a shake of the head and a mouthed 'No, thanks'.

Penzance was busy, far busier than it had been for many

seasons, which was good for local trade, including her own. Yet it was always a relief when the tourists had gone home and things reverted to normal.

On the dual carriageway Rose accelerated, noticing the slow response to her foot on the pedal. The car needed what her father called a 'blow-out'; a long run, he claimed, was good for the engine. It was also time she had the Mini serviced.

Her destination was Gwithian. Rose turned off at the roundabout in Hayle and silently repeated the directions she had been given by her client. Mrs Milton's house was off the beaten track, but easier to find than she had been led to believe.

As she turned in through the gate Rose saw that the cultured voice she had heard on the telephone was well suited to the property. Both exuded power and money. Rose would have preferred to be photographing or painting the scenery but the bills had to be paid.

She parked to the side of the house; Mrs Milton would not want a rusting yellow Mini in the forefront of the photographs. Seagulls wheeled silently in the air currents as she walked the thirty or so yards to the front door and the occasional chirrup of a cricket was the only sound to break the otherwise perfect silence. Heat rose from the drive and melting tar sucked at the soles of Rose's espadrilles. Her cotton shirt was damp between the shoulders.

From here, the sea was no more than a distant sparkle. A few stunted trees, bent to the direction of winter gales, stood in the grounds. Beyond lay nothing but sand dunes, their grass-tipped peaks motionless. Rose's critical eye took in the building. It was two-storeyed, solid, built with local granite and pleasing to look at. But the hanging baskets and tubs spilling over with purple lobelia and pink and purple pelargoniums were too garish against their starker surroundings.

There had been no response to the slamming of the car door and all the windows were closed. Rose wondered if she had made a mistake with the date. She rapped the metal knocker loudly and waited.

A middle-aged woman in an apron opened the door. She had a grim expression and a no-nonsense demeanour which

6

seemed to suggest she had better things to do than admit strangers. 'Yes?' She screwed up her eyes suspiciously.

'I'm Rose Trevelyan, the photographer. Mrs Milton's expecting me,' she said, wondering why she felt obliged to offer an explanation.

'You'd better come in then. Mrs Milton's in the lounge.' She opened a door to the right of the wide hall and, if she did not quite announce Rose's presence in the way of an eighteenth-century footman, it was the next best thing. The door was shut firmly as the woman left.

'Mrs Trevelyan, I'm very pleased to meet you. You were highly recommended.' Gabrielle Milton did not say by whom, she simply extended a hand adorned with four rings. Rose took it and realised that, from where she had been sitting, her client could not have failed to notice her arrival.

'Would you like some tea or coffee, or a cold drink, before you start?'

'Nothing, thanks, I'm fine.' Rose smiled. She did not want to waste time indulging in small talk. The sooner the job was done the sooner she could get on with the things she enjoyed. 'Would you like to tell me exactly what you want?'

'Of course.' Gabrielle Milton bent to pick up a long-haired cat which was curled on a settee. Rose watched her supple movements and tried to estimate the size of the price-tag which had once hung on the kaftan affair she was wearing. Mrs Milton obviously took great pains with her make-up and her hair, which was dark and coiled on top of her head. But she was not vain, Rose realised: no attempt had been made to disguise the grey strands above her ears. Surprisingly, her skin was pale and clear. Mrs Milton had not moved down here simply for the benefit of the sun.

'This is Dilys. Ridiculously named after my mother-in-law.' Gabrielle smiled self-mockingly and Rose was sorry she had refused the offer of a drink. She suspected she would enjoy the other woman's company. However, she guessed what was coming next. Pets were worse than children when it came to photographing them. 'I'd like her in the picture, if it's possible. On the terrace wall, I thought.'

'Of course.'

Outside, Rose set up her tripod, chose a wide-angle lens and adjusted the focus of her camera. 'OK, I'm ready. Put Phyllis where you'd like her.'

Gabrielle did so, stroking the soft fur and murmuring an endearment which seemed to work because the cat arched and stretched, then curled up in the sun. 'It's Dilys, actually.'

'Sorry.' Rose decided to take the shots head on, not a view she normally favoured but one which would achieve a good balance. To one side of the house were several palm trees of differing heights, to the other, slightly set back, was a creeper-covered outhouse. She used various exposures and half a roll of film: there had to be something there which would please her client. As the shutter clicked for the last time there was a slight movement. Dilys had disappeared.

Mrs Milton required a hundred and fifty copies for person-alised Christmas cards, first having toyed with the idea of Rose sketching the house. She told Rose they had only been in Cornwall for seven months and thought it would be a way of letting their friends see where they lived – 'without actually having to invite them down.' Unlike the people Gabrielle was used to mixing with, Rose had struck her as calm, a soothing person to be with, one in whom you could confide. Her mis-take, she realised, had been to fill her life with people to relieve the boredom and futility of her own life in the city but who, in turn, bored her further.

She would, she thought, as she opened her book later, like to talk to Rose Trevelyan, to have her as a friend.

But Gabrielle Milton never got the chance.

The small amount of air that was circulated through the open car windows was warm and offered no real relief. Rose was tempted to pull in at the first pub with a car-park and treat herself to a lager and lime but decided against it. Procrastina-tion had been her downfall on other occasions. She had, she realised, felt a little uneasy in Mrs Milton's company although there seemed no reason for it. She smiled, remembering David's words. 'You're more superstitious than the Cornish,' he had told her.

'You should know, you're one of them,' she had replied, laughing, but flattered because it was another sign of acceptance into a part of mainland England which was like no other. The climate, the people and the way of life were more reminiscent of southern Europe.

The sky was no longer blue but white and hazy. Heat, shimmering above the road surface, made the tarmac appear to undulate, mirage-like. There were few pedestrians about; locals would be at work, and holiday-makers were already on the beaches enjoying two weeks of what Rose had all year round.

She did a mental calculation of outstanding jobs. If the weather remained hot she would work outside, leaving the developing of the Milton film until one evening because the dark-room was stifling in the daytime. Five new views were required for a postcard company for whom she worked freelance and Barry Rowe had asked when he could expect some new water-colours which he would reproduce for his greetings card firm. The photographic work paid the bills, but it was painting Rose loved. However, she had learned early on that although she was good it was impossible to sell enough paintings to make real money.

Rose decided to take the car home. It was too hot and too busy to remain in it longer than was necessary. The Promenade was packed as couples and families enjoyed a light sea breeze, a breeze which now gently lifted the loose strands of hair around Rose's face and cooled her burning cheeks.

She parked in her driveway, facing the wall, on the off-chance that it might rain later. The Mini was a bad starter when the engine was damp. Once the camera was unloaded and the gear back in its cupboard, Rose picked up a sketch-pad and left again, on foot. The walk to Mousehole took just under half an hour and the road, at times without a pavement, held a continuous stream of traffic. Every visitor went there at some point of their holiday, delighted with the narrow rabbit warren of streets, none forbidden to traffic, which formed the ancient fishing village.

The local bus was making its complicated manoeuvre in order to be facing the right way for its return journey to

Penzance. It was full, with passengers standing. Leaning against the harbour rails, the overflow from the pub stood with drinks in their hands. There was a smell of grilling fish as she passed the restaurant window.

On the far side of the village, and high above it, was a vantage point from which Rose had decided to sketch. Views of Mousehole and Newlyn were always popular but she tried to vary them as much as possible.

Absorbed in her work, she hardly noticed the time passing and only when she saw how far the sun had moved round did she decide to call it a day. Besides, she was thirsty, having forgotten to bring a flask, and her stomach told her it was time to eat.

Cars were crawling back along the road, their drivers slowing to admire the curve of Mount's Bay. They would return to hotels and guest houses to shower away the sand and salt before a drink and dinner. Rose, too, would do the same.

Laying the four sketches she had made on the kitchen table, she felt pleased with the results. Now complete with pastel water-colours they were just what Barry had said he wanted. It was one more job out of the way.

Rose let the jets of water run over her body for ten minutes, easing her joints, stiff from the long walk, then she washed her hair. Clad in a robe, with her head wrapped in a towel, she went downstairs to open the white wine she had put in the fridge that morning and which she sipped as she prepared a salad to go with a salmon steak.

Dennis Milton left his office carrying his suit jacket folded over one arm. As soon as he was in the street he jerked his tie to one side to loosen it and undid the top button of his shirt. London, in a heat wave, was unbearable. Gabrielle didn't know how lucky she was.

He made his way through the crowds in Regent Street and joined the throngs in Piccadilly. The traffic, at a standstill, allowed him to cross the road against the pedestrian lights. The air was filled with diesel fumes belching from buses and the sound of irate taxi drivers' horns. He turned the corner and found relative peace in the bar of the Duke of Norfolk.

Dennis was meeting a colleague with whom he was in the habit of having an early evening drink. He did not like to admit that since Gabrielle had become ensconced in Cornwall what used to be a couple of pints now usually developed into quite a session. At least he no longer had to rush home to change for one of the numerous social events his wife used to arrange. She seemed to have slowed down, he thought as he raised his hand in greeting, to be content with her own company.

'Usual, Dennis?'

He nodded.

Gordon Archer summoned the barman and asked for a pint of bitter. 'How's it going? Haven't seen much of Gabrielle lately. Isn't she coming up for a spot of shopping, or the theatre? I would've thought she missed being in town.'

'What?'

'Your wife, old son. Doesn't she miss the city? Mine would, I know that.'

'No. She loves it down there. She's taken up all sorts of new hobbies. Besides, I can take her any of life's luxuries she can't get locally.'

Gordon glanced at him quizzically. Had he detected a hint of vituperation in Dennis's tone? 'Anything the matter?'

'No, nothing. Difficult day, that's all.'

'Drink up then, we'll have another. This heat's getting to everyone.'

Dennis tried to smile and contribute to the conversation but he was worried. He had heard that his firm were after young blood, that those not coming up to scratch were to be given the elbow. It was silently implicit that target figures were not simply to be reached, but exceeded, if employees wished to retain their positions. They were only rumours, but rumours in the music business in which Dennis worked were usually founded on certainty. Of course, he had been with the firm long enough for there to be the offer of a substantial redundancy settlement – there was no question of his being dismissed – but it would mean living on Gabrielle's private income and he was not sure he could cope with that. At fifty it was unlikely he would get another job. Ageism, he thought, was more rife than any of the other isms but no one seemed to take up the cause. Probably because they're past it, he silently but cynically said to himself. The solution would be for him to move to Cornwall where they could survive on less money. The house was paid for – not by himself – and they could sell the London flat. At least he and Gabrielle had reached the point where they could survive a whole weekend without their discussions degenerating into a slanging match.

'My shout,' Dennis said, seeing Gordon's glass was empty. He took some keeping up with.

'I don't know how you do it, up and down every weekend. Is it worth it, all that travelling?'

'It is to me. The golf's good, the air's clean and the scenery is terrific. And there's the added advantage of mild winters.'

'I still say it's a hell of a way to go for it. Why not Surrey or Sussex like the rest of us?'

Dennis shrugged. He could hardly say that was precisely why it wasn't the south coast, nor did he explain how relaxed he was able to be once he had crossed the Tamar. Tired of Gordon's company and especially of the way he denigrated his wife, Dennis left early. No matter how annoyed with her, he would not dream of speaking to anyone about Gabrielle the way Gordon did about Helen.

He was still not used to the emptiness of the flat when he returned in the evenings. The large house in Wimbledon had been sold once their son, Paul, left home. It had always been too big but they used to entertain at home more in those days, instead of in restaurants, and they had wrongly assumed there would be more children. Gabrielle's sudden decision to buy a place in Cornwall had come as a complete surprise but Dennis could hardly tell her how to spend her money.

He missed her. Even when they argued she was company and now he saw less of her he realised that, paradoxically, he had enjoyed their rows, that life had never been dull. Certainly it was better than Maggie's farcical compliance. She was a fool if she thought he didn't see through her.

12

The cleaning lady had restocked the freezer but there was nothing which tempted him enough to bother to cook. Dennis poured a stiff drink and added a splash of soda, then sat down, resting his head against the back of the leather settee, welcoming its coolness. He put his involvement with Maggie down to what people chose to call the male menopause and now he was sorry he had let it go on so long. Maggie was sending out messages he did not want to receive and he was not sure how to end the relationship. She was single and independent and, initially, she had been fun to be with, but Dennis felt he was being drawn into a trap. Maggie, he sensed, would very much like to replace Gabrielle.

The telephone rang and his hand holding the drink jerked. He had been on the point of falling asleep. Another bad sign: too much booze and not enough food.

'Hello, darling. I'm surprised to catch you in.'

'Gabrielle.'

'Are you all right?'

'Fine. You?'

'Yes. Look, I thought I'd better let you know I've organised the Christmas cards from this end. Tell Fiona, or she'll go to the usual people.'

Christmas cards? Christmas was four months away. But Gabrielle was right, his secretary Fiona took rather too much upon herself, to the extent once of buying a silver and crystal rose bowl she thought suitable for his wife's birthday present. Dennis would not have chosen it himself but felt obliged to reimburse her. If he was given the push, would Fiona be out of a job as well? Gabrielle was telling him something about some photographer she had commissioned.

'How much is that little lot going to set us back?'

'No more than if you get the usual printers to do them. It's not like you to question me over money, Dennis. I don't waste it, you know that.'

'I know. I'm sorry. I'll ring you tomorrow. Take care.' Dennis replaced the receiver. Tomorrow was Thursday and he had agreed to take Maggie out. Perhaps he ought to ring her now and cancel. Surely she'd get the message if he did it often enough.

13

Then Friday. How he looked forward to it these days. Gordon was wrong, he loved the four and a half hour journey, relaxing on the train with a drink and a sandwich, the evening paper and a book. It was a kind of no-man's-land, between the city and work and the slow, easygoing atmosphere of Cornwall. He had a regular booking on the Golden Hind from Paddington which reached Redruth just after ten. Gabrielle met him in the car – Dennis had no need of one in London – and dropped him back for the first train on Monday morning.

He would, he decided, make it up to her this weekend, take her out somewhere special, maybe, instead of playing golf.

With a wedge of Stilton and a couple of crispbreads serving as his evening meal he poured one more drink and took it with him to bed.

2

Eileen Penrose and her sister, Maureen, were sorting piles of clothing and bric-à-brac into appropriate groups ready for the church jumble sale on Saturday. It was a task they had once taken on several years previously and it had become expected of them that they would continue with it each year.

'Just look at this,' Maureen said, holding up a dirty shirt between thumb and forefinger. 'It's only fit for the bin. I'd be ashamed to send it.'

Eileen sniffed disdainfully and pushed her limp dark hair back off her face with a thin hand.

'Still,' Maureen continued, used to her sister's uncommunicative ways, 'Mrs Milton did us proud. I knew we'd get some good stuff from her.'

'Ah, yes. The lady of the manor.'

'Come on, Eileen, it's all in a good cause. Besides, you don't object when she asks you to help out, you said yourself she pays generously.'

Eileen sniffed again and folded some sweaters roughly. The church hall was musty and smelled of old clothes. Motes of dust danced in the wedge of sunlight shining through the open door, but at least the building was cool. Eileen had no wish to discuss Gabrielle Milton.

'Look at this top, we'll get at least two pounds for it.' Maureen put the knitted garment with its leather appliqué work on a hanger where it would be more prominent. 'I don't know what you've got against her, she's quite nice really. Well, you should know that better than me, you see more of her.'

Eileen's face had reddened. Maureen decided to drop the

subject because she knew exactly what her sister's problem was.

Eileen Penrose's husband, Jim, was dark-haired and handsome and his deep brown eyes hinted at seduction. Women were easy in his company; he teased them and made them laugh and they enjoyed the mild but meaningless flirtation. He was not unfaithful to Eileen, partly by choice but also because if he so much as propositioned another woman it would be all over the village before she had time to answer. Eileen had lived there all her life and must have known it, yet she carried her jealousy almost to the point of obsession.

In early February, not long after the Miltons had moved in, Jim had been called out in his capacity as a heating engineer to make some adjustments to the central heating boiler. 'You should see what they've done to the place,' he told Eileen after that visit, 'it's terrific. Wood block hall and carpets up to your knees.'

'What's she like?' Eileen wanted to know, interested only in the woman, not her possessions.

'She's a looker, I'll say that for her. She could be on the telly.'

That was enough for Eileen Penrose and when Mrs Milton rang a second time her lips were compressed with rage as she handed the telephone to Jim.

Both Maureen and Jim had tried to reason with her, to explain that Mrs Milton's needs were genuine. No work had been done on the heating system since it had been installed by the previous owners and several of the radiators were leaking where the joints had rusted. Maureen realised she would be wasting her breath explaining to her sister that women like Gabrielle Milton would not be interested in the likes of Jim Penrose.

'She's having a party, some sort of big posh do.'

Maureen waited, smiling to herself, knowing how the game was played. If she asked any questions Eileen would clam up.

'A week Saturday. All her London cronies, I suppose. She's asked me to help out,' Eileen volunteered.

'What about Doreen?'

'Oh, she'll be there as well. One of us to serve drinks, the

16

other to see to the food. Finger buffet, she calls it. Whatever that might mean.'

'It's a few extra pounds in your pocket.' Maureen was unable to understand how Eileen could work for, and take money from, someone she so obviously despised. Maybe it was a way of keeping an eye on Gabrielle. She shrugged and glanced at her watch. 'Come on, that'll do for today. I could do with some fresh air.'

Maureen locked the door and pocketed the key and told Eileen she'd pick her up at nine on Saturday morning when they could finish the last few bits.

The salad was ready, the salmon brushed with oil ready to go under the grill. As Rose waited for the new potatoes to boil she was surprised to notice she was already half-way down the bottle of wine. She had better take it more slowly. The condensation on the bottle was no longer a mist but had gathered in droplets and run down the sides leaving a wet circle on the kitchen table.

It's the weather, she excused herself, although she was aware that it was more than that and that she was desperately trying to keep other thoughts at bay. The kitchen was stuffy with the heat from the cooker. She lowered the gas and took her drink outside. She felt the warmth retained in the metal bench through the fabric of her skirt.

People shouldn't die in the summer, she thought, it doesn't seem right.

But her thoughts were really more specific. She meant David, David whom she had wanted never to die at all. It was four years now yet the pain was not far from the surface. She missed him more than she imagined possible even though she had had months in which to prepare herself. There were still times when she expected him to walk through the door; when suddenly in the street she thought she heard his voice; when she would say to herself, I must tell David that. Tall, easygoing and loving, he had died in the prime of his life, wiped out as if he was of no consequence. The anniversary of his death was in two weeks' time.

17

Rose pushed her hair behind her ears, dry now after her shower. She felt a tightening around her skull, the beginning of a headache caused possibly by the wine, but hopefully, by the way the clouds were banking up, by an impending storm. There was a sulphurous yellow glow in the distance.

Recognising her mood and knowing the danger signs, she had two alternatives: work or ringing Laura. She opted for work, but first she must eat.

The wine was returned to the space for bottles in the fridge; she might finish it later. A brilliant flash of blue-white light illuminated the kitchen, followed by a loud bang. Within seconds the sky darkened further; rain hammered on the windows and bounced off the bonnet of the car. Rose took herself up to the attic which served as a dark-room and developed Mrs Milton's film.

Engrossed in what she was doing she took several seconds to realise the telephone was ringing and she had not set the answering machine. With the film drying it was safe to switch on the light. She wiped her hands and went downstairs.

'Mrs Trevelyan? I'm sorry to bother you in the evening, but I was wondering if you'd like to come over a week on Saturday. We're having a bit of a do. Family and a couple of friends from London, but really it's for the people I've met down here. I know we hardly know one another, but, well . . .' Her voice trailed off.

Rose immediately guessed that the invitation was issued out of loneliness and not because a last-minute replacement was required.

'Thank you. I'd love to come,' she heard herself replying before she had given herself a chance to think about it. 'What time?'

'Any time after eight. I'll look forward to seeing you. Oh, I'll see you before that, won't I? With the proofs. No, wait, bring them with you. Dennis can have a say in the choice then and it'll save you a journey.'

Rose agreed to do so, then hung up. A party. She had not been to one since David died – and what would she wear? When did she last buy herself something new? And whom could she take? Gabrielle had said to bring a guest if she wished. Rose shook her head. Ridiculous, she felt like a teen-ager going on a first date. Barry Rowe. She'd ask him. There was, she realised, no other male who came to mind.

Once she had cleared up in the dark-room, Rose poured out some more wine and dialled his number. Barry made no pretence of checking a diary or hesitating. He had known Rose since she first came to Cornwall and did his best to sell her work. Since David's death he had been her only escort. He had always hoped to become more than that but there seemed to be no romantic attachment on Rose's side. At least they shared similar tastes and found a sort of comfort in each other's company.

'I'd be delighted,' Barry told her. 'God, it's not evening dress or anything, is it?'

Rose laughed. 'No, Gabrielle said it's informal.' Although that still left her in some doubt as to what would be suitable attire. What the invitation had done was to take her mind temporarily off the looming anniversary. She finished the conversation by promising to bring in the water-colours she had completed.

Depressing the bar, Rose waited for the dialling tone, then rang Laura. 'Guess what?' she said. 'I've been asked to a party.'

'Oh? Anyone I know?'

'A lady called Gabrielle Milton.' Rose waited. Laura, born and bred in Newlyn, knew everyone, and the gossip sur-rounding them, for a ten-mile radius.

'Milton?'

'Mm. She lives near Gwithian.'

'Must be a newcomer.'

'Relatively.' Rose smiled. 'Anyway, I'm taking Barry.'

'Ah, the ever faithful Barry Rowe. Rose, why don't you go on your own? New people, new friends, you might . . .' Laura stopped, suddenly remembering the date and how tactless she would sound if she suggested it was an opportunity to meet a new man. 'Well, buy something exotic and have a great time. And if you need a chat, I'm always here.'

'I know. Thanks.' Rose did know. Laura had been the one to

get her through the bad times after David died. 'Why don't you come up for a meal? Tomorrow? If Trevor's not home.'

'Great. I'll bring the hooch.'

Rose hung up. She had a nagging feeling of guilt but realised David would not mind the fact that she had something to look forward to. It was selfishly gratifying to Rose that Laura's husband was a fisherman, away for days on end. It meant Laura, unlike some women, had evenings free which they could spend together without worrying about being late or having a meal on the table. Her solitude, Rose realised, had changed her.

It was a mystery how her and David's lives had meshed so well. He was a mining engineer, methodical and tidy in all he did. Rose was scatterbrained and messy. Over the years they had had together they had adopted some of each other's ways until a middle path was formed. And David, forward-looking in all things, had been adequately insured. The mortgage was paid up upon his death; she had a small pension and her own business was gradually building up, now she was putting more effort into it. Rose supposed she had treated it more like a hobby until necessity deemed it otherwise.

Could she, she wondered, spare half a day to go into Truro to find something to wear? It would probably be worthwhile. Her wardrobe consisted of jeans and casual clothes, her manner of dressing a remnant from her student days, encouraged by the informality of her surroundings. Her hair, still shoulder-length and straight, either flowed loosely or, more latterly, in deference to the passing years, was tied back or twisted and held in place with a toothed, sprung clip.

It was still too early to go to bed. Restless, the storm noisily making its presence known, and her anticipation mixed with sadness, Rose put on some classical music. It usually soothed her, allowing her thoughts to drift. Leaning back in the shabby chintz armchair she closed her eyes. Sometimes it seemed like yesterday she had stepped off the train at Penzance station and begun walking to the lodgings her parents had insisted she booked before she set off. Resting against the rails near the open-air swimming pool she had understood why artists flocked to the area. The colours of both sea

20

and sky were unbelievable and she knew she would feel at home.

Her parents had financed her for six months after she had finished college. When the money ran out she started painting in earnest. She did not want to leave.

Barry Rowe came into her life soon after. Rose had gone into the shop from which he sold the cards his small firm produced and asked if he would be interested in any of her work. He had liked it and said so. On a future visit she met David. He was looking for a birthday card and happened to choose one which Rose had originally painted.

'The artist's standing behind you,' Barry Rowe had said, grinning.

'Oh?' David had turned around and something passed between them. Rose could never recall exactly how it was that they ended up having a pub lunch – one of them must have started a conversation. A year later they were married.

Rose opened her eyes. The wind had dropped, apart from the occasional squally gust, and the rain had eased, or ceased altogether. Her neck was stiff and the music had finished. Glancing at the small carriage clock on the low stone mantelpiece she was amazed to see that it was two thirty. It was the best and deepest sleep she had had for some time.

Maggie Anderson chewed the corner of her mouth in frustration. It was the third time Dennis had let her down recently. His excuse was pressure of work but she knew by his tone he was lying. Gabrielle was safely out of the way, there was nothing to fear as long as they avoided places where Dennis was known. He refused to take her to the flat – which, she supposed, was understandable. His wife had chosen and furnished it and had lived there with him. But Maggie hoped she wasn't losing her hold over him.

Ten years younger than Gabrielle and her opposite in looks and temperament, she believed she was exactly what Dennis needed, especially if he was to stay at the top. A suitable partner was an advantage: a partner who was attractive and witty and fun, yet knew where to draw the line. One who enjoyed socialising, something Gabrielle seemed to have given up. It was unfair on Dennis to expect him to attend functions and entertain clients on his own. Once or twice she had partnered him, introduced as a colleague. She knew enough about the trade to be able to converse knowledgeably albeit not in depth.

She stood in front of the mirrored wardrobe in her bedroom, dressed ready to go out. Dennis had left it very late to cancel. Tomorrow he would be off to Cornwall again. Maggie was fed up with weekends spent alone. He had mentioned the party, only, she guessed, because he was surprised at Gabrielle initiating it. That was the following weekend. Maggie smiled at her reflection, satisfied with what she saw. 'Why not?' she said aloud. 'Indeed, why not?'

'Oh, Rose, it's just *you*,' Laura said when she arrived, breathless from hurrying up the hill in the warm evening air. The storm of the previous night had only provided temporary relief. 'Here.' She placed some wine which had been in her woven bag on the table as was their custom when they ate in one another's houses.

'Do you think it's dressy enough?' Rose held the outfit in front of her and looked at it doubtfully.

'Yes. No one goes mad these days.'

The skirt was of pastel swirls, chiffon over a silky under-skirt, the long, loose matching top of chiffon only. Beneath it she would wear a pale blue silk vest the same colour as in the pattern. 'I suppose if I put my hair up?'

'Rose, you'll look lovely. I wish you'd stop worrying. Where've you hidden the corkscrew this time?' Laura had pulled open a couple of drawers, knowing things could not usually be found in the same place twice. Discovering it beside the bread bin she yanked out the cork, holding the bottle inelegantly between her knees. 'What shoes are you wearing? Don't tell me, you forgot. You can borrow my white sandals, I've only worn them twice.'

'Thanks, Laura.'

The same size feet was all they had in common physically.

22

Laura was several inches taller than Rose, and thinner, her hair cut level with her ears, the dark curls awry. Laura hated her hair but Rose always pointed out that people paid a lot of money to have theirs done that way.

Wineglasses at hand, they settled down for an evening of serious conversation and gossip, and, in an hour's time, some food.

3

The weekend had passed unnoticed. That is, for Rose, the days were the same as any other. She took advantage of the weather and continued with outdoor work apart from a quick job in Penzance on Saturday morning. The mother of a boy about to start secondary school wanted a professional photograph of him in his new school uniform. 'Before he ruins it,' she had added with a resigned expression.

Barry took her to the cinema on Sunday evening but they parted immediately afterwards. Then, with the weekend behind her, Rose found the rest of the week slipping by. She gave the following Saturday afternoon up to pampering herself: a bath, instead of a shower, and a coat of pale gloss on her fingernails. Her hands, she realised, could have been better taken care of but, despite rubber gloves, photographic chemicals had taken their toll.

At eight fifteen there was a toot from the main road. Rose did not recognise the car. Peering harder she saw Barry getting into the back seat.

Picking up her handbag she went to join him. 'A taxi?'

'No.' The driver laughed. 'Barry here's conned me into driving you over. You'll be coming back in a taxi, though.'

Rose turned and raised her eyebrows.

'Sorry. This is Geoff, works on the printing side.'

'Ah.' And probably Geoff had been responsible for printing the rather formal greeting in Gabrielle's Christmas cards. She had remembered to bring the proofs with her. 'Hello. Nice to meet you at last.'

'You, too.' Geoff smiled into the rear-view mirror.

The printing was done in Redruth but Barry had suggested Geoff make himself useful by collecting some urgent artwork and, whilst he was at it, dropping them off on his way home.

'Nice bloke,' Rose commented as they walked up the drive.

'Yes. Nice house.' Barry nodded towards the granite building, the stone softened by the warm tones of the sun as it began to set. There would be few more evenings such as this one. Of course, Rose remembered – it was the bank holiday weekend. How on earth could she have forgotten with the Newlyn Fish Festival on Monday?

The same woman Rose had seen before answered the door. She was wearing a brown dress, like something out of *Rebecca*, Rose thought, guessing it was the woman's own choice, not Gabrielle's. The look she received was fractionally more pleasant than on her previous visit. They were shown into the long lounge which ran the length of the house and which had once been two rooms.

'My, my,' Barry whispered, holding her elbow.

Gabrielle had decorated the room with flower arrangements; their scent filled the air. In the alcove in the far corner a table had been set up, covered with a cloth and holding an array of bottles and mixers. There was also wine but, to Barry's disappointment, he could not see any beer.

Rose was more interested in the other guests, one or two of whom she already knew and smiled at. She studied them not as people, but as subjects to paint. However, portraits were her weak area; she was never able to capture the essence of a character in oils.

'Mrs Trevelyan, I am so pleased you could come. May I call you Rose?'

'Of course. This is Barry Rowe.' Rose briefly explained what he did. 'I know one or two people here.'

'I'm glad. I'll introduce you to my family. Dennis?' She turned to address a tall, suave man in a yellow polo shirt and cream trousers. The man approached, smiling urbanely, obviously used to social gatherings. He also had the advantage of being on home ground.

Rose realised two things: she was slightly nervous, and she had allowed herself to get into a rut. As they were introduced,

25

she hoped Barry did not feel out of place in a jacket and tie: no other male seemed to be wearing one.

'Ah, the photographer.' Dennis shook her hand. 'And I believe I'm to inspect your handiwork this evening.'

'Yes. The proofs at any rate.'

'Dennis, I'm sure our guests would like a drink first.'

'Of course. Over there.' He indicated the table, behind which a thin, scowling woman was pouring drinks. 'I don't think there's anything my wife's not got in.'

Was he, Rose wondered, being snide? Dennis had one of those impassive faces upon which emotions did not register.

'I don't see any food,' Barry said as they crossed the room.

'There's bound to be. It's probably in another room. Gabrielle won't want smoked salmon trodden into the Wilton.'

Rose asked for a glass of dry white wine with a splash of soda. If it was going to be a long evening she didn't want to drink too much. Barry took a chance and asked if there was any beer.

'What kind?' the woman said. Behind her were several crates of bottles, but, more importantly, a firkin of Hicks. His eyes lit up.

Glasses in hand they found Gabrielle at their elbow once more. 'I'd like you to meet my son, Paul. And his fiancée.' She led them to where the couple stood. Paul was undoubtedly his father's son. The girl with him was beautiful, her looks spoiled at that moment by the sullen downturn of her mouth. They were in the middle of some sort of argument and were only just polite. 'We might as well have a look at those photos now,' Gabrielle said, more to cover her embarrassment at her son's behaviour than out of real interest.

They went to a small room across the hallway and Rose laid them on a table. It was left to Dennis to decide; Gabrielle liked them all. 'May I leave them here until later?' Rose asked, not wishing to be left holding the envelope all night.

'Of course. They'll be quite safe. Come on, I'll let you get to know the others.'

Mike and Barbara Phillips were just arriving. 'Rose. Good to see you, and you too, Barry.'

'You know Dr Phillips?' Gabrielle seemed surprised, unused yet to the fact that it was a close-knit community.

'We're old friends, actually. Hello, Barbara, you look great.' Rose did not add that Mike had been responsible for David's hospital treatment and that it was he who had broken the news of the prognosis to her.

Guilt rose anew. What would Mike and Barbara think of her partying so near the anniversary of his death? And she wished Barry would not keep taking her arm in that proprietorial way. 'Excuse me, I need to find the toilet.'

'David,' she said, pressing her face against the coolness of the mirror. 'Oh, why aren't *you* here with me?' She stayed several minutes until she felt able to face the assembled company and make the required small talk. It had been a mistake to come.

There was no sign of Gabrielle but she made an effort to talk to strangers rather than huddle with people she knew. Barry, it seemed, was doing the same. Perhaps he sensed her earlier resentment.

'Doreen tells me the food's ready,' Dennis said, trying to make these new friends of his wife's at home although he barely knew anyone himself. There were two couples from London, real friends, not just acquaintances.

And Maggie.

And how he was coping with her presence was beyond him. Gabrielle seemed to have accepted that she was a work colleague Dennis had invited but who had had doubts as to whether she would be able to make it. Now was not the time to sort that little problem out. As soon as he was back in London he would make it clear to Maggie that the relationship was no longer viable. It had taken this semi-separation for him to realise how much he thought of his wife.

But where was she? Surely she should be presiding over the food? He grinned ruefully. If Doreen Clarke allowed it, he amended.

Most of the guests had already had several drinks and needed a base on which to soak up any more.

'Impressive,' Rose said quietly as she and Barry surveyed the trestle tables laid up on the patio at the back, the food protected by awnings which, when rolled back, were virtually invisible in their holders neatly slotted into the stonework.

'This is very nice,' Doreen commented.

'Oh. I'll try some then.' Rose gave Doreen the full benefit of her smile. The ice had been broken. 'Delicious. Did you make them?'

'Yes. It's easy though.' Doreen Clarke spoke sharply to disguise her pleasure. 'Mrs Milton and I did it all between us. She likes cooking.'

It was not easy to picture their elegant hostess up to her elbows in flour.

Barry remained silent, his mouth too full to speak. His plate, Rose noted, was piled high. She had never known anyone able to eat as much and remain so lean. Rose strolled across the grass. Paul and his young lady were nowhere in sight. Presumably they were too upset to eat. It was difficult conducting a row in a room full of people. She and David had done so once, hissing at each other out of the sides of their mouths. And the woman on her own, who was she? They had not been introduced, but Rose had noticed the grim glances Dennis Milton was throwing in her direction. Was there something not quite right going on there? Gabrielle didn't seem put out. Another one who wasn't hungry, Rose decided. Perhaps the sight of all that food as it was being prepared had put her off.

Relieved to see Barry in deep conversation with Barbara Phillips, Rose took advantage of his absence to study the garden. The neatly cut grass put her patch to shame. There were no dandelions and no humpy bits. Still, they probably had a gardener. To the side of the house was a walkway, about five feet wide, bordered by hardy shrubs. Projecting from the building was a balcony, the ornate iron rail newly painted. On the paving stones, Rose saw what appeared to be one of the white damask table-cloths. She really ought to wear her glasses more often although her slight short-sightedness was no real handicap.

Strolling towards it in order to retrieve it, Rose munched some celery filled with cream cheese and garlic. Then she froze.

28

'Oh, God. Oh, my God.' She threw the paper plate and its contents into the shrubbery and ran towards the crumpled figure of Gabrielle Milton.

Rose took three deep breaths to steady herself. There was blood on the ground, oozing slowly from a head wound but already coagulating. She felt for a pulse, knowing in advance she would not find one. Gabrielle was on her side; one glassy eye stared at Rose through the strands of her hair.

Her own pulse racing, she went to find Dennis who came outside at once.

His face white with shock, he rang immediately for an ambulance. It was the instinctive thing to do, even though his wife was dead. 'And the police, I think,' Rose said quietly.

Almost incoherent, Dennis had the job of explaining the situation to his guests. 'There's been an accident,' he said. 'Gabrielle . . . she's, well, she's fallen from the balcony. I think she might be dead.' Impossible to admit it was so.

Rose heard a small scream. A male voice said, 'Shit.' Then for several seconds there was utter silence.

Rose was amazed to hear her own voice, loud and authoritative. 'I think it would be better if we all stayed in here.'

Perhaps because she was alongside Dennis the guests assumed she was closer to the family than she really was. Whatever their reasons, those who had been about to go outside remained in their places. 'An ambulance and the police are on their way,' she continued, realising everyone was waiting for someone to say something, to take charge of a situation which was in danger of taking on nightmare proportions.

Doreen Clarke helped shepherd the people who were still outside into the lounge. She had seen Rose's pallor when she rounded the corner on her way back to the house. She had also seen the way the young woman named Maggie Anderson had been looking at her employer.

Doreen Clarke busied herself clearing away empty dishes and generally tidying up the area where the food had been served. It was unlikely anyone would want to eat now. Rose Trevelyan, she thought, wasn't at all what she had imagined. She had seen a couple of articles about her in *The Cornishman* and recognised her from the photographs. For some reason she had imagined she would be a bit above herself. In the flesh she seemed quite nice. And she'd certainly handled things sensibly. Doreen had spoken to her husband, Cyril, about the lady painter but he, in his usual way, had just grunted. Cyril didn't fool her, Doreen knew he took in every word she said even if he chose to ignore most of them.

Doreen knew that Mrs Milton had not fallen off that balcony.

She resisted the temptation to creep round the side and folded the table-cloths ready for the laundry, wondering if, or for how long, her services would now be required.

'Please, everyone, have another drink.' Dennis was becoming more agitated with every minute that passed, aware that no one knew quite what to say. And should he, as her husband, be keeping vigil by the body? Of course he should, but he could not bear to see his wife like that.

'Where's Eileen?'

As he spoke she came back into the room. By the puzzled expression on her face she was apparently oblivious to what had happened. 'Pour everyone a drink, Eileen. A large one.' Dennis's hand trembled as his own glass was refilled.

Detective Inspector Pearce had commandeered several rooms and the process of interviewing the guests individually had begun. It was late but no one had been allowed to leave.

Outside a team of forensic experts were at work and through the curtains of the small room at the side of the house the pop of flash-bulbs could be seen.

Rose, being the person to find the body, was the first to be interviewed.

Detective Inspector Pearce seemed to have no consideration for the shock Rose had received. His questions were direct and demanded answers. She had none to give. Barely able to remember what she had done or even if she had screamed, she described the event as best she could.

'Yes, I did touch her. I felt for a pulse. In her wrist,' Rose added hastily. She could not have fumbled beneath the thick dark hair for the carotid artery and endured the stickiness of Gabrielle's blood on her hands. She was, Rose realised, being treated as a suspect.

'You were a close friend of Mrs Milton?' Inspector Pearce studied the woman who sat opposite him. Mrs Trevelyan. And she wore a wedding ring. But there was no Mr Trevelyan on the guest list Doreen Clarke had provided.

'No. I hardly knew her.'

'Oh?'

'I did a job for her. Mrs Milton telephoned me and asked if I'd like to come tonight. I don't go to parties very often. I thought . . . well, I thought it would make a change.' I do not need to explain myself to this man, she told herself.

'This job, what was it exactly?'

'Christmas cards. Mrs Milton wanted a picture of the house to be mounted on personalised cards. I brought the proofs with me tonight.' Rose felt ashamed as she briefly wondered if she would ever be paid for the job. But it had been the same during David's illness: trivial things had worried her, she had been irritated by minor inconveniences and her thoughts, at times, had been irrational. All of it, she guessed, had been a defence mechanism at work to prevent her dwelling on the reality of what was ahead.

DI Pearce, Rose concluded when she finally met his gaze, had the eyes of a dead haddock. She was trembling, her hands clasped tightly together in her lap, and despite the warmth of the evening she was cold. A horrifying idea crossed her mind. Was this a punishment? Had Gabrielle died and Rose been the one to find her body because she was enjoying herself instead of staying at home grieving over the anniversary of David's death? Was she to be the harbinger of tragedy for everyone with whom she came into contact? Only now, almost an hour after the discovery of the body, did the enormity of the situation hit her. Her trembling limbs began to shake, her head and hands suddenly felt clammy and waves of nausea washed over her. 'I'm going to be sick,' she said and promptly vomited on the carpet.

'Get Mrs Trevelyan some water, sergeant.' DI Pearce addressed the man in jeans and a short-sleeved shirt who sat beside him. 'And something to clean up with. Do you feel better now?'

'Yes, thank you. I didn't mean . . . I'm so sorry.' Rose had no reason to apologise. It was not her interrogator's house, nor was it his carpet. Gabrielle Milton lay dead outside on the paving stones; her being sick was a small matter by comparison. And the man hadn't flinched. He had shown no expression of annoyance or disgust but accepted what had happened as if it was a daily occurrence. Rose decided his emotions matched his appearance.

Sipping the water she tried to hide her face behind the glass as Sergeant Walters got to work with a bucket and cloth. She would not humiliate herself further by offering to clean up.

It was strange. She had not wanted David to die but had cursed at death for being so leisurely because of his pain. Although she believed she was prepared for the end, in reality she had not been. This was so different, so unexpected and hard to accept. She would never get to know Gabrielle Milton now.

'What was the party in aid of?'

'Nothing in particular. I think Mrs Milton just wanted to break the ice with people, to feel a part of things. I think, perhaps, she was lonely.'

'You said you didn't know her. Did she tell you that?'

'No. It was just an impression I had.'

'I am not here to seek impressions, Mrs Trevelyan, only facts.'

'Then am I free to go? I've given you all the facts I'm aware of.' There was some satisfaction in the way Inspector Pearce's eyebrows arched fractionally. He was not completely devoid of feelings after all.

Before she left, Rose was made to go through it all again. To catch her out? she wondered. She said she was fit enough to go home. The taxi they had ordered earlier to collect them had been cancelled. Rose asked if she could use the telephone to

32

rebook it. 'Half an hour,' Pearce told her. He knew she had come with Mr Rowe but he still had to be interviewed.

'What's going on back there?' the driver asked when he arrived. He had been made to wait at the gate by a PC monitoring comings and goings.

'We're not allowed to discuss it,' Barry said firmly, which was true. Even in the poor illumination of street lights he saw how pale Rose was and took her hand and squeezed it, but he made no attempt at conversation. They were silent throughout the drive. Outside her house Barry waited while she found her keys, then asked if she wanted him to come in.

'I could stay if you like?' The offer was made from concern for Rose, there was no ulterior motive.

Rose understood that but she needed to be alone, to rid her mind of images she hoped one day would fade completely.

'No, thanks, Barry. I'll be fine. Really.'

'OK. But don't hesitate to ring if you need to talk, no matter what the time is.' Barry, too, was aware how close it was to the date of David's death. For the evening to have ended as it had was the last thing Rose needed when she was trying to socialise in the way she had when David was alive.

Once inside the kitchen Rose started shaking again. She had had three fair-sized glasses of wine but was totally sober now. Her hands were like ice as she uncorked the brandy and slopped some into a tumbler. And then, for reasons unknown to herself, she went into the sitting-room and unplugged the telephone.

The brandy warmed her, its effects, on her now empty stomach, felt immediately. She rinsed the glass and went to bed. But sleep evaded her. Rose had told Inspector Pearce she had last seen Gabrielle ten minutes or so before Doreen Clarke had announced that the food was ready. Because she did not know everyone present it had been difficult to say who had or had not been in the lounge or near the buffet table before she had decided to inspect the garden. Eileen, the thin woman serving the drinks, had disappeared, Doreen Clarke had presumably been seeing to the food, the tallish, slim woman with auburn hair who seemed to be on her own had vanished, likewise Paul and his fiancée, Anna. There were approximately

33

forty people present; she could not be expected to know all their whereabouts. Fortunately she had been able to confirm that Barry was at the end of one of the trestle tables chatting with Mike and Barbara Phillips and, as most of the guests knew the doctor, they would not be under any real suspicion. Suspicion? Rose suddenly realised what she had somehow known all along. Gabrielle Milton's death was no accident. So what, she thought as she tossed and turned, had the woman done to attract such dislike that someone wanted her dead?

Doreen Clarke's duties were supposed to end at ten thirty, by which time the guests would have eaten. Any remaining food was to be neatly rearranged and left in the kitchen to be eaten later, if required. Cyril Clarke had been turned away at the gates and told to come back for his wife later.

When she was finally allowed to leave she had remained silent throughout the drive home, mystifying her husband further. Once at the cottage she had said she felt ill and, after filling a hot water bottle, had gone straight to bed. She was asleep when Cyril joined her half an hour later. Doreen, he realised, coped with things her own way. Major catastrophes not only silenced her tongue but allowed her eight or nine hours' sleep, three more than she was accustomed to. Anxiety or stress caused some people to eat more or less than was usual, not so his wife, but the extra hours of rest did not make her any more tolerant.

Cyril rose at seven to another sunny day although the thermometer in his small greenhouse showed it had been chilly in the night and there was an autumnal feeling in the early morning air. Satisfied that no plague of destructive insects had destroyed his plants, Cyril inspected the last of the tomatoes growing against the side of the cottage. They were still green and hard, and he decided they probably wouldn't ripen now. Doreen might as well have them to make chutney. Cyril Clarke, ex-miner, had taken quite a few years to come to terms with things above the earth's surface. With the closure of Geever mine came the end of life as he, and his ancestors, had known it. For him, and many others, there was no work to be found. Moving away was not a consideration. He and Doreen were Cornish-born, had never lived anywhere else and could not bear the thought of doing so. It was Doreen who had kept things going by doing other women's housework. Now he had his pension things were a little easier. Cyril, for want of something to do, had taken to putting things into the ground rather than digging tin out. There was a sense of achievement in being able to hand Doreen a head of lettuce or some peas or potatoes. It was cheaper than buying vegetables and the excess he sold to local shops. His pocket money, he called it.

He did not hear Doreen get up. She watched her husband from the back door as he peered at the undersides of the leaves on the rose bushes. His grey, grizzled hair was covered with a cap which he wore winter and summer. Doreen reckoned all those years in a miner's helmet made him feel naked when his head was uncovered.

'Cyril!'

'Dear God, woman. You gave me a fright.' The secateurs had clattered to the path.

Doreen, despite the sleep, was pale through her tan, her eyes heavy and her fading blonde hair untidy. 'Cyril, we're not supposed to talk about it, but I can't not tell you. You won't say anything, will you?'

'Of course not, love. What is it?' He approached her and smiled gently.

'She's dead. Mrs Milton. She's been murdered. Oh, they say she might've fallen off the balcony, but I know better. The railing's waist-high. Besides, she doesn't drink, not more than the odd glass, so it wasn't that.'

'Murdered?' Cyril rubbed his newly shaved chin. It seemed impossible, with the sun shining and birds singing, that such a thing could have happened to mar the peace of the village. Despite his wife's foibles he loved her and he did not doubt that what she said was true. She had stuck with him through the bad times, put up with less money and his own frustration and occasional bouts of bad temper which were the result of having no job. Once he had reached the official retirement age when his job would have ended anyway, he had come to terms with life. He had also come to terms with Doreen. He saw now that this was no hyperbolic description of some incident she had witnessed.

'Come on, let's go in and we'll talk about it.' He took her arm and lowered her into a kitchen chair, then plugged in the kettle. It was cool inside, the sun not having moved far enough from the east to be visible from the windows.

'I couldn't keep it from you, Cyril. We've never had any secrets in the past. It's just the thought that someone there did it, that's what gets me. To think I may have served them food.' Doreen shook her head. 'What'll we do if Mr Milton doesn't want to keep the place and the new people decide they don't want me?'

'Oh, Dor, it doesn't matter. Really it doesn't.' He put an arm around her shoulder and kissed the top of her head. 'We'll cope.' But he had a rough idea of what she was going through, he had been through it himself. And on top of that was the thought that someone they knew might be capable of murder.

4

Inspector Pearce knew it would be foolish to assume someone who had attended the party was Gabrielle Milton's killer, although it seemed most likely. There was the possibility that the party, with guests and cars arriving randomly, had been used to disguise the arrival of someone else whose presence would have been noticed at any other time by curious, nosy or suspicious neighbours. Cornish himself, Jack Pearce was aware that strangers were summed up and not accepted until they had proved themselves to be not wanting.

The hardest part of the job was having to treat people he knew as suspects. Of those present at the Miltons' on Saturday night he knew only Dr Phillips and his wife personally. Barry Rowe he had met two years previously when his printing premises had been broken into. A case, he recalled, which had never been solved.

It would be up to his counterparts in the Met to make inquiries into Mrs Milton's London connections. She had not lived in Cornwall for long enough to rule them out. Meanwhile he had to concentrate on the guests and those with whom she had come into contact locally. And in seven months they numbered quite a lot. There had been builders and decorators, electricians and plumbers, delivery men and tradesmen, each of whom had helped turn the house from a draughty, expensive place to run into the luxurious residence it now was.

The expression 'house-to-house inquiries' seemed ludicrous in that the Miltons had very few neighbours, but someone had killed her and someone, somewhere, may have noticed something unusual. He sent the men at his disposal to find out.

*

Eileen Penrose was still recovering from her ordeal when someone from CID came to interview her husband. She had been uncooperative during her initial interview, claiming she had been too busy serving drinks and looking after the guests to notice anything that had happened during the evening. Asked where she had been when Mr Milton had decided everyone had better have another drink she had replied, 'Where do you think I was? Everyone needs to use the bathroom at some point.' But not upstairs, she had insisted, the facilities there were en suite with the bedrooms. There was a downstairs cloakroom for guests and staff. She had not lied but there were things she had omitted from her statement.

As far as Eileen Penrose was concerned, she would shed no tears over the death of someone she considered to be a rival.

'He's out,' she said sharply when the detective constable knocked on the door. 'And I've only just got in myself.'

It was now possible for the police to be more open in their questioning, having ascertained that Gabrielle Milton's only relations were all present at the party and no one else needed informing of her death.

Eileen narrowed her eyes and crossed her arms over her scrawny chest, partly to disguise the thudding of her heart which she was sure could be heard. Her sigh of relief was barely audible when she learned it was Jim the man wanted to see. 'He wasn't even there,' she told him.

'We know that, Mrs Penrose, but we have to speak to everyone who's been to the Milton place.'

'My Jim saw to their heating system, if that's what you mean. I can tell you where he is if you need to speak to him right away.'

The young constable already pitied Jim Penrose and bet his pinched-looking wife demanded to know where he was every minute of the day. 'I've got other people to see. What time are you expecting him back?'

'Twelve thirty. For his dinner.'

'Thank you.' Before he had taken the two steps down from the front door it was closed.

38

Eileen went straight to the cupboard over the sink and took down a bottle of sweet sherry which was only ever used in trifles and gravy and poured an inch or so into a glass. Had anyone else done this, taken a drink in their own home in the middle of the morning, she would have claimed they were two steps away from being alcoholic.

She prayed no one had seen her on that day and wished now she had kept her mouth shut instead of letting Maureen know she thought Jim was up to something with Mrs Milton. Feeling calmer, she hung out the washing, looking forward to watching Jim's face when it was his turn to be questioned. 'That'll give him something to chew on,' she muttered. 'Teach him to mess about with other women. Serves him right if he's arrested.' But what she had seen worried her.

Rose woke from a fitful sleep with a headache. Catching sight of her face in the dressing-table mirror on her way to the bathroom, she found it ironic that she had expected to look and feel this way after the party, but for different reasons. The headache, she guessed, was caused by lack of sleep and an empty stomach. Yesterday she had eaten little, not wanting to spoil her appetite for later, and what she had eaten had not stayed inside her for long.

Once she had showered and cleaned her teeth she felt marginally better. Downstairs she pulled back the curtains. A sea fret hung over the bay like a veil. Only the tip of St Michael's Mount was visible; Lizard Point was totally obscured. The unbelievable shades of blue of the sea were not in evidence. Today it was a milky green. Two trawlers were making their way of out of the harbour and in the middle distance a salvage tug, rolling fractionally on a swell, hovered like a vulture, its owners and crew hoping for the worst.

Rose never knew what to expect when she drew the sitting-room curtains. The light and shade were ever-changing, the bay might or might not be busy. Now and then numerous sails would fill the far end of the bay where the yacht club was situated. Here was where she had finally understood the meaning of the word chiaroscuro. Light and shade. Here was so different from the memories of her childhood holidays, spent with her parents out of season in resorts such as Brighton and Great Yarmouth where the sea was the colour of dental amalgam and layers of clothes were required to keep out the biting wind and bursts of rain.

Rose lit the grill of the gas cooker – the toaster had packed up several months ago – and allowed it to heat up. She felt she needed pampering so made coffee in the filter machine rather than instant. She opened the kitchen door, which was at the side of the house and led to the small garden. To the right was a rocky cliff face, ahead was the lawn bordered by hardy shrubs and tubs of plants. To the left was the open vista of the bay, seen from the sitting-room and her bedroom, but not from the kitchen. A herring-gull appeared to be performing some secret ritual as it side-stepped first one way then the other along the narrow ridge of the sloping roof of the shed, ignoring the mewing cries of the immature birds beside it. The gull and its mate had nested for the second year in the angle of the chimney stack on her roof.

Rose ate two slices of toast and butter and was drinking her second cup of coffee when the news came on. There were brief details concerning Gabrielle Milton's death which, the announcer said, the police were treating as suspicious. She had been right, then. Rose did not believe Gabrielle had simply fallen.

Poor Dennis, she thought. But it was the reactions of both Paul and Anna which she had found interesting. They were shocked, certainly, but not distraught and they had exchanged a look she could not guess the meaning of. And the auburn-haired woman – there had been a gleam of something Rose could only think of as satisfaction when Dennis had broken the news. No, she told herself, pouring a third cup of coffee. It is not my concern. The fish-eyed inspector would sort it out. He would, he had told her, probably need to speak to her again and had written down her address. Well, it won't be this morning, Rose decided, because I'm going out. She set off in the car.

The tide was perfect, on the turn, leaving bare the shiny mud of the Hayle estuary where many birds were feeding.

Barry Rowe liked her bird paintings. They were not accurate, detailed representations but shaded impressions of shape and line. She laid down a waterproof sheet and sat down to work.

A slight breeze lifted her hair and soughed through the grasses behind her. There were few people in sight from the spot she had chosen and after this weekend there would be fewer still. The holiday season was coming to an end. In the distance cars crawled along the narrow road but the only sounds were rustlings and the occasional whistling call of an oyster-catcher.

An hour and a half later, feeling stiff, Rose packed away her things and decided to walk along the bank. The tide was coming in now. She continued on to where the shops started and crossed the bridge over the estuary and followed the road up into the Towans. Here, steep banks of the well-advertised golden sand had been warmed by the sun and trickled down the backs of her calves as she descended a path trodden by other feet between the waving marram grass on to the flat sweep of the sands. The sky was clear, the sea a darker blue, almost turquoise; there was no sign of the damp mist which hung over Mount's Bay and which could do so for days on end whilst everywhere else remained sunny. A frill of white foam separated sea from sand. Rose walked until her legs ached and she realised she still had to get back to the car.

Yesterday's guilt had disappeared. Rose was thinking more of the murder than of David, and of the strangers she had met. She was hungry again so she decided to go straight home, stopping only once at the Co-op in Newlyn for milk and some tomatoes. She had to wait to be served. A crew from a fishing boat had two trolleys to be checked out but she was not in a hurry.

'Zat all you got, maid?' One of the older men nodded towards her two items. 'You gwon then.'

'Cheers.' Rose smiled and handed over the right money.

The shock of finding Gabrielle was wearing off but Rose knew it would take at least another twenty-four hours. Work had helped to take her mind off it and she knew Barry would be pleased with her efforts. The bird scenes he used on cards left blank for the sender to write their own message.

Taking a doorstep sandwich containing cheese and salad up to the attic, Rose decided she would continue to work. Hopefully she would be able to fall into bed exhausted tonight and sleep properly. It was an advantage of being her own boss that it did not matter if she slept late in the mornings.

Another idea of Barry's had been to photograph churches, buildings which abounded in Cornwall and ranged from picturesque to Gothic to the no-nonsense style of the Methodists. The singing of hymns by the whole congregation had appealed to the Cornish; consequently John Wesley, who had introduced this idea, had left his mark by adding to the Methodist influence. Rose had agreed to Barry's suggestion and had added that they would be more striking in black and white matt. There was a roll of undeveloped film awaiting attention. Barry required them for a trade fair and thought they would make alternative Easter cards. Although he was in business to make money, like Rose he hated the commercial aspects of the two main religious festivals. 'Go on,' he had urged. 'I know how much you despise yellow chicks and bunnies. The most you can lose is a film.'

Leaning forward to catch a slice of tomato in danger of sliding out of her sandwich, Rose remembered she had left the proofs of the Milton photographs at the house. She might not have been allowed to retrieve them, she thought cynically; DI Pearce might consider them as evidence.

The work completed, Rose slid the first of the church shots under the enlarger, then decided against it. The pictures would lose their stark impact if they were made bigger. Let Barry decide, she thought. Before she went downstairs again she took out her own copies of the photographs she had taken for Gabrielle. Something troubled her but she could not remember what it was. She kept copies of everything in clearly marked folders in a filing cabinet, both for her own reference and in case a client desired a further order.

The sun was an orange globe by the time she was seated in the armchair nearest the window, a small table beside it. She had neglected Laura, whom she had promised to ring to tell her how the party went – although she was surprised Laura had not contacted her. Surely she must have heard the news? But Laura was out.

Six thirty. It was not too early for a glass of wine. She poured one and returned to the sitting-room. The first shots of the Milton house were what she expected. It was the last one which puzzled her. It took several minutes before she realised what it was.

On the far right-hand side was a minute blur. Rose picked up a magnifying glass but whatever it was became no clearer. When she had released the shutter the final time she had registered a movement. When she stepped back from the camera Dilys had gone. 'But Dilys', she said aloud, 'must have fled immediately after the picture was taken.' Because in that picture Dilys was still there. Standing, it was true, ready to jump, but there all the same. Rose doubted the enlarger would clarify the blur if the magnifying glass had not done so.

'Barry,' she said, having dialled his number, ashamed that she expected him both to be in and to respond to her wishes. 'How about that drink I owe you?'

'I was just about to ring you. I thought I'd leave it until this evening to give you a chance to . . . well, to rest.' He wasn't sure what he meant, only that he had guessed Rose would prefer to be on her own.

'Rest? Oh, yes, I see.' Was it selfish to have been working all day under the circumstances? 'I need someone to talk to. Are you busy?' she added hastily.

'No. And I'm your man.' I'm never too busy where you're concerned, he thought, but he could never say the words aloud. He did not want to lose whatever he had with Rose, as little as it was.

'Look, why don't I meet you somewhere? Are you at the shop?' Barry's calls were automatically transferred from the shop to his flat. Throughout the summer he opened on Sundays.

'No. I closed at six. I can pick you up.'

'I need the walk.' Her earlier ennui had worn off.

They arranged to meet outside his flat.

*

Rose was pale with dark semicircles under her eyes. 'Where would you like to go?'

'I don't mind.'

Barry's flat was situated in a side street which led off the Promenade. They strolled down to the bottom and turned left, crossing the road at the pedestrian lights directly in front of the long glass frontage of the Queen's Hotel. Rose realised she wasn't as strong as she had believed. 'The Navy?' she suggested. It was a small, friendly pub just off the sea front.

To the left of the door was a pool table, tucked away in its own space. The bar itself formed three sides of a rectangle and there were individual tables around the walls. They carried their drinks to a secluded area at the back. Barry did not comment that Rose had offered to pay. It seemed she had forgotten.

'There's something not quite right,' she said. 'Look, what I told you about that woman, the one that Dennis kept looking at . . .'

'Maggie.'

'Maggie?'

'Maggie Anderson. She introduced herself to me when you went walkabout.'

'Did she?' Rose turned in her chair and stared at Barry with new respect. Maggie was an extremely attractive female. Barry could not be described as handsome but he had a nice face; a kind face, if a little lived-in. His hair was thinning on top and his heavy-framed glasses kept slipping down. It was a characteristic gesture of his to be constantly pushing them back in place. 'Well, do you think I should have said anything to the police? About my suspicions, I mean?'

'Good heavens, Rose.' Barry laughed. 'Certainly not. You've met Gabrielle Milton only once, you don't know her husband and you certainly can't go around accusing people you've never set eyes on of having an affair.'

Rose felt herself blushing. That was the trouble with Barry. Although she suspected he was half in love with her he had no qualms about putting her straight. 'All right, what about

44

this then.' From her handbag she produced the photograph of the house with Dilys ready to spring.

'What about it?' Barry nudged his glasses and frowned.

'There. Can't you see?'

'It's blurred, if that's what you mean.'

'Quite. And I'm sure I saw something move. And it wasn't the cat like I thought at first.'

'Rose, what are you trying to do? You can't get involved, you know, and you're seeing things that aren't there. I know this isn't an easy time for you but you know nothing about the Miltons and their friends, and a tiny blur in a picture doesn't mean anything. Probably it was the wind disturbing something.'

'There was no wind.' Rose stared straight ahead, annoyed with Barry and with herself for being stupid.

'Leave it to the police.' But Barry took a second look. Between the shrubs was what he thought might be, if he allowed his imagination a free hand, the blurred image of a female body in profile. 'It could be', he said, thinking aloud without meaning to encourage Rose, 'Gabrielle. You know, getting out of the way if she realised she might end up on the front of her Christmas cards.'

'She was in the house.' Rose replaced the picture in her bag. But she was smiling. Barry had seen it too.

'I did notice something last night.'

'Which was?'

'The son, Paul, he kept trying to attract his father's attention. Like he was agitated about something.'

'He probably was. He and Anna were rowing. Drink up, it's my round.'

Barry watched Rose as she approached the bar. Her figure was neat in a straight denim skirt and slimmer by half a stone, lost when David died and never regained. Her bare legs were brown and, from behind, with her faded auburn hair in an untidy pony tail, she looked like a much younger woman. He had been too slow in asking her out, he recalled. It was David who had stepped in and now it was too late. Rose treated him like a friend; he would never be more than that.

Barry was aware what people thought of him even if they

kept these thoughts to themselves. 'Boring,' he muttered. 'And it's true.' It was as if the burning passions which drove men to great heights or the depths of despair had passed him by, but he was still able to feel a twinge of jealousy when other men looked at Rose.

'Thanks,' he said when Rose returned with their drinks. 'Have you eaten?'

'I'm not hungry.' The sandwich lay heavily in her stomach, the nausea of the previous evening not far away. Work, and trying to make something out of a stupid photograph, had, she realised, been a way of trying to forget what she had seen. Delayed shock was setting in.

'Well, I am.' He studied the menu in its red leather cover. There was a large selection but Rose knew he would, as always, order one of Marg's, the landlady's, home-made pasties. She could only eat half of one herself.

'Rose,' Barry said later, when he had walked her home. 'Just try and forget what happened. It wasn't as if we knew them.'

But that, to Rose, was the whole point. It had been another missed opportunity in her life.

5

Dennis Milton had spent most of Sunday at Camborne police station where the questioning, along with shock and grief, had taken its toll. He knew that as her husband he was considered to be the main suspect, but surely enough people had been able to say he was either in the lounge or on the patio the whole evening?

He was allowed to return to the house but his bedroom was still out of bounds. Forensic experts had gone over it and would probably do so again. For the time being the door was taped.

It had been confirmed that Gabrielle had fallen from the balcony but the police refused to tell him why they were certain she had been pushed.

Anna had also been questioned at length but told she was free to return to London as long as she remained at the address she had given. She returned by train as Paul had volunteered to stay with Dennis.

On Monday morning Doreen Clarke telephoned and asked if her services were needed. Unable to think rationally, Dennis said yes, then spent the rest of the day sitting on the bench at the end of the garden, his eyes averted from the path leading down the side of the house. He was numb, but what was worse was that Gabrielle's death was no accident. And it was unbelievable that she had been there long enough to make an enemy of someone. He refused to face the alternative.

'I don't know what to do about Mrs Trevelyan,' he said to Paul as they picked at the meal Doreen had left for them.

'Do about her?'

'I feel I ought to speak to her. I mean, she found . . . she was the first . . .' He did not want to say it. 'She must be very upset herself.'

Paul shrugged. He had never been an emotional child outwardly but Dennis knew he suffered in his own way. His dark hair made a stark contrast to the paleness of his face and there was a slight tremor in his hands unless they were employed. As an only child the loss of his mother must have come hard. Dennis suddenly realised he had no idea how to comfort Paul.

'I'm sorry, I can't finish this,' he told Doreen when she came to clear the plates. She had taken it upon herself to stay for a couple of extra hours but she, too, realised there was little she could do for the Milton men except keep the place tidy and produce food at regular intervals.

'Shall I come tomorrow?' she asked.

Dennis nodded. 'Please.' He could not bear the thought of having only Paul for company.

Rose Trevelyan's number was listed in the telephone book. Dennis lifted the receiver, then changed his mind. The telephone was not a method of communication he favoured; it would be better to speak to Mrs Trevelyan face to face. And it would get him out of the house.

Rose was cleaning her brushes when she heard a knock on the door. She was puzzled – all her friends came round to the side. The police, she decided, as she wiped her hands on the old towel she had tied around her waist. For most of the day she had succeeded in blocking out what she had seen.

'Mr Milton!' She stepped back, surprised. 'I'm sorry. Come in, please.' She showed him into the sitting-room and apologised for her appearance. 'Excuse me just one moment.' There was a jacket potato in the oven, which she turned down, and a piece of steak marinading. She had intended clearing her working areas, then making some salad. On the table near where she had asked Dennis to sit down was a bottle of red wine, open, and a glass beside it. It was too late to hide it and she wondered why she felt she should have.

Ought she to have written a note of condolence? People had been so good to her when David died, but what did you say to a man whose wife had been murdered?

'Would you like a drink? I've just opened a bottle.' Rose bit her lip. This, then, was what you said.

'I . . . er, yes. If you're having one.'

Rose fetched another glass and filled both, stopping herself in time from saying 'Cheers'. They sat opposite each other, either side of the fireplace. Dennis was in David's chair but that did not hurt her any longer. Rose took the initiative and broke the awkward silence. 'I should have telephoned,' she said. 'I'm sorry. But I didn't know what to say. I know I hardly knew her, but I liked Gabrielle. How's your son taking it?'

Dennis ran a hand through his thinning sandy hair which he wore swept back from his forehead. His stubby fingers, Rose noticed, were freckled. 'I don't know. He hasn't said a lot. It's a terrible thing to admit, Mrs Trevelyan, but somewhere over the years we've drifted apart.'

'Rose.'

'Rose, then. I suppose it started when we sent him away to school. Gabrielle was against it. I . . .' He stopped again. He seemed unable to take a thought through to its full conclusion. Every now and then the reality that he would never see his wife again hit him. It was like being winded. 'I struggle to make conversation with him. What do you think I should do?' He made eye contact for the first time.

Rose found it odd that this recently bereaved virtual stranger should be sitting in her house asking her advice. She gazed out over the bay. A purplish dusk was falling and the lights of Newlyn harbour flickered on. There was no inspiration there.

'Perhaps if you sat down and really talked to him, told him what you've just told me. He probably feels the same.'

'Yes.'

But Rose was not sure if he had even heard her.

'I felt I had to come. To make sure you were all right.' Dennis meant it but underneath he saw that, because Rose had found Gabrielle's body, a sort of bond existed between them.

49

'Please don't worry about me, Dennis, you've got enough to think about. Have the police gone yet?'

'No. They're still in and out and they've got one of their van things parked at the front. They said it was fortunate that most of the guests were local. Fortunate.' He spat the word. 'For them, maybe. Not for Gabrielle.'

Rose studied his face as he sipped his drink. There were lines of fatigue and strain but it was a pleasant, almost handsome face. Something told her there was more than his wife's death on his mind.

'I'm in a bit of a mess,' he said, as if he had telepathic powers.

'Oh?'

'Who wouldn't be?' he said quickly, unaware he had spoken aloud. 'You have a nice place here. This is the sort of thing I imagined Gabrielle wanted, something with more of a family feeling than our London flat.'

Rose saw the room properly for the first time in ages. It was far too long since she had decorated and the floral covers of the suite were fading. She could never have drawn the curtains, shutting out the sun and the view, to prevent it happening. Now, she thought, was not the time to be thinking of soft furnishings.

'I love it here. So did my husband. He died four years ago tomorrow. Of cancer.'

Dennis's expression was sympathetic. He guessed she wanted to reassure him that he was not the only one to suffer, that life would go on regardless.

'Would you like some more wine?' Rose was thankful she preferred the skin of baked potatoes crispy. Dennis seemed oblivious to the warm cooking smell which was drifting in from the kitchen.

'Please. And the view. It's amazing. The whole bay. That was another thing I couldn't understand, moving down here and looking out at sand dunes and gorse. You can just see the sea in the distance. And the extra bedrooms when Gabrielle made it clear she didn't want people coming down from London all the time. God, listen to me. I didn't mean to criticise.'

'Perhaps it was the space she wanted.' Rose meant mentally as well as physically. She could understand it. When she had to spend a couple of days in London the first thing she did upon her return was to walk. She'd take a cliff path and surround herself with sea and sky and breathe in the clean air.

Dennis bowed his head. 'I loved her, you know. Despite everything, I really loved that woman. And now I shall have to sell the house that she loved.'

Rose braced herself. Had Dennis been drinking? Surely two glasses of mediocre wine was not enough to make him maudlin. She recognised the difference between that and genuine grief. Grief, she knew, had no time for sentimentality. Grief was hard and sharp, the pain almost physical. It was tempered with cleansing anger.

Dennis, she suspected, was working himself up to making a confession and she would put money on her assumption that he was having an affair.

'I didn't know many of the guests, they were mostly people Gabrielle had met, but I feel responsible somehow, for putting them through this, all these questions. God, what a mess.' Dennis shook his head. 'Look, I've taken up enough of your time already. I really must go.' He placed his empty glass on the table and stood. 'Thank you, Rose, for listening. I won't bother you again.'

She saw him to the door and watched as he pulled away, his headlights sweeping through the darkness until the car had disappeared.

Rose put the steak under the grill and wondered if it had been an act, if Dennis Milton had killed his wife and was trying to put himself in a good light with people. Her natural curiosity made her want to find out more about the Miltons. Something, definitely, was not quite right.

Maggie Anderson had provided the police with her home address and that of her place of work. Like Anna, after endless questions, she had been allowed to return to London. She had explained that she had known Dennis for about eighteen months, which was true, that they had met through business

51

and that her being at the party was probably to redress the balance. Almost everyone else was a friend of Gabrielle's.

'It's over,' Maggie told herself when she boarded the train on Sunday evening. She had not had to lie but she had omitted many points. If they checked, the police would discover that Dennis's company was once a client of the advertising agency for whom she worked. And they would check, she was sure.

The train swayed through the darkness, stopping at all the stations until it reached Plymouth. Leaving Cornwall behind, she sighed with relief.

Saturday night had been spent under Dennis's roof, as had been the case with several of the guests. By the time the police had finished with them it was too late to go to bed and no one felt like sleeping. Maggie, along with two couples she did not know, remained in the lounge, resting as best they could on the settees. She had reserved a room in a hotel although she had hoped she would be invited to spend the night – not that Dennis would have issued the invitation. The matter was taken out of her hands.

It was hard to feel sorry for Gabrielle. The obstacle to Maggie's plans had now been removed.

Analysing her feelings, Maggie knew she was not in love with Dennis but he represented everything she wanted from life. He had money and power and knew how to use them although he had been unaware of her manipulation of the situation. Inexpensive restaurants had been chosen with care, the better to show herself in contrast to what she imagined was Gabrielle's extravagance. Gabrielle's contentment with books and her renewed enthusiasm for broadening her mind were not known to Maggie. But Dennis refused to discuss his wife with her.

Now, of course, it was only a matter of time before she got what she wanted.

'What do you think?'

'I think you're crazy.' Laura was studying the enlargements Rose had made of the view of the Milton house, concentrating on the right-hand side of the photographs. 'It's just a blur. It could be anything.' But Laura was prepared to humour Rose today. She had not forgotten the date. 'Does it matter?'

'I don't know. Barry agrees with me, though.'

'Ah.' Laura grinned. 'Barry would.'

'Should I show it to the police?'

'What for? It was days before she was killed. Besides, it's probably the gardener or Doreen.'

The idea of a gardener had not crossed Rose's mind. 'You know Doreen?'

'Of course I do. She was at school with . . .' Laura ran a hand through her dark curls. 'I keep forgetting you weren't at school with us. Shows how you've become part of the scenery.'

'Doreen's the same age as you?'

'Yes. Hard to believe, isn't it?' She was not being vain – it was simply that Doreen looked years older than her age. 'Could be to do with marrying a man some years her senior, but she doesn't seem to bother what she looks like.'

Nor do I these days, Rose thought, looking down at the worn jeans. 'What's she like? The first time I met her she gave me the creeps.'

'What? Doreen? She's all right. She resents outsiders, that's all, and to her you'll always be one.'

'But she worked for the Miltons and they've only just moved here.'

'That's different. There's money involved. She's had to keep Cyril for years now since the mine closed down. Rose? You're not thinking she killed her, are you?'

Rose shrugged. 'Well, I didn't, nor did Barry. Why not her?'

'When I said crazy, I meant it. You're not thinking of acting detective, are you? Anyway, I don't see any signs of liquid refreshment. What's up with you, woman?'

Rose looked at her depleted wine rack. There was enough for tonight.

Laura was studying the few lines in a national newspaper which were all Gabrielle's death seemed to warrant. Once it would have made headlines. There were times when Rose

53

envied Laura, with three grown-up children and two grand-children; at others she was glad she had not had any. She was better able to enjoy the years she had with David alone.

'What is it?' Laura glanced up and caught Rose smiling.

'I was thinking of you as a grandmother. It doesn't seem possible.'

'Come on, we're supposed to be deciding where we're going at the weekend.' Trevor would be at sea, Laura and Rose would have a night out.

'There's a film – God, who's that?' Rose frowned. The front door again. Had Dennis Milton decided to pay another visit?

Standing on the bottom of the three steps, and thus appearing the same height as Rose, was Inspector Pearce. 'I wondered when you'd turn up,' she said, realising she sounded rude but not caring. 'Come in.'

'Well, well,' Laura said from her chair at the kitchen table. 'They've put you in charge, have they?'

Rose looked from one to the other. Was there anyone Laura didn't know?

'Another of your school chums?'

'No. But his sister was. How are you, Jack?'

'Fine. You?'

'Surviving. I was just leaving.'

'But . . .' Rose did not have time to complete what she was about to say because Laura had swung her handbag off the back of the chair and waved from the other side of the kitchen door.

Rose took a seat but did not invite her guest to do the same.

'These photographs,' Jack Pearce said without preamble, 'the ones you claim you delivered to Mrs Milton –'

'I did deliver them,' she interrupted. 'I left them in the small room opposite the lounge.'

'We can't find them.'

'What?'

'They're not in the house.'

'They must be.'

'Are you sure you didn't take them with you? You might've forgotten, you were a bit upset at the time.'

Was he being facetious? 'I did not.'

'Perhaps you left them in the taxi.'

'Look, I know the driver who collected us. I know them all at Stone's Taxis. If I'd done so they would have let me know. And I'm not in the habit of lying, especially to the police.' Rose bit her lip. The man had riled her to the point where she was talking nonsense. The second half of her sentence negated the first.

'Is that so?' DI Pearce's smile was mocking.

'Someone else must've moved them. Mr Milton probably. He wouldn't want a reminder of a Christmas he's not going to be spending with his wife.'

'We've checked.'

'Well, perhaps your men didn't search hard enough.'

The remark was ignored. 'Now you've had a chance to think about it, is there anyone you know who would wish to harm Mrs Milton?'

'I told you at the time, I didn't know her. I spoke to her on the telephone on two occasions and met her once on a business footing. At the party there wasn't much chance to speak to her, she was busy making sure everyone was all right.' But not herself, Rose added silently. 'Is that it? I have got things to do, you know.'

'Hint taken, Mrs Trevelyan. I can see you're very busy.' He dropped his eyes so they rested momentarily on the newspaper spread out on the table and the almost empty bottle of wine.

Rose felt herself blush and opened the kitchen door in a dismissive gesture.

Still annoyed and wondering why she should be, she was not fully aware of what she was saying when the telephone rang. She replaced the receiver, amazed to find she had accepted an invitation for dinner with Dennis Milton.

A stiff breeze rattled the fronds of the palm tree which grew close to the shed. Rose liked the sound they made. It was one of those brilliant September days but colder outside than it appeared. The bank holiday had passed unnoticed for Rose who had missed the Fish Festival, preferring not to have to answer the many questions she would be inundated with by all the people she would see there who knew her.

Whitecaps formed on the tops of the shallow waves as the sea rolled in to Wherrytown Beach. When the tide was higher spray would soak the Promenade and the people foolish enough to think they could time the waves. Sennen, she thought. It would be perfect today. She could paint the sea as it broke over the rocks. She filled a flask with coffee and was just about to leave when the telephone rang again. 'What now?' she said as she went to answer it.

'Mrs Trevelyan?'

'Yes?' She did not recognise the voice.

'It's Mrs Clarke. Doreen Clarke. From the Milton place. I was wondering if I could have a word with you.'

'Well, I . . . Yes, of course. What is it?'

'Not over the phone. Could I see you? If you're not busy, that is,' she added hastily.

Rose was not exactly busy but she was beginning to feel her life wasn't her own. She was used to solitude and enjoyed it, and she could not imagine that Doreen Clarke had anything to say to her; it was more likely prurient curiosity as to what Rose had discovered on Saturday night. Rather than let her become a nuisance she decided to get it out of the way. 'Where are you?'

'I'm at the Miltons' but I'm leaving in half an hour.'

It was early for her to be finishing whatever she did up there. 'Do you have a car?'

'No. Cyril drops me off. I can get myself over to Penzance easy enough.'

'It's all right. Can you get into Hayle?'

'I don't want to put you to any bother.'

'It's no trouble.' Rose named a tea-shop and cursed herself. She had never been good at saying no but at least she had prevented Doreen from coming to the house.

She loaded what she thought she might need into the car, remembering the flask, then set off.

Doreen Clarke was there before her. But she didn't have as far to come, Rose thought irritably as she entered the café. After the cool wind it was warm inside and smelled of coffee and bread and pasties. On the table was a pot of tea. Rose ordered a coffee.

Doreen concentrated on the contents of her teacup until the waitress returned.

'How can I help you, Mrs Clarke?'

Rose waited, watching various expressions cross the woman's face. Her body language suggested she was ill at ease, embarrassed even, but whether that was because she was taking up Rose's time or because of what she had to say, Rose had yet to find out. Doreen fiddled with a teaspoon then dropped it. It clattered against her saucer. Colour spread from her crepey neck into her face.

'Mrs Clarke?'

'I don't think I should be here. I shouldn't have asked you to come.'

Wonderful, Rose thought. A whole morning wasted. 'Well, I am here.' She managed to keep the exasperation out of her voice. Did she need a job, was that it?

'If I tell you, you won't say it came from me, will you?'

'Tell me what?' Until she knew, Rose couldn't answer.

'It's probably no more than stupid gossip.' She took a deep breath and pulled her short, plump body upright in the chair, tucking her straight, grey hair behind her ears. 'Eileen Penrose is a very jealous woman. I've known her for years and it's not just me that realises it. How her husband puts up with her is beyond me.' She lowered her voice as the café began to fill up. Two women with children in pushchairs sat behind them, the children making too much noise for them to be overheard. 'She follows him.'

'What?' Rose could not imagine someone doing that.

'She does. Jim did some work for Mrs Milton.'

'Jim?'

'Eileen's husband. He was up there twice. Eileen helps out now and again, but I saw her, you see, about ten days ago it was. I thought you might've seen her too.'

'Me?'

'Yes. You was there, taking the snaps.'

Rose did not explain that what she did was a little more complicated than taking snaps. 'No,' she said firmly. 'I didn't

57

see her.' But maybe she had captured her on film. And in which case, what was she doing there?

'She didn't see me,' Doreen continued. 'But you see, she'd overheard me telling someone in the village that Mrs Milton was having a visitor that afternoon. I think she thought it might be her Jim and she wanted to catch him out. The visitor was you, of course.'

Rose tried to visualise the sort of woman Eileen Penrose must be. Suddenly she realised who Doreen meant. 'Is that the lady who was serving the drinks?'

'Yes.'

Now she understood. Eileen Penrose had been missing around the time Gabrielle had met her death. 'Did you tell this to the police?'

'No.'

'Why ever not?'

'You don't understand what it's like. She'd never forgive me. Nor would anyone else.'

But Rose did understand. She had lived there long enough to know what a tight-knit community it was, how everyone knew everyone else's business. Doreen Clarke's position would not have been enviable had she mentioned her suspicions. But Rose also saw the advantages. If you weren't seen for a day or so someone would make sure you were all right. 'Why are you telling me?'

'Because you live far enough away. And you were there. And I thought, you being a local celebrity and all, they'd take more notice of you.'

Rose smothered a smile. A local celebrity. So Doreen Clarke already knew or had made inquiries as to who she was. But she did not see how she could bring herself to say all this to Inspector Pearce, although it now seemed likely that it was Eileen Penrose she had captured in that final photograph.

'I can leave it to you then?' Suddenly businesslike, Doreen stood up and fastened her short jacket. She picked up her own bill and took it to the cash desk, leaving Rose trying to decide what she ought to do. Gabrielle Milton's murder, now she was over the initial shock, was beginning to intrigue her.

Dennis Milton was not sure of his motives for asking Rose Trevelyan to dinner but at least it was a way of getting through another night. Paul remained uncommunicative. Dennis had taken Rose's advice and tried to get him to talk, admitting his own faults. Paul had ignored his efforts.

The house seemed larger than ever yet there was no peace. Two men were upstairs now, going through things belonging to Gabrielle that they had not taken away with them. The invasion of her privacy was sickening. Even her handbag was not sacrosanct. Were there, he wondered, secrets she had hidden from him? It was ridiculous feeling the way he did when he had been seeing Maggie, but he was unable to bear the thought that Gabrielle might have met someone else. It could, of course, explain who had killed her. The front door had been left open on the night of the party. It would have been easy for someone to enter the house and wait. If whoever it was was seen – no, Dennis realised that if it was someone local other guests would have known him. Unless it was someone Gabrielle had met in London, in which case everyone would assume it was one of his friends.

He held his head between his hands in despair. It was not his job to find the murderer.

Rose finally made it to Sennen but she was not in the mood to work. Instead she watched the sea. Long, rolling waves gathered momentum and crashed in plumes of white spray over jagged rocks, beyond which water and sky were an identical blue where they met on the horizon. The sight calmed her, made her forget Gabrielle's broken body. The sounds calmed her further: the hiss as the sea sucked at sand the texture of castor sugar, the thud as it hit the rocks. Overhead, gulls screamed like raucous schoolgirls and a black-backed, larger and noisier than the others, made its presence known from the top of the cliff. The wind, coming off the sea, flung her hair wildly round her head and minute grains of sand into her face.

Rose breathed deeply, enjoying the salty tang, and felt cleansed. For a few short minutes there was only the present. Then she remembered she was having dinner with Dennis Milton.

She walked back to where she had parked the car, arms folded across her chest, aware that she was chilled. In the driver's seat she poured coffee from the flask, a perfect circle of mist forming on the windscreen from steam from the cup resting on the dashboard. Why, she thought, did Dennis seek her company? Did he suspect she had seen more than she really had, or was he simply lonely?

Rose finished the coffee, tucked her hair, sticky with spray, behind her ears and drove home.

Doreen Clarke had, without consulting Dennis, rearranged her working day. Instead of starting at nine and finishing at one, she was up at the house at eight to cook breakfast and clean, then she went home until it was time to prepare an evening meal. The hours were roughly the same so she did not bother Dennis with discussions about financial alterations. Her motives were not entirely altruistic. She felt sorry for the Miltons and was upset herself but she was looking to her own future. If she made herself indispensable Dennis would want to keep her on. She could take care of the place whilst he was in London, an easy enough task, leaving her time to find other employment as well. She had been surprised when he told her he was expecting Mrs Trevelyan for dinner but had not expressed it. Rose, she was sure, would not mention their earlier conversation.

'Anything in particular you'd like to eat?' Doreen inquired.

'No.' Dennis did not seem to care and most of what she cooked he left.

'You won't say anything, will you?' Doreen whispered to Rose when she let her in at seven thirty.

'Of course not.' And before she could ask if she had spoken to the police yet, Rose opened the door to the lounge.

'I'm glad you could come,' Dennis said, stretching out a hand. It was cold and dry compared to Rose's. 'You remember Paul?'

'Yes. Hello.'

Paul nodded but did not speak. He seemed uncomfortable, for which Rose did not blame him. She should have refused the invitation. Surely tongues would wag when it was known that Dennis had entertained a single woman to dinner only a few days after his wife's death. And it would be known, she was quite sure. Doreen would not be able to keep it to herself. At least Paul was present too.

Dennis poured drinks and between them they managed to fill the half-hour until Doreen said the meal was ready with small talk relating mostly to art and Rose's business. 'Dennis,' Rose said, 'I brought some proofs up the other night. Do you know what happened to them?' It was not a tactful question but the police seemed suspicious of her and Dennis had looked at them with his wife.

'No. We chose what we wanted. I assumed you'd taken them with you. The police were asking me about them too.'

They went into the dining-room. Rose let the subject drop.

The house was quiet. Rose had seen the mobile unit outside and wondered if there were actually any men upstairs. Surely by now they would have searched every inch of the place for whatever it was they hoped to find.

The meal was plain but it was hot. Rose's appetite was blunted as she watched her male companions push their food around their plates.

'I'm off now,' Doreen said after she had served the main course. 'There's cheese if you're still hungry.' Rose did not blame her for going to no further trouble. Her efforts would have been wasted.

'Have you made any wedding plans yet?' she asked Paul to try to involve him in the conversation.

'We hadn't, but I spoke to Anna yesterday and we decided there's no point in waiting any longer.'

'Waiting?' It was an odd choice of words. She studied Paul. Straight-nosed, thin-lipped, with soft greyish-blue eyes which did not reflect whatever he might be feeling. His skin was waxen and his hands shook. He was difficult to age but assuming Dennis and Gabrielle were in their early fifties he was probably between twenty-five and thirty.

61

'Having seen you can never tell what's around the next corner, we thought we might as well go ahead.'

Paul seemed unable to refer to his mother or her death but at least he was making an effort to talk.

'Where will you live?'

'In London. Our work's there and it wouldn't suit us down here. It's too quiet.'

From that statement Rose thought Gabrielle might have left the house to her son rather than her husband.

'As long as Anna's happy, that's all I care about.' For a second there was a flicker of enthusiasm in Paul's manner. It did not last.

'And you, Dennis? Have you made any plans?' Rose was bored with treading around the subject. She had been asked here yet neither man seemed to have noticed she had actually arrived. Perhaps, she thought, Dennis, having been unable to speak to Paul himself, hoped she would break the ice. In which case Gabrielle's name could no longer be ignored. 'I know it's early days yet, but what will you do with Gabrielle's house?'

'I don't know.' He smiled wanly. 'I'm still coming to terms with her not being here. There are problems with my company at the moment, it may be that I'll decide to live here.'

'But you . . .' Paul stopped. There was a tinge of colour across his sharp cheekbones.

His father misunderstood him. 'I wouldn't miss London. I've had my share of the rat-race. If I could get fixed up with something, a lower salary wouldn't bother me. If not,' he wiped his mouth with his serviette, 'well, I'd have to sell and find something smaller. Something like your house, Rose.'

Paul stood up and went over to the table against the wall upon which Doreen had placed cheese, a jug of celery and a basket of biscuits. Rose saw his actions were to hide his feelings, to prevent him saying something he might regret, rather than because he was hungry.

She was right. Paul ate a cube of cheese, then crumbled the biscuit. He filled the silence by saying, 'It might not be yours to sell.'

'What?'

'My mother mentioned to Anna that she might leave us the house.'

Dennis's head jerked up. There was genuine fear in his face. 'When did she tell her that?'

'I'm not sure. Anna only mentioned it recently. It's not a problem, is it?'

Dennis could not believe Gabrielle would have changed her will without telling him. He had to remind himself of Maggie and the things he had not told his wife. 'Paul, you might as well know, it looks as if I'll be made redundant.'

'My God.' He paused. 'But you've still got the flat, that's worth a bit, and they'll pay you off, they'll have to, you've been there years.'

Rose looked from Dennis to Paul, the one so defeated, the other without sympathy. Here was another reason to be grateful she was childless. Paul's parents had brought him up and had, presumably, done what they thought was best for him. Now, when his father most needed support, he showed only callousness. Rose's elbows were on the table, her fingers steepled. Her hands jerked and she knocked her knife to the floor with a clatter. 'I'm sorry,' she said, bending down to pick it up. No, she said silently. No, it can't be. 'It was a lovely meal. I really must go, Dennis.'

He did not try to persuade her to stay longer. Both men stood as she got up; Dennis saw her to the Mini, waited until he was sure it had started, then returned to the house without waving.

Rose was vaguely aware of a light coming from the incident van and the faint purr of a telephone ringing. Although she knew little of police procedure, it crossed her mind that their conversation might have been recorded. So keep out of it, she told herself.

Winding down the window because her face felt hot Rose realised she must be mad to have imagined that Paul had killed his mother in order to inherit, even if his wedding plans had been brought forward. She tried to remember Anna and her first impressions of her, but they had hardly spoken and it would be unfair to judge her when she was in the middle of a row with Paul. Anna was tall and slim and pretty, her straight dark hair cut in a perfect bob, and she knew how to dress, but for some reason Rose did not think she was the type of woman men would kill for. Even from that brief meeting she sensed she lacked personality. However, her views were unimportant, Paul had admitted he would do anything to make Anna happy.

Rose slowed and pulled into a wide spot in the otherwise narrow lane. A car was approaching, headlights on full beam. It did not dawn on her until later that its only destination could be the Miltons' house.

6

A dim light filtered into the room through the unlined curtains. Rose had slept well and was comfortable in the double bed, the duvet enveloping her warmly. It had taken a second death to enable her to survive the anniversary of David's without enduring several days of depression. She hated herself at such times but listing all the good things in her life did not help and she gave in to the forces which made it seem each day was grey even when the sun was shining.

She heard the first drops of rain pattering on the window and decided to make coffee and bring it back to bed. I'll take the day off, she thought, read and slop around. I might even light a fire later.

But it was not to be. As she waited for the kettle to boil there was a tap on the window of the kitchen door. She opened it and a draught scattered the sheets of paper upon which she had jotted some notes the previous evening. Laura stood inside the door, her curls bejewelled with raindrops, her clothes dripping water on to the floor and an expression of abject misery on her face.

'Whatever's the matter?'

'Oh, Rose.' The tears came suddenly and rolled down her face. 'It's Trevor,' she said.

'Trevor?'

Rose froze. Had there been an accident? Had his boat gone down?

'We can't stop rowing. Every time he comes home I try so hard to make everything right, nice meals, you know. It's partly my fault, he can't say anything right.' Laura sat at the table. 'Then as soon as he's gone back I feel awful. He's gone off this morning after a blazing row and I keep thinking, if anything happened to him . . .' She stopped, not wishing to tempt fate.

'He'll ring you later,' Rose told her. 'He always does.' It was true. Each night he was at sea Trevor rang at an arranged time.

'I know. And I'll apologise. But how do I stop it?'

Rose had been aware that things were not quite right but this was the first time Laura had told her. A weight lifted from her shoulders, one she had been unaware of, a minor form of the depression she dreaded. She had been lucky. She and David had had all those months to say all the things that needed saying, to know where they stood with each other. But Rose could not offer the consoling platitude that nothing was going to happen to Trevor. The sea chose its victims randomly.

'And what makes it worse', Laura continued as she accepted the coffee Rose placed before her, 'is that he keeps saying it's my age. It's so bloody insulting. It's his answer for everything.'

'Well, is it?'

'Is it what?'

'Your age? The menopause?'

Laura looked up and smiled faintly. 'I suppose it could be. God, that would make the bastard right. No, it's more than that. He comes in and has a few drinks and he's tired and doesn't want sex, then I get annoyed and we argue. Do you know what he said this morning? He said I sounded like a fishwife. Rose, don't laugh.'

'I'm sorry. He probably didn't see the irony. He *is* a fisherman. Come on, don't sulk. We'll have some more coffee.'

Laura heaped in three spoonfuls of sugar, a sure sign she was upset. 'I'll have to keep trying, I suppose. Anyway, what's all this?'

It was one of Laura's less endearing qualities that once she had poured out her troubles she let other people worry about them, regardless of the effect it had, and was herself able to continue as if nothing had happened. In brightly patterned leggings, a T-shirt and a loose top, her hair curling more tightly because of its soaking, she now looked perfectly cheerful.

'Ah. Just some scribblings.'

'But this is all to do with Mrs Milton's murder.'

Rose chewed her lip as she gently took the paper from Laura's hand. On it she had written what Doreen Clarke had told her as well as everything else which had occurred to her. She would not, not even to Laura, break Doreen's confidence.

'I get it, you're trying to outwit Jacko. He fancies you, you know.'

'What on earth are you talking about?'

'Jack Pearce. It's obvious. I could see by the way he was looking at you.'

'Honestly, Laura, the things you think up.'

Laura grinned and held out her mug. 'Any chance of another, or are you busy? Anyway, what's our Barry going to say about it? Detectives and widowers vying for your favours.' Rose had mentioned the invitation to the Miltons' in a telephone conversation.

Trevor's right, Rose thought later. She's obviously going through some hormonal changes if she believes DI Pearce has anything other than a professional interest in me. And she knew she ought to go and see him.

If she had to go to Camborne – and she certainly wasn't going to present herself at the mobile incident unit in the grounds of the Milton house – then she might as well take her sketching things in case it decided to clear up. The disused mine-stacks, seen from the A30, had frequently been depicted in oils and pastels and sketches but to Rose they were displayed at their best in winter, outlined with low cloud, their crumbling brick stark against bracken and gorse. More than once Rose had felt a sense of utter isolation when working near one of them despite the hum of traffic, and even on the brightest of days she had experienced the hair standing up on the nape of her neck. It lasted only seconds until she heard the sound of a lorry grinding its gears or a crow, its black wings gleaming blue, cawed. Rose never questioned whether this was the product of an over-imaginative brain or whether such things as spirits existed. It was part of life there and she accepted it.

'I don't believe it.' She had picked up an oilskin, one appropriated from Trevor some years ago and never returned, and had her hand on the kitchen door handle when the telephone rang. The answering machine was switched on but Rose was not able to leave it to do its job if she was in the house.

'Do you fancy coming over for something to eat tonight? I've got a rep coming to the shop at six, but any time after seven thirty.'

'Thanks, Barry,' Rose answered guiltily, having mentally gone through the contents of the fridge. It would save shopping.

The fish market was packing up as Rose drove past. She waved to several of the men she had met through Trevor and Laura and who recognised her car. By the time she reached Penzance station the rain had eased and she put the wipers on half-speed, noticing the smears of salty grease on the windscreen.

Maggie Anderson had decided to front it out. Why leave Dennis with an opportunity to extract himself? He could use many excuses for not seeing her, for not returning to London for some time. It was a double risk under the circumstances but she felt sure she could handle the police, if necessary. The advertising agency had allowed her three days' compassionate leave; she had said there had been a death but did not qualify the statement. As none of her clients was clamouring for attention, and as she did not allow anyone to get close enough to know her family background, what she said was accepted without comment.

Maggie had been more than surprised to see the temporary hut-like structure in front of the house but not as surprised as she was at the reception she received.

I should've phoned, Rose thought as she asked if she could leave the car where it was until she returned. She had expected DI Pearce to be seated behind a desk, which was, she knew, unreasonable. But he was over at Gwithian and would be returning within the hour. Rose was quite firm when she was asked if anyone else could help her and said it was the inspector she needed to speak to. Why? she asked herself, but could not come up with an answer.

Camborne, a granite-built town, dour and uncompromising, was bleaker still in the light drizzle which showed no signs of stopping. Recession-hit, many shops were boarded over and if it wasn't for South Crofty, the last working tin mine, she did not know how it or Redruth, the neighbouring, almost adjoining town, would survive. But South Crofty had been saved from closure by the injection of capital from a Canadian company and by local, individual investment.

She could have shopped but instead took refuge in Tyacks, a central hotel in Commercial Street, where she ordered coffee. It was brought on a tray by a cheerful waitress. As Rose looked up to thank her, her mouth dropped open in astonishment. In the doorway, shaking an umbrella, was the auburn-haired woman she had seen at the party. She must have been mistaken in thinking it was one of Dennis's friends from London and could not remember why she had had that impression.

The woman walked towards her, pausing for a second before going on to the bar. Rose was not sure if she had been recognised or not. Turning slightly in her seat she waited until the woman had been served then, as she made her way to a table, said, 'Excuse me. Haven't I seen you before somewhere? Were you at the Miltons' party?' Close up, Rose saw fine lines in the translucent skin radiating from the eyes, under which were dark smudges.

'Yes.' Maggie hesitated, unsure if she wanted to become involved in conversation. She had a lot to think about. Finally, having decided that Rose might be an asset to her plans, she asked if she might join her.

'Of course.'

'Maggie Anderson,' she said.

'Rose Trevelyan.'

'Ah, yes. I heard someone mention you. You're the painter, aren't you?'

The painter. It made her sound more important than she was. 'I do paint, yes, but mostly I do photographic work these days. That's how I met Gabrielle.'

'The poor woman. I couldn't believe it. I mean, I'd never even met her before that night. I'm a friend of Dennis's,' she added quickly. 'We met through work.'

'Have the police made you stay down here?'

'No. I . . . well, I didn't like to think of Dennis being left on his own. I was due some leave so I took a few days off.'

To Rose it sounded like a well-rehearsed speech. 'But Paul's there.'

'I didn't know that. I thought he'd go back to London with Anna.'

So Maggie knew enough about the Milton family to realise Paul was capable of being that selfish, of leaving his father alone. Had Dennis told her? 'It seems', Maggie said honestly, but with some anger, 'that my presence is not required. I stayed here last night. I was going back first thing this morning.'

Rose did not ask why she had changed her mind, she could read the answer in her face. Maggie wanted Dennis and was not going to give him up easily. But how could such a relationship last? One which had begun before Gabrielle's murder? There would be too many painful memories, at least for Dennis, and a constant reminder of his guilt. 'Can I get you another drink?' Rose glanced at her watch. There was time, before she returned to the police station. Let DI Pearce think what he liked if he smelled alcohol on her breath. She would be under the limit if he chose to query it.

'Thank you. A gin and tonic, please.'

Rose ordered a half of bitter for herself and paid the barman. The same waitress was placing a plate of sandwiches on the table. 'I don't know why I ordered this, I'm not hungry.' Maggie stared at the food. 'You've guessed, haven't you?'

'Yes.'

'I always hoped Dennis would get a divorce. His wife had moved down here, I assumed it was because they weren't happy together. I thought I could talk him round in the end. There's nothing I wouldn't . . .' She stopped and picked up a sandwich.

'Do the police know? About you and Dennis?'

'If they do, I didn't tell them. What difference would it make?'

What difference would it make? Rose wondered if Maggie was stupid. 'Did Dennis invite you to the party?' She was beginning to form an assessment of Maggie Anderson's character. It was not a pleasant one.

'No. I wanted to see what his wife was like. He could hardly make a fuss once I was there. And she seemed to accept it. That's not true.' Maggie had seen the expression on Rose's face and had guessed what she must be thinking of her. 'Gabrielle invited me.'

'Gabrielle?'

'She knew. I think she knew from the start. I don't know how she found out – I expect she had enough contacts to make the right inquiries. Unless Paul told her.'

'Paul knew too?'

'We bumped into him by accident once.'

Rose found all this new information hard to assimilate. 'But why would Gabrielle ask you down?'

Maggie smiled for the first time and Rose saw her attraction. 'You obviously don't play the same games, Rose. Think about it. There is Gabrielle as the hostess, in her own home, with her husband. My being there would show the affair up as shabby compared with what Dennis already had. His guilt and fear and anger at seeing me there would be enough for him to end it. Gabrielle was not going to let go, you see.'

Rose felt sick. Did many people carry on in this way? She decided to drop her own bombshell. 'Did you know Dennis is about to be made redundant?'

'What?'

'He told me the other night. When I was having dinner with him.'

Maggie's face reddened but whether it was from anger or some other emotion was not clear.

'Look, I'm sorry, but I've got to go. I've got an appointment.'

Rose would have liked to stay longer, but Maggie now knew her name. If, for any unlikely reason, she wanted to speak to her she could look the number up in the book. She was not going to get involved further.

My God, Rose thought as she went out into the cool air. Maggie? Had she realised that evening that she stood no chance, and had she decided to wipe out the opposition? Leave it to the police, her subconscious told her.

'Have a seat, Mrs Trevelyan.' DI Pearce was smiling and polite, perhaps deliberately in contrast to the way she had treated him in her own home. 'Tea or coffee?' Rose shook her head. 'Well, what can I do for you?' Jack Pearce leant back in his chair, relaxed and easy, his hands resting on his lap.

'I . . . well, it sounds daft, but this . . .' She slid a copy of the photograph across the desk.

Jack glanced at it for less than a second, then raised his eyebrows inquiringly.

'Can't you see it?' Rose leant over and pointed to the blur.

'Hmm. Just like in the film.'

'The film? You mean the negative.'

'No. The film. *Blow Up*, I think it was called. You must remember it.'

Was that a deliberate insult? She would have to find out when it was released. She and David had not been great cinema-goers but she often went with Laura now. 'I think that blur might be part of a woman, someone that Mrs Milton did not realise was there.' It was said with cool dignity.

'Could be. Probably Eileen Penrose.'

'Oh.' Rose could think of nothing further to say and she was not going to apologise for doubting the efficiency of the police.

Jack Pearce studied the woman in front of him. She had not, he thought wryly, dressed for the occasion; a yellow T-shirt, faded jeans and a denim jacket were more suitable attire for the cells. Her hair was twisted up and held in place with a tortoiseshell clip resembling a buckle and her pleasant, no, let's face it, he admitted, attractive face looked tired.

'You know.'

'Yes. Several sources told us Mrs Penrose was in the habit of following her husband. He himself admitted he had heard she was up at the house that day, and the lady in question has held up her hand.' He did not add that there was still the matter of her absence around the time Gabrielle was killed. That was not Rose's business.

Rose swallowed. She might as well go the whole way no matter what sort of fool she appeared. 'There's something else which I'm sure you're also already aware of.' It was harder than she had anticipated, this running to the police with tales, and it made her feel disloyal, although to whom she wasn't sure. 'I've been speaking to a lady named Maggie Anderson.'

'And?'

'She and Dennis Milton were having an affair.' No village gossip could have felt worse than Rose did at that moment. She sensed the colour rise into her face.

'You know Miss Anderson?'

'No.'

'Then how come she thought fit to confide in you?'

'I don't know. I met her by chance and we started talking.'

'Before the night of the party?'

'Oh, no. I don't think I even heard her name that evening. Today, I meant.'

'Today?'

Rose felt a moment's satisfaction. Pearce did not know she was back. 'She's staying at Tyacks.'

Jack Pearce tapped the desk with the end of a biro, his mind elsewhere. He had not known about the affair although there had been speculation. Miss Anderson's background had been checked and it was true that the firm Milton worked for had once used the agency's services. Having questioned Milton in depth he was certain he had had no intention of leaving his wife but he had not broken down and confessed to his adultery. Why? To protect himself or his wife's memory, or even the other woman? Or was there a more worrying reason? Rose Trevelyan had been far more helpful than she would ever know but what she had told him was no more than hearsay, if it was true. Anderson may have lied to her for some reason of her own, perhaps to make her jealous.

73

Mrs Trevelyan had, after all, been to the Milton place for dinner.

'Anything else, Mrs Trevelyan?'

'No.' She saw him lean forward and open the top drawer of his desk, stare at something for a second or two, then seem to change his mind. He slid the drawer shut and stood up in one motion, his body, in the small room, appearing taller and better muscled than she remembered it to be. He ran a hand through his dark hair as he held the door open.

'Goodbye.'

''Bye,' Rose said, unable to help seeing his face. He was laughing at her and not doing a very good job of disguising it. 'The bastard,' she hissed as she left the building.

7

'Did I do the right thing by telling her, Cyril?'

'Leave it, Doreen. That's the third time you've asked me. You've done it, you can't change that.'

'But supposing I was wrong?'

'How can you be? You told me at the time what you'd seen.' Cyril gazed anxiously out of the window, eager to be outside or, failing that, in the greenhouse, not that there was much to do at this time of year. Once the rain starts in these parts, he was thinking, it can go on for weeks.

'I didn't sleep a wink last night, worrying about it.'

Cyril ignored this exaggeration, realising that the real problem was not what she had told Rose Trevelyan: Eileen's antics were known to everyone. It was the thought that the job might be coming to an end and so far she had not had any luck in finding a replacement. 'Do you need any veg, love?'

'No, I don't think so. I might even start on the chutney this afternoon. What time do you want dinner?'

'Oneish.'

Doreen started chopping the tomatoes. Dinner, to her, was the midday meal. Up at the house they ate it in the evening but she always kept the two vocabularies separate. Toilet and lavatory, lounge and front room, napkins and serviettes. Still, she thought, each to their own. Her mind was a storehouse of clichés.

At least she had done her bit and saved Mrs Trevelyan from more bother.

Jim Penrose had had more than enough. He slammed out of the house without touching the food Eileen had prepared for him. It was no good arguing, he always lost. He had never met anyone as expert as his wife at making the smallest omission or the slightest grievance sound like a major crime. Why he stayed with her was beyond him and if everything he did upset her so much, the reverse was also true.

He returned to work, having decided he would not go straight home when he had finished. 'I'll give her something to think about,' he said, his anger mounting when the van refused to start until several attempts later.

'Did you drive here?'

'No, I got the bus most of the way.' Rose shook out her jacket and hung it over the door knob.

'I didn't realise it was raining that hard again.' Barry turned back to the saucepan in which he was stirring something.

'What're we having?'

'Pasta. With my own special sauce.'

'How unusual.'

'Don't be ungrateful, woman. You know it's one of the few things I don't ruin.' He pushed his glasses up, unheedful of the steam which had rendered them useless. 'And if you're rude to the chef, you won't get any wine. You may as well open it, I'm sure you're ready for some.'

Whilst the sauce simmered they sat on the two unmatching chairs either side of the formica-topped table. Barry made enough money for somewhere better but claimed his surroundings didn't bother him. The flat was small enough for him to manage, but to Rose it seemed cramped and inconvenient.

'What's in there?'

Rose had produced an A4 envelope from her bag. 'Just some notes. Tell me what you think.'

Barry saw immediately what she was up to. His instinct was to tell her to stop at once, to leave things to the relevant people, but it might be that she was trying to exorcise a ghost, David's ghost, by facing another sort of death. If she did, would he have a chance?

Rose waited for the verdict. Now she was warm and dry and

76

sipping Barry's wine, which was always superior to what she bought, she began to relax again, forgetting the humiliation Jack Pearce had inflicted upon her. Barry stopped reading once, to place a large pan of water on the cooker to boil, then again to ease in several handfuls of spaghetti.

Rose watched his serious face as he continued to read. The flat was at the back of a building, the only sounds the plopping of the boiling water and a dripping tap, both of which were restful. Condensation covered the windows and the room was aromatic with garlic and tomatoes and the faint smell of soap powder from Barry's shirts which were drying on an old-fashioned wooden pulley strung from the ceiling.

'You're in the wrong trade,' he said at last, jumping up as he remembered the spaghetti. 'You should've joined the police.' He was thoughtful as he strained the pasta. That bit about the trains, it fitted. If it had been someone from Gabrielle's circle in London they would have needed to arrive and depart by car. No trains left the area that late at night and a taxi was out of the question. How could the person, assuming the murder was premeditated, have asked a taxi to wait? It was a ridiculous idea. Nor could one have been called – someone would have remembered if a guest departed early. Besides, as Rose had noted, everyone, according to what she had overheard that night, who was on the guest list was still present when the police arrived. She had ruled out someone on foot; they would have been conspicuous on the narrow lanes, and no one in their right mind would be walking over the cliffs and dunes at night. So, she had concluded, it had to be one of the guests.

They ate in silence for several minutes. Rose was hungry, she had not eaten all day. First Laura, then Maggie, and by the time she got home from speaking to Inspector Pearce she had gone past wanting anything. 'It's excellent, as always.'

'Thanks.' At moments like that, seeing her smile, he was tempted to ask if Rose would like a live-in chef but Barry knew he would not be able to take the disappointment her reply would cause.

'Have the police been back to see you?' she asked after a few more mouthfuls.

'No. Should they have?'

'I don't know. I suppose it means they don't consider you to be a suspect.' She had not told him they had been to see her and did not want to discuss it now.

'Rosie, do you think you know who might have done it?'

'I'm not sure.' She looked down. David used to call her Rosie. Barry did so now occasionally but she didn't have the heart to tell him not to.

'Here, your glass is empty. Did I mention that I'm going to London soon?'

'No. Trade fair?'

'Yes. And if it's all right with you, I'm taking some of your work.' Barry's firm, small as it was, also supplied other outlets. Soon, he realised, he would need to take on a couple more staff. He liked things as they were; expansion scared him and he knew he would not have survived in a city. 'Want to come with me?' he asked casually as he cleared away the plates.

Rose calculated quickly. She was as up to date as she was ever likely to be. 'I'd love to,' she answered. But she hated herself when she saw his face light up. She had her own reasons for wanting to go.

'I'm glad,' Rose said when Laura, during their daily telephone conversation, told her she had spoken to Trevor.

'He was a bit cool, but I don't think I've driven him away completely yet.'

Rose told her about the trip to London. 'With Barry? Is that wise? He might get the wrong idea.'

'No. He went out of his way to let me know he had booked separate rooms.'

'Oh, Rose, I wish we could turn the clock back. We used to have such fun, the four of us.'

'I wish we could too.' But she was not in the mood for Laura's reminiscences. Laura still had a husband. Just. But life had been fun. It was an element which was missing from Rose's present existence.

Replacing the receiver, she was on her way back to the

kitchen when her plans were disturbed once more. This time, with the sun behind him, Rose recognised the shape of DI Pearce through the dimpled glass of the front door. 'Yes?' she said abruptly, wishing she didn't look such a mess every time he saw her.

'May I come in?' He followed her into the kitchen and conspicuously eyed the filter machine through which coffee dripped slowly.

He had been polite to her and offered her a drink. 'Would you like coffee?' she heard herself saying ungraciously.

'Love some.'

Rose's mouth was a grim line as she got out milk and sugar. She had intended having half an hour with the paper before setting off for her first appointment of the day.

Jack Pearce leant against the worktop, arms folded, legs crossed at the ankles, as relaxed, apparently, here as he was in his own office. He was in jeans, a blue and white striped shirt and a grey leather jacket. The uniform of the CID as it appeared on television, Rose thought sneeringly, allowing that it did suit him.

'We were concerned about those photographs you took, Mrs Trevelyan, for the very reason you came to see us. We thought they might contain something incriminating and had therefore been stolen. However, there was an innocent explanation for their disappearance. Here.' He handed her the envelope. 'Mrs Clarke had taken them home with her. She thought they would be an upsetting reminder for Mr Milton.'

Rose was pouring milk into the coffee. She turned to look at him, her head on one side. Doreen had not mentioned it to her. 'And she's just remembered and handed them in?'

DI Pearce ignored the question. Rose guessed they had already been in his possession the previous day. Was that what he had been deciding when he looked in his drawer? So why the visit now? 'Thank you. I don't know what I'll do with them. I don't suppose Dennis will want them now. Sit down,' she added belatedly. But Jack Pearce, it seemed, preferred to stand.

He sipped his coffee and asked if she minded if he smoked.

She found a blue glass ashtray with the Courage Brewery logo and placed it on the worktop beside him. He glanced at it with a wry grin.

'It was left here by the previous occupants,' she said, annoyed that she felt she had to make an excuse. If he wanted to think she was in the habit of nicking things from pubs, let him.

'Mrs Trevelyan, you seem to be taking quite an interest in this case. Have you now got any ideas as to who might have killed Mrs Milton?'

'No.' She was surprised at the question but she did not know DI Pearce was aware that she was the type of person people confided in and that she might actually know more than she thought she did. Her answer was not strictly honest; she was beginning to have a vague idea but it was based on instinct rather than elimination or facts.

'Ah, well. I'd better be going. Thanks for the coffee.' Rose noticed he had left half a mugful as he let himself out through the kitchen door.

There was just time to hang out the washing that had been in the machine overnight. She was taking a chance but it didn't look like rain at the moment. Her first assignment was a portrait for a local writer whose publisher required a new picture for the jackets of his books. It was straightforward work: a few shots in his own home. She made sure she had the background sheet which folded down to nothing in its metal frame. It would not be worth coming back again because at twelve thirty she was due at the offices of a firm of solicitors where one of the partners was retiring. He had been with the firm for thirty years and a surprise party was being held during the lunchtime. She was to take a photograph of the presentation of whatever it was they had decided to give him.

The author was charming and did not interfere or make suggestions. Rose told him he could expect the proofs in a week to ten days' time, then left his terraced house. Because they had been chatting, Rose asking questions about his books, she had only half an hour to kill. She might as well get there early and be prepared.

There was space for the car in the firm's small car-park. Taking her equipment with her, she asked the receptionist which room was to be used for the presentation. 'In there, the senior partner's office.' She pointed to a door across the passage. 'It's all right, you can go in. They're just laying out the food.'

Rose introduced herself and was handed a glass of wine. A cold buffet had been set out on a white sheet covering the large desk. She shuddered, recalling the last buffet she had attended.

Finally most of the staff were assembled and a smiling man was led in by a secretary. Rose captured his expression as the door opened but guessed, by how hard he tried to look surprised, that he could not have missed all the activity that had been going on during the morning.

She took two shots of the wrapped gift being handed to him by the senior partner and another of the retiring man holding the gift box open. It contained a carved wooden pipe rack and two expensive-looking pipes and, by the smile on his face when he opened it, the contents would give him far more pleasure than the ubiquitous clock.

'One more, please.' The senior partner paused. 'Ready?'

Rose nodded and focused on the two men. This time an envelope was involved but she did not get to see the amount written on the cheque it contained.

She was duly thanked and left with the rest of the day free. There were two exposures left on the roll of film; she would, as she often did, waste them. Rose tried to keep one job to one film but today, each client needing so few shots, she had used the same one.

The sky over Newlyn was darker, grey clouds banking up behind the houses built in the side of the hill. With luck she would get back before it rained and if the washing was dry she would iron it.

Maggie Anderson did not want to cut her losses but if she stayed she would antagonise Dennis further. His reaction to her arrival was violent. 'How dare you?' he had shouted when Paul had shown her in. She had not been allowed the chance to explain that her invitation to the party had been issued by Gabrielle, that she had not gate-crashed. But why should he believe it? She had not mentioned it in London. She had kept the invitation, it was still in her handbag, and it stayed there because, before she could utter another word, Dennis had gripped her by the elbow and virtually thrown her out of the house.

Later, after her encounter with Rose, Maggie had telephoned the house and left a message with the housekeeper to say where she was staying, asking Dennis to ring her. He had not returned the call and, after a second night in the hotel, Maggie knew there was no alternative but to return to London.

She paid her bill, her face gaunt, her auburn hair dull. The loose-cut trousers and blouse which hung perfectly could not make her attractive after two nights without sleep. She threw on an olive raincoat, picked up her holdall and left, unaware that an hour later Inspector Pearce came looking for her.

Once on the M5 she settled into the driving. The conditions were good; no rain to cause spray, no sun slanting at an awkward angle. The greyness overhead suited her mood. She felt bad about Rose Trevelyan; she had been arrogant in her company, behaved badly, and the woman did not deserve it. She had been the one to find the body and had probably not recovered from the shock. But why had Dennis had her to dinner? Surely he wasn't deceiving Maggie the way he had his wife? She couldn't leave it alone. She must find out.

The Cornwall she had left behind was drab and dreary, so different from the warmth of her arrival. She did not want to go back again. London was the place for her with its theatres and cinemas and restaurants and shops, where it didn't matter if it rained.

'Yes,' Jim Penrose had admitted when Eileen placed his midday meal in front of him. 'I went up there a third time. I don't know why you're making such a fuss. Mrs Milton simply wanted me to show her where the stopcock was. It was well hidden, it wasn't an excuse. Besides, I've told the police all this. Anyone'd think you suspected me. You've got more reason than me for killing her, with your nasty, jealous ways.'

'You can't deceive me, Jim Penrose.'

'The woman's dead. Let it be.'

'Attractive, wasn't she, with all that black hair? And you, touching her arm like . . .' Eileen had stopped, knowing she had gone too far.

'Touching her arm? When?' Realisation dawned. 'You bitch, you've been following me.'

Eileen turned away and busied herself at the sink. That was when he had walked out. If she had gone to those lengths, was she capable of murder? He could not bear to think of it. But the police had been back again to see her. She had not said so but he had seen them drive off as he returned the previous evening. His own interview had gone on long enough but he understood the reason. He had been on the premises three times and knew his way around. His wife was working there on the night of the party and would be otherwise occupied; if he had reason to kill Mrs Milton it was a perfect opportunity, especially as no one would be surprised to see him with Eileen being there. Mrs Milton had mentioned the party to him and, although she had phrased it subtly, he understood why he was not to be a guest. It might lead to awkwardness between husband and wife if one was present in a social capacity and the other as an employee. Had Gabrielle also had an inkling of Eileen's suspicions? If so, she had definitely done the right thing. Eileen would never have forgiven him if he had accepted an invitation.

After he had installed a shower unit in a newly converted cottage it was still only four thirty, and Jim had no more work that day. He left the van quite close to the house, handy for the morning, then took himself to the nearest pub. He did not intend his drinking to be limited by what Eileen thought was good for him, nor would he be home in time for the supper which was always on the table at six thirty.

And, he thought defiantly, I shan't go home until she's back from Bingo. That'll give her something to think about. Jim Penrose ordered his second pint of Hicks bitter.

Satisfied that the clothing she had chosen as suitable for London was ironed and in the airing cupboard, Rose wondered exactly how she would go about what she planned to do. Barry had telephoned to say he would pick her up at ten so they could reach London in time to shower and change and have a couple of drinks before dinner. The trade show was not until the day after. Barry would attend for all of the first day but only the morning of the second. It was all over by then anyway, and most of the stalls started packing up around lunchtime.

Still not having shopped, Rose drove down to Newlyn and got a Chinese take-away. It would also save washing up and she would, no matter who tried to interrupt her, have an evening at home with a book.

Only half her mind was on the radio programme she had switched on to listen to whilst she ate. Presumably the police had spoken to everyone who had been at the Miltons' that night but they didn't seem to be getting anywhere. Not that they would tell me, Rose reflected. And presumably, if more questions needed to be asked of the few people from London, the Met would deal with it.

Barry was exactly on time and Rose was ready. For the journey she was wearing trousers; her tan suit was carefully folded in her overnight bag. 'I'm looking forward to this,' she said. And she was. The prospect of two days away from work and all that had been happening was a welcome one. She would, of course, be pleased to come home again when it was over.

'Are you coming to the fair with me?'

'Not the first day. I want to do some shopping.' Of a sort, she added silently, still unsure why she was so obsessed with Gabrielle Milton's death. Perhaps it was because she had found the body and because she felt she had lost a possible friend. 'Do you know, this is the first time I've been up since David died?'

Barry glanced at her briefly, then returned his eyes to the road. It was not said with any trace of pain.

With a shock Rose realised how parochial she had allowed her life to become.

Barry took one hand off the wheel to brush back the strands of hair over his balding scalp. He had timed it well, the roads were not too busy at this hour. But shopping? In the twenty-odd years he had known Rose she had never shown the least interest in shopping. It crossed his mind she might want to purchase new clothes to impress Dennis Milton.

Rose was also thinking of Dennis. If her efforts came to nothing she would invite him over, with Paul and Anna. Paul had said she would be down again for the weekend. And what was it that Paul did that allowed him so much time off work? At dinner, Dennis had said he was staying down at least another week. Strange she had not thought to ask, she was naturally curious.

'Do you want me to drive?' Rose asked when they stopped at Exeter services for petrol and a cup of coffee.

'Think you can handle it?'

Rose narrowed her eyes. 'I've driven bigger and better cars than yours.'

'Only teasing.'

Rose took the wheel and switched on the radio. It was tuned to Radio 4. She fiddled with the knob and found a music station. She was in the mood for something livelier.

They had taken it steadily and, with the stop, reached London a little after five o'clock. The hotel had an underground car-park with a complicated security system which they finally worked out. Having registered at the desk they went up to their separate rooms. 'See you in the bar at – what? Seven? Is that too early?'

'That's fine, Barry.'

'You don't want to do any shopping first?'

'They close at five thirty!'

'I appreciate that, Rosie, dear, but I suspect it's not retail shopping you were talking about.'

'I . . .' But Barry was already striding down the corridor, turning once to smirk at her over his shoulder.

She was downstairs first and sat at the bar on a stool, absent-mindedly picking at the peanuts and olives in dishes in front of her. Showered, her hair pinned up neatly, and dressed in the tan suit, a cream shirt and heeled shoes, she had thought she would blend in with the other clientele; however, some of the women strolling through the marbled reception area, which she could see through the wide doorway, and those who entered the bar with their escorts, made her feel provincial. Suddenly she grinned. The barman smiled back and asked if she wanted another drink.

'No, thanks.' It had occurred to her, perched as she was in full view, a single female with her slim legs crossed, that she might be sending out all the wrong signals. Two businessmen came in, briefcases in hand, but they did not give her a second glance. Rose was not sure whether to be pleased or disappointed.

'Been waiting long?' Barry asked.

'No. Ten minutes.'

'Sorry. Had to make a couple of calls. What're you drinking?'

'Vodka and tonic. I didn't want to get stuck into the cocktails.'

'Have what you like, it's all going on the bill.'

'I'm paying for myself, Barry.'

The barman watched with amusement as they argued amiably about how they would settle the account. Rose finally convinced Barry that she was not prepared to let him pay but agreed the drinks could go on his room. At times like that she saw why a relationship, other than the one they had, would not have worked. Barry could be peevish at times, almost petulant, like a small child, and she became exasperated with him. He pushed his glasses firmly on to the bridge of his nose and turned away, not speaking for several minutes.

'Where shall we go to eat?'

They had glanced in at the hotel dining-room and studied the menu on the board outside but it did not appeal to them.

Rose would let him pay for the meal; she did not want any more sulking.

Enjoying the sights and sounds they strolled around and found a restaurant which they both liked. When they returned to the hotel Rose fell asleep immediately.

'Come on the train, Anna, there's no point in us having both cars here. I'll pick you up from the station.' Paul had studied the timetable Gabrielle kept handy. 'I love you,' he said, once the arrangements were made.

'Me too,' Anna replied. She replaced the receiver. With Gabrielle dead everything had changed. Paul had been fond of his mother, more than fond, unlike the way she had felt about her own parents. She had never been able to forgive them for what she thought of as their sins. She had not seen them for ten years.

Anna picked up the telephone again, dialled the number of the shop where her wedding dress was being made and arranged a time for a fitting.

At the weekend she would return to Cornwall and take stock of exactly how much Paul had inherited. It had taken her a long time to come this far.

Rose and Barry breakfasted early as Barry was due at the exhibition centre at eight thirty to get set up. 'Shall we meet back here?'

'Yes. That's easiest. About the same time? And it's my turn to pay for the meal tonight.' Rose had agreed he could pay for her room, otherwise she would never hear the end of it, but she would not allow him to pay for everything. Barry did not have time to argue.

Hoping she appeared more confident than she felt, Rose got a Tube to the area where the music company Dennis worked for was based. She found it easily and made her request to the receptionist, expecting to be asked a lot of questions or to have to see someone else. She held her breath as the girl put through a couple of incoming calls. She had got the address from Yellow Pages having remembered the name from the night of the party when Gabrielle mentioned it as they were going through the proofs. It was a company even Rose had heard of.

'Thank you, that's very kind.' Rose left the building without having to speak to anyone else. How easily she had lied and how quickly the girl had believed her. Rose had told her she was an old friend of the Miltons and had only just heard the news. She pretended to be disappointed to hear Dennis was not in the office.

'I'm not sure where he is. All I know is that he won't be back for a while yet.'

'Oh dear,' Rose had said. 'I've tried their address in Cornwall and he's not there either.'

Without having to ask, she was provided with the number and street of the London flat. The girl, presumably, thought that if Rose knew the Miltons well enough to possess one address there could be no harm in letting her have the other.

What do I expect to find there? she thought as she waited to cross the busy street. Studying the Tube map she saw the journey only involved one change.

Luck was with her. The woman who cleaned for Dennis answered the door. 'I'm only here twice a week at the moment,' she said, asking Rose in. 'Just to keep an eye on the place really. I still can't take it in, you know. Such a lovely woman.' She stopped and studied Rose suspiciously. 'We haven't met before, have we?'

'No. I've been away for quite a long time. I've only just heard myself. I thought Dennis might be here, they said at his office they weren't sure where he was.'

'He's still down there. I don't know what he'll do about the funeral.'

'Well, I'm sorry to have troubled you. Perhaps it would have been a bit much for Dennis, me turning up out of the blue. I know . . .' She paused as if the idea had just come to her. 'I could get a message to him via Paul. That way, if he doesn't want to see people there's no harm done.' She rummaged in her handbag. 'Damn it. I haven't got my diary with me.'

'I can't help you there, dear.' The woman, who had not given her name, sniffed and brushed back stiff blonde hair. 'I don't know where he lives. I know where his office is, though.'

'Fine. I'll leave a message there.'

'You can phone from here if you like. I'm sure Mr Milton wouldn't mind.'

'No, don't worry. I'd prefer to write a note.'

She listened to the directions and memorised them. Wandsworth was not an area she knew. By the time she got there it was almost lunchtime.

Standing outside the run-down premises she thought Dennis's cleaner must have been mistaken, but the sign on the fascia board confirmed that it was the right place. Paint peeled from the woodwork where the sun had blistered it and the window, through which could be seen revolving cards displaying properties, was dirty. It might be that the place was leased and the landlord responsible for outside upkeep, but surely Paul had the money for a coat of paint?

The inside was a little better.

'Can I help you?' A young man jumped up from his seat behind a teak-veneered desk.

'I'm not sure. I'm looking for a flat really, but I wasn't sure where to start.'

'Renting or buying?'

'Renting.' Rose did not want to raise the man's hopes; perhaps he would simply say they did not deal in rented accommodation.

'Actually, we've got a couple of places on the books. I'm not sure they'll be what you're after, though.' He seemed to be sizing her up. 'Of course, if you did decide to buy you wouldn't be wasting all that rent.' He turned and pulled open the drawer of a filing cabinet. 'Are you from around here?' Rose shook her head. 'You do realise how expensive things are in London?' He had detected a West Country burr. 'How many bedrooms were you thinking of?' There was a wedding band on her finger; there might be teenage children.

'Oh, two, I suppose.' How adept she was in deceit, but how mean it made her feel. 'I'm a widow,' she added, just to add some particle of truth.

'I'm sorry.'

89

'It's all right.' People always said they were sorry. How could they be, when they knew neither her nor David? But the young man was pleasant enough.

'Did you just walk in on the off-chance or did you hear of us through somebody?'

'I was passing, but I had heard of you. One of my friends knows Paul Milton. That's not you, is it?'

'No. Paul's the boss. He's away at the moment. Family problems.'

Rather an understatement, Rose thought, but he might only be aware that Gabrielle was dead, not that she had been murdered. No, impossible. The police would have made their own investigations: if this was the state of Paul's business, he might be more than keen to inherit earlier than was anticipated. She gave the man credit for his circumspection.

'May I take these with me?'

'Of course. I could take you to look at them this afternoon if you like.'

Rose was at the door. 'I'd like to study the details first. I'll let you know.' How ridiculous to imagine she could swan up to London and hope to find anything. Did she really think she was smarter than the Met? Possibly smarter than DI Pearce, though. Pearce with the laconic expression and mocking eyes who never seemed to be in a rush and was surely getting nowhere in finding Gabrielle's killer.

'Mrs, er . . . just a minute.'

Rose was surprised to see the young man in the shop doorway, locking up.

'Look, I haven't been strictly fair with you. It's just . . . well, I feel I may have wasted your time.'

'Oh?' She was not the only one who wasn't playing straight. 'Look, it's almost one. Do you fancy a quick drink and a sandwich?'

'Yes. Why not? There's a good place about a hundred yards down the road.' He turned the sign to closed and locked the door.

They walked in silence, both surprised at the situation they had found themselves in. 'My name's Gareth.'

'I'm Beth.' Rose crossed her fingers. At least it was her

mother's name. She did not want Paul or Dennis to find out she'd been snooping.

Rose insisted on paying for the drinks and they took them to a table near the frosted window. A plush bench seat ran along the length of the wall. The tables were solid, with heavy iron legs. It was a typical city pub and filling up rapidly.

The extractor fans were prominent and noisy but had little effect on the stale, heavy air or the cigarette smoke which drifted upwards in spirals. All was overlaid with the smell of chips.

'I don't know what to say really, Beth.'

He was not afraid of using her name. It was probably a good selling technique.

'Beth,' he repeated, causing her to smile. 'It suits you.' He studied her unselfconsciously. When she had been with David she had been pleased to be the object of complimentary glances because she was in a position of being safe and loved. These days, if she received them, she did not notice. What did Gareth make of her from a distance of about twenty years?

'You said you'd heard of us. How well do you know Paul Milton?'

'Not that well at all. Why do you ask?' The positions had been reversed. Rose was supposed to be asking the questions.

'It's just that if you were a friend . . . no, never mind.'

'What's bothering you, Gareth?'

'God, it's awful. I don't know what to do, and now with the police . . . Look, Paul is the boss in real terms although he persuaded me to go into partnership with him. His share of the business is the greater. To be honest, I was happy enough working for him. I like meeting people and the salary was acceptable. I wasn't going to be an estate agent for ever, I go to night classes. We were doing well and I changed my mind. Then the recession hit. And now . . . well . . .' He left another sentence unfinished.

'And now?'

'I'm not sure.'

Rose guessed he was deciding how much he could tell her without being disloyal but it was obvious he needed someone to talk to. Who better than a stranger whom he would never see again?

'I've been sitting there hour after hour in that bloody empty office and I can't get hold of Paul. There's no answer from his flat and I don't have the number in Cornwall. I'm tempted just to lock up and dump the keys through the letter-box.'

'Are you in some sort of trouble?'

'Yes. Financially, that is. We owe money all over the place. If something isn't done about it within a few days the bailiffs'll be in. Not that there's anything much for them to take. The fax and most of the electronic stuff is on lease. Paul does all the bookwork, you see. I had no idea how deeply we were in, not until the police came to speak to me about Mrs Milton's death and they began looking into Paul's financial status.'

Rose had expected it would be so but she was disappointed to hear it. Did they suspect Paul, then? Perhaps that's why he was still in Cornwall, maybe he had no choice but to remain there until the investigation was over.

'But I thought I'd heard his parents had money, couldn't they have helped him out?'

Gareth shook his head. The mid-brown hair, brushed back and gelled, remained motionless. 'They've bailed him out before. From what I gather they've refused to do so again. At least I haven't got a girlfriend at the moment. Paul's got Anna to think of. They're supposed to be getting married.'

Things were falling into place. No wonder they had brought forward their wedding; Anna did not look the sort to put up with making do. If Gabrielle had left them the house it would sell for a lot of money, enough probably for Paul to start up in something else.

'I was so worried,' Gareth was saying. 'You see, initially, I thought . . . well, I thought Paul may have done it. Killed his mother.'

Only when spoken aloud, and by somebody other than herself, did the enormity of one of the possibilities Rose had been considering hit her.

It was strange how looks and a certain sort of upbringing could lead to misconceptions. Paul dressed and spoke nicely and exuded confidence even though he was not very talkative in her presence. She had put his manner down to grief, not realising how many other worries he had; Paul's careful upbringing had not done him much good.

'Beth? Another drink?'

'Oh, yes, please.' Barry would have been amazed to know how long she had been sitting nursing an empty glass.

'I'm sorry, I've been boring you. I just wanted you to know that if you had decided on any of those flats I'm not sure that the deal would've gone ahead.'

'Thank you for being honest,' Rose said, knowing what a hypocrite she was.

'Well . . .' He grinned. It was a nice smile. 'You've helped me make up my mind. I'm not going back there. I'll post the keys to Paul's house and write him a letter. As soon as I get another job I'll start repaying whatever my share of the debt is. Thanks for listening. You're a nice lady. You remind me of my mum.'

'Cheers.' Rose raised her glass sardonically. She could have done without the last comment.

The conversation moved on to more general topics, then Rose said she had to leave. There was time, after all, to do some shopping. Maybe a dress which she would wear this evening – that would make Barry eat his words.

'Nice meeting you, Beth.' Gareth shook her hand. 'Poor old Paul, there's nothing he wouldn't do for Anna and I think the reverse is also true. They idolise one another.'

Was it intended, Rose wondered, to be a deliberate parting shot? Was Gareth trying to tell her something? He did, she noticed, walk away in the opposite direction from that in which the shop lay.

As she stood on the pavement orientating herself she recalled what Barry had said about Paul trying to gain his father's attention. Had he been trying to talk Dennis into lending or giving him more money? And, having failed, had he taken things into his own hands? And if he was so devoted to Anna – if, as he claimed, there was nothing he would not do to make her happy – wasn't this another motive? So why had he and Anna been arguing?

The dress was of pale-blue wool, fully lined and so very soft to the touch. Rose saw it and had to have it. She only shook a little as she signed the credit card slip but it flattered her and brought out the colour of her eyes.

Not until she was half-way down Regent Street did she realise she had no shoes to match. The court shoes she had brought to go with the suit were tan.

With a little shrug she returned to Oxford Street to find a shoe shop. It's only money, she thought, and heard the oft-repeated phrase used in West Cornwall for any and every eventuality: 'Madder do er?' It had taken her several weeks to discover this meant 'It doesn't matter, does it?' and only the upward inflection at the end had given it away.

Back at the hotel she had enough time for a soak in the bath, much needed after the grime of the city. The dress was on a hanger, the navy shoes by the bed. She had taken the precaution of rubbing soap around the heels. Her tendency to wear espadrilles or sandals all summer made winter shoes rub initially.

Why, as she soaped herself, Jack Pearce should come into her mind was a mystery, but she saw his face clearly. Ought she to say where she had been? No, there was no need. The police had already spoken to Gareth.

'Wow. Terrific,' was all Barry said when she met him that evening.

Too late Rose realised Barry might believe she was all dressed up for his benefit.

Doreen Clarke, clad in a raincoat and with a woollen hat pulled down over her straight grey hair, got into Cyril's car feeling like a schoolgirl let out early. The Miltons were going out in the evening and she need not return that day.

'Can't make that girl out at all,' she said, strapping the seat belt around her. 'Doesn't say much. Nervy sort, if you ask me. Still, if there's a big wedding coming up it's hardly surprising.'

Cyril waited patiently for traffic to pass before he negotiated the roundabout at the bottom of the hill.

'*He's* all right, Mr Milton – not quite as classy as his wife, but his heart's in the right place. I heard them talking about the will. Seems the solicitor's been on the phone. Apparently they were going to do it proper, like – you know, have it read out after the funeral, though God knows when that'll take place. Seems the police've got there first. They wanted to know what was in it, who'd benefit.'

Cyril waited. He wondered how his wife had been privy to this conversation. It was not the sort of thing discussed in front of the daily. He did not put her in an awkward position by asking.

'Cyril? Aren't you interested?'

'Yes. I was waiting for you to go on.'

'Well, I couldn't hear the rest of it because of all the shouting. All hell was let lose, I can tell you. Do you think they'll put it in the paper? How much she left?'

'I doubt it. They usually only do that when there're no beneficiaries or if one person receives an enormous figure.'

'Well, they might, if it's relevant to the murder. I hope they do.'

Cyril let her continue talking. No doubt Doreen would find out what the sum was through one means or another.

'You won't mind if I go to Bingo, will you?' Doreen had not been for several weeks. Mostly she went with Maureen but since Eileen had started going too, she had taken to going with a neighbour. Maureen was a laugh; she could not understand how two sisters could be so unalike.

'You enjoy yourself, love. You haven't had a night out for ages.'

By his complaisant smile Doreen guessed there would be football on the television.

She rang the neighbour, Teresa, and arranged to call for her. They always had one drink first, a whisky and lime for Doreen, and a bottle of Pils for her friend. After the session, in which Teresa shared a win and picked up four pounds, they returned to the pub. It was much busier now with only half an hour or so before last orders were called. It was Teresa's turn to buy the round.

They watched the other customers, easy in each other's company. A group of men were discussing rugby; there were several couples and a pair in their late teens in the corner. 'Look at them,' Doreen said. 'It's embarrassing to watch. I don't know why they've wasted their money on drink. They might as well go home to bed and get on with it.'

'Doreen!' Teresa laughed and turned to see if she knew who the couple were. 'Jesus! Don't look now, but you'll never guess who's just come in.'

'Who? My, my. Fancy that.' Doreen stared openly at Jim Penrose and Rita Chynoweth as they entered the bar, arm in arm and both, she guessed, the worse for wear.

'Wait till Eileen hears about this. Still, it won't be from me.'

'Nor me,' Doreen said. But she would have liked to be there when Eileen did hear.

Barry was startled when Rose produced a small plastic bag and handed it to him. 'A gift,' she said.

'Isn't it a bit . . . well . . . modern for me?' He held the loudly patterned tie away from him as if it was offensive.

'No. Everyone's wearing them. It'll go with that jacket you got in Burton's sale. You should splash out more, you've nothing else to spend your fortune on.'

I'd spend my money on you, Rosie, he thought. 'Thank you.' He kissed her cheek, which was the only intimacy she ever allowed him. 'Ok. Let's go and eat.' Barry was too moved to add anything further.

'I could get hooked on this.' Rose stirred the cocktail she was drinking.

'You'd get hooked on tap water if someone told you it was alcoholic. You still coming with me tomorrow?'

'Yes.' She had had enough of the Miltons. Her obsession, she realised, was fading. And it would be interesting to see if anyone was keen to buy any of her work in its finished form.

The following day left them both exhausted, and Barry drove off as soon as he had delivered Rose to her door. The trade fair had been busier during the second morning than Barry had anticipated, then there was the packing up and the long drive back.

Rose had looked around the fair but had to admit, after two hours, she was bored. She whiled away the time drinking coffee. They had toyed with the idea of staying a third night and driving back slowly the next day but it would have been unfair on the woman who had come in to run the shop in Barry's absence.

Rose drove for the first part of the journey home and they stopped again at the same services; she was fascinated by the crowds of people and asked Barry where he thought they could all be going. It was warm and they were surrounded with the smell of food. Rose could see how tired Barry was and insisted they drive with the radio on and the windows open.

It was with a sense of relief that she let herself in, threw on the light switches and dumped her holdall on the bottom stair. 'We'll get our priorities right here,' she said aloud, reaching for the corkscrew and a bottle of claret. They had not had a drink as both of them were driving. She carried the glass through to the sitting-room. The light on the answering machine was flashing twice rapidly in succession before a short pause. She clicked it on. 'I don't particularly wish to leave a message,' Laura's voice told her, 'but as your social life's so full lately, I suppose I'll have to. I'll call round in the morning. I want to hear every sordid detail of your two nights in London.'

Rose smiled. Typical Laura. Straight in with what she wanted to say and no clue as to who was calling. Except that, after all those years, Rose could not mistake her voice.

'Mrs Trevelyan,' the second message started. This was a voice she did not know. Rose sat on the chair nearest the telephone with a pen and paper handy. 'It's Maggie Anderson. I'd hoped to catch you at home. It's now six thirty. If it's convenient I'll try again later.'

But six thirty when? Tonight or yesterday? If it had been the previous day Maggie may have got tired of getting nothing but the machine. No, it had to be tonight. Laura knew when she was due back and had said she would see her in the morning. Maggie's call had come after Laura's.

With a second glass of wine beside her, Rose ate some cheese on toast which was all she was up to making and thought over the events of the last two days. Tomorrow, maybe, she would commit those thoughts to paper.

At eleven thirty she pulled the duvet up around her ears and turned on her side with the intention of reading. When she woke the bedside light was still on and her book was on the floor, pages splayed. Maggie Anderson had not rung back.

Laura did not stay long once she had learned that Rose and Barry had remained in their separate rooms. Chewing her lip as she wondered if it was wise to invite Dennis to her home, Rose dialled the number anyway. He accepted the invitation on behalf of the three of them, having spoken briefly to Paul – he must have been in the same room for Rose heard a muffled conversation. Anna, who had not yet arrived down from London, was not to be consulted, it seemed.

It was a blustery day, the windows rattled and the first of the falling leaves were swept across the lawn. Rose made coffee and took it up to the dark-room where she developed the film containing the two jobs she had done the previous week. As she worked she planned what she would cook for the Miltons, a task she looked forward to. Apart from the occasional visit from Laura or Barry she had only herself to cater for and, although she ate well, she would enjoy having to make a real effort.

Mid-morning it began raining again. Rose flicked the switch and the kitchen was bright, the overhead fluorescent light dispelling the shadows. With a dog-eared cookery book open in front of her she made a shopping list. When the phone rang she half expected it to be Dennis, cancelling the arrangement.

'Mrs Trevelyan? It's Maggie Anderson. I'm sorry I didn't get back to you last night. I . . . well, I wanted to apologise. I was rude to you that day in Camborne. I hope you don't mind me ringing.'

'No.' Rose was puzzled. She had known something wasn't quite right when they had that one drink together and it had crossed her mind that the woman might try to contact her. But why? 'I was surprised at what you told me, I didn't think you were particularly rude.'

'I shouldn't have said anything. There was no reason for me to involve you.'

'It's all right. I shan't say anything.' Not to Dennis or his family or anyone else, but she had already told DI Pearce. To have hidden it, she excused herself, might be classed as shielding a suspect. Both Dennis and Maggie might have wished for Gabrielle to be out of the way.

'Thank you. It's too late for that, though. The police came to see me again last night. That's why I was unable to call you back. It's the second time since I've been home.'

During the pause Rose sensed her anxiety. 'Do they suspect you?'

'Yes. But I didn't do it. God, if only I could turn the clock back. I should never have accepted that invitation. And Dennis won't have anything to do with me, I believe he might suspect me too.'

Maggie Anderson was paying for her sins and Rose felt some sympathy. There was little she could say to her, and she was not really sure why Maggie had rung. Why apologise to someone you had spoken to once and you were not likely to come across again? Unless it was a ploy – perhaps Maggie hoped she'd put in a good word for her with Dennis. But Rose was not going to interfere. A bit late for that, she thought, when the conversation had come to a faltering end. Why else had she invited the Miltons over?

When the rain stopped she walked down to the shops and purchased what she would need for the following evening plus staples for the fridge. Not fancying a struggle up the hill with the groceries she stood at the bus stop where several other people were already waiting. When a car she did not recognise tooted, Rose did not, at first, realise that DI Pearce was behind the wheel. He leant across to the passenger side. 'Need a lift?' he asked through the partially opened window.

She hesitated, feeling curious eyes upon her. 'Thank you,' she said coolly and got into the car.

'Home, I take it?'

'Please.' She remained silent, wondering why he was in Newlyn and hoping it was not because he needed to speak to her again.

He pulled in off the road but was unable to get into the drive. His car was too large and Rose's was parked there anyway. 'Do I get invited in for coffee? You do make nice coffee.'

'Really? You left it last time. I do have things to do.' She had imagined his tone was playful.

'I, too, have things to do, Mrs Trevelyan,' he replied, letting her see her mistake. 'I have to find whoever killed Gabrielle Milton. Can you spare me a few minutes?'

'Yes.' It was an official visit then. How stupid of her to have thought otherwise. She tried to ignore her disappointment.

DI Pearce did not offer to carry her shopping. She dumped it on the back doorstep and unlocked the door, leaving him to follow and shut it behind him. Silently she filled the kettle. It would be instant this time.

'Mrs Trevelyan –'

'Oh, for goodness sake, call me Rose.'

'Rose, then. I asked you before if you knew of anyone who would wish Mrs Milton harm. You assured me you did not. You claim you barely knew the lady. You also claimed you had never set eyes on Miss Anderson before the party either.'

'It's true.' Rose jumped to her own defence. Jack Pearce irritated her.

'All right. But I find it hard to understand, if you have so little interest in the family, why you've been poking around in London, turning up at the Miltons' flat and questioning Paul Milton's partner.'

Rose felt the colour flooding into her face. Put like that, she sounded like an interfering old bag.

'What you told us, about Miss Anderson, has been very helpful but I find it surprising that she confided such a matter to a stranger. Can you enlighten me?'

'No. I don't know why she did it. And she telephoned to apologise for doing so. Perhaps she just wanted to get it off her chest.' Better to admit to the call; the way Pearce was getting at her she wouldn't be surprised if he had tapped her line.

'Possibly. Another possibility is that she thinks you know something; that she is trying to cultivate your friendship in order to find out what it is.'

'You have a nasty mind, inspector.'

'It's a nasty job, Rose. What were you aiming to do? In London?'

'I don't know.' She tightened the band around her hair for something to do with her hands, feeling like a scolded child. 'Maybe you think I killed Gabrielle. Is that why you keep coming here?'

'It crossed my mind.'

She had, she realised, asked for that. Naturally everyone who had attended that evening would be under suspicion. And she had found the body. 'I never went upstairs.'

'Upstairs?'

'She was pushed from the balcony.'

'Was she? Now who told you that?'

'Well, I assumed . . . we all assumed . . .' She stopped, knowing each time she opened her mouth she made herself appear more of a fool in DI Pearce's eyes.

'Assumptions are dangerous things, Rose.' Absent-mindedly he heaped four spoonfuls of sugar into his coffee and stirred it. 'However, I have it on good authority you would not be capable of murder.'

'Oh?'

'Your friend, Laura.' He smiled. 'I bumped into her the other day.' Rose Trevelyan, he thought, is extremely uncomfortable in my presence, but her feelings do not arise out of guilt.

Rose, as if realising the impression she was making, sat down, glad she was wearing a Viyella checked shirt and a newish pair of cords. She was not at quite such a disadvantage as the other times he had seen her. She had forgotten about first impressions, and that Jack Pearce's initial sight of her had been when she was dressed for the party. 'I see. You make a habit of discussing suspects or witnesses with their best friends, do you?' She was furious to think Laura had chatted with him in such a manner.

'We make a habit of speaking to anyone who knows anyone at such times. But if it makes you feel better, it was a chance meeting and your name came into the conversation.'

Rose stood up and began unpacking the groceries, hoping he would take it as a hint to leave. She had not done anything illegal, he must know that.

'You like a drink?' He nodded at the wine rack and at the two bottles she had bought at the Co-op to go with the meal she would cook for the Miltons.

'Is that any of your business as long as I don't go out in the car?' She could not be civil to him. He seemed to fill the kitchen and, always, he seemed to be enjoying a private joke at her expense.

'No offence meant. I like wine myself.'

'It's for a dinner. I have asked the Miltons over. It's easier for me to tell you now, it'll save you another journey.'

Jack surprised her by ignoring the comment. He stood up to leave. 'The filter coffee's better,' he said, 'but thanks anyway. And Rose?'

'Yes?'

'Don't get involved. I don't think you realise quite what you're dealing with.'

So that was the reason for this appearance; to warn her off. Did he already know something? He had not said she was not to socialise with the Miltons, therefore there was no reason not to go ahead.

When she lay in bed that night she went over all she had learned, but it was what she had not found out that puzzled her. It might be that tomorrow evening would provide the solution.

Before she fell asleep she thought about sex. She missed it, missed David's warm body next to hers, although she had not done so during the months of his illness. Too many other things had taken priority then. Since his death she had been out with only one man – apart from Barry, with whom her relationship was platonic – and Rose knew she had been rushing things. Lonely and miserable, she had tried to find a replacement. Within a fortnight she knew that a husband could not be replaced, that one day, in the distant future, she might meet someone whom she wanted to live with or even marry, but he would not be a substitute, he would be someone she loved.

Living alone had made her selfish, made her think it would be ideal to have a man for company when she required it and who would fulfil her baser needs when necessary without making any demands on her. She smiled to herself. But I wouldn't like a man who allowed me to treat him that way, she thought.

She had no idea how sex had come into her head. And she didn't even like Jack Pearce.

Rose hummed as she worked with the radio on, enjoying the distraction of preparing three courses. Hopefully Dennis and Paul would have regained their appetites. Would they notice if she wore the same outfit she had bought for the party? Anna might, but not the men, surely, and it did not matter, as long as it did not act as a reminder.

'Come in.' Rose held open the front door, suddenly experiencing nervousness at entertaining three people she hardly knew.

'I brought some wine,' Dennis said. 'And it really is very kind of you to have us. I didn't know as many people as Gabrielle, but I get the feeling we're being avoided,' he added as she showed them into the sitting-room.

'People don't always know what to say. They feel embarrassed.'

'I expect you're right.'

'Anna, I didn't get a chance to speak to you before. I'm glad you could come.' Rose's social graces seemed to be in order. She poured drinks and explained they would be eating in the kitchen. Then she excused herself to attend to the food. Anna, she thought, was polite enough but not a great conversationalist. With her figure and colouring she was stunning but seemed a little ill at ease, although that was understandable. Satisfied that the table looked elegant and that there was nothing lying around which shouldn't have been, she told them that the meal was ready.

Dennis initiated the conversation once they were seated, commenting again on how comfortable and welcoming Rose's home was. He was more relaxed, less grey-faced than before; Paul, too, had lost some of his tenseness and was, on this third meeting, almost animated.

'Anna's had the last fitting for her dress,' he informed Rose. 'It's had to be taken in again. Pre-wedding nerves, on top of everything else, I expect.' He smiled fondly at his fiancée. 'At least she's enjoying your cooking tonight.'

'I'm not a very good cook,' Anna admitted, 'but I'm learning. If we find someone like Mrs Clarke she won't be there all the time. Still, I expect as Paul makes more and more business contacts we'll also eat out quite a lot.'

There was an uncomfortable pause which Anna misinterpreted. Father and son exchanged a quick glance but neither spoke of Paul's financial difficulties.

They had eaten a sea-food salad. Rose cleared away the plates and poured more wine before dishing up roast lamb spiked with slivers of garlic and several bowls of vegetables. She had not prepared a roast for years; as Doreen Clarke had produced a plain and simple meal she had not risked anything too rich in case it was not to the Miltons' taste. Hopefully she had not overdone the garlic.

Saturday night and I'm jollying along a bereaved man, his virtually bankrupt son and his beautiful but edgy girlfriend, Rose thought as she carved the meat, not very neatly.

Handing around the plates she smiled at the irony. It was herself she had believed needed cheering up. Perhaps she should take up good works as a full-time occupation, it must be good for the soul.

'What is it you do, Paul?' Only when she had asked the question did Rose realise Gareth may have mentioned her visit. She had given a different name but DI Pearce knew about it: presumably Gareth had provided a description.

'I'm in the property business. In London.' It sounded impressive put like that.

'And you, Anna?' Rose handed her the mint sauce.

'I'm with a firm of fashion buyers. We're working on the summer collections now.'

'It must be difficult, always being several seasons ahead.'

'You get used to it.'

Rose wondered how the pastel outfit stood up to inspection. Anna was wearing a coat-dress. 'So, has anything been decided about the house yet?' No mention had been made of the photographs she had taken. Rose would have to cut her losses.

'I'll have to sell,' replied Dennis. 'I've been on to my office. Well, to be frank, I took the bull by the horns and asked if the rumours were true. I explained I needed to know my position. It'll be put in writing, but I shall, as they phrased it, be taking voluntary redundancy. With that, and what I make from the sale of both properties, I'll get a small place down here and take my chances. I wouldn't be happy in London now.'

'But Gabrielle said –'

Dennis interrupted whatever Anna had been about to say. 'Whatever Gabrielle said doesn't count. She has left everything to me.'

'No!' Anna thumped the table. 'No. That's impossible.'

Rose stared from one to another, her hand reaching out to steady her wineglass.

'Anna.' Dennis and Paul spoke together. Her face was scarlet.

'It's true,' Dennis said quietly. 'The police needed to know what was in the will.' There was no need to elucidate; they all knew the reasons for that. 'Maybe she intended changing it and was killed before she could do so, but I think not.'

The pallor had returned to Paul's face. 'Hasn't she left me anything at all?'

'I'm afraid not. You see, your mother and I felt we had

bailed you out enough times, that you'd never be a success if we continued to do so. I think she did it for your own good.'

'It's all right, Paul.' Anna laid a hand on his arm. 'Your father won't let you down.'

'Let him down? What do you mean?' Dennis was puzzled.

Rose watched the interplay silently. It was hard to believe that she was in her own kitchen, harder still to accept that her guests were so freely discussing Gabrielle's will in front of her. Curiosity was one thing but she felt embarrassed although she did not interrupt.

'Paul needs an injection of cash if he is to succeed. Gabrielle always promised she would do the best for Paul. I'm sure you won't go back on her word, Dennis. She told me we had nothing to worry about. It won't be easy getting married if we haven't any money.'

'Other people manage.' Rose was surprised to hear her own indignant voice. 'David and I started from nothing.'

'But I expect you were used to not having very much.'

It was true but Rose still felt it was no justification for Anna to try to manipulate her future father-in-law. At least by the way the couple were looking at each other they seemed to be in love.

Paul stepped in. He could not bear to see Anna distressed and he felt he owed an explanation for what seemed to be a mercenary streak. 'Anna's not had an easy life, I wanted to repair that damage. She found out accidentally that she was adopted but her sister wasn't. Her parents claimed they wanted to wait until she was older to tell her. You can imagine the shock.'

Rose could, but others survived unscarred, and money would not heal that particular trauma.

'After that she lived with an aunt and then, just when she thought she'd finally found security, the person she was going to marry let her down. You can see why money has become important.'

I can understand, Rose thought, but she's also using the past to gain sympathy. She wondered if Anna realised the pain she must have caused her adoptive parents who had cared for her and loved her. But she would not judge too harshly even though Anna seemed to show little grief or sorrow for the dead woman's family. It was obvious that she loved Paul.

Their plates were not quite empty but the food had gone cold so Rose removed them from the table; she regretted issuing the invitation. Turning back from the draining board she saw the faces of all three before they had a chance to compose themselves. Dennis was staring at the young couple with a mixture of bewilderment and despair; Anna was tight-lipped, upright in her chair, while Paul reached out and took her hand. There were two spots of colour across his high cheekbones yet he did not seem angry.

'Would anyone like coffee?' Rose wanted them to leave and decided not to offer them the fruit salad she had made.

'No, I think we ought to go.' Dennis stood. 'It was a lovely meal, Rose. Thank you. I'm sorry if we appeared rude.'

At the front door Paul shook her hand and thanked her too but was obviously anxious to get Anna on her own. Anna smiled weakly and waited for the men to walk on to the car. Then she turned to face Rose. 'I enjoyed the meal and I appreciate your concern for the family but I don't think you're being very fair to Dennis.'

'Oh?' Rose blinked in surprise.

'It's too soon after Gabrielle's death to expect him to be interested in other women.' Before Rose could answer Anna had hurried down the path.

Rose stood motionless in the doorway. Was that how Anna saw her? As a single woman who was only interested in Dennis for his money, perhaps hoping to marry him for that reason? She shook her head in disbelief. It had been a disastrous evening and one she did not intend to repeat. Besides, Anna seemed unaware of Dennis's own financial position. Unless he managed to find another job locally he would have to invest whatever he inherited wisely. Then another thought occurred to her: just how much did Gabrielle have to leave? There might be a considerable sum as well as the house.

'Don't,' she said aloud as she scraped the food from the plates into the bin. 'Don't think about it.'

She could not face the washing up. Once the remains of the

107

joint were in the fridge and the fruit salad dish covered with film she went to the sitting-room and sat in the dark looking out over the soothing aspect of the harbour and the bay until some sort of peace returned.

8

'I'm going to bed,' Anna said as soon as they reached the house.

'I need to talk to you.'

'Not now, Paul. In the morning.'

Paul went to join his father in the lounge but there was nothing to be gained there either. Dennis sat staring moodily towards the drawn curtains unable to cope with the conflicting emotions he was experiencing. For the first time the real magnitude of what had happened hit him and he realised he would never see Gabrielle again. Maggie no longer counted, she would not be part of his future. She must have guessed that by now but when Paul had gone to bed he would telephone her to make it clear. It was only fair. Strange, he thought, now it was too late, he wanted to do the right thing by everyone.

'The police don't seem to be doing very much, do they?' Paul wanted to get his father talking. He had tried, on the night his mother was killed, to ask him for a loan or for payment in advance of whatever money he was due to inherit later. But he did not want to dive straight in with a request for cash.

'They wouldn't tell us if they were. We're all suspects. Why do you think they keep coming back? Look, Paul, I'm not in the mood for conversation, on this or any other topic. If you don't mind, I'd like to be alone.'

Paul shrugged and left the room. Tomorrow would have to do, although he had hoped to be able to tell Anna everything was sorted out.

Dennis poured a brandy, knowing he did not need or want

it. What he did need was a night's sleep but the bedroom he was using felt wrong. At first he had been forbidden use of his own room but now the police tape had been removed he could not face the double bed he had shared with Gabrielle. Sometimes he stood in the doorway and, although he was sure it was not possible, he thought her perfume lingered in the air. What he did know was that all pretence of being a happy family had gone.

Rose woke to a clear blue sky and a boisterous wind. She opened several windows, thinking that a through-draught would rid the house of the contamination of last night's visitors.

Studying her face in the bathroom mirror she thought she looked tired, but otherwise the same Rose. She had never been beautiful, but she had grown into her looks and men considered her to be attractive. She had always been comfortable with her body and face and had not really given them much thought. She groaned as she remembered the dishes waiting to be washed. And there was a baby to be photographed. Sunday was the only time that was convenient for the family, which Rose found odd. However, work was work.

Dishes done, she threw on an old jacket and drove into Penzance. That was the only problem with the photography side: the equipment was too heavy to lug about on foot.

The baby was plump and dimpled. 'She's born to it,' Rose told the mother as the child gazed straight at her, gurgling and beaming. It was to be a record of her first birthday.

The wind was dying down and there were quite a few people enjoying a walk along the front. Further out were several white-sailed yachts. She promised herself a long walk after lunch, a lunch which would consist of cold lamb and salad.

She had been tempted to have a quiet word with Dennis, to let him know Gabrielle had sent the invitation to Maggie Anderson, but that would be playing into Maggie's hands. And it might not be true. Rose had guessed Maggie wanted

110

her to put in a good word for her. And Gabrielle was no longer around to defend herself.

Rose braked suddenly. She had almost crossed the roundabout without giving way to an oncoming car. What if Dennis knew that his wife knew about Maggie? What if Dennis also knew that his wife was about to change her will in Paul's favour for that very reason? How much more of a motive did that give him, especially as he was concerned about losing his job?

Stop being melodramatic, she told herself. The police had to be aware of these facts. Yet they had not arrested Dennis. She reminded herself that there were about forty people present that evening, apart from anyone who might have arrived unseen.

She seemed to recall that the inquest was to be held soon. How long would it be before Gabrielle was allowed a funeral? Rose was not sure if she would attend: they were not close, but it might be rude not to. It would be the first since David's.

She should have known that she would pass Laura, who was on her way up to see her. Trevor had been home for several days but was now back at sea.

'You've been out early for a Sunday,' Laura said as she climbed into the passenger seat.

'I had a job.'

'How did it go? With the Milton clan?'

'Don't even talk about it.'

'That bad?'

'That bad. How's things with you?'

'Improving. I tarted myself up and persuaded Trevor to take me out for a meal. We've had a long talk and we've both agreed to make some compromises. It's not exactly bliss, but it's one hell of a lot better than it has been.'

'Good.'

Laura looked at her slyly. 'Jack Pearce was asking about you.'

'I heard.' They had reached the house. Rose pulled on the handbrake and killed the ignition. She turned to meet Laura's eyes. 'And what exactly did you tell him?'

'Only what he wanted to hear. That you aren't a murderess.

111

Like I said, he fancies you. Now come on, woman, I'm gasping for a cup of coffee.'

There were no messages on the answering machine, for which Rose was grateful. An hour with Laura, then she would have the afternoon to herself. If it didn't rain she would clear the tubs of the summer flowers which were becoming brown and untidy.

Laura sensed her friend was not in a communicative mood. 'You're not upset, are you?'

'About what?'

'About me discussing you with Jack. I didn't say anything that you couldn't have listened to.'

'No, I'm not upset.' She smiled to show it was true.

Laura got up to leave. Rose watched her bob down the path, her long legs thin in her leggings, her hair blowing this way and that in the blustery wind. She looks better, Rose thought, happier. She wondered just how serious her problems had been.

She was staring into the fridge when a tap on the side window made her jump. 'Oh, sodding hell,' she said, hoping it was loud enough for Jack Pearce to have heard her. 'Yes? What is it now?'

'May I come in?'

Rose did not answer. He took this to mean yes. 'I'm not staying. I was on my way to my mother's actually. Mr Milton asked me to give you this.' He handed her an envelope. Rose took it from him, frowning in confusion. It was unaddressed. She tore it open with her thumbnail. Inside was a cheque, made out to her and for a sum which meant nothing.

'He said it was for the photographs.'

'But he's only had the proofs.'

Jack shrugged. 'Nothing to do with me. He simply said he remembered you hadn't been paid for your work and apologised for leaving it so long.'

'He could have posted it, or brought it personally.'

'He wasn't sure if that was possible.'

'Why? What's happened? Where is Dennis?'

'He's in Camborne at the moment.' He waited to see what her reaction would be.

Rose realised the implications of what he was saying. Dennis, then, was helping with inquiries or whatever euphemism it was they used for hauling someone in. His remembering she had not been paid could be interpreted in converse ways: a guilty man wishing to repay any debts before being locked up, an innocent man remembering a chore because he had nothing else on his conscience. She was not going to ask.

'In case you believe we're not doing anything, we're going through a process of elimination.'

'Like Sherlock Holmes, no doubt.'

'I'm sorry?'

'You know, when you've ruled out the impossible, whatever remains, however improbable, must be the answer. Something like that, I can't remember.'

'Are you a Conan Doyle fan?'

'Not particularly. And I don't wish to spend Sunday afternoon discussing literature. Besides, your mother'll have your dinner on the table by now.'

Jack Pearce's mouth tightened. He exhaled slowly, then said, 'I do not expect my mother to run around after me. I'm taking her out to lunch. Then I shall spend the afternoon playing cards with her. She's almost eighty and half crippled with arthritis and she's lost most of her friends. I suspect she's lonely and I am unable to see her as often as I'd like.'

'I'm sorry.' Rose turned away. What a bitch I am, she thought, and a hypocrite. She had shown no mercy to Anna either.

'It's OK, you weren't to know.' And then he spoiled it. 'I did use to have a wife to run around after me, though.'

When Rose looked up she saw he was smiling and changed her mind about the retort she had been about to make. And now he had made his marital status clear to her. Why? 'Used to?'

'She left me.' There were no excuses, no explanations, just the honest statement.

'I'm widowed.'

'Yes, I know.'

Of course he did, he would have made inquiries into the background of everyone who was at the party. 'Well, you'd better not keep your mother waiting.'

'Hint taken. I don't know why you're so prickly with me,

113

Rose. I find it strange when everyone tells me what a nice person you are.'

She did not rise to the bait. No way was she going to ask who else he had been discussing her with. 'Inspector Pearce, I hope you're not going to formally arrest Dennis Milton. He didn't do it, you know.'

'Oh?'

'I'm sure he didn't.'

'Ah, the old gut reaction. Still, it's often right. Now, I really must go.' He managed to make it sound as if she had deliberately been trying to detain him. 'You'll be pleased to know we no longer consider you to be a suspect.'

'I –'

'But you are still a witness. However, I'd like to take you out to dinner, as a friend. And if anyone asks, I'm making further inquiries. May I telephone you tomorrow for your answer?'

'I –' For the second time Rose was lost for words. The door crashed behind him before she could speak.

Later that afternoon she telephoned the Milton house. Doreen Clarke answered. 'No one's here at the minute. Can I take a message?'

'No, it's all right, thanks, Doreen, I'll call back later.'

'Have you heard?'

'Heard what?' She might have to explain from whom she had heard if she admitted anything.

'All hell's broken loose over this way. First Mr Milton gets taken away in a police car, then Eileen Penrose's shot her mouth off and got Jim dragged into it too. Well, there's nothing in it, of course, we all know why she's done it.' Rose had lost track of the conversation but knew Doreen would continue anyway. 'Eileen found out Jim had taken another woman out. She must've told the police he was always at it and coupled his name with Mrs Milton's. Me and Cyril think she's probably gone and told them he was up at the house that night. He *was* out with someone though, me and a friend saw him.'

'I expect the police'll sort it out. "Bye now.' Could it be that simple? Rose wondered when she replaced the receiver. Was this Jim Penrose a womaniser, one with a jealous wife, one who needed to kill his lover to prevent her from dropping him in it? For now Rose had other things on her mind. What answer was she going to give Jack Pearce tomorrow?

Jim Penrose had walked brazenly and deliberately into the pub knowing that at that time of night there would be quite a few customers he knew. He had met Rita Chynoweth by chance in another pub. Although there was no proof that she shared her sexual favours with anyone who asked, rumour declared it was so. Rita was unperturbed and had taken to dressing the part: tight jeans over amply fleshed thighs were complemented by a white knitted top which stopped short of her midriff, exposing a comfortable roll of brown flesh which rested on a studded leather belt. Around her shoulders was a red leather jacket. On her arm was Jim Penrose.

Seeing Doreen and Teresa in the corner had prompted her to clutch at her escort as they came through the door. She flung back her hair, which was dyed a reddish purple.

Jim had noticed the women too. It would be interesting to see what Eileen had to say when presented with what she would assume was unquestionable proof of his guilt.

It took several days before it got back to Eileen when she overheard, as she was meant to, a conversation in the green-grocer's. She purchased her vegetables and went home planning Jim's punishment.

When he came in for his evening meal he saw by her face that things were not right but, surprisingly, she said nothing. An hour later the police arrived.

Rose telephoned the author she had photographed and asked if it was convenient for her to bring around the contact sheet from which he could make his choice. It was ready but there was no hurry, Rose simply wanted to be out of the house in case Jack rang early. She had not made up her mind what to say to him.

She was out no more than an hour. The light on the answering machine glowed but was not flashing. No one had telephoned.

It was not until six fifteen whilst she was clearing up watercolours and brushes from the table where she had been completing some sketches that the telephone rang.

'Hello?'

'Rose? It's me, Jack.'

She waited.

'Are you free this evening?'

'This evening?' She hadn't washed her hair. Which means, she thought, that I intended saying yes.

'I know it's short notice, but I can't guarantee another night this week.'

'I . . . er . . . OK.'

'Good. I'll pick you up about eight. Anywhere you particularly like?'

'No.'

She ran a bath and looked through the small cupboard in her bedroom which served as a wardrobe. She picked a skirt, gathered at the waist, in striking shades of orange and red and black. It wasn't really the weather for boots but she had no suitable shoes to go with it. Her top was a black leotard.

She was ready by seven thirty and tried to read but found herself watching the minutes ticking by on the carriage clock on the mantelpiece.

Jack Pearce was fifteen minutes late.

'I'm sorry. Work.'

'It's all right.' Rose was cool; she was not sure whether she would have preferred him not to have turned up. It was all too unsettling.

'Can we call a truce?' Jack asked as they headed towards Penzance. 'And I would appreciate your opinion on some of the people involved.'

'I see. You want me to be your . . . what's the word? Grass? Informer?'

Jack laughed loudly. 'You slay me, Rose Trevelyan. I just meant that, being an artist, you must have an eye for detail.'

'Oh.'

'I bought my wife one of your paintings once.'

116

'You did? Which one was it?' Rose, like many artists, had her work on display in local shops and cafés. Occasionally she sold a few that way, others were commissioned through word of mouth or sold via galleries which handled several artists' work.

'I don't know. It was a view of Land's End. Before it was ruined,' he added, referring to the theme park.

'You feel the same as me, then. I suppose tourists need things like that but I liked it as it was. Just the cliffs and the sea.'

'And the signpost.'

'Oh, yes, and the signpost.' Under which visitors could stand and have a picture taken. Inserted would be the name of their home town and the distance away in miles. Rose realised it was the first time they had had any sort of interaction which did not involve the Miltons in some way and was not tense with undercurrents.

'Marian – that's my wife, ex-wife – she said, now don't take offence, she said it was a little on the crude side but that's what appealed to her. She said it showed feeling and you probably enjoyed painting it. I don't know anything about art myself, but I liked it too.'

'Thank you.' Was the flattery genuine? 'It was done a long time ago, not long after I came down here. I love wild landscapes. Unfortunately I can only make a real living out of photography.'

'Will a curry suit you?' Jack had slowed the car. He needed to know where to park.

'Yes, fine.'

'A drink first, though – I can't imagine you refusing.'

She glanced at his face – lined, pleasant – but could not see his eyes as he turned to reverse into a space on the sea front.

They walked up the hill, several feet apart, Rose wishing she had brought a jacket. The evenings were cooler now and the heat of the previous weeks seemed to have become a thing of the past.

'Barry Rowe told me you do a good line in greetings cards too. That you paint them and he reproduces them.'

'Did he now?'

117

'He's very fond of you.'

'And I of him. I've known him for over twenty years.'

'Your boyfriend?'

'Boyfriend? At my age? No, just a good friend.'

They entered the Union Hotel and Jack went to the bar leaving Rose to pick a table.

'Is there one?' he asked when he returned with a pint of bitter and a glass of red wine. 'A boyfriend?'

'Not at the moment.' Let him make of that what he liked, she thought as she sipped the red wine she had not asked for. He was taking a lot on to assume he knew her tastes.

There was silence for several minutes. Jack was taller than her with dark springy hair, plenty of it for his age, she considered, guessing that he might be older than herself but that there were not many years between them.

'Me neither,' he volunteered. 'I've been divorced for twelve years, I don't seem to have the time for women somehow.'

Was this another veiled compliment?

'Anyway, as I said, what do you make of the Miltons?'

Not a compliment, Rose realised. She was here to give him information, information he supposed she possessed but was keeping to herself. 'I feel sorry for Dennis. He regrets his affair.'

'No doubt he does. Now.'

'I think he was manipulated into it. Maggie gives the impression she knows how to handle people. Paul? Well, to be honest, I think he's just a fool.'

Jack smiled as she took another sip of wine. So far, their opinions coincided. Enough of work, that was not the real reason he had invited her out. 'How long have you lived here?'

'Since I left college. I've never imagined being able to leave.'

'I didn't realise how much I loved it, either, not until I moved away. Come on, I'll tell you about it while we eat.'

They walked on to the Indian restaurant, where they ordered a main course each and opted to share a portion of rice and a couple of vegetables. 'Why did you leave?' Rose asked.

'Usual story. I was young, thought life was lived elsewhere

and that there was nothing here worth staying for. I went to London, then north. Leeds. I was in the force by then and that's where I met my wife. We got married, had a couple of kids and then, sounds daft, but I was homesick. I requested a transfer and finally got it. Marian wasn't keen, she's a city girl, but she was prepared to give it a try. I pointed out the benefits of bringing the children up down here. Well, it all went wrong. I'm not blaming her. I think she felt the same way about her home as I did mine. Anyway, we decided to call it a day.'

'And your children?'

'The boys? They were fourteen and thirteen when Marian left. They took it better than we'd imagined. They'd spent most of their lives in Leeds so it wasn't an entirely new start for them.'

'Do you see them?' Rose hoped she wasn't asking questions which might cause pain.

'Oh, yes. They used to come for holidays, begrudgingly at first. My mother looked after them if I was working, then they got involved in water sports and surfing and, of course, in the summer, there were girls. Funny to think they're men now. Twenty-five and twenty-six. Makes me feel ancient.'

'So you're about fifty?'

'Exactly. Had the big birthday last month.'

'Equals us up a bit.'

'What?'

'You got all my personal details from that first interview.'

A waiter placed hot-plates on the table, then brought the food. Jack watched. Yes, he was right. Rose, having been told they were very hot, was one of those people who just had to touch. She drew her finger back quickly and placed her hands in her lap. 'I know it's daft,' she said, aware he had seen her, 'but you're no different.'

'How come?' He leaned forward, elbows on the table.

'When you sat down you automatically pushed your knife and fork in a bit. You watch, loads of people do that.'

'*Touché*. Like I said, you're a very observant lady.'

'I was trained to be.'

'So was I.'

Stalemate, Rose thought as she helped herself to prawn dopiaza.

Jack Pearce ran her home, watched her safely to the door and departed without getting out of the car. Rose Trevelyan, he thought, as he made his way back to his flat, knows more than she is saying. What made him so sure was not what she had told him, but what she had not mentioned. And how come, if she was on friendly terms with the Miltons, she had not asked whether Dennis was still being held?

9

Rose's mood the following morning was carefree and she knew she was now not going to fall into the pit which threatened each year. The anniversary was behind her. She had wanted to ask Jack what was going to happen to Dennis but did not wish to spoil the evening by referring back to that subject.

She wrote a receipt for the cheque she had received, although it was not necessary, and used it as an excuse to visit the Milton household. Anna's rudeness still rankled; it would be interesting to meet her on her own ground. But she was genuinely concerned about Dennis.

Ignoring Jack Pearce's warning to keep out of things, she drove to Gwithian and pulled into the driveway. The mobile police unit was no longer there, which made her think an arrest might have taken place.

'Mrs Trevelyan.' Doreen Clarke dried her hands on an apron. 'Mr Milton's out. I don't know what to do.' Her round face was creased with worry. 'Come in. Come out to the kitchen for a minute. No one'll disturb us there. Least of all madam.'

The kitchen had every appliance a cook could wish for. Rose was impressed.

'I expect you'd like some coffee.' Doreen obviously wanted to detain her. 'I don't know whether to go in there or not.' She nodded vaguely towards the hall. 'The two of them were shouting at each other.'

'Who?'

'Anna, and the other one. Maggie something or other.'

'Maggie?'

'Turned up demanding to see Dennis. She said she had something she wanted to tell him. Anna asked her to leave, she said whatever it was could be done over the phone. She refused to go, said it wasn't Anna's house. That's when the shouting started.'

Rose wasn't surprised. If Anna had been expecting the house to be left to Paul she would wonder how Maggie knew otherwise. 'Where are they now?'

'I don't know. I heard footsteps on the stairs. I suppose Anna's gone to her room. Can you do anything?'

'Me? Like what?'

Doreen held out her hands in a gesture of helplessness. 'I don't know. Talk to them? I don't want poor Mr Milton to walk back into this. They let him go, you know. I don't know how they could've thought he'd done it. Maggie or no Maggie,' she added firmly.

So Doreen, too, was aware of the affair. 'Where's Paul?'

'He's gone into Redruth for something. He didn't say when he'd be back.'

Just as Doreen handed her a cup of coffee the kitchen door opened.

'Good heavens. What's going on? There seems little chance of much privacy in this house.'

'I didn't mean to intrude,' Rose replied.

'That's what the other one said.'

Rose placed her cup and saucer gently on the table. 'I'm not sure why you don't like me, Anna, but it wasn't you I came to see.'

'No. Dennis again, of course. I'd prefer it if you left.'

'You're right, it is Dennis and it's up to him to decide whether or not he wishes to see me. He needs friends at the moment, not histrionics from young girls.'

Doreen gasped, half in shock, half in pleasure. Good for Mrs Trevelyan, she thought.

'I'm sorry,' Anna managed to say. 'It isn't easy at the moment.'

'It isn't easy for anyone, knowing that there is still a murderer out there. Their grievance may not rest with Gabrielle alone.'

'Oh, really? And how come you're such a damn expert?'

'I do not claim to be an expert, I'm simply here to offer Dennis assistance because it's obviously not forthcoming from his future daughter-in-law.'

'Get out.' Anna hissed the words.

Rose hesitated, then, feeling Doreen's hand touch her arm briefly, stood her ground. 'I'm staying until Mr Milton returns.'

The door slammed behind Anna, and Rose and Doreen exchanged a look of relief mingled with uncertainty. 'See what I mean?' Doreen said. 'I don't know what to do, who to let in or anything. Mr Milton left me no instructions.'

'And he's going to return to find two uninvited women in his house. Doreen, would it be all right if I went through to the lounge? I might as well chat to Maggie.'

'Of course, Mrs Trevelyan.'

'Oh, call me Rose, it's too much of a mouthful.'

Doreen was pleased. She would be able to tell her friends she was on first-name terms with a real artist.

'Maggie?' Rose had opened the door quietly. The woman was seated on the edge of a settee, head bowed. 'Sorry, I didn't mean to startle you.'

'What a mess it all is. It's crazy, I can't keep away from the place. Despite that girl. At least they've let Dennis go but from what I've heard, it might not be for long. And it's all my fault. The police suspected me and all I've done is to make them think it's Dennis.'

'How was that?' Rose joined her on the settee.

'Other guests have confirmed that at one point we were both missing from the room. It's true, and I told the police. I followed him because I wanted to put him straight, to let him know Gabrielle knew. The looks he was giving me! I thought if she did know and hadn't made any fuss, she might be willing to let him go.'

'That's not what you told me, Maggie. You said Gabrielle had invited you to put you at a disadvantage, to let Dennis see what he'd be losing if he went off with you.'

'I know. And that's true. I'm sure that's why she did it, but what I just said holds true as well.'

'You really did receive an invitation?'

'Yes.' She looked surprised.

'You haven't exactly stuck to the truth, you see.'

'No. I was only trying to protect everyone, including myself.' She reached for her handbag which was on the floor beside her. 'Here.' She handed Rose the deckle-edged card, still in its envelope.

Rose had not seen one; her invitation had come via the telephone. The printing was done in black sloping letters, only the name of the recipient had been filled in by hand. The address on the envelope was typed. 'Did you show this to the police?'

'Yes. Once they knew about me and Dennis, and Dennis denied he'd asked me, I had to. They thought I'd gate-crashed.'

It wasn't Dennis's writing. Even though there were only three words from which to judge they were not written by the same person who had written out the cheque she had received. Dennis wrote in large, sprawled characters and there was hardly enough room for him to sign his name on the bottom.

'You said Paul knew. About you and Dennis.'

'If he didn't know, he must have guessed. He saw us together. We were in a restaurant. Unfortunately we were holding hands at the time. God, you don't think Paul sent it? Why would he do that?'

'I don't know. To show his father what he was doing was wrong, maybe?' But Rose did not think so. She had other ideas. 'There's a car. That must be Dennis.'

'Stay with me, will you, while I talk to him?'

'I don't think that would –'

'Please, Rose.'

Maggie had become agitated and the appeal in her eyes could not be ignored.

'All right.'

They heard voices in the hall, one male, one female. Doreen Clarke must also have heard the car and warned her employer.

'Hello.' Dennis came into the room. His face was expressionless and he looked exhausted.

'Maggie has something to say to you. She asked if I'd stay while she did so.' Rose then clasped her hands together and closed her mouth. She had done her bit.

'Dennis, I appreciate your telephone call the other night. I understand how you feel.'

'Do you? I doubt that. Your wife hasn't been killed.'

'No. I meant about me. I just wanted . . . Jesus, this isn't easy. I just wanted to say that I never meant to hurt anyone. I didn't give Gabrielle a thought when it started. I'm sorry. And I'm sorry if I said anything to the police which misled them. I couldn't telephone, I wanted to say it to your face. Besides, I thought you'd hang up. I accept it's over, Dennis, and I won't trouble you again.'

'You came all the way down here just to tell me that?'

'Yes. I didn't want it to end the way it had.'

Rose was as surprised as Dennis appeared to be. She had imagined Maggie was going to come out with something a little more earth-shattering. However, it had probably salved her conscience a little.

'And in the process I've upset Anna.' But Maggie did not offer an apology on that count. 'I'll go now.'

Dennis nodded and held the door open for her. From where she was sitting Rose saw Maggie look back once. She thought she might have been crying.

'Rose?'

'I just happened to be here. I came to see if there was anything I could do to help. I didn't know if they'd kept you at Camborne.'

'No. But they've asked me to remain here. It doesn't matter. Paul's not back yet?'

'No. Dennis, Anna asked me to leave, but I said I'd prefer to wait and see you. I hope I haven't added to your problems.'

'Anna has no right to do that. Ignore her. She's neurotic at times and I think she's very frightened. Despite what Paul told you the other night, she's led a sheltered life. This has upset her, and she's getting in a state about the wedding.'

'It's still on?'

Dennis glanced at her sharply. 'Yes. Of course. Thank you, Rose.'

'For what?'

'For coming. For taking an interest. I'm very much in need of a friend right now. Paul's got Anna to consider and my colleagues in London don't seem to be returning my calls.'

No, Rose thought. She had seen it before. People felt threatened in such situations. Dennis's wife had been murdered, he himself was being considered as a suspect, and he was about to be made redundant. He was probably regarded as a loser and no one wanted that sort of luck to rub off on them. How lucky she had been in her own friends when David died. 'You've got my number. I'd better go now.' She had forgotten the pretext of the receipt in her bag.

There was so much to think about. Ought she to tell Jack what she suspected? No, he would be annoyed. Jack. Already she had dropped the Inspector Pearce bit. And tonight she was repaying Barry for the meal he had cooked and the two he had insisted on buying in London. On the second evening he had outwitted her by asking for the bill on the way out to the toilet and paying it upon his return.

Barry arrived promptly at seven thirty and she poured him a can of beer she had got in especially. 'Go and sit down while I finish out here,' she told him. It was dusk; the table lamps were already on and the artificial coals of the gas fire glowed, although there was no need for the fire itself.

Ten minutes later Rose joined him. 'I went to see Dennis today.'

'How nice.'

'He doesn't have anyone else to turn to.'

'He's got a son, and the girlfriend, and a housekeeper. Three more than I've got.'

'Whatever's the matter with you?'

'You might've told me.'

'Told you what?'

'Not only are you hob-nobbing with the Miltons, which doesn't look too good so soon after Gabrielle's death, but you're going out with the bloke who's running the case.'

'I see.' Rose stared at her drink. Wherever she turned lately people started having a go at her. 'My social life is my own affair, Barry. I don't have to answer to you. And I am not going out with Jack Pearce, as you put it. He took me for a meal because he wanted to discuss a few things.'

'I bet he did.'

'If you're going to be like this all evening I can't see there's much point in your staying.'

'Sorry, Rosie. I just hate it when you get obsessed about things. I feel I'm losing you. I value your friendship, you see, more than you may realise.'

She understood but said nothing. This was not just about friendship; Barry was jealous. Seeing his familiar face, the hair brushed over his scalp, the glasses already slipping, she wondered if a different kind of relationship was possible. He was attentive and kind and understanding and punctual. Not once in either business or pleasure had he let her down. But look how he was tonight, and how he had been on other occasions. If they were together permanently she suspected he would want to know where she was every minute of the day. No can do, she thought, as a picture of Jack Pearce's face came into her mind.

'And I'm worried about you, Rose.'

'Worried?'

'When you get your teeth into something, you won't let go. It's unhealthy. And', he added, sitting upright as if the thought had just occurred to him, 'you could be in danger.'

Rose frowned. She had told Anna that the murderer had not yet been caught. Barry might be right. And was that why Jack had warned her off? But what did anyone have to fear from her?

'OK. We won't talk about it any more. Have you had any come-back from the trade fair yet?'

'A couple of orders have trickled in. It takes a while. Don't forget, I picked up several while we were there.'

She had forgotten. She had been too busy thinking about other things. 'How did you know about Jack?' That subject could not be dropped until her curiosity had been satisfied.

'You were seen.'

Rose laughed. 'You make it sound so ominous. *You were*

127

seen.' She mimicked his tone. 'I wasn't doing anything people can't know about.'

'They'll know all right.'

'Right. The food's almost ready. If you're going to sulk you can go, if not you can join me. Now act your age and drink that beer. There's three more cans in the kitchen.'

He smiled sheepishly. 'What've we got?'

'Bacon, with apple and red cabbage. It's Polish, I think.'

'And the wine?'

'The Co-op's finest. But plentiful.' Rose sighed. The status quo had been restored.

An hour later it was completely dark and there was a stillness outside. The window was open because the kitchen was over-warm from the oven being on. They both looked up when they heard the first drops of rain hit the glass. They were followed by a clap of thunder which made Rose jump. Lightning illuminated the garden for a split second. The storm had started almost immediately overhead. Sometimes they would last for hours, just rolling round the bay, not affecting other areas. The lights flickered. Rose got up and fetched a couple of night-lights from the drawer, along with a box of matches. They were safer than candles and had originally come with a food warmer she never used. She would not be badly affected if the electricity did go off; both cooker and heating were gas and the water in the immersion heater would stay hot until at least the morning.

They went through to the sitting-room and stood in the window, watching the violence which was taking place outside. The lights flickered again and went out. At one point Rose thought Barry was about to speak. He touched her shoulder, then changed his mind. She was glad. If he made any sort of romantic declaration their relationship would change.

'Come on, there's still some more beer. I'll finish the wine.'

'You've had most of the bottle.'

'Oh, don't you start! Jack . . .' but she, too, did not complete what she had been about to say. She had bitten her tongue too late.

'Are you seeing him again?' Barry asked quietly.

128

Only then did it occur to Rose that no mention of a further meeting had taken place. 'I don't think so.' She hid her dismay by pouring out the last of the wine. 'He might need to ask a few more questions, I suppose.'

It was an appropriate time for power to be restored. It would probably go again. The fluorescent tube buzzed and lit itself with a twang. The flames from the night-lights seemed paltry by comparison. She blew them out, liking the acrid tang of the wisps of smoke from the burnt wicks.

'See you over the weekend?' Barry asked as he left.

'Not Saturday. I'm going out with Laura.'

He shook his head but refrained from commenting, other than to say good-night.

Rose had said to Barry that the rain was too heavy to last. Her prediction was correct. Puddles lay on the lawn and in the pot-holes of her drive but they reflected a watery sun. She needed some fresh air, to get away and paint in solitude. First she did some overdue housework. Surfaces dusted, carpets vacuumed and the bathroom gleaming, she pinned her hair up, put on a waterproof jacket and loaded what she needed into the back of the Mini. It refused to start.

'Bugger it.' Rose got out and sprayed the relevant parts of the engine with Damp-Start. When she turned the ignition it whined but refused to kick into life.

Back inside she rang Laura's number. There wasn't an engine that baffled Trevor, on land or at sea.

'Of course he will,' Laura said. 'But he won't be back for two more days. Can you manage? If you need a lift I'll take you.'

'No. I'll cope.' It was a nuisance, but she'd walk somewhere. Trevor would sort it out when he came home. She tried the ignition once more on her way out but it sounded worse, just a slow whirr, then nothing.

It took about half an hour to walk to Abbey Basin. Rose had decided to get a bus somewhere. The harbour was to her right. She changed her mind: she would sketch that, then have a coffee somewhere in the town. Would Jack be like Barry? she thought, as she began to work. Surely not. With his irregular hours he could not expect anyone else to be at his beck and call. It was hypothetical anyway, he was not going to ring her again.

When she returned she found there had been three calls in her absence. Two were jobs, the third was from Jack. 'You're busy, I'll catch you some other time,' was all he said after he'd given his name.

Jim Penrose had been allowed to go home but only after he had spent several hours being questioned. Eileen may have thought she was paying him back but she had only made herself look a fool. On the night of Gabrielle's party, knowing his wife would be working at the house, he had arranged to do a job for a friend in St Erth. He had run into difficulties and it had taken an hour longer than he had estimated. Afterwards, as thanks for his efforts, his friend had bought him a drink. It would be checked, but Jim Penrose could not have been at the Milton place that evening if what he claimed was true.

'Well?' Eileen sniffed when he returned. 'I'm surprised they didn't lock you up.' She moved across to the cooker and stirred something in a pan.

'Don't bother cooking on my account. Has anyone ever told you what a bitch you are?'

Eileen turned to face him, an expression of shock on her face. He was leaning against the fridge, his eyes hard.

'All those years, Eileen, and I've never laid a finger on another woman.'

'What about Rita? You can't deny that.'

'I bought Rita a few drinks. No more than that. Whether you believe me is up to you. I'm sick of making excuses for innocent things. In fact, I'm sick of you. I'm leaving you, Eileen. Oh, don't worry.' He raised a hand to stop any protests or recriminations. 'I'll make sure you don't suffer financially.'

'You can't leave me, Jim,' she whispered as he walked towards the stairs.

'I can't stay. Not with a woman who'd do that, who'd try and get the police to believe I'd killed someone.'

'I only meant –'

130

'It doesn't matter what you meant, you did it. I'll never forgive you for that.'

Eileen did not move. Above her head she heard his heavy tread on the worn carpet, the opening and closing of drawers and cupboards and, finally, the flushing of the toilet cistern. She loved him in her own way. The problem had been that she was never able to understand what he had seen in her. She had never been pretty and Jim was so handsome. She wasn't even really sure if she had suspected him of seeing other women.

But for once in her life Eileen Penrose could not think of a single thing to do or say to defuse the situation.

The front door closed quietly. Jim had left without even saying goodbye.

'I've changed my mind, Paul, I think we should wait. What'll people think if we get married so soon? I mean, your mother isn't buried yet.'

'You've never cared what people think, Anna. I love you, that's the only thing that matters. Don't you know I can see how all this has affected you? The sooner you're my wife, the better.'

'But, the thing is . . .' She paused. Her shiny black hair fell forward, covering her face.

'What?'

'Nothing, Paul. It doesn't matter. Look, I think I'd like to return to London.'

'Please, not yet. Just stay until the weekend. They're not expecting you back at work yet.'

Anna contemplated her fingernails. It might be better to remain. She had told the police she would be staying and the idea of being alone in her flat was not so appealing now she thought about it. 'All right.' She made an effort to smile. 'Until the weekend.'

'They'll probably have arrested someone by then. They're still going around asking a lot of questions.'

'Paul, what if they don't find who did it?'

'Of course they will.'

'Supposing it was a stranger, someone who just came by chance?'

'By chance? With a houseful of people?' But as he thought about it, he realised it was a possibility. It was not a pleasant thought, but who else could it have been? Realistically, it was worse to believe it was someone known to them who had killed Gabrielle.

10

'We have no proof and only one piece of circumstantial evidence, which certainly isn't going to satisy the CPS. They'll laugh their bollocks off.'

'Succinctly put, Jack,' his chief inspector told him. 'That's why I want you to find the proof. I can't believe no one at that party saw anything odd or suspicious. And the victim didn't struggle, wasn't expecting to be toppled over that balcony, so it was someone she knew. Someone she trusted, more than likely.' He sighed. Like Jack he had hoped to have it neatly wrapped up by now. They knew all about the husband and his bit on the side, they knew what was in the will. They had also discovered that Mrs Milton may have intended altering that will, which left Dennis Milton firmly in the frame in view of his forthcoming redundancy. It had seemed perfect. Husband clobbers wife, inherits more than enough not to have to worry, then runs off with the bimbo. Better still, the bimbo's present, they'd planned it together.

But they wouldn't crack, neither of them, and he was beginning to feel Jack Pearce's theory was right. Only one little problem: the question of proof.

'Leave 'em long enough and someone'll make a mistake,' he told Jack. 'They're ringing each other up, visiting each other willy-nilly, there'll be a slip-up. Ease off on the pressure for a day or two. At least, let them think you have. Go on, shove off, you look tired.'

Jack was relieved. Initially he didn't think his superior had believed him. There was a way he thought he might be able to get that proof. It might be the only way. He didn't want to do it. It meant involving Rose Trevelyan.

*

'Shall I make a fresh pot?'

'No, thanks, Eileen, I must be going.' Maureen touched her sister's arm but there was no response. Eileen was staring at the seersucker table-cloth, trying not to cry.

'Come up for supper tonight.' Maureen didn't know what else she could say.

'No, I'll be fine. I'd better be here, in case he comes back. He'll want feeding.'

Eileen watched her sister leave and envied her her easy-going attitude. Jim had not been in touch for several days now and she did not know where he was staying. Pride prevented her from asking around.

It was a very odd thing, she reflected later, that it was on Doreen Clarke's shoulder she had finally cried when she turned up with a pot plant from Cyril's greenhouse to offer a bit of comfort.

Paul Milton and Anna were the next to be requestioned. Individually. They had both so far refused to say what their argument had been about. More people than Rose and Barry had noticed they were barely on speaking terms. Paul now insisted that it was nothing more than a disagreement, that Anna was wound up about the wedding. The detective constable made a note of this. Jack Pearce would be interested. From what he knew, no wedding date had been set at that point.

Anna claimed that whatever it was was so trivial she could no longer remember.

They, too, were allowed to leave.

When Rose heard Jack's voice on the end of the line she was pleased. She listened to what he had to say and was puzzled. 'I wouldn't ask if I didn't think it . . .' He had been about to say 'necessary'. 'It would be helpful. You're good at getting people chatting. Will you give it a go?'

'I suppose so. It shouldn't be difficult.'

'Good girl.'

Rose replaced the receiver. Good girl? How patronising. And no mention of seeing her again – apparently Jack Pearce simply wanted to use her. She would do as he wished, for her own satisfaction more than his. It was a very strange request he had made but he obviously had his reasons. And it had to be tomorrow.

She rang the Miltons' number. It was Dennis who answered.

'I hope I'm not being a nuisance –'

'Of course not,' Dennis interrupted.

'Only I'm doing some work on churches.' So far it was true. 'The thing is, I believe Gabrielle had some books on the history of Cornwall. I wondered if I might borrow one. You see, I thought I might try ancient monuments next.'

'Certainly. She would've been pleased to think you shared an interest.'

'Thank you. Would it be all right if I called in for them tomorrow? About three?'

The arrangement made, she hung up. Why Jack Pearce wanted her to borrow books she either already possessed or could get from the library was beyond her comprehension, but she had agreed to do it. Dennis would be fixing the car in the morning.

When the appointed time came Rose was shown into the lounge and Dennis asked if she wanted tea.

'No, I've just had some, thanks. I won't keep you, I feel I've taken up enough of your time.'

'No trouble. And there's no hurry to return them.' His face dropped as he realised they would no longer be needed. 'Ah, here's Paul. Paul, would you show Rose where your mother keeps her books?'

'I'd like to borrow a couple,' Rose explained.

'This way.' Paul preceded her up the curved staircase which ended in a gallery off which rooms ran. Rose had not been upstairs before. Paul opened one of the doors. 'This was Mum's studio.'

One wall was entirely of plate glass with a view over the garden and the sand dunes. There was nothing and no one to overlook the inhabitants.

The floor was wood block and there were two bright rugs. A

couch was covered in tough cloth, pattered with zigzags in primary colours. There was also a table holding a sewing machine and an old wooden kitchen table. White walls were adorned with pieces of patchwork.

'Mum had several hobbies,' Paul said.

'It's a lovely room to work in.' It had a foreign feel, Mexican maybe. There was no sign the police had ever been in it but they must have searched everywhere thoroughly. Rose studied her surroundings, enjoying the smell of the new fabrics which covered the furniture but wishing she knew what she was doing there.

'Look. Mum did this.' Paul held out a cushion he had taken from a shelf. The cover consisted of many layers of material, slashed at random, letting the various colours show through, the edge of each gash neatened with minute stitches and, here and there, tiny beads, so small that Rose could not imagine a needle passing through them. But, more importantly, she was taking note of how Paul spoke of his mother. There was regret and fondness in his voice as he showed her the almost completed piece of work.

'Would you like it?'

'What?' Rose's head jerked up.

'This. You might even finish it, there's only a corner to do.'

'Oh, Paul, I couldn't. I'd mess it up.'

'No, you won't. You paint, don't you? You must have a steady hand. Here, go on, take it.'

Rose did so. Of course she would love to possess it. She thanked him but wondered what Dennis would have to say about it.

'The books don't seem to be here, not the ones you wanted. They must be in the bedroom.'

Rose followed Paul across the landing. Gabrielle's bedroom was spacious and well furnished without being fussy. It was a room in which either sex could be comfortable. On the bedside table on the left of the bed were the two volumes Jack Pearce had asked her to borrow. Then he knew, Rose thought. He knew they were in here and guessed that no one would have removed them. But why? Unconsciously her head turned towards the tall windows which opened on to the balcony which ran around two sides of the house. Jack had wanted her to be in here, not in Gabrielle's study or work-room. She let Paul pick up the books and hand them to her, then they went back downstairs.

Dennis was on the phone so she smiled and waved and let herself out. The cushion and books she placed in a plastic bag she found under the dashboard. She saw many cars during the journey home but did not realise two of them held police officers.

Rose began seeing Paul in a different light but she suspected he was weak. Anna was the strong one, someone Paul could look to to tell him what to do, who would sort him out emotionally as long as the cheques kept coming in. What am I supposed to do now? she thought as she turned into her driveway. Did Jack expect her to ring him or would he be the one to make contact? She decided to leave it to him.

It had not crossed Doreen Clarke's mind that someone up at the house might be the murderer. It was Maureen who pointed it out to her over an afternoon cup of tea.

'Mr Milton? Don't be daft. He's too soft.'

'Paul then,' Maureen suggested.

Doreen shook her head. 'I'd know. You can always tell a killer by his eyes.' Not that I've ever seen one, she thought, but she'd know somehow or other. 'Besides, they've both spent hours with the police and they haven't been arrested.'

'There you are. They could be in it together. Dennis could have his bit on the side and they could share the money.'

Doreen had not meant to mention Maggie Anderson's name in relation to Dennis, but in the excitement it had come out. 'I don't know about that. I heard Paul asking his father for a loan the other day and Mr Milton said they couldn't do anything with the money until the probate was sorted out. I thought they'd have gone back to London by now, but they're all still there, the three of them. Madam expects me to wait on her hand and foot.'

Maureen smiled. She could imagine her friend's reaction to that. Doreen was quite capable of acting deaf or simply ignoring something if it was voiced as an order. 'Well, they seem to be taking long enough to find out who did it.'

'Yes, but think how many people were in the house that night.'

'Yes, plenty of suspects. Including you.'

'You're daft at times, you are. Still, you make a nice cup of tea.'

'Want another?'

'Please.' But Doreen's mind was elsewhere. She hoped Mrs Milton had not taken it upon herself to leave her anything in her will. With her and Cyril's present financial position, even a small amount might be considered as motive enough.

Routine had been so much disrupted lately that Rose went to answer the door without feeling in the least irritated. Dennis Milton stood on the step, the wind blowing his thinning hair across his scalp.

'They've arrested Paul,' he told her without preamble.

'Paul?' Rose tucked her hair behind her ears as if seeing him better would belie what he was saying.

'I don't know where else to turn. Anna's no good, she's shut herself in her room.'

'But I can't . . . I'm sorry. Come in.' The wind was whistling around the side of the house and there was a through-draught as the kitchen window was open.

Dennis was defeated, it showed in his face. In the kitchen she plugged in the kettle before thinking something stronger might be called for. Dennis accepted a small glass of whisky, and Rose poured herself a glass of wine. Underneath her concern for the man was an underlying feeling that people were dumping their burdens on her indiscriminately. She had to remind herself that it was her own interest which had encouraged it. And, if Paul was under arrest, Jack Pearce had beaten her to it. Her own feeble deductions were wrong. She could not see how her presence at the Milton house and that strange thing with the books had anything to do with it.

'What'll happen now?'

Dennis shrugged, his head bowed. 'I don't know. I'll get him a lawyer, I suppose, but he'll be lucky to get away with it.'

'Get away with it?'

'Oh, Rose! Surely you didn't think . . .? No, no, it wasn't anything to do with his mother. Fraud. He was up to all sorts in London. God knows why he didn't come to me sooner. No, I do know.' He paused. He and Gabrielle had agreed after the last time they had bailed him out that they weren't doing him any good. 'I don't understand exactly what he's been up to but they'll be seeing his partner as well.'

Rose just stopped herself from saying she didn't believe Gareth was dishonest. She was not supposed to know him.

'As far as I can make out it's something to do with taking commission from property owners, showing them a signed lease then saying the lessee has backed out. Only eighty per cent of the commission's repayable.'

'But how can that happen? The people who sign can't just back out.'

'Quite. But it's worse than it seems.'

'Oh, no.' Rose realised what Dennis was saying, that it was Paul who had forged signatures on the agreements between his firm and the landlords, drawn up without the services of a solicitor.

'I'm afraid so. When questioned, Paul would give false details of the non-existent customer who obviously couldn't be traced.'

'You mustn't blame yourself, Dennis. You've done more than many parents would have.'

'I don't. It's Anna I blame. She puts so much pressure on him. Oh, I know that sounds as if I'm making excuses, but Paul's weak, he always has been. And he loves the girl – whatever she says goes.'

Rose had been right in her estimation of Paul's character. If he was that weak was it possible Anna had persuaded him to kill his mother?

'Another drink, Dennis?' She hoped she had said it in a tone which suggested she would prefer the answer to be no.

'I'd better not. I've got the car. I just hope that the engagement's off now. That would be one good thing to come out of it. I'm so sorry, Rose, to bring all my troubles to your door-step. I wish I knew more people here.'

'You will, in time. If you decide to stay.'

Once he had gone Rose poured out a second glass of wine. I must eat, she thought. Later there would be more drinks with Laura; even if they decided to have a meal somewhere, Rose needed some food inside her first. A buttered roll filled with salad and corned beef took the edge off her hunger. This was followed by coffee, then a bath. Closing her eyes, Rose lay with suds damping the back of her hair as images of Jack Pearce, Paul, Dennis and Anna floated through her mind. And Jack's request. Was it of vital importance? What if he rang whilst she was out? And why did it matter so much?

Forget it, she told her reflection in the full-length mirror as she towelled herself dry. Turning sideways she thought, all in all, what she saw wasn't too bad. There was still a waist even if there was a little more padding on the hips than there once had been.

Because she had the hairdryer on its strongest setting, she did not hear the telephone ringing. When she went down-stairs the light was flashing on the answering machine. The message was from Jack; he would try her again later. There was no clue as to whether the call was personal or not. Tempted to put Laura off, Rose decided against it. She was not about to make the mistake of losing a friend for the sake of a man. If it was that important Jack would keep trying until he got an answer.

The evening was not a success. Laura was not her normal vivacious self but rather withdrawn. Rose did not like to ask if it had anything to do with Trevor. Her own mind was preoccupied, too. So many ideas were jumbled and she was unable to concentrate on one thing at a time.

'Do you mind if we go now?' Laura asked at ten fifteen. They had walked as far as the Queen's Hotel on the front, had one drink there, then retraced their steps to Newlyn. It was a landing day, the harbour a mass of masts, the pubs reflecting the number of boats in by the persistent ringing of the tills. Mostly they enjoyed the noise and laughter but the two women needed solitude and a chance to think.

They parted outside the fish market, the shutters down now on the concrete building. 'I'll ring you tomorrow,' Rose said as she turned to make her way up the hill.

She had left a light on. The path was uneven and it was easier to see to fit her key in the lock. No danger of burglars tonight, she thought, seeing Jack Pearce's car outside, Jack himself at the wheel.

'Where have you been?' he asked as soon as she was parallel with his window.

'Out. Is it allowed?'

Jack got out of the car.

'I'm tired.'

'So am I. Did you get my message?'

Rose could not deny it. Had he looked, he would have been able to see through the front window that the message had been played back. The light was no longer flashing. Opening the kitchen door she realised he was right behind her. Without invitation he followed her inside.

'You've arrested Paul, then,' she said immediately, hoping to put him at a disadvantage.

'Not much escapes you, does it, Rose?'

'But not for the murder?'

'Dennis Milton's been sniffing around again, I take it.'

Rose resented his terminology but ignored it. 'I got the books. Had I known it was to be a wasted journey, I wouldn't have bothered. Did you just want to borrow them or something, and not like to ask yourself?'

'My, my. We are in a mood this evening.'

'Are we? I'm simply very tired.'

'Listen, it wasn't a wasted journey. I can't say more than that. I'll go now. I only wanted to make sure you did what I asked.'

'Do I get expenses?'

'Pardon?'

'Expenses. Petrol money? Loss of earnings? And I'll have to return them at some point.'

Jack's smile did not reach his eyes. Rose saw he really was tired. The lines around them seemed to have deepened.

'Make sure you lock up,' he said before he left. 'Oh, I wondered if you were doing anything tomorrow evening?'

'I am, actually.'

'Barry Rowe?'

'I don't think that's any of your business, Inspector Pearce.' She smiled sweetly and shut the kitchen door before he could say anything else.

'Feisty little madam,' he muttered as he slammed the car door.

Rose heard nothing from Jack the next day. She did some housework and ironing before printing a dozen copies of the photograph the author had chosen from the contact sheet. There were two jobs in the diary for the following morning. After checking she had enough film and cleaning the camera lenses Rose sat down with a cup of coffee and a book. Her intention was to have a quiet evening alone, to simply relax and forget all that had happened. It was not to be.

'She what?' Anna was amazed that Rose Trevelyan had returned to the house on the pretext of borrowing some books. It was obvious what she was after. Dennis. Dennis would be a nice meal ticket for a single woman who had to work for a living. And Paul, the stupid fool, had encouraged it by giving her one of Gabrielle's bits of sewing. And now Paul had been arrested. Of course, he would be released – he didn't have it in him to kill his mother.

Dennis, sick of Anna's attitude, had not bothered to tell her why he had been arrested. She had been out at the time, shopping in Truro.

Anna thought very carefully about what she must do. First, so as not to arouse suspicion, she must sit with Dennis and try to eat the meal Mrs Clarke provided. The woman, she thought, had no idea of sophisticated cooking. Dennis, she knew, would push the food around his plate. If she were Doreen Clarke she wouldn't bother.

*

'Do you want a divorce?' were the first words Eileen Penrose uttered when Jim returned for more clothes. She had seen him approach from the window.

'I haven't had time to think about it yet.'

'So I just sit here and wait for you to come to a decision?'

'It isn't easy. Not after all this time.' He was weakening, he knew that, but he did not want Eileen to know yet. They had been through a lot together and he had supposed that once the children left home his wife would relax, that her jealousy would become less of a problem. Living in a mate's back room was not his idea of a home life and Eileen could not be faulted on how she ran their home. But it was more than that – he loved her. Loved, not in love with, and Jim knew the difference. He saw her properly for the first time in years. She was too thin, eaten up by her anxieties, but she still had a nice smile. Not that she had smiled for ages. The expression in her eyes was not one he had noticed before, half pleading, half angry. She would not make the first move, of that much he was certain. 'Give me a few more days, love.' And with that he was gone.

Eileen did not move. He was coming back, she knew it. He had called her love.

The following evening he was back again, letting himself in with his key. He threw his bag into a corner. 'All right,' he said, 'we'll give it another go. But there's going to be some changes. For a start you're going to stop checking on my every movement. You could have got me locked up, you realise that, don't you?'

'I wouldn't have let that happen.'

Jim ignored her. 'And I won't be answering any of your endless questions from now on. If I want to take a drink, I'll do so. If I want to eat my supper in the pub, I'll do that too. And if you ever accuse me of going with another woman again then it will be a divorce. Do you understand that?'

'Yes,' Eileen said, turning her back so he would not see the gleam of triumph in her eyes.

But Jim was enjoying his own little triumph. For three of the

143

nights he had been away he had shared the bed of Rita Chynoweth – and what made it even better was that, although he was sure no one knew, if the news did filter back to Eileen there was nothing she could do about it, not if she wanted him to stay.

Jim felt no guilt. For too many years he had been made to feel guilty over things he had not done. It was his own small revenge.

The gossip spread rapidly. Eileen was aware of halted conversations when she entered a shop and the nudges of women chatting on the pavement but she assumed they were discussing the split-up and Jim's return. Let them talk, she thought, head held high. The irony was that she had always believed him unfaithful when others hadn't and now the reverse was true.

DI Pearce had explained to the superintendent that the plan had not worked.

'I think you should give it another day, Jack,' he was told. 'After all, you can't guarantee the position's been made clear. We dare not take any risks now.'

Jack was glad to hear this. He was also glad to be operating from headquarters rather than from the Milton premises. He was never as comfortable on away ground.

Anna telephoned her office and said she would be back at work soon. Once the police realised Paul was innocent, he would be released. Meanwhile she had to make sure Dennis was not influenced by anything Mrs Trevelyan might say or do. Several times she had broached the subject of money with Dennis, playing on what she believed to have been Gabrielle's wishes, that she would have wanted Paul to be all right. Dennis had not said much but at least he had not given a refusal.

Anna was unaware that he was not even listening, that his thoughts were of Gabrielle and of the trouble his son was in.

Doreen Clarke was amazed when she learned that Paul had been arrested. She, too, made the wrong assumption. 'To think I was under the same roof as a murderer, Cyril. I can't believe it. I could've had my throat cut any minute. And Cyril, I do wish you'd take that cap off when you're in the house.' She stirred a dollop of cream into the cauliflower soup she had made. Doreen believed a generous portion of the clotted variety every day never hurt anyone.

'Will you stay on?'

'Of course. No point in leaving now, when the danger's over.'

'There's a girlfriend, isn't there?' Cyril asked, finally removing his cap.

'Anna. Madam. God knows what she'll do now. They won't be engaged any longer, you mark my words. She tried to get round me this morning, she did. Came into the kitchen and tried to get me into conversation. She was asking about that nice Mrs Trevelyan. Rose, the artist.'

'Oh?' Cyril was studying the paper. It would not have taken much trying to get Doreen into conversation, he thought, but was wise enough not to say.

'I soon put her right. I said I was busy and that I wasn't going to discuss a friend of mine, especially one as nice as that. I told her, I said, "She's got a good head on her shoulders, she knows more than most around here." And then when she said she wanted some coffee I told her where the kettle was.'

Dennis and Anna sat in silence at the dining-room table and toyed with mushroom soup. Dennis had crumbled a bread roll but had not eaten any of it. He had arranged for a solicitor to be present while Paul was questioned but the man had told him not to be optimistic.

Chicken casserole and broccoli followed the soup. Anna ate most of it, not wishing to seem in a hurry to leave the house. Doreen nodded in satisfaction when she cleared the plates. It was a shame that Anna refused to eat cream, she looked as if she needed a few more pounds on her.

'I don't believe it.' Rose threw her book to one side and heaved herself out of the armchair. She was comfortable and pleasantly tired and well into the plot. Although she was tempted to let the answering machine do its job, she knew that would be daft. If she refused to answer the phone each time it only meant ringing back whoever had called. It was hardly an economical way of doing things.

'I thought you'd be out.' The surprise in Jack Pearce's voice was genuine.

'I changed my mind.'

He was thrown. He had planned a carefully worded message. Instead he said, 'Well, in that case, do you fancy meeting me for a drink later? There's a couple of things we need to discuss.' He paused. 'And I would like to see you again.'

How could she resist? 'All right,' she said. 'What time and where?'

'Eight thirty? I can't make it until then. Somewhere in town?' Normally he would have offered to pick her up but he did not want to compromise her as far as her neighbours were concerned. He named a pub. 'There's a chance I might be a few minutes late. It's unavoidable in this job. I hope you'll wait.'

'See you later.'

Jack was pleased. There was something he needed to tell her, which he could have done over the telephone, but he wanted to see her, to have her to himself on neutral ground. Last time they had got along fine.

There was time to finish the novel. Rose made another coffee and decided what, out of her limited wardrobe, she would wear. It was a mild evening but almost dark. The few remaining flowers took on different hues in the half-light and the grass was a bluish green where the fluorescent tube cast a

146

paler rectangle on the lawn. Rose shut the back door but did not lock it.

Later she cleaned her teeth and changed into a sage-green pleated skirt and a cream blouse, then put on some make-up. She gathered her hair at the back and clipped it in place with a large wooden slide.

· Downstairs she picked up her book to finish the last four pages before she set off for Penzance.

11

Jack Pearce, fresh from the bath, was only running a few minutes late. He had, he realised, overdone the aftershave and rubbed off the surplus with a towel, wondering at the wisdom of taking Rose out. They were not teenagers, he could not buy her a couple of lagers or a few glasses of wine and leave it at that. Rose would expect more of him. Besides, he thought as he grinned at himself in the steamed-up mirror, she might easily outdrink me. For the first time in many years he studied his face. Was he good-looking? He did not know. He was used to what he saw, but what did Rose see?

Trousers, clean shirt and jacket, but no tie, that would be overdoing things . . . He checked his pocket for keys and wallet and left his flat.

Jack liked Rose – more than liked her – but just why, he wasn't sure. She was pleasing to look at and took no nonsense from anyone. She was talented and intelligent and moved around with the energy of someone half her age. But God help anyone who got her back up.

Since his wife, Marian, had departed, Jack had taken out several women but once the sexual attraction had waned they had bored him. They lacked something he needed by being too compliant or too obviously seeking a husband. Rose was interesting. There were depths to her he was sure he would never reach.

Jack whistled as he walked down the hill towards the sea. Lights from the salvage tug anchored in the bay rippled over the water and, to the west, a fishing boat chugged out of the harbour. It was a calm evening; the faint slap of water against pebbles was the only sound apart from an occasional passing car. Above the harbour the tiered lights of the houses of Newlyn twinkled. He paused and breathed in the air with its hint of kelp. An oyster-catcher called as it flew from the shore.

The Mount's Bay Inn was less than a hundred yards away. Rose would be sitting there, a drink in front of her. Jack anticipated her smile.

He pushed open the door. To his right, in the small dining area, a couple and a man on his own were eating. At the bar were three men, two of whom he knew. The window table was occupied by an elderly couple with a dog. There was no Rose. He ordered a drink and exchanged a few words with the solicitor at the bar, a prosecutor, with whom he had come into contact several times, then he sat down.

Rose used the pub, she would know the people present, but he could not bring himself to ask if she had been in. He was only fifteen minutes late. Surely she would have waited that long? He lit a cigarette. The obvious explanation was that he had told her he was likely to be late so she had not hurried herself.

Each time the door opened he glanced up expectantly. At nine fifteen, two pints later, he knew she wasn't coming.

'Similar?' the landlord asked when Jack placed his glass on the bar.

'No, thanks. I'm off now.'

He crossed the road and leant against the railing, staring at the sea, kidding himself that he was enjoying the view: hoping that Rose would appear, walking quickly from the direction of Newlyn. A youth cycled past him. Jack could not be bothered to challenge him – let him ride on the pavement if he wanted to.

'Sod her,' he said aloud, and started walking back towards the town. Not wishing to go home, he stopped at the London and began some serious drinking. Something stirred at the back of his slightly befuddled brain. He went to the telephone and dialled Rose's number. The answering machine came on. 'Rose,' he said. 'Rose, it's me. Jack. I'm in the London. I'll be here for another twenty minutes. Come in the car. I'll wait.'

He returned to the bar and ordered one more drink. If she did not arrive he'd get a cab and go over there. If Rose didn't want to see him, fine. But he had to make sure she was all right. Maybe she hadn't stood him up. There might have been an accident, or perhaps some relation had been taken ill. Rose did not have his home telephone number and it was unlikely she would have tried to contact him at work. Her parents might have needed her. If she still had parents. There were so many things about her he didn't know.

After twenty minutes there was no sign of Rose. Jack rang for a taxi and was told one would be there in five minutes. He gave the driver the directions, feeling slightly ridiculous, like some love-struck youth hanging about for a glimpse of a girl. He knew the registration mark and make of Barry Rowe's car and dreaded seeing it outside the house.

'Just here. Hold on a minute.'

The driver pulled in, the engine running. Rose's house was higher than the road. Jack leaned over. There was a light on in the front room but the curtains were drawn. No sign of Rowe's car. Then his stomach tightened. In the gap between Rose's Mini and the road was a car he recognised. Gabrielle Milton's car. It now belonged to Dennis.

'Back to Penzance, please. Drop me in Greenmarket.'

The driver shrugged, unconcerned at his passenger's strange request.

So that's the way it is, Jack thought. I should've seen it coming. Rose hadn't wasted any time. She had taken him for a fool. She might even have known Dennis before she met Gabrielle, might even have been having an affair with him. Why not? Dennis was no saint.

There were approximately thirty pubs in Penzance. If he couldn't get drunk tonight, he never would.

Rose had not heard the tap at the door. She was half-way down the stairs when she began to feel uneasy, to sense that she was not alone in the house. Laura would have called out. Whoever it was was not going to delay her – she was looking forward to the evening.

She pushed open the kitchen door. Anna stood leaning against the outer door, her hand behind her, still on the handle. 'I need to talk to you,' she said.

150

'Oh? You might have telephoned. I'm just on my way out. Perhaps you'd like to come back tomorrow.'

'I think we'd better get this over with right away.'

Rose hesitated. Anna's eyes were narrowed. Something was definitely troubling the girl. 'Five minutes then. In here.' She led the way into the sitting-room; it seemed more formal that way and Jack would probably be late. 'All right, what is it?'

'I want Gabrielle's books back, and I want you to stop asking so many questions about my future family. Why are you so interested?'

'Is that really any concern of yours?' Rose flushed, annoyed with herself for doing so. She had taken too much upon herself; she saw how it must appear from Anna's viewpoint.

'Is that any concern of mine?' She mimicked Rose. 'It is, when it's blatantly clear you're after Dennis, that you want to take what's rightfully mine.'

'Yours? I don't understand.'

'Gabrielle promised she'd leave everything to Paul. Of course it would be mine as well.'

'But she didn't change her will.'

'She would have. Now it's Dennis's and you're after it.'

'Oh, Anna, honestly. I can't see what you're getting so excited about. I'm not after Dennis, as you put it.' She smiled to show how silly she thought Anna was being, yet underneath she was wary. The girl showed all the signs of being mentally unbalanced.

'Excited?' Anna swung round. Her coat flew open to reveal an expensive dress. 'You're trying to steal what's mine and you're going around like some bloody amateur detective attempting to put me in the wrong. You leave us alone, do you hear? Or I'll go to the police.'

And Jack would just love that, Rose thought. Her mind was working on two levels, coping with what was happening at the moment and analysing what she had previously suspected. As an intellectual exercise it had been one thing; this was something quite different.

I'll redecorate, she thought irrationally, once this is over – I really will. She was unaware that she was doing what she had

151

done throughout David's illness, concentrating on trivia, not allowing her mind to accept reality.

'Why don't you sit down, Anna, and we'll discuss this sensibly.' Rose glanced at the carriage clock: the minutes were ticking away. How long would Jack wait before he rang or came to look for her? How long before he gave up and went home, the logical part of her brain said. She must keep Anna talking, defuse the situation if at all possible. Something else struck her: Anna was wearing gloves.

'There's nothing to discuss. You're a bitch, Rose Trevelyan.'

Even with the gloves Rose was astonished at the amount of pain the stinging blow to her face caused. She raised a hand and felt the heat. No one, she realised, had ever hit her before, not since the days of the school playground anyway. She had no idea how to react and could not bring herself to deliver a blow in return. 'As I said, I was on my way out. I'd like you to leave now. Or *I* shall call the police.'

'Do you know what you're doing, you stupid, stupid woman?'

Rose flinched at the fury in Anna's face. She was no longer attractive.

'You're stupid and crass and boring, living your parochial little life down here. As soon as a real man comes on the scene you're after him like a bitch on heat.'

Rose cursed herself for having become involved, for listening to Dennis in the first place and for not doing as Barry suggested, leaving it to the police.

'Did you hear me? You're a bitch.' Anna was screaming as she threw herself at Rose, her hands grabbing her hair, her arms strong from regular exercise.

Rose's eyes filled with tears from the pain. She pushed at Anna, realising her twenty years' seniority for the first time. All the times she had heard or read of ways of protecting yourself – kicking at a shin or poking fingers into an opponent's eyes – and still she could not bring herself to do it. She couldn't even scream.

Anna had backed her out of the room but Rose couldn't remember getting to the kitchen. The small of her back was against the sink, their faces were almost touching, and Anna's hands were around her throat. Rose had her hands on Anna's, trying to grasp the little fingers, to wrench them back and break them if necessary, because now she really knew the danger she was in. Anna had nothing to lose. The room was spinning. There was a harsh pain in her chest obliterating the other pain from the ridge of stainless steel cutting into her spine.

Anna's grip relaxed but one hand grabbed for her hair again. Rose knew, without doubt, that she had seen the bread-knife. If she got out of this Rose knew she would never leave dishes unwashed again.

Anna pulled back her arm. Fleetingly Rose was puzzled. Something dripped from the knife. Had she been stabbed and not felt it? She had heard that pain could be delayed. No, it was water, not her own blood.

Only then were all inhibitions gone. In a split second she acted instinctively, the need for survival an all-encompassing emotion. Had she really wished herself dead when David died?

Rose kicked out, hard, glad of the low-heeled court shoes with their solid uppers. The blow hardly unbalanced Anna.

'No,' she shouted, and with every ounce of strength she possessed Rose bent sideways and grabbed Anna's wrist, kicking out again as she did so. She was free. In one movement she turned and picked up a kitchen chair.

Anna shrieked obscenities and raised the knife. Rose felt hot tears run down her face. 'No, oh please God, no,' she sobbed as she raised the chair and brought it down hard on Anna's head.

There was a sudden silence and then a strange noise. It took Rose several seconds to realise it was coming from herself. Her breathing was ragged and caught at her chest. Her whole body felt limp. She clutched at the table to steady herself.

Anna lay on the floor, her stockings and pants visible where her clothing had caught on something. Rose covered her. She was breathing. There was no blood. Rose knew that was bad, that gaping wounds and flowing blood always looked worse. It was internal injuries which were dangerous. What if Anna died? But what if she didn't do something quickly, if Anna revived, picked up the knife and plunged it into her before she had a second chance of defending herself?

Rose kicked the knife away, then picked it up and placed it in a drawer. In the sitting-room she picked up the telephone. 'Jack,' she said, 'come quickly, I need help.' The words sounded slurred to her own ears. There was no reply. She stared at the receiver wondering why she could only hear the dialling tone.

Shock, she thought, I'm in shock. Some normality returned. She punched out three nines with shaking hands, her index finger sliding off the last one. 'There's someone in my house. They're injured. I think they've killed someone.'

'Fire, police or ambulance?' the impersonal operator demanded.

It seemed an age until Rose was certain that they understood, that help was on the way. She wanted to stop them talking so they could get there faster.

She had to get out of the house. Her handbag was in the kitchen. Only afterwards did she realise how ridiculous it was to have felt she must have it with her, how many times people had endangered themselves for a few bits of paper and a couple of pounds.

Anna was stirring, trying to push herself to her knees. Her face was grey. Rose shoved her, knocking her to her side, then fled. She was half-way down the hill before she saw the blue light in the distance. She stopped then, and leant against the wall, unable to move. A breeze rustled the hedge behind her and she jumped but she did not have the strength to care if Anna had somehow caught her up. She sank to the ground, arms across her chest, head on her knees . . .

'Mrs Trevelyan?'

Rose looked up and saw the concerned expression on the face of a WPC.

'Come on.'

A blanket was wrapped around her and she was driven the short distance back to the house. 'I can't go in.'

'It's all right. You're safe now. The young lady's going to have a headache, but she's not badly injured.'

Rose allowed herself to be led inside and past the figure who was being attended to by another officer as they waited for the ambulance.

The next half-hour was a blur. At some point Anna was taken away but the kitchen still seemed to be full of people. Rose sat at the table and drank the tea someone had made. Each time she raised the mug to her lips some spilled. There were spots on her skirt. The blanket was still around her shoulders.

Then the questioning began. Rose told them everything she knew and all she had done. At some point she thought she heard the telephone ringing but no one else seemed to notice so she might have been mistaken.

'Is there someone you'd like to stay with tonight?'

'No. I have to stay here.' Rose knew that if she left, if she did not face what had happened, she might not want to return. She could not leave this house where she and David had been so happy.

'Someone who would stay with you, then?'

'Laura. No.' She shook her head. Trevor was home. They had enough on their plate already. 'Barry. Barry Rowe. He'll come.'

'What's his number, love?'

Rose stared at a man in plain clothes. How long had he been present? 'I don't know.' How many times had she dialled it? Yet she could not recall any of the digits. 'In my bag. My diary's in my bag.'

Someone handed it to her. She fumbled and pulled it out. There was more confusion but she ignored it. Then, it seemed seconds later, Barry was standing in the kitchen. 'Oh, Rosie, what have you been up to?' He put an arm around her and she started to cry. Long, gulping sobs that came from deep inside.

'Do her good,' a disembodied voice said. 'Delayed reaction. Can you stay the night, sir?'

'Yes. There's a second bedroom.' Even in such circumstances Barry was careful for her reputation. The police might have imagined they were lovers.

Not that night, nor at any other time, did Barry say, I told you so. He did not know the details of what had happened; in time Rose might tell him. What he did know, what he guessed from the number of police present, was that Gabrielle Milton's murderer had been caught.

Jack carried on drinking until closing time, the effect of those drinks beginning to tell. He was mellow. Past caring. In fact he was so far past caring that he might just walk over and tell Mrs Trevelyan exactly what he thought. No point in telephoning, she probably wouldn't answer when she heard his voice.

Not as steady on his feet as he believed himself to be, he reached Newlyn and lumbered up the hill. Something was wrong. He paused. There were no lights on in Rose's house, but that was to be expected, it was after midnight.

'Jesus Christ,' he muttered. Dennis Milton's car was no longer there. Parked in its place was the estate car Barry Rose drove.

Unable to believe the evidence of his own eyes, he began the walk home. Fortunately, he was unable to recall Rose's number and couldn't be bothered to look it up in the book or he would have left a less than pleasant message for her.

Instead, fully clothed, he got under the duvet and fell asleep.

'I'm sorry, Barry.' The spare bed had not been made up.

'It's OK. I was warm enough. Anywhere's warmer than my flat. It's not me we should be worrying about but you. How are you?' There was a slight air of embarrassment between them. It was the first time either of them had stayed in the other's house. Hotels in London didn't count. This was far more personal. And Barry was flattered and relieved it was him Rose had turned to.

'Numb,' Rose replied. 'Bruised but otherwise numb. I suppose I look a mess.'

Barry smiled gently. 'I've seen you look better.'

Rose smiled back. Typical of Barry to be truthful.

'I'm going to make something to eat. Is there anything in the fridge?' He opened it. There were eggs and not much else. Scrambled eggs it would be then. He found bread for toast and made more coffee for Rose who, he noticed, was trembling.

'Barry? What about the shop?'

'Don't worry. I rang Clare before you were awake. She's opening up and she's prepared to stay all day if necessary.'

'No, I'll be fine.'

But she did not look it.

'There's a message on your machine, you know.'

Rose did not know. She had forgotten she thought she heard it ringing the previous evening. But she could not be bothered to see who it was. Not much seemed important any more. The smell of the bread warming under the grill filled the room. Rose was hungry. She thought she had never been so hungry and forced herself to eat slowly.

'I was right, Barry,' she finally said. 'I always believed it was Anna.'

And you nearly got yourself killed for it, Barry thought, but did not say. 'Do you want to talk about it?'

Rose shook her head. 'Not yet. Later maybe.'

When they had finished eating Barry washed up and dried his hands on the tea towel. 'Would you prefer me to leave?' he asked.

'Yes. I'm so tired. I can't thank you enough for being here.' She stood painfully and reached up to kiss him on the cheek. She did not see the expression of anguish on his face as he turned away, knowing that that was as much physical contact as he would ever receive from Rose.

'Take it easy. You know where I am if you want me,' was all he said before leaving.

'I'm going back to bed. The police're coming back later, I believe. I don't suppose I made much sense last night.'

'You're great, Rosie, you know that? And you'll be fine.'

Yes, she thought as she closed the door behind him, and locked it. I am and I will.

Two CID officers returned in the afternoon, one male, one female. Rose went over everything again, from her very first meeting with Gabrielle: this time in chronological order. She

157

was still not sure why Anna had attacked her; she had not told Anna she suspected her, or anyone else for that matter. She was disappointed it was not Jack who was interviewing her but perhaps it was forbidden, like a professional/client relationship. There had been no telephone call either, apart from the one she had now played which was obviously left last night. Maybe he was off duty, unaware of what had happened, or he might think she had simply changed her mind and was too proud to inquire. Rose was wrong on both counts.

Alone once more she thought she had better eat. She had had nothing since breakfast. Pulling open cupboards she could not find anything she fancied, nor could she face going down to the Co-op or getting a take-away. With a mug of tea in her hand she switched on the television for the local news. She was too exhausted to do much else and she was interested to see if there was any mention of Anna's arrest.

There was, but it was only a mention and no one was named.

A sound jolted her awake. On the screen was a half-hour comedy programme. She had fallen asleep again. The sound was repeated. Someone was knocking at the door, but timidly. There were no lights on and she couldn't be seen from outside where she was sitting; she was tempted to ignore it. However, the flickering of the television may have given her away. If it was Dennis she would not ask him in, she could not cope with that man's problems tonight.

Turning down the sound on the set she went wearily to the door. Her body ached all over with a feeling akin to flu. Outlined through the frosted glass was a shape she did not recognise. Only when she opened the door did she see why. Jack Pearce stood holding an enormous bouquet wrapped in cellophane and tied with a bow.

'Hello,' he said tentatively.

'Hello.'

There was a pause of a few seconds. 'These are for you,' Jack told her, holding out the flowers. 'And this.' From the pocket of his jacket he pulled out a small box of chocolates awkwardly, the corner catching in the lining.

'Thank you.' Rose thought he looked worse than she must. His eyes were slightly bloodshot, his skin was sallow, and there was a slight stoop to his shoulders. 'You'd better come in.' She led the way to the kitchen. 'I'm sorry about last night. I was otherwise engaged.' She took the bouquet and began undoing it, averting her face as tears filled her eyes. There was no reason to cry but her GP, whom the police had called, had explained it was likely to happen for a day or two.

'I don't usually bring women flowers.'

He was ill at ease and Rose was pleased their roles were reversed. Did he feel guilty for not coming to make sure she was all right?

'How are you, Rose?'

'Recovering. Bruised and shaken, but otherwise all right. Jack?' Rose indicated the gifts. 'Why all this?'

'Guilty conscience.'

'Ah.'

'Because I doubted you, I thought certain things about you which I should have had the sense to know couldn't be true. I cursed you all evening. Then I got very drunk. I wanted to make it up to you.'

'It shows.'

'What does?'

'Your binge. You look dreadful.'

Jack laughed then. This was the Rose he had come to admire. 'Say no if you want, but are you up to going out? Nothing wild, just a quiet meal somewhere. I'll drive, I won't be doing much drinking.'

Rose did feel like going out. The tiredness had not worn off but she had spent the previous forty-eight hours under the same roof and had slept most of the day. A change is as good as a rest, she thought. 'Am I all right like this?' She indicated her jeans and thick jumper, under which was a shirt. She was still cold.

'You'll do.'

Rose trimmed the stems of the flowers and put them in a bucket of water. 'I must make a phone call first.' She went through to the sitting-room.

'Barry Rowe,' she explained a few minutes later. 'He was

159

good enough to stay with me last night. He said he'd call in later to see how I am.'

Jack did not ask for further elucidation. He was in possession of the facts now. She need not know how he had misinterpreted them. Barry was her friend and she had had the decency to let him know she would be out rather than cause him anxiety or a wasted journey.

'I'm ready.'

Together they went out to the car. Rose felt the weakness in her legs after all those hours of lying down, but it would pass.

The restaurant Jack had chosen was expensive and, she noted, he had already reserved a table.

'I didn't do it with the assumption you'd accept,' he said, seeing her expression. 'It's just that it's popular and you need to book. I'd have cancelled if you said no.'

Seated, they ordered their food and some wine. Jack poured himself half a glass. Rose took a few sips and felt its effect at once.

'I always thought it was Anna,' she confessed. 'But I was wrong not to consider myself in danger. I might've caused you even more work. Jack, why did you want me to borrow those books?'

'We knew from Anna's background that she was unstable and we also knew that people are inclined to tell you things they won't tell us. I knew the books were in the bedroom and I knew Anna considered you to be a nuisance, she believed you were moving in on Dennis Milton. I'd hoped she'd be at the house and take you up there herself, to the scene of the crime, as it were. I wanted your reaction to her own. I wanted you and Anna together in the room where Gabrielle was killed. Irrational, really, but I felt you'd, I don't know, sense something or get her to talk. If that failed I assumed Anna might well come to collect the books from you herself, to prevent Dennis doing so or you returning to his house. We, too, believed it was Anna, but how to prove it was the problem. She had free range of the house so fingerprints didn't count, and she often chatted to Gabrielle in the bedroom. We couldn't break her with our questioning but we thought if you could build up some sort of rapport with her, or, alternatively, if she hated you so much, she might say things she had not intended to say. We used you, Rose, I'm sorry, but you did seem to get yourself involved from the start.'

'Didn't you have her followed or put under surveillance or whatever you call it?'

'Yes. That's how help arrived for you so quickly.'

'What're you talking about? I had to ring the police myself.'

'I know.' Jack looked down and rearranged his cutlery. 'We had a man follow her to your house. He was parked outside. He saw Anna enter and waited. No lights were extinguished, there was nothing to show you were in any danger. Only when he heard someone scream did he radio in. People were already on their way before you rang.'

At the time, even when minutes and hours meant nothing, Rose had been surprised how quickly she was surrounded by people. 'He must have seen me, the man in the car.'

'He did. But he realised you were at least in a fit enough state to run. His concern was with the lady inside the house. He went in immediately.'

The starters were served. Rose dug her fork into the hot chicken liver salad and began to eat.

'I still don't understand it,' she said after several mouthfuls. 'This business with the will. Did she really kill Gabrielle for money?'

'Yes. Or at least, that's the obvious motive. There's more to it than that. No doubt the psychological reports will tell us. But she was a very mixed-up young woman. Always has been. She claims she was adopted, that she only found out when she was fifteen. Not true. Her natural parents are alive and well. She despised them for being ordinary, for not having money. It didn't help that she was considered to be beautiful, boys and men falling at her feet. It gave her inflated ideas of her worth.'

'It doesn't sound as if she needs a psychiatric report. You seem to have worked it out for yourself.'

'I can't claim that, Rose. We knew about the parents as soon as we began our investigations. They, and people her own age she used to know, told us. When she found out Paul's true financial state it sent her over the top.'

'But the will?'

'I was coming to that. From what she told us it seems she totally misconstrued what Mrs Milton said. They'd had a heart-to-heart. This took place soon after she became aware Paul was virtually broke. Anna went to Gabrielle to try to wheedle some money out of her, to keep Paul going. Gabrielle said that she wanted to do her best for Paul, that it was time she helped him properly, and that she had changed her will.'

'But she hadn't. Dennis implied . . .' Rose stopped. She, too, had misinterpreted things. Dennis had been surprised everything had been left to him. Of course, Gabrielle *had* changed her will, but in favour of Dennis, not against him as a punishment for his infidelity. And someone had told her that the Miltons were tired of bailing Paul out. Gabrielle, it seemed, had stuck to her word, had tried to make it possible for Paul to stand on his own feet. If he thought nothing was coming to him he would have to make much more of an effort. 'Maggie Anderson?' Rose continued. 'Did Gabrielle know of her existence?'

'We'll never know for certain.'

Rose leant back to allow the waiter to clear the plates. 'That was good. Very filling.'

'I hope you've still got room.'

'I have. I'd like to think she didn't know. That invitation, it wasn't Dennis's writing. Maggie would have known that. She told me Gabrielle sent it, but the more I thought about it the more I felt that it was Anna who did.'

'Correct.' Jack raised his glass. 'It wasn't difficult finding out. The two women had shared the job of addressing them and sending them out a couple of weeks before the party. Anna took an extra one.'

'How did she know about Maggie?'

'Paul told her. He was worried his mother might get hurt. He'd seen his father and Miss Anderson in a restaurant somewhere or other. He confided in Anna, as anyone would their fiancée, just to get it off his chest, I suppose. We don't know how she found Maggie's address but maybe Paul told her the name – Dennis had no option but to introduce them at the time of their unfortunate encounter. He may even have said

162

what she did – it would have been an excuse for their being together.'

'And Anna wanted her under Gabrielle's roof, to make sure she did find out, to show her she was doing the right thing by leaving everything to Paul.'

'Seems likely.'

'And she killed her because she found out otherwise?'

'Oh, no. It was far more cold-blooded than that. That would have been heat of the moment. She killed her because she couldn't wait for the money. Money which wasn't going to Paul anyway.'

'That's why she agreed to get married so quickly. She was sure Paul was about to inherit and she didn't want to give him a chance to change his mind.'

'That's about the sum of it. A lot of this is supposition at the moment but we've got a confession. Thank God.'

There was a pause as they both realised it might have cost Rose her life for them to be absolutely certain of having a case. Jack felt vaguely ashamed but he had believed Anna would say something to Rose, something which would give them a lead. He had had confidence in Rose's ability to make her talk.

Rose could hardly blame him. Had she not insisted on becoming involved, on dealing with matters she knew nothing about, Jack would not have come to her for the favour. The best thing was to try to forget it, to concentrate on the meal which had been placed before her.

'Damn it.'

'What is it?' Jack looked up, the pepper grinder in mid-air.

'I had appointments today. I forgot to cancel them. I'm not so affluent that I can lose business.'

'No need to worry. It's taken care of.'

'What?'

'Your friend. Barry. He cancelled them for you first thing.'

'He did what? How did he know?'

'Apparently your diary was lying on the kitchen table. He checked it.'

It had been, Rose realised. She had got it out to find his number the previous night. 'Hang on. How did you know he'd done so?'

'I called into the shop. Once I knew he'd been looking after you, I asked if he thought you were up to going out tonight.'

'He knew?' So many things seemed to be going on around her, concerning her, yet she was not aware of them. Barry had not mentioned this when she rang him earlier. But, on second thoughts, he hadn't sounded very surprised either.

'He was kind enough to tell me to have a good time.'

Rose wasn't listening. 'Paul,' she said. 'How is he taking it?' He had lost his mother and his girlfriend in a very short time.

'At the moment he's denying it to himself. He relied on her for everything. Emotionally, that is. He was pleased to have someone to do things for. There was nothing he was able to do for his parents.'

'He could have tried harder, to get on without running to them for help.'

'Rose?'

She pushed the remaining pheasant to the side of her plate, too full to finish it. 'What is it?'

'Rose, promise me you won't do anything? I know you've a penchant for lame ducks, but let this be.'

'I will.' The last thing she wanted was to become embroiled with any more of the Miltons' problems. 'I wonder if it will bring them closer together? Dennis and Paul.'

Jack doubted it. The two men only seemed to have their grief in common. Once that passed – if it passed – things would revert to how they had been before.

'What's going to happen to Paul?'

'I'm not sure. It's not our case. The Met are dealing with it.'

'Will they take into account what's happened?'

'No. Paul was in trouble long before any of this. Can you manage a sweet?'

'No way. Not another thing.'

'You'd better knock back the wine, then I'll take you home. You look shattered.'

Poor Dennis, Rose thought when Jack went to ask for the bill. His wife dead, his son in prison, his son's future wife also locked up. What on earth would he do? Survive, that's what he'll do. She answered her own question. She had managed to survive.

'Jack? How did Anna know Gabrielle would die from that fall? I mean, she did push her over, didn't she?'

'Yes. But the PM showed that certain injuries were received before she hit the ground.' He lowered his eyes and Rose knew he would tell her no more. There were things that he could not reveal in case Anna changed her story, in case there was a trial after all, not just a hearing. Still, she couldn't help herself, couldn't leave it alone. 'But there would have been blood in the bedroom, surely?'

Jack grinned ruefully. 'There wasn't any when you dealt with Anna, Mrs Trevelyan.'

She felt the hot flush creep up her neck and decided it was time to keep quiet.

Rose cancelled her appointments for the next few days. She was still not up to working and, as people heard, one by one they were telephoning or coming to see her. Laura, tactfully, gave her a chance to recover but kept in touch by phone every day. Jack, too, rang daily.

At the end of the week he asked her out again.

'And whose car was that parked outside early this morning?' Laura asked when she called in for coffee on Saturday.

'You know perfectly well whose it was.'

'Well, how was it?'

'Pardon?'

'You know what I mean. What's he like in the sack?'

'None of your business.' But Rose was smiling, she did not need to tell Laura.

Laura was pleased. Rose had been without a man for far too long. Things were still not certain between her and Trevor but she had made an appointment to see the doctor. There might be something in this hormonal business after all.

'I'm not going to get the lurid details then?'

'No chance. It'd be all over Newlyn before lunchtime.'

165

'It's all over Newlyn already, my girl. Everyone knows a copper's car when they see one. And a lot of people know Jack. Don't forget –'

'Yes, I know. You all went to school together.'

'Seeing him again, are we?'

'Oh, bugger off, Laura, I've got things to do. I'll ring you tomorrow.'

Rose remained at the kitchen table. It had seemed natural, inviting Jack in for a nightcap and ending up in bed with him. She had felt a small pang this morning when she heard him swear as the shower attachment fell out of its holder, just as it had done when David was alive. The low ceilings of the house were fine for someone of Rose's dimensions, but there was nowhere to install a shower unit suitable for use by a tall man.

Jack was no replacement for David, she had known that from the start. They were different, and each attracted her for different reasons. And she had changed. Jack was like her now, there was always going to be a part of each of them that the other couldn't touch. For now she was content to take every day as it came.

He had not stayed for breakfast, not even for coffee. For that, too, Rose was grateful. It smacked of too much domesticity too soon. She had no illusions. There would be broken dates when work interceded, and the flowers and chocolates were a one-off. Jack was not a man to operate in that way.

Later, she got into the Mini and wondered why it wouldn't start. It seemed a lifetime ago she had asked Laura if Trevor would fix it. Laura, too, must have forgotten. She picked up the telephone to remedy the situation. Leaving the keys under the seat she strolled down to the sea and sat on a sandy bit of beach, her back resting against the high Promenade wall, the weak sun warming her face. She smiled at her indolence. Next week it was back to work.

Her parents, in their early seventies, were still full of life. They visited two or three times a year and, since David's death, had persuaded her to spend each Christmas with them, away from the memories. Rose knew that it was for her sake, that they did not enjoy the traditional celebrations. How nice to be able to tell them that this year she might have other plans. Either way, whether or not Jack was still around to accept her invitation, she was spending Christmas in Cornwall. She was not going to run away from possible pain again. They would make objections of course, but she knew they would sigh with relief when they put down the phone and rush off to book a cruise or a foreign holiday. They had the money to do so – why should she prevent them from enjoying whatever time they had left together?

Taking a paperback out of her bag Rose settled back to read, mentally waving two fingers at the still rumpled bed and the unpaid bills which would soon need attention.

Several small clouds drifted apart, exposing the whole of the sun. Herring-gulls paddled at the edge of the water, the tide far out. The salvage tug, which had been in the bay for weeks, had disappeared, maybe to refuel or maybe to be in on the kill. Rose felt a surge of optimism. David would understand her grieving days were over.

FRAMED IN CORNWALL

1

Dorothy Pengelly sniffed the top of the carton of milk and shrugged. The expiry date had elapsed but it smelled all right and the cats wouldn't notice. One of her uncles used to drink a pint of sour milk every day of his adult life and he had lived to be over ninety. Dorothy did not use milk in her tea or put butter on her bread, she could not abide dairy products.

She had three cats and two dogs, one of them a retired racing greyhound an old friend up Exeter way had given her, the other a snarling Jack Russell.

Her granite-built house was none too clean but only because she refused to admit that her eyesight was not as good as it once was so she was unable to spot the cobwebs or the spills on the flagstone floor. The place was too large for her but she would never move. It had been her home all her married life and she intended dying in it. Besides, she knew the number of years left to her were limited and she could not bear the idea of upheaval.

She filled the three saucers which were lined up in front of the metal legs of the ancient cooker. They had concentric circles of cream in them ending in yellow crusts. Peter; she smiled wryly. Her son couldn't wait for her to die. He and Gwen would sell their house in Hayle and move into something far too grand for them. Her son had married unwisely. Gwen was a schemer and tended to forget that Peter had a brother. Martin might not be as bright as Peter but he was her flesh and blood and she loved him dearly. Oh, well, she thought, they would all find out in time.

Her will, made on a visit to Truro with Martin, would give several people a shock. Her assets were worth a lot more than many imagined and Rose Trevelyan had put her wise as to the value of her paintings.

The house was situated on sloping ground between outcrops of boulders. The grass between them was tough, seasoned by the blistering sun and the harsh winter storms which swept mercilessly over the terrain. One or two stunted trees, bent to the angle of the winds, barely survived but the low gorse thrived and flowered twice a year when its almond scent filled her nostrils and made her nostalgic for her youth. In the distance was the glimmer of the sea although, on dull days, it merged greyly with the sky on the horizon.

There were two outhouses, one of which was almost in ruins. The other was only suitable for storing junk as the corrugated iron roof leaked. At one time the dogs had slept there until Dorothy had finally relented and allowed them into the house. The cats were never to be seen at night.

Once a week she got a lift into Camborne or Penzance with Jobber Hicks, a neighbouring farmer she had known since childhood, and whom she had once seriously considered marrying. Apart from those shopping expeditions she rarely went out. Fred Meecham used to share a pot of tea with her when he dropped off her groceries, but not so frequently now that Marigold was so ill. In fact, although he had called in two days ago she hardly saw him at all and she had an uncomfortable feeling she knew the reason why. But there was a lot for Fred to come to terms with, she did not know how he would cope when Marigold finally went. Rose's visits were awaited with pleasure. If the weather was fine, they would take a stroll or go out in the car and have tea in a café. Dorothy decided to give Rose a ring and ask if she would mind bringing over a couple of pints of milk when she came tomorrow.

Rose stood in her lounge window in the manner of someone waiting for a guest. In her hand was a mug of coffee. She stared across the wide expanse of Mount's Bay trying to make up her mind what the weather was going to do.

The view was spectacular and ever-changing. On clear days she could see the white sands of the beaches of Marazion and the whole of St Michael's Mount rising majestically, almost menacingly, out of the sea. To her left was Newlyn harbour where beam trawlers and netters came and went without pattern. On some days a jumble of masts could be seen, on others there were few. It was landing day. The tuna season was over but she had returned from the fish market with two large monk tails which had cost her next to nothing because she knew most of the fishermen.

In the kitchen she rinsed out her mug and inverted it on the draining-board. Through the window which looked out over the sloping garden she could see more and more patches of blue appearing between the clouds but, knowing the inconsistencies of the weather in West Cornwall, she decided to take a waterproof jacket anyway.

Leaving the house by the side entrance which led directly into the kitchen, Rose got into her Mini which was parked on the steep narrow drive beside the house. It started first time because it had recently been serviced. Trevor, the husband of her best friend, Laura, fished out of Newlyn. He had his engineer's ticket and could make sense of any machinery. Rose's car was child's play to him. As he refused payment Rose had bought him a bottle of Jack Daniel's and a packet of his favourite tobacco. Despite the service Rose knew it was time for the Mini to go. For a painter a vehicle was not indispensable, but in her other role as a photographer it was essential. Her equipment with its heavy lenses was impossible to lug around on foot or by public transport.

She backed down the precarious drive with the ease of years of practice, negotiated the bend at the bottom and waited for the Mousehole bus, along with a stream of cars held up behind it, to pass. When it was safe to do so she pulled out and drove down into Newlyn village and turned left for Lamorna Cove.

She was fully aware of her hesitation in changing the car. David had bought it for her. But David was dead and although he had died five years ago it would seem like a betrayal of sorts. He would have wanted you to be practical not sentimental, she told herself, recalling how very different they had been – yet the marriage had worked, had been happier than most.

Rose planned to make some sketches of the cove. She had been commissioned to do a series of watercolours of some of the small Cornish bays. Once complete they would be reproduced on the front of notelets which would be packaged along with

9

envelopes, ten to a box. She had decided to depict each from a high vantage point so that she could include the granite cottages which sloped down to the bays. It did not matter at this stage if it rained for Rose would only be concentrating on the outline and scale.

The car-park on the quay was busy. Lamorna, with its one hotel and its one pub, the Lamorna Wink, was always popular with holiday-makers and walkers. There were still plenty of people around although the children had gone back to school. In the gently moving water protected by the harbour wall were several divers. Sitting on the wall, legs swinging into the void, were others, their wetsuits gleaming.

Rose turned and began walking. In the distance three people could be seen making their way up the steep cliff path which led back to Newlyn. Glancing at her watch she saw that she had two hours before she was due in Penzance. She slung her canvas bag over one shoulder and began the ascent which would make her calves ache but would lead her to a sheltered vantage point. Her hair, the lighter strands mingling with the auburn, was tied back against the breeze which became stronger the higher she climbed. Twice she stopped to allow walkers to pass in single file.

Between two boulders covered with rough green and yellow lichen, Rose laid down a waterproof sheet and removed an A5 sketchpad and pencils from her bag. She wriggled into a comfortable position, resting her back against a smooth patch of the cliff. The drawings would be smaller than the paper size so she made the necessary allowance. Dressed in old jeans which were faded and threadbare at the knees and a thick checked shirt which had been David's, she was warm enough in the lee of the rocks towering above her.

The patches of blue had all but disappeared and within half an hour the sky was a uniform grey but the rain held off. Herring-gulls glided overhead and occasionally swooped, squawking noisily when they spotted people in the car-park who were foolish enough to produce food. The birds had become a nuisance in recent years and signs had been put up in many resorts entreating visitors not to feed them, but Rose liked their arrogance and aggression although she was doubtful if they knew any longer what a herring was. Their staple diet consisted of chips, pasties and burgers. She would include their graceful flight in the sketch; two of them, she decided, their lateral feathers spread as they soared effortlessly.

An hour and a quarter later her back ached. Getting to her feet she stretched then picked up the sketchpad to study it. Satisfied with what she had produced she packed up. In no particular hurry she stayed for a while, relaxing under the changing sky. Lying on the waterproof she linked her hands behind her head and gazed into nothingness, emptying her mind. It was something she rarely had a chance to do. By the time she left the sea had changed from grey to green with a silken sheen where a ray of sunlight was reflected off the surface. A warm stillness had settled over the cove.

She knew she had been in danger of falling asleep. Many of her nights were restless since she no longer had the security of David's body beside her. It was not fear of living alone as much as simply knowing he wasn't there. They had not had any children but to Rose it was no longer a matter for regret. They had had each other.

Before she reached the car she went over the things she had planned for the next couple of days. This afternoon she had arranged to see Barry Rowe and later she was to photograph a Mrs Morgan's daughter whose eighteenth birthday it was. Informal shots would no doubt be taken at whichever night club the girl ended up in but her mother wanted one which she could frame. Tomorrow was Friday and she would be seeing Dorothy Pengelly. Rose smiled. What a character that lady is, she thought. And tonight, Jack Pearce. The smile faded. She had been seeing him on and off for more than a year. The relationship had not followed the usual form of progression and Rose was not sure of her feelings, only that they were ambiguous. They met when it was mutually convenient and enjoyed each other's company when they did so. But Jack, she knew, wanted more from her than she was able to give. Alone for so long, Rose had grown used to her independence and, in a way, so had Jack, whose hours were erratic, but she suspected he was one of those men who would prefer to live with a woman than without one.

Heading back along the country roads she was glad of the easy familiarity she felt with Barry Rowe. He was an old friend and the only person she allowed to call her Rosie, because he had given her her first break when she came to Cornwall all those years ago and because he had always been in love with her. What she had offered was friendship, no more than that, but she was vain enough to be flattered by his attentions.

Detective Inspector Jack Pearce had had a busy summer. From the moment the season proper had started crime had escalated. Not that he kidded himself that this branch of the Devon and Cornwall police had quite as much to contend with as the city boys who were stationed in Plymouth or Exeter. And he should know. He had spent several years in the force in Leeds. Of course the warm weather brought an influx of visitors and more people meant more crime. It also brought a lot of drop-outs to the area. This was not to say that the locals could not make just as much of a nuisance of themselves but the police generally knew where to find them. Recently he had been involved in one of the biggest drug hauls in the West Country.

Tapping a pen against his teeth he wondered what Rose was doing at that moment and if she was thinking of him. He smiled his wolfish smile. That was extremely doubtful. She had probably taken herself to some isolated spot and was immersed in the scenery. Even on a day like today she could find beauty in something. Was she viewing it with her artist's eye or through the lens of a camera? Jack found it hard to believe she was only two years his junior, she was so petite and youthful. He towered over her by eight inches. He was solidly built with the typical dark Cornish colouring. Although his accent had been diluted by the years he had spent away from the area it was still strong enough to identify his origins.

Petty crime annoyed him. The perpetrators were rarely caught and the victims suffered out of all proportion to what the criminals gained. He sighed. He couldn't wait to see Rose that evening and wished he could see her more often. But at least he knew where he stood with her. Rose had made it quite clear that she would not give up her friends to spend more time with him. He accepted there was no choice but to make the best of what little he had. It was, he realised, little enough.

It had finally happened, the dreaded time when Marigold needed to be hospitalised. For months Fred had coped, running the shop but relying more and more on his staff, keeping the flat clean and seeing to Marigold's needs. As she weakened he had received outside help. Cheerful nurses were in and out of the upstairs flat several times a day.

Tears ran down his face as he thought of Marigold in that high bed, intravenous fluids running into her wasted arm. It had been so hard to leave her there. Barely able to speak she had managed a few whispered words. 'No one could've done so much for me. I love you, Fred.' It was the first time she had said it and he would remember it for ever. All he had done had been worth it in the end. Yes, he decided, even ... but he would not allow himself to complete the thought.

He stared at his surroundings. The flat was cold and empty without Marigold. Kneeling, he tried to pray but no words came. Not since his boyhood had he missed church on Sunday but he thought he would stop going now. Sometimes he found it hard to believe he worshipped the same God as the rest of the congregation. The one he knew was a personal friend with whom he held conversations. How could He have time for all those others, for the women, some of whom still wore hats and who gossiped outside after the service? His parents had been strict Methodists, bringing him up to fear shame and dishonesty, to act in a way which could not offend or cause gossip. He had not caused gossip, he had been very careful on that score.

Fred had offered his soul in return for Marigold's health. All he had ever desired was someone loyal and kind, someone worth loving, someone worth living for. Whilst many paid lip service to the familiar words of the litany Fred silently communed with God. He had suffered and he had paid the price of his sins. She

13

would not pay the price of hers, he had seen to that, but without
her he was nothing.

Dorothy Pengelly's younger son, Martin, had just passed his
thirty-fourth birthday but looked much younger. He knew what
people said about him, that he was simple, that he wasn't all
there, and it hurt. Worse, it made him self-conscious and
confused in strange company, which only served to perpetuate
the myth. Alone he was a different man. Only his mother
understood him fully and accepted him as he was. In return he
loved her unconditionally.

Martin lived in a caravan which had been abandoned some
years ago. Technically he was a squatter but it was unlikely
anyone would return to claim it now. He had been out walking
one day when he first discovered it about a mile from his
mother's house. It was on rough ground, surrounded by clumps
of bramble and obviously uninhabited. Many times he had
returned but it remained empty and was becoming dilapidated.
One day he had plucked up the courage to try the door. It was
unlocked but the handle was stiff. On closer inspection he saw
why it had been abandoned; it was fit only for the scrap heap.
To Martin it was a challenge. He spent a month making repairs
which may not have been aesthetic but which were effective. A
few weeks later, when he was certain no one was going to lay
claim to the van, he packed up his belongings and moved in,
knowing that his mother would be pleased at this first step
towards independence.

His income came solely from government benefits because
despite his efforts to find work there was nothing at which he
was able to succeed. The few employers who had given him a
chance mistook his insecurity and shyness for stupidity and he
had been asked to leave.

The caravan was comfortable and equipped with a battery-
operated radio, Calor gas for cooking and heating, an oil lamp
and a pile of pornographic magazines which he bought surreptitiously when he went to Truro. To Martin the women were not
sexual objects but real people who would not laugh at him and

14

snigger behind his back in the way in which the local girls did. His only downfall was drink. He couldn't handle it in the way other men seemed to. When he had money he walked into Hayle or Camborne and drank pints of cider and let his mouth run away with him. It allowed him to feel normal, part of a society from which he mostly felt excluded. When people spoke to him when he had drink inside him he was neither tongue-tied nor confused but he always suffered for it the next morning.

Once a month Peter, his brother, would invite him for Sunday lunch. No one particularly enjoyed these visits, least of all Gwen, Peter's wife, but none of them seemed capable of breaking with tradition. The invitations had originally been extended to please Dorothy because she had suggested it would be good for Martin and there was her inheritance to consider. Martin had not known how to refuse. He felt uncomfortable in the almost sterile atmosphere of Peter's house but his niece and nephew enjoyed the hour he spent with them, playing, before they ate.

He had woken yesterday unable to remember quite when Mrs Trevelyan was coming to see his mother; the days were all the same to him. But she hadn't turned up. It would have been nice to have a friend of his own but where would he find one?

By the evening the air was heavy and oppressive. Martin studied the horizon as dusk fell. Tomorrow it would rain and there would probably be thunder. He sensed it and it made him restless but he had no money for a drink. Dorothy would lend him some, she often did. It was never begrudgingly, never handed over with anything other than a simple 'of course'. He always paid her back. This was one of the reasons why he was her favourite, one which Peter, who was encouraged by Gwen to push for all he could get, could not understand.

Martin kicked at the springy turf with the heel of his shoe and stared in the direction of the house. Its squareness and the two tall chimneys were outlined blackly against the darkening sky. He walked towards it, his hands in his pockets. Pressing his forehead against the kitchen window he saw Dorothy sprawled in her high-backed chair over which a knitted patchwork blanket had been thrown to disguise the threadbare fabric. Voices from the radio reached him faintly but Dorothy was sound asleep, her mouth partly open, her knees apart and one of the cats curled into the cradle made by her skirt.

George, the Jack Russell, bristled then relaxed when he saw it was Martin. The greyhound did not stir. She was going deaf.

Martin had let himself in with his own key and helped himself to a ten-pound note from his mother's purse then left her a note in his rounded block capitals to say he had done so. 'I've lent ten pounds. Martin,' he wrote on the back of an envelope. There were six other banknotes of the same value in her purse so he knew he was not leaving her short. He kissed Dorothy gently on the forehead and made sure the lock on the back door clicked shut behind him.

Beads of sweat formed on his skin as he trudged across the scrubby slopes until he reached the main road into Camborne. There, in one of the pubs, he had spent all but a few pence of the ten pounds before he was bought a drink by a man whose name he could no longer recall. It was after midnight before he'd got back to the van and he'd fallen asleep, fully clothed, on top of his bunk. When he opened his eyes it was daylight and his head was thumping.

Barry Rowe's shop was in a prominent position in Penzance. He made his living producing greetings cards which sold throughout the country as well as locally. He also stocked maps and films and other bits and pieces that appealed to tourists. In the summer he kept the shop open until trade dropped off because the season was so short yet, surprisingly, he also made a reasonable income during the winter. Much of what was on display was based on the work of local artists or, at least, depicted local scenery. Rose Trevelyan provided him with two things: original watercolours, which he reproduced, and a sense of joy whenever he was in her company. She also photographed landscapes which he sold on to postcard companies.

He had known her since she first arrived in Cornwall, having just completed three years at art college. She had come to study the Newlyn and St Ives artists for six months before taking up a career but she had never gone back. Oils had been her favourite medium and she'd initially sold one or two each year through the cafés and galleries which served as outlets, although photography had taken over now.

It had been love at first sight on Barry's part. He would never forget the day she bounced into the shop, her long flowing hair burnished copper by the sun which streamed through the open door. Her enthusiasm and vitality were almost tangible. Then she had been pretty; now, with maturity, she had become more than that.

Barry pushed his glasses up his nose. Every pair he had ever possessed worked loose and the habit, so strongly ingrained, caused him to do so when there was no need. He knew he was no great catch. His hair was greying and rather thin, his shoulders were stooped and he was underweight but his devotion to Rose had not ceased. He was long over the pain he had felt when David Trevelyan had walked into his shop to buy a birthday card. Rose had been there at the time and Barry bitterly regretted telling David that the artist was standing behind him. The look which Rose had given David had been identical to the one he had given her a few short months previously. With that simple introduction Barry had known that his chances were nil.

When David died Barry had been genuinely distressed because he had liked and admired the man and knew that he had made Rose happy. Shamefully he struggled to stifle the thought that Rose might now come to accept him as more than a friend. It had not happened. Then Jack Pearce arrived on the scene. At least Rose hadn't dropped him completely in favour of the arrogant Inspector Pearce.

At precisely one o'clock Rose walked through the door, surprising Barry who was used to her tardiness. He grinned. 'It's all yours,' he said to Heather who was the latest in a long line of temporary or part-time assistants.

'Oh, I expect I'll cope,' she said wryly, rather liking the serious man for whom she worked.

'We're going out?' Rose had only expected to collect payment for some work.

'Just up the road for a quickie. There's something I want to

17

discuss with you so I thought you might as well buy me a pint.'

'Fair enough. As long as you're about to hand me an envelope containing a cheque.'

'Mercenary bitch.'

Rose laughed. 'It's taken you long enough to find that out.'

They strolled up to Causewayhead and entered the London Inn. The front bar was busy where a group of fishermen who had landed that morning, along with their women, had been making an early start. Rose acknowledged the ones she knew before following Barry around to the small back bar where he was already ordering their drinks. Rose handed over the money.

'Okay, I've kept to my side of the bargain.' She held out her hand.

Barry shook his head and reached into his jacket pocket, taking out the cheque which Rose had been expecting.

'Thanks,' she said, glancing quickly at the figure before stuffing it into her shoulder bag. It had taken her a long time to become businesslike about her transactions. Initially she had imagined a sponsor or agent would deal with the monetary side of things. Her financial position was now secure but without her work she would be lost. The house had been paid for upon David's death and the capital from his insurance policies paid the bills. What she earned gave her freedom. 'What was it you wanted to discuss?'

'How are you at wild flowers?'

'I can tell a daisy from a buttercup.'

'Honestly, Rose, you know what I mean.' He wished she would not grin at him in that way, it always made him want to kiss her. 'I'm talking about notelets, the usual, ten to the box and packaged nicely.'

'It's been done to death.'

'Yes but they're popular and I was thinking of a different angle.'

'Go on then.'

'This time with an appropriate background, something simple, say a cliff or a disused tin mine, something which shows where the plant can be found with the location printed on the bottom.

Take a look at this.' He slid a sheet of paper across the table and pointed at it with a thin finger. 'See, like this. Western Gorse, common enough down here and in Wales, I believe, but rare elsewhere and there's – '

'All right, all right, I get the drift. You've obviously done your homework,' Rose interrupted before he could get too carried away, as he tended to with new projects. 'But isn't it a bit late in the year to be starting on something like this?'

'Aha, that's where you're right. I have done my homework. Most of the plants on the list flower until October. If you're not too tied up with other work you could make a start and finish the rest in the spring.'

Rose was impressed. Scrawled in Barry's untidy hand were the names and locations of over twenty wild flowers. She raised an eyebrow. 'Usual rate?'

'Of course.'

'Oh.' Rose chewed her lip thoughtfully. 'October? I might get wet feet.'

'Honestly, woman. Okay, plus five per cent.'

'It's a deal. Now I can't sit around all day drinking, I've got to go. Things to do, you know.'

Barry shook his head, grinning at her cheek. He rarely indulged in more than one or two pints, Rose enjoyed a drink far more than he did. The smile faded as she walked away and he was left to wonder if Jack Pearce was on her agenda.

Since the time Fred Meecham had taken over the shop in Hayle he had spent an hour or so with Dorothy Pengelly at least once a week. But that was before Marigold's illness had taken hold and he had discovered his secret might not be safe. Despite the difference in their ages they got on well. It had started when Dorothy had given up the car and begun sending in an order for heavy goods such as a case of cat or dog food which he delivered free of charge. A strange kind of friendship had developed. He knew she did not buy everything from him but he did not resent it. He understood how much she enjoyed her trips to Camborne or even Truro with Jobber Hicks.

19

It was Dorothy to whom he had confessed that his wife had run off with a rep from a biscuit company who used to call at the shop. 'She took all she could carry,' he had told her, 'but she didn't take the boy.' Fred had been left to bring Justin up as best he could. Five years later, at the age of sixteen, Justin, too, had left home.

'Where did they go?' Dorothy had wanted to know.

'To hell as far as I care.' Fred had left it at that. He had tried hard to make the marriage work. Divorce was against his religious principles but Rita had gone away, waited the stipulated period and filed the papers without any resort to him.

He thought about what Dorothy had said a few years afterwards, when Marigold had moved in. 'Time you took over your own destiny, Fred. It's all very well your sister running your home and helping out in the shop but a man like you needs a wife.'

He had nodded and smiled and gone on to talk about the chrysanthemums he grew in the small garden behind the shop. Dorothy had made a joke about them being the wrong sort of flower, they ought to have been Marigolds.

She had been deeply sad when he came to say that Marigold had been diagnosed as having cancer. 'It's so unfair, she's so young.'

'I'd spend every penny I've got to find a cure,' Fred had continued. 'Every bloody penny. I want the best treatment money can buy.'

Dorothy had reassured him that she was probably getting it anyway and that he would be wasting his time by paying for private care.

But Fred had not been able to let the matter go. 'I could send her to America. You read about people who get sent to specialists over there and get cured.'

How hopeful he had been in the early days of the disease. He had had an estate agent look over the shop and give him a valuation but even with his savings and any other money he could scrape together he knew he would never get Marigold to the States.

Was it too late? Wasn't there something he could do? Of course

20

there was. He should not have allowed the pessimistic thoughts to arise.

Most days his staff would mind the shop whilst he paid a mid-day visit to Marigold in the hospital but he always spent a couple of hours with her again in the evenings. He pulled on his jacket. Tonight, once she became too tired to bear his company any longer, he would make his final attempt.

Fred Meecham locked the shop door knowing that things would turn out all right.

2

It had taken Martin most of Thursday to recover from his hangover. He spent the morning cleaning the caravan and washing out his socks and underpants. It was therapeutic, a way of cleansing himself, ridding his mind of the shame he felt at disgracing himself. They were chores which would have taken most people far less time but he always worked slowly and methodically, never undertaking more than one simple task at a time. He polished the windows inside and out, using newspaper soaked in vinegar as he had seen his mother do. As the morning wore on the chill of the past few days evaporated under a hot autumn sun. Martin removed the long seat cushions which doubled as mattresses at night and lugged them out to air, propping them against rocks.

In the afternoon he walked down to Hayle and cashed his unemployment cheque then bought a bagful of groceries, enough to last him the weekend. He got a cheap cut of meat, a loaf of bread and some fresh vegetables. It was after three when he had finished and he realised that he had enough money left over to repay his mother and just still be able to have a drink. Just one, he told himself. Hesitating only briefly he crossed the road, walked past the lane he should have taken to go home and went into the pub.

Glancing around he was relieved to see that there were only

21

three other people present, none of whom he recognised. The two men he had spoken to on his previous visit must have gone back to wherever it was they came from. They had not been local but he could not place their accent. Martin had not set foot outside Cornwall and things which occurred on the other side of the Tamar Bridge were of no interest to him. He decided they had been holiday-makers and left it at that.

He jangled the coins in the pocket of his jeans and resisted the temptation to buy a second pint of cider. He felt worse rather than better for the one he had drunk.

The walk home helped to clear his head. Instinctively his feet picked their way through gorse roots and scattered stones. For a big man he moved lightly and easily and all the walking kept him fit. He stowed his groceries in cupboards in the caravan then walked down to the house.

'What's up, son?' Dorothy asked as soon as she saw his face. No answer was necessary, the way he was trembling and refusing to meet her eyes said it all.

'Nothing, Ma.'

'You've bin drinking again.' It was a statement. She wiped her hands on a tea towel and studied him carefully before turning to stir something simmering in a pot. 'You'll end up in trouble if you don't look out.' Martin was not dishonest, nor was he a fighting man, but he was easily taken advantage of, especially when he had drink inside him. How unlike her boys were. Peter was much the brighter but he lacked compassion. Martin was insecure, easily hurt and quickly ashamed yet he intuitively offered comfort whenever it was needed.

Peter imagined that, because she insisted on his repaying loans, she thought the less of Martin. This was far from true. She was trying to teach him a set of values and how to look after himself financially, preparing him for the time when she would no longer be around. 'Well, now you're here you may as well eat with me. Cut some bread, son.'

Martin got out a loaf and hacked off four thick slices then they sat down to eat. Saliva filled his mouth as he took the first mouthful of beef stew. The remains from yesterday having been reheated, the flavours had mingled appetisingly. They ate in companionable silence; they were close enough not to feel the need to make inconsequential conversation.

When they had finished Dorothy cleared away the plates and made tea. She wished she knew what was troubling her son.

'Anyone been here?' Martin asked so abruptly that she jumped and the tea leaves on the spoon scattered over the wooden draining-board instead of into the pot.

Dorothy bit her lip. 'No,' she said hesitantly for there were some things she did not want Martin to know, not just yet. 'But Mrs Trevelyan's coming tomorrow. Why?'

'Oh, 'er's all right. I mean anyone else?'

'No. You know only Fred Meecham and Rose come, and Jobber Hicks to give me a lift now and then. What's got into you, Martin?'

'That's all right then.' He avoided an answer but seemed to be relieved as his shoulders unhunched and he pushed back a lock of brown hair. He drank his tea and thanked his mother for the meal then left by the back door, heading up over the rough ground in the direction of his caravan where he intended getting his head down for at least eight hours.

Dorothy remained at the table, her hands clasped around her pint mug as if she was cold. She felt vaguely sick. She had never lied to Martin before. There had been a visitor and she now understood what had brought that particular person to her door. Martin had not been able to keep his mouth shut. However, inadvertently he had done himself a favour and now Dorothy was returning it by keeping quiet.

Outside the night enveloped the house like a cloak. All that could be heard were the familiar creakings of the building. Through the kitchen windows the outlines of boulders became shadowy shapes until they merged completely into the blackness. Clouds hid the stars and there was no street-lighting for a long way. In a couple more days she would need to light a fire. There was a good supply of wood stacked against the side of one of the outbuildings. Martin had cut it for her in the spring and left it there to weather. Fresh wood with the sap still running burned longer but was no good for giving off heat. Dorothy smiled. She liked the winter when gales made the windows rattle and the wind relentlessly but unsuccessfully pounded away at the house which had stood undamaged for the best part of two hundred years. Only once had she needed someone to come and replace a couple of roof slates.

When the dark evenings arrived Dorothy took herself to bed early and read, her mind always partly aware of the screaming elements outside. When a strong westerly brought rain it lashed against the bedroom window but the sound was comforting, a part of all she had ever known. She would lie contentedly beneath the sheet and blankets and the patchwork quilt her mother had stitched and give thanks for her life.

She was, she realised, a woman of extremes. She liked summer and winter, understood only good or evil and had no time for people who dithered because they couldn't decide the best thing to do. Everything in life was black or white to her and this outlook reflected both her character and her surroundings. She loved the harshness of the scenery outside and could never have lived in one of the picturesque villages which attracted tourists. Even as a girl she had avoided crowds, walking the cliff paths alone or with friends from the village. They would lie amongst the rough grasses and the thrift, its pink flowers bobbing in the soft breezes, and plan their futures, futures modelled on their parents' lives. They knew only open spaces and the moods of the Atlantic Ocean as it battered the coastline or caressed the golden sand. Time was measured by the storms and the baking heat of summer. Their food came from the sea and the surrounding farms, their bread from their mothers' kitchens and their only entertainment was listening to the stories passed down through the generations or hearing one of the choirs sing in the church.

Progress, she thought. What has it brought us but people in a hurry with their fast cars and their televisions and computers which were called, she believed, technology communication? 'Communication!' she spluttered. 'They things does the opposite. Nobody talks any more, not proper. Just tap, tap, tap in they machines. Bleddy tusses.'

She was still at the table, deep in thought, talking aloud as she often did lately. A knock at the door jerked her into alertness. Tap, tap, tap. The sounds were real, not an echo of her thoughts.

24

She was surprised to notice it was now completely dark. 'I'm coming,' she called as she pulled a cardigan around her shoulders and wondered if her visitor had returned.

Peter Pengelly worked on the railways and enjoyed the life although he was not sure how he felt about privatisation. He had recently been promoted to senior conductor on the Inter-City line from Penzance to Paddington although he never completed the whole journey. Mostly the trains changed crews at Plymouth or Exeter. They could manage on what he earned but with two school-age children it wasn't easy, at least according to Gwen.

'Why don't you get a job?' he had asked more than once. 'Just something part-time. You'll probably enjoy it, it'll get you out of the house.'

'I don't want a job, I want to be a proper mother.'

He knew this was not the real reason. Gwen hankered after a life where money was no problem and where she could lord it over others. But she did not want to have to work for it. Sadder still, she had no real friends. Lately he had pressed her harder but she had given him one of her cool glances and made him feel inadequate again.

'There isn't much point now, is there? Your mother won't last for ever. Think about it, Peter, it'll make such a difference to our lives. We can have a bigger house and when all her bits and pieces have been sold – '

'For God's sake,' he had hissed in exasperation, dropping his mug in the washing-up bowl before leaving for work.

'I'll never live out there. Never!' Gwen had shouted after him, almost in tears. All she had ever wanted was a life to make up for her miserable childhood and Dorothy Pengelly was the only thing standing in her way.

That same morning Gwen drove into Truro and bought some new underwear. To her mind Peter was a highly sexed man and she thought she knew exactly how to get what she wanted.

At home, an hour before she was due to collect the children from school, Gwen pulled the flimsy garments out of their plastic carrier and admired them. Her figure was good enough that they would flatter her. Once the children were in bed she would shower and dress in her new things then come downstairs, the lacy garments covered only by her thigh-length robe.

Rose finished the day's work early and returned home at four. The light was blinking on the answering machine. She dropped her camera cases into an armchair and flicked the switch.

'Rose, dear, is that you? It's me, Dorothy. Can you bring some milk with you tomorrow? Oh, be quiet.'

Rose grinned. The short, sharp barks were unmistakably those of George, the Jack Russell. The greyhound, Star, whose name had been shortened from her racing name of White Star Dancer, did nothing but sleep or rest her lean, greying muzzle on your lap.

'Anyway, if it's not too much trouble. I'll see you all right when you get here.'

Rose knew better than to refuse the money. She had no idea of Dorothy's financial position but had learned her lesson some time ago when Dorothy had expressed her views on charity. She had, on that same occasion, rather slyly asked Rose's opinion of a painting which hung on her bedroom wall. It was an original Stanhope Forbes and there were, she had hinted, one or two more by various members of the Newlyn School. She had come by them by way of her mother who had mixed with the artists and who had, according to Dorothy, known one or two of them intimately. In those days they had been regarded as bohemian and rather shocking with the women drinking and smoking as well as the men and with their unorthodox lifestyles. Now, of course, they were regarded with admiration. Rose wondered just how intimate the relationships between Dorothy's mother and the painters had been and whether Dorothy might actually be the daughter of one of them.

The picture she had been shown was badly in need of a clean but Rose's experienced eye saw immediately that it was worth a lot of money. It had struck her at the time that this might be

Dorothy's way of saying that she could well afford to pay for her shopping. After that incident Rose had taken stock of the contents of Dorothy's house and had realised that amongst the outdated junk there were some good pieces of furniture but her interest in antiques was limited and therefore she had no idea what their value might be. However, it was Dorothy's company she enjoyed, not her possessions. She decided to ring her back.

'It's Rose,' she said when Dorothy finally came to the phone.

'Sorry to keep you, dear, but I was trying to find they blasted cats. Wild, they be, I don't know why I bother with 'un.'

Wild is right, Rose thought, they would as soon scratch and spit as be touched. 'How are you?'

'Fine. A bit tired but the blasted wind kept me awake last night and my shoulder aches. Trouble is, I always fall asleep listening to the radio of an evening then when it's time for bed I toss and turn all night. Makes me teasy, it does. But you don't want to be listening to my moaning.'

Rose frowned. She knew Dorothy refused to consider the possibility that she might be ill. Not once in her life had she been troubled by anything other than minor ailments and she would not give in to them. No doctor had set foot in her house and a midwife had delivered her sons in the wooden-framed bed upstairs.

'How're the grandchildren?'

'Don't see 'em much, really,' Dorothy admitted without self-pity. 'Gwen leads what she calls a busy life, though how that can be with washing-machines and all is beyond me. They're both at school now, and, selfish old woman that I am, I've never volunteered to look after them. Real modern kids they are, into the telly and computer games. They'd be bored silly out here with nothing but fresh air and God's own country all around 'em.'

Rose laughed. She heard the irony in the words. She knew that Dorothy's own children had been content to make their own amusement and had been allowed to run wild over the unin-habited countryside. In his teens Peter had taken to going to friends' houses but Martin had always remained content with his surroundings. Dorothy had shown Rose the treasures she still possessed; small things which Martin had carved out of wood although some of them were unrecognisable as objects.

'Martin's bin drinking more'n's good for him,' Dorothy said as if she had read Rose's mind. 'It's not so much that which bothers me, my husband liked a drop hisself. Ah, well, not much to be done about it. How's that young man of yourn?'

'Jack?' Rose laughed. 'He's not exactly young, and he isn't mine.'

'Got shot of him, have you?' Dorothy cackled down the phone.

'No. We still see each other.'

'Time you was married then. I can't understand you. With me it were all or nothing. Sorry, maid, take no notice of me.'

'It's all right. Really it is.' Dorothy knew that for Rose, too, it was all or nothing. It had been with David. 'I still don't know how I feel about Jack.'

'Early days yet, it's not hardly a year, is it?' Dorothy contradicted herself. 'You'll know, right enough. One day you'll wake up and say he's the right one or he isn't. My, my, listen to that. Can you hear it down your way?'

Rose could. The wind had strengthened and an unexpected rattle of rain hit the window. 'Yes. I hope the electricty doesn't go off again.' It was a common problem. 'I must go, I'll see you tomorrow.'

'I'll look forward to seeing 'e, maid.'

Rose hung up. She could already smell the familiar mixture of dogs and cigarettes and Pear's soap which was Dorothy.

In the attic which she had had converted into a dark-room Rose developed two rolls of film and left them hanging in the drying cabinet prior to taking prints from them. Jack was coming over. He said he was tired and fancied a quiet night in but he was prepared to provide supper in the form of an Indian takeaway and some alcoholic refreshment. Rose had taken pity on him and had offered to cook provided he brought the drinks.

'And will I get to rest my weary head on your pillow?' Jack had half teasingly wanted to know when he rang her. Despite his brashness and his inability to deal with certain matters tactfully he made up for his deficiencies with his offbeat humour and Rose was aware that his show of masculine superiority was only a disguise for his need for reassurance. Jack Pearce, she thought, was as vulnerable as the next man. But do I really want a vulnerable man? was a question she often asked herself.

A crack of thunder made her jump and the rain became a torrent of water which streamed down the side of the house, taking with it mud from the flower beds. The tide was high. By now the waves would be breaking over the Promenade. Rose did not know whether she preferred the vibrant colours and heat of the summer or the violent but spectacular storms of winter.

She showered and washed her hair and changed into a dress, spraying her wrists and neck with perfume which Jack had bought for her last Christmas but which she rarely remembered to use.

Jack could be unpunctual when his job prevented him from being otherwise but tonight he arrived on time, sprinting around the side of the house to the kitchen door, the entrance which all her friends used. She let him in, water dripping from him on to the floor.

'See, I didn't forget.' He kissed the top of her head as he placed a bulging bag bearing the logo of an off-licence on the table. 'Aren't you cold?' He nodded towards her short-sleeved dress.

'Not really.' But soon the dress would be put away for the winter. The evenings were noticeably pulling in and twice in a week she had had to close the bedroom window at night. Jack did look tired but it did not detract from his dark good looks. In jeans and shirt and raincoat, left unbuttoned, his powerful body was shown to advantage. Beside him Rose felt tiny and was never able to get over her surprise at the way in which he seemed to fill a room. But Jack was also trying to fill the life she was building without David. She wasn't quite sure how she had allowed it to happen.

The following morning Rose told Jack she was going to visit Dorothy. 'I'm worried about her. She was a bit pale last time I saw her.'

'Can't you get her GP to call in and see her?'

'I doubt if she's got one. Besides, she'd be furious. God, look at the time. Push off, Jack, I've got loads to do.' He was not on duty until the afternoon but she didn't want him under her feet any longer. She was already regretting letting him stay.

'Is that all the thanks I get for my superb performance last night?'

'Oh, Jack.' He had meant it as a joke but she knew he tried to please her in every way. What was missing was on her side alone.

'I do believe you're blushing, Mrs Trevelyan. I didn't think I'd live to see the day.' He bent to kiss her but something in her eyes warned him not to. 'It's all right, I'm going. Unwillingly, but I'm going. I'll give you a ring later.'

She nodded and watched him leave, his bulk blocking the light from the kitchen window as he passed it.

It was going to be one of those days. No sooner had she washed the dishes which had been left after the previous night's meal than Laura's figure replaced Jack's, although hers was of different dimensions. She too was taller than Rose but thin, naturally so. As she bounced up the path her corkscrew curls bobbed around her shoulders, restricted as they were by a towelling band.

'Don't worry, I won't keep you long,' Laura said, laughing because she had seen Rose's dismayed expression. 'I know you're busy but as I was passing I thought I'd let you know that film we said we'd see is now on in Truro. Fancy going some time?'

Rose did not point out that it would have been easier to telephone but she did understand that on Trevor's first day back at sea Laura felt the need for company. Her three children were grown up and had left home. Two of them had made her a grandmother which, looking at Laura, seemed hard to believe.

'Yes. But not tonight. You might as well put the kettle on now you're here.'

'You obviously had company last night,' Laura said as she nudged Rose out of the way and ran the tap. 'Was it the ever faithful Barry Rowe or the delectable Jack Pearce?'

For the second time that morning Rose blushed. Laura had not failed to notice that there were two sets of crockery and cutlery on the draining-board and had probably guessed the reason why the dishes had not been seen to until just now.

'No need to answer, your face says it all.' Laura grinned again and creases formed in the tight skin of her face, but instead of ageing her they had the opposite effect. She reminded Rose of an oversized imp.

Rose did not begrudge her the time. Her friend had seen her through the months of David's illness and the awful year which had followed his death. Not once had she told her to pull herself together and she had listened patiently throughout the stage where repetition becomes monotonous and most people get bored. For half an hour they chatted amiably then Laura said she must go.

Bradley Hinkston and Roy Phelps, his associate, had paid a visit to Hayle where they had taken bed and breakfast accommodation at a pub. Two days after their conversation with Martin Pengelly they were on their way back to Bristol where the business was based. Roy was driving the van although Bradley was none too comfortable in the passenger seat, preferring the comfort of his Jaguar.

'It was worth it, then?' Roy took his eyes off the motorway winding ahead of them for a split second. The van had no radio and Roy was not a man at home with silence.

'Oh, yes. It was defintely worth it. The old dear's got a treasure trove there.' From the corner of his eye he saw Roy's thin-lipped smile.

'What's she like? A proper Janner if her son's anything to go by.'

Bradley's arms were crossed. He raised a hand and smoothed his cheek with a forefinger. 'No. Oh, she's got the accent, all right, but I don't think much escapes Mrs Pengelly's notice.'

They had reached the M5 and both were anxious to be back in the city. Since his divorce Roy had lived alone, over the shop, an arrangement convenient to them both and to Bradley's insurers who were pleased to have the rooms over the business occupied. The premises were not the sort that generally passed for an antique shop. There were no oddments of china, no broken chairs and no boxes of junk scattered on the floor. The items he sold were genuine and well cared for. Mostly they consisted of large pieces of furniture along with the occasional bit of porcelain or silver. Everything was displayed under bright lights and there were grilles which pulled down over the windows at night. Roy was never sure if any of Bradley's deals were crooked because he was not privy to them all, like the Pengelly woman, for instance. Still, it was best not to ask. One or two sales a week were enough to keep them both but they usually made far more than that. 'What if she talks?'

'Oh, she won't talk, sunshine, I can guarantee that.'

They reached the outskirts of Bristol and were heading for the centre just as the rain that was sweeping from the west hit them. They drove past Temple Meads Station and continued on to the shop where they unloaded what they had managed to purchase in Cornwall.

'Fancy a drink before I drop you off?'

Bradley nodded as he padlocked the door grille. 'A gin and tonic would go down a treat. I can't be long because I promised the wife I wouldn't be late tonight.' His voice was cultured, his manner urbane. 'All in all a good trip, wouldn't you say?'

Together they walked quickly through the city streets. The shops were closed but the traffic was still heavy. The rain hit the pavements with a steady hiss and the drops bounced up again. They began to walk faster.

After a single gin Bradley glanced at his watch and said it was time he was going. Roy drove him to his house in the suburbs which, he estimated, was worth more than he would ever be able to afford. He bore no grudges because he liked the man with his silvery hair and the twill trousers he favoured who was so very different from himself but who treated him like a father. But he felt unsettled that day. Within him was a sinking feeling that Bradley might have gone over the top back there in Cornwall. He wished he would confide more in him. No, he amended, there had been no need for confidences. Roy knew exactly what Bradley had planned to do.

Bradley's wife welcomed him with an absent-minded kiss on

the cheek before carrying on preparing a tray of canapés. 'I won't be long,' she said, 'but you can use the bathroom first.'

Bradley went upstairs anticipating an excellent meal.

As he shaved for the second time that day and got ready to receive their guests he mentally listed the deals he had made during his visit to the West Country and calculated how much money they would make. The Cornish, he thought, are a strange lot. But strangest of all had been the time he had spent in the company of Dorothy Pengelly.

3

Rose intended making a start on the wild flower sketches after she had seen Dorothy. She drove out of Penzance and joined the dual carriageway, taking a left at the roundabout.

The rain had eased off but the road was still wet and drops of moisture clung to the long grass in the verges, glittering in the sunshine. Behind her was St Michael's Mount, Rose caught a glimpse of it in her rear mirror, and around her was countryside. It would be a nice day after all. But something was wrong, Rose knew it. David had once said she was more superstitious than the Cornish and that her sixth sense was developed enough for her to be classed as one of them. Please let him be wrong, she prayed as she neared Dorothy's house.

There was no ferocious barking from George as she swung into the drive nor did Dorothy come to the door at the sound of the Mini's engine. A car passed on the main road, but other than that there was silence. Not even a bird sang. Anxiety gripped her as she approached the front door. On the grass to one side of her a crow, busy shredding something with its beak, paused to glance at her then hopped a few paces away before flying off. The front door was slightly ajar. Rose stopped, her heart beating faster. She could hear something now, some faint sound coming from within the house. It might have been someone in pain. At least she would be able to do something about it if Dorothy had fallen over. She knocked and called out but there was no response. Pushing open the door she called again. 'Dorothy? It's me. Rose.'

The sounds were coming from the kitchen. Rose hurried towards them then stood in the doorway trying to make sense of the scene before her. Dorothy lay on the floor, her head cradled in Martin's lap. It was Martin she had heard. He was gently rocking his mother and making crooning noises as tears ran down his face. Star was asleep in her basket and George, normally so volatile, whimpered quietly, curled up in Dorothy's armchair.

'What's happened? What's happened to her?' Martin asked Rose, seeming unsurprised to see her there.

'I don't know, Martin. Have you called an ambulance?'

He shook his head. Rose quickly took over. She bent over Dorothy and touched her. She was stone cold and her eyes were slits, the half-moons of her irises dull. Dorothy Pengelly was dead. Rose knew that at once. It was too late for an ambulance but she was not qualified to presume that. She rang for one anyway. Mike Phillips, she thought, Mike who had cared for David, he would tell her what she ought to do. No wonder Dorothy had been pale the other day, she had obviously been ill. Too late, Rose wished she had taken Jack's advice and sent a doctor anyway.

One of the hospital switchboard operators bleeped Mike and he came to the phone quickly, knowing that Rose would not disturb him unless it was necessary.

'Mike. My friend . . . Dorothy . . . oh, Mike, she's dead.'

'Stay calm, Rose. Have you rung for an ambulance?'

'Yes.'

'Who's her GP?'

'She doesn't have one.'

'Look, I think you ought to call the police as well. The paramedics'll probably do it anyway. If she's always been fit the police surgeon will want to take a look at her.'

'Thanks, Mike.' Rose replaced the receiver feeling stupid to have telephoned but it had been reassuring just speaking to him.

Martin had not moved, he was still rocking Dorothy. She wondered whether she ought to make him some strong sweet tea but felt a sense of repugnance at the idea of moving around Dorothy's kitchen and using her things whilst she lay there on the floor.

It seemed a long time until she heard a vehicle turn into the driveway although it could not have been more than a few minutes. The police arrived first. She had contacted Camborne station as it was the nearest.

One of the PCs made a quick examination of Dorothy and nodded to his colleague who turned away and spoke into his lapel radio. Martin ignored them all.

'Are you a relative?'

Rose shook her head. 'A friend. Martin's her son.'

They all stared at him. 'There'll be a doctor here soon. I think the lad needs attention too.'

The ambulance arrived, its siren shattering the subdued silence. The crew assessed the situation and saw that their services were unnecessary.

By the time the police surgeon had joined them the kitchen was crowded. 'There'll need to be a PM,' he told Rose, realising that Martin was in no state to take in anything. 'I'll arrange for her body to be collected. Is there anywhere Martin can go?'

'He can come back with me.'

'Good. And I suggest you get his GP to have a look at him.'

Rose nodded. It would have to be her own. He could not be left alone now and she could not begin to think what the loss of his mother would do to him.

'We'll need to ask you some questions,' one of the officers said. 'And Mr Pengelly in due course.'

There was little Rose could tell them. She described the scene as she had come upon it and they were told they could leave. 'What did she die from?' Rose asked.

'I'm not sure. Heart maybe?' The surgeon shrugged. He wasn't sure but there was a smell of alcohol and an empty paracetamol bottle which one of the police officers had picked up and shown him discreetly. The post-mortem would show if his suspicions were correct. It was not for him to blab to all and sundry that Dorothy Pengelly had taken her own life.

With the help of one of the policemen she got Martin to his

35

feet. Taking his arm she led him out to the car. Tall and big-boned as he was, he allowed himself to be gently settled into the front passenger seat. Rose took a quick look at him as she started the engine. His dark hair grew long over his collar, his face was tear-stained and his brown eyes were unseeing but Rose did not think he would do something stupid, like trying to jump out of the car while it was moving. 'Martin?' she tried tentatively, touching his arm. 'We're going back to my place. You can stay the night with me.' Her voice was firmer now. She had to take control, not let her own grief surface until she was sure Martin was all right. There were still some of David's things in the airing cupboard, it was ironic that it had taken another death for them to be put to use. Driving home she was glad that they would not be there to see Dorothy's body taken away.

When Martin finally spoke his words frightened Rose. 'She'll be all right soon, won't she?' he asked, making it clear that he had no idea of the finality of it.

'She's dead, Martin,' Rose said quietly, but she could not bring herself to say that she would never be coming back. Once they were safely at home she would try to get through to him.

She parked on the small concrete patch at the top of the path alongside the house and let them in. In her handbag were Dorothy's spare keys which the police had told her to take as someone would need to feed the animals. She had told them that Martin lived elsewhere and that there was another son who needed to be informed. Thankfully, that would not be her job. As she placed the keys on top of the fridge tears filled her eyes. Shock had worn off and she felt the loss of her friend badly. With her back to Martin she waited until she was more in control until she turned to face him. She had noticed there were four keys on the ring, two Yale, two Chubb, and realised that she had two identical sets. Presumably Peter would have a third.

Tomorrow the police wanted to question Martin. Rose owed it to Dorothy to ensure that he was ready and able to face up to their questions. She pulled out a chair and sat next to him.

'Peter,' he said before she had a chance to begin. 'You have to tell Peter.'

Rose nodded. It was a good sign. He understood that his

brother needed to know which meant he was aware that something was dreadfully wrong. 'The police will go and see him, there's nothing to worry about.' Useless words, Rose knew better than most. But there were no words which could ease the pain or change the situation. 'Would you like something to drink?' Dorothy had mentioned her anxiety on this count but these were exceptional circumstances. She barely remembered the three days after David's funeral when she had locked herself in the house, refusing to answer the door or the telephone as she sat drinking one bottle of wine after another, unwashed and without food. The long months of nursing and the final days spent at the hospital had taken their toll. Only then did she allow herself the indulgence of obliteration. It was Laura who had finally shouted at her through the letter-box, saying that if she didn't open the door she'd break the bloody thing down. If Martin now needed the temporary comfort of alcohol she would not deny him it.

'I'd like some tea, please. Can I smoke?'

'Of course you can.' She got out the only ashtray she possessed and placed it on the table. Rose smoked occasionally but no longer got through a packet a day. As she made the tea with shaking hands she wondered if Dorothy had left a will. As far as she was aware there were no relatives other than her two sons. It was an uncharitable thought but she hoped that Peter and his wife did not hold another set of keys because she suspected they might remove anything of value before probate had been finalised.

Impossible to work now. Even if she'd been up to it Martin needed someone to be with him. He was, she realised as she placed his tea before him, the same size as Jack but he appeared to have shrunk somehow.

Catching sight of her wrist-watch she saw it was already mid-afternoon. Without asking if he was hungry Rose made some sandwiches but Martin did little more than take a few mouthfuls and crumble the bread between his fingers. His grief was plain to see but he seemed ill at ease. Rose watched him as she tried to eat her own sandwich. She had a habit of skipping meals and recently her jeans had become looser. She kicked off her canvas shoes and hooked her hair behind her ears. She must eat to

37

encourage Martin although she gagged on the bread, and then she had to get him to talk.

Without warning he stood up. 'I think I killed her,' he said. 'I want to go home.'

At that moment the telephone rang. 'Sit down, Martin. I won't be a minute.' Rose went to answer it, too dazed to think straight. It was Doreen Clarke, a woman she had met some time ago when she had been commissioned to take photographs of the house of a wealthy family. Doreen cleaned other people's houses and was a great source of gossip, a pastime for which she was renowned. But surely even Doreen couldn't have heard the news yet?

'Rose, dear,' she began, 'I was wondering if you'd open the Christmas bazaar for us this year? I know it isn't until December but you can't leave these things until the last minute. Only, you see, we tried to get whatshisname, the MP, but he's got other commitments and we can't find anyone else who's willing.'

Despite everything Rose felt a flicker of amusement. The two women's initial dislike of each other had mellowed and turned into mutual respect until they had finally become friends. Doreen now considered her to be a minor celebrity but it was apparent that she was by no means first choice for the job. 'What's the date?' Rose flicked through her diary knowing that she had nothing booked that far ahead. 'Yes, that's fine. But I hope people won't be disappointed, I'm sure no one will know who I am.'

'Of course they will,' Doreen assured her firmly. 'I'll make sure your name's on all the posters and in the adverts in the paper. Here, why don't you bring along some of your stuff? You might make a sale or two?'

'I'll think about it. Doreen, I've got a visitor at the moment, I'll have to go. Thanks for asking me.' Rose replaced the receiver and went back to the kitchen. Martin hadn't moved. He remained standing behind his chair, his large-knuckled hands gripping the back of it, his eyes staring. For a second Rose wondered if he was mad.

'I don't think you ought to be alone, Martin. Why not stay here tonight?'

'Please, Mrs Trevelyan, I want to go home.'

'I'll drive you, but first you must tell me what you mean.' Martin was frightened. Perhaps Dorothy had still been alive when he found her and he now realised he ought to have called for help.

'I told 'un.'

'Told who, Martin? I don't understand you.'

'They men.'

'What men?' She couldn't guess how the police would deal with him.

'In the pub.' He clamped his mouth shut. 'I want to go home.'

Rose hesitated then nodded. He was in shock, he didn't know what he was talking about. Dorothy had told her how he drank too much, it was highly unlikely he'd remember anything he'd said to someone in the pub. Assessing him she saw that perhaps he was better on his own. Men like him, used to solitude and uncomfortable in other people's homes, would heal quicker if left alone. Tomorrow she would go and talk to him again.

Reluctantly she drove him back, praying that she was doing the right thing. Martin had been so close to his mother that she feared for his state of mind. If anything happened to him it would be on her conscience for ever. Already she had ignored the advice to get a doctor to see him. It would be pointless, a doctor couldn't bring Dorothy back, nor could he ease Martin's pain. All he could do was prescribe pills to blot it out temporarily. Besides, she tried to reassure herself, she could not force a grown man to remain under her roof.

The working day was coming to a close and the traffic heading in the opposite direction was building up. Although there was little on her side of the road she got stuck behind a tractor piled high with bales of hay. It turned sharply into a farm gateway, the rear end of the trailer swinging behind it. The clouds were moving faster, building up from the west until they were banked in a grey mass. Rose wound up the window as the wind changed direction. On the slopes the heather was beginning to flower. Walking through it, hand in hand, were a couple. Had Martin ever had a girlfriend? she wondered. It would have been nice if there was someone other than herself to comfort him. She doubted his brother and his wife would trouble themselves.

Stopping as near to the caravan as she was able she watched him climb slowly up over the rough ground, his head bowed, his arms hanging limply at his sides. She had no idea what was going on in his head. For a second she had a maternal urge to run after him and hold him tightly but it would embarrass them both. When he had disappeared over the brow of the hill she turned the Mini around and went home to find another message on her answering machine. It was Barbara Phillips, the wife of Mike Phillips whom she had rung earlier in the day. 'Rose, are you there? Never mind. It's me, Barbara. Mike told me what happened. You poor thing. Give me a ring when you can. Look, I know this isn't a good time but I'm having a bit of a do to celebrate Mike's fiftieth. Saturday week. You've got to be here, and I won't take no for an answer. Ring me when you can. We'll be thinking of you.' Dear Barbara, who had during that awful year gently but persistently encouraged her to go out more but who now did so forcefully. Here was a chance to meet new people. I'll go, Rose thought. Alone. No Jack and no Barry.

Barry. Suddenly she remembered that she was supposed to be meeting him that evening for a long-standing dinner date. She would not ring him to cancel, it would be too hard breaking the news over the telephone. Let him come, then she would tell him.

There were three appointments in her diary for the next day. Rose did cancel them. Tomorrow she must make sure Martin was all right and she needed time for herself, time to grieve for Dorothy. It had not really hit her yet. Aimlessly, she wandered around the house which she loved and where she had always been so happy. What had happened to her youthful dreams? Was the woman who drew and painted wild flowers and pretty bays for commercial purposes the same girl who had had such high hopes for herself? Having gained a place at art college and having been told she had talent, her ambition had been to make a living in oils; wild, dramatic oils of rugged seascapes and rocky promontories. After a brief flirtation with contemporary art she knew it was not for her. Rose's work was representational, alive and real.

She hadn't given herself a chance. Just because her initial attempts had not created a storm didn't mean she could not have

40

improved. Few artists were instantly recognised, many not at all. Up until David had died she had painted one or two oils each year, after his death there had been only one. And now Dorothy's death had shown her how tenuous the grip on life was. It was time she made some changes.

Jobber Hicks had been farming since the day he left school at fourteen and by that time had already completed his apprentice-ship by way of the various tasks he was allocated each evening and which he did as soon as he had changed out of his uniform. Only then could he wash and sit down at the table with the rest of the family and eat the large meal his mother prepared for them every day. Of the five children he was the only one who had remained on the farm. When his father died he had taken over his role. By that time his mother had been dead for five years.

The money that Harry Hicks had scrupulously saved had been divided equally between the children but Jobber's three sisters and brother showed no interest in making any claim on the farm itself. They were all married and comfortable in their different ways and they knew that if the property was sold Jobber would be out of work and have nowhere to go. They were not interested in a fifth of its worth because the whole place had fallen into disrepair since Mrs Hicks's death and the land surrounding it belonged to the Duchy anyway. The deeds were transferred to Jobber and he began the long task of renovating the farm.

Jobber was also the only one to remain single. From his youth he had always hankered after Dorothy Pengelly, or Trelawny, as she had been then. She was different from the other girls he knew, having guts and spirit from an early age. When her husband died his hopes were renewed. He waited for a decent interval then began to woo her in his own steady way. Dorothy disappointed him by saying that she had no intention of marrying again, one husband had been enough. Jobber never knew how close to saying yes she had been. He had had to content himself with the farm and her friendship but he had wanted more.

His work usually took up ten or more hours a day so he

employed a married woman to come in and cook and clean. During school holidays she would bring her small daughter whom Jobber would sometimes take out with him. He was touched by her devotion and by the way she would slip her hand in his without prompting.

He had been christened Joseph Robert Hicks but when Florrie, the baby of the family, first began to speak she could not master his names and ran them into one. Jobber, she had called him and the name had stuck.

He sat in the kitchen in an armchair beside the range which burned all year to serve the back-boiler and the ovens. He was ashamed, he could not remember when he had last cried, but Dorothy's death had rocked his world. His own mortality did not bother him, death would come at some point and occasionally it seemed welcome. But how he would miss those jaunts into Camborne and being able to go up to the house and discuss all manner of things with her. The last time he had seen her he had had the strong impression there was something she wanted to tell him.

He thought of Martin. As soon as Rose had rung him he had driven over but the boy was neither at the house nor in his van. Mid-evening he had found him, sitting on a rock, the setting sun giving his pale face a rosy glow. He had barely responded to Jobber's questions.

Jobber dried his eyes and pulled out his pipe, sucking at the stem and spitting out the sticky blackness which lined it before tamping the bowl with strong-smelling tobacco. Once it was lit he applied himself to the question of Dorothy's younger son. He decided to go and see him and ask if he might have Star, the greyhound. It would be nice to have something of Dorothy's to which she had been attached. Niggling at the back of his mind was the worry that he had put too much pressure on her. If it was heart trouble the last thing she needed was his persistent efforts to get her to marry him.

4

'What do you say, Peter?' Gwen stood with her hands on her hips, her head on one side, waiting for an answer. She had already half extracted a promise that he would sell his mother's house when the time came. Her husband slowly chewed a piece of toast, his face as yet unshaven, as he sat at the kitchen table where all their meals were taken because they did not have a dining-room.

'It sounds like a reasonable idea, but she'll not agree.'

'You don't know unless you ask.' Gwen sat down, her elbows on the table as she leant forward enthusiastically. She did not tell Peter that she had been up to see Dorothy, nor could she ever admit what had happened. 'Look, it might be just what she's waiting for. You know how proud she is, she'll never admit she can't cope up there by herself. I bet she's just waiting for you to suggest it. Besides, she'll be far better off in one of those warden-controlled places.'

Peter was not prepared to argue so for the sake of peace he agreed to put the proposition to his mother although he knew the outcome in advance. Gwen had changed her tune, she was, by her standards, talking quite reasonably. But something was wrong, he could tell by the excitement in her eyes. Excitement? Or was it agitation? He never really knew what was going on in his wife's mind. He supposed that she imagined his mother would simply hand over the money. In which case she was a fool. The state would want the proceeds of the sale for taking care of her.

'She's never spent a penny on any of us – she's selfish, you know that. We could do with the money while we're young enough to enjoy it.'

'That's enough! I've said I'll mention it, now leave it.' He shook his head in exasperation. He was still a young man with a young family but Gwen was wearing him out and today he couldn't fathom her at all. Still slagging his mother off but without the usual venom, almost like a cat that's had the cream, he thought, resorting to clichés because he was unable to think straight when his wife's behaviour confused him.

Satisfied that she had done all she could, that she had covered her tracks, she slipped a hand inside Peter's shirt and massaged his chest. The children had been dropped at school by a friend, there was time enough to go back upstairs before Peter had to leave for work.

Later, when Gwen was about to collect them from school, she saw, from her bedroom window, the police car pull up. 'Oh, God,' she whispered as the two officers got out and approached her door. 'What have I done?'

Ashen-faced and with trembling legs she made it down the stairs just as they rang the bell.

'Mrs Pengelly?'

Gwen nodded, unable to speak, her fingers clutching at the buttons of her dress.

'May we come in?'

'Yes.' Her voice was hoarse.

PC Tregidgo ushered his female companion ahead of him. It was she, as Gwen had expected, who said that Dorothy was dead. Gwen's legs finally gave out. Her knees buckled and she slumped back into an armchair. The WPC offered to make tea.

'No. No, thanks, I'm fine. Really. It was just such a shock. I mean, she was old, I knew it would happen at some time, but, well, you never do really expect it, do you?' She was babbling and she knew it. 'My children. I've got to fetch them from school.'

'Can't a neighbour go? I really don't think you ought to drive. Can we ring someone?'

Gwen capitulated. She, too, thought it doubtful that she'd be able to control the foot pedals. PC Tregidgo also rang the school to let them know that someone else would be collecting the Pengelly children.

'What did she die of?'

'We don't know yet for certain. There'll be a post-mortem.'

'Oh, I see.'

44

The two officers exchanged a glance. Most people were upset when they heard this news, Mrs Pengelly's daughter-in-law actually seemed pleased. An empty paracetamol bottle did not necessarily prove that the old lady had swallowed the lot, she may simply have taken the last two because of chest pains for all they knew. It was up to the pathologist to find out. For the moment their instructions were that the cause of death was as yet unknown.

'Can we go ahead with any arrangements?'

'I'm afraid not, not until after the inquest.'

'Inquest. Yes, I see.' Gwen pressed her lips firmly together. In a minute she'd lose control, she'd felt her teeth knocking when she relaxed her jaw. 'And the post-mortem, why's that necessary?'

'It's quite normal under the circumstances if someone dies suddenly and they're not under medical supervision.'

'Yes. Good.'

PC Tregidgo raised his eyebrows and tilted his head towards the kitchen. The WPC took the hint and went to put the kettle on. Mrs Pengelly seemed to be in shock, her reactions were not those they usually experienced in such cases.

'What time'll your husband be home?'

Gwen looked up. The policeman did seem young, it was true what they said. 'Not until about ten. He works for Great Western.'

'Is there someone who can sit with you?'

'No. I'll be fine, and I'll have the children.'

By the time they had drunk the tea the children had returned home, dropped by one of the neighbours. They were unnaturally quiet at the sight of the two uniforms and went upstairs to their rooms.

Alone at last Gwen went straight to the kitchen cupboard and pulled out a bottle of whisky. She half filled a tumbler and drank most of it standing by the sink. It was an unprecedented action but never more needed. Five minutes later she started to prepare tea for Kirsty and Michael. Breathing deeply to steady herself she realised that now she would be able to buy some more dresses. She never wore jeans or trousers, they were unfeminine and she knew what men liked. Better still, they could move to a large house. But first she had to deal with the guilt and the fear.

Rose was staring out of the window; her face was wet with tears so she did not immediately notice it was raining. 'Oh, Dorothy,' she said sadly. 'How I'm going to miss you.' She brushed at her face impatiently and went to the kitchen and out into the garden to retrieve the washing which flapped furiously in the spray-laden wind and rain. Hurriedly she unpegged it and threw it into the basket. From the comparative warmth of the kitchen she could hear the loose brass knob on her bedroom door rattling because the windows were open.

As she placed the washing basket on the table a wave of exhaustion swept over her. Delayed reaction. As long as there had been Martin to consider her own feelings hadn't come into it. And now she was dreading telling Barry Rowe. Rose could not see that Dorothy's death was that simple. Yes, she was old and not quite as strong as she liked to think, but she was tough and she hadn't shown any of the symptoms of heart disease. Yes, Rose knew it could happen, a sudden massive coronary, but not to Dorothy, surely? Barry would struggle to hide his annoyance because he was always angry when she became too involved with other people. Jealous, more like, she thought. But Barry Rowe and Jack Pearce no longer seemed to matter much. At some point during that apparently fruitful staring out of the window she had made up her mind about her future.

With a glass of wine in her hand she waited in the sitting-room in her favourite armchair for Barry to arrive. The suite was covered in fading chintz, there was an open fire, lit in the winter to supplement the central heating, and cosy table lamps, and nothing was quite straight. Rose's house, like its detached neighbours, was built of Cornish granite and the rooms were small, although comfortable. The floors sloped imperceptibly and the walls were uneven. Upstairs they were emulsioned but the sitting-room walls remained in their original state, the glittering granite cold but enduring. On the floor was a deep claret carpet which continued through the hall and up the stairs.

Restless, Rose picked up their framed wedding photograph and studied it, unable to understand how she still felt mentally as young as the girl who smiled back at her. Like Dorothy she did not think she would remarry but she had not ruled it out entirely. Sometimes Jack stayed overnight but she could not envisage living with him on a permanent basis. There was a frisson between them which could lead to laughter or, equally, to an argument, but that wasn't enough. And if she was honest, the novelty was wearing off. She replaced the photograph as she heard Barry calling from the kitchen.

'Oh, Rosie, I don't know what to say.' Barry Rowe stood in the kitchen looking so pitiful that Rose almost laughed. His thinning hair was damp and so were the shoulders of his jacket. His glasses were misted with rain and had slipped down his nose and he seemed not to know what to do with his hands.

'Some wine?' Rose poured him a glass, aware that he had wanted to reach out and put his arms around her, but they rarely had any physical contact. 'I don't feel like going out, I hope you don't mind.'

'Of course I don't. You should've rung me.' He watched her slender figure as she moved around the kitchen. In jeans and T-shirt, her hair tied back untidily, she hardly looked more than a child. Jack Pearce or not, he thought, he wouldn't have stood a chance.

'I can't believe she just died like that.' Rose raised her hands, palms uppermost in disbelief. 'I mean, not Dorothy.'

'No one ever believes it at first.' Barry stopped. He had been about to add, You should know better than most.

'Well, it'll be interesting to hear the result of the post-mortem.'

'You've got to stop doing this, Rose.'

'Doing what?'

She spun around to face him, irritation making her tone sharper than she had intended. Unless she slapped him down now and then Barry had a tendency to be dictatorial.

'Getting involved.' He shrugged. 'Finding problems where there are none.'

'I thought the world of Dorothy, you don't know how much I'll miss her.' She felt the tears starting again. 'And just because

47

you don't give a damn about the human race doesn't mean we're all the same.'

'I'm sorry, Rose. I think it's best if I go now.'

'So do I.' Rigidly she watched him leave, pulling his jacket collar up against the rain, then she sank into a chair. Poor Barry, she thought. He had never been close to anyone. Orphaned young and with no siblings he had been unable to form real relationships. His total emotional output was expended upon herself and she had been mean to him. How could she expect him to understand that she and Dorothy had been kindred spirits? Both had lost their husbands and through their losses had grown into strong, independent women. Rose knew how fiercely she protected this independence. Whatever Barry thought, she knew there was something wrong. And then the real pain began. 'Oh, David, oh, Dorothy,' she gasped before laying her head in her arms on the table and sobbing.

Rose woke at six unable to recall going to bed. Sleep had not revived her, she felt listless and depressed. Outside the rain continued to pour down, drenching everything and bouncing off the glass roof of the porch. In a way she was sorry she had cancelled her appointments.

Trying to make use of her time she spent the morning in the dark-room developing and printing several rolls of film. At a little after midday Jack rang. He, too, sounded tired.

'I would've rung last night but I thought you'd rather be left alone.'

'Thanks, Jack.' Of course he would know about Dorothy. It was to Camborne that she had telephoned.

'Want me to come over?'

'No.' She did not offer any explanation.

'Rose?'

She waited, knowing by the tone of his voice that there was more to come, that he hadn't only telephoned to see how she was.

'Rose, the post-mortem took place today. The path bloke wasn't busy so he fitted it in.'

'And?'

'And ... Well, the final results aren't available yet ... Look, this is confidential until after the inquest, OK?'

'You don't need to ask, Jack.'

'No. I'm sorry. Dorothy committed suicide.'

'Don't be ridiculous.' Rose was actually laughing.

'The stomach contents say so. An overdose. There was an empty paracetamol bottle at the scene and – '

'At the scene? Come off it, Jack, it's me you're talking to. Not in a million years would Dorothy kill herself, she loved life too much.'

'It wasn't paracetamol.'

'All right, what was it then?'

'Something stronger. We don't know yet. She confided in you, was anything worrying her?'

'She didn't kill herself so just sod off.' Rose hung up.

Fred Meecham drove away from the hospital in a state of numbness finally acknowledging that Marigold was going to die.

Lying in the high bed, her skin grey against the white sheets, emaciated and almost fading away before his eyes, she had seemed like someone else, someone he had not met before.

He was so preoccupied with Marigold that the realisation that Dorothy Pengelly had been found dead hardly touched him. As he parked the van behind the shop he began to think of her, wishing, too late, that he had heeded her advice instead of carrying on unrealistically. Throughout his life Fred had been unaware that his own actions could affect others. He lived in a world where he believed things were done *to* him, that he was moulded and altered by external events, rather than having any influence over his own destiny By nature he was insecure. Until Marigold came back into his life his only comfort had been in God. But Marigold had changed everything and for the first time in his life he had acted out of character. Fred could not see that if people knew of some of the things he had done before she had come to live with him, they would consider them to be so unlike him as to be impossible.

Upstairs in the flat he sat in the darkness. The wind was rising, the trees at the back swaying, their leaves shaking off droplets of water as the glow from the street-light flickered between them. Soon it would be winter, really and metaphorically. Without Marigold there could be no spring or summer. There was no hope, nothing to assuage the loss he had coming. All Fred had ever wanted was a faithful companion, someone to share his life, someone who would not let him down like all the others. Marigold had been that person, worthy of all the love he had to give. They had, he saw, saved each other. There wasn't a customer who didn't declare what a devoted brother and sister they were. Now she, too, was leaving him and there was nothing he could do to stop it happening.

As he tried to come to terms with the future he realised that the past did still matter. He had imagined that once he was alone again he would not care. Instead of wishing himself dead, hoping that he, too, could join Marigold as quickly as possible, a strong sense of survival was emerging and, with it, a need to protect everything he had fought so hard to attain.

Some time during the small hours he took himself to bed. He slept uneasily and dreamed of Dorothy. It was her he saw in that hospital bed, not Marigold. There was blood on the sheets, seeping slowly and brightly down across the counterpane, but Dorothy was smiling, mocking him. Clutched in her hands were bundles of fifty-pound notes, around her were his customers making the same sounds they made in his shop, muttering the same banalities, avoiding the word cancer as if it was contagious. 'How is she?' they would whisper as if by speaking quietly they could lessen the horror. He saw in their faces pity and sympathy but also relief that it wasn't themselves or one of their own who was suffering.

In the dream they, too, mocked him as if they could see into his soul and knew the secrets hidden there. Everyone seemed to be there, huddled around that bed, standing or sitting, admiring the flowers on the locker, yet still there was room for the nurses and the doctor who came rushing to Dorothy's bedside as a long, soft 'Oooh' was breathed in unison. Dorothy had flung the bloodstained money at Fred before falling back, her mouth open as she died. Rose Trevelyan stood at the head of the bed, smiling.

The money floated weightlessly above their heads like confetti taken by the wind. His customers reached up, trying to grab it, ignoring Fred who became aware that he was invisible. They were as one; he was, as always, on the outside. He walked through the heaving mass of bodies without feeling contact.

When he woke he was sweating although a chill breeze blew through the window he had forgotten to close. His mouth was dry and it took him several seconds to realise that it was a dream and that, although Dorothy had really died, Marigold was still alive, but he rang the hospital just to make sure.

He prayed as he dressed: Please, God, not today, don't take her away from me yet. As he fastened his tie he nodded slowly as if responding to some unheard voice. Good. It wouldn't be today.

The bathroom cabinet seemed bare now since the hospital had asked him to bring in all of Marigold's medication when she was admitted. There had been so much of it as the long days passed. He had kept it there although it was not as convenient as beside her bed but he didn't want her room to look like a sick room. By her bed had been flowers and a pile of the romantic novels she liked to read. Only she hadn't read much lately, her arms were too weak to hold the books. Fred had gone back to the library and exchanged them for paperbacks. Marigold had smiled and thanked him and had finally explained that she couldn't see too well. Each day added to the burden of her infirmities and the doctor had told him it was only a matter of time.

'How long?' Fred had asked.

'Days. Maybe less.'

He was going straight there. Days. Fred wanted every second with her. When it was over would be the time to think about the other things, to think about what Dorothy had said. But Dorothy was dead; when Marigold died too he would be the only one who knew.

51

5

Like most people, Doreen Clarke learned of Dorothy's death within twenty-four hours and spread the news as quickly as she had come to hear of it. On Sunday she was going to visit her sister in the village of Paul and Rose had invited her around for coffee first. Gossip though she was, Doreen was tempted to cancel the arrangement because, knowing how close to Dorothy Rose had been, she did not want to be the one to break the news if she hadn't already heard. It was her husband, Cyril, who talked some sense into her, saying she could not turn her back on a friend and, besides, young Jack Pearce would've put her wise.

Rose was ironing when she arrived. It was one of those deceptively warm September days when it seemed as if summer was beginning rather than ending. A vivid blue sky arched high over Mount's Bay, framing the Mount itself. Beneath it the sea shimmered as silver ripples skimmed its surface. Ozone hung in the air with the ever-present tang of fish. Even the gulls were quiet.

Rose had the back door open; her face was flushed with the heat of the iron. She was dressed in faded jeans and a T-shirt. Doreen studied her for a second, aware of how much younger than herself Rose looked although there was less than a year's difference in their ages. Doreen favoured sensible skirts and jumpers and her straight grey hair was cut level with her chin.

The kitchen was filled with the aromas of domesticity, of coffee and clean cotton clothes, the starchy steam of the iron and the toast Rose had made herself eat earlier.

'Come in, Doreen. I'm glad you're here, I hate this job.'

'Don't we all,' Doreen replied as Rose unplugged the iron. She saw at once that Rose knew. Her friend's face was drawn and there were dark circles beneath eyes which had recently shed tears. Doreen clutched her large black handbag to her stomach with both hands as if for protection. 'So you've heard about Dorothy. Poor old thing, I could hardly take it in.'

'Yes, I know. I was there. On Friday. I brought Martin back with me but he didn't want to stay. He was here when you rang, actually.' Rose chewed a thumbnail hoping that Doreen was not offended.

Doreen nodded. She did not need further explanation, she could imagine how upset Rose would have been. 'Poor lamb. Real fond of his mother, he was. I wonder what'll happen to him now? Still, the other one'll be pleased, no doubt. Probably rubbing his hands with delight, if you ask me.'

'Have a seat, Doreen, for goodness sake.' Rose busied herself with cups and saucers. Doreen knew the Pengellys better than Rose did because she lived in Hayle herself, but Rose did not want to discuss them, nor did she mention that Jack had been pumping her for reasons why Dorothy might have killed herself. Doreen could read it for herself in the *Cornishman* after the inquest.

'That Gwen thinks she's better'n all of us, got her heart set on a big house, that one has. I hope she's disappointed, that's all I can say. Fat lot of attention she paid her mother-in-law when she was alive, I don't rightly know if she even took the kids out to see her. Wouldn't surprise me if Dorothy left the lot to a dogs' home. Serve 'er right, it would.'

Dropping a sweetener into her cup and placing the sugar bowl on the table for Doreen, Rose was barely listening. She could have predicted the conversation. All she knew, all she instinctively felt, was that the police report was wrong. But what could she do about it?

'I've heard she'd got a few good bits and pieces up there,' Doreen continued confidentially, leaning forward to speak as if there was a chance of being overheard. 'Well, you'd know more about that than me, you being an artist and all. Wouldn't surprise me if that Gwen doesn't go up there and help herself because I don't suppose Martin realises what her stuff's worth.'

Coming from Doreen it sounded callous but the same thought had crossed Rose's mind, although Martin had reassured her when she dropped him home. 'Ma had three sets of keys. I've got one. I'll need it to feed the dogs.' So, surprisingly, Rose was in possession of the only other keys. Had Peter not been trusted with them? He had not contacted her to ask for a set and she was glad if what Doreen said was correct. *It's none of your business,* she chided herself and offered Doreen more coffee by way of changing the subject. As they drank it Doreen caught Rose eyeing the ironing still waiting to be done.

'It's all right, dear. Violet's expecting me any time and she gets in a right to-do if the dinner's served up late. I'll be on my way if I can get the car out of the drive. I don't know how you do it.' Doreen patted her hand. 'Give me a ring later.'

Rose watched her rounded figure plod down the path and out to where she had parked the ancient vehicle which took her from one cleaning job to another. Apart from Cyril's pension it had been their only income since the mines had closed. With a sigh Rose picked up the iron. No sooner had she finished one blouse than a shadow fell across her. It was Jack.

'Can I come in?' He looked sheepish.

'Yes. If you want coffee help yourself. I'm awash with it.'

He did so and sat down, uninvited. 'Look, Rose, I apologise if I upset you, but are you really convinced she wouldn't kill herself?'

'One hundred per cent.'

Jack stretched out his long legs and stroked his chin. 'We'll have to wait for the inquest but we're making discreet inquiries.'

'Oh?' Rose continued ironing, annoyed that he should turn up unannounced.

'Mm, very discreet because there was no sign of forced entry and from all accounts nothing seems to have been taken. Her purse was there with money in it and . . .'

Rose stood still. 'You mean you believe me?'

'I'm not saying that, I'm simply saying that nothing points to it being anything other than suicide except that she wasn't registered with any local doctor and it wasn't paracetamol which she swallowed. And it seems a bit extravagant to find a doctor out of the area if you intend taking your own life because there're enough drugs behind the counter of any chemist's shop to do the trick.'

'So?'

'So, is there any chance of you nosing around? You know the family.'

'I see. Once more I'm supposed to do your job for you.' She flung her hair back over her shoulder angrily.

'Oh, Rose, you're always so defensive. I thought you'd be pleased. Do as you wish. I really came here to see if I could buy you a drink. I thought you'd need cheering up.'

He is very handsome, Rose thought, and I'm attracted to him, but if he can irritate me this much now, how much worse would it be if the relationship were more serious? She unplugged the iron, wondering if the job would ever be done. 'All right then, but somewhere local.'

'The Star?'

'The Star's fine.'

They made no overt signs of affection in public, it would have been out of character for them both. Instead they strolled down the narrow pavement of the hill in single file, stopping for a minute to watch a fishing-boat turn in through the mouth of the harbour. There was a cat's cradle of masts alongside the north pier and the smell of fish was stronger there.

The bar was basic, designed for working men who came in in their boots, but the walls were covered with photographs of local boats, the sea sweeping over their bows or engulfing them altogether, white spume flying, seagulls in their wake.

Rose knew many of the customers, as did Jack, who had been to school with some of them, and they were both at ease amongst these men. Their lives were dangerous but their living depended on the sea. They were loud, boisterous and often crude but this was one of their pubs and if others didn't like it they could leave. To the uninitiated the events which took place in the local bars would seem bizarre but Rose knew she would never be happy anywhere else.

They stayed for two drinks then Jack offered to walk her home. He noticed there was more colour in her solemn face. 'I've got next Wednesday off, fancy going out somewhere for the day?' He sometimes got the impression that she was about to say she didn't want to see him any more but she said yes, if a little distractedly, and he said he would pick her up at ten.

At her kitchen door he hesitated. Rose's head was bowed as she unlocked it. 'Thanks, Jack. 'Bye.'

'Yeah. See you.'

Rose closed the door and leant against it. 'Oh, Dorothy,' she whispered as she tried to stem the tears. Life seemed such a mess at times. Barry and Jack, both demanding her attention, Martin, left basically on his own, and Dorothy dead. 'Oh God.' She had not rung Barbara back and she was supposed to be going out with Laura that afternoon. At least she could sort one day out. Picking up the phone she chatted briefly to Barbara saying she was all right and that she would love to come to the party. How callous it sounded but Rose knew she had to start living properly, she had to start making things happen. Barbara sensed her need to be alone and did not keep her talking.

'Laura? It's me. Look, do you mind if we don't go today? I'm really not up to it.'

'Of course not. Want me to come over instead?'

They had planned to go to a car boot sale which was one of Laura's current crazes, then to a film in Truro.

'I, uh . . .'

'Rose, I'm coming anyway. I won't stay long, I just want to see for myself how you are.' Laura hung up. From the tone of her friend's voice she feared she might be slipping into a similar depression to the one she had suffered after David's death.

Although it wasn't far, Laura took the car, parking it untidily in the drive.

'What's it all about?' she demanded as soon as she arrived, dressed in ubiquitous leggings over which she wore a long silky shirt. Her hair was curling wildly around her shoulders. 'It's not just Dorothy, is it?'

Rose shook her head. 'No. It's everything.'

'Then sit down and tell Auntie Laura all about it.'

Rose did so, pouring out her fears that someone had murdered Dorothy and that Martin, who was confused, would get the blame and Gwen and Peter inherit everything. 'Jobber phoned me this morning. He's keeping an eye on Martin. I meant to go over myself but he doesn't know me that well.'

'Well, you can trust Jobber to see he's all right.'

'I know.'

'And?'

'Oh, Laura, it's Jack.'

'Yes. And dear devoted Barry, no doubt.'

Rose smiled weakly. 'How well you know me.'

'Just tell 'em both to bugger off. You're usually quite good at that sort of thing.'

And although Laura had promised not to stay long it was over two hours before she left and Rose was decidedly more cheerful.

It had been a dreadful weekend for Gwen and Peter Pengelly. Peter had arrived home on Friday to find his wife white-faced and almost incoherent. 'I'm sorry,' she kept repeating although he didn't know why. She had never liked his mother. 'I didn't want to contact you on the train – I mean, there was nothing you could do until you got home.'

He understood that. He'd have had to stay on the train anyway, even if they found another conductor to join it.

'Do the children know?'

'No, I thought it'd be better coming from you. They're next door. I didn't want them to overhear.' Gwen wondered how they would react to their first encounter with death although they had not known their grandmother very well. She had given no thought to Martin or to Dorothy's pets, her only concern was for Peter and how this would affect them all. Herself especially. Especially, she thought, after what she'd done.

Nothing mattered to her but her own family. From the time her own mother had died and left her and her brother in the care of a brutal, drunken father she had vowed that when she got married things would be very different. Peter, she adored, and she had made a career out of caring for the children and maintaining the solidarity of her family. Nothing was going to get in the way of that or stop her achieving her ambitions of a better life for all of them.

Only one thing nagged at her conscience. Peter was unaware of the visit she had made and it had to remain that way. Surely out there no one would have seen her car? But it was too late now to alter things, what had happened had happened and it just meant the money came to them sooner. I'm strong, she thought, strong enough for all of us. I must keep telling myself I didn't kill her and everything will be all right.

There had been no easy way to tell him. She had told the police she would do it herself, that he would want to hear it from her.

Peter's eyes were still wide with shock, he hadn't taken it in at first. 'When? When did she die?'

'They think it was some time last night.'

He shook his head in disbelief. 'No, not Mum, she can't be. It's a mistake. Mum was fitter than most women half her age.' He sank into a kitchen chair.

'It's true. They think it was probably her heart.' Gwen reached over and touched his hand.

'Don't.' He jerked it away as if she'd struck him. 'Don't. Just leave me alone.'

Startled, she drew back. Peter had never spoken to her in such a way.

'Oh God,' he muttered as he staggered to his feet. 'Oh, God, what have we done?' All the guilt rose up. 'We never went to see her, she hardly knew her grandchildren.'

No, Peter, what have I done? Gwen thought, ignoring his outburst. Visiting her more often wouldn't have prevented what had occurred on Thursday. 'Peter, wait.' Gwen watched in horror as he left the house, slamming the door behind him. It was the first time he had rebuffed her and it hurt all the more because her tactility had not been sexual. Suddenly the future was uncertain. This was a time she should be sharing with her husband but it seemed he did not need her.

'Is anything the matter?' Louise Hinkston whispered to her husband as she served the cheese course after dinner. They had guests again. Louise was very fond of entertaining and Bradley could usually be relied upon to ensure they were entertained. He had a fund of amusing anecdotes but he had been quiet throughout the meal.

He winked at her but did not reply. At the time, perhaps because of the influence of his surroundings, the oddly captivating atmosphere of a county where anything seemed, and often was, possible, he had not given much thought to the requests made of him. Only when he was back in familiar territory did he start to feel concerned. Bradley was not a man to worry unduly, his philosophy was that problems were simply there to be solved. Monday would be time enough to sort it out. And sorted out it must be. He was still unsure what Mrs Pengelly's motives had been and he could not afford to damage his reputation. What had happened could not be undone. He hadn't wanted to hear all the details but she did not spare him. If they find out, if they find out, he kept thinking.

'Bradley?' Louise was talking to him with her eyes, she was good at that. The message was, we have guests. Feeling more than one pair of inquisitive eyes upon him he forced himself to grin and began to charm his dinner guests.

Louise relaxed visibly and got up to bring in the coffee and brandy.

On Sunday he and Louise had lunch with their son and his wife who had just produced her second baby. It did not seem appropriate to closet himself in their library and make long-distance telephone calls when he was expected to make a fuss of the new child, but there were certain things he needed to verify. In the long run a weekday was better, he decided as Louise unobtrusively squeezed his arm. The bundled-up baby was passed to him. He smiled fondly at his grandson, wishing he had listened more carefully to what Mrs Pengelly had muttered as she had unwrapped newspaper from around a porcelain figurine. And how had a woman like that come to possess so many valuable items? The baby started to cry. Temporarily Bradley was distracted.

DI Jack Pearce decided to speak to each member of the Pengelly family. Just a casual chat, a few simple questions as to why Mrs Pengelly might have taken her own life. Although he usually trusted Rose's sixth sense, it seemed more likely that Dorothy had decided to end her life before she could no longer manage on her own. Rose had said her eyesight was failing. But she wasn't ill, Jack reminded himself. The pathologist had been surprised at how fit she had been. Martin was a strange boy and he drank. No, if alcohol had made him violent he'd have hit her or strangled her – and, according to Rose, he loved his mother. Peter, then. Had he got tired of waiting for his inheritance? There were few other people in Dorothy's life but he would have a quiet word with each. He was risking his neck. There was no evidence of any description, no suspicious circumstances at all, the verdict at the inquest would be suicide or death by misadventure if the old lady had swallowed more pills than she had intended. The latter seemed the most probable theory. Then where did she get the stuff?

He made himself concentrate on more pressing matters with the knowledge that he would have a whole day with Rose on Wednesday.

When Rose woke on Monday morning she felt as if a weight had been lifted from her. Since David's death she still had occasional bouts of depression but each time she seemed to recover more quickly. Energy flowed through her and she felt able to face the world and everyone in it. First there was work to be done. The proofs of photographs she had taken of a silver wedding anniversary were ready for the clients. She had put them in an album, a sales trick she had learned because people tended to order more that way. Over coffee she worked out some figures. The album could be delivered on the way over to see Martin. She ought to have questioned him further about the men and how he thought he had killed his mother. Smiling because she knew what was happening, that she was, as Barry would say, about to poke her nose into other people's business, Rose left the house, swearing mildly as it began to drizzle. Ten minutes earlier there had been no sign of a cloud but already a sea fret was swirling around the base of the Mount leaving only the highest point visible. The sea had turned a steely grey and a heavy swell pushed it shorewards. She went back inside for the jacket which hung inside the pantry door. Once the small whitewashed room had been just that, now it housed the washing-machine and boxes of David's engineering textbooks which she could not bring herself to part with.

Grease streaked the windscreen as she drove away. Rose pressed the washer switch and cursed further as foam replaced the diesel smears. She had put too much washing-up liquid in the water.

Along the Promenade spray hit the car as the first waves of the high tide flung it up over the railing along with slimy bits of seaweed and a shower of small stones. It was early in the year for such weather but it would be far worse in February when gale force winds and torrential rain would cause the fishing-boats to lie idle far too long for the liking of their owners and their crews.

Stopping at a neat bungalow on the outskirts of Penzance, Rose hurried to the door and handed over the boxed package which contained the proofs. 'I'll let you know which ones I want within a couple of days,' Mrs Harvey told her. Rose refused the offer of a cup of coffee and returned to the car. The rain was coming down heavily and splashed against the back of her bare legs. Droplets of water ran down her face as she turned the ignition key, praying the engine would jump into life immediately. It did.

Leaving Penzance behind her she tried not to think of the scene which had awaited her on her last visit to Dorothy.

The sea fret had rolled inland and hung depressingly over the countryside and shrouded the house. Two stunted trees shed a deluge of water on to her as a gust of wind hit them. With a shudder Rose reached for the door handle. It didn't turn. Martin had locked the door. She suspected Jobber had told him to do so. Rose let herself in. To her surprise everything was just as it had been when she had found Dorothy and Martin in the kitchen.

The cats were nowhere in sight but they had the freedom of the flap on the back door. Star was in her usual place, in her basket, and took no notice of her entry. Even George seemed to have lost some of his vitality: he did not growl at her or pretend to nip her ankles as she nervously crossed the kitchen expecting him to change his mind and remember to protect his territory. There was no sign of Martin but there was food in the animals' bowls and water in dishes. Feeling like the intruder she was, Rose checked the cupboards. There was a good supply of tins for both cats and dogs and an unopened sack of biscuits.

Feeling disorientated in Dorothy's empty kitchen she sat down in the seat where she had last drunk tea with her friend. She wondered if the dogs had been out but was not certain they would respond to her in the way in which they once had to Dorothy when she called them back. She took a chance and left the door open because the room smelled stale. Breathing in the moist air perfumed with gorse and heather, she watched Star stagger out of her basket, sniff the air herself then, in her less than youthful manner, lope up the side of the hill. George followed, yapping excitedly.

Through the kitchen window she watched the rain hitting the flagstones of the small yard where Dorothy used to hang her washing. Beyond it was the towering hill which always cast the room in shadow. A figure was approaching. Rose breathed a sigh of relief. It was Martin. He stood straighter and had more colour and if she failed, he'd get the dogs back in.

'I saw you,' he said, pointing over his shoulder as he stood in the doorway. 'I saw from up there that the door was open. I didn't know it was you, though, I thought they might have come back.'

'Who might have, Martin?' Rose stood, her hands at her sides, waiting. He knew something, of that she was sure, but whether it was relevant was difficult to tell. Outwardly he seemed to have accepted Dorothy's death. It was a mistake to have invited him to her house; Martin's solitude was not an enforced situation, it was one which he preferred and which she now saw would enable him to come to terms with his grief in much the same way as she had done.

'The men I spoke to.'

'I still don't understand, Martin. You told me you spoke to some men in the pub. Are you saying they came here?' She was, for the first time, alone with him in that large house with no one else around. For some reason she was afraid to ask him again why he thought he had killed his mother.

He nodded dumbly and looked at his feet then raised his eyes to stare at Dorothy's empty armchair. 'I didn't see 'em, but I know they came.'

Rose frowned in bewilderment. She had no idea what he was talking about. His next words made her catch her breath.

'Will you come upstairs with me?'

Rose inhaled deeply, trying to steady herself. There was no one for miles around and Martin was twice her size. Without meaning to she glanced at his muscled forearms before realising she was behaving neurotically. Martin would not hurt anyone. 'What for?'

'To see if they've taken anything.'

'Of course,' she said with relief.

She followed him up the uncarpeted stairs, their footsteps echoing. There was a sharp angle half-way up where three steps were triangular-shaped as the stairwell changed direction. Rose was careful to keep to the wider bits. The upstairs corridor was quite light as it reached a level with the brow of the hill. Martin, it seemed, believed that someone had come to the house with the intention of robbing Dorothy, but if that was the case why hadn't the police followed it up and why had he told her he thought he had killed her? There was the additional problem that although the police would not be able to tell if anything had been taken it was not certain that Martin would know either.

Rose had only been on the upper floor once, on the occasion when Dorothy had shown her the painting. Presumably Martin wasn't expecting her to recall what had been there but had needed company to make this search.

He opened the door of what used to be his own bedroom and stared around vacantly. It was sparsely furnished but had a panoramic view over the landscape with a distant hint of the sea. He shook his head. 'Nothing gone,' he said, closing the door. The next room, slightly larger, had been Peter's when a child but had long since been turned into a storeroom. Boxes were piled high on and around the single bed. Most were sealed and covered with dust. Only one had been opened, the cardboard flaps upright and yellowed newspaper lying crumpled on the floor as if something had been removed. To Rose it looked as if nothing else had been touched for years. Martin closed this door too but did not speak.

Outside the third one he hesitated. This was where his mother had slept, where she had slept all her married life and where she had given birth to both of her sons. 'I never went in here,' he offered and Rose saw that she had been right. This had been his mother's sanctuary, her one place of privacy, and he did not want to invade it alone. It was Rose who opened the door.

It was by far the biggest room and had two windows which looked out over the rainwashed countryside. The top of a minestack could be seen lower in the valley and cars, like small insects, wound their way along the main road. Opposite the window was the wooden-framed bed with its patchwork quilt. The pillowslips were white and clean, as was the edge of the sheet which was folded back over the blankets. On the chest which also served as a bedside table was a fringed reading lamp and a pile of books, Dorothy's place in the top one marked with an old envelope. The unread novel saddened Rose and she had to look away.

There was a wardrobe, probably Edwardian, and a small table beneath the windows. Everything was neat, everything seemed just as it ought to be. The Stanhope Forbes hung in its rightful place and there were no lighter patches on the faded wallpaper to indicate other paintings had been removed. 'Everything looks all right to me, Martin. Can you see anything wrong?'

He shook his head and stroked the patchwork quilt. Like Rose he was able to smell Dorothy's presence. Martin, she thought, was confused about the conversation in the pub which may or may not have taken place. He might even have dreamed it. 'Come on, let's go back down.' It was affecting them both, being in her room.

Rose turned to leave, her artist's eye naturally settling again on the Stanhope Forbes. Then she froze. 'Martin,' she finally said as calmly as she was able, 'did your mother keep her special things somewhere safe?' His brow creased with non-comprehension. 'I mean her paintings, did she put them somewhere safe and hang copies on the wall?'

'No. Not 'er. She liked her bits where she could see 'un.'

Rose stepped slowly towards the painting. It was identical to the one she had seen before, even down to the frame. Only this one was a print; not a copy, she had only used the word so as not to confuse Martin further. Had Dorothy noticed? Despite her pretence to the contrary, her eyesight wasn't good. But had Dorothy had time to notice? Was she dead even before it was swapped? Martin may not have been mistaken in thinking that the men he had spoken to had come to the house. Now you'll take me seriously, Jack Pearce, she thought. 'She hasn't changed this painting?' Rose pointed towards it; she had to be sure.

'No. 'Tis the same one.'

To Martin it probably seemed so. She had to let Jack know. If Dorothy had decided to put the original away for safe-keeping it was not her place to make a thorough search of the house. But the police would need to speak to Martin and that worried her. If he repeated his fears that he had killed his mother they would question him endlessly and he would probably say things he didn't mean. There were other items to be considered, ones which Rose had not been shown and which might also be missing. She guessed that more valuables were stored in the boxes in Peter's old room. And one of those boxes had been opened.

Retracing her steps she peered into the other rooms. Her expert eye told her that what was on the walls had not been tampered with. There were one or two local scenes from some of the lesser known painters. Strange, then, that only one had been replaced, and why bother unless it was meant to conceal a crime? She smiled at Martin. 'I'll make us some tea. Do you think I could use the telephone?'

'Course you can. 'Er won't mind.'

As she preceded Martin down the narrow staircase she asked what he intended doing about the animals. For the time being they gave him something to do, a reason for getting out of the caravan rather than dwelling upon his mother's death.

'Well, I can't leave 'em starve. Me an' George've never got on too well but I expect he'll treat me different when he knows it's me what's going to feed him. I can't have them at the van, though, there's no room.'

Rose let it go. The house would be sold, or Gwen and Peter might live in it – either way, at some point a decision about the animals would have to be made. 'Martin, I've still got the keys. Do you want them back?'

He frowned with concentration. 'No, you keep 'em. I don't want Gwen out here.'

'All right, if you're sure.' She made tea and took out the mugs, pint pots that both Dorothy and her husband had favoured. 'What you told me,' she began, 'about those men. We're going to have to tell the police.'

'They'll lock us up, they buggers.'

Rose sipped her tea. By us he meant himself, and he might be right. 'Martin, you don't have to answer me but did your mother ... well, was she short of money?' It had only just occurred to her that Dorothy might have sold the painting and replaced it with the print by way of consolation.

'No, 'er always said she'd got more than she could possibly need.'

'All right, but we do have to let them know. If they need to ask you any questions I'll stay with you, all right?'

'I s'pose so. Ma said you was a sensible woman.'

Rose bent her head to hide an amused smile then stood and reached for the old-fashioned telephone. Jack wasn't at Camborne nor was he at home. She could have informed someone else but it did not seem appropriate and they might not have any idea what she was talking about. It could wait an hour. Martin's relief was obvious.

Rose looked around the kitchen and found a scrap of paper upon which she wrote her telephone number. 'Ring me any time you like. If there's anything at all you want, just let me know. Oh, if I'm out I've got an answering machine. All you have to do ...' Seeing the hurt expression on Martin's face, Rose stopped.

'It's all right, Mrs Trevelyan, I aren't stupid. Your phone number's in the book and I know how to leave a message.'

Rose felt herself blushing under his scrutiny. How patronising she must have sounded. She would not compound her mistake by offering an apology. 'That's fine then,' she said briskly. 'Oh, and Martin, will you let me know about the funeral? I'd very much like to be there.'

'She'd want you to be and no mistake. She said you was 'er friend.'

'And she was mine.' Rose looked away, afraid she might cry. 'Don't forget, if you need anything, let me know.'

'I suppose Peter'll see to the arrangements an' that. He never trusts me to do anything.'

'Yes, I expect he will. Shall we call the dogs in, it's getting late?'

Martin stepped out of the back door into the rain and gave a long, low whistle which brought the dogs, one bounding a little painfully, the other scurrying, but both saturated, to the back door. He held them away whilst they shook themselves. Star went straight to her basket, George stared balefully at Dorothy's chair then, reluctantly, leaped into it. He looked brighter now but Rose hoped not too bright to recall he was supposed to growl at visitors. She said goodbye to Martin and left him to lock up.

It was now impossible to sketch even under the protection of waterproofs and her golfing umbrella. The best of the light of a miserable day had already gone and the rain was falling in sheets, obscuring everything beyond a few yards' distance. Rose drove home slowly, peering through the windscreen as the wipers did their best to clear the spray the traffic in front was throwing up. It was an afternoon to be spent in the attic where she would start on the watercolouring of some previous work. The northern light would be of no use today but the lamps which she had had fitted and which gave off the next best thing to daylight would have to suffice.

Sodden and wet-footed, Rose kicked off her shoes inside the kitchen door and hung her jacket on its hook in the pantry where it dripped over the floor. The fluorescent light buzzed as she flicked the switch and its brightness illuminated the room. Water from the gutters gurgled down the drainpipe, rain lashed against the window and the sea rolled relentlessly towards the land. She seemed to be in a liquid world with wetness everywhere.

Leaving the kettle to boil she went up to shower, throwing her clothes into the wicker laundry basket. She would not be going out again so dressed only in underwear and a long towelling robe. Feeling rather like a schoolgirl playing truant she ignored the kettle which had already boiled and pulled a bottle of dry white wine from the fridge. Jack often made sarcastic remarks about her having more alcohol than food in store but, she thought, Jack could do the other thing. She poured a glassful and took a sip before carrying it upstairs where she succeeded in doing a couple of hours' work uninterrupted.

Three small paintings complete Rose had the satisfaction of knowing that they were better than she had anticipated. The sky was lighter now. Without her noticing the rain had eased considerably and the blackest of the clouds had rolled eastwards. 'Rain heading from the west,' she muttered. Someone elsewhere was in for it. She conscientiously cleaned her brushes then went down to her bedroom to study the view because there might be a rainbow.

Fingers of sunlight lit up the white windmills which produced electricity on the hills far across the bay. It was not often she could see them. The sea was now aquamarine in the foreground and deeper blue in the distance. You are procrastinating, she told herself, you know you really ought to tell someone about Dorothy's painting even if you do make a fool of yourself. Before ringing Jack's direct line at Camborne she poured another glass of wine to give her courage. There was no answer. She sighed. But at least temporarily it solved the problem. Half an hour later she tried again. 'It mightn't mean anything, Jack, but – '

'When you come out with things like that my nerves start jangling,' he interrupted.

She could hear the smile in his voice but there was no sudden desire to see him although she knew that she must. 'I think it might be better if we spoke face to face.'

'Is that a veiled invitation, Mrs Trevelyan?'

'It might be important,' she snapped, sorry he had misinterpreted her words.

'Put like that, I can hardly refuse. I won't get away until eight,
is that too late?' His tone was mildly sarcastic.

'No.' Wearily she relented. 'You can share my supper if you
want.'

'Is it something I like?'

'For goodness sake, Jack, I – '

'Only teasing. See you later.' And with that he hung up.

Jack Pearce is no one's fool, she thought, and although Rose
liked to keep him at arm's length, he was quite adept at the same
game himself. She busied herself preparing the meal then
remembered she wasn't dressed. She did not want Jack to get
the wrong idea. Remedying the situation she put on tan tailored
trousers, a cream shirt and a brown cord waistcoat. She loosened
her hair to brush it. There were waves where the band had
constricted it and the dampness had dried and shaped it. Rose
turned her head in front of the mirror and decided it looked
quite nice.

It was a quarter to nine before Jack's car pulled into the drive.
She had poured him a glass of wine before he reached the kitchen
door.

Fred Meecham sat at Marigold's bedside holding her hand. She
had been in a coma when he arrived but he whispered softly to
her. The nurse had said she might be able to hear him. The
words he used were gentle and loving and he carried on talking
even after he knew she could no longer hear him.

'Mr Meecham, come away now.'

'What are you going to do with her?'

'We're going to put on a clean nightdress,' the nurse explained
tactfully. 'I'm really sorry, you were so close to your sister,
weren't you?' She touched his hand, knowing there was nothing
he could say. 'Is there someone we can telephone to take you
home?'

Fred shook his head. Home. The word was meaningless now.

69

He shuffled out of the ward, turning back too late because the curtains had been redrawn around Marigold's bed. No! he wanted to scream, but he knew it was no use. Down in the car-park he sat cocooned in the car watching the rain stream down the windscreen. It was as if with the final closing of Marigold's eyes his own had been opened. He saw himself for the hypocrite he was, his whole life a lie. Yes, he believed in and prayed to God but he had broken many of the commandments. He took no comfort in the fact that none of it had been for himself; it did not lessen the wrongness of the deeds. Had Dorothy been right all along? Now was not the time to think of Dorothy.

He drove home and sat in the flat with the lights off, his head in his hands. If he had been a drinking man he reckoned he would have got drunk. But he wasn't, it was one of the vices he did not have.

Later that evening when Fred went downstairs to answer the summons of the bell at the side of the shop door he initially thought that it might be a customer in urgent need of something. Then he wondered if his thoughts had somehow transmitted themselves to the rest of the world. Why else should the police be standing on his doorstep? All that other business was years ago.

'What a great welcome. Cheers.' He took a sip of wine. He had been expecting Rose to behave coldly towards him. Pulling out a chair he sat down and leaned back. Rose wondered what it was that made people more comfortable in her kitchen than anywhere else in the house. 'Now, are you going to tell me what it is that might or might not be important?' Quite relaxed, he crossed his legs.

Rose explained about the painting, adding the alternative possibilities she had worked out for herself.

'But the others are still hanging, you say?'

'Yes. And there're a couple that are worth a few bob.'

Jack was thoughtful. 'So why not take them all? Look, Rose, a thief isn't going to bother to swap a painting.'

'Why not? What if he knows Dorothy can't see too well, what then?'

'You have a point, but how would he have had access to her bedroom?'

'You're supposed to be the detective.'

'Yes, but you think like one. Answer me this one, then. If the drugs were not self-administered, how come she didn't notice them being forced down her throat or taste them in something or other?'

Rose shrugged expressively, causing her hair to fall forward. Jack reached out to push it back, touching her face as he did so. Rose's head jerked up, startling Jack.

'What is it?'

'Alcohol.'

'Alcohol?'

'You said the police surgeon noticed the smell, I did too. Dorothy didn't drink. Well, not really. A glass of sherry on special occasions. If someone gave her, say, whisky, she wouldn't have noticed.' Her face was animated. Whatever Jack Pearce decided, she was going to discover the truth. 'Perhaps whoever it was didn't mean to kill her, just knock her out for a while. Perhaps they didn't realise she wasn't used to drink or medication of any sort.'

Jack was only half listening. What had happened to the paracetamol bottle? If it had contained the means of Dorothy's death there might be fingerprints. 'Rose, as I said, I'd already decided to ask a few questions. I think I ought to start tonight. But tell me one thing, you're certain that what you saw the first time was an original?'

'Yes.'

Then it was worth a considerable sum and, with the way things were in the county at the moment, enough to consider murdering for. Fishing-boats were being decommissioned whilst foreign ships trawled British waters and the Government as well as the EU thumbed its nose, South Crofty, the last working tin mine, was on the verge of shutting down unless something truly drastic happened and the towns and villages that had relied upon both industries were fast losing their identity as the once proud miners and fishermen became no more than statistics in the unemployment figures. Jack ground his teeth. And the beef crisis was causing farmers to tear their hair out. Their three main industries were being wiped out and Cornwall, his birthright, was being sanitised for the sake of the emmets who littered the place with their fast food containers and ignored the signs telling them not to feed the gulls and who preferred the tourist attractions and visitor centres to the unspeakable beauty all around them. He was angry, with himself as well as the world, because he was powerless to change the way things were going, angry also with the people who brought to Cornwall or expected to find here all that they had come to escape. One bloody great theme park, that's what we'll be, he thought. Youngsters were moving away because the average wage would have been laughed at elsewhere. Yes, he decided, an original Stanhope Forbes was definitely worth killing for.

'Jack?'

'I'm sorry, Rose, I was thinking.' The scowl left his face because of the concern showing in hers. 'Well, not thinking exactly, more like conducting a mental diatribe against the human race.'

'Me included?'

'No, Rose, never you. I'll have to go. I'm sorry. I hope you didn't go to too much trouble with the meal. What was it anyway?'

'Monkfish with fennel.'

He groaned. 'Just my luck. I'll make it up to you.'

'No need.' Just get to the bottom of this, Jack, she thought as she bolted the kitchen door behind him.

'Shall I come back later?' he called through the partly open window.

Rose looked down. 'No, not tonight.'

She might as well eat, and eat a proper meal. As she slid the monk into the pan she tried to see if she could be wrong, if there had been anything different about Dorothy on her last few visits. There hadn't, not unless she counted that business with the envelope. 'Oh, no!' The fish slice clattered to the floor. All that fussing around with the envelope – had that been a pantomime she was meant to remember? The last time she had been to see her, Dorothy had slipped something into an A5 envelope, written ostentatiously on the front, sealed it and tossed it into a kitchen drawer in a rather dramatic manner. Surely it wasn't a suicide note? There's only one way to find out, she decided. But it was too late that night.

Fred Meecham's sister, Marigold, outlived Dorothy Pengelly by only a couple of days. Naturally it was Doreen Clarke who rang Rose the following morning to tell her. 'I know you never met her, but you know Fred and I thought you might want to write a note or something. The shop's shut, he's put a sign on the door. It'll be a double blow for him. First Dorothy, now this. It's awful, isn't it, both of them going in a week?'

Going. Typical Doreen, Rose thought. If there was a euphemism available Doreen would use it. Rose had met Fred Meecham on several occasions when he had stopped at Dorothy's place to deliver a case of dog food or a box of heavy groceries, and once or twice she had been into his shop. With her painter's eye, in the way she did with all interesting faces, Rose had committed the details of his to her mind. He had a shock of red hair which seemed to have a life of its own. With his washed-out blue irises and pallid complexion he was far from attractive but his lean body and sensual mouth made him seem so. His Cornish accent was not pronounced and bespoke his Truro origins. Dorothy had told Rose about the sister, Marigold, and had said she thought it was time that Fred faced up to the gravity of the situation. 'He won't allow himself to believe she's dying. And he should have more sense than to think money can solve everything,' she had said. 'It's going to hit him hard when it happens.' At that point Dorothy had clammed up, realising – too late – that it was another painful reminder for Rose.

'I'll be going to the funeral,' Doreen continued. 'I'm sure most of Fred's customers will be there. I wonder if he'll close the shop that day, too? Out of respect, like. Dear me, it's ages since I've been to one, do people still wear black? Doesn't seem right somehow, not for someone so young. She was only in her forties.'

'Wear whatever you feel comfortable in, Doreen,' Rose answered, allowing her chatter to drift over her head. Face to face she enjoyed her company but it was often difficult to end a telephone conversation. Rose finally replaced the receiver. Having met Fred on so few occasions she wondered if it was appropriate to send a message of condolence. On the other hand they had both been friends of Dorothy so there was a mutual, if tenuous bond. She got out a pen and some paper.

Twice during the course of the day Rose heard the telephone ringing but she did not bother to answer it – she rarely did if she was working. There were many jobs to catch up on and she wanted them all out of the way before she sat down and made some serious plans, which she intended doing that evening.

Later she carefully rewrote the note to Fred Meecham, realising as she did so what the many people who had written to her during her bereavement had gone through. Almost satisfied she put down her pen. The phone rang again. Unthinkingly she reached out a hand and picked up the receiver, resting it between her shoulder and her ear. 'Hello?' she said cheerfully.

'Keep out of it. Just keep out of it or you're dead.'

'But . . .? Who are you?' But the line had been disconnected. Rose sat very still as she tried to work out if she had heard that voice before. She did not think so. And keep out of what? Dialling 1471 she learned that the caller had withheld their number. She was not easily frightened but that evening she turned on the lights before they were strictly needed.

Fear turned to anger. She would not be intimidated by anyone, least of all an anonymous caller. Despite her intentions not to do as Jack had requested and speak to the Pengelly family, she changed her mind. Whoever had threatened her knew something which could only be connected with Dorothy's death. But why the threat? What had she done to induce it? Nothing, as far as she knew. Not yet.

6

The unexpectedness of his mother's death had shocked Peter
Pengelly more than the event itself. When Gwen had told him,
he had had to get out of the house. The overwhelming grief he
felt was genuine, worsened by his sense of guilt. None of this hit
him at first. Since then the police had been back, wanting to
know if Dorothy had complained of feeling ill or depressed or if
she had expressed any financial worries or any worries whatso-
ever. Shamefully Peter had admitted that they did not see much
of his mother.

For the first time in his life he viewed his childhood days
objectively. He had never been as close to his mother as Martin
and, since the day he had started school, he had steadily grown
away from her. He wondered if this was because Martin had
remained at home for another two years and therefore he was
jealous or if he had always suspected his brother was the
favourite.

As a child and a young man Peter had found his mother odd,
even eccentric, although he wasn't sure why. She was a good
deal older than most of the mothers who collected their children
from school, some no more than girls themselves who had
married at sixteen or seventeen. Peter could have borne the age
discrepancy if Dorothy had not gone out of her way to disregard
generally held opinions and to distance herself from his friends'
mothers who huddled in groups outside the school gates.

On the death of his father her grief had seemed disproportion-
ate. His limited experience of such things told him that people
quietly wiped away the tears and suffered stoically until a
normal life could be resumed. Not so his mother. She had sobbed
and screamed and shouted, waving her fists in the air and railing
against God. Now and then she had thrown things, but never at
her sons. With them she had been loving and understanding. In
the privacy of their home Peter was able to shut out these scenes

by going to his room. To drown out the sounds he would play his transistor radio loudly and pretend it wasn't happening. He did not know how to cope with such an excess of pain.

Martin had either been impervious to it or had instinctively known how to deal with it. He would remain at his mother's side, quietly playing with his toys or struggling with homework he could not understand. When Dorothy was calmer he would climb on to her knee and stroke her face.

It became embarrassing for Peter at school. Dorothy had inherited their father's car and she had learned how to drive it. Instead of coming in on the bus to meet them she would sit behind the wheel, parked some distance away safely out of reach of any words of sympathy that might have been offered. This alienated her from the other mothers further.

Then one day, as if some dramatic catalyst had occurred whilst they were all asleep, Peter came downstairs to find his mother cooking a proper breakfast and humming as she did so. Neither his father nor God were mentioned again and an old photograph of Arthur Pengelly, which Peter had not known existed, appeared on Dorothy's bedside table, framed in wood.

And now she was gone and he could understand what she must have felt but it was too late to tell her so. Bitterly he wished he had spent more time with her, told her that he loved her, because now he realised that he did. All those years she had lived up at the house, alone after Martin left, and he had no idea what went on in her head or if she thought of him at all.

He had used Gwen and the children as an excuse, as a reason for being too busy to visit. He loved them, too, of course. Gwen could be overpowering at times and usually got her own way. She also had a far greater need for sex than he did, which wore him out. Her insecurity in such matters was exhausting. He tried not to disappoint her but it was difficult at times, and he knew she bought the underwear because she thought it would please him. He did not have the heart to say it didn't matter, that he did not expect her to be like a film star all the time. He would have liked to come home one day and find her in a pair of jeans, her hair tousled, like other young mothers. He suspected Gwen was compensating for what she considered to be his own mother's sloppy ways, trying to prove what a good wife she was by comparison. She had nothing to fear, there was no competition.

He had walked miles on that Friday evening, tiring himself physically but unable to still his thoughts. Very quietly he had let himself into the almost silent house. The children were in bed but a few faint sounds came from the kitchen. He had sat in his armchair in the small lounge and leant back against the cushions. Without warning his throat began to ache and hot tears filled his eyes. He had not cried for years and he wondered if his own tears were a substitute for the ones neither his wife nor his children had shed. It was a sad reflection on them all that they had hardly known their grandmother.

Gwen had opened the door, a dishcloth in her hand. 'I thought I heard you come in,' she said gently. 'I've kept our meal hot.' She hesitated in the doorway. Peter's shoulders were bowed and she did not know how to go about comforting him because she was afraid of another rebuffal. She was glad the children could not see him like this. 'Peter?' She advanced slowly.

Reaching out blindly he had pulled her to him, sobbing wetly into the thin cotton of her dress. Without warning his grip tightened and Gwen fell on top of him. Before she could protest he had tugged at her buttons and pulled the dress open.

'Peter,' she had protested, but it was useless, he had pinned her down and was inside her, moving frantically as if the act could expurgate all the guilt and sorrow he felt. Gwen was too stunned to struggle. It had never been like that before.

When it was over Peter sat up and ran a hand through his hair without looking at her. 'It's what you've always wanted, isn't it? Just like you've always wanted my mother dead.' He turned to see her face, her mouth open in horror. Getting to his feet he adjusted his clothes and left the house again with no idea where he was going.

Tireder still, he had walked fast and without thought, trying to numb all emotions. Heedless of the dewlike moisture which clung to his clothes he headed towards the soft white sand of the

Towans and walked down to the water's edge where it was damp beneath his feet and the soles of his shoes left impressions in the sand. It seemed as if he might walk straight into the sea.

The rhythmic slap of the shallow waves against the beach had soothed him. The tide was receding and through the still night air the calls of oystercatchers feeding on the estuary carried over the water. Two gulls huddled nearby, facing the breeze, shifting slightly as he approached.

Not once had he wished his mother harm. Yet look what he had just done to Gwen, proving he was capable of violence. His face reddened with shame. 'Goddammit!' he shouted. 'I should have revelled in my mother's differences.' All he had done was to pretend they had not existed.

It was very late by then and Gwen would be worried. Peering at the luminous dial of his watch he saw it was after midnight. He had to face her at some point so he began the long walk home, his footsteps dragging through the dunes. Below him the harbour lights winked. The drizzle had eased but in the distance a fine mist hung beneath the lights of the bypass. By the time he got home he felt a tiny surge of optimism. It was not too late to become a decent human being.

Gwen had been too shocked to cry or to question Peter's behaviour, which was beyond her comprehension. As soon as he had left she went upstairs to shower, glad that both children were asleep. Feeling dirty and defiled she let the hot water run over her body for fifteen minutes yet she had to admit that Peter was right in a way. She was sexually demanding but she had been brought up to believe that that was what men wanted, that if you were not available and willing they would find someone who was. Her father, when he had hit her, used to say that it was for her own good, that it was because he loved her. Gwen had grown up requiring endless proof that she was loved and desirable.

There would be no repeat performance that night. Her hair damp and wearing only an old T-shirt of Peter's, she had gone back downstairs to wait. She was anxiously chewing the skin around her nails when he returned. Whatever happened the police must not find out about that evening. If they thought that Peter was a violent man what else might they think? Gwen decided she would never mention it.

When Peter came into the kitchen she felt as though she had been holding her breath. He looked her up and down and took in the unmade-up face, the bare feet and the tatty T-shirt. She had not blow-dried her hair and it lay flat against her skull. Never before had she looked so young and so vulnerable. 'Oh, Gwen,' he said, reaching for her and pulling him to her. 'I don't know what to say.'

'Let's forget it, shall we? I'll make us some tea.'

Peter nodded. 'That'd be nice.'

Gwen pulled away from him and in a businesslike way got out the cups and saucers. The temptation to tell him what she had done had completely disappeared.

Two days later things were back to normal until the police had returned with their questions. Peter, grey and old-looking, had only shaken his head when they mentioned the word suicide. Gwen had become hysterical and if one of the detectives hadn't calmed her down he was sure he would have slapped her. Peter's guilt increased with the knowledge that his mother had been unhappy enough to take her own life. He was unable to see in which direction the questions were heading.

Rose stretched then sat up in bed, brushing the hair out of her eyes as she squinted at the alarm clock. Seven thirty-five. She had had a good night's sleep after all. Sliding back down under the duvet she felt warm and comfortable, until she remembered the telephone call and what she had determined to do.

She slipped out of bed and went downstairs to make tea. The sun slanted in through the sitting-room window where the curtains were never drawn. Rose could not bear to shut out that view. As the kettle boiled she scanned the sky with its promise of a fine day, although she knew how often those promises were not fulfilled. The warning horn of a beamer boomed out as it negotiated the gap between the two piers and left the harbour.

Out in the bay it gathered speed, bowing and dipping, spray flying along its sides although the sea was cellophane smooth from where she stood.

The kitchen was cool. Only when the sun was setting did the golden rays reach the side window. Rose poured boiling water on to the tea leaves in the pot and lit the grill to make toast. She had never possessed a toaster and guessed that she and David must have been the only couple not to have been given one as a wedding present. Sadly she got out the last jar of orange marmalade, one of a batch which Dorothy had made and given to her.

Opening the door to enjoy the weather Rose realised how few such days were left before the storms of winter set in for real. After the rain the grass was verdant once more. She stood and watched a blackbird who, head on one side, was also watching her as he finished his business of stamping on her unkempt lawn to bring the worms to the surface. She smiled. He must have been hungry for her presence did not deter him. Finally he succeeded in his task. Watching him eat reminded her that Barry Rowe was cooking her a meal that evening. It was quite a while since she had been to his flat.

Rose took her breakfast upstairs and ate it in bed, having drawn back the curtains and opened the window fully in order to watch the beamer's progress. It was already passing in front of the Mount. She cursed when the phone rang as she had to go downstairs to answer it. She kept meaning to get an extension for the bedroom.

'Rose, it's Jack. I've got to cancel, I'm afraid. There's someone off sick and they want me to go in. I'll make it up to you, I promise.'

'It's okay. Really.' Wednesday. She had completely forgotten they were supposed to be spending the day together. You don't love him, girl, Rose told herself, you've got to do something about him. Yet she had remembered her date with Barry. Barry she did love, but as a friend, one she would not let down if she could possibly help it.

'Sure?'

'Positive.'

'Yes . . .' Jack paused, unsure what to say. 'Well, goodbye then.'

Rose knew she had not sounded disappointed. She shrugged. There was no point in encouraging him.

She ran a bath and whilst it was filling opened the cabinet to get out a new bar of soap. On the shelf were the disposable razors she had bought for Jack because she did not want to see his own where David's had once lain. Or so she had thought. Now she realised that was not the sole reason, it was also because Jack's own razor in her bathroom would have smacked of a permanence she did not want. Is that how I see Jack, too? she thought. As disposable?

She bathed quickly and tidied the kitchen, throwing more washing into the machine in case the weather held. 'He's got a nerve,' she said aloud, unfairly blaming him when she knew she could have called a halt to the relationship at any time. And then to suggest she had a word with the Pengellys on the feeble pretext that she was offering condolences – who did he think she was? He had said that Peter and Gwen had already been questioned but he would be interested in her opinion. She would do it but on her own terms, for herself but, more importantly, for Dorothy. Then she would have to decide whether or not to mention any of it to Barry whose reaction she could predict. The threatening telephone call was still on her mind. Only Jack and Barry were aware of her suspicions. And Martin. She stifled the thought. Barry would not have discussed them with anyone so how could anyone know what was on her mind? Laura? No, not Laura and not Doreen Clarke either. Besides, she was sure it was a man's voice. It didn't make sense, it was as if someone was already outguessing her. Foolish, maybe, to ignore the threat but her stubbornness dictated that she would try harder to find out why Dorothy had died.

One of the wild flowers listed by Barry grew close to the Hayle estuary. Rose took this as a sign. She would call upon the Pengellys because she had reason to be in the area. Jack had told her that Peter worked shifts but had taken some compassionate leave and was almost certain to be at home. She had met him only once; Gwen she had never met.

Throughout the short drive she tried to plan what she would say but her mind kept returning to the phone call. It was silly not to have mentioned it to Jack. If there was another one she would do so.

The house was exactly as Dorothy had portrayed it on an occasion when she had tried to describe her daughter-in-law. 'Typical Gwen,' she had said. 'Neatness means more to 'er than anything.' It was one in a terrace which stepped down towards the estuary. The lower halves of the buildings were brick, the tops pebble-dashed and painted white. Each had a small shed to the side of the front door with its entrance at right angles to the house. There were spotless net curtains at the windows. In front was a small patch of grass. Tiny wooden fences divided the gardens.

Rose rang the bell. She knew from Dorothy that Gwen did not go out to work so it was likely that both Pengellys would be in. 'Mrs Pengelly?' Rose smiled warmly then realised it was a mistake. The woman in front of her was slender and beautiful in a waif-like way but her features showed signs of misery. She had not expected this reaction, not after what Dorothy had led her to believe. But Rose did not know about the events which had shaken Gwen to the core. Sizing her up quickly, Rose took in the expensive haircut, the straight blue skirt, soft blouse and high-heeled shoes. It seemed an incongruous outfit for a housewife and mother on a weekday, one who was recently bereaved. 'I'm Rose Trevelyan. Dorothy may have mentioned me.'

'Yes. Yes, I believe she did. You paint or something, don't you? Won't you come in?'

Rose nodded. This was a far cry from Doreen Clarke's extravagant praise of the way in which she earned her living. Doreen had obliquely let it be known that she did not like Gwen Pengelly but Rose would not let her opinion cloud her own judgement.

'Would you like some coffee?'

'If you're not too busy. I only came to say how sorry I was. Dorothy was a good friend to me.'

Gwen seemed surprised to hear this. 'I see.' She plugged in a percolator. 'Please sit down. Excuse me, I must put these in.'

Gwen picked up a pile of children's clothes and bundled them into the washing-machine.

It was such an ordinary, everyday domestic task yet Rose would have been less surprised if she had said she was about to leave for a modelling engagement. In her faded denim skirt, a pink and yellow checked shirt, frayed rope espadrilles and her soft hair already escaping from the wooden clasp at the nape of her neck, Rose felt a complete mess beside her. One day she really would do something about her wardrobe. The sound of running water filled the sunlit room as the machine filled then began its cycle.

Gwen stood up and looked at her hands as if she was unsure what to do with them. 'We were going to see her on Sunday. Dorothy.'

'I'm sorry. It must have been a dreadful shock for you.'

'It was.'

'Do you know when the funeral will be held?'

'It'll be at Truro Crematorium but we haven't got a date yet. We can't do anything until after the inquest on Friday. If you leave me your phone number I'll let you know.'

'Thank you.' Rose rummaged in her shoulder bag for one of her business cards.

Gwen took it and read it slowly. 'Look, I apologise. I didn't mean to sound offhand. It hasn't been easy lately.' She paused. It would have been pleasant to confide in another woman but she did not know Rose Trevelyan. 'At least Dorothy had a reasonably long life. We must be grateful for that. Oh, Peter, I thought you'd gone out.'

Neither of them had heard the door leading to the hall open. There had been no other sounds in the house and she, too, had imagined Peter was out. It was him she had come to see but she had the feeling that Gwen had been about to confide in her. She watched them both: there was tension between them.

Standing in the doorway, looking unsure of himself, Peter's hand was still on the handle. 'I heard the bell. I came down to see if it was the police again. It's Mrs Trevelyan, isn't it?' Rose nodded. 'I thought I remembered you.' Dressed far more casually than his wife, in jeans and a sweatshirt, Peter had not yet shaved. His hair showed the first signs of thinning in small indentations at each temple.

'I came to say how sorry I am about your mother.'

'We meant to telephone. We said we would, didn't we, Gwen? The police told us you did what you could to help. Martin wouldn't have been capable of coping on his own. It was a good job you were passing. Thank you.'

Rose saw that Peter was right. Martin was not stupid but, left to his own devices, he might have sat there, rocking Dorothy, for hours. 'Thank you.' Gwen had placed three cups of coffee on the table.

'I'm just glad the children are back at school. It's better for them. If this had happened during the summer holdiays . . .' The sentence trailed off and Gwen shrugged.

'God, nothing seems to make sense,' Peter said, ignoring his wife's comments. 'First they lead us to believe she had a heart attack, then they tell us it's suicide, but when that inspector bloke turned up on Monday night we didn't know what he was getting at.'

So Jack had come here after leaving her place. He had not mentioned that when he rang earlier. And she hadn't mentioned the threatening call. If they were back to playing those games Rose was determined to win.

'Who could possibly wish her harm? She was just an old lady. I mean, no one went out there, did they?' Peter had slumped into a chair.

Rose knew that Dorothy had more friends than he realised. He was, she saw, genuinely upset whereas Gwen almost shrugged it off. Something different was troubling her; she seemed to be under a lot of strain. Women use drugs and poison far more than men. The thought flashed through her mind. Don't be so stupid, she told herself.

'It must have been awful for you, walking in on it.' Gwen decided it was time she made a contribution.

'It wasn't very pleasant. How's Martin?' Rose could have predicted the answer.

'Martin?' Gwen glanced briefly at her husband.

'He prefers to be up at the caravan,' Peter put in quickly, ashamed that he had only tried once to find him despite his intention to behave decently. But Martin had not contacted them either. 'I expect you know that,' he continued with a ready excuse. 'I heard that he went home with you but didn't want to stay.'

'He doesn't feel things the way most people do.' This was from Gwen. Rose thought it was the strangest comment she had heard in a long time. Gwen sighed. 'There's such an awful lot to do and we can't start until the police give us the go-ahead. We can't even put the house on the market yet.'

Rose raised an eyebrow in surprise. Gwen was taking a lot upon herself unless she knew for certain that it had been left to her. And poor Martin, it was as if he did not exist. It was not her place to bring it up but Jack, damn him, had encouraged her. Besides, she liked Dorothy's younger son and someone had to be on his side. 'Won't Martin have some say in the matter?'

Gwen made a sound which Rose could not interpret. 'Oh, he's just fine up in that van of his. He won't be interested in the house. Anyway, Dorothy told me she'd left a will and that she'd done the right thing by us. We've got a young family to bring up. After all, Martin's only got himself to think about.'

'Mm.' Rose was non-committal. Dorothy could be cryptic at times and it was extremely doubtful that she would let Martin lose out financially. But perhaps she was wrong.

Peter had clammed up and seemed content to let his wife do all the talking. He blew on his coffee and avoided making eye contact with either of the women. Rose did not know how or whether she should bring up the subject of the Stanhope Forbes. To her surprise Gwen did it for her.

'She's got some lovely old pieces up there. And her paintings. There're some very good ones. We'll probably keep a couple, I expect, but the rest will have to be sold.'

Peter seemed unperturbed by the mercenary turn in the conversation. He might have been in a world of his own except for what he did next. He got up abruptly, almost knocking over his chair. 'It's my mother you're talking about,' he hissed at Gwen then left the room, banging the door behind him. Rose had listened carefully, trying to think how the voice on the telephone had sounded, but she couldn't be sure. Taking her cue she stood too. There was nothing to be learned from Peter and whatever Gwen had been about to tell her earlier she would not find out now. 'Thank you for the coffee. If there's anything I can do, well, you've got my number.'

'Thanks. I won't forget to let you know the date of the funeral.' Gwen walked her to the door and closed it as soon as Rose had stepped outside. She had learned little other than that Gwen was neurotic, and whether or not there was a will it was up to a solicitor to sort out. She could not see Martin switching that painting, but if Peter suspected he had been left nothing could he have done so? There would have been no problem in gaining access to the house, Dorothy would have let him in unquestioningly. Was that why Gwen was so anxious? Did she know something? Rose shook her head. Nothing seemed to make any sense. She got into the car and drove down the hill convinced that there was more to it than a missing painting. There were undercurrents in the Pengelly household which she could not define. And she had taken an instant dislike to Gwen which might interfere with her objectivity. She would sketch the damn flower then go and see Martin.

Bradley Hinkston told his wife that he would be away overnight again. She seemed not to be listening. Seated at the breakfast bar, both elbows resting on its surface, she held a magnifying mirror in one hand and a mascara wand in the other. Clad in cream leather trousers and a scarlet silk shirt Louise was preparing for a morning's shopping and lunch with a girlfriend. The breakfast dishes lay scattered around – they and the rest of the chores would be left for the woman who came in to see to them. 'Louise, did you hear me?'

'Sorry, darling.' She looked up and smiled. 'Can't talk when I'm doing my eyes. Just tonight, is it?'

'I think so. I'll let you know either way.'

'Good. I don't like it when you're not here.' Her actions

seemed to belie her words because she immediately turned away and stretched her lips to apply lipstick.

Cursing mildly as the sleeve of his jacket brushed spilt tea on the work surface, Bradley reached down and picked up his briefcase. He could not really blame Louise. She ran her own beauty business, although nowadays she mostly left the manager in charge, and she had as little inclination towards housework as he had himself.

It was mild but overcast as he left the outskirts of Bristol behind him and, as the holiday brochures optimistically promised, the nearer he came to his destination the warmer it was and the brighter the sun shone. He knew from experience that this was not always the case. Twice before he had driven into heavy rain. Depressing the switch which activated the electronic windows he felt the breeze produced by the speed of the car cool his face. It was more subtle than the consistent air-conditioning. With luck he would get accommodation at the same place. It was clean and comfortable, the room was attractive and the food was plentiful and good. Better still, the landlord did not hurry him upstairs once the bar was officially closed. Bradley had stayed in hotels which were of a lower standard. By himself he was quite happy with bed and breakfast. When Louise accompanied him she preferred more luxurious surroundings.

Dorothy Pengelly was an interesting woman and she had made him an interesting proposition but he hadn't trusted her to keep quiet about it. Initially it had crossed his mind that senility had taken a grip but, on reflection, he sensed that she was an extremely acute old lady and knew far more about what made people tick than he did himself and he was no fool.

The season may have been over but there was still plenty of traffic heading towards the south-west. A caravan swayed dangerously ahead of him and as soon as he had an opportunity he overtook it. The driver of the car towing it was travelling too fast. He tooted his horn and gestured towards the rear vehicle as he passed it but the driver ignored him.

First things first, he decided as he left the A30 at the Hayle junction. He pulled up in the car-park of the pub where he had stayed before and went into the bar. Lunchtime customers were ordering food. Bradley was flattered to be remembered by the landlord.

'Same room if you like,' he was told. 'The missus'll show you up. Let her know if there aren't any towels. We weren't expecting much more trade.'

Bradley entered the low-ceilinged bedroom with its tiny *en suite* bathroom. There was a shower stall, a lavatory and a small hand basin. The plumbing was efficient and it was adequate for his needs. He hung up the spare clothes he had brought and placed his toilet bag on the glass shelf above the sink. After splashing his face with cold water he went down to the bar for a quick drink before going over to the Pengelly place. It was a risk returning, he knew that, especially if what he had learned about the daughter-in-law was true. Gwen Pengelly was angling to get Dorothy into an old people's home in order to get her hands on her possessions. It was too late now for Gwen Pengelly to have her way; Dorothy had made other arrangements.

Marigold's funeral was not taking place until the following week. Fred had needed time to let everyone know and he felt it would have seemed like rushing her departure from the world if he took the first date which was offered. He could not contemplate how he would get through the intervening days. It was unbearable in the shop receiving the pitying glances and hearing the well-meaning words of his customers. 'She's no longer suffering,' was the most oft repeated. Fred wanted to shout at them, to say that she shouldn't have been made to suffer at all. It was even more unbearable upstairs in the flat with nothing but his own thoughts for company and Marigold's possessions all around him.

Out of a perverse desire to please, he had lined up the condolence cards he had received from his customers on the shelf behind the counter. All the crosses and lilies made him feel sick. A thousand sackfuls of cards couldn't bring Marigold back. But he, Fred Meecham, was going to preserve what they had had together and protect their secret until his own dying day. At any cost, he told himself.

The police had been to see him, turned up on the very night of Marigold's death. He had had no idea they could be so insensitive. Of course, later he realised they could not have known. They were polite and respectful and had not come to question him about the past at all but about Dorothy. He had told them when he had last seen her and that she had seemed in good spirits. What else was there to say? Then they had expressed interest in the drugs Marigold took. There were none in the house now, of course, he had handed them over as he had been asked to do, but he had had no trouble listing them. For two years he had supervised the taking of them. Then they had left. Fred had been shaken but also relieved. It was Dorothy they were interested in, not that other thing.

Fred was still convinced that money could have saved Marigold. He had not had enough of it and blamed himself rather than fate over which he had no control. Dorothy could have lent him some but she had refused.

Now it was over and Dorothy was dead too. In an odd sort of way he missed her because she was a good listener and might have helped him deal with the pain. She was the one person who knew more about him and Marigold than anyone had. Both women had taken the secret with them to the grave.

Rose parked in a gateway, guessing that the farmer would not need to use it because there was stubble in the field and no more work would be done there until it was time for ploughing. Below her was the estuary, the tide low, the waders and gulls, settled in the middle, too far away to make out clearly. How Barry could be so sure she'd find the plant was a mystery but he must have done so himself or got someone else to because, after a wasted fifteen minutes, she finally saw the tiny delicate head of it and settled down to work. Not for much longer, Rose told herself as she held the drawing away from her to check it was exactly right.

She sat with her arms hugging her knees and looked at the small church on the brow of the hill, visualising it painted in oils. All right, she would finish all the jobs she had taken on then she would start again, see if she still had it in her to be a real artist. It had been too easy to accept the praises of Doreen Clarke and Barry Rowe. What was it Jack had said once? Yes, that his ex-wife had bought one of her oils because she had liked it, because it had feeling even if it wasn't technically a great piece of work. The technical side could be developed. Will be developed, Rose thought as she packed away her pencils. I will get my life sorted out and I will do my best for Dorothy.

Filled with determination she strode back to the car, her hair flying in the wind. Water was flowing back into the estuary and many of the birds had disappeared in large flocks. A solitary egret proceeded to the waterline with queenly grace, its white plumage unmistakable. Once rare here, they were now often to be seen.

She reached the car and headed towards the main road, racking her brains as to what the warning had meant. It has to be somebody close, she thought, someone who knows I won't settle for less than the truth, someone who knows how much I cared about Dorothy.

It got her nowhere, less than a handful of people fell into that category and they were all people she trusted. Which reminded her, she had not been in touch with Jobber Hicks since their one conversation regarding Martin. He, too, would be lonely and missing Dorothy, his lifetime companion.

She sighed as she changed gear to pull into Dorothy's drive and the engine missed. 'You'll really have to go,' she told the Mini. There was no sign of Martin at the house so she walked over to the caravan. He wasn't there either and could be anywhere so it was pointless to wait. Standing on the hillside in the unnatural silence, Rose shivered. Clouds scudded across the sky, intermittently obscuring the sun. Their shadows passed stealthily over the grass, deadening its colour; their shapes sliding over the boulders seemed almost human. For the first time she began to wonder if Martin had anything to do with his mother's death: if someone had given her alcohol laced with enough drugs to kill her where had the mug or glass been? The table had been clear and the sink empty when she came upon the scene. Fear rose in her throat and she stifled an exclamation as a huge black cloud blocked out the light and turned the moorland into a place of evil where unseen eyes watched her. The cloud was blown southwards and she blinked in the sudden brightness. It was time to leave.

She did not see Peter Pengelly passing in the opposite direction as she made her way to where she intended to finish a piece of work because she did not recognise his car.

For two hours she continued without interruption. The threat of rain had passed and she could feel the autumnal warmth of the sun on her head. Gorse was still in its second flowering and bees hummed around the clover amongst which she was sitting. Putting aside her watercolours she lay back and closed her eyes, enjoying nothing but the colourful patterns which formed behind her lids. They reminded her of a kaleidoscope she had had as a child. A bee, black and gold like a Cornish rugby shirt, landed near her ear. Rose remained motionless whilst it went about its business. When it had flown off she sat up and poured coffee from her flask. Traffic was a distant murmur, not enough to disturb the peace. Ahead and surrounding her was nothing but scrubland with a few scruffy trees, but she felt no fear now. If it had not been for the brightness of the gorse she might have been on a hillside in Italy or Greece. Ah, yes, she thought, the gorse and the crumbling stack of a copper mine. Scattered the length and breadth of the county the old mines were so much a part of it, it was as if nature and not man was responsible for their presence.

With bent legs, knees splayed, Rose sat with the plastic cup of the flask held in both hands between them, her posture that of an unselfconscious teenager rather than a mature woman. Her denim skirt had slipped up her thighs exposing her tanned legs, the muscles toned by all the walking she did. Overhead a flash of silver caught her eye. It was a plane, reflecting the sun, too high for its engines to be heard and only visible because of the clarity of the air. In its wake was a vapour trail which was breaking up into white balls of fluff. 'Time to move,' she told herself, screwing the lid back on the flask and putting away her equipment. She shook dry seeds and grass from her clothes and strode back to the car. The almost smooth-stemmed Western Gorse, its flower more delicate than the everyday kind, had challenged her which was good, because she had a tendency to become complacent at times. The series would be complete before Barry actually required it. Tempting as it was to stay out of doors Rose knew there was more to be done at home. And the sooner it was done the sooner she could get out her oils.

There had been no message from Jack who was either still tied up at the station or too tired to want to see her. She did not contact him. Leaving the house at a few minutes to seven she arrived at Barry's promptly at seven thirty. He was flushed with a sheen of perspiration on his forehead. The sleeves of his white shirt were rolled up showing pale, freckled forearms gleaming with golden hairs. Over one shoulder was a tea towel and his glasses, perched on his nose, were faintly misted. He pushed them into place impatiently and kissed Rose chastely on the cheek. She was cool and smelled clean from her recent shower. He recognised the pale blue dress as the one she had bought on a trip to London with him and was flattered that she had worn it because he had said how much he liked it.

'I wish I hadn't attempted something so complicated. Help yourself to a drink, Rosie. This won't be ready for a while yet.' Barry turned back to the small counter upon which was a pile of dirty utensils.

'What're we having?' Rose reached for the wine bottle.

'Beef Wellington,' Barry replied with a touch of satisfaction as he wrapped shop-bought pastry around the meat he had spread with pâté.

'What? No pasta?'

'It's not the only thing I can cook,' he replied defensively.

'No, but it's the only thing which turns out right.'

'I shall ignore that. I'm simply trying to pay you back for the lovely things you cook for me.'

Rose handed him a glass of chilled white wine. 'Have a slurp of this before you explode.'

He did so, his fingers leaving greasy prints on the stem. Rose watched him struggle with the beef but was tactful enough not to say he could have bought the whole thing ready-made.

The kitchen was cramped and ill equipped. She took one of the two unmatching chairs and sat at the rickety table. Barry had lived in the one-bedroomed flat over the shop since she had known him. His financial status was of no concern to her but she knew that he could have afforded somewhere far better. He was, she decided, in a rut, but one in which he seemed content to remain.

'There! Or should I say *voilà*? It's in the oven. It might be an idea to drink ourselves senseless in case it's a disaster. Right, now you can tell me what you've been up to.' The chair creaked beneath him as it took his weight.

'What makes you think I've been up to anything?' He looks so boyish and helpless at times, she thought. It's a shame no woman's got hold of him. 'I'm well ahead with the wild flowers. I did the Western Gorse this afternoon. It won't be long until they're all done. Why're you looking at me like that?'

'You're babbling, Rosie, and I know what that means.' He reached across the table and touched her hand. 'I didn't mean to upset you the other day, I know how you felt about Dorothy.'

Rose nodded and a loose hair fell on to her lap. She picked it off the material of her dress and wound it around her finger. 'I shall miss her. I'm already missing her.'

'I know.'

'The police said it was suicide, now they're not so sure but . . .' She shrugged and picked up her wineglass.

Barry's mouth tightened. By the police he assumed she meant Jack Pearce.

Correctly reading his expression Rose added, 'She didn't kill herself, Barry, I don't believe that for one minute. You don't think that, do you?'

'Oh, Rose.' Barry rubbed his forehead as if he was tired.

It had been best to get it over with before he heard from other sources and accused her of having secrets from him. This was the one aspect of his character which infuriated her. If she told him things he accused her of meddling, if she did not he called her secretive. Rose then announced that she would not be readily available for commercial work, she was reverting to oils. The expected outburst did not come.

'At last,' Barry said, smiling.

'Don't you mind?'

'Mind? Good God, Rosie, why should I? It's your life, your career and, to tell you the truth, I was disappointed when you didn't keep going. You see, I always thought you'd improve. Each one was always slightly better than the last. Go for it, that's what I say.'

She could barely believe what she was hearing but the encouragement was worth more than any commission. Her desire was now not to let Barry down. 'Oh, and I've been invited to a party on Saturday.'

'Oh? The glasses were pushed up once more, this time the gesture was deliberate, to disguise what would show in his face when Rose said that Pearce was taking her. 'Why're you grinning?'

'Because I can read your mind.' She twirled her glass between her fingers knowing that she was teasing him. 'I'm going by myself.'

'I see.' No Jack, he thought, but no Barry either.

'My social life's becoming as restricted as yours. I miss the times when I was mixing with other artists and writers. I have to do something about it.'

Barry nodded. She was right. They talked of general things until it was time to serve the meal. It was far better than either of them had anticipated and they ate the lot. 'I think I'll walk home rather than get a cab,' Rose said.

'And I shall accompany you. I need to walk it off, too.'

There was a three-quarter moon illuminating the bay. Pale ripples spread into the surrounding blackness of the water. The lights of Newlyn were to their right when they stopped to lean over the railing to absorb the sound of the sea sucking at the pebbles. Rose thought she could listen to it for ever. The distinctive cry of a curlew reached them as it took off from Larrigan rocks which were completely visible now the tide was out. 'Come on, we'd better make a move.'

Arm in arm they walked along past the Bowls Club, situated right on the front and exposed to the elements, past the Newlyn Gallery and around to the Strand and the now shuttered fish market then up the hill. To their left the harbour was lit by moonlight and the lifeboat, *Mabel Alice*, lay slightly on one side as the incoming tide lapped at her hull, gently nudging her upright.

Barry left Rose at her door then began the return journey. He chewed his mouth thoughtfully, knowing that if there was anything unusual about Dorothy Pengelly's death Rose would not rest until she had found out what it was. Better to think of that than Jack Pearce or whom she might meet at Mike and Barbara's party.

Rose threw her shoulder bag into an armchair. The clasp had been undone and the contents spilled out on to the floor. She ignored them and kicked off her shoes, always preferring to be barefoot in the house. The evening had gone well and Barry's reaction to her involvement with the Pengelly family had not been as censorious as she had expected. In fact, he had surprised her in several ways.

The sitting-room was half lit by the moon and the light from the hall. Rose turned to take one last look at the bay as she did every night. As she left the room she saw the red light of the answering machine winking in the corner. Jack, she thought. Her brow creased in a frown when she heard Jobber's voice. He had started the message twice, the second time was clearer. It was too late to contact him or Martin now so she would do as he had asked and meet them in the morning. Was it too late to ring Jack? She was surprised he had not been in touch, if only to find out if she had been to see the Pengellys. 'No, bugger him,' she muttered and went upstairs to bed.

Jobber Hicks had got into his ramshackle van and made his way slowly to Dorothy's house. He had not wanted to burden Martin with his request too soon because the boy might give him an answer he would later regret. He always drove at a leisurely pace because he saw no reason to rush through life. The end would come at some point. Happily ignoring impatient drivers behind him he slowed to take the bend then indicated right, turning into Dorothy's drive.

Jobber's calloused and roughened hands gripped the wheel at precisely ten to three, the way his father had taught him, and his head, tortoise-like, jutted forward from the loose collar of his shirt as he peered through the windscreen. His lack of height did not bother him. All his family had been short. The skin of his face, neck and forearms was weathered but the rest of his body had not seen the sun since childhood. Only in repose did the starburst of lines around his eyes relax enough to reveal the paler skin in the creases. His grey hair was cropped short and he wore whatever happened to be nearest when he got dressed. All his clothes held a faint suggestion of manure.

The van was worse. It stank of animals. Often a single sheep or pig was loaded into the back of it to be taken to market. For more than one he used the horse-box.

He killed the ignition and let the silence fill his ears, half expecting Dorothy to come to the door. Jobber studied the sky and nodded knowledgeably. It would rain before the day was out. He, like his father before him, could predict the weather with more accuracy than any satellite station.

Leaving the van where it was, he walked around the side of the house and peered through the kitchen window. The dogs were there, in their usual places. Star was scratching behind her ear in an ungainly fashion. They looked restful and their bowls were empty. Martin must have seen to them already.

Jobber continued on up the hill, his pace so steady his heartbeat did not alter. In the distance, slumped against a boulder, he spotted Martin. He waited until he was near enough to talk in a normal voice before he spoke.

Martin raised his face. He looked haggard. 'He came back,' he said.

'Who did? Who came back?'

'The bugger I saw in the pub.'

Jobber's eyes narrowed. What had Martin been saying to this stranger? 'Have you told the police, son?' Jobber, too, had been questioned and was aware that things might not be as straightforward as everyone had initially believed.

'No.' Martin got to his feet. His nostrils were pinched and he was white around the mouth. 'Won't bring 'er back, will 'un?'

'No. Nothing's going to do that. Why don't us go on down to the house. There's something I want to ask you.' He thought Martin looked in need of a strong mug of tea.

Together they negotiated the irregular route back down. The dogs greeted them both in a friendly way and Jobber put the kettle on. They drank the tea black. 'Are you coping?' Jobber nodded towards the animals.

'They're no trouble. I take 'em out twice a day and feed the cats.'

Jobber leant forward. 'Martin, do you think I could have Star? I'd look after her proper, like, you can rest assured of that. I'll even pay you for 'un, if you've a mind.'

Martin stared at the greyhound. There was no room for her in his van and if she went to the farm she'd have company. 'All right. I don't want no money, though.'

They sipped their tea in silence. Both were men of few words. 'I should stay here, at the house. He'll come back again else.'

'Who is this man you keep on about? If you think he's trouble you've got to tell the police.' Jobber's hands shook. If Martin was right he had no need to feel any guilt. He had cried in the belief that he might have driven Dorothy to her death, unaware that he had not been as persistent as he thought, that a lot of it had been in his head.

'No. I'll tell Mrs Trevelyan. 'Er'll know what to do.'

97

Jobber nodded. Rose Trevelyan was a sensible woman and had been more than a good friend to Dorothy. Good-looking with it, too, he thought. He nodded again and ran a hand around his badly shaved chin. Although he had had few dealings with the police he had an inborn prejudice against them. 'We could telephone her now.'

'You do it.'

Jobber glanced at his watch. It was getting on for seven o'clock. Mrs Trevelyan would probably be at home. He found the number in the book beside the telephone and felt a sharp pain in his chest seeing Dorothy's large, rounded writing. He began speaking before he realised he was talking to a recorded message. 'Damn things,' he said, feeling stupid and self-conscious. Clearing his throat he stood straighter as if Rose's disembodied voice was able to see him. He said that Martin had something important to tell her and asked if she was free to come to Dorothy's house at ten the next morning. 'Thank you,' he said politely at the end of the message. 'There, all done. That just leaves the problem of Star.'

They loaded half of the tins of dog food and her blanket and basket into the back of the van, then finally Star herself. Martin patted her fondly and watched as Jobber turned around and drove to the end of the lane.

Star whined and fretted and rested her front paws on the back of Jobber's seat where he had left the dividing window open. He spoke to her soothingly and quietly. Star would settle down in a day or two. Jobber had had many dogs in his life and knew their ways well.

Fred Meecham sat with his head in his hands, his red hair sticking up untidily. The vicar had shown no surprise that his sister's surname was different from his own, it was known that she had been through a bad marriage. Marigold Heath was the name on her death certificate. No one had yet asked to see this certificate. The woman who had issued it at the register office had needed nothing other than the form from the hospital doctor who had pronounced her to be dead.

Her headstone would be simple, bearing only her name and her dates and his own contribution, 'always loved'. Fred did not know what to do about her other relatives, or even if they were alive. Time was running out and many things were preying on his mind. Both Marigold and Dorothy would have known what to do but they were no longer in a position to help him.

Jack Pearce was not in the best of moods, which irritated him as much as anyone else. The whole thing was shambolic but he couldn't blame the officers who had been the first at the scene. Dorothy Pengelly had been an old lady who had died accidentally or deliberately from an overdose. The police surgeon had seen it almost immediately and this had been confirmed by the pathologist. There had been no need for the murder team. He still wasn't as convinced as Rose that it was anything else and any evidence, if it was evidence, had been destroyed. The paracetamol bottle had disappeared and any container in which the drug had been administered would have been washed up. They could still fingerprint the place but what would that show? Martin and Rose had keys, old prints were likely to have been disturbed or smudged and they only had Rose's say-so on who might have been in the house.

Was there a will? Was money the motive? If there has been a crime, Jack reminded himself. If Dorothy was intestate both sons would inherit equally, if there was a will it might be a different matter but murdering her would not alter its contents. If one or other son stood to gain little he would want her alive in order to have a chance of persuading her to change it. But the reverse was also true. Supposing Dorothy had left everything to one son but had been about to change her own mind? And where was the painting? One of her children must have it. He shook his head in exasperation. Here, too, was information based only on Rose's opinion. Jack warned himself to be careful. He must not let his professional judgement be clouded because he trusted the instincts of Rose Trevelyan.

Interviewing the family had been a waste of time. No one had a decent alibi but why should they have if they were innocent?

Peter and Gwen claimed to have been together watching television all evening and had gone to bed around eleven. With two small children this was more than likely true. Martin said he had been alone, in his van. Either he was totally honest or he knew they would not be able to prove otherwise.

Jobber Hicks and Fred Meecham, apparently Dorothy's only other friends, had also been questioned. Meecham's sister had just died and he was understandably too upset to be of much help. Jobber, Jack knew from Rose, was Dorothy's ardent admirer and he could see no reason why he should wish her dead.

I'm wasting my time, he thought as the day drew to a close. The old lady decided she had had enough of life. It's as simple as that.

Three times during the evening he dialled Rose's number only to get the answering machine. He could have left a message but what he really wanted was to speak to her in person. Strange that she should be avoiding him, unless she knew something she didn't want him to know just yet. That wouldn't surprise him at all. But he was unaware that Rose was spending the evening in the company of Barry Rowe, the man whom he considered to be his rival.

Fred Meecham was trying desperately hard to get on with the everyday running of his shop. It was a delivery day and, at least for the morning, the added work helped take his mind off Marigold. He checked the forms against what he had ordered then unpacked the goods and re-stacked the shelves although this was usually the job of one of his part-time assistants. Beneath his red hair his face was whiter than usual. He realised that these were still early days, that at some unspecified point in the future he would come to terms with it all and live normally again. For now his grief and anger were eating away at him.

When customers spoke he answered them as best he could, aware of the glances which passed between them and the assistant behind the counter.

Life had dealt him two harsh blows where women were concerned, first the departure of his wife with the young sales rep and now Marigold. On top of this his son was an ingrate, unappreciative of the sacrifices Fred had made for him. He had not seen him for years now and Fred was not sorry.

He had always stuck to the rules, done things by the book, and it had got him nowhere. During those first years with his ex-wife he had borne with stoicism the endless rows and her avarice, never resorting to violence or taking consolation elsewhere. She had repaid him by moving out and leaving their son behind. That son, too, had gone.

Abandoned now for the third time Fred went through the motions. He collected up the empty cardboard boxes and took them out to the back where he would later burn them. He needed some air and to spend a few minutes away from the shop. Pounding away in his head was the idea that he had deserved all he had got, but there had only been two aberrations in his life. One had given him immeasurable pleasure, the second nothing but a fleeting minute's joy followed by a hopeless rage.

He returned to the shop, picked up a price gun and began marking tins of corned beef.

Biting her lip, Rose tried unsuccessfully to arrange her hair in a neat roll at the back of her head. She claimed she kept it shoulder-length because there was so much more she could do with it, something about which Laura teased her. 'You've either got it loose or in a pony-tail,' she said. But Laura wasn't there to admire her effort when she finally got it right.

It was not so much her hair which bothered her at that moment but herself. She was sometimes gregarious and other people's lives and personalities fascinated her but, like Martin Pengelly, she required stretches of isolation. This was one of the reasons she had not been able to make a commitment to Jack and she recognised it as a fault. She had known she would not mourn for ever and had enough insight to see that she had used Jack as the first stage in her recovery. Laura had it both ways. Trevor, at home to enjoy and fuss over, then periods of a week or ten days when he was at sea. And now, when she needed some breathing space, she would not allow herself any because she was worried sick about Martin. Yet her feelings were ambiguous. One minute she wanted to protect him, the next to put as much distance between them as possible. She was, as Barry would have pointed out, becoming too involved. Martin worried her in various ways but Jobber would be there too.

It had rained overnight and the road was still damp. The clouds, a curving canopy of grey, domed over the sea. The salvage tug which came and went was once more anchored in the bay after refuelling in Falmouth. It pitched and tossed on white-capped waves.

The Mini was buffeted as she picked up speed on the main road and the canvas cover of a high-sided lorry flapped noisily as it passed her going in the opposite direction. Knowing flocks of gulls drifted inland and took refuge in the fields.

The blank windows of Dorothy's house reflected the car as she drew up in front of it. Jobber's old van was already there, parked on the grass to allow her room.

He appeared at the side of the building as she stepped out into the blustery morning. 'We've made the tea,' he said by way of greeting. 'I'm glad you could make it, Mrs Trevelyan. Martin's in a bit of a state.'

She followed him around to the back door, neither of them wishing to presume to use the front one. The wind whipped at her clothes as they turned the corner.

Martin was sitting at the kitchen table. He seemed to have shrunk further and there were dark shadows under his eyes. Despite his spartan living conditions he kept himself clean and tidy. He wore jeans and shirt and a V-necked jumper and his durable boots. His brown hair was neatly combed. 'Where's Star?' Rose asked, surprised to see that the space her basket usually occupied was empty.

'I've taken her. She's a bit restless, but she'll soon get used to the place. I didn't bring 'un this morning, though, it'd only confuse her.'

It was Jobber who poured Rose's treacle-coloured tea, adding milk which he had brought from the farm. She waited, wondering which one of them would be the first to speak. Martin's eyes were dull, his expression flat as he stared at the mug in front of him. 'Martin? Was there something you wanted to tell me?' she asked, half expecting another admission.

He finally looked up but remained silent. Jobber nudged him. 'Go on, tell her, tell Mrs Trevelyan.'

'They're back. The two men I told you about. One of them was hanging around outside the house. He didn't know I was about. I told 'un, I said if I ever caught him here again I'd kill him.' Some colour had returned to his face. 'I nearly hit him.' He picked up his mug and drank deeply.

'Who are these men?' Rose looked at Jobber who raised his shoulders to show he knew no more than she did.

'I met them down Hayle. In the pub. We had some drinks.' Martin's face darkened further as he recalled just how many drinks and how he had been foolish enough to let one of the men pay for some of them. 'We got talking. I said . . . I said Mum had some nice stuff an' he told me he went round buying off people.' He stopped, ashamed that the drinks had made him boastful. 'If I hadn't said that, they wouldn't have killed her.' He bowed his head and Rose finally understood what had been troubling him.

'Do you think they were con men, Martin? Do you think they came here and frightened your mother?'

'Yeah. Something like that, I suppose.'

'Mrs Trevelyan?' Jobber had seen the look of horror on Rose's face. She was thinking about the Stanhope Forbes and what men like that might do to get hold of one. Realising his incomprehension she explained to Jobber about the painting.

'Dorothy owned one?'

Martin was watching them both. He had no idea why they were making such a fuss over one of Dorothy's pictures. It had hung on the wall ever since he could remember and, as far as he knew, no one had commented on it, least of all his mother. And if it was worth so much money, why hang it in the bedroom where only she could see it? Martin had known about the bits of china but he had been unaware that paintings could be expensive. Of course, Mrs Trevelyan would know because she was clever in that way.

'But there's a reproduction hanging in its place now,' Rose concluded. There was no reason why Jobber should have known, Dorothy was not a boastful woman.

'I knew she had some valuable paintings, but she never mentioned no names. Did you tell the police, Mrs Trevelyan?'

'Yes. I had to. Martin hadn't realised because he never went in that room.'

'Don't matter now, boy, we've got to tell the police.'

'I already did, the first time. I told 'un I thought I'd spoke out of turn because they were strangers.'

Rose frowned. She did not know they had been to see Martin at all. But she saw why he was upset. He believed himself responsible for bringing the men to the house in the first place, if that was what had happened. It was all conjecture, of course – they may not have been near the place and if they had, they may have left Dorothy in perfect health. She was beginning to wonder if she had made a terrible mistake only because she didn't want to believe it of Dorothy. But Rose still couldn't help asking, 'Did you tell these men where the house was?'

His blush answered the question. Rose met Jobber's eyes and each knew what the other was thinking. 'And you saw one of them again. When was that?'

'Yesterday. That's when I threatened 'im.'

It was puzzling. If someone had cheated Dorothy and, in the process, felt the need to silence her, it was unlikely that they would return. 'Martin, when did they come? The first time, I mean?'

'I don't know. I never saw them then.'

'Look, we have to be very careful. If you didn't see them, yesterday might've been the first visit. The man would have no reason to know that...' She stopped. There was no point in making things harder for Martin.

'Could be. Could be that he came back for more of what wasn't 'is.'

Martin had a point. 'Would you know them again, boy?'

'Course I would.' He gave Jobber a strange look. He wasn't daft. But he did not realise that Jobber had had an idea.

'He says they're not local, so if they're not from round here and he met them in the pub and now they seem to be back again, well, you can see how the land might lie.'

Rose thought she was following what Jobber was getting at. 'You think they might be staying at the same place in which case we could find them?'

'That's exactly what I was thinking, Mrs Trevelyan.' He sucked his unlit pipe.

'Oh, Jobber, please call me Rose.'

'An' as pretty as one too, to my eyes.'

Rose was more flattered than she would have been had another male offered her the banal compliment. Jobber did not waste words on things he did not mean. 'Thank you. Look, why don't we meet later, say about six, and see if Martin can point them out to us.' Rose swallowed the guilt she felt knowing that she ought to have told Jack about the men even if they had been a figment of Martin's imagination. I will, she promised, later this evening.

They arranged to meet at Jobber's farm. Rose would collect the two of them there as the van only had the two seats in the front.

'And that'll give Martin a chance to take a look at Star. Here, why don't you come a bit earlier, boy, and have a bite of supper with me?'

Martin said he would and Rose was touched by the older man's concern. 'What's going to happen to George?'

'Well, now, I've had an idea or two about that, too,' Jobber replied but refused to expand upon it. The Jack Russell growled as if he was aware he was under discussion but since Dorothy's death and now the disappearance of Star some of his aggression had left him. The dog was the most unlovable pet Rose had come across but the cats were even worse. They were almost feral and hissed and spat if anyone but Dorothy went near them.

No further words were exchanged as they each went their separate ways. Rose wondered when she would hear from Jack and how much she would tell him if he rang before she left home again that evening.

Several hardy souls were battling their way across the Promenade, heading into the wind on the raised pavement opposite the Mount's Bay Inn. Their lightweight jackets billowed around them. If the wind was coming from the west there was a chance of more rain but she would be home long before it started.

There were two messages from Jack. The first said he would try again later, the second asked her to contact him at the station as soon as she got home. She tried but was told he wasn't available. Rose left her own message with a sergeant then went upstairs to develop some rolls of film.

'Goddamm the woman,' Jack said when he returned to his office and found the note on the desk. He still had no idea how her meeting with the Pengellys had gone or if she had been there at all. Once more he rang her number and was relieved to hear her voice.

'That's it?' he asked, disappointed when she had given her explanation.

'Yes. Sorry, Jack.'

'You did your best.'

Rose was glad he could not see her. He would have known by her face that there was more but she was not ready to tell him yet. After the trip to Hayle later would be the time to tell him whether or not anything came of it.

Perverting the course of justice? Obstructing the law? she asked herself, having replaced the receiver. No, she amended, more like bloody-mindedness. If Jack was doing his job properly he would know all about the nameless men in Hayle.

Rose was unaware that the landlord of the pub had already been questioned but was unable to supply the names because they had paid for their accommodation in advance, in cash, which might indicate that the transaction did not go through the books but was of no help in identifying them.

8

Bradley Hinkston stood at the bar with a brandy and soda in his hand, more shaken now than he had been yesterday. How right his initial instincts about the Pengelly family had been. Eccentric was not a strong enough word to describe them. The old lady must have been having him on in some way, although he couldn't quite see how, not after his first visit. Then, out of the blue, he had been physically threatened by the son. The only thing to do now was forget all about it and pack up and go home. Too late tonight. He'd been drinking and Louise was not expecting him because he had telephoned to say he was staying on. Besides, he'd already paid for a second night and he couldn't expect the landlord to give him his money back.

Tomorrow he intended visiting a village near Plymouth for a house clearance sale. From the catalogue he did not think it would be very profitable but there were a few nice pieces he wouldn't mind if he could beat the other dealers to them. What annoyed him most was that if he had been able to get his hands on Mrs Pengelly's other paintings and that rather nice commode it would have added to his reputation as far as his customers were concerned. With a mental shrug he decided to put it all behind him and enjoy the home-made steak and kidney pudding and fresh vegetables which were offered on the menu. He would have another drink to settle his nerves before he ordered. Louise tended to go for exotic foods or things which would not harm her figure. Alone, Bradley allowed himself to indulge in large helpings of plain cooking.

He moved away from the bar as more customers came in. He wanted to be sure of a table at which to eat. When a gust of wind told him that the door had been opened again he looked up automatically. 'Oh, Lord,' he whispered. It was the Pengelly boy and he had come with reinforcements. He hoped there would not be some awful public scene. However, the short, grizzled man and the extremely attractive middle-aged woman posed no real threat. It was the son who might be out for trouble. He placed a finger to his lips as he wondered what the disparate group wanted.

As they went up to the bar and ordered drinks he saw them whispering.

It was the woman who approached the table first, the two men close behind her. In the car they had decided that they had been stupid, that there was no chance of the men being there. Now they were actually facing one of them no one was sure what to do.

Rose quickly took in the debonair man who looked completely at ease. He reminded her of a fifties film star she was unable to name. The silver hair and well-defined features were attractive. Neither Jobber nor Martin appeared to want to initiate conversation so it was left to her. 'Excuse us interrupting, but we're friends of Mrs Pengelly. Well, two of us are,' she began uncertainly. 'This is Jobber Hicks. And this is her son, Martin. I believe you've already met.'

Bradley had not been expecting such polite introductions. He turned on his full charm. 'Jobber, what an interesting name. And Hicks. Don't tell me you're responsible for that excellent local beer by the same name?'

'No, I'm a farmer. We'd like to know who you are.'

'Forgive me. Won't you sit down?' He waved a hand over the empty seats surrounding him. 'It's so relaxing down here it's easy to forget one's manners.' He stood as they joined his table. 'I'm Bradley Hinkston and I'm very pleased to meet you.'

Rose introduced herself as his eyes slid appreciatively down to her legs.

Bradley sipped his drink. 'Mr Pengelly, I'm pleased that we're now on better terms. Unless, of course, this is your hit-team?'

The incongruity of the comment and the man's wry humour amused Rose. Jobber took it more seriously. 'Martin meant nothing by his behaviour, sir. Naturally, he was upset.'

'Yes. It must've appeared as if I was trespassing, but Mrs Pengelly – '

'Just a minute.' Rose stopped him. Unless he was a true con artist he did not know that Dorothy was dead. 'Mr Hinkston, Martin's mother died on Thursday night.'

'What? Oh, my goodness. I'm so sorry. No wonder – ' but he stopped himself that time. 'Oh, dear, I should've telephoned first.'

'Wouldn't've been no point. She couldn't have answered,' Martin stated philosophically.

'I can't believe it, she was fine when I last saw her.'

So he had been to the house before and he was making no attempt to hide the fact. This, Rose knew, would be important to the police, more so in view of his next comment.

'Thursday! I was with her on Thursday. I didn't know she was ill, she really showed no signs of being so. Oh, dear. If only she'd said.'

'Would you mind us knowing what it was you went to see her about?' Jobber had taken the initiative.

'I don't know what all this is about, but would you allow me to freshen your drinks before we continue?'

Rose and Jobber said yes but Martin put a hand firmly over his glass. He knew what had happened the last time. 'Why not, 'e looks like 'e's got a few bob,' Jobber whispered but Martin shook his head.

Bradley returned with the glasses then leant back in his seat ready to answer their questions, not admitting that he was as baffled as his interviewers. They listened, astonished, to what he had to tell them. Later, in the car, Martin surprised them. A will existed and he knew where it was.

It was nine thirty before Bradley got to eat his steak and kidney pudding, and it gave him indigestion. Foolishly he had ignored his instinct which had told him not to return.

'No,' Peter Pengelly stated firmly. 'You are not going up there. The solicitors'll sort it out. Knowing Mother, everything will be in order.'

'But it needs a good clean.'

Peter knew Gwen's intention was to remove anything she thought to be of value, small things, maybe, but nonetheless, they were not hers to take. He still could not understand the urgency: they both believed that the bulk of the estate was coming to them. If Gwen feared Martin had the same intention as herself she need not have worried. His brother was completely trustworthy.

Peter turned his head as he heard the swish of his wife's legs crossing. Her skirt had slid higher up and the top of one stocking was visible, as he knew it was meant to be. He sighed. Did she really think her blatant methods would work now? Was she incapable of seeing that he was still grieving? Even allowing for her miserable childhood he was impatient with her.

Peter's grim face showed Gwen she had made the wrong move. She tugged her skirt into place and sat up straight. 'I didn't mean anything by it, Peter, I just thought if the house had a good clean it would be easier to sell. I keep meaning to ask you, do you know where the will actually is?'

'No. But her solicitors or the bank probably have the original.'

'I don't mean to sound mercenary, but they won't necessarily know she's dead, not unless we tell them.'

He frowned. It was true. It was the first sensible suggestion she had made. It was up to the relatives to make it known. 'I'll see to it in the morning. Failing that I'll get the key off Martin and we'll look for it together.'

Gwen's face relaxed.

'Me and Martin, I meant.'

Gwen saw there was no point in arguing.

Rose unlocked the kitchen door. She was much later than she had anticipated. The hall was lit, the timer switch had come on a couple of hours ago. It had been Jack's idea and he had installed it for her. It was yet another reminder of the way she had allowed him into her life.

Locking the door behind her she reached out for the kitchen light switch then boiled a kettle for tea. At the moment the idea of sleep was impossible. There was so much else to think about and she ought to ring Jack immediately. There were several messages for her but they all concerned work. Rose made a note of the numbers. She would return the calls but it was doubtful if she would take on the jobs. Leaving a message for Jack on his answering machine she went to bed. Her sleep was patchy and she dreamed of the life she had stayed in Cornwall for, where her friends were talented or bohemian or both, and their minds were intellectual. Deep sleep only came before dawn and she awoke feeling drained, but the first thing she did was to get out her oil paints.

At eight she rang Jack's flat only to find she had missed him. He was not at his desk at work either. She did not leave a message.

Rose made a list of the things she needed to do: a trip to the library, some grocery shopping, a dozen rolls of fast film and some business cards to collect from the printers; mundane chores after her grand plans, but they had to be done. After that, coffee with Laura whom she felt she had been neglecting.

With her books in a carrier and her bag slung diagonally across her body, Rose set off for Penzance. Once all the items were ticked off her list she still had twenty minutes to spare so she decided to call in at the book shop in Chapel Street to order an illustrated art book she had seen reviewed in the paper. It was her favourite street. Dog-legged at the bottom and steeply sloped, it was lined with historic buildings, including the Union Hotel from where news of the death of Nelson was first announced. Further down, the pavements were high and cobbled and so narrow that two people could not walk abreast.

She ordered the book then walked up Causewayhead where they were to meet. Ahead of her were three young people, travellers, as they were now called. It was the way in which they were dressed which caught her eye, the multi-coloured layers of the girls' clothing and their beaded plaits. She had dressed in a similar manner in her own youth.

'Look.' Laura nudged her and smirked.

Rose jumped, she hadn't seen her approach. She followed Laura's gaze.

'Why do they do it?' A middle-aged man in loud Bermuda shorts was accompanied by a woman his own age in a pastel lemon towelling tracksuit through which the bulges of her flesh were visible.

'Holiday gear.' Many tourists were so predictable. Rose saw the parallel with her own life.

'Why the dark glasses?' Rose asked when they were seated in the café and had ordered their coffee. 'Afraid you'll be recognised?' Trevor was at sea so they had not had one of their rows which left Laura tear-stained.

Laura removed them. 'That's why. Both my sons arrived last

111

night and we had a bit of a pub crawl. I feel a little poorly this morning.'

'You look it. But it serves you right.'

'Don't be smug, Rose, dear. You're not exactly abstemious yourself. It wouldn't surprise me if you've got shares in a vineyard. Shall we have something to eat?'

'Not for me.'

'Are you okay? I didn't mean to be flippant.' She knew Rose must still be thinking about Dorothy.

'I'm worried, Laura, none of it seems right. Anyway, I've got other things to tell you.'

'You want to prove something to Jack.'

They had been friends for years, since they were in their early twenties, and could say almost anything to each other without causing offence.

'Maybe, but it's more than that. However, Jack's no longer part of the equation.'

'What? He's quite a dish, Rose. Why not just enjoy what you've got?' Laura replaced the sunglasses to hide her astonishment.

'I don't want to any more.'

'He's crazy about you, Rose. Are you afraid of taking a second chance? I've noticed that every time you seem to be getting closer you distance yourself from him. He'd try to make you happy, you know.'

'Yes, he'd try but it wouldn't work if I don't want it. And you're always saying you shouldn't rely on other people to provide your happiness. So, how are the boys?'

Laura began to understand that her friend had finally pulled through. It had been a long haul but she had got there. She chatted about her sons and their families, animated when she spoke of their achievements. Watching her, so full of vitality even after a heavy night out, Rose found it hard to believe that there were two generations growing up behind her. Laura's life was full and she was contented, but in a different way from the way Rose wanted.

When they left the café Rose found an outfit to wear to Barbara and Mike's party and said she would have it without looking at the price tags. It was unlike any of the clothes in her existing wardrobe.

The phone rang as soon as she got back. Jack wanted to see her immediately. Rose plugged in the percolator but she did not offer him anything to eat when he arrived just before one.

'We seem to keep missing each other. Did you have a chance to speak to Martin?'

She leaned back against the rounded edge of the worktop and folded her arms. No hello, no kiss, nothing but The Job. Under the circumstances her annoyance was ridiculous. 'Yes. I ran your errands for you, Jack.'

He squinted at her quizzically. 'Teasy today, aren't we?'

'Are we? I don't know. What I do know is that I'm sick and tired of not having a minute to myself.' She turned her back and fiddled with the coffee pot. He had not really deserved that and she disliked herself for her sharpness, it was out of character. It was going to be difficult to finish it. 'Sugar?' Unable to soften her tone she pushed the bowl towards him, then sat down herself. 'I told you on the phone that seeing Peter and Gwen was a waste of time. She didn't seem particularly upset although I'm pretty certain she is worried about something. I think Gwen's main concern is what's in the will.'

'The will?' Jack looked surprised.

'Yes. And they're not just guessing. I know for a fact that one exists.'

'All right, Rose, let's hear it all.' He leaned forward, his deep blue eyes on her face. She lowered her head because when he looked at her like that it did something strange to her stomach.

'We'd just finished talking to Bradley Hinkston when Martin told us he knew where the will was kept. Dorothy's solicitors have it, and Martin seems to think they're the executors too. He says his mother didn't keep a copy in the house but he doesn't know why.'

'Martin told you? I would've thought – never mind. But who the hell is Bradley Hinkston?'

'Well, it was like this.' She took a deep breath then carefully

113

explained from the beginning, from the time Jobber had telephoned her. Jack listened in amazement at the plan they had formed and how successful it had been.

'The Three bloody Musketeers. As I've said before, you really do slay me, Mrs Trevelyan. Go on.'

There had been admiration in his voice. 'The will first. Martin's positive about it because he went with her to Truro when she drew it up and again when she signed it, although he was made to wait outside.'

Jack wrote down the name of the solicitor in question. 'That's great, we can take it from there. Now this Hinkston bloke.'

Rose drained the last of her coffee and went to pour more. Jack held out his mug. He was familiar with all her actions and this one, the ritual refilling, was, in Rose's case, much the same thing as someone rolling up their sleeves ready to get stuck in.

'Bradley Hinkston is an antiques dealer from Bristol. He has an assistant called Roy Phelps. Someone else usually runs the shop while they go out buying and selling. Occasionally they are asked for a specific object and Bradley says that's the part he enjoys most, the search for whatever it is a customer wants. They also do valuations.'

Jack sat back, crossed his long legs at the ankles and folded his arms. He was impressed.

'Purely by chance, or so he says, they came across Martin when he turned up at the pub in which they were staying. They got chatting and Martin, a bit the worse for wear, started boasting about his mother's possessions once he knew what line of work they were in. They bought him more drinks. Now I don't know whether this was to loosen his vocal chords further or whether there was a more innocent explanation.' Rose looked thoughtful. 'He didn't strike me as a dishonest man, but that's only my opinion, for what it's worth.'

Your opinion is extremely valuable to me, Jack thought, and you're a damn good judge of character. 'So Hinkston hot tails it out to the Pengelly place to do Dorothy out of her paintings or whatever.'

'Not according to him. He says after he spoke to Martin he looked up the number and address in the phone book and contacted her first. He put his cards on the table and she invited him out there. Naturally Bradley was interested, who wouldn't be? But he wasn't sure if Martin was telling the complete truth. Dorothy gave him a warm welcome and said something along the lines about his having come at the right time. He couldn't believe his luck. He said she offered him the Stanhope Forbes and that she had a pretty good idea how much it was worth. There was, however, one proviso. He had to find her a replica. He got one that day, they're not hard to come by.'

'Come off it, Rose. You surely didn't fall for that?'

'Why not? He says he paid her by cheque. There'll be a record of it somewhere.'

'But why did she want the picture replaced?'

'That's the thing. She wanted him to come back as soon as he could and buy more stuff from her but all under the same conditions. She didn't want her family to know anything was missing. And again according to Bradley, it was to do with her will.'

'I don't understand. If she'd made one, however she divided her estate, selling her possessions wouldn't make any difference.'

Rose shrugged and brushed back her hair. 'I know. You'll have to get the will to find out.'

'We'd already asked questions at the pub,' Jack said to fill the silence which followed Rose's last statement. He vaguely resented it, it was as if she was telling him how to do his job. 'The landlord wasn't any help. He knew we wanted to speak to those men – he should have got in touch when they came back.'

'Only one of them came back and he went out to Dorothy's for a second time.' Rose paused. 'The day before yesterday.'

Jack's mouth dropped open and Rose could not help smiling. One to me, Jack Pearce, she thought, and here comes a second one. She opened her bag which was hanging over the back of her chair. 'Bradley Hinkston's business card. In case you wanted to speak to him.'

Jack stared at it, then at Rose who was unable to hide a smirk. He nodded as he placed the card in his inside jacket pocket. 'I suppose you know how grateful I am?'

'Naturally, and with justification.'

115

'Then you also know you should have told me all this before, as soon as you went to Dorothy's and Martin told you Hinkston had come back.'

'What difference would it have made?' Trust you, she thought. Maybe he'd like to charge her with something. But deep down she knew he was right.

'It would have saved us a day. Is there anything else you haven't told me?'

'No. That's it. I thought I ought to leave some of it to our wonderful boys in blue.'

'Sarcasm doesn't become you, Rose.'

'No. But you were the one who suggested I go and see Peter, you're the one who got me involved and you obviously know a lot of things which you can't tell me. One day won't make any difference, Jack, not to Dorothy anyway.' To her consternation Rose found she was crying. The tears came without warning because it had suddenly hit her that she would never see Dorothy again.

'Oh, Rose. Don't. Please.'

He got up and went around to her side of the table where she sat with her face in her hands and gently touched the back of her neck beneath her hair. He had forgotten that feelings were involved, that Rose had been Dorothy's friend. Nothing seemed important other than that she stopped crying and told him it was not all over between them. Hinkston was an honest man, Dorothy had killed herself, Dorothy had been murdered, he would believe anything if it meant not losing Rose.

Rose straightened up. 'I'm sorry. It's a long time since I've made such a fool of myself.' Her voice was cold. 'There's nothing else I can tell you so you might as well leave.'

'No.' He knelt on the flagstone floor. 'No, Rose, I won't leave until you say I can see you again.'

'And if I don't?'

He raised his palms helplessly. 'Then I don't know what I'd do,' he said very quietly.

Rose wiped away a last tear with her index finger. 'Give me a ring this evening. I need to be on my own right now.'

He stood and walked slowly to the door. It wasn't a definite no, he had to be content with that.

When he'd gone Rose cried again, her head on the table as the hot tears of release flowed down her face. She had not realised how tense she was and how hard it would be to say goodbye to Jack. Not that she had done so yet. It was also a relief to hand everything over to him. But she had forgotten to tell him about the telephone call. She had almost forgotten it herself. Bradley Hinkston? Why not? Perhaps Dorothy had mentioned her name, or Martin for that matter. More likely Martin, who may have built her up out of all proportion. But why would Bradley think that Rose would not be satisfied with a suicide verdict? And hadn't she told Jack she thought he was honest?

Nothing made sense. She promised herself a long, hot bath and an evening with a book. Apart from the party, there was nothing in her diary for tomorrow; she would find a suitable card and present for Mike.

Bradley Hinkston had stopped off in Plymouth as arranged but the house clearance sale had been a waste of time. He had left half-way through the bidding which he had watched just as a matter of interest. When he arrived home he was not surprised to learn that someone from the Avon police was coming later to ask him some questions.

Jack had arranged this and he remained at Camborne until the transcript of that interview was faxed through. Every few minutes he was tempted to pick up the phone and ring Rose but he knew it was best to leave it until he went home.

He studied the fax. It corresponded with what Rose had said almost verbatim, except she had omitted the threats Martin had made to Hinkston. Her loyalty had never been in question; she would not have wanted Dorothy's son to be under the slightest suspicion. It did, however, show that Martin was capable of threatening behaviour, although this was hardly unusual if he was protecting his mother's property.

The will surprised him. The lawyer in question had been more co-operative than some and Jack had been allowed to read the contents in the privacy of the older man's office.

Peter Pengelly was to inherit the house. 'It won't fetch a great deal,' the solicitor had told Jack. 'Its isolation will only appeal to a few, there's no central heating or double-glazing and it needs an awful lot of work done to the interior. A new kitchen and bathroom for a start.'

Even so it was a house with a saleable value and Jack would not have turned his nose up at it. What was interesting was that Dorothy Pengelly had left the remainder of her estate to Martin. This would include the house contents and her not inconsiderable savings which had now come to light. Why, then, had she been trying to sell off Martin's inheritance? Had she been worried that Peter and Gwen would get their hands on her valuables and sell them off or did she believe that Martin would not realise their worth and be duped out of them?

He studied the list again. It contained over thirty items. Alongside each was a detailed description and an approximate valuation. Jack whistled through his teeth. The amount in question made Martin Pengelly an extremely wealthy man and was motive enough for anyone to commit murder. Martin Pengelly would be as rich as a lottery winner.

Only one thing was wrong: the cheque Bradley Hinkston claimed he had given Dorothy for the Stanhope Forbes had not been paid into either of her accounts.

The bank had a record of a telephone call from Dorothy but the cheque had not, as Hinkston believed, been subjected to special clearance. Dorothy had only gone as far as to verify that there were enough funds to meet it. Therefore, he concluded, she at least had had it in her possession at some time. Had Hinkston somehow retrieved it? Surely he wouldn't have bothered writing it out if he had intended harming her.

And what of Martin? Had he killed his mother for the money because he couldn't wait for her to die? Did money actually mean anything to him? He drank too much but otherwise his needs were basic.

Jack shook his head in frustration. The timing didn't fit. Hinkston had visited Dorothy on the Thursday morning. Dorothy had had enough time to contact the bank and although an exact time of death was impossible to pin-point she certainly had not died that early in the day. There was no reason for Hinkston to have waited, to have gone back later – he could have done whatever he intended whilst he was there. Unless, Jack thought, Dorothy had said she was expecting someone. Maybe Hinkston thought she would not have had a chance to pay the cheque in, which now seemed likely. With the man's consent they were now checking Hinkston's account to see if the relevant sum had been debited or transferred elsewhere.

He was too tired to think straight and Rose kept intruding upon his deliberations. He had not seen her cry before and, if he had his way, he would never let her do so again. But with Rose Trevelyan it was not a case of having his own way. He picked up the telephone and dialled her number. There was no reply but he had already steeled himself to that probability.

9

Rose woke at a quarter past four. The previous evening she had unplugged the telephone and enjoyed a long soak in the bath followed by a decent meal. At nine o'clock she had collapsed into bed and fallen asleep immediately, her unopened library book sliding off the bed unnoticed. Consequently she was awake early.

She opened her eyes and listened for sounds. There were none, not even the soughing of the wind in the chimney breast. Not a noise, but a dream, she thought, realising what had woken her. But it was rapidly dissolving, slipping away from her as easily as the sun burned off an early morning mist. She tried not to think about it, hoping it would come back, but whatever pleasant memories it had evoked had now disappeared.

She padded downstairs, barefoot, and made a pot of tea. To her side were some notes she scribbled down; her own thoughts which could in no way be construed as evidence or facts. She studied them until the yellow light of dawn appeared on the horizon then decided to complete the work she had begun yesterday. She was rapidly approaching her goal but the jobs still on hand would be done to the best of her ability. Her own dissatisfaction, she thought, was nothing compared with that of Gwen Pengelly. Hooking her hair behind her ears she wondered what had made her think that. The downward turn of the mouth, maybe, the nervous energy? Or was it guilt? Still in her towelling robe she mounted some photographs under the enlarger. It was only six thirty. Ahead of her was a whole new day and she was going to take a walk along the beach. Rose, like almost everyone in Newlyn, knew the movements of the tide as well as most people know the days of the week.

As daylight rose into the eastern sky she stepped down on to the pebbles below Newlyn Green. All the rocks beyond the shore were exposed, dark and jagged against the limpid sea. There was no one in sight, which surprised her for she was not alone in taking early morning strolls. She wanted to speak to Doreen Clarke who would not have thanked her for a call before 7 a.m., even if she was an early riser.

Her shoes scrunched into the the shifting mounds of stones until she reached the hard, wet sand left uncovered by the tide. She stood quietly, watching the waders as they fed along the shoreline and in the crevices of rocks. Most of them had returned now for the winter. A crow, unintimidated, scavenged alongside herring-gulls, dunlins sank their beaks into the yielding wetness and a flock of sanderlings scurried along the edge of the lapping water like miniature road-runners. A man approached and let his dog off the lead. In unison the birds took off and circled until they felt safe to land again. The air was full of their wings and their calls. The labrador stopped to sniff at something then ran on further, barking gruffly at a row of gulls further along the tide-line. They squawked indignantly, rose as one then settled down again as soon as the dog had passed.

Rose walked the full length of the beach until the walls of the Jubilee Pool were towering above her. It was closed for the winter but she was fond of the 1930s art deco construction and had been pleased when it had been restored for use.

The tide crept slowly in. There was no way now around the pool whose foundations were built out on to Battery Rocks. She mounted the slope which led up to the Promenade, stamped the sand from her shoes and retraced her steps on firmer ground.

Doreen Clarke usually left the house at eight thirty; if she walked quickly Rose would just have time to catch her before she set off for work. She could not understand how anyone could choose to earn a living cleaning other people's houses, especially on a Saturday morning. Facing her own housework was bad enough for Rose.

'Anything the matter, dear?' Doreen inquired, surprised to hear the hesitancy in Rose's voice.

'No, not really. But there's something I wanted to ask you. Fancy coming over for coffee later?'

'Suits me. You know I always love a bit of a chat with you. Besides, I can't get any sense from Cyril at the moment, he spends half his time guarding those blasted vegetables of his. Don't ask me why, he hardly ever wins a prize.'

Rose was smiling when she replaced the receiver. Doreen was a good soul and down to earth but it was easy to see why her husband spent a lot of his time in the garden or greenhouse. He had suffered the same fate as many others when Geever mine closed but he had taken up gardening and Rose often benefited from his gifts of produce.

Armed with her painting things she set off on foot again. Going down through the village, she stopped for a moment to watch the auctioneers in the market as they gabbled the prices for boxes of fish. After choosing a birthday card in the paper shop she carried on up the Coombe, worrying about whether her choice of gift for Mike was acceptable. The river, to her right, flowed steadily, bubbling over the stones and under the bridge and spreading around the stems of the giant rhubarb which flourished there. To her left the fish shops were preparing for the day ahead.

When the pavement ended she took the path between two rows of trees and tried to remember exactly where Barry had told her she could find Saw-wort. It was, apparently, common in the south-west but scattered elsewhere, preferring damp, grassy

121

places with woods nearby. Having taken the precaution of checking in one of her reference books she knew what she was looking for. It was a thistle-like plant but without spines and flowered until October. I'll say one thing about this, she thought, my knowledge of natural history's increasing.

As always when she painted, time passed quickly. Only the altered angle of the sun told her how long she had been working.

Regretting she had not brought the car Rose began the walk home. Some fishermen she knew were heading for the pub. 'Absolutely not,' she told them, smiling, but with a firm shake of the head when they tried to persuade her to join them. There would be enough to drink later.

Taking her canvas bag up to the attic Rose paused on the way back down to look at her new outfit which was on a hanger hooked over the top of the bedroom door. Yes, she thought, it's definitely me.

Turning away she pulled open the bottom drawer of the wooden chest set against the wall opposite the window. With shaking hands she lifted out a flat, rectangular object wrapped in clean sacking. It was the oil painting she had started when David first became ill and which she had completed in the dark months after his death. It had not been out of the drawer since.

'My God.' She almost dropped it. Finishing it was a vague memory yet now she saw it she clearly recalled almost attacking the canvas with her brushes. The strokes were strong, the colours vivid.

She propped it on the chest and stood back. As if her circulation had been sluggish Rose suddenly felt the blood pulsing through her veins. 'Bloody hell, Rose Trevelyan, it's good.' And it was. It was exciting and real: the picture lived. Had that been the missing ingredient of her youthful attempts? Were pain and experience necessary to produce decent work? No, she rationalised, not always, but they are with me.

The idea had been to give it to Mike but now she hesitated. Only when she conceded that if the past was to be completely behind her she needed to make this final gesture did she go down to the kitchen and wrap it in tissue and sheets of shiny gold paper.

122

Doreen arrived at twelve, straight from her Saturday job and before going into Penzance to shop. 'Like I said, you can't have a proper chat with Cyril under your feet,' she complained although Cyril was rarely in the house.

She sat down heavily and placed her bag neatly on the floor beside her, surreptitiously studying Rose's face. 'You look different, somehow, if you don't mind me saying.'

'Do I?' It was typical of Doreen that she had noticed. Rose felt different; alive and full of an enthusiasm that even Dorothy's death could not dispel. Or maybe her death was partly responsible for it, having made Rose aware that life should not be wasted. 'Well, I'm going to a party tonight.' Explanation enough for Doreen who would not understand the complexities of Rose's mental metamorphosis, or her decision concerning Jack.

'Ooh, lovely. Where?'

'Blast.' The telephone was ringing, Rose regretted plugging it back in.

'Keep away from Dorothy's place. Understand?' The voice was gruff, unrecognisable. The line went dead before Rose could say she would not be intimidated by someone too cowardly to give his name. 'I will not give in,' she said. 'I will not.' She returned to the kitchen determined not to let Doreen see that anything was wrong. Had she been watched that day when she couldn't find Martin? Perhaps it was not imagination after all.

'How's Martin? Have you seen him recently?' Doreen asked as she spooned two sugars into her coffee and stirred it vigorously.

'I think he's beginning to come to terms with it.' Rose hesitated. 'Doreen, what you were saying the other day, about Gwen and Peter, is there anything else you can tell me?' Rose wished she had listened more carefully at the time.

'Maybe. Hey, you're not trying to do your young man's work for him, are you?' There was a glimmer of amusement in her eyes and her round, red face lit up expectantly, but Rose did not answer.

'Well, if you want my advice, and I don't suppose you do, he's a decent enough bloke and if he's any sort of a detective he ought to realise what a good catch you are.'

Rose appreciated the flattery but realised that it was useless discussing Jack with Doreen, who was of the opinion that a woman should be grateful for any man she could get hold of then make it her duty to keep him.

'What were we saying, dear? Oh, Gwen. Well, let me think.' She leaned forward, elbows on the table, and lowered her voice conspiratorially. Rose knew more coffee would be required.

Jobber Hicks had taken it upon himself to become Martin's mentor. Dorothy was gone and the boy needed someone and, of all the people in the world, the two of them would never forget her. When he used to visit Dorothy, Martin was often absent or, if he did appear, soon took himself back up over the hill. Of course, in later years he had taken to living in the van and Jobber had seen even less of him. Star had settled down quite quickly but she, like Jobber, was getting on a bit. He felt there ought to be more he could do for the son of the woman he had loved. Yes, he thought, I did love her. It was the first time he had verbalised his feelings. Before, he had described her to himself as a fine woman, a strong one, and the only one he had wanted to marry. Perhaps if he had expressed his feelings rather than merely pointing out the benefits of their getting married things might have turned out differently. It was time to make amends.

The more he thought about it the more certain he became that his idea was a good one. The outcome would depend on Martin but he intended asking him if he would like to bring the van down to the farm. Jobber could find work for him, something manual, something which would not confuse or intimidate him. George could move into the farmhouse if Martin didn't want him in the van and they could, if Martin was willing, share some of their evening meals together. It would be company for them both. He did not want to admit that he wanted someone he could talk to about Dorothy.

Jobber had made up his mind but he was afraid to ask in case the answer was no.

*

Mike and Barbara Phillips lived in a rambling house out near Drift Reservoir. The façade was shielded from the narrow road by a hedge of evergreen shrubs but few cars or people ever passed the place.

Rose got out of the taxi and walked towards the front door, which was open. Light flooded from the house, spilling on to the uneven path and turning the leaves of the hydrangea beneath the windows a purplish blue. Its flowers had turned from pink to green and many were already dry and browning. The sound of music and conversation and clinking glasses made her realise how much she had been missing. She was just about to ring the bell when Barbara appeared in the doorway, chic in a straight silvery dress which would have made most people look shapeless. Her blonde hair was wound into a complicated chignon.

'Rose! Wonderful to see you. Have you come alone?' Barbara peered down the path before kissing her. 'Good. I'm glad.' She stepped back. 'My, my, you look great. What have you done to yourself?'

'Oh, it's the new clothes.' Rose smiled. There was a light in her eyes which had not been there for some time. She felt good in the muslin skirt with its black satin lining which caressed her bare legs as she walked. Tucked into it was an emerald silk blouson. Her auburn hair lay in soft waves around her shoulders and there were gold hoops in her ears, gold sandals on her feet. Under her arm was her gift.

She followed Barbara into the lounge which was softly lit. More than twenty people had arrived before her. Rose recognised several faces and, during the short journey across the room, was introduced to several more. 'Ah, here's the birthday boy.' Barbara laid a possessive hand on Mike's arm. Of medium build and with short brown hair and glasses, he was not good-looking but there was an air of gentleness about him and a kind curve to his mouth. He, too, kissed Rose and said how pleased he was to see her.

'About Dorothy – I'm really sorry.'

'It's all right.' Rose did not want to spoil the mood of the evening. 'Here, this is for you.' She handed him the parcel. 'Happy birthday.'

Mike turned to find a space in which to unwrap it. Placing it on a small side table he carefully removed the shiny paper and pulled away the tissue then he stood back. 'Oh, Rose,' he whispered. 'Oh, Rose, I never knew. Look, Barbara.'

Barbara came to his side and frowned before straightening up. 'Did you do this?' Rose nodded. 'Stella, come over here a minute,' Barbara called, waving an impatient hand to a black-haired woman in the corner. 'And you, Daniel.'

The couple approached them but no introductions were made until the painting had been examined.

Within three or four minutes Rose knew that her life had changed. Stella Jackson, whose own work was highly rated and who was rarely without an exhibition somewhere, expressed her genuine admiration, as did Daniel Wright, who was her husband and a sculptor. Daniel whistled through his teeth. 'It's terrific, Rose. Have you always painted?'

'Yes, but not like that.'

No one commented because they suspected what had happened – that Rose, like many artists, had become side-tracked along the way.

Stella was rounding up others to view the work. 'Are there any more?' she finally asked when Mike went to find a safe place for it.

'Not yet.'

Stella nodded. 'When there are, come and see me.' She wrote down her telephone number, then grinned. 'Come and see me anyway. We're in St Ives.'

'I know.' It was Rose's turn to smile at the woman's modesty.

'We'll have coffee, or something stronger. Now, let me introduce you to Nick Pascoe.'

The evening passed so quickly that Rose couldn't understand why people were beginning to leave. Glancing at her watch she saw it was after one thirty and rang for a taxi. Despite the wine she felt sober and clear-headed although she over-tipped the driver in her euphoria. It was hard to recall that it had been Mike's celebration rather than her own, but that was what it had felt like.

She ignored the messages on the answering machine and got

126

into bed, not really wanting to take off her new clothes and spoil the magic of the evening.

Fred Meecham survived the weekend although he could not recall what he had done during the few hours that the shop had been closed. The world had become an alien place, or else he was an alien in it.

Monday arrived, bringing rain which swept depressingly across the harbour. It gurgled along the guttering and ran down the drainpipes noisily; appropriate weather for a funeral. In retrospect he could not recall attending one where it hadn't been raining, with the congregation huddled beneath dark umbrellas and the church smelling of damp wool. Or perhaps it just seemed that way.

He could not face the drive. It would have seemed disrespectful to turn up in the delivery van but he didn't accept any of the many offers of a lift. For the first time in years Fred organised himself a taxi.

He was numb, physically and mentally, but beneath that numbness lay fear and guilt. How wrong he had been to assume that the two deaths would close a chapter of his life. Other agencies were at work, dangerous ones. Rose Trevelyan for one, and Gwen Pengelly for another. Gwen with her avarice and her dislike of her mother-in-law, Gwen with her ambition and her pushy ways who would stop at nothing to lay her hands on Dorothy's money. And he had heard rumours about Martin, that the police wanted to question him again because he had easy access to the house and all that was within it. Why couldn't people believe that Dorothy had just decided to end her life? Dorothy had acted strangely on his last visit. Furtively was the word which came to mind. Someone had been there ahead of him, that much he guessed by the two cups and saucers on the draining-board. Dorothy only ever offered him a mug. Things were going on which Fred didn't understand and had no chance of understanding until Marigold was laid to rest and the sedative the doctor had given him had worn off.

The taxi driver was local and therefore made no attempt at

conversation. What could he say to a man who was about to bury his sister, one to whom he had been exceptionally devoted? His passenger sat in the back which also precluded the opportunity to hold a proper conversation. He accepted the fare and the tip with a nod and a thank you and asked if Fred wanted collecting.

'No. I . . .' Fred shrugged. It didn't seem to matter what happened afterwards. He walked up the path towards the church. Organ music floated through the open doorway. He was almost overcome by the number of people standing around outside, nearly all of whom were his customers. Tears pricked behind his eyes. The cards of condolence had been one thing, this was overwhelming.

He nodded to acquaintances who stood back to let him pass as he entered the church. He sat in the front pew to which he was directed, his hands between his knees, quietly waiting. Most of the mourners remained outside, some of them enjoying a last-minute cigarette as if they thought it might be their last. Fred understood what such occasions did to people and he did not blame them. He dreaded the finality of the ceremony ahead but at the same time wished it to be over. As far as he could tell none of Marigold's relatives were present. There was no reason for them to be, it would have been strange if they had known. Out of the corner of his eye he saw Gwen Pengelly. He did not like her and he almost asked her to leave but a scene would be unthinkable.

As one the congregation turned when the organ music changed and they were asked to stand. At the back of the church was Rose Trevelyan.

Jack had telephoned on Sunday morning but Rose's cool tone discouraged him from making the conversation more personal. The Pengellys, Bradley Hinkston and anyone else, she said, were now his concern. Mentioning the party and the new acquaintances she had made, Rose hoped that she had thrown out enough hints for him to realise that the affair was coming to an end. All that remained was for her to see him face to face and tell him so but she despised herself for postponing it.

Her clean sweep as far as work was concerned was almost complete. Rose decided to emulate Doreen and clean the house before starting on the garden and the shed. Many of the summer flowers needed tidying and the grass required cutting. The final task, getting rid of the junk that had accumulated over the years, would be a painful pleasure. She knew there were still some of David's things in the shed but there was also a lot of rubbish. Once it was empty Rose would paint there. There were windows in the front and side, filthy now, but they could soon be washed, and they overlooked the bay. If she could succeed a second time, as she had with the one simply entitled 'Storm' which she had given to Mike, she would venture further for scenery.

Tired and grimy with soil and dust and cobwebs, Rose longed for a shower and a large gin and tonic. She had just undressed when the telephone rang. If it was Jack she would tell him there and then. The female voice was unfamiliar but Gwen Pengelly had kept to her word. She had rung to give the details of Dorothy's funeral. 'It's on Wednesday. Two fifteen at Truro Crematorium.' Rose did not ask the outcome of the inquest when Gwen said that the body had been released for burial.

'Thank you for letting me know.' She replaced the receiver and stood looking at it for several seconds. For Dorothy's sake she hoped there would be more than the direct family and one or two friends in attendance. Two funerals in one week, she thought sadly. Tomorrow Marigold was to be buried. Because Dorothy would have gone had she been alive, Rose decided to go in her stead. It was the least she could do.

In the shower Rose washed her hair and soaped herself twice but dirt was ingrained in the skin around her nails. Wrapped in her robe, her hair still wet, she sat in the window with a drink thinking of landscapes she wanted to paint. It was a peaceful evening and Rose enjoyed her own company. When she saw the black clouds building up in the night sky it seemed one might be directly above her. Remembering the telephone calls had shattered her tranquillity.

129

Because of the downpour dawn was a long time coming. Newlyn was a blur through the wetness. The forecast promised more of the same. There were no appointments for that day and there would be fewer and fewer if her new venture succeeded.

There was nothing black in Rose's wardrobe. After David's funeral she had vowed not to wear the colour again. She chose a brown suit and matching shoes, which hardly seemd to matter as whatever she wore would be covered by a raincoat.

Seated at the back of the church she concentrated on the other mourners. Gwen Pengelly was there, which was surprising.

When the service was over and Marigold's body had been committed to the ground she stood alone, half hidden by a tree, watching the vicar move from group to group and exchange a few words with each. Fred Meecham, she concluded, was going through the motions. Numbness allowed him to accept handshakes and whatever words of comfort he was being offered. The disbelief and misery in his eyes moved her. Rose trod carefully across the slippery grass and touched him lightly on the arm. 'Mr Meecham, I'm Rose Trevelyan. I met you a couple of times at Dorothy's house.'

She waited, puzzled at his odd expression, as if recognition was slow in coming yet she knew he had seen her earlier. 'Oh, yes. Yes, I remember. Thank you for coming.' Fred did not question her reasons for doing so. Rose put his peculiar manner down to despair.

'I'm so sorry. You'll miss her dreadfully.'

Fred nodded slowly. 'You don't know how much. I loved her,' he added forcefully, glaring at Rose. 'I loved her from the moment I first saw her.' He bit his lip. 'I – oh, please excuse me, everyone seems to be leaving. Are you coming back to the hotel?'

'Thank you, but no.' Rose would be an intruder amongst the people who had known Marigold better.

Fred nodded again, looking relieved that she had refused. Just in time she stopped herself from mentioning Dorothy's funeral. Under other circumstances Fred would have wanted to be there but she doubted he would be able to face it this week. She patted his arm once more as she turned to walk away then wished she hadn't when he flinched.

For several minutes Rose sat behind the wheel of the car and waited as people drove off. The rain had started again, becoming heavier until it was beating a tattoo on the roof. Fred's words came back to her again and by the time she had realised their possible implication the windows had misted over. 'I loved her from the moment I first saw her,' he had said. Of course, Marigold was a good deal younger than Fred: it could be that he, as an older brother, had loved her from the minute she was born. But Rose did not think so, and she was also beginning to believe that Doreen's idle gossip may have contained a grain of truth.

Many siblings, after death or divorce, lived with one another. Fred's wife had deserted him long ago and, according to Doreen, the same thing had happened to Marigold. 'But I wonder?' Rose muttered as she turned the ignition key and thankfully heard the engine splutter into life. Instead of going home she turned left when she reached the main road and pointed the Mini in the direction of Truro.

'You've got to tell him, Rose.'

'Why should I? It's only guesswork.'

'Come off it, you wouldn't have told me if you really believed that.' Laura pushed back her dark curls which were hanging loose about her shoulders. They were sitting in Laura's living-room in front of the log effect gas fire. Rose had gone there upon returning from Truro. Outside it was almost dark although it was not much after six o'clock. Staccato bursts of squally rain hit the windows.

Laura had known that Rose was going to Marigold's funeral as well as to Dorothy's and she had been worried that too many reminders might be harmful so she had insisted that Rose came over for a meal and some wine afterwards. They were sipping a good claret and the effects of that and the warmth from the fire were relaxing. But Rose was not in the least depressed, if anything she was animated.

'I could have been mistaken. Doreen could have been mistaken.'

'You'll come to a bad end, as my mother was fond of telling me. Oh, wait a minute, I get it. It's not that you don't think it's important, it's because you don't want Jack to know what you're up to. Am I right?'

Rose's face was hot. Laura was a little too perceptive. 'Jack doesn't come into things any more.'

'But you haven't told him yet.'

'No.'

There was silence as Laura digested this information. 'All right, let's leave Jack out of it. What makes you think it's anything to do with Dorothy Pengelly?'

Rose sighed. 'I'm not saying it is, it's just that I feel there's some connection. Something which ought to be obvious but I'm buggered if I can see it.' She wanted to change the subject and wished she had not brought it up in the first place. But Laura was her friend, the one person in whom she could confide completely. All she had been able to discover were negatives but to Rose's mind that proved something because there were far too many of them to be pure coincidence.

'I'll see to the food, it should be almost ready,' Laura said, glancing at Rose and seeing that she was in a world of her own.

Rose was thinking about Fred Meecham. He had been born in Truro. Dorothy had told her that and Doreen Clarke had been able to supply the details of which street he had lived in. Fred was a churchman and never missed a Sunday service, logical then to make inquiries at the church nearest to Fred's old address. It had taken no more than twenty minutes to go through the parish register and find Fred's christening recorded. Both his parents had been buried in the churchyard. Marigold was younger than Fred so she used his dates as a starting point, working forwards from there. Marigold's name did not appear. Rose went back over the entries and checked the name Heath. Marigold had not been married there either. The incumbent vicar was unable to supply any information because he was new to the district.

Three times Rose checked the register but there was no entry for Marigold Meecham or Marigold Heath. She had thanked the vicar and complimented him on his place of worship then returned to Newlyn and Laura's house.

Either Marigold had not been christened or Fred was being economical with the truth when he said that she had spent the whole of her life in Truro until she had moved in with him. But so what? And is it any of my business anyway? she asked herself. Then why had Doreen said, 'If they're related, then I'm the Queen of England.' The expression had made Rose smile. Someone less queenlike than Doreen was hard to imagine. 'You've only got to look at them, no way're they brother and sister. Now listen to this,' she had continued, 'and don't forget, I never repeat nothing 'less I'm pretty sure of my facts.' This had given Rose cause to hide another smile.

'Come on, Rose, let's eat.'

Laura's comment pierced her concentration. Rose got up and followed her to the kitchen where steaming bowls of fish stew and crusty bread awaited them.

Rose picked up a spoon and studied her face in the back of it. 'Everything's changing, Laura.' And as they ate Rose began to tell her what she intended doing with her life.

'And about time. Your watercolours are good, but you're capable of a damn sight better.'

Rose stared at her. This was the reaction from all her friends. Why had it taken her so long to discover it for herself? She grinned. 'This fish is delicious. But, Laura, dear, the service is a little slapdash this evening. My glass is empty.'

'Fill it up yourself, Mrs Trevelyan. You're not usually so coy.'

Once the dishes were stacked in the sink Laura fetched a second bottle of wine. 'I wouldn't want to risk being called inhospitable,' she said, waving it in the air.

Feeling that she had bored Laura with talk of Dorothy, Rose changed the subject. But just as she was leaving she couldn't help saying, 'Laura, I've been getting some odd phone calls.'

'Oh?' Laura's eyes narrowed. 'You mean threatening ones, don't you? And you haven't told Jack.' Rose shook her head. 'You must. Apart from any danger, don't you see that it proves there's something to hide?'

'Jack knows that. He's come round to my way of thinking.'

'You've always been the same, too bloody stubborn for your own good. Tell him, Rose, for goodness sake.'

Ignoring the advice she continued, 'If you wanted to find someone, someone who had disappeared, how would you go about it?'

'Ask someone who knows them.'

'I can't do that. Besides, I don't want anyone to know what I'm doing.'

'Is this some sort of parlour game? No, don't tell me. And you can't ask Jack, of course. I don't know what's got into you, Rose. Perhaps Dorothy Pengelly is really a royal Russian exile and that Fred's sister, Marigold, was Mata Hari. Oh, God, I'm sorry, Rose, I know how much you cared for Dorothy. Forgive me, put it down to the vino. But please, please be careful.'

'It's okay.' Rose kissed her on the cheek. In a way the comment was no more than she deserved. She was inclined to get carried away. 'Ah, I must go.' They had both heard the toot of the taxi as it pulled up outside.

Rose's journey home was no more than half a mile but she did not want a soaking before she went to bed. She would not allow herself to admit how much the telephone calls had scared her. Thanking Laura for the meal she left.

10

Martin Pengelly told Jobber Hicks he would think about his offer. He could not bear the idea of leaving the only place that had ever been his home until after his mother was buried. He was not unrealistic enough to imagine the house would always be there for him, nor did he want to live in it alone. Having overheard enough of Peter and Gwen's conversations he knew that if it was up to them they would get rid of it at the first opportunity. At least his mother had been able to live her life out there. He still went to see to the cats and to feed George but he had not contemplated what would happen or how he would feel when someone else finally moved in. Peter would have to see to the paperwork and the will, Martin knew it was beyond his capabilities. The legal world was as much a mystery to him as technology would be to Star.

He did not know that Peter had been looking for him or that the police wanted to speak to him again. Most of his waking hours he spent tramping over the countryside that he had come to think of as his own. Jobber had found him, but Jobber always knew where to look. Only when it rained would he return to the van, soaked to the skin, and towel dry his longish hair. His body grew even firmer with the extra exercise but he was trying to walk off feelings he was ill equipped to deal with. He had not suffered pain like this before because Dorothy had always protected him. And now Jobber's idea was making him reel. It seemed too good to be true. He would have someone to talk to and he would see George and Star every day. What frightened him was that he was not used to being treated as normal. He could not understand why Jobber should want him around.

Martin no longer cried but the awful ache somewhere inside him wouldn't go away. He had no idea that Peter was also suffering, because his brother had never shown any interest in their mother. Gwen, he knew, disliked her intensely. At school Peter had run ahead or lagged behind when she came to meet them yet seeing her at the school gates had been the highlight of Martin's day. He had been very upset when Dorothy said they were old enough to catch the bus by themselves.

The tightness around his chest sometimes threatened to suffocate him, making him want to lash out. He knew the dangers of that so kept himself away from people. He had come very close to hitting Mr Hinkston the day he had found him snooping around but was glad now that he hadn't. When they met him in the pub he found he quite liked him. And Mrs Trevelyan thought he was all right, so he must be.

He trudged across the open land and the fields, mile after mile, until George was so tired he had to carry him. Suddenly he stiffened. In the distance, way down below him, he saw Gwen's car in his mother's driveway. Starting to run, he felt the panic subside. It was all right, she didn't have a key. He crouched beside a boulder and watched and waited. Gwen came away from the front door and walked around the side. Had he locked the kitchen door? Yes, he must have done. A few minutes later Gwen got back into the car. He heard the reverberation of the slamming door before she drove away. Martin did not know what to do but the one person who might be able to help him was Mrs Trevelyan. Although she was a lot younger and prettier than his mother she reminded him of her, and her house, although smaller, had the same feel about it. When she'd taken him there it seemed right sitting in her kitchen, not saying much, but letting go of some of the grief which the welcoming atmosphere seemed to absorb.

Bypassing the caravan he took George back to the house and opened some food for him. George ate half-heartedly then scrabbled at the armchair where Dorothy had once sat, managing to make it into the sagging seat on his third attempt. He fell asleep immediately. Martin watched him then gave him a gentle pat. He checked there was water in his bowl then went to the telephone and found the book with Rose's number in it. He dialled the digits slowly and carefully as his mother had taught him because he became confused if he got a wrong number. With relief he heard Rose's voice and not a recording of it.

As he listened to her calmly saying it was fine for him to come and see her any time he wanted, some of the tightness in his chest slackened. Tired from his long walk Martin knew he would have to catch the bus. One passed hourly along the main road on its way back from Truro. It would take him to Penzance bus station. From there he would walk the rest of the way. He had a handful of change ready and waited at the bottom of the drive. Despite the circumstances of his one and only visit to it Martin recalled exactly how to find the house in Newlyn.

Rose lay in bed for several minutes. Would she be able to paint before the mystery of Dorothy's death had been solved? She bit her lip and brushed the hair out of her eyes. Instinct told her to continue, that she was close to something even if she had no idea what.

Dorothy had left a will, which Martin knew about and, unbelievably, so did Bradley Hinkson. Bradley met Martin by chance, learnt of the Stanhope Forbes and then it disappeared. No, to be fair, Rose recalled, Bradley said he still had it and admitted leaving a print in its place as per Dorothy's instructions.

Marigold Heath was dead, although there was nothing suspicious in those circumstances, only sadness. She had been ill for a long time and everyone had known the only possible outcome, everyone except Fred who would not admit it; Fred who admitted that he loved her. But Fred had also known Dorothy, had spoken to her about the possibility of getting hold of a substantial sum of money for treatment for Marigold. Rose dared not continue with that line of thought, and she did not have a single fact to substantiate any of it. To mention her suspicions to anyone would be foolhardy and irresponsible and possibly cause irreparable damage to an innocent person. She had formed an hypothesis which was probably wildly off the mark. But to continue would be satisfying – except that she needed a copy of a birth certificate and without a name, date and place of birth, and other details such as the father's occupation, she would not be able to procure it. Only one thing was out of place. Why, in this day and age, would anyone care? That was the question which had revolved in her subconscious all night.

Now it seemed she might have the answer. Fred Meecham was a church-going man, he lived the life of a good citizen nothing was too much trouble if he could help someone out. Too good to be true? Rose wondered. Or did he have something to hide? Yet it still seemed impossible to imagine that Fred had killed Dorothy because she would not give him the necessary funds to send Marigold to America. Rose was very much afraid she was fitting the circumstances around the facts rather than the other way around.

Dorothy had hinted that there was more to Fred than met the eye. And there was something else, some hint, some small clue, something which might mean nothing. 'I tried to talk him out of it, I said he should spend time with Marigold, not waste it seeking the impossible.' Dorothy had told Rose how she tried to convince him of the wildness of his scheme. Had Fred then helped himself to Dorothy's painting and, noticing the switch, had she called him to task and had he then killed her? Too far-fetched, Rose, she told herself, and how would he know it was there? As far as Rose was aware few people had known. But what about that envelope? Had she misread what she took to be Dorothy's way of telling her something? Stop it, she told herself. This isn't getting you anywhere.

An aunt, Dorothy's last surviving relative apart from her sons, had left her the money. The proceeds had come from the husband's business, coffee, she thought it was, somewhere in Africa when times had been good. That was no longer important. Laura was wrong, Rose thought, I don't believe Marigold Heath was Mata Hari but I don't believe she was Fred's sister either. She was trying to rationalise something that was no more than a gut feeling and she hoped it was not simply a way of avoiding facing Dorothy's death in the way she had done with David's. Tell Jack, her conscience kept saying. Sod him, her emotions retaliated. Her better nature dictated that matters should be left alone but curiosity and stubbornness were not so easily conquered.

Rose had half a dozen photographic assignments left to fulfil and she would not let her customers down. Soon she would be mixing with artists again; she was impatient, but she did not want to give up one area of her life leaving a bad taste behind. One of the messages which had been waiting on her machine was an invitation to dinner at Stella and Daniel's place in St Ives on Sunday. There would be eight of them.

Rose wondered who had been invited to partner her.

Piling her equipment into the car she suddenly knew what her next move would be. She returned home just in time to take Martin's call.

A knock at the front door an hour and a-half later puzzled Rose because she wasn't expecting anyone and most people came around to the side. 'Martin!' she exclaimed when she saw him standing on the doorstep, his face sorrowful. She was astonished that he had taken her up on her offer so quickly. 'Come on in.'

He followed her, pleased that they were going to the kitchen and not to some other room. There was a pile of clothes in a basket on the table waiting to be ironed and a strong smell of coffee. Martin only drank tea but he thought he wouldn't mind trying whatever it was Mrs Trevelyan had in the machine that spluttered and hissed.

Rose followed his eyes, smiled, and got out two mugs. She offered him milk and sugar, moved the clothes basket to the floor and sat down with him. Martin was not the sort to pay a social visit but he seemed reluctant to break the silence. 'Is something the matter, Martin?'

Martin pushed back his thick hair and nodded. 'I don't feel right. I hurt and nothing looks the same any more. Am I sick?'

Rose's own emotions were in turmoil as he described what he was feeling. 'No, you're not sick. It's what happens to people when they lose someone they love. It'll pass, Martin, I promise you it will. But it takes time, sometimes a very long time. Have you told Peter any of this?'

'No. I ain't seen 'im. Nor 'er, not till today. She was snooping up at the house. And now I don't know what to do.'

'About what?' Gwen, up at the house? She would think about that later. She listened as he explained about Jobber's proposal and once more she felt a great warmth towards the man who was prepared to step in and take over where Dorothy had left off. At the same time she was disgusted with Peter for ignoring his brother. 'I don't want to be there when there's new people.'

'Is the house being sold?'

'It'll have to be.'

'Is Peter seeing to all that?'

'I dunno. But I don't know if 'e knows about Mother's papers. I don't think she told 'un where they was. She told me, though.' He folded his arms across his broad chest as if to underline the importance of what he was saying.

Rose frowned. She had told Jack where the will was, surely someone should have contacted Peter and Martin by now. But perhaps someone had and that was why Peter was keeping out of his brother's way. If only she knew what was in it.

'I wasn't to tell, see, about the papers.'

Rose understood. The will had been a secret between Martin and Dorothy but he realised it was time his brother knew although he was not prepared to tell him himself. 'It's all right, the police know all about it. I had to tell them, Martin.'

He surprised her by smiling. 'I knew you'd do the right thing. I never thought of that.'

'Would you like some more coffee?'

'Yes, please. 'Tis lovely.'

As she poured it Rose recalled the tension between Peter and Gwen and wondered again what might have been the cause of it. 'Would you like me to speak to your brother?' She had uttered the words before she had a chance to think of the wisdom of them. Whatever the response, it was Martin she was thinking of. He nodded enthusiastically.

The telephone conversation was brief and to the point. Rose was sure that Peter knew of the existence of a will by now but it would put Martin's mind at rest.

'Dorothy's solicitor has been in touch,' Gwen Pengelly said coldly. 'Not that I think it's any concern of yours.'

'It isn't,' Rose replied mildly, 'but Martin wasn't sure if you knew.'

'Martin! Oh, I suppose he was told first.'

Rose mumbled something and said goodbye. Gwen could think what she liked, at least some unpleasantness had been avoided. What infuriated her was that no mention had been made of Martin, no inquiry as to how he was or even where he was. Rose walked stiffly back to the kitchen trying not to let her anger show. She explained to Martin what would happen now but that these things took time. There was nothing he need do, the solicitor would see to it all. 'You might have to go and sign some papers but if you like, I'll come with you.' Satisfied that he understood and saw there was nothing to fear she gently broached the subject of his mother's funeral and offered him a lift to the crematorium. That was something else which seemed not to have crossed Gwen's mind, how he would get there or even if he knew when the ceremony was taking place. It had been Jobber who told him, who had gone to the trouble of ringing up to find out when the service was to take place. 'Look, why don't we do as we did before? You go to the farm and I'll pick you and Jobber up at the same time. I'll ring him to let him know.'

'Like the other night?' He seemed to take comfort in the fact that the three of them would be together.

'Yes, something like that. Now, shall I run you home?' But Martin would only take a lift as far as the bus station. He showed her his return ticket so Rose let it go at that. 'Hang on, I'd better make that call first.' She did not want Martin turning up at Jobber's only to find he'd got a lift with someone else or taken his old pick-up truck. 'That was lucky, he'd just popped in before seeing to the hens.'

'Don't you keep no pets?' Martin looked around the kitchen for evidence of one.

'No. Not since I was a child.'

Martin thought about this. 'You ought to. Where's your husband then?'

For a split second the pain came back. 'He died, Martin.'

'Like Mother.' There was another pause. 'So we're the same, you and me. You ought to get yourself a pet though. I'll tell 'e what, you can have one of the cats if you want.'

Rose smiled, touched by the kind offer, but she did not have the heart to say that there was no way she would give one of Dorothy's cats house room. 'Thank you. But I'm used to being on my own and I go out a lot. It wouldn't be fair. They're happier out in the country.'

As they drove down to the station Rose chatted casually about the following day, wanting to make sure Martin understood exactly what was to take place.

'Mr Meecham might be there,' he said. 'He used to come up and talk to Mother. He's got someone dead as well. Marigold.' Martin gave a small giggle. 'Silly name. Mother always reckoned she weren't his sister. Why would he say she was if it weren't true? Seems daft to me.' His face was flushed. He was unused to making conversation and felt he might have said too much.

Nothing Dorothy told him was ever repeated but it was some-how all right to tell Mrs Trevelyan.

'She told you that?' Rose took her eyes briefly from the road.

''Ezz, course she did. Who else would tell me? Mother always talked to me, I reckon she thought I wasn't listening half the time. She knew lots of things, did Mother. She knew Marigold wasn't no Cornishwoman.'

·'She wasn't?'

'No. Couldn't understand it myself. I knew Mr Hinkston wasn't from round these parts, 'twas obvious, but I wouldn't have known about Marigold. Mother did. She said to me, "if that's not a Plymouth accent, I don't know what is."' He nodded several times, pleased with his fairly accurate mimicry of Doro-thy's voice.

Plymouth. The accent was a lot different, just as local accents varied in different parts of Cornwall. If Dorothy had spotted it then others must have done too. Was that what Doreen Clarke had alluded to? 'Are you sure?'

'Course I'm sure. Mother was never wrong. She said it weren't broad because Marigold had picked up the way we do talk, but she knew, Mother knew.'

All thoughts of forgetting her theory were wiped out. This new information gave her something to work on. But surely it would be impractical, if not impossible to go searching in Plymouth. Or would it? A perusal of the telephone directory for Heaths could do no harm, it covered the whole of Cornwall and Plymouth. If that failed it really would be the end of it.

Rose made a quick calculation. Marigold had been younger than Rose and both Rose's parents were still alive, which reminded her she must ring them. It had been over a week since she had last done so. She smiled as she thought of their busy lives. Unlike many of their contemporaries retirement had not made them less active. They treated it as an opportunity to do all the things they previously did not have time for and they were rarely to be found at home. So far they had both been spared the inconvenience of the infirmities of the elderly and she hoped it would remain that way. They were close, but not in a cloying way. After David died they had done all they could

142

before returning home. It was Laura who had threatened to get them back down if Rose didn't start living again. For a long time they had insisted upon a daily telephone call, made by one of her parents each evening. Four Christmases they had given up to be with her. Until the last one. Then they had taken a cruise, happy in the knowledge that Rose was to be spending the day with Jack Pearce.

There was a strong smell of kelp in the air as they reached the Promenade. A wind had picked up and was drying the brown weed where it lay in heaped piles along the beach, washed up by the high tides.

She saw Martin on to the bus then went home. There was a lot to think about, including Gwen's visit to Dorothy's house, and she wondered if she had been gullible in taking Bradley Hinkston at face value. Wasn't he a little too urbane, too sure of himself? And what ready replies he had had to all their questions.

DI Jack Pearce had done all he could and was becoming more and more convinced that he was wasting time on a matter which did not merit it. Roy Phelps had now also been questioned by the Avon police.

Jack ran through Phelps's statement once more. Both he and Hinkston claimed the former had not been near the Pengelly premises. More than likely this was true otherwise Phelps could have been used to alibi Hinkston. Once, or if, the cheque came to light then the picture might be a little clearer.

Half-way through the morning he received a call from Dorothy's bank manager. 'I only became aware of it today,' he told Jack, 'but Mrs Pengelly had a meeting with our financial adviser on Thursday afternoon. It was arranged rather hurriedly but he managed to squeeze her in. Apparently she was in the process of setting up a trust fund for her younger son, Martin, using the cheque you were inquiring about. We have a copy of the forms with her signature on but the papers from the trustees won't yet have reached her address. Mr Rowe, that's our financial adviser, is here with me now if you want a word with him.'

Jack did, but he only received confirmation of what he had just been told. Mr Rowe, he thought after the call was over. It was a common enough name in Cornwall but it still had the power to disrupt a good mood. He believed Rose when she said there was only friendship between herself and Barry, but what Jack envied was the long-standing relationship, the years which the two of them had had to get to know one another. He was, he supposed, plain jealous but he could not expect her to stop seeing Barry. At least he had the answer to the missing cheque, but why Dorothy Pengelly had gone about things in such an unusual manner was beyond him. Surely people set up trust funds when their children were small? Then he began to understand. To make the necessary arrangements had meant selling off her valuables. Dorothy had probably wanted to enjoy them for as long as she could and only as she reached what soon would naturally have been the end of her life did she decide to provide for Martin in this way. Martin would not be able to handle a large sum of money, nor would he have known how to go about selling the house contents. Even if he had done so there was the danger of his brother, or his brother's wife, persuading or cheating him out of his inheritance. This way Martin was guaranteed an income that could not be misused by himself or Peter. Another point crossed Jack's mind. Rose had said that Dorothy was concerned about the amount of alcohol Martin sometimes consumed. A regular income would prevent him blowing the money on drink in a few years whilst ensuring her son's needs were met for the rest of his life. Another motive out of the window.

So what next? As he ran a hand through his dark hair Jack realised it needed cutting. Too often lately the job seemed to come before all other things, especially Rose. Not that she complained. Not that she seems to care at all, he added silently but bitterly. 'What next is that I forget the whole thing.' The words were addressed to the empty room in which he was sitting. Hinkston and Phelps were surely in the clear; Dorothy Pengelly's death might have been untimely but it no longer seemed suspicious.

It was after six before he got the chance to ring Rose. His

144

stomach knotted with disappointment when he heard the click of the answering machine. He was missing her more than he liked to admit. He was about to leave a message when he heard what he thought sounded like 'Oh, bugger' over the top of the recording. Then 'Hold on.' He smiled as he pictured Rose running down the stairs to answer the call but getting there too late. The line cleared. 'Hello?'

'Hello, it's me.'

'Ah, Jack.' There was a pause. 'I'm sorry about that, I forgot the stupid thing was still on.'

'How are you?'

'I'm fine.'

There were times when he wanted to shake her. She sounded so offhand and not in the least pleased to hear from him. He could not recall knowing a more infuriating female. 'Are you free tonight?'

'Actually, I was going to ask you the same thing. You see, there's something I need to talk to you about.'

'Oh?'

'Not on the phone. Can I meet you somewhere?'

'Yes,' he said as his stomach churned. 'Wherever you like.'

Somewhere quiet, Rose thought, somewhere where we won't come across any of the numerous people we know between us. But in West Penwith that was almost impossible. In the end she decided on the Cutty Sark in Marazion. Jack agreed to be there at eight. Whatever happened he would not be late.

Later, under the shower, he felt as though his life was on the line. Unlike Rose he did not possess intuition or what was often referred to as a sixth sense, but that evening Jack would have bet money on what she was going to tell him.

Rose was nervous, unable to think of the best way of breaking the news. There is no best way, she decided, I'll have to take it as it comes. Beneath her anxiety was the anticipation of the dinner with Stella and Daniel and the knowledge of her next move as far as Dorothy was concerned. I still have the keys, she thought, but she was reluctant to use them. It had to be more

145

than coincidence that after each visit to the house she had received an anonymous call. Someone was watching the place. Her pulse raced. Or me, she amended.

But crowning everything was the sight of the canvas, primed and ready for her to start work.

At seven thirty she went out to the car. It was a balmy evening, the wind had dropped and the sky was clear. It would not be too long before the clocks went back and the rhythms of winter were set in motion.

Because she was early, Rose left the car in the car-park some way down the road from the pub and strolled, hands in the pockets of her jacket, up towards it. People were eating at the polished wood tables at the front of the premises but over their heads she saw Jack standing against the bar which ran at right angles to the door. She swallowed.

'Dry white wine?' he asked, his voice carefully neutral.

'Please. With soda.'

Having paid for the drinks Jack turned to face her. 'Well, Rose?' Towering over her all he could see was the top of her head because she was studying the contents of her glass.

She sighed, shoulders drooping, before she met his eye. 'Jack, I'm sorry. I'd like us to be friends but . . .'

'I see. So it was just a fling.' His voice was like ice.

'No, it wasn't that, it was much more than that.' She felt near to tears seeing the pain and bitterness in his face. 'I'll never forget what you've done for me. You see, after David I thought there'd never be anyone else. And then I met you and you proved me wrong.'

Jack nodded slowly. 'Yes, I see. I was the trial run, the practice before you got back into the swing of things. Thank you so much for telling me.' He threw back his drink, emptying the glass. 'Well, sod you, Rose Trevelyan.'

'Jack, wait, I'm scared.' Rose spoke quietly but it was too late. His glass was on the bar and there was an empty space beside her. Briefly his large frame filled the doorway and then he was gone, a few heads turning inquisitively to follow his departure.

Rose smiled stiffly at the barmaid who could not have helped but overhear their conversation then she finished her drink, taking her time because she did not want anyone to see how upset she was.

As she drove back to Newlyn a few spots of rain hit the windscreen but she would be home before it started in earnest. Jack, she thought, would no longer bother about Dorothy Pengelly. All the time she had believed he had taken an interest only because she, Rose, was involved. Suicide. And why not? Except, through her own foolishness, she had not told Jack about the phone calls. Laura was right, they proved there was more to it than that. It's up to me now, she thought, standing in the space between the parked car and the kitchen door. Heedless of the rain she was unwilling to enter the house just yet. She inhaled deeply. The air smelled different. There was the usual salt tang and the rich smell of damp earth but there was something else. Rose realised it was the scent of freedom.

Marigold was at peace. Fred, with the assistance of some of his customers, had had to organise drinks and sandwiches in the function room of an hotel in Hayle. He would not have bothered but the two women who came to help serve in the shop had been shocked and told him it was expected. It was ironical to be paying for the sort of food he could have provided from the shop but he had had no intention of inviting people back to the flat.

The day after the funeral he felt exhausted, as if he had been awake for many more nights, but sleep eluded him.

Tomorrow was Dorothy's funeral but he would not be attending. It was too soon after Marigold's for it to mean anything.

With a jolt he realised the relevance of this. His face, which for so long had been creased with misery, altered. What he had started had been a waste of time. It didn't matter now. Whatever Dorothy had in the house didn't matter, no one could possibly find out now. The knowledge should have brought comfort but as the hours passed it had the opposite effect. He required certain knowledge and he wouldn't rest until he had it.

11

Rose, too, tossed and turned. She felt bad about Jack but her life was changing. Ever since she had arrived home from Marazion she had been expecting him to ring. He had not. Perhaps he remembered it was Dorothy's funeral the next day and thought better of causing an argument.

Her body heavy with lack of sleep she dragged herself out of bed in the morning. What she was about to do was against her better judgement but for Dorothy's sake she would do it.

Half an hour before she was due to pick up Martin and Jobber she pulled up outside Dorothy's front door and let herself into the house. Standing still she listened. She was alone and there had been no sign of life outside. Holding her breath she opened the drawer beside the sink in the kitchen. There was the envelope she had seen Dorothy place there. She picked it up. It was sealed and her own name, in Dorothy's spindly writing, was on the front. 'Well, well,' Rose said as she slipped it into her handbag. There was no time to think about it now.

Martin was waiting anxiously at the end of the lane when Rose's Mini came into sight. He knew what to expect but he could not have faced it alone. The anger was still there, burning away inside him, but Jobber had said that that was all right, that soon it would go. He was very glad that Mrs Trevelyan would be with them, nothing could go wrong. The only other funeral he had attended had been that of his father but he was too young to remember anything other than the sun which had beaten down on his uncovered head and the solemnness of the adults which had seemed out of place on such a lovely day.

Rose saw Martin standing apprehensively in the gateway. It seemed impossible that it was only yesterday afternoon he had come to her house with all that had intervened. She had returned from dropping him at the bus station and gone straight up to the

148

attic to attend to some paperwork, forgetting to switch the answering machine off. When she ran down to intercept the call which she had hoped would be from one of her new acquaintances it had been Jack. As soon as she had heard his voice she had known that the time for procrastination was over. There had been no word from him since.

Rose waved and tried to smile, putting herself in Martin's position. 'It'll be all right, you'll see,' she told him as she got out to let him into the back seat. 'Where's Jobber?'

'He's just coming.'

Rose got back behind the wheel. Without anyone suggesting it Martin had dressed in grey trousers, a white shirt and a tie. She had no idea where the tie had come from but guessed it was an old one of Jobber 's. Over this he wore a waxed jacket which was the only coat he possessed. The sky was a clear blue but a cold wind blew from the east. Rose suddenly realised that the weather was irrelevant, Dorothy was being cremated, they would not be out in the open.

'Ah, here he is.'

Jobber walked down from the farmhouse towards them, his bent legs working quickly. He, too, was dressed in his best clothes, in his case a dark suit, shiny with age. Rose was surprised to notice the black tie and armband. She did not realise that people still wore them.

'Morning,' he said solemnly.

'Hello, Jobber,' she replied as he got into the front passenger seat. She did not know which of the two men looked the more despondent. 'Shall we go?' It was an inane question, only intended to break the tension but no one answered.

At first they thought that Dorothy's funeral had attracted a crowd until they realised that the mourners milling around were from the previous service and had gathered to look at the flowers which were laid out for inspection. Their own party consisted of the three of them, Peter and Gwen, and two elderly strangers Rose did not know. There was no sign of Dorothy's grandchildren. At the last minute Doreen Clarke hustled into one of the pews, her face red beneath her tea-cosy hat. 'I managed to get an hour off,' she whispered as the music stopped playing.

149

''Tis a sad day,' Jobber said, wiping his eyes when they filed out. 'Are you all right, boy?'

Martin nodded. He seemed stunned.

After the short service Peter came over to them and thanked them for coming then, after a noticeable hesitation, invited them back to the house. Rose did not know what to say. She had provided the transport, if she drove Jobber and Martin back to Hayle who would take them home? It was Peter's duty to see to it but she doubted if he would.

Jobber met Rose's eyes and gave a small shake of the head before he looked at Martin. 'Do 'e want to go back to your brother's?'

'Of course he does,' Gwen said, taking his arm.

'No. I'm going along with Mrs Trevelyan.'

'Are you sure?' Rose asked, noticing the disparaging look Gwen gave her, as if she alone was responsible for Martin's decision. Peter showed little interest in the interchange. There were dark shadows under his eyes and his skin seemed to be sagging. He stared into the distance somewhere above their heads. Gwen's attitude was entirely different. She seemed brisk and efficient, trying to organise people, but Rose noticed she was trembling and unable to meet anyone's eye.

In the car Rose suggested that they ought to do something in the way of seeing Dorothy off. She invited Jobber and Martin back to her cottage.

'Naw. 'Tis out of the way, girl. You both come back to me. I've got a drop to drink and Angela's there with the kiddie, she can soon knock some sandwiches together.'

Rose had not been inside the farmhouse before. It was warm and comfortable and not a bit as she had imagined it to be from the outside. The furnishings were shabby but it was a home, one which was loved and lived in. Star was livelier than she had ever seen her. She got out of her basket clumsily and licked Jobber's and Martin's hands. George growled, which made Rose smile. Something was as it should be. The Jack Russell had been adopted into farming life in advance, Rose suspected, of Martin's joining them.

'I heard they was wanting to talk to Mrs Pengelly again,'

150

Jobber commented innocently as he poured three glasses of port. 'They say 'er car was seen up at your mother's place the same day as she died.' The words were addressed to Martin but Rose knew they were meant for her. She supposed by 'they', Jobber meant the police but she had no idea how he came by the information. That was one of the quirks about Cornwall, everyone seemed to know everything without actually being told. It was as if knowledge was absorbed by osmosis. But this piece of information did not fit in with the picture she was building up. Was she so wrong, was it Gwen Pengelly who was watching her?

Rose stayed for only half an hour. The port was strong and she had to get the car home and catch up with some work. Martin was having supper with Jobber so she knew he would be in safe hands for what was probably the worst day of his life.

Once home Rose felt the sudden need of someone to talk to. She rang Barry. 'Are you busy?'

'No. Hardly anyone about today, surprising as it's turned out fine. Mind, it's bloody cold in the wind. And you know I'm never too busy for you, Rosie.'

How she wished that Barry would not make his feelings so obvious. He was bound to gloat when he heard about Jack.

'How did it go this morning?'

'As well as these things can. There were only a few of us there.'

'I think you need a bit of cheering up. Look, let me take you out tonight. Put your glad-rags on and we'll go and have a decent meal somewhere.' And please don't say you've already arranged to meet Jack, he prayed.

'I'd love that. Thank you, Barry.' They arranged a time and she hung up, picturing him in his white shirt, the sleeves rolled up as he worked his way through the ever-increasing mound of paperwork which littered his desk in the back office. He reminded her at times of an absent-minded professor. Perhaps it was the thick-rimmed tortoiseshell glasses which did it. He's a good friend to have, she thought, as she settled down to some paperwork of her own.

Barry's main downfall was the lack of a sense of humour. He

151

took life and himself too seriously, which was the opposite of what Jack had accused her of. But that evening he excelled himself. Sensing Rose's grief over Dorothy and something else he was unable to define, Barry went out of his way to entertain her and he managed to succeed.

'So, what plans for the immediate future?' he asked as he helped her on with her coat prior to taking her home.

'I'm having a shopping trip to Plymouth. It's ages since I've done that.'

Barry knew Rose's aversion to shopping but refrained from commenting. Perhaps Jack was taking her out for the day which might make it more appealing. He did not want to know. When she changed the subject he decided he was wrong, that Rose was probably off on one of her crusades, and he wanted to know even less about that. Of course, it might all be innocent; Rose rarely bought new clothes but perhaps the trip was intended to cheer herself up after losing a friend. At least he could credit himself with having helped a little in that direction.

Neither of them mentioned Jack. Rose knew that to make a point of explaining the situation would only lead Barry to build up his hopes. She thanked him for the meal and left him wondering what was going through her mind.

Thursday morning dawned crisp and bright. Too crisp for September. Rose shivered as she pulled her dressing-gown around her waist and belted it tightly before closing the bedroom window. Twisting a towelling band around her hair she went downstairs.

In the garden the leaves were beginning to show signs of red and gold. Autumn was usually late in Cornwall, but not that year. The climate, despite the rainfall, was suitable for sub-tropical plants to flourish. Rose could only ever recall one occasion where frost had damaged them.

While the water trickled through the coffee machine she fingered the envelope which still lay on the table. Addressed to herself it contained no letter, only a street map. A few days ago it would have meant nothing, now it told her that her suspicions were correct. That Dorothy had left her a message, cryptic though it might be.

Plymouth, she thought, as she gazed out upon the now tidy garden. There were plenty of trains and there was no point in going through an endurance test with the car. She checked her timetable and picked an early one. Penzance being the terminus there would be plenty of seats. Half an hour later she set off on foot, enjoying the level walk along the Promenade and the crisp wind in her hair.

She bought a day return ticket and a coffee to drink on the train. For the first half-hour she looked out of the window, emptying her mind of all that had gone before that week. The sea was rolling in over the sands of Marazion beach. Shallow breakers with white crests broke along the shore. The causeway leading out to the Mount was still covered. Later, when the tide turned, people would be able to walk across.

Rose had made sure her credit card and cheque book were in her handbag. Whatever else happened that day she was determined to buy some more new clothes. But before she did that she was having coffee with Audrey Heath.

The simplicity with which she had found Marigold's mother had been astonishing. Her number had been listed in the telephone directory, although it was not the first Heath she had rung. She was not certain who Mrs Heath believed her to be. Rose had been vague over the telephone and allowed her to draw her own conclusions. Having ascertained that she was related to Marigold Heath, and Rose did not think there could be two people of that name, she had said she wanted to ask her some questions. Mrs Heath had said she would be pleased to talk about her daughter but, in her own way, had been as enigmatic as Rose.

The train pulled into Bodmin Parkway before Rose realised where they were. It would not be long now. Mrs Heath lived in St Budeaux, on the outskirts of Plymouth, but the Inter-City train on which Rose was travelling passed through the small station there without stopping. This meant catching a local train or getting a taxi as she was uncertain of the bus routes.

Loud tannoy announcements greeted Rose as she stepped on to the platform. Hurrying across the brightly lit concourse she had to swerve to avoid passengers gazing up at the arrival and departure screens. Outside a row of black cabs stood waiting. The driver of the front one was reading a paper but he reached out of the window and behind him to open the door without looking up as if he had sensed Rose's arrival. She gave him the address and folded herself into the back seat. The driver chatted as he negotiated the city traffic. She was only half listening because they were driving down streets she did not know and she was curious, taking everything in.

Soon she was knocking nervously on Mrs Heath's front door. The house was identical to the others which lined the road. Muffled footsteps were followed by the sound of a bolt being drawn. A round face peered out through a gap of a few inches before the door was opened fully. 'Mrs Trevelyan? You found me all right then?'

'Yes.'

'Come on in. I didn't know what to think when you rang, but if it's to do with Marigold, well, I thought it was time I knew.' The Devonshire vowels were rounded, the speech slower and more drawn out than Rose was used to hearing. She did not have a good ear for accents but the difference was obvious. If Marigold had retained a trace of her origins then Dorothy would not have missed it.

She followed Mrs Heath down a narrow hallway, the carpet of which was protected by a clear plastic runner. There was to be no formality, she was shown into the kitchen. It was clean but untidy. A bottle of milk stood on the table alongside a plate of toast crumbs. Mrs Heath made no excuses nor did she remove the plate. 'I more or less live out here. It's warmer in the winter and I get a better reception on the telly. Take a seat. I'll put the kettle on then we can have a chat.'

Audrey Heath tipped the used tea-bags from the pot into the sink. As the kettle boiled she lit a cigarette and offered Rose the packet. Rose accepted one, it was the brand she smoked. It was a useful prop, something with which to occupy herself as she thought how best to approach the subject. It was quite clear that her hostess did not know her daughter was dead.

Rose noticed that beneath the shapeless grey skirt and pink sweater Mrs Heath wore elasticated stockings. Her feet were swollen and a small roll of flesh hung over the sides of her slippers. Rose was unable to put an age to her, she might have been anywhere between early sixties and mid-seventies. This, then, was Marigold's mother to whom Rose had to break the news. She did not think she could possibly leave without doing so.

'Sugar?'

'Sorry? Oh, no thanks, I've got sweeteners.' Rose dug into her bag to get them out, still unsure what to say.

'It's nice having a bit of company. I don't get out much, with my legs, you see. Where did you say you were from? My memory's not what it was.'

'Newlyn.'

'Down Penzance way. That's a fair old way to come.' Audrey looked pleased, as if the length of the journey was more important than what her visitor had come to talk about.

Rose knew she had to make a start. 'Mrs Heath, as I explained, the questions I want to ask are for my own interest only, nothing will go any further without your permission. I'm not from the press, or anything like that.' She paused, thinking what a mess she was making of it. Perhaps, from the strange way in which she was being observed, Mrs Heath may have been expecting payment or to hear good news. Stalling was useless and she could not continue until the truth came out.

Audrey nodded. 'Whatever you say can't hurt me, dear. I've got nothing to hide.' She sipped her tea noisily, the cup held in both hands because her joints were gnarled with arthritis.

'I don't know how to put this. There's no easy way. Mrs Heath, it's bad news, I'm afraid.'

'Concerning Marigold.' The statement was flat. 'I can't say it surprises me.'

Audrey's reaction was nonchalant and therefore unexpected. For a minute Rose thought there might be another Marigold

155

Heath. She had to make sure before she continued. 'When did you last see your daughter?'

Audrey squinted through the smoke. 'Some years ago now. Not since she left home.'

'Where did she go?'

'Where she was destined to go. Downhill. Oh, don't look so upset, that girl was trouble from the minute she was born. By the time she was sixteen she was on the game, nothing I could do to stop her, she never took a blind bit of notice of me. I suppose it's true what they say, about kids needing a father. Hers was killed when she was small. She used to pick up seamen, did Marigold. There's enough of them in Plymouth. Sometimes down Union Street, sometimes down the Barbican, but that was before they done it all up. It's real nice now. Next thing I heard was that she'd taken off for Cornwall. Not even a goodbye. Don't ask me why, she didn't know anyone down there. Still, we were never what you could call close, not really. Marigold always kept her distance, even as a little girl.'

Rose swallowed. It felt painful. 'Mrs Heath – '

'Oh, Audrey, please.'

'Audrey, Marigold died last week.'

'Died?'

'Yes. I'm so sorry. And I wish there was someone closer to you who could have broken the news.' Rose half stood, ready to put a comforting arm around her shoulders. It was not necessary.

'I always said she'd come to a bad end. Someone strangle her, did they? Wouldn't surprise me, I was tempted to myself many a time.' She paused and stared at Rose. 'No. Can't be that, the police would've come round.'

The words were harsh but there was no other way to put it. 'She was ill. Marigold died of cancer.'

'Oh!' Audrey's face registered a mixture of emotions. Shock and pain and regret but no grief. That would come later. 'I wouldn't have wished that on her, no matter what she did.'

'I went to her funeral. I naturally assumed all the family knew, I can't think why someone didn't tell you.'

'It was very kind of you. Thank you. But I don't think I'd've gone if I had known. We fell out badly and she said she never

156

wanted to set eyes on me again. I'm glad there was someone like you there to say goodbye.'

'There were an awful lot of people, over a hundred.'

'What?' Audrey's eyes bulged in disbelief, then she laughed. 'Maybe all her clients turned up. How was she, I mean did she do all right for herself?'

Rose saw Audrey reach into her pocket for a tissue and make a pretence of blowing her nose. 'Yes. She did all right. Did she have any brothers or sisters?'

'No, she was the only one. I couldn't have coped with two like that.'

Rose was safe to carry on. 'Marigold had a boyfriend. They were together for some years. They ran a shop and from what I know she was happy enough. She didn't want for anything and her boyfriend adored her.'

'Marigold turned respectable? My God. Running a shop, you say? I never thought I'd live to hear such a thing.' Audrey sighed deeply. 'I wish she'd let me know, I wish she could've just telephoned me. Perhaps she was afraid I'd tell this bloke about her past, but I wouldn't have, I wouldn't have said a word.'

Rose saw that it was a double loss. First her daughter had walked out on her then she had lived the sort of life Audrey would have wished for her.

'Were there any children?' She held her breath.

'No.' At least she had not missed out on that.

The tears still held at bay, she asked Rose to talk about her, to tell what Marigold was like.

'I didn't know her, but I met the man she lived with. He was quiet and, as you said, respectable, a church-goer, a warden, I believe. They had the shop and until Marigold became ill they both worked there. She was well liked by the customers.'

Audrey was shaking her head as if Rose was talking about someone else. 'She wasn't a bit like that at home. I tried everything I could think of to keep her on the straight and narrow, but by the time she was fourteen I knew I was wasting my time. Then just before she left the police wanted to see her. Something to do with a man who was stabbed in the street. Three o'clock in the morning, it was. Of course, she wasn't here, she'd left home ages before

157

that. Turns out he was her pimp. No great loss to the world to my mind. All the girls were questioned and once they knew he was dead they were more than willing to speak. I don't condone the way they earned their living but I did feel sorry for them knowing how he treated them. Marigold had been seen with him that night – mind you, she'd been seen with other men too. Not long after that she went away. I heard they were satisfied that she wasn't involved after some man came forward and said how he'd spent the whole night with her. She didn't come home, not even then. Later I heard she'd moved to Truro.'

'Why there?'

'Beats me. Another city, maybe, although not so big as this one.' Audrey pushed back a lock of hair. It was grey except at the front where nicotine had stained it yellow. 'I always wondered if she'd taken up with one of her men, one of the ones that used to come up here to get what they weren't getting at home, if you see what I mean.'

Coincidence? Rose did not think so. Fred Meecham originally came from Truro but he already had the shop when Marigold moved in with him. She may have said that Truro was where she was heading but it was not where she had ended up.

As for Fred, that was the part which puzzled her. He made such a big thing of acting the perfect citizen and of being deeply religious. Had he really come to Plymouth to visit prostitutes? And could a girl like Marigold have changed so drastically? Or had it been what she had wanted all along, a man and a life of domesticity? They would never know now. 'What happened in the end, about the man who was stabbed?'

'Oh, I don't remember now. You know how it is, big news one minute and the next everyone's forgotten all about it. I can't recall hearing they got anyone, but good luck, I say, if it prevented other girls getting beaten up. Here, if this chap was so fond of Marigold, how come they didn't get married?'

Rose shrugged. 'I've no idea.' It was a good question. Both of them were single, perhaps Marigold did not want it. But why pose as brother and sister? Surely even someone like Fred would not be embarrassed in this day and age. There might have been gossip to begin with but, as Audrey had said, things soon blow over. Rose was certain there was an explanation which had nothing to do with the conventions.

They talked for a little while longer then Rose said she must leave. She felt she knew a great deal more about Marigold Heath now than she did about Fred Meecham. Audrey tried to persuade her to stay to lunch but Rose refused. She held out her hand. 'Thank you for seeing me, and I really am sorry.'

Audrey clutched her hand in both her own. 'You've nothing to be sorry for, dear. It's me that should thank you for coming. And it's easier now I know she found a man to care for her.' Audrey shut the door but Rose saw that as she did so she was pulling the tissue from the sleeve of her jumper.

There was a bus-stop at the end of the road. Rose had given no thought as to how she was to get back to the city centre and there was no telephone box in sight from which to ring for a taxi. As she was deciding on the best course of action a young woman with a push-chair arrived at the stop. Rose asked her how to get back into the centre of Plymouth.

'There's a bus in a couple of minutes, it'll drop you in Royal Parade.'

Rose thanked her and smiled at the toddler who was smacking at the plastic hood protecting him from the wind. They were high up and Rose could see the gantries of the huge cranes in the dockyard. When the bus arrived she carried the push-chair on to it, leaving the mother's hands free to cope with the child and to pay for her fare.

Alighting in the city centre Rose crossed at the lights and studied the posters displayed inside the plate glass windows of the Theatre Royal. If she had thought about it in advance she could have booked a matinée seat but that wouldn't have left any time to buy herself something to wear. With her new-found freedom there were many things she could do.

Strolling through the pannier market she eyed the colourful stacks of fruit and vegetables, noted the cheapness of the meat and fingered the swinging bundles of pungent leather handbags. The mixture of aromas was almost exotic but over all was the warm, meaty smell of pasties, Devon pasties, with the crimped crust running along the top instead of around the edge.

Leaving the market she walked up New George Street towards the main shopping area. The wind off the sea, stronger now, gusted up Armada Way. In a department store she bought three sets of matching underwear but did not see a dress or suit she wanted.

Rose liked the spaciousness of the city, rebuilt after the heavy bombing of the war with its added attractions of the Hoe overlooking Plymouth Sound and the Barbican, steeped in history with its cobbled streets and eating places and art galleries and where she and David had once done the tour of the gin distillery. It was housed in a building which had been a monastery and a prison amongst other things. It was after three and she had almost given up. In desperation she went into a boutique from whose doors throbbed rock music. And there she found exactly what she was looking for; bright, flamboyant clothes, items which reminded her of her youth. But it was not her adolescence she was trying to recapture, it was the freedom of spirit she had once possessed. As she came out of the changing room a flowered dress caught her eye. She tried it on and bought that too. Her purchases wrapped and paid for, she left the shop.

With a smile of satisfaction she walked the last couple of hundred yards back to the station and was just in time to catch the London train, Inter-City.

It was dark when she arrived back in Penzance and there were damp patches on the pavement where a passing shower had occurred in her absence. Although she had walked a fair distance in Plymouth she needed to stretch her legs after the two-hour journey. As always, each time she returned she felt as though she had been away longer and it was a pleasure to fill her lungs with the fresh salty air.

She walked briskly, carrier bags swinging as she looked forward to a drink and a meal. She had not eaten anything since breakfast.

It had been an odd but enjoyable day. Rose was thinking about what Mrs Heath had told her but nagging at the back of her mind were Jobber's words, about Gwen Pengelly having been seen at Dorothy's place on the day of her death. Gwen was aware of her involvement with the family and must surely have been suspicious of her reasons for calling on her and Peter. That's it, she thought, remembering the details of the neat kitchen and the immaculate appearance of her hostess. Beside the kettle had been a brown plastic container of pills. Tranquillisers? Rose wondered. Gwen had struck her as the type of woman to resort to them. And if so? No, Jack would have made inquiries. It was not up to her to speak to the woman. Wrapped in thought she had not seen just ahead of her, leaning on the railings, a man whose profile, even outlined against the darkness, she recognised. Smoke trailed from a cigarette as he tapped ash over the sea wall. It was Jack. She was about to cross the road when he turned his head and saw her. It was too late to avoid him and it would have been childish to pretend she had not seen him. She carried on walking, more slowly now.

'Rose?'

'Hello, Jack.'

They stood looking at each other. 'Are you on your way home?'

'Yes.'

'I was just taking a walk. Rose, I've been out of my mind since I saw you. I wanted to ring you. Every minute I've wanted to but I told myself it was no good, you wouldn't speak to me. I owe you an apology, I was very rude. Are you still angry?'

'No, Jack, not angry. Disappointed, though, because I'd hoped you'd understand. Believe me, it wasn't your fault.'

He threw the end of the cigarette to the ground and stepped on it. 'I'd like to remain friends. I've had time to think about it and I promise you there'll be no pressure.'

She was ashamed to acknowledge a new disappointment. Jack Pearce seemed to have got over her very quickly. 'Good. I must get home, I've had a long day.' She swung the carriers. 'I've been up to Plymouth.' It would mean nothing to Jack. Marigold's death was not the one he was investigating but she felt a mean streak of smugness that she knew things of which he was completely unaware. Her white plastic bags glistened under the street-lights as she began to move away.

Jack's eyes moved over her face. Rose had enjoyed herself, he could see that. He would not have been able to if their roles were reversed, but there was something else, an undercurrent of excitement which had nothing to do with her day out or seeing him. 'Can I buy you a drink?' he asked quickly before she had taken more than a couple of steps.

She hesitated before agreeing. It would be a test, a way of seeing if Jack would keep to his word. 'Yes. But it'll have to be a quick one.'

He did not ask why, he was too pleased that she had not refused. They crossed over and walked back to the Yacht which was set back from the front, a Union Jack and the Cornish flag flying from its turreted roof. Like the Jubilee Pool, it had been built in the thirties.

Rose ordered a gin and tonic, Jack had a pint of beer. They took their drinks to the curved seat in the bay window.

'Have you eaten?'

'No. But I've got something planned at home,' Rose said firmly. Seeing Jack unexpectedly had unsettled her. There were things she knew now which she ought to tell him and things she had guessed at, but it would mean spending more than half an hour with him to discuss them and she was not ready to do that.

'Okay.' His tone was light and almost relaxed. Rose wondered if he thought he'd won a minor victory.

They spoke little, neither sure what would now offend the other. One thing was certain, the relationship was on a different basis. To emphasise this Rose told him about the party and the dinner to which she had been invited and then she said she must leave.

He nodded and stood as she picked up her bags but he was not going to make the mistake of offering to walk her home. Instead he went back to the bar.

Peter Pengelly had taken the rest of the week off. After the funeral he and Gwen had returned to the house with the two elderly friends of Dorothy's whom neither of them really knew but who, having participated in many such events, expected to be fed. Gwen had done her best to be charming but was relieved when they left. She was aware that their departure quickly

162

followed a comment about collecting the children who had gone to a neighbour's straight from school.

Now it's over, she thought, now we can get on with our lives. She had cleared away the plates and glasses and thrown the paper serviettes in the bin. It would have been a mistake to discuss anything with Peter that evening. She knew he had struggled through the day, trying to be polite when all he had wanted was to be alone with his thoughts. Now, twenty-four hours later, he sat in his chair in the living-room facing the blank television screen. She had no idea what was going on in his head.

Gwen gave the children milk and biscuits although they would be having their tea soon. She was trying to silence them because they were noisily demanding to know what exactly had happened to their grandmother. She looked at them fondly. They and Peter were her life. Would there be enough to be able to afford to send them to private schools? But not as boarders, she couldn't bear that. Guilt did not tarnish her anticipation of the money that was to come although waves of it kept taking her unawares. With her back to the children she swallowed one of the tablets prescribed for her although they did little to reduce her permanent anxiety. No one could have seen her go to the house that day or the police would have questioned her about it. No one need ever know.

Shushing them once more she left the children at the table with instructions not to disturb their father. Rearranging her features into what she hoped was a semblance of sorrow she went to see what comfort she could offer Peter.

The shop was closed and had been for over an hour. Illuminated only by the street-lights Fred Meecham's face was pudgy and jaundiced. He did not know how long he had been standing there, only that his legs had stopped trembling, but they ached. He peered around in the gloom and pulled a plastic milk crate towards him, upended it and sat down, oblivious to the discomfort of its hard moulded surface.

All this was his. The shop, the goods, the living accommodation overhead. His kingdom, as he used to joke with Marigold.

His kingdom, and she was the queen. She used to like it when he called her that. It might not be much by some people's standards but to Fred it represented a lifetime's work and loyalty to his customers which they had repaid. So many shopped at supermarkets these days. Now there was no one with whom to share it all and this saddened him. One day everything would go to his son who would sell up and it would be as if Fred Meecham had not existed.

It shouldn't be this way, he kept thinking. Marigold was so much younger than himself. He should have been the first to go, she would have been left in a comfortable position. Now he would have to change his will. He supposed he ought to do the right thing by Justin even if they did not communicate. Marigold had given him more happiness than he had believed possible although he had been aware that his love was not reciprocated in quite the same way. Until the end her feelings had been those of gratitude and fondness. That did not matter. Having her under his roof had been enough for Fred. The first time he met her on one of those shameful visits to Plymouth he had recognised a need in her, one that he believed he could fulfil. To the best of his knowledge he had done so. The security she had craved he had provided in the only way he knew how and he had removed her from danger, protected her to the end. He would continue to protect her for ever. His only regret was that they had not married, but they had been agreed upon that because it was too much of a risk. The bond that united them had been secrecy.

His life loomed ahead, stretching endlessly into nothingness, the days marked only by the opening or the closing of the shop. He jumped when he heard someone tapping on the window. Peering in, hand shading her eyes, was one of his regular customers. Wearily he got up to open the door. 'You couldn't let me have half a pound of butter, could you? I wouldn't have disturbed you, but I saw you there and, well . . .'

'It's no trouble.' The words came automatically, he used them almost every day of his life. He took the money and gave change from the float in the till. It made no difference how long the hours he worked, there was always someone who had run out of

164

something. Knowing that in some small way he was needed, he had decided to keep on the shop. There seemed little point in selling, he had nothing else to do with his time.

He knelt on the cold floor and prayed. 'Forgive me, God,' he said. 'Forgive me. It was all for Marigold.'

Sometimes God answered him, Fred could hear His voice, but more and more lately there seemed to be no response.

He double-locked the shop door and went up to the empty flat.

As Martin walked past his mother's house he ran his fingers along the rough granite wall, almost enjoying the scrape of the stone in this farewell gesture. The sun was rising behind the hilltops but there was a low-lying mist in the valley above which everything else was crystal clear. Dew sparkled on the grass and stained the leather of Martin's boots as he breathed in the richness of damp vegetation. There was time to kill until Jobber came with his tractor to tow away the van. Everything was ready, Martin's few possessions were stowed away in the over-head lockers or firmly tied down. The previous afternoon they had made a thorough check of the vehicle because it had not been moved for many years. Jobber had seen to the tyres and inspected the tow-bar and between them they had made the necessary adjustments.

George had already gone to the farm, Jobber had come for him the day before Dorothy's funeral. There had been an ecstatic reunion between the two dogs until they each remembered their respective positions in life and settled down to ignore one another. The cats, too, had gone with him, spitting and scratching until Jobber had them safely in the back of his truck, the sliding glass windows firmly closed behind him as he drove for fear they would go for his scrawny neck. Back at the farm he had opened the rear doors and all three cats had fled screeching across the yard. Whilst they were seeing to the caravan Jobber had said they had disappeared, but he had found the remains of several rats and mice so he knew they could not be far away. They would be useful. His own cat, Mathilda, had never shown the slightest inclination to do what should have come naturally and Jobber had had to resort to poisons to keep vermin at bay. Mathilda preferred the comfort of the hearth, an armchair and regular supplies of food which she did not have to catch herself.

Jobber had thought it best to remove the animals first. It would be less of a wrench for Martin when the time came and they would be there at the farm to welcome him.

Martin stopped. A pane in the window of the back door was broken. It was no accident. The glass had been knocked out and the door was unlocked. Had George still been on the premises the intruder would not have got away lightly. His face paled. If it wasn't Peter or Gwen trying to get in without a key then it had to be Hinkston come back to get his mother's things. Hinkston knew that his mother was dead and that the house would be empty.

Carefully stepping over the shards of glass which glinted in the weak sunlight he went inside. Puzzled, he walked from room to room. Nothing seemed to be missing.

Martin was sitting on the step of the caravan when Jobber arrived. He was pleased to hear the noisy engine of the tractor as it made its lumbering progress up the side of the hill.

Jobber stepped down, nodding seriously when Martin told him what he had discovered. 'All right, boy, let's go over to the house and tell the police.' He had a good idea who might be responsible but kept his thoughts to himself.

Despite their preparations it took until the late afternoon before they were on the move. First they had to wait for the arrival of a patrol car then they had questions to answer. As nothing was reported as missing the two officers suggested it was a case of vandalism, kids who had heard that the place was uninhabited and who had probably been scared away by the hoot of an owl or headlights which played over the hillside as cars rounded the bend. DI Pearce had been making inquiries about the sudden death of Mrs Pengelly, so they decided to inform him of the vandalism, if that was what it was. It could be that someone had smashed the window in order to remove evidence or, if it was Martin himself, who held keys, in order to make it look that way. The police officers left them to it.

Just as they thought they were ready, one of the tyres went down and as they began their descent the sound of grating metal caused them to stop and investigate the underside of the van. Finally they were on the road and began the painstaking journey to the farm. Jobber was watching the road and the traffic coming from the rear, Martin sat sideways in the front of the tractor, looking over his shoulder, keeping an eye on the movements of the vehicle they were towing. Neither of them saw Peter's car as it headed towards Dorothy's house once more, this time in search of Martin to tell him about the appointment on Monday.

Gwen had received a telephone call from Dorothy's solicitor in Truro asking if she and Peter could go in and see him on Monday regarding the contents of her will. She agreed readily although she was not certain of Peter's shifts. Martin was to be there too although Henry Peachy had been unable to contact him. Gwen offered to let Martin know or to get Peter to do so. Silently she made plans for the future, their future. Hiding her excitement was not easy.

'The van's gone,' Peter said when he returned that evening. Only as he said it did he realise that he had passed it. It was unremarkable, old-fashioned and painted cream, but he had not been expecting to see it being towed behind a tractor. It had not crossed his mind that Martin would ever go anywhere else. The first person he thought of was Jobber Hicks. He telephoned the farm and was surprised to learn that Martin had taken up residence there, then he waited until his brother came to the phone.

'He'll be there,' Peter told Gwen. 'He said he'll make his own way.'

Gwen nodded, hoping that Rose Trevelyan was not involved with Martin's transport arrangements.

The answering machine was blinking furiously as Rose opened the sitting-room door. Nine calls, she calculated, watching the flashing light in disbelief. But only three messages had been left.

Jack's was the first, a tentative 'Rose? Are you there?' followed by a pause and the clunk of his receiver being replaced. The next came from Jobber who asked apologetically if she could ring back as soon as possible. 'You've let yourself in for it,' Rose told herself. The final message she replayed twice, forgetting the six non-existent calls.

'You may not remember me,' a smooth male voice said. 'My name's Nick Pascoe, we met at Mike and Barbara's. I wondered if we might meet again. I own a gallery just outside St Ives and I was impressed with your work. I was hoping there are some more like that.' The pause lasted for so many seconds that the first time she listened Rose thought he might have been cut off. 'Look, what I said is absolutely true, but I'd like to see you anyway, Rose.' She grabbed a pencil to write down the number he was dictating slowly then she sat down to think about it.

Stella and Daniel had introduced her to Nick, who had said little at the time. She recalled the lanky man of an indeterminate age, dressed in jeans, a fisherman's shirt and a frayed denim jacket. His greying hair hung over his collar. But his face was what she remembered best. It was a strong face; uncompromising, lined, firm-featured and weathered, but his eyes were unreadable, the grey pupils speckled in a way she had not encountered before. In her excitement at meeting new people she had supposed he had taken little notice of her. She knew his work but she had not met him until that evening.

It was after nine and Rose had no way of knowing whether the number was that of the gallery or his home address but she refused to get out the phone book to check, nor would she appear too eager by ringing back at once. Just as she was deciding what an appropriate time might be, the phone rang again. She reached for it immediately thinking it might be Jack, that he had not accepted what she had said and was going to start pestering her. 'Hello?'

'I warned you. This time – '

'This time, nothing. You're wasting your time.' Rose slammed the receiver down so hard she thought the plastic might have cracked. Too late she realised how foolish she had been. She was alone in the cottage, unprotected, and she had not told Jack

168

about the threats. And she could not, would not ring him now. He would misread the situation and think she had made it up just to get him over there. Three times she had been to Dorothy's empty house, three times she had been threatened. And instead of keeping the caller talking, trying to recognise the voice or background sounds, she had hung up. Desperate to hear a friendly voice she rang Jobber.

'Dorothy's place's been broken into,' he said without preamble, 'but young Martin sez nothing's gone missing. We called the police and I've boarded up the window as best I can. Martin's here with us now. You don't think it's our fault, maid, do 'ee?'

'How can it be?' Rose sank into a chair. Bad news followed bad news lately. She had been up to the house herself, she might be in some sort of trouble. With a sickening feeling she knew that whoever had also been up there had been looking for what was now in her possession. But why? Why had Dorothy made such a thing of it? Why not just tell Rose and be done with it? Then she knew. It was typical of Dorothy. She wanted justice to be done but not at the cost of additional pain.

'That there Hinkston fellow, we told 'un Dorothy was dead. Martin thinks he came back to help hisself.'

'But you just said nothing was missing. Besides, I just can't see it.'

Jobber was silent. Rose imagined him scratching his grizzled head or rubbing his unevenly shaved chin.

'I 'spect you're right. Oh, there's something else.' Rose held her breath. 'Martin's got to go to Truro on Monday. Peter rang to say so.'

'About the will?'

'Tha's right.'

'And he wants me to go with him.' Well, she had offered, she couldn't back out now and he would need someone on his side.

'If it's not putting you out.'

'Of course not. What time?'

The arrangements made, Rose poured a stiff gin and tonic. Tomorrow, no matter what, she must face the situation. She could not live with threats and the danger was real, she knew that now.

169

That night, for the first time since she had lived there, Rose drew the curtains and shut out the view of the bay. Then she made sure every door and window was firmly locked. When she went to bed she left the downstairs hall light on in case anyone was watching. They might believe she was still up.

The enormity of what she had done hit her as she lay, wide awake, beneath the duvet. She had removed what might turn out to be a vital piece of evidence, even if it was addressed to herself. Tomorrow she would know for sure.

12

Dorothy Pengelly was very much on Jack's mind despite several other pressing cases. If Rose's premise was correct, and Dorothy had not taken her own life, then who had? It was peculiar dealing with something he could not put a name to. This was no clear-cut murder, it might not be murder at all. However, certain things did not fit. The paracetamol bottle Martin had explained away. His mother kept them for his use. Jack did not need an explanation, he assumed they were for the times when Martin had over-indulged, and although the bottle had been lost along the way it was not paracetamol which had caused Dorothy's death. Nor was it any of the drugs which Marigold had been prescribed: he had not just taken Meecham's word for it, he had checked with her GP, the same GP who prescribed the mild sedatives for Gwen Pengelly. And, as Rose had said, Dorothy herself was not on the list of any local doctors. So where had the Nardil come from? The pathologist had said it was not a common drug and rather old-fashioned now, though still useful in certain cases. Phenelzine was its proper name and it was used in the treatment of depression and phobic states. More importantly it was an MAOI, which to Jack had meant nothing. 'Monoamine Oxidase Inhibitor. Risky to give to depressives because it reacts badly with certain foods and alcohol and it shouldn't be prescribed for the elderly.'

'So someone in their seventies who's never taken medication could swallow these MAOIs with alcohol and die.'

'You swallow enough of anything with alcohol and you're not going to be too healthy,' the pathologist had replied.

Fine. But who, if not Dorothy, had got hold of the stuff? And who had now broken into the place? They had been back once, with Martin who had let them in on the occasion when they had questioned him. There had been no sign of anything containing alcohol yet the PM results showed that Dorothy had been drinking. This alone was enough to convince Jack that Rose was right. Someone had been there and someone had removed the bottle. He had cursed himself for not realising this sooner but, on the other hand, there could still be another explanation. Dorothy may have accepted a drink knowing what was likely to happen, and whoever had provided it was innocent and had simply thrown the bottle away or taken it home with them because she had said she would not drink it. It didn't hang together, though, not when he thought about it. It was hardly likely that Dorothy, receiving a visitor bearing alcohol, had suddenly thought, I'll kill myself.

Who was the visitor? Who was it who had removed the bottle and washed up after them? Martin? Peter or Gwen? Rose? She was a welcome visitor and Jack knew that she had not been left out of the will. Jobber Hicks and Fred Meecham were her only other friends. Bradley Hinkston? The first transaction seemed genuine but had he gone back for another look or for some other reason beyond Jack's imagination?

Several times he had gone through the statements taken from those who had known Dorothy. He was not entirely happy with Gwen Pengelly's account and Rose had expressed suspicion of the woman. Now there was more evidence – if it could be so called, for it had been given anonymously and was, as yet, unsubstantiated. Gwen Pengelly had been seen at the house prior to the death. He must speak to Peter's wife again.

All the time he sat at his desk the telephone remained silent. Now and then he would glance at it as if he could will it to ring and Rose to be on the other end. He had left a feeble message on her machine.

Sighing, he picked up his jacket, felt for his car keys and drove over to see Gwen Pengelly.

She had worked it out, she was sure she knew what had happened to Dorothy. Once she had proof Rose was going to contact Nick Pascoe. When she met him she wanted nothing more on her mind than art and the pleasure of his company. It was as if she was keeping him as a reward for her efforts.

She needed someone to accompany her because of the risk involved and did not listen to common sense dictate that Jack was the answer. Was Barry or Laura more suitable? It was Barry's number she finally dialled, having stood by the phone chewing a nail for several minutes.

'But why?' he wanted to know, sounding surprised.

'If I told you you wouldn't come.'

'What on earth can I do with you, Rosie? All right, what time? Seven's fine. No, don't argue, if we're going, we're going in comfort. I'm not risking my neck in that bone-shaker of yours. I'll pick you up.'

'Thank you.' 'Thank you,' she whispered again as she stared at the phone. All she had to do now was to get through the rest of the day.

Nick Pascoe's words echoed in her mind. There were no more oils, not like the one she had given to Mike, only the immature attempts of her youth and the not very interesting ones she had painted after her marriage.

Rose went up to the attic and got out her easel. It was adorned with cobwebs; it was a very long time since it had been part of her equipment. At the back of the cupboard, carefully wrapped in clean sacking, were several canvases but she would need more. Having packed the one she had already prepared, plus the easel, paints and brushes, into the back of the car she went back into the kitchen and filled a flask with strong coffee. She pocketed an apple and a banana and set off. Could she execute another oil as good as the one she had given Mike Phillips? Yes, she kept telling herself, yes, you can. And all the time she was conscious of what she was going to do later and wondered what she was letting herself in for, how much danger she was in.

It was many months since she had been to St Agnes but the journey was worth the trouble. She had needed to get away to paint and to try to forget and the steep ruggedness of the landscape suited her mood. Surf rolled into the bay and covered the sand in long sweeps, and droplets of spray caught the sun like prisms. From where she sat on her canvas seat, partly sheltered by the bonnet of the Mini, the wind still took her breath away. She tied a scarf around her hair and pulled a heavy jumper on top of the one she was wearing, then she got down to work.

The sky was clear but it remained cold. Only when Rose's fingers were too numb to continue did she stand back from the easel which she had stabilised with metal pegs and study what she had achieved. Excitement flooded through her. The painting was nowhere near finished but she had blocked out the background and fixed the perspective and the initial brush strokes were confident. But it was more than that, she saw that she had painted with her emotions as well as with her skills. Instead of limiting her, fear and anger had set her free.

It was a pleasure to be out of the cold. Rose let the car engine warm up then began the drive home.

She said nothing to Barry about where she had been and why, that would come later, when the painting was finished. He was punctual, as she had known he would be.

'You're right, you know. I really ought to get out more often,' he said as they drove smoothly down through Newlyn, his car engine purring quietly, the padded seats comfortable behind their backs.

Rose glanced across at him. He sat with his head jutting forward, both hands on the wheel, as he peered through his glasses at the road ahead. For once they remained firmly on the bridge of his nose.

'Pull in here,' Rose said as they approached the car-park of the pub where she and Martin and Jobber had met Bradley Hinkston. 'I thought we'd have a drink first, we've got plenty of time.' She had told him that if he was prepared to accompany her she

173

would treat him to a meal but there was something she had to do first.

There were other customers waiting to be served and not many spare seats. 'I know this is your treat, but you must let me buy you the first drink, by way of celebration.'

'Celebration?' It was the last thing on Rose's mind.

'Mm. Your new life?'

'I see. Thanks, I'll have a white wine, please. Look, you order it, I'm just going over the road. There's something I want from the shop. You'll be served by the time I get back.'

Half puzzled, half amused, Barry nodded and held out a five-pound note to attract the attention of the busy bar staff. The smell of the food wafted out from the kitchen at the back of the building and he began to feel hungry. He wondered where Rose was taking him, he was more than ready to eat. At last it was his turn to be served. He got the drinks and moved to the corner of the bar where there was more room.

Rose hurried from the pub, looked both ways and crossed the road. The tide was out and fishing-boats leaned against the harbour walls, seemingly stuck in the mud and shadowy in the darkness. There were no other pedestrians in sight.

Fred Meecham's shop was open, as she had known it would be. Dorothy had told her that winter and summer he did not close until nine.

It was more than a grocery store. Apart from the shelves and cold cabinets stocked with food there was now a pile of wire baskets to enable customers to help themselves. There were the usual postcards and toiletries and a small rack of paperback books. At the back, in heaps, ready for the colder weather, were bags of coal and logs. In the spring their place was taken by bags of compost.

Rose swallowed, it was now or never, then she progressed slowly down the aisle to the far end of the elongated shop. Fixed to the wall was a slotted wooden box which held free pamphlets advertising local places of interest. She flipped through them idly. Fred was busy at the till serving a woman with a basket full of goods. When she left they were alone.

174

'Can I help you?'

Rose had not heard him approach but she was unaware he had been able to see her in the curved mirror which hung over the counter from where whoever was serving could watch for shoplifters. Her actions may have seemed suspicious for she had not taken a basket and did not seem to know what she wanted. She forced a smile. 'I've brought you something. From Dorothy. I think you were looking for it.' She reached into her shoulder bag, almost dropping it because she was trembling. As she looked up and met his eyes she knew with certainty that she was right. Dorothy had known but she had left it to Rose to do whatever she thought was necessary. When Marigold was dead, Rose realised. But had Dorothy had some sort of premonition that her own life would end prematurely?

Fred took the envelope she held out to him, glanced briefly at her name on the front of it then withdrew the street plan of Plymouth. He froze when he unfolded it and saw the cross, marked in red felt-tipped pen at the corner of two converging streets.

Whatever reaction she had been expecting, Rose was totally unprepared for the one she got. Colour drained from Fred's face and his skin acquired a clammy sheen as he clutched at the edge of the counter, his knuckles white. He swayed and she thought for a second he might faint.

'She told you. I knew she had. I knew you wouldn't let it go. I saw you out there snooping around at the house.' His voice was strangled and rose several semitones as he spoke. He pulled his shoulders back and came towards her, menacingly slowly, a peculiar expression on his face which had turned almost as red as his hair.

Rose flinched and took a step backwards, unable to scream. 'I don't know what you mean,' she croaked untruthfully, realising what an idiot she had been not to confide in anyone. She saw that he did not believe her. Fear turned to terror. It was so stupid to have come alone, especially when Barry was only a matter of yards away. For God's sake, she thought, come and find me. And then, as Fred swung around and she saw what he was

175

about to do, a voice in her head shouted, Jack, for Christ's sake where are you?

Gwen was serving supper. The radio was on to dispel the gloomy atmosphere of the household. Peter had hardly spoken to her all week. She called him and he came through from the living-room and sat down. She stemmed her irritation at his refusal to discuss what they would do with his inheritance and tried to get the children seated and quiet.

Sensing their father's mood, the children picked up their knives and forks and began to eat.

Gwen sighed. She had had enough. 'Peter, we've got to talk. We can't go on like this. Oh, now what?' Whoever was at the door could have chosen a more convenient time to call. Gwen went to answer it.

'Yes?' She tossed her head and the short fair hair fell immaculately back into place.

'Gwendoline Pengelly?' She nodded and bit her lip. She did not know the man but she guessed who he was. 'Detective Inspector Pearce. I'd like to clarify a couple of points. May I come in for a minute?'

'We're just having our meal.'

'I won't keep you long.'

'All right,' she said begrudgingly and flung open the living-room door. She stepped aside and followed him in. The room was gloomy, the light had faded. Gwen impatiently flicked on a table lamp.

'Who is it?' Peter called, getting up from the table.

'It's the police. I've got to answer some more questions. You go and finish your supper or you'll be late for work. You can put mine in the oven. What do you want?' she asked rudely when Peter had returned to the kitchen.

'One of my officers called before, not long after Mrs Pengelly's death. You said at the time that you hadn't seen her for weeks. We now have information that you were seen turning into the drive on the day of your mother-in-law's death and that you were there again afterwards. Perhaps you'd like to clarify this?'

176

Out of the corner of his eye Jack had seen a small movement in the gap of the door. Peter Pengelly was listening outside. So be it, he thought.

Gwen's hand was at her throat, nervously fingering a silver Celtic cross on a chain. She licked her lips. 'I did go there but I couldn't get in. I thought the back door may've been unlocked.'

'And the reason for your visit?'

'I thought I'd clean the place up a bit.'

'So why not ask Martin for a key?'

'I didn't know where to find him.'

Jack took this at face value. If she had intended helping herself to some of Dorothy's bits and pieces she had not succeeded. 'And the first time?'

'It was about tea-time. Peter was at work and the children were next door.'

'And you spoke to Mrs Pengelly?'

'Yes, of course I did. Oh, I see what you mean. She was fine. Really she was.' Gwen bowed her head. 'I wanted to persuade her to give up the house, to go into a home. It's far too big for one old lady, and Peter and I could have done with the money. Anyway, I was worried about her.'

Jack ignored the lie. If her daughter-in-law had been in the least concerned she would have visited far more frequently. 'Did you argue?'

Gwen decided there was nothing for it but to tell the truth. Neither she nor Jack knew that it was Jobber who had seen her and made the call to the station. He had mumbled his name, passed on the information then hung up before he could be questioned further.

'No more than usual. She wasn't an easy woman to get on with.'

'Can you clarify that statement? What were you arguing about?'

'I think I can do that for you.'

'Peter!' Gwen spun around. 'How long have you been listening?'

'Long enough. My wife couldn't stand my mother, Inspector. All she was interested in was getting her hands on her money.

You see, Gwen always thought my mother was beneath her. She wouldn't even take the children up there.'

'Oh, Peter, don't, please.' The redness of her face showed her humiliation.

'You see, my mother once told us we would get what we deserved. I think I understand now what she meant. I think I can even guess what she's done.'

Jack said nothing. He knew what the will contained. What interested him was the conversation which had taken place that Thursday tea-time. 'I need to know exactly what was said,' he continued.

Gwen swallowed hard as tears filled her eyes. 'I shouted at her. I called her a selfish old woman. But she was all right when I left her, I swear it.' She turned back to her husband. 'You must believe me, Peter, you must.'

Peter remained rigid and avoided her eyes but Jack believed her. From what he knew of Dorothy it would not have surprised him if she had given the younger woman a run for her money.

'Have you ever taken Nardil, Mrs Pengelly?'

'Nardil? What's that?' Her astonishment was genuine.

'It doesn't matter. That's all for now. I'll see myself out and leave you to get on with your meal.'

He was about to step outside when his bleeper went. 'I'm sorry, may I use your telephone?' Peter waved a hand to indicate where it stood.

'Sir? Where are you? We couldn't get you on the car radio.'

He heard the words 'Fred Meecham', the name of one of Dorothy's friends, but when he heard Barry and Rose's names too he felt sick. Slamming down the handset he was out of the door and into the car in almost one movement. With tyres screeching he drove to the shop.

Barry was studying the other drinkers and found he was enjoying doing so. No wonder Rose took so much pleasure in watching people. Because he was beginning to unwind he did not, at first, notice how long she had been gone. He looked at his watch.

Something was wrong. He placed his drink on the bar and left the pub.

Outside he looked left and right and wondered which shop she could possibly have gone to. Surely they were all closed now. The street-lights were on, the pavements and road illuminated, but there was no sign of Rose. His stomach knotted in apprehension. How stupid he had been, he ought to have known that there would be more to their outing than a meal. If only she would confide in him more. And why had he not questioned her sudden need for something from a shop when she had had all day in which to buy things? He wiped his forehead and breathed deeply then began walking swiftly in the direction she had taken.

Ahead he saw a couple, hand in hand. It was no use asking them if they had seen a small, auburn-haired woman because they were oblivious to everything but each other. No lights spilled on to the pavement, each shop he came to was in darkness, the closed sign on the door. Until he came to Fred Meecham's premises. There were lights on there and the door was partially open. Unable to see inside because of the display unit behind the window, Barry pushed open the door. It took several seconds for his eyes to adjust. 'Rose,' he cried. 'Oh, Rosie.' With an enormous effort he swallowed the bile which flooded his throat and went inside. 'It's all right, it'll be all right,' he repeated several times as he stepped around the pools of blood and reached for the phone.

Jack's car skidded to a stop as he parked at an angle against the kerb. If Barry Rowe had made the call he knew with a sickening certainty that Rose was hurt or in danger. He could taste the tuna roll he had eaten hours earlier and the coffee he had drunk too quickly. Rose did not want him, Rose only wished to see him as a friend. That was okay, that was good, that was fine by Jack Pearce, but to live without ever seeing her again? For the first time since his father had died he felt as if he might cry.

He was walking through treacle, everything was in slow motion. Ahead of him was an ambulance, its blue light casting

179

its eerie glow over the buildings on either side of the road as it revolved silently. The paramedics were loading a stretcher into the back of the vehicle, the patient invisible from where he was. His knees sagged.

Barry Rowe emerged from the shop doorway pushing up his glasses in that irritating manner. Then, behind him, deathly white and with bloodstains on the front of her dress but apparently unscathed, came Rose. Jack's fear and anguish instantly turned to fury. He ran towards her.

'You stupid bitch, what the hell do you think you're playing at?' He towered over her, his anger coming from relief in the way a mother's does when a child runs into the road.

Rose took a deep breath and controlled the trembling which threatened to start at any second. 'Inspector Pearce, I was merely doing your job for you. Excuse me, Barry's going to take me home. You can send someone else over to ask your questions.' With as much dignity as she could manage, Rose took Barry's arm and they walked unsteadily back to where he had left the car, neither caring that she was bloodstained.

Her own anger at Jack's treatment of her had prevented her from passing out. As it drained away she clung more tightly to Barry's arm. He helped her into the car and got the key into the ignition on the third attempt. He was shaken himself and thankful that he had had no more than half a pint of beer. And however small a gesture, driving Rose home was at least something he could do for her. Putting the awful scene to the back of his mind he realised he was pleased at the way in which she had spoken to Jack. He did not allow himself to hope that the relationship was over, that would be too much to ask.

Neither of them spoke until they reached the cottage. Staggering, Rose made it inside. 'Please, go, Barry,' she said. 'I'll be all right.' But before he could answer she had fled upstairs and was violently sick.

At her insistence Barry had left. Rose lay in bed, shivering despite the two hot water bottles she had taken up with her. The fear she had felt when Fred grabbed the knife resurrected itself when she thought how close to death she had been. He had screamed at her, cursing her and Dorothy and saying other things which she did not understand. His bereavement, she thought, had sent him mad.

Jack spoke briefly to the two officers who had arrived at the scene before him. Only after Barry and Rose had gone did he step into the shop. Barry, it seemed, had had the sense after he'd rung the emergency services to switch off the shop lights and turn the sign on the door to closed whilst Rose had remained with Fred, trying to stem the bleeding. The ambulance crew had said they believed he'd survive. Jack would have to wait to find out what had preceded their arrival. As Barry had done, he stepped around the pools of blood. From the floor he picked up the knife which Fred used to slice the joints of meat which he kept in the refrigerated counter if customers wanted them thicker than the slicing machine could provide. At some point someone would have to go and see Barry and Rose but he doubted they would be up to answering questions that day and he knew he could not face her himself so soon.

The first thing Rose did upon waking was to ring Laura. She was still shaking and needed to talk to someone before the police arrived, which she knew they would.

'I'll be right over,' Laura said.

Rose replaced the receiver, knowing that what she had said must have come across as gibberish. She was still standing by the phone when she heard the tap on the kitchen door and Laura was there holding out her arms. 'What on earth have you got yourself into this time, girl?'

As Laura made tea Rose explained all that had happened, from the time Jack had told her it was suicide up to his abysmal treatment of her when he had turned up at the shop. She looked up: a figure had passed the kitchen window and Jack Pearce stood in the doorway. Laura let him in. 'I'm off now, Rose. Trevor's sailing this afternoon.'

'I'm sorry. I forgot.'

'Hey. It doesn't matter. What're friends for.' As she turned

181

slowly, Laura's eyes travelled the length of Jack's body. 'You're a bastard,' she said and closed the door quietly behind her.

'She's right,' Rose added in a voice so low he hardly heard her. 'What do you want?'

'Several things, Rose, but firstly and foremost to apologise. You see, I saw the ambulance, I thought it was you, I thought something had happened to you.' He stood just inside the door with his hands in his pockets. Rose was still pale and her eyes were dull. 'I didn't mean to shout. I was scared, scared I'd lost you completely.'

'If you're here to take a statement you'd better sit down.' She refused to look at him, to be influenced by what she knew she would see in his face.

'I am. I have another officer waiting in the car, I just wanted you to know how I felt first.'

Rose closed her eyes and nodded. The sooner it was over with the better. Jack went outside and signalled for someone to join him. It was a female.

When they were all seated Rose spoke of her visit to Audrey Heath in Plymouth and about how Marigold's disappearance had coincided with the stabbing of a man. She went on to say that Marigold had moved to Cornwall and that, for reasons of her own, Dorothy had wanted her to find the map of Plymouth which she had marked with a cross.

'He did it, you see. Fred Meecham killed that man and Dorothy somehow found out about it. I went to the shop and showed him the map. He thought Dorothy had confided in me – she hadn't, but he wouldn't believe me. He went berserk, I didn't really know what he was shouting but, but . . .' She stopped, inhaling deeply. 'He picked up the knife and I thought he was going to kill me.' Rose squeezed her forehead between her thumb and forefinger. She felt exhausted. 'I was trying to get out of the shop when it seemed he'd changed his mind, that it wasn't me he meant to harm any more, it was himself. It was so quick I couldn't stop him. He slashed both wrists. It was horrible. He dropped the knife and staggered around and fell to the floor. I grabbed some tea towels from one of the shelves and wrapped them round his wrists. I should've acted faster but the knife was there beside him and I thought he might pick it up again and go for me. Then Barry was there, he turned off the lights and shut the door to stop any customers coming in. The knife . . . the meat knife – Oh, God, it had ham fat on it and blood. I . . .'

'It's all right, Rose. It's all right.' Jack wondered how much of it was his fault. He had told Fred Meecham that it was Rose who had given him his name.

'Rose, can I use the phone?'

'Yes.'

Jack was away for several minutes and she was unable to hear what he said. 'Is there someone who can stay with you? Barry or Laura?'

'No. I'm all right. I'd prefer to be alone.'

'If you're sure. We've got to go now, Rose.' He reached out as if he was about to touch her but either the presence of the female detective or Rose's change of heart stopped him. His own heart was behaving peculiarly. Wrapped in an oversized robe Rose looked very young and very vulnerable and he was partly to blame for the latter because he had helped to get her into the situation.

Rose watched them leave but then remained at the kitchen table, unable to drag herself upstairs to dress.

13

The morning passed and the shock was beginning to wear off. Gratefully Rose remembered that Stella Jackson's dinner party was that evening. She had accepted the invitation with alacrity, delighted to hear that other artists would be present. She wondered if Nick Pascoe would be one of them but although she had rung him back and arranged to meet him for a drink on Tuesday, he hadn't mentioned the Jacksons. It didn't matter, whether he was there or not it was bound to be an interesting evening: her social life was finally starting to expand.

Rose decided to find out how Fred Meecham was faring but

she was not sure if the hospital would give her information as she was neither a relative nor a friend.

As she showered in preparation for the party she began to see how much she had to look forward to although she would also like to know the whole story behind Dorothy's death. At least she had proved to Jack Pearce that she had not taken her own life.

Rose decided to travel to St Ives by the branch line train. It was too dark to appreciate the view from the rails which ran high up along the coastline and overlooked miles and miles of powdery sand running from Hayle and Carbis Bay to St Ives.

The Jacksons lived above their studio and gallery and immediately she entered their apartments she was back in the sixties. The floors were uncarpeted, the boards sanded and polished. Sofas lined the walls, deep and comfortable and half hidden by hand-made cushions and woven blankets. Rose saw immediately that the furnishings were not those of her own youth, items purchased or borrowed because of lack of finances. Stella and Daniel had deliberately created this atmosphere but it had not come cheaply. A table held an array of bottles and glasses and from the kitchen came the unmistakable smell of chilli. In an A-line calf-length denim skirt, a cream frilled shirt and a waistcoat Rose blended in with the other guests as if she had known them all her life.

Stella put an arm across her shoulders and led her around the room, stopping at the table to hand her a drink. 'We're so pleased you could come,' she said, smiling. Her teeth were uneven and one pupil did not move as quickly as the other but beneath her straight black hair, cut just below her ears, her quirky face portrayed a lazy sexuality.

Rose had had time to study the other guests and felt only a slight disappointment that Nick Pascoe was not one of them.

When one of Stone's taxis came to pick her up Rose felt exhilarated. The conversation had ranged from art to politics, from literature to the theatre, and she knew that soon she would host such an evening of her own.

In the morning she sang as the kettle boiled, not very tunefully nor very loudly, but she was out of practice lately. It did not matter that a gale force wind was rattling the windows and bringing down more leaves. To Rose they looked beautiful as they skittered across the grass, their reds and golds colours she would capture in oils.

In the sitting-room she stood in the window, steam from her coffee misting the glass, and watched the waves battering the reinforced wall of the Promenade as they had done since it was built and would continue to do as long as it stood.

So many new and exciting people had entered her life that it was difficult to feel sorry for Fred. But it still hurt to think of Dorothy. There was plenty of time until she was due to collect Martin and take him over to Truro.

'Oh, no.' She backed away from the window but it was too late. Jack had seen her and waved as he strode up the path. She pulled her dressing-gown more tightly around her and went out to the kitchen.

'Don't be angry,' were his words of greeting. 'Knowing your curiosity I thought you'd want to hear the outcome.'

'Come in. Coffee?'

'Please.'

Rose made instant and handed him a mug, omitting to ask him to sit down.

'Meecham's going to pull through – it wasn't as bad as it looked.'

Rose nodded, biting her lip, guessing that Fred would have wished it otherwise. 'I think all he wanted was someone to love him, someone of his own.' She was sure he had begun life as a decent man but circumstances and insecurity had changed him. Looking up she saw what was going through Jack's mind. She ought not to have mentioned love.

'Yes. He lost his first wife, then his son. We now know he paid regular visits to Plymouth to visit prostitutes, one in particular. Marigold Heath. It was the old story. He fell for her in a big way and wanted to take her away from it all, to save her, if you like. The irony is that, in a way, he did, despite the fact that he, a church-going man, was frequenting such a woman.' Jack took a

185

few sips of his coffee. 'You should've told us about the map, Rose, and you were extremely foolish not to mention those threatening calls.'

She remained silent although she had noticed the use of the plural pronoun which depersonalised the conversation. 'What'll happen to him?'

'Psychiatric reports. All that.'

'He won't last, you know.'

'He may not go to prison.'

'I didn't mean that. I don't think he wants to live, not now. He spent all those years with Marigold, firstly protecting her from that pimp of hers, killing him for her sake, then protecting her from gossip. That's why they didn't marry, isn't it? Because he, or they, thought that it would draw attention to themselves and that someone might make the connection. A sister's always a safe bet.'

'You're probably right. He's confessed, Rose, to the murder of Harvey, that's the man in Plymouth and to murdering Dorothy. You understand that this mustn't go any further, there's his trial to come yet and – '

'You don't need to tell me, Jack.'

'No. I'm sorry. It's . . . well, it's the new circumstances, I'm not sure how to deal with you.'

Rose turned away to hide a smile. Deal with her? Was she that awkward?

'Marigold was involved too. She'd told him how Harvey treated her, he was a sadist, and there was no way he was going to let her walk off into the sunset. They set it up together. Heath led Meecham to him. It was as easy as that. Then he provided her with an alibi. Heath made sure she was seen with Harvey earlier in the evening, as she would have expected to have been, and he was fine when she left him. Meecham wasn't known in Plymouth and there was no reason why he should have come under suspicion. He'd booked a hotel room, a double, and made a show of taking her up there but they slipped out later. When he got back to Cornwall the next day he put it around that his sister was coming to live with him.'

'Dorothy knew all this, is that why he killed her?'

186

'Yes, Dorothy knew, or guessed. She'd been unpacking some china with a view to selling it. It was wrapped in old newspaper. She happened to come across a report and put two and two together.'

Rose frowned. It was unlike Dorothy not to have done anything. Then she remembered that the unpacking would have been recent and she had done something, she had put the map in an envelope for Rose to find, trusting her not to do anything until Marigold had been buried. Maybe Dorothy suspected how Fred would react if he was confronted, maybe she was trusting him, too, to do the right thing.

'But why was Dorothy selling her things?'

'This is strictly between you and me. She was setting up a trust fund for Martin. She wanted Hinkston to provide prints or replicas of everything she sold him in case Peter and Gwen noticed the missing items and made life difficult. She was terrified they'd get a doctor in to say she was unfit to live on her own. We know that the daughter-in-law went up there and an argument took place, but I suspect Gwen Pengelly got her money's worth from your friend.'

'I'd like to think so.'

'Anyway, Meecham went up there as well, a couple of nights before her death. It was late in the evening. He was intending to make one last attempt at squeezing money out of Dorothy and to soften her up had taken along a bottle of decent whisky. He knew it wasn't something she normally drank and he imagined, quite correctly, that a few glasses would do the trick. But again she refused his request, as he'd expected she would, but then she made the fatal mistake of telling him what she knew, what she had read in that old report in the *Western Morning News*. He denied it and left, forgetting to take the whisky with him. He knew he had to act quickly or Dorothy might go to the police. We now know that whilst he was in Truro and had begun seeing Marigold he'd suffered from severe depression, caused by guilt, the psychiatrist believes, because he was frequenting prostitutes, and also because he knew he was going to kill Harvey, that at some point he would have to. Meanwhile he moved to Hayle and life started to improve so he didn't get around to taking the

Nardil that was prescribed for him. Like Dorothy, Meecham didn't sign on with a doctor here, that's why we couldn't trace where the drug came from.'

'Poor Dorothy, first Gwen has a go at her, then Fred kills her. But how did he do it?'

'Ground up the pills to powder and went out there on the pretence that he wanted to apologise. He said they might as well have some of the whisky. It affected Dorothy very quickly and he topped up her glass, adding more of the Nardil. He watched her die.'

'Oh, Jack!'

'On his previous visit he had called her a hypocrite, saying she didn't spend any money and she begrudged it to a dying woman. That's when Dorothy had explained that he was the bigger hypocrite with his church-going ways when she knew what he had done. She was probably already exhausted on that final visit after having dealt with Gwen earlier.'

'Thank you for telling me.'

'That's okay.'

She stood. 'I have to get ready to go out. Goodbye, Jack,' she said quietly but with a certain finality.

Jack didn't reply. He turned to leave, knowing that what he had had with Rose would never be again.

The wind howled, rocking the car. Through the windscreen his vision was blurred for several seconds but it wasn't raining. He sighed. Yes, they would meet from time to time but Rose Trevelyan had become a different person.

At eleven she picked Martin up at the gate of Jobber's farm. He was dressed in his best, his hair slicked down with water. Making general conversation they drove into the city and parked the car. Martin was still pale and his hands shook but the blankness had gone from his eyes. Being with Jobber was the best thing that could have happened to him.

Together they entered the old building which was smartly decorated inside, and were asked to take a seat. Peter and Gwen arrived seconds after them. The words of their greetings were cordial but Rose sensed an underlying hostility on Gwen's part.

She had promised to stay and give Martin a lift back as the solicitor had said he would not detain them long.

'Ah, good morning.' Henry Peachy was tall and thin with deep lines etched in his face. He wore a suit which was by no means new and his shoulders were stooped but what struck Rose was his warm smile and something about his eyes which suggested that he was content with his lot and that there was little which could disturb his equanimity. Shaking hands with them individually he glanced inquisitively at Rose.

'I gave Martin a lift,' she explained. 'I'm Mrs Trevelyan, I was a friend of Dorothy's. Can I wait here or shall I come back later?'

'Mrs Rose Trevelyan?'

'Yes.'

'In that case, my dear, you might as well join us. This involves you too.'

Rose felt Gwen's eyes on the back of her head and was glad she could not see the expression in them. They followed Mr Peachy to a room at the end of the corridor. It was not an office, it housed only a large walnut table and eight chairs.

'I thought we'd be more comfortable here.' Henry Peachy placed some papers on the table and invited them to sit down. 'I knew Mrs Pengelly for many years,' he began. 'I suppose you could say that she was more than a client. I can't tell you how sorry I was not to be able to attend her funeral.

'Now, before we get down to business I've asked for some coffee to be sent in.'

There was a strained silence while they waited for it although the solicitor seemed not to notice as he continued to study what was in front of him. When it arrived he indicated that they should all help themselves.

'I think it'll be easier if I read out Mrs Pengelly's instructions first, then if there are any queries I'll be happy to answer them for you.' Methodically he went through the heading of the will. Then, '"To Peter James Pengelly I leave the property known as Venn's Farm."'

Rose's head was tilted slightly as she tried to gauge Gwen's reactions without appearing to. She seemed to be smirking but hid it by raising a hand to her mouth then pushing back her fair hair. Rose, having been through something similar, began to see that Gwen had misunderstood the statement.

'"To Joseph Robert Hicks I leave one thousand pounds and the Queen Victoria Jubilee mug of which he is so fond. To my friend, Rose Trevelyan, I leave one thousand pounds and a Beryl Cook original of her choice of three."'

But Rose wasn't listening. She was delighted at Jobber's bequest although it had taken her a couple of seconds to realise who Joseph Robert was. But there had been no mention of Martin. Had Jack been wrong? Something registered. She looked up, her mouth open. Henry Feachy was smiling at her, he repeated what he had just read out.

'*And* a Beryl Cook? Oh, how wonderful.' She grinned around the room. Only Martin grinned back. He seemed unconcerned or unaware of the way things were going.

Mr Peachy coughed and continued. '"The residue of my estate I leave to Martin John Pengelly."'

Another silence followed until Gwen had worked out what this meant. 'No, that can't be right.'

'It is perfectly correct, Mrs Pengelly. Your mother-in-law's wishes are quite clearly stated. You may see for yourself if you choose.'

'But what's he going to do with it all?'

'That is for Mr Pengelly to decide. Of course, none of this takes place with immediate effect. Probate has to be proved. Now, is there anything you'd like to ask me?'

Rose and Martin shook their heads, Peter stared down at his hands. 'Mother's done the right thing,' he said.

Gwen jerked around in her chair. 'Don't be ridiculous. Can't we challenge this? She can't have been in her right mind when she made this will. What about us? We've got the children to think of.'

Henry Peachy hid his indignation well. 'My client was of perfectly sound mind when she came to me with her instructions and we have discussed the matter again recently regarding a trust fund when she provided me with a list of all her valuables and their estimated worth. We also have a record of her savings.

As executors my firm has been instructed to arrange for the sale of any goods Mrs Pengelly has not been able to dispose of, the proceeds of which are to be placed in the said trust fund for Martin.'

There seemed to be nothing more to say. Gwen and Peter left first, followed by Martin and then Rose who had stopped to thank Mr Peachy. At the door she took Martin's arm. 'Great, isn't it? You'll never have to worry now.' But Martin was too bemused to reply.

Back at the farm she went in with him to tell Jobber the good news. Tears filled his eyes. 'I always had my tea in that mug, she never cared that it was worth a bit. Still, the boy's taken care of, that's what matters.' They had a celebratory drink then Rose drove home planning where to hang the painting and what sort of car she would exchange the Mini for.

Peter and Gwen did not speak on the drive back to Hayle. When they reached the house Peter remained in the car. 'I'm going for a drive. Alone,' he said. At some point since his mother's death he had come to see how much Gwen had influenced him where Dorothy was concerned. 'You're sick, do you know that? Martin deserves it, he deserves the whole bloody lot if you ask me.'

'I'm sorry, Peter. Look, at least we'll be able to move.'

'Will we?' He crunched the gears, prior to pulling away from the kerb. 'You're forgetting that the house was left to me. It's my decision whether we stay here or move to Venn's Farm. When I've made up my mind you can decide what you're going to do.'

With a sinking feeling Gwen watched him drive away. She knew what his decision would be and that she would have to spend the rest of her life in that awful place without enough money to restore it for years.

Rose stopped at the Co-op in Newlyn and bought a bottle of champagne. It was far too early in the day to be drinking but she didn't care. Once home, she placed it in the freezer section of the fridge to chill quickly. A new car and the painting, a new life and a date with Nick Pascoe tomorrow – and the mystery of Dorothy's death had been solved. So had another, one which had taken place years ago, Harvey's, and she, Rose, had helped to solve it. 'I deserve it,' she said as she popped the cork and watched the pale gold liquid effervesce in her glass.

On Monday night Nick Pascoe lay in bed, his hands clasped behind his head. He was smiling. Tomorrow he was seeing Rose Trevelyan. He did not know which excited him more, the woman herself or her painting.

BURIED IN CORNWALL

'You've made a real fool of yourself this time.'

Rose Trevelyan closed her eyes and took a deep breath. No need to ask who was calling, she knew that voice well enough. Anger and humiliation fought for supremacy.

'Especially now. God, you must've read enough articles in the *Western Morning News* about time-wasters. You know, people who ring triple nine when they break a nail or can't find their glasses. People like you, Rose.'

'End of lecture?' she asked sweetly, trying to show how little she cared for his opinion of her.

'Why on earth did you do it? Do you know how much that whole exercise cost?'

No, she thought, but you're about to tell me. He did, and it was an awful lot of money. How many emotions could she cope with at once? Guilt had now joined in the struggle with humiliation and anger. Never explain, never apologise, someone had once said. Rose had no intention of doing the latter but she still felt an unreasonable need to do the former, to justify herself to the man who had once promised her so much and whom she had wrongly blamed for not living up to her expectations. It was she who had not been ready to make a commitment. Rose knew what he was thinking, that in this, as in their personal life, she would refuse to take the blame. 'I heard something, I really did.'

'Too much red wine, I expect.' And with that the line went dead.

Anger won. It was more than anger, it was rage. Red-faced, she paced the room, chewing at a fingernail. 'Sod you, Jack Pearce,' she said aloud, feeling the prickling of tears behind her eyelids.

With a shake of her head, she went to the kitchen and, to spite Jack, opened a bottle of Médoc. She took the glass into the sitting-room and sipped the wine as she surveyed what had become her world from the window. Warmth from the fire she had lit in the grate complemented that of the small radiator beneath the curved window which overlooked Mount's Bay. Darkness was already descending, coming earlier each day as Christmas drew nearer. St Michael's Mount in the distance was no more than a sinister jagged rock outlined blackly against the striated colours of the sky. The horizon was tinged a whitish yellow as the sun sank further into the west. The clouds were purple, a shade deeper than that of the heather which bloomed on the cliffs that ran down to the sea. The last fingers of light edged them in brilliant orange.

A few cars, unseen below Rose's steeply sloping garden, passed from Mousehole down into Newlyn, but she could see the tops of those coming up the hill. One slowed, and the arc of its headlights briefly illuminated the front of the house as it pulled into the drive. She swore aloud in the language of the fishermen with whom she often drank. The view which, day or night, winter or summer, was always able to restore her equanimity had done its work. The appearance of Jack Pearce, Inspector Jack Pearce, had destroyed it again. She heard a rapping on the kitchen door. It was at the side of the house and opened on to the garden. She could, of course, refuse to answer it even though the door was unlocked and the kitchen light was on. Jack knew that she was in and that the door was rarely locked but he also knew better than to walk in uninvited. It would be cowardly to ignore him. Her affair with Jack was over, although he found it hard to accept, but that was no reason to behave in anything other than an adult manner. She had nothing to fear from him. Besides, in a way she owed him something. It was Jack who had shown her that she was able to feel again. Five years after David had died he had come into her life and proved that there could be someone else. The months of David's lingering death were not a period of her life she would ever forget but she had learned to accept the finality and had put it behind her as belonging only to her memory. Initially she had thought that to get involved with another man would be to diminish what she and David had shared, which was over twenty years of happiness. Later she had learned that no one or nothing could take that away from either of them. In retrospect it seemed calculating to admit that Jack had served his purpose. Metaphorically he had brought her

7

back to life and made her strong enough to live it alone. Jack had wanted permanency, Rose only wanted to feel alive again. There was no question that she had enjoyed his company: the laughter and the arguments, the spark which had existed between them and the nights they had spent together. But that, too, was in the past.

She let him knock a second time before crossing the narrow flagstoned hallway and going to open the kitchen door. Through the glass she saw Jack's large, familiar figure as he stood rubbing his hands together. She let him in. With him came cold air so she quickly shut the door. That indefinable feeling, that *frisson* which had existed between them, had not completely disappeared, Rose realised as his bulk filled the room and she looked up, allowing herself a brief glimpse of his dark, handsome Cornish face.

Warmth flooded her neck and cheeks when his own eyes dropped pointedly to the glass she still held in her hand. It was so unfair. Most evenings when she had finished work she opened some wine. Why did Jack always have to catch her in the act and make it seem like a sin? 'Why are you here?'

'I wanted to make sure you were all right.' In a manner which suggested he was more than at home in her kitchen he folded his arms and leaned back against the cooker. Rose wished it was on. Full on.

She snorted and flung back her thick, shoulder-length hair with her free hand. In the evenings she untied it and brushed it loose over her shoulders. There were a few strands of grey amongst the auburn waves but she chose to ignore them, as she did the fine lines around her eyes. She was not vain and she had no idea how attractive she was as she neared her fifties, but she was comfortable with herself, physically and mentally, and it showed in her character. In jeans and low-heeled shoes she only reached Jack's shoulder. She had bought her shirt in Waghorn Stores in Newlyn Strand. It was a shop where anything could be purchased, from hardware to hard-wearing clothing, from crockery to gardening tools, from light bulbs to pet food, and if what you wanted wasn't on display they were sure to have it upstairs. The shirt was thick and heavy, checked in blue and black, and although the smallest size it was meant for a man and therefore swamped Rose's petite figure. She was out in all weathers for most of the year and her fashion sense was non-existent during the daytime. Over the shirt she wore a baggy sweater, streaked with paint and fraying at the hem, beneath which the tails of the shirt could be seen. To Jack Pearce she always looked vulnerable and desirable but, to his cost, he had learned she was only the latter. She lifted her arms as if to display herself, being careful not to spill her drink. 'Well, as you can see, I'm fine. Why shouldn't I be?' She did not want to hear the answer.

'Because it was so unlike you, so completely out of character for you to panic and to act the way you did, if you don't mind me saying so.'

'But I do mind, Jack.' She smiled sardonically and sipped the wine, making a point of not offering him a drink. 'Are you here officially? Am I to be charged with anything?'

'Of course not. Mistakes happen. I just thought...'

Rose was already moving. She had placed her glass on the table and opened the side door. 'Goodnight, Jack. Thank you for calling.' His mouth dropped open in surprise. 'I said goodnight. Now go. I'll catch pneumonia standing here in this draught.'

With an angry shrug he thrust his hands into the pockets of his reefer jacket and stomped out of the house. Rose locked the door with a decisive twist of the key but her satisfaction didn't last. She slumped into a kitchen chair and played with the stem of the wineglass, which was cold between her fingers. It would have been the perfect opportunity to explain. Once his anger had abated Jack would have listened, she was sure of that. He had always believed and trusted her in the past. It was too late now, and she had no intention of telephoning him. An awful end to an awful day, she thought.

It had been one of those balmy days with which the area was often blessed in winter. Late October and most of November had been wet, heavy rain had been accompanied by gale force winds, then, just when it should have been getting colder, the temperature started to rise. Indian summer days were followed by spectacular sunsets and chilly evenings. It was difficult to believe Christmas was so close...

Thinking back over the events of that day led to nostalgic memories of her youth. Having left art college, Rose had arrived

9

in Penzance at the age of twenty-one with no idea of what to expect. Her intention was to remain for six months whilst she studied the artists of the Newlyn School and did some painting herself. But fate had other things in store and she had never gone home. Lodgings had been organised before her arrival and she had soon settled down to work but, unable to sell many of the oils she completed, she had turned to watercolours. A chance meeting with Barry Rowe, the owner of a shop which sold greetings cards and postcards amongst other things, had altered the direction of her career. Needing a map, she had gone into the shop. Barry, noticing her sketchpad, politely asked if she was an artist. Rose had shown him some of her watercolours and before she knew it he had employed her on an almost full-time basis, using her designs on his notelets and cards. He had a printing works in Camborne where they were produced. Later Rose had taken up photography and sold much of her work to postcard manufacturers as well as taking portrait pictures. The oils, which she had so loved painting, had long gone by the wayside. Until recently, that is. Her new friends, met at a party thrown by Mike and Barbara Phillips, a couple she had known for many years, had given her so much encouragement that she was now relatively successful in marketing and selling her work. A single painting had done it, the one she had started immediately after David's death, one she could not recall finishing. Recovering it from its hiding place because she had an idea it might make a suitable gift for Mike's fiftieth birthday, she had been startled by how good it was. Anger and grief and experience had lent her work the maturity it had previously lacked and had added something which even she was unable to define. Mike and his guests had been genuinely impressed with her talent and things had continued from there.

Today she had gone back to capture the barren ruggedness of the countryside rather than the dramatic coastline or the prettiness of the villages which nestled in the coves. The work depicted the ruins of an old engine house at a disused mine. With the trees and the undergrowth still in autumnal colouring, it was the perfect place to test her ability in her new medium. Sitting there in the early afternoon, she had heard a scream: the high-pitched scream of a woman.

She rested her head in her hands. No, she had not imagined it. Superstitious and able to sense things almost as well as the Cornish could, she knew the difference between reality and fancy. Nor was it some trick of acoustics, the countryside was well known to her. She knew how many areas of open country could be dangerous with hidden and uncovered mine shafts which might suddenly subside. Still, she saw how it must appear and was annoyed to think that those who had answered her summons, made from the mobile phone she now carried with her, probably thought her an hysterical female. An ambulance and the cliff rescue team had turned up. At least they hadn't sent a helicopter from Culdrose as well. There was nothing she could do now but to put it from her mind and live with the humiliation: despite a thorough search no one had been found.

She glanced at the cooker clock. It was time to get changed. Nick Pascoe was taking her to a classical concert at the Methodist church in Chapel Street, and afterwards they were going for something to eat. This was to be their third meeting. So far they had done no more than to share a few drinks, once in Newlyn, and once in St Ives where Nick lived and worked.

Rose knew of his reputation as an artist both locally and nationally yet she had hardly noticed him at Barbara and Mike's party where they were introduced. This, she realised, was due to the excitement she had felt at the more than favourable reception of her painting which she had wrapped and presented to Mike. It showed a wild, storm-ridden coastline which reflected the state of her mind at the time she had worked on it. Only when he telephoned to invite her out did Nick's face come clearly to mind. It was a nice face, lined and rugged and weatherbeaten. His hair, completely grey, was the colour of her filing cabinet and he wore it brushed back from the forehead and long over the collar. His green eyes were peculiarly speckled and changed with the light. At the party he had worn jeans, a shirt and a denim jacket and, having seen him twice since, Rose wondered if he possessed any other clothes. Only the shirt had been different. On the first occasion it was black, worn over a black T-shirt; the second time it had been similar to the one she was now wearing herself. Mounting the stairs, she smiled as she imagined what her mother would have to say about him. 'Honestly, Rose, he might have put on a jacket and tie.' Rose's parents were conventional and were still bewildered by their artistic only child who had adopted the lifestyle and dress of her own kind.

Rose showered and washed her hair. Bending her head she flung the wet tresses forward over her face to give them more body as the drier buzzed noisily. From the wardrobe she took a black dirndl skirt with an embroidered hem and a silky green shirt. Over this she wore a black jacket. Shoes were a problem so she settled for her one good pair of boots in tan leather. At least they matched her handbag.

They had arranged to meet in the Admiral Benbow, a pub and restaurant in Chapel Street in Penzance. The drinking was done upstairs, at the long bar or in the room which overlooked the sea; the restaurant was on ground level, behind a door with a low lintel. The building dated back to the days of smugglers and a tunnel was supposed to run from the building to the sea. There were ancient beams and nautical artefacts and unmatching furniture made from heavy wood.

Rose had no intention of driving as she had already had a glass of wine and there would be more drinks with Nick, but thanks to Jack Pearce it was now too late to walk. She glanced at her watch. If she hurried she could catch the next bus; failing that it would mean a taxi. She was surprised to feel anxious that she might be late.

Just as Rose reached the nearest stop the lights of the bus appeared over the brow of the hill. She shivered, glad she had not had to wait. I'm soft now, she thought, recalling the weeks of snow and ice she had regularly endured as a child. The slightest drop in temperature and the inhabitants of West Penwith complained that it was freezing. However, she admitted, handing the driver the exact money, by local standards it was cold. She sat at the back of the small single-decker and unbunched her winter coat from beneath her. She did not want to crease it. It was a recent acquisition, pure wool in a rusty colour which, with her hair resting across her shoulders and the tan boots below, made her as autumnal in appearance as the countryside. Rose rarely bought new clothes. When she did, she looked after them excessively well for about three months then they received the same treatment as older items: they were thrown over the backs of chairs, dropped on to the bed or even left to slide off their hangers in the walk-in cupboard which served as a wardrobe.

She shifted again, trying to keep the material smooth, and caught the eye of a rheumy old man with a stick. She smiled but he turned away, clearing his throat and hawking into a tissue. Rose averted her eyes.

The bus lumbered down the hill and towards Penzance. Along the Promenade was a continuous string of plain lights which were now a permanent fixture. They went well with the new Victorian-type lamp-posts. The festive lights were already strung in Penzance and would be shining brightly. There were only two weeks until Christmas and she had made no plans. Other years, since David's death, her parents had arrived and taken over. Last year she had spent in the company of Jack Pearce. They had enjoyed a quiet day by themselves. Rose had cooked a joint and Jack had provided champagne, wine and whisky. In the evening Laura and Trevor had joined them and they had played cards and got merrily tipsy. There would be no Jack this year and she had persuaded her parents they were not to cancel their own plans.

Despite the distance between them, they kept in touch regularly by letter and telephone and knew their daughter well enough to understand that the past was behind her and that even if she was alone her memories could no longer make her sad. Laura Penfold, her best friend, had invited her for lunch but Rose would not dream of imposing when Laura's own family were coming to stay. 'They're arriving on Christmas Eve and leaving on the 27th,' Laura had said. 'Just right. Not long enough to try my patience.' Rose knew the Christmas Day procedure in the Penfold household: Laura would do all the preparations in advance but it was Trevor and their daughters-in-law who cooked the meal, allowing Laura to go to the pub with her three sons. They had all moved away, none having followed their father into fishing. Perhaps it's just as well with the way things are going, Rose thought, as the bus pulled in opposite the post office. She alighted and thanked the driver then crossed the road, stopping at the top of the street to glance in the window of Dorothy Perkins. Across the road a shaven-headed model stood in the window of a boutique. Posed with its legs wide apart, knees bent inwards and an aggressive grimace on its face, it caught Rose's attention. She stood back and studied it, wondering why ugliness could sometimes be appealing as well as eye-catching.

A vicious wind caught the hem of her coat and lifted her hair as she rounded the corner and made her way down Chapel Street to the Admiral Benbow. Upstairs in the bar Nick Pascoe was half seated on a tall stool, one foot on the ledge below the counter. A pint of beer stood in front of him. He rose as she approached, swept back his hair with his long, narrow fingers and leaned over to kiss her cheek. Apart from shaking hands at Mike's birthday party it was the first tactile gesture on either side yet it felt perfectly natural. 'Wine?' he asked.

'Please. You're sure this starts at seven forty-five? There're people going in already.'

'Positive. Don't panic. I didn't think to book anywhere to eat, I'd forgotten about the Christmas party crowds.'

'Oh, we'll get in somewhere. It's Wednesday, it shouldn't be a problem.'

They sipped in silence for a few minutes. Nick made a roll-up and lit it, blowing smoke from the corner of his mouth. 'Rose, is something bothering you?'

'No!' She was astonished. It was astute of him to realise anything was wrong, but she had been trying to forget her earlier foolishness. There was no time to tell him now, maybe later, after the music had worked its magic. She checked the time. 'Ten minutes. Shall we walk over?'

Nick downed the last two inches of beer. He wore jeans again, his best pair, Rose assumed, as they weren't threadbare nor were they covered in paint splashes. Over them was a fisherman's jersey with the collar of a pale blue shirt poking over the top. He wore no jacket so probably had a T-shirt underneath as well. Rose blinked in surprise. She had been undressing him mentally.

Nick took her arm as they mounted the steps to the broad-fronted church, whose interior was more ornate than its outward appearance suggested. It was filled with the rustlings of programme sheets and muted conversation. Discreet coughing continued until the orchestra filed down the far aisle. The musicians

14

took their places in front of the altar and began to tune their instruments.

Only once did Rose look at Nick. He had his eyes half closed as a Mozart piano concerto washed over them. This was followed by a movement from Beethoven's Second Symphony and then a soprano whose pure notes filled the church and made Rose shiver. The fourth piece was by a composer of whom Rose had not heard. To her ears the music sounded discordant and she wasn't sorry when the interval came. They left the church as Nick wanted a cigarette, then, giggling like teenagers, they dived over the road to the Turk's Head where they just managed to get a drink before it was time to return.

'Enjoy it?' Nick asked when the concert was over.

'It was lovely. I should make the effort more often. There're so many things going on if you bother to look. I usually get to see one of the male voice choirs every month or so, though.'

'Ah, you can't beat hearing Cornishmen sing. Can you sing, Rose?'

'Not a note.'

They were heading up the hill along with many of the audience who would be making for one of the car-parks. 'Where're we going?'

Rose shrugged. 'Chinese as we're up here now?'

They decided upon the nearer of the two almost adjacent restaurants, both situated on the first floor above other premises. It was surprisingly busy but they were given a window seat. 'So, let's hear it. What has upset my painter in oils?' Nick asked, having recalled his earlier impression of Rose's strange mood.

Unsure of the significance of the possessive pronoun – was he making fun of her because she was only just finding her feet whereas he had been established for years, or was it a sign of affection? – she felt awkward and almost kept her counsel. But knowing how the grapevine worked he would hear within a short time anyway. Feeling the heat in her face, Rose said, 'I did something incredibly stupid. I was so... Ah, well. I must've been wrong.'

Nick was sitting back in his chair with his arms folded. He raised a hand and rested his index finger against his lips. 'And from that short garbled paragraph, the penultimate sentence, if you don't mind me pointing out, lacking a complete predicate, I'm supposed to deduce exactly what piece of stupidity you have been engaged in.'

Rose smiled. He *was* making fun of her now. 'All right, I'll explain. I was out painting. I heard a scream. It came from near an old mine shaft. I went to investigate. I heard a second scream. I ran back to the car and rang the police from my mobile phone. The emergency services turned up in force.' She shrugged. 'They didn't find anyone.'

'Most comprehensible, and not a sub-clause anywhere.'

'Pedant.' Rose was playing with her chop-sticks as the waiter arrived with the wine Nick had ordered. She opened the menu and studied it, choosing her main dish immediately because she knew that if she hesitated she would keep changing her mind.

'Seriously, though, if you did hear a scream you did the right thing. I didn't know you had a mobile phone.' He raised an eyebrow but Rose did not take the hint and give him the number. Nick placed a hand over hers but only to stop her fiddling. He removed it as soon as he saw the closed expression on her face.

'No. Well, I mostly forget to take it out with me.' As with the time-operated light in her hall, it was Jack who had suggested she got one.

'It was handy today.'

Rose snorted. 'Handy to have everyone arrive a bit sooner, that's all.'

'Yes, but when you're out by yourself at night, it's safer.'

Rose chewed the side of her mouth. He was right, of course. The West Country, for so long always a step behind and a reminder of a more gentle age, was now no stranger to crime and seemed to be catching up with everywhere else. 'So, I'm walking up Causewayhead and about to be mugged or attacked and I say, "Hold on a minute while I get out my phone to ring the police"?'

'Now who's being pedantic? You know perfectly well what I mean.'

'Well, it's heavy, I could always use it as a cosh.'

Nick shook his head, smiling as the waiter brought several dishes and arranged them on the hotplates. Nick indicated that Rose should begin before he helped himself to food. Having tasted it he nodded approvingly then continued, 'It could've been the wind.'

'No. I can't expect you to believe me but it was a scream. A woman's scream. Oh, let's forget it, it's one of those things that happen round here, that'll never be understood.'

'Did anyone know where you were going today?'

'What difference would that have made?' Rose, her carefully loaded chop-sticks half-way to her mouth, felt a fleeting panic.

There was a strange expression on his face as he said, 'I'm not sure.' He paused. 'I just wondered.'

'I told Stella and Daniel. In fact, I think it was Stella who originally suggested the scene. I'm so grateful to them, Nick, they've really taken me under their wing. They're all so nice. I expected, well, I'm not sure, not jealousy, I'm nowhere in their league, but perhaps resentment at a new face amongst the recognised.'

'We're not like that, Rose. I'm surprised you should have thought so.'

'I apologise, I meant no offence. It's just that after coping on my own for so long and allowing myself to settle for second best . . .' She shrugged again and pushed her hair back over her shoulders, tucking it neatly behind her ears so as not to get it in the way of the food as she leant over the bowl.

Nick remained silent. He guessed wrongly that she had been suffering from a lack of confidence. Having lost the husband she had loved deeply and with whom she had been so happy that her talent had taken second place, she must have needed courage to change direction so late in life. He was annoyed for having underestimated her. It had been easy for him, he had been one of the lucky ones, his work had been shown and bought almost from the beginning. Unlike Rose he had not married, although there had been several long-standing relationships. The last one had ended six months ago. Jenny was an artist's model, one of those wild-looking creatures with olive skin and a tangle of black hair and eyes that could seduce with a glance. Nature, he thought, could be very deceptive. Jenny had wanted nothing more than to settle down and have babies and she had believed Nick would oblige on this score. After three years she had flung

17

her few possessions into a bag and walked out, slamming the door, shouting recriminations about her wasted youth and his having used her. Initially too stunned to retaliate, Nick had remained standing in the kitchen, spatula in hand, and continued to fry the mackerel that was to have been their supper. Used? he had thought. She lives with me free of charge, off my earnings, and eats my food which I generally end up cooking. If she'd got out the hoover once in a while it might have helped. He had flung down his cooking implements and rushed to the door. 'Used?' he bellowed down the narrow alley from the cottage door, much to the astonishment of locals and holiday-makers alike – although the latter had probably lapped it up as a piece of local colour. 'Who's used who, I wonder?' But Jenny had already disappeared around the corner.

Rose was completely different. She was lovely but more mature, she had known pain and had learned to deal with it and he admired what little he had seen of her work. He sensed that she would not play games, that whatever occurred between them she would be straight with him. That would make a change from Jenny's prevarications. And, he realised, as he watched her picking expertly at the dishes with her chop-sticks, she did not feel the need to talk constantly.

'What?' Rose looked up just in time to catch his grin.

'You're enjoying that.'

'I am.'

There was no way he was going to say he had also been thinking how much he desired her. But were these things enough? And why was he even thinking them? It was far too soon to tell how or if the relationship would develop. At least he would like her as a friend, if nothing else.

'I'm going to Stella's exhibition tomorrow. It's the opening, she invited me.'

'Then you'd better not drive. She'll press wine on you till it's coming out of your ears.'

'Doesn't sound like much of a hardship to me.'

'Wait and see.'

'I can't say I've noticed she drinks a lot.'

'No, that's the point. She doesn't. It's nerves.'

'Stella?'

'I know. Hard to credit. But it's the same every time she has a new show. She's always terrified each one'll be the last.'

'Right now I'd settle for one.'

'Then you'll need more canvases. How many have you done now?'

'Oh, several decent ones. It's odd, the ones I liked least have sold. You're grinning again. What is it this time?'

'You're learning. You're beginning to recognise what's good and what isn't. How do you tell?'

Rose frowned. 'I don't know. It's just a feeling.'

'Then you're probably right. Can you finish this?' Nick indicated the beef in black bean sauce.

'No, I think we over-ordered.' There was still a dish of spare ribs hardly touched.

'Shall I get the bill?'

'Yes. Look at the time, it's almost eleven thirty. We'll split it.'

'I wouldn't dream of it.' This was definitely not something Jenny would have offered to do. Another plus point to Rose Trevelyan.

The waiter arrived to clear their dishes. 'Do you think you could put the ribs in a take-away container, please?'

Across the table Nick's jaw dropped. 'Have you got a dog?'

'No, they're for me, unless you want them.'

His laughter caused heads to turn. 'Do you ever waste anything?'

'Not if I can help it. Besides, if I wake in the night I'm always hungry.'

'You eat them cold?'

'I do. You should try it sometime.' She pursed her mouth in amusement. 'I have other habits you might find disgusting.'

'Please, spare me them tonight. Let's get your coat. Taxi home or shall I walk you?'

'A taxi, it's miles out of your way.' Rose stopped, her arms half in the sleeves of her coat. 'How will you get home?'

'I'm staying with a friend in Penzance.'

'Oh, I see.'

The waiter rang for a taxi and they stood in the doorway at the bottom of the stairs out of the wind until it arrived. Clutching the tinfoil container of ribs, Rose was thinking about his throw-away comment. Had he already arranged to stay with this friend or had he been expecting to go home with her? He had offered to walk her back. Too late now for speculation, she thought as the familiar shape of a Stone's taxi hove into view. Nick opened the back door then felt silly as she got into the front passenger seat and greeted the driver by name. 'Thanks. I really enjoyed this evening,' she said, winding down the window. 'My treat next time.' Then, wishing she had not been so forward, she asked the driver to take her home.

She walked up the steep path which led directly to the side door of the house, which was set into the cliffside. To reach the front door she would have had to turn right and pick her way in the dark along the uneven path, alongside which overgrown shrubs sloped down to the road. Like her friends, Rose rarely used this door and after the last heavy rain she discovered that the wood had swollen. Letting herself into the kitchen, she was thinking what a strange sort of day it had been. Still that lingering cry echoed in her head. Perhaps she was going mad or her imagination had been working overtime, although she could not recall thinking about anything other than her work when she had heard that eerie sound. The embarrassment lingered and Jack Pearce's reminder had been unnecessary. And what had Nick said about anyone knowing where she was? What on earth had he meant by that? Was there someone who wanted to scare her or make her look a fool?

Too tired to care, she went upstairs and got ready for bed, taking one last look at the bay and the lights of Newlyn harbour below. The moon was partially obscured by a cloud but there was still light enough to undress by. No one could see in: passing cars or the unlikely pedestrian at that time of night would be too low down beneath the overhang of her garden and any seaman would need a high-powered telescope if they had a sudden desire to watch a middle-aged widow undressing.

Rose was wary about returning to the mine but more work was required on the painting. Stella had seen it in its early stages and had confirmed Rose's own opinion that it was good. She could not abandon it because of some imagined noise but there would not be time tomorrow. Laura, whom she had been neglecting, was coming for coffee and there was Stella's preview in the evening. There were also a few things she needed to do in Penzance.

There was Maddy, too, another of the St Ives crowd, whom Rose felt she would like to know better. She sensed they shared something in common, something deeper than mutual acquaintances although she had not yet worked out what. Madeleine Duke was self-supporting and could turn her hand to many things. She made ceramics and pottery and was skilful at textile printing, and she sold her goods from a little shop in a back lane in which she worked as she waited for custom. She had placed a small sign on the street corner, propped against one of the tiny cottages which made up the village of St Ives. Rose had to admit that it was a beautiful place. The sand was fine, the colour of clotted cream, and the sea, beloved by surfers, was bluer than the Aegean. If you arrived by train the breath-taking view was framed by a fringe of palm trees at the side of the line. But to live there was another matter. Unable to move for tourists in the summer, Rose would have felt claustrophobic. St Ives had its fishing history but Newlyn was still very much a working village, no quaintness unless you knew where to look for it, nothing but the concrete edifice of the fish market and the ice factories. Most visitors drove straight through on their way to the picturesque village of Mousehole.

There was at least another half-hour until daylight when Rose opened her eyes at seven. Switching on the bedside lamp she pulled on the towelling robe she used as a dressing-gown in the winter, tied the belt and went downstairs, shivering. Something must be wrong with the heating. It was timed to come on at six and although it was set at a temperature low enough only to take the chill off the air, it was missed that morning. She opened the door off the kitchen which led into what had once been the larder or pantry but now served as a laundry and store-room. The light had gone out on the boiler.

'Damn it.' Rapidly losing patience, she saw that it needed more skill than she possessed to get it to work again. Laura's husband, Trevor, was home from sea and there was little in the way of engines or appliances that baffled him. She'd ring before Laura came and see if he could help her out. Meanwhile coffee was needed. Filter coffee, she decided. Whilst it was running through the machine she went into the lounge and knelt in front of the grate. There were a few embers beneath the ashes of the logs – with a bit of luck she could get the fire going quickly. Stuffing newspaper concertinas in its midst and adding a few bits of driftwood which she had picked up from the beach and which burned so well and so brightly because they were seasoned and salty, she lit a match. The flames caught immediately. Adding a few lumps of coal she waited until they, too, caught then balanced a dry log on top. Sitting back on her heels she felt the heat on her face as she listened to the snapping and hissing of kindling and solid fuel while the sparks flew up the chimney.

Outside the sky was clear, the last of the stars less brilliant as dawn approached. The moon had set an hour ago. The hydrangea bushes with their spiky twigs were bare but had borne new shoots since October and, she had read, there were camellias flowering in a nearby country house garden. As if to prove the clemency of the weather there was a jug of narcissi, flown over from Scilly, on the mantelpiece and the first daffodils would soon be appearing in bud in the shops of Penzance. There was no hint of a frost. It probably wasn't much colder outside than inside the house at the moment. Bank, post office, library, hairdresser's, she reminded herself. A twice-yearly trim was something she endured rather than enjoyed.

Sporadic spluttering from the kitchen told her that the coffee was ready. It was rich and strong and just as she liked it. Gratefully she sipped the first mouthful, her hands clasped around the mug for warmth. Thankfully the immersion heater was independent of the boiler and she was able to have a bath.

In jeans and shirt and a heavy knitted sweater, she found some old woollen socks which had holes in the toes but were nonetheless warm and put them on before stuffing her feet into the leather hiking boots she wore for most of the winter. Not only were they comfortable but they were a necessity as her outdoor work often took her over rough terrain.

At eight thirty she dialled Laura's number and was answered by a yawning female voice.

'Did I wake you?' Laura was usually an early riser.

22

'No, I was up, but we didn't get to bed until two. We had some friends over and – you know how it is. How did it go, with Nick? He's not there, is he?'

'No, Laura, he isn't here,' Rose said firmly. 'Nor was he last night.'

'Don't get teasy, you know I have to know. Why're you ringing, can't you make it this morning?'

'Actually, I need a favour. Is Trevor busy today?'

'If you call lying about with the newspaper before wandering off to the Star for a lunchtime drink busy, then yes, he is. What's the problem? Surely not the car?'

'No. The central heating boiler.' The car was relatively new, bought with a legacy of a thousand pounds an old friend had left her. It had replaced the yellow Mini which had been a gift from David and which she had hung on to for far too long for sentimental reasons. Now she was the proud owner of a blue Metro which started first time and had only had three previous owners. Mike Phillips had gone with her to choose it, claiming he knew about such matters. It seemed he did – doctor or no doctor, he had proved he knew almost as much about the internal workings of the combustion engine as he did about the patients upon whom he wielded his scalpel.

'No problem, I'll bring him with me. See you later.'

Rose hung up. She had known Laura since they were in their early twenties but it felt as if they had always known one another. There were times when Laura would preface a remark with something along the lines of 'Remember Miss so-and-so who taught us in the third year?' or quote the name of a schoolfriend as if they had actually been to school together. Laura had never left Newlyn and had vowed that she never would. Before marrying Trevor she had travelled but she had always been glad to return. It had shocked her when her boys, one by one, had moved away.

Rose had finally been accepted. She had, after all, married a Cornishman and kept his name and she had not tried to impress but had made a slow integration into the community. Doreen Clarke, a more recent friend, once told her, 'You'm all right, maid, you don't give yourself no airs and graces like they London people.'

Rose did not bother to explain that she came from Gloucestershire and had lived in the middle of nowhere, surrounded only by verdant English countryside and cows and sheep, and that trips into Swindon or Cheltenham were a rare treat. Her father had been a country farmer who had lived through the good times before BSE and European intervention; he had hunted to hounds and had, so her mother told her, been on a protest rally against the anti-hunting campaign. Rose found it hard to believe that her conventional, rather self-effacing father had put himself so much in the limelight. He had retired whilst still in his fifties and sold the farm. He and his wife had then bought a small stone cottage with a manageable garden and spent the intervening years doing all the things they had not had time for before. Rose saw the problems other people her age had with elderly parents who were frail or senile and knew she was lucky. On the other hand she suspected a lot of it was to do with their attitude. They did not believe themselves to be old or incapable of doing anything they chose. There was, she had long ago realised, no point in discussing her past at all with Doreen, who would not recognise the difference between London and the Gloucestershire countryside because anyone from across the Tamar was 'one of they' and therefore a Londoner.

As Rose loaded the washing-machine, changed the bed and tidied up, the sun came up, a wintry yellow but promising another fine day. She finished some paperwork until the washing-machine had ended its cycle then piled the clothes into a basket and took them outside to hang on the line she had strung from the shed to the highest branch of a tree. Towels flapped in the breeze coming off the sea, an easterly breeze, she noticed, no wonder it was colder.

The shed at the back of the garden had been cleared out and the rubbish taken to the dump. Anything serviceable she had given to the charity shops in Penzance. With a Calor gas heater installed and the door and windows made draught-proof, it was where she had recently taken to working if the light was right. At other times, if she wasn't painting in the open air, she used the attic which she had had converted many years previously. One half had been partitioned off to use as a dark-room for her photography work, although it was little used lately, and the other half with the sloping window in the roof was perfect for colouring her sketches as it was at the side of the house and therefore faced north.

The last item of clothing had been pegged firmly to the line just as she heard the familiar voices of Trevor and Laura, who had arrived on foot. Their faces were pink and they were both in heavy jackets. Laura, despite her height and thinness, was typically Cornish in appearance. She possessed deep, dark eyes and naturally rosy cheeks and her long dark hair, loose today, flew about her face in untidy clumps. She had never been able to control the natural wave. Trevor was an inch shorter than his wife, his face weathered with lines radiating from his brown eyes. His hair, too, curled and was worn long although of a lighter brown than Laura's. Through the beard he had not shaved off in all the years that Rose had known him, his lips were red and full. A tiny silver cross dangled from his left ear.

'What've you broken this time, Rose?' were his words of greeting.

'The boiler won't light. It just went out. I didn't touch it,' she added defensively although she had fiddled with it that morning.

'I'll take a look.' With the familiarity of an old friend Trevor let himself into the house and went straight to the boiler and removed its cover. The two women followed. Rose shut the door and put the washing basket on the draining-board before getting out milk and sugar. She reached for the tin of biscuits she kept for guests, knowing that Trevor would eat some. Laura, too, had no mean appetite but she never gained an ounce of weight. Rose was also naturally slender but tended not to eat at all at stressful times.

There was a whoosh from the laundry room. Rose and Laura exchanged a complicit glance. Trevor had fixed it. Water gurgled in the radiators and just the sound of it made Rose feel warmer. 'A well-earned coffee,' she said, handing him a heavily sweetened mugful. 'Do you want more milk?' Trevor shook his head. The job had only taken minutes but over the years Rose had learned that Trevor was offended if she offered remuneration. Instead she repaid him with a packet of tobacco or a few cans of his favourite beer.

He sat at the table and got out the makings of a roll-up, scattering tobacco as he did so. Not a man for conversation unless it was necessary, he left the talking to the women. Years at sea had taught him to keep his own counsel. Cooped up in a confined space with a crew from whom there was no escape until you landed had made many a man taciturn. He listened, all the same, and took in all he heard.

'Rose,' he said, licking the adhesive strip of his cigarette paper and dextrously twisting it around the tobacco, 'what happened yesterday?' He looked into her face with his shrewd brown eyes.

She sighed. 'You might as well hear it from me as from anyone.' The explanation already sounded tired to her own ears.

'That's just about how I heard it.' Trevor inhaled and blew out smoke with his eyes half closed.

'You didn't say anything to me, Trevor.' Laura was indignant. She flung back her hair as if she had suffered the worst possible affront. Not knowing things, for Laura, was unbearable and for her husband to withhold information was an unthinkable insult.

'No. Not till I heard it from the source. Strange goings-on, that. Where was this?'

Rose told him. Trevor shook his head. 'It was no echo then.'

'No.' Rose wished everyone would stop discussing it, but only because she was still convinced that what she had heard was real. However, the area had been searched thoroughly, and she could only question her sanity.

Trevor crossed his legs and folded his arms, one hand with the cigarette hovering over the ashtray Rose had placed before him. 'You might be artistic, but I wouldn't call you sensitive or fanciful. If it wasn't an echo or a trick of the wind and no one was found, then there still has to be an explanation.'

Rose was later to recall those words and to see that she ought to have made more of them. 'That's just it, Trevor, but I can't come up with an answer. At least you know me well enough to realise I believed what I heard at the time.'

He shook his head and the wavy hair moved with it. 'The way I see it is like this, if you're not breaking things you're landing yourself in trouble. Were you accident-prone as a cheel?'

Rose slapped his arm affectionately, knowing he was sending her up. 'No. I've never even broken a bone.'

'Well, mind you don't now. Take my advice and keep away from they places. If you're right, and I'm not saying I disbelieve you, then there'll be trouble in it for you somewhere along the line. You know what you're like, Rose Trevelyan.'

What he said made sense but she had no intention of letting her friends know that she planned to return to the mine tomorrow. That painting was good, too good to relinquish now, she had to finish it. Pouring more coffee, she listened to Laura's plans for Christmas.

'Are you sure you won't come to us? You know we'd love to have you. Besides, it'll be such a houseful one more won't matter, and the boys worship you.'

That was, Rose thought, putting it a bit strongly, but she did get on well with them.

'Come on, girl, if you want a hand with the shopping.' Trevor stood up. Like many local families they did not possess a car. If the men were at sea they didn't travel far when they returned home and there were ample buses into Penzance and from there to other places. There were also enough people who did have transport and who were prepared to offer lifts. They walked down the path in single file and waved before disappearing from view.

Rose knew that many villages and small towns comprised the same mix of pubs and small shops which served the locals, but in Newlyn there was a difference. It was in both the people themselves and the one thing which bound them together: the sea. The sea and its produce and the dangers it held, proven by the tragedies which, when they occurred, affected not one person but many in such a close-knit community.

She rinsed the mugs and inverted them on the draining-board before glancing at the sky, which could change in seconds. There were still no clouds. She slipped on a jacket, picked up her large leather handbag and went outside. The walk along the sea front would do her good and she could change her library books on the way up to Penzance. Breathing in the clean air, she made her way down the hill, waving to a fish buyer as she passed the market. It was busy but the auctioneer's voice could be heard above the clattering of fish boxes.

Library, bank, post office, hairdresser's, she reminded herself again as she reached the level surface of Newlyn Green.

2

Stella Jackson paced the honey-coloured, highly polished sanded boards of her living-room floor, cigarette in hand. Daniel Wright, her husband, ignored her. He was used to the first night nerves from which she suffered as much in St Ives as in one of the big London galleries. And tonight they were to be honoured by the presence of a well-known art dealer. Daniel was not alone in admiring his wife's work as well as the woman herself and was therefore unable to understand her insecurity. It was some years now since he had stopped trying to reassure her; this anxiety was part of her, something which she had to endure and which, he realised, helped her artistically. If she lost the desire to improve, to be the best, if she took her talent for granted, it might slide into mediocrity. In many ways they were worlds apart but their marriage worked and they allowed one another plenty of freedom.

Daniel had been commissioned to produce a sculpture for the gardens of a government property in London. Twice he had travelled up with plans and then the model from which he would work. It was now under way. The basic shape had been formed and sat in his studio wrapped in damp cloths. It would take months to complete and he couldn't afford a mistake. Some days he didn't touch it at all but merely stared at the plans and his initial drawing. Then he would run his hands over the clay. When he could feel in his fingertips the form which would finally emerge and picture it as well as he knew his own body, then he would continue. For now he was happy enough to offer whatever support he could to Stella at the private viewing of her exhibition.

The flat over her gallery in St Ives had once been a net loft. They had moved there from Zennor five years previously, although Daniel still preferred the old granite house despite its relative inconvenience. The loft had been partially renovated before they moved in but they had decided to leave the rafters in their original form rather than build a ceiling. They sloped up to the roof, forming an apex and creating a sense of spaciousness. The decor appeared very casual but the effect had taken Stella a long time to achieve as she searched for just the right material for cushions and curtains and the rugs that were thrown over the settees. The television and video recorder were hidden in a cupboard built into the wall, as was their collection of CDs and the player. Against the longest wall was a dining-table made of oak, with matching chairs. It was second-hand but had cost more than the modern equivalent they had looked at. Basic wooden shelving, made by Daniel, held their numerous books. At the bottom were the heavier, glossy tomes containing pictures of the great works of artists and sculptors. Above were dictionaries and reference books, while the top three shelves held novels. It was an eclectic collection. Many of the paperbacks were Penguins with their original covers and priced at half a crown or less. The edges of the pages were orange with age and the books still retained the smell peculiar to the roughish paper on which they were printed.

The kitchen was small and adjoined this room. It was extremely functional, space being at a premium, and had been designed by a seafaring friend who had worked within the limitations of a ship's galley. The bedroom and bathroom had not required much improvement; the latter some modernisation, the former only redecoration. The previous occupants, who had carried out the initial conversion, had had their main rooms downstairs.

The gallery ran the length and breadth of the building with only a small cubicle blocked off for office-work and a kitchenette alongside it. A selection of Stella's new paintings, carefully framed and kept from the public eye, were now hanging on the walls and the six-foot removable partitions she had erected down the centre. Daniel had placed an order with the wine merchant, hired glasses and made sure there was at least one spare corkscrew and some whisky for those who didn't drink wine. There were also soft drinks and plates of food which were covered in foil and waiting in the fridge. There had been produced by Julie Trevaskith, the daughter of Molly who did their cleaning. Julie was at Cornwall College learning the catering trade. To earn some spending money she helped out in the gallery during the holidays.

'Want to go for a walk, burn off some of that nervous energy?' Daniel asked, irritated by her restless pacing.

'No.' Stella shook her head, causing the straight black hair, cut to chin length, to swing. It looked unnatural, it was as dark as a string of jet beads except for a shock of grey springing from the crown. She was lean and willowy and dressed mainly in black but always with some splash of brilliance. Today, over the black ski-pants and satin tunic top she had slung a shawl of scarlet and emerald. The green was reflected in the huge ear-rings which dangled against her neck. She looked at Daniel and smiled. 'I know you're doing your best, I can't help it.'

He smiled back, wondering how a woman with slightly crooked teeth and a bit of a squint could be so sexy. Apart from her lissom body, there was something about her face which made men look twice. Maybe it was the bone structure or the fact that the two flaws, if they could be so called, cancelled each other out. It did not matter that her breasts were small, the whole effect added up to a beauty similar to that of a panther. Daniel wanted to take her to bed right then but she was too uptight to contemplate an act which might actually relieve her tension.

'I've asked a few people for drinks before we officially open.'

He liked the way she said 'we' although it was her gallery and her work on show. He tended to exclude her from his own artistic efforts, not letting her see anything until it was finished. Stella was far better at sharing than himself. 'Who's coming?'

'Maddy, Jenny, Barbara and Mike and Rose.' She counted them off on her fingers.

'No Nick?'

'He can't make it until later.' Stella smiled her feline smile. 'I didn't tell Rose he was coming.'

'She'll know, won't she? I thought they were seeing each other.'

'They are, as you put it, seeing each other, but I think that's as far as it goes. Don't start match-making.' She pointed a slender finger at him. Like the other seven it was bedecked with heavy silver rings and her nails, long and carefully filed, were scarlet, without a chip, the polish gleaming beneath its coat of clear varnish. No one would realise it had taken her an age to remove the paint from her hands and nails and wrists. Her lips, in the same shade, were pursed as she recalled it was Daniel who had paired Jenny off with Nick and that had turned out to be a disaster. It was now far enough in the past that it was safe to have them under the same roof.

'I won't. Cross my heart.' He did so as he stood up and stretched. 'Ought I to change?' He looked down at his brown cords. The nap on the knees had disappeared but his Viyella shirt with its tiny brown and white checks was perfectly presentable as was the matching brown V-necked sweater.

'You know I don't mind.'

'I think I will, trousers, anyway. You look so smart.'

She turned to hide a smile. Stella knew that had she insisted he tidy up he would have refused, stating that people must take him as he was.

'Hey, take it easy.' He patted her shoulder. Stella had jumped when the door bell chimed.

'Someone's early.' Brushing the cold metal of the rail with her hand she went down the circular wrought-iron staircase to see who it was. 'Jenny! It's unlike you to be so punctual.'

'I was hoping Maddy would be here. She's always the first to turn up.'

'Maddy? No, you're the first. You should've called for her on the way.'

Jenny put on her helpless face, her head on one side. 'I need a job.' She still modelled for artists, clothed or unclothed, having the sort of looks which transposed well to canvas, but it was by no means a full-time job and many couldn't afford to pay her at all. Sometimes she was rewarded with a meal or a painting that didn't sell or a few drinks in one of the pubs.

'Well, I don't see how Maddy can help. Oh, come on up. You look as if you could do with a drink. I certainly could but I promised myself I wouldn't start until someone arrived.'

Jenny smiled behind her back, knowing the state her hostess needed to work herself up into before she could begin to enjoy the evening. 'I just thought she might like someone to work in the shop. She could spend all her time at her craftwork then.'

'Be realistic, Jenny. All right, she's doing okay in the run-up to Christmas, but January and February? Even in the summer she just scrapes by.'

'I know. But I'm desperate, anything's worth a try. I don't suppose you...'

Stella raised her hands, palms facing forward. Her face was stern. 'No chance, Jenny. Sorry.' Stella could have afforded to employ the girl but for some reason, when Jenny was involved, there was always trouble. She wasn't dishonest or rude, she was just one of those people who was always caught in the vortex of other people's problems and managed to exacerbate them. But Stella was honest enough to admit that the main reason was that Jenny Manders found it difficult to keep her hands off other women's men. The door bell rang again. 'You'll have to help yourself. On the side there.' Stella indicated the drinks that were kept for their personal use before clattering down the stairs to admit Mike and Barbara Phillips and Rose whose cars had converged in the car-park simultaneously.

Stella frowned. 'Barbara, you know Jenny, don't you?' Her life was hectic and there were occasions when she couldn't remember which of her friends and acquaintances already knew each other.

'Yes. Nice to see you again.'

Rose grinned at Jenny and accepted a glass of wine. Two would have to be her limit as she had come in the car. She knew nothing of Nick's three-year affair with Jenny, only that there had been someone until six months ago. These were new friends, more personal details had not yet been exchanged, although the basics of their lives were no secret.

'Ah, here already.' Daniel had changed and shaved. He greeted their guests whilst keeping an eye on Stella who was now chain-smoking. He liked the Phillips. Mike was a surgeon at Treliske hospital in Truro and his wife worked there as a physiotherapist. Rose Trevelyan was another woman he admired, and not only for her looks. She was a survivor. He wondered how Stella would fare if she did not have his constant support.

Maddy was the last to arrive. Her accent instantly placed her as an 'outsider', as someone from the Home Counties who had moved to Cornwall in search of the simple life, where she believed her dreamy manner and craftwork would be more appreciated. Having arrived only three years ago she was still considered to be an outsider, although she had made friends amongst the locals. Barbara, never less than elegant, smiled at Maddy's chosen ensemble. Over thick black tights she wore brown lace-up boots and a billowing smock in royal blue with embroidery across the tight-fitting chestband which flattened her curves. Beneath the smock was a striped T-shirt in olive green and white, over it a quilted jacket in squares of differing colours. On her head was a Paddington Bear hat with a large red flower stitched to the side. Long hair cloaked her shoulders. It was fair with a slight wave but of the dryish texture which did not shine even when newly washed. She resembled a character in a nursery rhyme.

Stella, a cigarette balanced in the corner of her mouth, replenished their drinks. Rose put her hand over her glass. 'Not for me, thanks.'

'Sure? Okay. I'm beginning to feel better already, Rose. You wouldn't believe what these evenings do to me.'

Rose nodded. Stella didn't know how lucky she was to be hosting one. Turning to speak to Barbara and Mike, acquaintances once, then firm friends from the start of David's illness when Mike had been his consultant and Rose's confidant, she studied Maddy Duke. Rose had met her at Stella's on several occasions and had found her to be amusing company, if a little zany, but beneath her cheerful exterior Rose guessed there was hidden pain.

Daniel circulated with the wine bottles but Rose told him she was saving her rationed second glass for the official opening.

'How's it going?' Mike Phillips, in causal trousers, shirt and sweater, finally got a chance to speak to Rose. He looked tired.

'I'm fine.'

'I can see you're fine, I meant the painting. Your oil has pride of place in our lounge. Did Barbara tell you?'

'No. I'm flattered.'

'How typical. We're the ones who're flattered. We had no idea you were that good.'

'Hidden talent,' Maddy said, joining them with a glass containing what appeared to be neat Scotch. 'I bet we don't know of half the local painters with hidden talents.'

'We?' Jenny had joined them. By her tone it was obvious she resented Maddy counting herself as one of them.

'I do think of myself as local, you know. I felt at home from the minute I came here.'

Rose sensed an animosity which she had not noticed between the two women before.

Jenny chewed the inside of her lip but said nothing. Instead she played with her thick black hair, which hung around her face like a frame. Her skin was good and her eyes were large and luminescent but it was her mouth which attracted. Full and pink, it hinted at both innocence and sensuality. She was about to move away and speak to Stella when Maddy asked Rose how Nick was. Jenny hesitated, her shoulders stiff. Rose replied that she had no reason to suppose he was other than well, but she had seen the give-away gesture and guessed that there had once been something between Nick and Jenny – and still might be, she thought, not liking the feeling this produced although she and Nick were no more than friends and there was certainly no commitment on either side. She decided to ignore her feelings and enjoy the rest of the evening although she continued to be aware of the vaguely hostile undercurrents in the room.

A few minutes later they all went downstairs and Stella unlocked the door. Guests were by invitation only. Stella stood at the front to welcome them into the brilliantly lit showroom whose lights now spilled out into the blackness of the narrow street. Earlier Stella had hurried her friends through the darkened gallery, allowing them no chance to glimpse her work.

Daniel went to the back to open the wine for Julie who had just arrived and had begun to take the foil off the trays of food. This was Stella's night, she must be allowed to enjoy the credit due to her whilst he and Julie handed around the food and drinks.

Spotlights had been switched on and the early arrivals, glasses in hand, wandered around admiring the paintings. Rose stopped in front of one she particularly liked. If only, she thought, almost able to feel and see the waves as they crashed over the headland.

'You will.' Stella, having silently positioned herself behind Rose, seemed to have read her mind. Ash from her cigarette sprinkled the front of Rose's blouse as Stella placed an arm across her shoulder. 'It's in you. Really it is. Of course there's a long way to go yet, and a lot of hard work in store for you. It isn't that easy to make it to the top.'

Rose nodded. Could it be possible that one day she would be in Stella's position? She was about to answer when she saw Nick's lanky figure duck through the doorway. He came straight over to her and Rose was glad there was a partition between her and Maddy and Jenny who were in conversation on the other side of it. His face lit up. 'I didn't say I was coming because I wasn't sure I could make it. Once you said you'd be here I had to come.'

'She's good, isn't she?' Rose ignored the compliment because there was a sudden silence on the other side of the partition.

'Better than she realises. You like this one?'

'Very much.' Rose accepted her second drink and took a canapé from one of the trays Julie was handing around.

'How're you getting home?' Nick didn't seem at all interested in the exhibition but he had probably attended so many, including his own, that it wasn't much of a thrill for him.

'I've got the car.'

'Ah. Never mind. Are you all right? After yesterday, I mean?'

'Yes. Must've been my imagination.' She paused, and was unsure what then made her blurt out, 'I'm going back tomorrow if the weather's fine. I really want to finish that painting.'

'Yes, you must,' Stella insisted, having heard the last remarks as she approached them.

Rose moved away, intent on seeing the rest of Stella's new work. Nick followed, knowing that two pairs of eyes were on their backs.

Rose stopped to admire a small canvas, as yet unframed. It was an amusing piece showing a half-naked woman of a certain age; a little raddled, a little overweight but, judging from the smirk on her Picasso-style face, completely uncaring as she painted her own portrait from a full-length mirror. Rose wondered whether Stella intended it to make a statement or whether it was a work of pure fun. Her own smile faded as she overheard Jenny's words.

'Oh, there's no doubt about it, he'll have to take me back. How can he not? I am his responsibility, after all.'

'Is that what you *really* want?' Maddy asked, her voice clipped. 'Think about it, Jenny. You're the one who's always saying there's no going back. And there's... well, there's you know who to contend with.'

Rose felt suffocated and wanted to leave. With a determined stride she went out to the little kitchen and placed her glass on the fridge and her paper plate and serviette in the bin-liner put there for the rubbish, before returning to thank Stella and Daniel for inviting her.

With what she hoped was a cheerful wave to the others she walked out of the shop and straight back to the car. He's making a fool of me, she thought. And for the first time since she had met them Rose felt that maybe she didn't fit in with these exotic people after all, that there were things about them she didn't understand, and that she had no desire to join in their sexual games. For a moment she felt a pang for the faithful, reliable Barry Rowe who had yearned for her since before she had met David but who could never be more than a friend. Like Laura, he had been neglected lately and Rose wondered if she was becoming selfish. By the time she pulled into her drive she realised she was being melodramatic, that what had happened at the mine shaft had left her edgy and more than a little suspicious. On the other hand Nick had offered no more than friendship and if it was Jenny he wanted they could still remain friends. Rose had done nothing to jeopardise his relationship with the younger woman.

Both Laura and Barry had been delighted that she was finally doing what she had been born to do. She was not deserting them, she was simply picking up a career where she had left it off.

Turning her key in the lock she decided she was glad to be home.

3

Jenny Manders was one of the last to leave the gallery. She was quietly seething. How dare Nick be so obvious about Rose in front of her and the people who had known them as a couple. Maddy hadn't wasted any time before making one of her bitchy comments. And what did Rose Trevelyan have that she didn't? She could paint, that was all. I may only be a model, Jenny thought, but I'm fifteen years her junior and better looking. But despite an excess of wine which had made her bitter, she acknowledged the unfairness of her thoughts. Rose was a nice woman. Even Alec Manders, her father, known for his taciturnity and meanness of manner, had seemed drawn to her on the one occasion all three had met in the street. And who the hell does Maddy think she is to be so judgemental when all she produces is tat for the tourists, and she has the gall to imagine she's one of us.

Jenny's pride in her roots was genuine. Unlike many of her contemporaries she had tried life in London and had also spent two months in Paris, mixing with artists on the Left Bank and posing for them. Something in her cried out to be accepted by such people. Although she recognised that she had no talent herself, she fed on those who did. Disappointment had followed disappointment. The Frenchman with whom she had lived for seven of those eight weeks had thrown her out as soon as he was satisfied with the work he had produced using Jenny as his model. Good work, too, for which she would get none of the credit. She had sat shivering for hours in the daytime and shared his bed at night, and all for nothing. With Nick, because it was the longest relationship she had sustained, she had believed it would be different, that he would eventually marry her or at least keep her as his mistress. She would have had the best of all worlds; being amongst the people she admired and both working for and living with an artist, one who could provide a proper home for her.

Her mother had disappeared when she was three years old but she did not learn of the circumstances until she was seventeen. Renata Trevaskis was a beauty, descended from true Romany stock. She had married Alec Manders on her eighteenth birthday but soon became restless and dissatisfied with married life and a small child whose upbringing was mostly taken over by her mother-in-law with whom they had had to live. She started drinking, encouraged by Alec's mother who had never liked her. A year later rumour had it that she had run off with another man, a holiday-maker from somewhere up country. It had surprised no one, knowing the awful restrictions she had had to live under in the strict Chapel environment of the Manders' home.

Agnes Manders was a martinet and had brought her son up to attend two church services every Sunday. He had, over the years, acquired his mother's views and opinions on everything. Oddly, considering that he believed that women should obey their menfolk, he had always been dominated by his mother. She was the strong one, the one who put food in their mouths and clothed them after his father had died in a mining accident. Because she told him so often, he had grown to believe that she was almost a saint.

Jenny, too, had been brought up on discourses of her grandmother's virtues along with constant reminders of how much she resembled her own mother and that, therefore, she had bad blood in her.

'Why did you marry her, then?' she had asked her father defiantly when she was told her mother's history. The reply had come in the form of a stinging blow across her cheek. Her grandmother, who had been in the room, had hands like steel hawsers.

Once Renata had gone, Jenny's father and his mother tried to curb her natural exuberance but no punishment worked for long. Apart from the time she spent in school she mostly roamed the streets, avoiding the house whenever possible. She suspected it was a relief to both of them when she went away.

As she strolled up the hill, moonlight shining on the cobbles, Jenny pictured her father. He was a squat but well-muscled man, handsome in a lived-in sort of way. A bit like Charles Bronson, Jenny thought, having recently seen a video of one of his films at Stella's. It was easy to see why Angela Choake, a divorcee, had been attracted to him. As soon as Alec's mother had been buried she had moved into the house as her father's wife. Jenny was still in Paris at the time. She had not returned for the funeral, neither had she grieved. She had not loved her grandmother and knew that her own existence had been a thorn in the old woman's side.

Jenny had tired of the sanctimonious ramblings knowing that, for a very long time, it had been her father who was the real provider. He had turned his hand to anything; fishing, mining and back to fishing until he had finally established himself as a reliable jobbing builder.

It was not until a fortnight after her return to St Ives that Jenny learned that her father had been seeing Angela Choake for many years, but until the demise of her grandmother they had not been out together in public. This led Jenny to understand the power the old woman had had over her son. She had alienated him against his wife and his own daughter. Angela, she thought, was all right. She could have done far worse for a stepmother. Naturally her father had legalised the relationship before allowing Angela to move into the house.

Jenny's return to Cornwall had not been a success. She had moved in with a friend and her husband but, uncomfortable in the midst of their obvious happiness, she left after a month, taking work wherever she could find it and sleeping wherever there was an available bed, occupied already or not.

Then she met Nick and life took an upward turn. That, too, had ended in disaster. She was penniless once more but too proud to let on that she was sleeping in a squat with three other homeless people whom she barely knew. Jenny did not blame anyone else for her position, nor did she blame herself. She put it down to fate. If she could just get some work things might be better. Work – or a man who was prepared to keep her, that would be even more favourable. All she required was a bit of comfort. But maybe it wasn't too late with Nick. He had not ignored her tonight and was usually friendly if they met by chance and he had gone out of his way to ask how she was. After Rose Trevelyan had left, it was true, but perhaps that meant more than if he had done so whilst she was present. Failing Nick she would fall back on her original plan.

Jenny had drunk all that was offered and had filled up on the food, which solved the problem of that evening's meal. Leaving the gallery she had decided to go and see Nick, a decision she would not have taken with less alcohol inside her.

In the shadows of the old, cramped buildings she felt buoyant. Not one, but two choices, she thought, and clutched her woollen charity shop coat closer to her as she made her way through the deserted streets. Her long skirt flapped around her ankles as the wind funnelled down the narrow alleys she had to negotiate to reach Nick's house. The night held no fears for her; not once had she felt afraid in the place of her birth. It wasn't late, a little after nine thirty, but she had passed the area where there were pubs and restaurants. Now there were only quiet lanes, each one becoming narrower and narrower and progressively steeper and darker.

Behind the tiny paned windows of the cottages the occasional light showed through thin curtains or those not tightly pulled together. She shivered, pleased to see Nick's porch light shining in welcome. From inside she heard his voice and stood, undecided, before knocking. No other voice replied so she assumed he must be on the telephone, which was near the front door. She lifted the metal ring and let it drop. The dull thud reverberated through the street. Nick let her in, smiling and nodding his intention that she should sit down. He closed the door behind her whilst cradling the telephone receiver between ear and shoulder. 'Okay, I'll see you then. 'Bye,' he said, giving Jenny no clue as to whom he had been speaking.

'Jenny? What brings you here?'

She would not beg but she wanted to make her position clear. 'I was lonely. I wanted to talk to someone. Well, you, really.'

'Drink?' Nick turned his back and opened the door of an old-fashioned sideboard from which he produced a cheap bottle of brandy. 'Of course we can talk, there was no need for us to fall out at all.'

Jenny thought this was a good start. She took the brandy glass and sat down on the sagging sofa which he had still not got around to replacing and on which they had made love many times. The thought made her maudlin. 'I miss you, Nick,' she said, already aware that she *would* beg if absolutely necessary. 'What went wrong?' She bowed her head submissively. 'Please tell me.'

Nick frowned. If he told her, she would become even more insecure than before; if he didn't, she would think he wanted her back. 'Nothing really went wrong, we just weren't suited.'

'How can you say that?' Her voice was raised. 'We were everything to each other.'

'Jenny, listen. This might come out all wrong, but if I was everything to you, you had a strange way of showing it.'

'What do you mean?'

Nick swirled the brandy in his glass and kept his eyes averted. 'I kept you, Jenny, and I didn't resent that one bit. I was fully aware of your financial position. However, despite my earning both our keep, it was still me who looked after this place and cooked most of our meals.'

'Oh, Nick, I'll cook for you. I'm quite a good cook, you know. And I'll do the cleaning.'

He was embarrassed, not for himself, but for this proud girl who was metaphorically on her knees before him. There was no option but to be cruel. 'It wasn't just that. You never forgave me for going to London alone. That was business, I couldn't have spared the time to entertain you as well. For months after I returned you accused me of all sorts of things. I, apparently, was allowed no freedom, whereas you had as much as if we weren't together at all. Jenny, you, of all people, know how everyone gossips. There were other men during the time you were with me. That bloke who came down from Cheshire, the one you claimed you were posing for –'

'I did pose for him.'

'Accepted, but that's not all you did. He made it pretty obvious in the pubs he drank in. No, Jenny, I'm more than happy to remain your friend and I'll do anything I can to help you, but that's as far as it goes.'

'Because of Rose Trevelyan.'

'No.' He paused. It was true, but since they'd split up he'd used Jenny. He now saw how stupid he had been.

'I suppose she cooks you meals before she lets you screw her.'

Nick stood and walked over to where she was sitting. For a split second Jenny thought he was going to hit her. She flinched but she knew that Nick would never hurt her. He took her by the elbow and lifted her to her feet. 'You're going home now, Jenny.

41

You've had far too much of Stella's excellent wine. Let's both forget this ever happened.'

'I won't forget,' she shouted from outside the closed door. 'I won't forget,' she repeated in time to her hurried, stumbling footsteps as the tears ran down her face.

Ten minutes after she left the telephone rang. It was Maddy. 'Nick, have you seen Jenny since the opening?'

'Yes. She just left here.'

'Ah, I thought so. I was upstairs looking out of the window and I saw her go by coming from your direction. She looked pretty wild, if you ask me. Is she okay?'

'Yes, I think so. She's much tougher than she lets people believe.'

'I just thought I'd check. Hey, why don't you come over tomorrow? I've got four mackerel here which I've cleaned, seems a shame to freeze them. Any time after seven would suit me.'

'I'm not sure, Maddy. Can I let you know in the morning?'

'Of course. No problem.'

Nick hung up. Life was strange. He had been speaking to Rose when Jenny arrived, although she hadn't sounded all that thrilled to hear his voice. The brief conversation had ended by Rose telling him that she was busy until the following weekend. Now Jenny wanted to come back into his life and Maddy, out of the blue, had invited him around for dinner. 'All or nothing,' he muttered, recalling the many months of his life when there had been nobody.

Rose had intended to telephone Barry Rowe upon her return from the gallery but after Nick's call, which had unsettled her for some reason, she had decided to leave it until the morning.

'Rosie! I was beginning to wonder what had happened to you. You're almost a stranger these days.'

She pictured his lean, stoop-shouldered frame, a bony hand pushing his heavily framed glasses up his nose as he answered the phone in the shabbiness of his small flat. He claimed to like where he lived although he could easily have afforded somewhere far nicer. Was he dressed yet or was he wearing the rough woollen dressing-gown with its silky girdle that she had seen hanging on the back of the bathroom door? 'I wondered if you'd heard about...?'

'Your most recent escapade? Of course I have, you know how fast news travels here. At least it didn't come to anything. Wait a minute, that's not why you're phoning, is it? Don't tell me that you, in your indomitable way, think there's more to it?'

'No. I made a mistake.'

'Jesus! Did I hear right? Is this the Rose Trevelyan I've known and, well, known for many years? An admission of error, no less.'

Rose smiled. He may have stopped in time but she knew what he had almost said. But had she made a mistake? Logic told her yes but her instincts said no. 'I'm trying to forget it. Anyway, the reason I'm ringing is to invite you for dinner tonight.'

'I'll be there. Seven thirty okay? I've got to go to the Camborne factory at five.'

'Fine. See you later.'

The forecast had proved to be correct. The sun was rising in a cloudless sky, the air was fresh and clear with a hint of an offshore breeze. Rose went out to the car. It was still a pleasant surprise to turn the car key in the ignition and hear the engine catch immediately. She hesitated before putting it into reverse gear and backing down the drive. I have to go back, she thought. I have to finish that painting.

She barely noticed the drive or the other traffic but anxiously chewed her lip, wondering if she was a fool for being so nervous or a worse one for returning to the old mine. She parked, aware of the sudden silence as she cut the engine, then headed to where she had sat two days ago. Nothing had changed except that some of the scrub had been flattened where the tyres of the emergency vehicles had crushed it. The bracken was crisp, more russet than brown, but the undergrowth still showed signs of green. Lichen-covered rocks, hidden in summer, began to show through as the plants died down. Rose stared at the old engine house, now in ruins, then across to where the adit of the mine lay. She listened but there was no sound apart from the whisper of the bracken and the sighing of the wind as it swept over the bleak landscape and through the bare, twisted trees which had bent to its will and stood no higher than Rose herself. She shook her head. It had to be a trick of acoustics, she thought as she set up her easel and began to work.

Was it Stella, or had Maddy originally suggested this particular location? she wondered. And did it mean anything?

Mortification washed over her again as she recalled the false alarm she had raised. Uneasily she worked, mixing oils on her palette and lining up the scene using the wooden end of a brush. An hour passed and she became absorbed in what she was doing, fascinated with the ruins as they stood in silent testimony to the proud mining history of Cornwall. A kestrel, which she recognised by its long tail, distracted her for more than ten minutes as it soared then hovered high in the sky, head down in typical manner as it searched for prey. Three times it plummeted but Rose did not think it caught anything. She shook her head. There would be no exhibition like Stella's if she didn't get a move on. Swirling the brush in the colour she had mixed for the brickwork which was in shadow, her arm jerked and paint splashed her jeans. 'Dear God, no.' Her voice was strangled as she jumped to her feet. A scream had pierced the air. She swung around, terrified. Had she been mistaken before, there was no doubt about it now. Her hands shook and her legs felt weak. It was hard to judge where it had come from yet it did not contain the thin quality which open air ought to have given it. And, more to the point, what to do now? Impossible to ring for assistance, the only help she could expect would be in the form of men in white coats come to take her away. Rapidly she packed her things, leaving the wet painting on the easel. Then, sick with fright and aware of the risk, Rose picked her way towards the engine house feeling like an actress in a horror film when the audience will her not to go into the empty building. She stood still, listening. Nothing, not a sound except her thumping heart and ragged breathing.

She looked in every direction but there was no sign of life other than the kestrel, now further away looking for richer pickings.

'I've got to get out of here,' she said. 'I must be going mad.'

Panic overcame her. Staggering and half tripping, she turned and ran, grabbing her equipment and throwing it into the back of the car, remembering just in time the wet canvas which she placed, face up, on the front passenger seat. Her foot slipped off the clutch and she reversed jerkily before starting to make her way home.

Never was she so relieved to see her house looking so normal at the top of her drive. It was a little after two and already the sun was less bright. It would set by four o'clock. Not caring what time it was or what anyone might think, the first thing she did was to pour a gin and tonic. If Jack Pearce walked in and called her an alcoholic she wouldn't care. Gin slopped on to the worktop as the bottle clinked against the glass. Ice slipped on to the floor. Rose left it there and took a large sip before switching on all the lights.

The shaking began to lessen but it was an hour before she felt able to clean her brushes and the palette knife and stand the canvas against the wall in the attic studio out of the way of the central heating. Since she rarely used the room now she had turned off the radiator. Thank goodness for the down-to-earth solidity of Barry Rowe, she thought as she lit one of the five cigarettes she allowed herself each day and sat down at the kitchen table to finish her drink and to plan what to cook him for dinner. Something special, she decided, to make up for her neglect. The crab season was over but she had some which she had frozen earlier in the year. She got it out of the freezer, it wouldn't take long to thaw. White and dark meat. She could mix it with soft cheese and make pâté with crudités. This would be followed by lamb kebabs marinated in lemon juice, olive oil, garlic and some of Doreen Clarke's redcurrant jelly. Served with rice and a green salad it would appear to have taken more effort than it really had. Rose knew that concentration on the food was a way of subduing the thoughts that wanted to rise to the surface; if she kept calm a perfectly logical explanation would come to mind.

As she crushed the garlic its pungent aroma overrode the fruity smell of the redcurrant jelly which was melting slowly in a small saucepan. Rose enjoyed cooking and the automatic, familiar gestures as she moved around her kitchen soothed her. Outside the night clouds began to gather and soon it was completely dark. Once the table was laid, the pâté in individual dishes in the fridge and the rest of the meal ready to cook, Rose went upstairs to change.

She was sitting quietly listening to some music when Barry arrived, his head jutting forward as if he was unsure of his welcome. Rose kissed his cheek, accepted the bottle of wine he had brought and asked him to open it.

'You look a bit pale, you're not going down with something, are you?'

'No, I don't think so.'

He stood, arms folded, and studied her face. 'Rose, tell me what's happened.' It wasn't a question.

Her head jerked up. Had she spoken her thoughts aloud or was he telepathic?

'You're involved in something, Rose, I know it.'

'No. Not involved. Oh, it's ridiculous.'

'You didn't go out there again?'

'I had to, Barry. The painting's good, I know it is. In fact, I'm certain it's the best I've ever done. I couldn't not finish it because of some wild auditory hallucination.'

Barry shrugged and pulled the cork from the bottle. 'The mind can play strange tricks.'

'Yes. You're right. Perhaps I need a holiday.'

'I could do with one myself.'

Rose turned away to put the skewered lamb and peppers under the grill, unprepared to follow up the obvious hint. 'It won't be long.'

They were half-way through the meal. Rose was struggling to eat as Barry regaled her with stories about his customers and complimented her on the food. He knew something was very wrong and was hurt that she wouldn't confide in him, but to press her would be a waste of breath, she would dig her heels in further. All he could do was to offer assistance if she required it. 'Rose?'

She looked up and tried to smile. He was a decent man, solid and dependable, and she often wished she had been able to offer him more. He could also be irritating, domineering and possessive, she reminded herself as the telephone rang causing her to jump. She went to the sitting-room to answer it. It was Nick. Rose shuffled backwards, trailing the lead in one hand, and, with the heel of her shoe, nudged the door closed behind her. This is silly, she thought, there was no reason she shouldn't receive a call from whomsoever she pleased. However, she had to take Barry's feelings into consideration. Nick asked how she was. Rose wondered why he was ringing again. Only last night she had told him that she was busy. Was he the sort of man to pester, not to take no for an answer? If so, there was no future for them. That was not the sort of relationship she wanted. A more sinister thought crossed her mind. He knew she had been going back to the mine that day – had he called to find out her reaction to what he may have known would happen?

'No, I haven't,' she answered, puzzled, when Nick asked if she'd seen Jenny. 'Not since we were at Stella's. Why? What's wrong?'

'Probably nothing. She came to see me afterwards. Rose, I ought to have told you sooner, we were once...'

'Yes. I thought so. You don't have to explain, Nick.' And she meant it. At least he was being honest with her.

'Well, good. Anyway, as I was saying, she came up here wanting to make a go of things again. It was all over more than six months ago and there was no chance of my agreeing. In retrospect I see I could've been kinder. She was in a bit of a state when she left. Maddy rang me to say she'd seen her running down the road in tears.'

Rose couldn't see where this was leading.

'I felt bad about it. I mean, I loved the girl once. Did you know she's staying in a squat?'

'No. I didn't.'

'Well, nor did I until today. I went down there. The crowd she shares with haven't seen her since yesterday morning. We know she was all right when she left my place. I'm probably worrying about nothing, Jenny can look after herself. If she was that upset she may not have fancied facing her friends.'

'But why would I have seen her?'

'Oh, God. Look, I just thought, well, she made one or two insinuations about us. She was drunk and upset. I thought she may have come to see you, to persuade you to give me up or to put you off me. Besides, you're out and about a lot, I thought you may simply have run into her somewhere.'

'No, Nick, I'm sorry. The last time I saw her she was still at Stella's.'

47

'Okay, thanks anyway. I expect she'll turn up when she's got whatever it is out of her system. I hope I'm not interrupting anything?' he asked with a question in his voice.

Rose hesitated. 'I've got a dinner guest.'

'I see.'

No, you don't, she thought, but was not prepared to explain.

'Rose, can I still see you next Saturday? We could make a day of it, go to Truro and shop and have a meal.'

She was surprised that she didn't hesitate in agreeing. 'I shall look forward to it,' she said. And that was as much encouragement as Nick Pascoe was getting. If he was so worried about Jenny, a girl, or woman, with whom he had once been close, one who now chose to live or sleep wherever she pleased, then he must still care for her. It was none of her business. She still loved David and always would. You don't necessarily stop caring for someone just because you're no longer together, she reminded herself.

Putting on a cheerful smile she returned to the kitchen to find Barry cleaning his glasses on the edge of the tablecloth in a manner so nonchalant she guessed he had made a determined effort not to eavesdrop on her side of the conversation. She felt exhausted and was glad when he said he must go because he was seeing another of his artists early in the morning.

As she lay in bed the weather began to echo the turmoil of her thoughts. The breeze, which had sent tremors through the shrubs as Barry was leaving, gained strength and whistled in the chimney breast. The windows rattled as the wind increased to gale force. The house was taking the blasts from the front. Rose was unconcerned about damage. The place had survived numerous storms, worse ones than this, and the roof had been replaced a couple of years ago after slates had been ripped off and flung into the garden.

In the end she had decided against telling Barry what had happened. For once she would have welcomed the listening ear of Jack Pearce and almost found herself missing him. Perhaps, she admitted, that was only because he was a foil for her eccentric friends.

Rose did not believe that Jenny was the sort of girl to do a disappearing act simply to gain the attention of a man, but she didn't know her well enough to be certain. And there was, she decided as she turned over to find a more comfortable position, little enough for Jenny to be jealous of. If anything, it ought to be the reverse. Jenny was young and beautiful with a softness of body and face few possessed.

When she woke the violence of the wind had not abated although it had veered to the west and, with it, brought squally rain. The sky had hardly lightened by the time she had showered and dressed and by nine thirty it was obvious that the weather was set for the day. The view Rose so loved was obscured. The Mount, shrouded in rain, might not have existed. To cheer the place up she lit the fire, which smoked infuriatingly for half an hour before finally catching properly. There was no reason for her to leave the house. The fridge was well stocked and she could put the final touches to the painting in the attic where she had splashed out on an overhead light fitting which produced the next best thing to daylight.

Against her better judgement Rose still took the odd photographic commission, which Laura had told her was a sop to her insecurity.

'I don't want to lose my touch,' Rose had argued.

'What you mean is you're afraid you'll fail and you'll need something to fall back on.'

Is she right? Rose wondered as she carried a mug of coffee upstairs to develop the one roll of film that was outstanding. Twice she was interrupted, once by Stella who had now heard that Jenny had gone into hiding, although this was not the main reason for the call. She was ringing to ask if Rose would come to a party they were having on 23 December. 'It's the only effort we make,' Stella added. 'All our friends come in one go. After that we lock ourselves in and ignore Christmas. I suppose if we'd had children it might've been different. Do come.'

'I'd love to. Thanks.' Rose scribbled herself a reminder note then, without time to think about what she was saying, said, 'In which case I hope you'll come to me on New Year's Eve.'

'I'll check with Daniel but I'm sure the answer'll be yes. Goodness, we haven't done that for donkey's years.'

And neither have I, Rose thought, wondering what she had let herself in for. A party? Not since the early years of her marriage had she thrown one. It was an exciting thought.

'Did you do any work on your painting yesterday? I managed to get out for an hour or so and make the most of the weather.'

'Yes.' Rose waited but Stella made no further comment. For the first time she wondered how genuine her friend's interest was.

On her way back upstairs she realised that there wasn't much time. If she was seriously going to throw a party she must organise the invitations quickly before people made other arrangements, if they hadn't done so already.

The second call was from Barry to inform her that they had sold out of the wildflower notelets and he wanted her permission to do a reprint. Rose said yes, knowing that he need not have asked, she always agreed, but that he often found excuses to talk to her. When she mentioned the party, Barry stuttered his acceptance. He was as amazed as Rose had been at the idea.

Leaving the film to dry prior to making prints, Rose stared at the almost complete oil. It disturbed her because of its associations and if it wasn't so good she might have destroyed it. But it is good, she thought, very good. Ought I to tell someone, even if it does make me look ridiculous? she asked herself as she began mixing colours which would put the final touches to the painting.

It was early evening and she was cleaning her brushes when she thought she heard a noise downstairs. Standing still, she listened. From two flights up she could not always be sure if it was the wind or a knock on the kitchen door. She wiped her paint-stained hands on a rag and went to see. Leaning against the jamb, soaking wet, was Inspector Jack Pearce. Rose bit her lip. What now? Why did he keep having to bother her? Seconds later she saw that he wasn't alone.

'May we come in?'

'Yes.' Rose stood back and held the door open, shutting it quickly as rain gusted in. She switched on the fluorescent light to dispel the gloom, knowing that this was no social visit.

'Just a few questions,' Jack said in a voice more official than she had heard before.

'Please, do sit down.'

Jack pulled out a chair and introduced the younger man as Detective Sergeant Green. It was he who took notes whilst Jack asked the questions. 'Three days ago you rang the emergency services regarding what you thought was a scream coming from near or inside the old mine shaft.'

Rose waited. If this was another game to humiliate her further she would threaten to make an official complaint. She was certainly not about to mention the second occasion.

'What made you think there might be someone there?'

'Look, Jack, I've better things to do with my time than play games with you. I admit, I was wrong. I thought I heard a scream, later it was proved that I couldn't have done.' Sergeant Green's eyebrows shot up at her use of his first name.

Jack did not fail to notice Rose blushing. 'That's not what I meant. Have you any reason to believe anyone uses the place for whatever activities they think fit? You know, drugs, orgies, painting, like yourself? Witchcraft?'

Rose laughed. 'None at all. That place is always deserted.'

'Thank you. Just one more thing. When did you last see Jennifer Manders?'

'Two nights ago. I was at the opening of Stella Jackson's latest exhibition. Jenny was there as well.'

'Not since?'

'No.' So Nick had been more than a little concerned if it had reached the stage of police involvement.

'And you wouldn't have any idea where she might be staying?'

'Jack, I hardly know her. I've met her less than a dozen times, mostly at Stella's, once with her father. We haven't reached the stage of exchanging confidences.'

It was Jack's turn to raise a sardonic eyebrow as if he found this unlikely. His next words confirmed her suspicion. 'I'd say that was unusual, wouldn't you? People do seem to have a tendency to confide in you.'

'I don't know where she is,' Rose replied firmly. 'Nor do I have any idea why she's disappeared.'

It was a mistake. She knew that as soon as she had uttered the words.

'I didn't say she's disappeared.'

'Then why are you asking these questions? Her friends in St Ives will be far more use to you than I could be.' Damn him, she thought, feeling his dark eyes on her face: he probably believed she knew more than she did and was holding something back. The fact that this was true made her uncomfortable.

'If you do hear anything you'll let us know, won't you?' It was an order rather than a polite request.

'Her father,' Rose added, recalling the firm, interesting features of Alec Manders. 'Have you tried him? She might be staying there.'

Jack didn't answer. Instead he stood, nodded to his silent companion and made his way to the door. 'Sorry to have troubled you, Mrs Trevelyan.'

Rose closed the door behind him. The formality hurt and it shouldn't have done. The agreement was that they remained friends but Jack didn't seem to want it that way. She peered into the fridge trying to decide what she fancied to eat. Jenny Manders had only been missing for a few hours short of two days. Rose thought it odd that so much was being made of her disappearance. So soon, anyway. She shrugged. There were probably factors she knew nothing about and there was no way she was going to allow Jack to involve her. 'But I think I'm already involved.' She spoke aloud as a terrible thought crossed her mind. Could it possibly have been Jenny whose screams she had heard? No. Jenny had been at Stella's after that first occasion. She shook her head. The painting was finished, there was no need to go there ever again.

4

Jack Pearce was thoughtful during the drive back towards Camborne. It had been a deliberate policy to take someone with him because whenever he encountered Rose he was unsure how he would react. Her rejection still hurt. And, he admitted, he had made the visit in an official capacity although someone of lower rank would normally have done so.

Rose was not inclined to panic. After his initial anger he had realised that some good reason must have prompted her to make that call. Now Jennifer Manders was missing – and Rose knew the girl. He was sure there was more to it than a lovers' tiff or whatever they called it these days. Jenny may be hiding out, sulking, or she could have taken off, alone or with another man, but from what they had learned it was unlikely that she would have left the area.

Madeleine Duke, Stella Jackson, her husband Daniel Wright, and the girl's father and his wife had all been questioned; all had expressed the opinion that she would not have strayed far. If it wasn't for the suspicions that were aroused every time Rose came into the equation he doubted if he would have paid much attention to Nick Pascoe's telephone call despite the fact that the man had sounded genuinely worried.

The three with whom she shared the squat had been unhelpful. They resented the police and, not knowing Jenny well, neither knew nor cared what might have become of her. All they were prepared to say was that they hadn't seen her for a couple of days. It might be worth paying Pascoe a personal visit, he thought. 'Take the St Ives turn-off,' he told DS Green who was driving.

According to Pascoe, Jennifer Manders had been after a reconciliation but he wasn't having it and had sent her away. But had he sent her somewhere permanently? Now who's being fanciful? he asked himself. Had he done so, Pascoe would hardly have drawn attention to the fact.

Nick was upstairs in the room he used to store his work, sorting through frames for a forthcoming show in which he was to be one of half a dozen exhibitors. He was still deciding on the last two of the ten canvases he was expected to display when he heard the crash of the knocker.

'You'd better come in,' he said, frowning, when he learned who his visitor was. DS Green had been asked to wait in the car.

Jack wiped his feet on the coarse doormat and stepped straight into the living area of the low-ceilinged dwelling. Its small windows and the proximity of other similar properties rendered it dark even on a sunny day. Now, on a wet winter's evening, it was positively gloomy despite the two table lamps. The room was chilly but not damp. Pascoe was a hardy man; the sash window was open six inches. Ahead was a wooden staircase, beside it an open door leading to the kitchen. To Jack's right was the back of the settee with its sagging springs and against the wall by the window stood a table and four chairs. On it were the remains of a single meal. There were no shelves. Pascoe's books and cassettes were stacked on the floor beside the player. Neither was there a television set, possibly because there was no room for one, or maybe it was kept in the bedroom.

Jack had surveyed the room in seconds, and now turned his attention to the man. His mouth tightened. He could understand why Rose was attracted to him. Not only was he an artist but he possessed rugged good looks and he had a way of moving which suggested that he was totally comfortable in the world.

Standing with his hands in the pockets of his denim jacket, Nick asked if there was any news.

'No. None.' Fighting for objectivity in the face of the man who had replaced him, Jack asked him to go over the night in question again. It would be all too easy to apportion blame here and thus effectively remove the opposition. But blame for what?

'Certainly.' Nick hooked out a chair with the toe of his suede boot and sat down. Jack chose the settee when it was indicated that he should do the same, then regretted it as he sank low into the cushions. 'Jenny turned up at Stella's exhibition. She was there before me. I wasn't certain if I could attend.'

'She was invited?'

'Jenny? Yes, definitely. She was there for the drinks upstairs before the official opening. I didn't see much of her in the gallery, there were too many other people there, but we managed a few words. I left before she did and came straight home. About forty-five minutes later, possibly more, she knocked on the door and I let her in. I was on the phone at the time to Rose Trevelyan.'

Jack flinched. He could have hit the man but he listened carefully as Pascoe went over the events of that evening.

'That's it. It's exactly as I said before on the phone. Oh, then Maddy rang. Madeleine Duke.'

'For any specific reason?'

'Out of concern for Jenny. She knows Jenny can be a bit highly strung, if that phrase is still in fashion. She also wanted to invite me to supper the next night.'

Jack nodded. The man was certainly in demand and he wondered if Rose knew. But he would not lower himself to ask if he had accepted the invitation. 'And yesterday morning?'

'Yesterday morning I began to worry about what Maddy had said. Jenny's impetuous, the sort of girl who is capable of doing something stupid to draw attention to herself, but I didn't know where she was staying. I asked around and when her three – what shall we say, room-mates? – said they hadn't seen her either I decided I ought to call the police.'

'You went out of your way to find her?'

'Naturally. I wouldn't waste your time if I thought I could locate her myself.' Nick had felt the right thing to do was to report Jenny missing but he had not expected any action to be taken. Now he asked himself why an inspector was involved. It worried him.

'And who did you ask?'

'Everyone who was at the exhibition. The people I know, that is.'

'Including Mrs Trevelyan?' He couldn't help it even though he knew the answer.

'Yes.'

'Why?'

Nick's frown deepened but did not detract from his good looks. 'Just in case she'd seen Jenny.'

'Mrs Trevelyan lives in Newlyn. What made you think she might have done?'

'Nothing made me think so, Inspector. It was just that she was there and, well, Jenny knew that we'd been seeing each other.'

'But your affair with Jennifer Manders was over. Why should it concern her who you're seeing now?'

'Look, I don't really know. I've already explained she wanted to come back here to live. If she was jealous, I thought she might have gone to Rose's to cause a scene. Really, I'm not a mind reader, it was only a guess.'

He has a temper, Jack thought, as Nick got up and strode around the room, sweeping back his hair impatiently as he did

55

so. And what had caused Pascoe to think Jenny had been to see Rose? He sighed, knowing there was little more he could do. But as he stood he thought it worth a try to ask, 'Did Mrs Trevelyan tell you she called us recently? She – '

'When she was out at the old engine house? Yes.'

'Was anyone aware she'd be there that day?'

'How on earth should I know?' Nick stopped pacing. He picked up a paintbrush and slapped the bristles against the palm of his hand. 'Actually, now I think about it, quite a lot of people. It was Stella who suggested it as a starting place. There was a crowd of us there one night when the subject came up.'

'By which you mean?'

'Rose has gone back to working in oils, and not before time if what I've seen of her work's anything to go by. Stella thought it'd be a test for her. So many artists have painted just that type of scenery but if Rose could do it, and do it well, or better, it would prove that she wasn't run-of-the-mill. Stella thought it would give her the confidence to carry on.'

'I'll need the names of the guests that night, if you don't mind.'

Nick provided them and Jack left, more puzzled than when he had arrived. Had those screams had anything to do with Jenny's disappearance even if she had been seen afterwards? There was one way of settling something which bothered him and he believed he could arrange it with very little outlay. He was owed a favour from several years back. One he decided it was time to call in. This was unofficial business. If nothing came of it he would not, like Rose, have made a public fool of himself.

Madeleine Duke's past life was mostly unknown to her Cornish friends and this was part of the reason why she hadn't been accepted with as much enthusiasm as she had expected. True, invitations came at regular intervals, such as the one to Stella's exhibition, and there was never a shortage of visitors to her shop or the flat above it, but she still felt she was treated differently. Already she was beginning to realise that her past, good or bad, didn't matter here. What did matter was that she refused to talk about it. What she had failed to understand was that she would have been welcomed more warmly if the details of her life were common knowledge. The Cornish possessed a need to know but for no reason other than to satisfy their innate curiosity. Nothing would have been held against her.

Maddy had had a child, a daughter, and for this sin, because she had been unmarried, her parents had disowned her. She had realised too late that she was pregnant, and a termination was out of the question. The baby had been adopted. It was some years ago now but she still regretted it and the pain remained. How happy the child would have been in Cornwall if only she'd been allowed a chance to think things through. But it was too late now. An only child herself, she had been the centre of her parents' world, only to be told how cruelly she had let them down in the end. Having Annie, as she secretly called the little girl, adopted had not healed the breach between them as she had believed it would. Her parents had refused to have anything more to do with her. Maddy had given away her child for nothing. She had moved down to Brighton and mixed with a crowd her parents would have loathed until it dawned on her that they were losers like herself. From there she had moved from town to town along the south coast, never finding the sense of belonging that she was searching for. Finally she had come to Cornwall where, after two years of constant grind, cleaning and serving in cafés and pubs, she had saved enough to add to the small sum her grandmother, who had secretly sympathised with her, had left her and rented the tiny shop and the premises above it. In the little spare time she had had Maddy had worked at her crafts and, although initially her stock was sparse, she had continued to add to it, buying in when necessary.

Just over a year ago, after a particularly successful summer, she had spoken to her landlord and made him an offer to buy which had been accepted. Now she had a mortgage hanging over her head but instead of worrying her it gave her the sense of security which she had been lacking since the adoption of her baby when her life had been turned upside down. She lived frugally but was almost content. Only one thing really mattered: tracing her daughter. But that was not her prerogative, legally it must be the other way around. Maddy realised she was nest-building in case of that happy eventuality.

Her need to belong was so desperate that even she realised it was unnatural. Other women, women like Rose Trevelyan, seemed quite content to go it alone and regarded being accepted as neither here nor there. Perhaps that was the secret, not to care too much. Rose Trevelyan was an outsider, too, although she had married a Cornishman and had lived in the area for over twenty-five years.

She had been rearranging the stock on the shelves during a quiet period when a policeman had arrived to question her about Jenny Manders. Maddy had been unusually withdrawn and barely spoke other than to confirm that she had seen Jenny when she went past in tears but had no idea where she might have gone. 'If she was that upset she could've come here, she'd have seen the light on,' she had added. 'She knows me well enough for that.' A customer looking for Christmas presents had come in and the policeman had gone.

Later that afternoon Stella, who had closed the gallery early, dropped in for a chat. There was still no news of Jenny. Maddy Duke did not know how she was supposed to react but she managed to keep her feelings hidden. She was still smarting from the disappointment at Nick's refusal to share her mackerel.

The following morning, after a fitful sleep, Maddy stood behind the glass of the shop door and watched the teeming rain. Water ran over the cobbles and down towards the harbour. Some of the galleries were open. Last-minute Christmas shoppers huddled beneath umbrellas and stepped back, pressing against the buildings to avoid being splashed, when a car passed through the narrow lanes. She sighed. What's done is done, she thought. It's too late to change things now. She had not lied to the police, except by omission. Wanting Nick, she hoped he would show his gratitude in the way in which she desired once he learned how she had protected him from what might have been a potentially awkward situation.

Rose stared out of the window. It was Sunday evening. 'It's still raining,' she commented unnecessarily.

'It was forecast,' Laura said, getting up stiffly from the floor with a groan. 'It'll probably last through Christmas now.'

58

The two women looked at each other and smiled. Long wet spells were very much a part of their lives and the conversations that were conducted in the local shops. The sharp, cold weather, if it came at all, never lasted and Christmas Day was almost always mild, if not warm.

They had been sharing a bottle of wine in Rose's sitting-room and talking about the Newlyn lights which had recently been switched on. Then, on the night of 19 December, they would go off in memory of the crew of the lifeboat *Solomon Browne* who, in 1981, lost their lives in a desperate bid to save those of others.

The switching on of the lights was an event and crowds came to witness it, along with the fireworks, and to listen to the male voice choir, although it was to Mousehole the coach parties went to see the displays, some of which floated in the harbour or were fixed high up on the hills.

Unlike most places, Newlyn and Mousehole preferred to wait; their lights were lit mid-December during the Christmas season proper, not two months in advance.

'I haven't heard one word about Nick Pascoe this evening,' Laura commented slyly as she refilled their glasses.

Rose, curled in an armchair, shrugged.

'Are you going to see him again?' Laura rewound the band restraining her hair before resuming her position, cross-legged on the floor in front of the fire. She had taken off her boots because the toes were damp and, despite the horizontal stripes of her Lycra leggings, her legs still looked thin. Rose couldn't remember the last time she'd seen her friend in a skirt.

'Yes. On Saturday.'

'You don't sound over-enthusiastic.'

'I'm not.'

'Come on, Rose. Tell Auntie Laura.'

'Oh, I don't know. I just don't want to rush into things.'

'Dear God, woman, you waited five years to get involved with another man, I wouldn't call that rushing. Okay, I accept that you and Jack wasn't to be, but Nick's an artist and you've got lots in com – Oh, Rose. Don't!' Laura was on her feet, pulling a tissue from the sleeve of her thigh-length tabard. 'What have I said? Me and my big mouth.'

Rose wiped her eyes and sniffed. 'It's not you, Laura. It's me. I don't know what I want any more. I don't even know if I want anyone else. I enjoy male company but it was David I loved. You see, I was lucky, I had the best. I don't see why there needs to be anyone else.'

'There doesn't,' Laura said decisively, perching on the arm of Rose's chair. 'No one can replace David but you mustn't close your mind to the possibility that there could be someone else out there who would be equally right. Different, yes, but still right.' Laura pursed her lips and stared over Rose's head. 'I think you're talking to the wall, Laura Penfold.'

Rose managed a smile. 'I'll bear in mind what you said. It's just that I thought I was finally over it. It's a long time since I cried.'

Laura hugged her. 'No harm in that. And you'll cry again. There'll always be times when you feel like this, but you still have to live, my girl.' She took Rose's glass. 'Come on, we'll never get drunk at this rate. Now, what else is bothering you?'

'Honestly! Can't I have any secrets?'

'You should know better than that when I'm around.'

'You've got to tell Jack,' Laura said when Rose had told her what had happened on her return visit to the mine. 'Especially if this girl has gone missing. There might be a connection.'

Rose knew she was right, but now she would have to endure his wrath for *not* reporting it. 'Okay, I'll do it.'

Laura said she was going home because there was something she wanted to watch on television. After she left, Rose debated whether to have a bath and an early night with a book or to watch the programme herself. She did neither because Jack turned up ten minutes later. She swallowed hard. She had not kept her promise to Laura to ring him immediately. Still, she could rectify that now in person.

'Rose, I need to talk to you. Nothing personal,' he added quickly, seeing the sceptical look on her face. 'May I come in?' She looks pale, he thought, and troubled, but still lovely despite that baggy old jumper.

'I'm very tired, Jack, as long as you're quick.'

Jack sighed and sat down, uninvited. 'We've found the remains of a female.' He paused, wondering what the rest of the news would do to Rose. She was frowning. 'In the shaft.'

'What?' Rose's hand flew to her mouth as she sagged into a chair. 'Is it Jenny?'

'Not a body, Rose, remains.'

Her eyes widened with realisation. 'You mean bones? A skeleton?'

Jack nodded.

'Well, obviously it's not Jenny then. She's only been missing for three days. And it can't have anything to do with the other screams I heard.'

'What other screams?' Jack leaned forward, glaring at her.

'I think I'd better explain, Jack.'

'I think you better had, Rose.'

She did so, aware of his anger and knowing how impossible what she was telling him sounded.

'How the devil do you always get into these situations?' he said, but it was a rhetorical question.

Rose squeezed her forehead between her outspread fingers. 'Wait a minute. The rescue team checked the mine. How come they didn't find anything?'

'They looked at the bottom of the shaft, not further in along it.'

Rose did not seem to be listening. 'Found? What do you mean found? Did someone just decide to pop down there for a quick look?'

'No. I got a rock-climbing friend of mine to do me a favour. Look, don't take this amiss. I know you, Rose, you're not inclined to dramatise and it seems now that there *was* something going on out there. What you heard may have been genuine or some sort of attempt to scare you off. However, what we need to do now is to identify the woman.'

Rose was genuinely tired and emotionally exhausted and none of what she was hearing made sense. She wished Jack could explain it all away and she could forget about it. 'Will you be able to?'

'We don't know yet. It's been a long time. We'll have to go back over missing persons and hope the pathologists can give us something to work on. I just thought I'd let you know. I wanted to tell you myself rather than you hear it through the grapevine.' He was worried about Rose on two counts. Firstly because he did not believe she had imagined she'd heard something. Although nothing or no one had been found, Rose was too level-headed to have panicked for no reason. And, secondly, if the long-dead woman turned out to have been murdered there was a chance that Rose might be in danger for having drawn attention to the place.

He was suddenly aware that she had been crying before his arrival. She certainly looked as if she had had enough for one day. He got up to leave. Glancing back over his shoulder as he opened the back door, he saw Rose sitting motionless at the table, her head in her hands. Leave it, Jack, he thought, wanting nothing more than to comfort her. 'Goodnight, Rose.'

'Goodnight.' She barely raised her head.

Rose sighed deeply. She was tired and knew that she ought to eat but could not face doing so. Instead she locked up and switched off the lights and went upstairs to get ready for bed. Lying beneath the covers she tried to think of anything other than the body of a stranger lying forgotten at the bottom of the shaft. Cornwall was full of superstition and there were stone circles and ancient places of worship where people claimed to feel power if they touched the stones. This had not happened to Rose but she did wonder if she had experienced some sort of supernatural episode.

The sound of gulls woke her. Above the rattle of rain on the window she heard their noisy squawking as they fought over scraps. Rose drew back the curtains and confronted the gloom of another wet morning. She showered quickly and dressed before making coffee. She intended to buy Barry's present and organise her New Year's Eve party, although at the moment it was the last thing she felt like doing. It puzzled her that Jack had said little regarding her having heard a second scream but she doubted he would leave it at that.

The wipers flicked effectively back and forth across the windscreen as she drove along the sea front. It was mild and muggy, the sort of atmosphere in which germs bred easily and would bring about the misery of colds and flu. The windows steamed up. She started winding down the one beside her before remembering that the demister in this car worked.

Christmas trees twinkled in windows as she made her way towards the Jubilee Pool and Ross Bridge which spanned Penzance harbour. *Scillonian III*, the ferry which made daily trips over to St Mary's, was now laid up for the winter. Rose pulled into the large car-park which had once been part of the harbour before it was filled in and where a space was always guaranteed.

The drizzle was gentle on her face and misted her hair as she walked up Market Jew Street. At the top she turned down into Chapel Street and was cheered by a lively conversation with Tim and Katherine who ran the bookshop where she called to collect the two hardback novels she had ordered as her Christmas present to herself. There was still the question of what to get for Barry but that would have to wait. Although the rain had stopped Rose no longer felt like shopping and she had a sudden desire to be on her own.

At home, coffee beside her and pen and paper at hand, she made a list of friends and acquaintances. Planning the food and drink for the party would provide a welcome distraction from her muddled thoughts. She chewed the mangled cap of the biro. Barry Rowe had already accepted, as had Laura and Trevor. Stella had not yet come back to her so she made a note to ring her and Daniel again. There was Mike and Barbara, Maddy Duke and Nick. And Jenny? Well that would depend upon whether she turned up by then. Nine people, apart from Jenny, ten with herself. It was not many. On the other hand, had she been asked to draw up a list of her friends a year ago there would have been even fewer names. Jack? She shook her head, unsure how he would react to such an invitation. A fleeting smile crossed her face. How about Doreen and Cyril Clarke? They were nice people. Doreen was the same age as Rose but dressed and acted as though she might be her mother. Cyril was an ex-miner who now threw all his energies into his garden. She added their names. I will ask Jack, she decided. I want him to be my friend. Thirteen people. It couldn't be helped, and not everyone might be available.

Half an hour later she had completed a suitable menu. All she had to do now was to plan the location of her next piece of work. St Michael's Mount had been photographed and painted from every conceivable angle and in every type of light and weather.

Rose did not think the market could bear another canvas of that famous view. Besides, it was time to experiment. She preferred rugged scenery or rough seas but she wanted to attempt something more gentle, a country setting, where there were trees and maybe running water, the type of thing she had always been able to capture in watercolours but had not attempted in oils.

Taking the guest list to the sitting-room she received affirmative replies from everyone, along with gossip and speculation over the finding of the unknown female. With the exception of Jack, whom she was nervous of asking, Maddy was last on the list. She asked if she might bring a guest.

'Peter Dawson,' she explained. 'Do you know him?'

'Only by reputation. I'd love to meet him.'

As soon as she replaced the receiver, the telephone rang. 'Who on earth have you been talking to? I thought I'd never get through. Rose, can I ask you a favour? Terry and Marie have decided to stay on until after the New Year. Any chance of them coming on the 31st?'

'Of course. I'd love to see them.' Any of Laura's sons was guaranteed to liven up a party should it show signs of flagging. If Jack accepted, that would take the number to sixteen, enough to fill the small house and create a proper party atmosphere. Rose shivered. It was not Jack who made her nervous but his alter ego, Inspector Pearce, who had eventually believed her when she said she had heard screams and who had, because of this, discovered a dead woman. And somehow she was involved, or would become involved – she knew that instinctively. 'Laura, they've found someone in that shaft. Whoever it is, she's been there for years. Jack told me last night.'

'That's a bit too much of a coincidence, isn't it? And how come they didn't find her before?'

Rose explained as much as she knew. 'Look, why don't we meet for a drink tonight if you're not doing anything?'

'Okay. Sevenish in the Swordfish?'

Rose hung up. Arms folded, she wandered across to the window. A widening band of blue was gradually pushing upward from the horizon. Above, clouds parted and spokes of sunlight fanned down to the sea. How odd, she thought, watching the changing vista, a girl goes missing but another female body turns up. But there was work to be done. Upstairs that roll of developed film was waiting to be printed. She decided to get that task out of the way.

Later, having typed out the invoice and boxed up the prints, Rose left them on the hall table to remind herself to deliver them. It was too early to meet Laura so she switched on the television to watch *Westcountry Live*, the hour-long regional news programme. Half seated, she aimed the remote control at the screen and changed channels just in time to hear the newscaster say, 'The body of a woman was discovered this morning near Godrevy Point. She has been identified as Jennifer Manders from St Ives who was recently reported missing. The cause of death is uncertain as the police have not yet issued a statement but they are appealing for the public to come forward with information as to her whereabouts if she has been seen since Thursday night. This is the number to ring.' It appeared at the bottom of the screen. 'We will repeat that number later in the programme. And now we move on to the latest dilemma facing West Country fishermen.'

But Rose was no longer listening. Jenny was dead. It was impossible to accept. The telephone rang. Rose ignored it, the answering machine would pick up the call, she was not ready to speak to anyone yet. Poor Jenny, she thought, so lovely and far too young to have died. Selfishly, Rose felt glad that her body had not been found anywhere near the mine. She would not have been able to cope with that.

Hardly aware that the television was still on, she wondered whether it was suicide or an accident. She might have fallen from the rocks or drowned in the sea. The bulletin had given no clues. The phone rang again. She let it, hearing the machine click into action once more. The sound was down so she had no idea if it was the same caller or a different one.

The small clock on the mantelpiece with its brass base and domed glass cover chimed the hour. Seven o'clock already. She would be late for Laura. Throwing on a raincoat she grabbed her handbag and left the house, slamming the kitchen door behind her.

The street lights were reflected in the water of the harbour and on the glistening pavements which had not yet dried after another brief shower. Three cars came up the hill, thumping

65

music pulsating from one. Another, badly corroded by the salty air, spluttered noisily and belched fumes from a faulty exhaust. The driver of the third tooted but had passed before Rose had a chance to see who it was.

She reached the Strand and hurried to the pub. The Swordfish was unusual in that it had retained two bars. The smaller lounge was carpeted and cosy and might almost have been someone's front room. The long public bar was far more basic with its wooden floor and juke-box. Laura was perched on a high stool talking to two of Trevor's friends. Rose knew them by sight and smiled. They moved away after saying hello.

'The usual?' Laura asked, getting out her purse. She ordered a glass of wine and paid for it then looked Rose full in the face. 'What is it? Are you still upset about last night?'

'No.' Rose turned and dragged a spare stool nearer to Laura. Both women were in jeans and sweatshirts, their hair feathery from the damp atmosphere. 'They've found Jenny.'

'Oh, that's good.' She paused and met Rose's eyes. 'Jesus, not good, I take it.'

'No. She's dead. It was on the news this evening.'

Laura shook her head and her hair, held high on her head in a band, danced wildly. 'What happened?'

'They didn't say, only that her body had been found.'

'Has Jack said anything about it?'

'No.' Rose wondered if it had been him on the telephone rather than one of the St Ives crowd.

They sipped in silence for a while, oblivious to the rock music blaring out and the crashing of the table-football game in progress. 'Laura, I think I'll go home if you don't mind.'

'Of course not. You shouldn't have come, you could have rung me.'

They parted company in the street and went their separate ways. Rose had a lot to think about. Why, for instance, had Jack made such a point of searching the shaft and who was the woman they had found? What relevance, if any, did their findings have to Jenny's death?

But most puzzling of all were those screams. Why would anyone wish to draw attention to the place even if they hadn't known what lay beneath the ground?

5

Maddy Duke had rung Peter Dawson to ask him to accompany her to Rose's party. He had agreed to do so. When she rang a second time to invite him to her own party, arranged on the spur of the moment for Boxing Day, he had been surprised to hear himself accept another invitation because he was not gregarious.

He was considered to be eccentric, even by Cornish standards. Yet as an artist he was far from flamboyant; he cared little whether his work sold or not because his love was the act of painting, not the income received from it. He lived alone in a two-bedroomed house perched high overlooking the sea between St Ives and Zennor. His abstracts sold for a lot of money, maybe only one or two a year but he knew the danger of flooding the market. Many of his pieces were kept from the public eye until he believed it was time to produce another. He had investments which provided an adequate income for his basic lifestyle and he preferred to live where he did rather than in a better property which would be too big for a single person. He had no intention of sharing his home with anyone and, although many might not agree, it was comfortable enough for him. Now and then he needed a woman but usually went out of the area to find one because the local available females knew better than to expect more than one night in his bed. If he succeeded in seducing Maddy Duke he knew that she was unlikely to prove to be the exception. However, there was something about her which appealed to his baser instincts. She struck him as a passionate woman, one who, involved in her own business, would not make demands on him or expect more than he had to offer. This, he supposed, had been at the back of his mind when he had accepted the invitations. Dress was informal, she had told him, but then it usually was. Peter only bothered with a suit on his rare trips to London.

His house was built of granite and was simply furnished but was not without its touches of luxury. A modern heating system ensured that it was always warm in winter and that there was a constant supply of hot water. He ate well and the cigars he smoked were bought from a specialist shop in Truro. His single malt whisky was delivered by the case from an off-licence in Penzance. With an occasional woman thrown in, Peter Dawson could not imagine what else any man could possibly wish for.

He stood gazing critically at his latest, as yet incomplete, work which was propped on a chair. Whatever the cynics may think, the shapes and colours displayed on the canvas made perfect sense to him. His head on one side, his chin in his hand, he decided that there was a definite pattern in what seemed like randomness.

He moved languidly across the room, cigar smoke trailing behind him and masking the smell of oil paint and turpentine. From his window he saw the lights of a fishing-boat as it returned to the harbour and a scattering of stars which promised a cold night. He would be warm, not so Jenny Manders who would now be in the mortuary in her refrigerated container. He had heard the news on Radio Cornwall as he pottered around in the kitchen making a list for his next visit to the shops.

Jenny had spent the occasional night in his bed and he had fond memories of her. She had been undemanding, accepting that all that was in it for her was the chance to share a few drinks, a simple meal and his body. The arrangement had suited them both and neither of them was offended when they spoke of other lovers. In fact, he thought with a grin, between us we knew enough to make a lot of people sweat.

He sighed and ran a hand through his short hair. It was greying now, but not noticeably so because it was fair and had once been the colour of ripening wheat. Poor cow, he thought, knowing that in reality Jenny had only ever loved Nick. But I understood her, he realised. Loving Nick had not stopped her from sleeping with other men, but her conquests had been born out of insecurity. With Jenny, nothing ever lasted although the fault had lain with her. She had the male trait of being able to compartmentalise her life; love and sex were not the same thing. She ought to have been a man, he concluded, before walking over to the table which held his drinks and pouring another half-tumbler of Scotch. He sat back in the brown leather settee which had altered its shape to suit his and speculated upon how Jenny could have antagonised someone enough to kill her. In Peter's mind there was no doubt it was murder. Jenny was no fool, apart from which she loved life. And, being so much a part of the place where she was born, she knew the dangers, she would not have been walking along perilous clifftops when the wind was off the land. Yes, she could be irritating, but so could most people. Revenge for an illicit love affair? It seemed unlikely in this day and age although men and women had been known to kill for less. No, Jenny may have been casual but she was careful and no one could accuse her of avarice. Initially it had crossed his mind that she may have stooped to blackmail but he soon saw how out of character this would have been. And as far as men were concerned, apart from one indiscretion with Daniel Wright, married men were not on her agenda. On the other hand Stella Jackson was an unknown quantity. She may well be financially independent of her husband and feminist enough to prefer to keep her own name but would she have tolerated an affair? Peter shook his head. It was highly unlikely she had found out. Nick Pascoe? he mused. No, too level-headed, he decided, and he had nothing to gain by it. Or had he? Had Jenny, who wanted him back, been making a nuisance of herself? And hadn't he occasionally sensed that violence lurked beneath the surface of Nick's urbanity?

He would miss Jenny and her contrary ways. As awkward as she could be at times, she still had had the capacity to mock herself and to make him laugh. Rumour had it that Nick was now seeing a woman from Newlyn, a fellow artist called Rose Trevelyan, one who, apparently, had allowed her talents to lie idle for too long. Naturally this might have upset Jenny but she was a fighter. It was six months since their relationship had ended but if she had set out to win Nick back, Peter doubted if the small matter of another woman would have troubled her.

In a couple of weeks he would meet this Mrs Trevelyan, possibly sooner if she was at Maddy's on the 26th. A widow. He grinned. 'You never know,' he said with a contented smile as he nudged the compact cylinder of ash off the end of his cigar with his little finger.

With his drink beside him he tried to calculate how long it would take the police to discover his relationship with Jenny. Perhaps, he concluded, they never would.

'Dead? She can't be dead.' Nick stared around the room as if it was strange to him or else the walls might provide the answer to what seemed like the present madness.

All three men were standing: himself, Inspector Pearce and another man whose name he had already forgotten. Despite the horror and outrage at what he had heard, Nick saw that some strong emotion also gripped the inspector beneath the grimness of his expression.

Jack Pearce was assessing his man, unsure how genuine the shock was. Everyone who had known Jenny would be interviewed although they would not yet be aware that this was a suspicious death. Her body had been found by a couple out walking. It had lain on the shoreline, her clothes and hair saturated, and the initial assumption had been that she had drowned. With the arrival of the police surgeon, a reliable man from Redruth, this had become less certain. He expressed his doubts and suggested that higher powers than his become involved. Jack had not digested the medical technicalities but had put the wheels in motion anyway. They had been lucky to find a pathologist to do the post-mortem early that afternoon. The police surgeon's suspicions had been confirmed. Jenny was dead before her body was immersed in water. Two blows to the back of the head had killed her. They had been barely detectable as the bleeding had stopped quickly in the icy salt water which had also washed away the blood. Her mass of hair had concealed the injuries which had not had time to swell. Tests on her lungs and stomach proved conclusively that she had not drowned.

A suspicious death, Jack thought, but not necessarily murder. There was the slim possibility that she had fallen, landed on rocks, then been washed out to sea and brought back to land when the current was right. It was unlikely, though. A fall serious enough to kill someone ought to have produced other injuries and there were none: no bruises or scratches anywhere else on her body. She had been dead for at least three days.

Nick Pascoe had been asked to make a formal statement. As her most recent lover and the man who had reported her missing, he was the obvious starting point, if not, Jack thought, the most obvious suspect in view of the fact that she had tried to revive their relationship. Nick Pascoe had not been interested. Because of Rose? Jack asked himself.

And Rose knew these people, had known Jenny, and had been one of the last to see her alive. What sickened him was that she, too, had a motive. If she was desperate for Pascoe she might have felt the need to remove the younger, more attractive competition. Not that he believed that himself, Rose was far too pragmatic, but he knew how it might look to his colleagues. He could not protect her, she would have to be interviewed along with everyone else.

Those screams, what did they mean? Rose had reported them; Nick had reported Jenny missing. Were they in something together?

Almost in imitation of Nick Pascoe, who was near to tears, Jack ran a hand through his thick, dark hair and sighed. He wanted nothing more than to go home and shower and get something to eat. But that luxury was hours away yet.

Stella Jackson was unaware of a conversation which had taken place between Daniel and Rose some weeks previously. Daniel had already forgotten it. He was not a man who had much recall when it came to things he had said.

'It's for the best, I think. Don't you agree? Under the circumstances,' she added with a touch of spite.

Daniel merely nodded. What a mess it all was. What a fool he had been. Thank goodness only the two of them knew. He was not a natural liar and neither was Stella but this lie was more than necessary. They agreed to stick to the same story. The only person who could have invalidated their story was dead. Having listened to the news they knew it would not be long until the police arrived.

Rose stepped into her brightly lit kitchen, removed her raincoat and reached for the half-full bottle of wine she had opened for Laura the night before. It seemed more like a week ago. Then she lit a cigarette. Armed, as she called it, she went to the sitting-room to listen to her messages, cheered by the chintz of her upholstery and the low lighting. She depressed the PLAY button.

'Stella here. Will you ring me?' A bleep was followed by a second voice. 'Hi, it's Maddy. Your having a party gave me an idea. I'm having one Boxing Day afternoon. Do come. Let me know. Cheerio.'

About to erase the messages, she realised there had been a third call in her absence. 'It's Jack. Did you listen to the news? I can't talk now but I'll be in touch later.'

Rose knew he used the word later in the local way. It might mean this evening or any time during the next month. Am I up to returning these calls? she wondered, then decided she might as well in case people rang back when she was in bed. She longed for another early night and couldn't understand why she was so tired lately.

Stella answered on the second ring as if she had been hovering by the phone.

'I got your message,' Rose began.

'Have you heard?'

'About Jenny? Yes.'

'Isn't it awful? What on earth can have happened?'

Rose wished Stella hadn't bothered to contact her if all she wanted to do was speculate.

'And poor Maddy. She was the last one to see her alive. And to think she seemed fine when she left here.' Rose assumed she was now talking about Jenny. 'It's hard to imagine something like that happening while we were tucked up in our beds.'

'They didn't say when she died.'

'No, but it seems logical. Why else wasn't she seen after Thursday night? Anyway, don't let all this affect your work. You've got a long way to go yet.'

Rose made some excuse and hung up. It was true that things occurred in threes: the screams, the unknown woman in the shaft and now Jenny. Jenny had certainly been knocking back the drink at Stella's; if she had taken a walk along a cliff path she might have lost her footing, especially on the narrow muddy path. But it hadn't been raining then, Rose remembered. Stop it, she told herself. It isn't your problem. But something Stella had said was playing on her mind. 'When we were tucked up in our beds.' Surely Daniel had told her that Stella, nervous beforehand and wound up afterwards, always went for a long walk after a preview because she was unable to sleep. Rose shook her head. Stella was her mentor and an intelligent, highly talented woman. Why would she wish harm to an innocent girl? This is ridiculous, she thought. I don't even know how she died.

She felt a rumble of hunger. It was almost nine and time to think about food. As she opened cupboards it dawned on her that this would be her first Christmas alone. She planned to make it a hedonistic day, a day of small luxuries, and she would save her new novels until then.

Bone weary, her limbs feeling heavy, she had decided that scrambled eggs would have to suffice, but they would also have to wait. The phone rang again. It was Jack. At least he hadn't arrived in person. He, too, sounded exhausted and said he was ringing to warn her she would be required to make a statement.

'Yes, I was expecting to have to. Jack, does this mean what I think it means?'

'Rose, you know I can't...'

'Sorry. I shouldn't have asked.'

There was the slightest hesitation before he said, 'Maybe I could arrange to interview you myself. You knew them all.'

'They know each other better.'

'But they don't have your knack of seeing things that others don't.' This was not flattery. Rose had an eye for details, in what people said as well as in the way they looked. And she might be more forthcoming with him than in a formal interview.

'When?'

'Soon. I'll let you know.'

Rose said goodnight and returned to the kitchen where she had got as far as cracking the eggs before she realised that, without actually saying so, Jack had let her know that Jenny Manders had been murdered. She threw the shells in the bin. I forgot to invite him to my party again, she thought, then wondered how she could possibly be thinking about such a thing after hearing the awful news.

'Oh, don't, love.' Angela Choake, now Manders since they had married quietly in Penzance register office, sat down beside

73

her husband and put her arm around his shoulders. She hated to see a man cry, especially one who was as outwardly tough as Alec. His body was firm, his muscles taut, and his face showed strength of character. She could not begin to imagine how he must feel because she had no children herself. She had not wanted them and this was one of the reasons her first marriage had ended. She did not like to admit that childbirth terrified her and she had had no intention of losing her figure.

Patting Alec's shoulder she got up and searched in the sideboard, unexpectedly finding some brandy. Alec rarely drank and his mother had not allowed alcohol in the house, or so he had told her in the days when their relationship had been a secret, although not as well-kept a secret as they had supposed. Probably the brandy was for medicinal purposes. Either way she needed it even if Alec refused it.

In the kitchen which her husband was in the process of modernising she fetched two glasses and poured generous measures, taking a sip from one of them before returning to the living-room.

Alec wiped his eyes, blew his nose loudly and gave her a watery smile. With unexpected insight, Angela saw that he was confusing grief with guilt because he had largely ignored his daughter over the years. His mother had a lot to answer for: she had bound Alec to her with ties far stronger than apron strings and had prevented him from enjoying his marriage and loving Jenny.

Jenny was all right. From the little Angela knew of her she had recognised her as a survivor despite the lack of affection from her small family.

After the passage of years it was hard to recall how their affair had come about. Angela supposed the attraction had been there from the day Alex came to fit a new sink at her old place. She had made him tea, aware that he struggled to keep his eyes from the contours of her body in tight-fitting jeans. It had been summertime and her large breasts, out of proportion to her figure, had pushed against the restraints of her T-shirt. Angela was striking rather than beautiful. She was aware that her face was quite ordinary but her figure could have belonged to the models who posed for top-shelf magazines and her long, straight red hair caused other heads to turn. She hoped no one realised that she now coloured it because the natural red was fading.

At forty-one and over a decade younger than Alec she still retained a carefree attitude to life. But only when her first marriage had ended had she really begun to enjoy life. Freed from the boredom of housekeeping and entertaining John's rather dry friends and their dull wives – whom, she suspected, he cultivated for these qualities because they provided a foil for his own charm and exuberance – she had started many projects, none of which had lasted. Finally she had taken a part-time job in a baker's where she still worked. Around the house she did as little as possible and spent the afternoons with friends or, in the summer, on the beach.

Alec was all that she wanted: a mixture of father, mother and lover. He could cook, he was tidy, far tidier than herself, and he was skilled with his hands which meant he could alter or repair anything in the house. Despite his rather stern demeanour and his lack of experience with women he was a good lover.

Watching him fighting back tears she felt a momentary disgust. It weakened him in her eyes because what she required from him was his particular maleness. She had no idea that what had attracted him was not so much her looks but her similarity to Agnes Manders, his mother. Angela was, without being aware of it, the head of the household and always managed to get her own way.

The police had come to break the news that Jenny was dead but they would be returning once Alec had had time to accept it. There were questions they needed to ask. Angela could not imagine her stepdaughter being stupid enough to go wandering over the cliffs at night, but maybe she had been drunk, maybe she was following in her mother's footsteps.

Alec had hardly tasted his drink but Angela's glass was empty. She refilled it in the kitchen hoping that he wouldn't notice. Running a finger over the smooth wood of the cupboards he had built for her she realised there would soon be no trace of the woman who had ruled this house for so many years once this last room had been modernised.

She frowned. Renata Manders had been a drinker. But had she been driven to it? If what she had heard about Agnes Manders was correct then it would not surprise her. But what am I doing now? she wondered as she stared at the dark gold liquid in her glass. Was there something about *Alec* that made women want to drink? It was a ridiculous idea, brought on by the shock she had received upon hearing of Jenny's death. But, as she stood in the still unfinished kitchen, she asked herself why, when they had both been free agents, she had gone along with his desire to keep their relationship a secret for so many years. For an independent woman it had been a strange way to behave. 'Is his attraction that strong?' she whispered. It was. She had never tired of his muscular body and his habit of saying little but thinking much. There was also the anomaly that, although he possessed an animal-like strength, it was Angela who was in control.

Well, she was his wife now and nothing could alter that. And she did not regret it either. Once the police had been back and the funeral was over life would revert to normal. They had nothing to fear.

Alec was not an intellectual man, he acted instinctively and only thought about what he had done afterwards. He did not know why he was crying, only that he was. His only child was dead but he hadn't loved her because he hadn't really known her. Odd, he thought, that he had not cried when his mother had died. But then, she would not have expected him to.

He had had no dealings with the police before and therefore no idea how they worked. Their questions would be answered, although there was little he could tell them about Jenny, and Angela, who had gone to Truro with a friend to see a film, did not know about Jenny's recent visit to the house. No one knew and there was no reason for them to do so. What had been discussed between father and daughter concerned them alone and the third party involved lived too far away for any connection to be made. He gulped at the brandy. It burned unpleasantly but it did make him feel better.

Angela returned, a little flushed, her eyes over-bright. She sat beside him and took his hand in hers.

'I'm all right now,' he said. 'In fact, I think I'll plumb in the washing-machine.'

Later that Monday night Angela gasped in surprise when Alec grabbed her before she was undressed and made love to her. It was as if she wasn't there. Normally their couplings were beneath the sheet and the duvet which had replaced Agnes Manders' scratchy blankets. Afterwards, he seemed at peace, as if by that one almost violent action he had got his daughter's death out of his system.

'Good evening, Inspector. Do come in.' Stella Jackson held open the plate glass door of the gallery, which had been closed for several hours. She ignored the sergeant at his side. Outside the Christmas lights glittered in the rain and were echoed in a much smaller way by the string of fairy lights on the minute tree in the corner of Stella's window. It was a sop to the season and did not detract from the carefully arranged display of her work. 'Shall we go upstairs? It's more comfortable.' The heating in the gallery went off at five thirty and it was chilly.

Jack and his colleague followed the streamlined figure, tonight dressed entirely in black, up the spiral staircase. Stella Jackson reminded him of a sleek cat; a wild cat, he amended, although he could not say why the adjective had come to mind. Daniel Wright, the woman's husband, appeared in the doorway of the lounge as they approached. The room took Jack by surprise with its tasteful uniqueness. He received another surprise when Daniel moved away and he saw the small figure of a woman sitting on the striped settee.

'This is Maddy Duke,' Stella said. 'Maddy, Inspector Pearce and, er...?'

'Detective Sergeant Green,' Jack told her, thinking they might be able to kill two birds with one stone. Madeleine Duke was, apart from the killer, the last person to have set eyes on Jennifer Manders. As far as they knew. No one had come forward in response to the television and radio broadcasts but only hours had passed since the announcement. 'I know someone spoke to you at the time of Miss Manders' disappearance but I'm afraid it's necessary for us to go over the last time that you saw her again. I'm sure you're already aware of the news?' Maybe with three witnesses present one of them might jog another's memory. Some small fact, some forgotten line of dialogue could make all the difference.

'Yes. Of course we know. In a community this size...' Stella spread her hands. There was no need to finish the sentence. 'Sit down, Daniel, for goodness sake,' she snapped.

Jack observed her without seeming to. There were undercurrents here – had there been some disagreement between husband and wife? Was something troubling them? However, Maddy Duke appeared to be at ease so he had to assume the couple had not been in the middle of a blazing row immediately prior to their arrival.

The half-hour spent in the room over the gallery proved to be a waste of time. Jennifer Manders' three friends merely repeated what they had said when questioned about her disappearance; Stella and Daniel confirmed that she had been one of the last to leave. She had left alone and they had not noticed which direction she had taken. They had not seen her since. Stella, exhausted, had gone straight to bed and Daniel had made a half-hearted attempt at clearing up and followed her fifteen minutes later. Maddy had gone home earlier. She had not seen Jenny head towards Nick's place but had later observed her running down the hill, in a distressed state. Assuming she had come from Nick's she had telephoned to see if everything was all right. That was the last time she had seen Jenny. But later, although she did not say so, she had seen Nick walking in the same direction.

Jack wondered why Maddy was blushing. Was it the mention of Nick Pascoe's name? She had invited him for a meal, he recalled. Was he a womaniser? If so, he felt sorry for Rose. He thanked them for their time and noted their relief when he left. But he was far from satisfied. One or all of them were holding out on him.

It was just after nine on Tuesday morning when DS Green and a WPC turned up on Rose's doorstep. She heard the bell and frowned. The front door meant business. She struggled to pull it open, breaking a nail in the process, and wished she wasn't wearing her working clothes when she saw who her visitors were. She could hardly make a good impression in tattered jeans and a paint-splashed jumper. They refused the offer of coffee, which did not deter Rose from pouring one for herself before she joined them in the sitting-room where she had shown them.

It was soon established how long and how well she had known Jenny, which was no more than a few months and hardly at all.

'Mrs Trevelyan, it is our understanding that you've been seeing Nicholas Pascoe. Were you aware he had been in a long-standing relationship with Miss Manders?'

'Yes, I was.'

'And that, recently, she decided she wanted this relationship to resume?'

'Yes.'

'I see. How did you feel about that?'

'I didn't think much about it, really. Nick said it was over and that he wasn't interested in renewing it.'

'And you believed him?'

'I had no reason not to. Besides, although I see him, as you put it, he's no more than a friend.' But Rose got the feeling that they did not believe *her*.

'Forgive my asking, but were you jealous of Miss Manders?'

Rose stared at the detective, her eyes wide. Then she laughed but wished she hadn't. She was being too flippant. 'Of course not. I liked her, in fact. Anyway, I knew their affair was over. Other people confirmed it, too.'

'You needed confirmation?'

Rose was annoyed. Sergeant Green was no fool but he was beginning to make her look one. 'No, I didn't actually ask anyone, it just came up in conversation. Gossip, if you like.'

'Yet on the night Miss Jackson held her preview Miss Manders was present, along with Mr Pascoe, and later she turned up at his house. They were obviously still friends.' Before Rose could speak he continued, 'When you left the gallery where did you go?'

'I came straight home.'

'And later Mr Pascoe telephoned. Did you know Miss Manders was with him at the time?'

'No. Not then.' Rose closed her mouth. Not then? Not at all, she thought. He certainly hadn't mentioned it. But she had heard the knock on the door and subconsciously registered that it was probably Jenny. But why? Rose frowned in concentration.

79

Because of the flirtatious way in which Jenny had been behaving at the gallery, she realised.

DS Green was relentless. 'Who might have seen you after you left St Ives?'

'No one. I told you, I came straight home.'

'So we only have your word for it that you didn't go out again that night after you received the telephone call.' It was a statement.

'Yes, you only have my word for it,' she replied with resignation.

DS Green leaned back in his chair. It was his colleague's turn now. WPC Sanderson had a flawless face with a mask-like expression. Her looks were classic but cold. 'Miss Manders was young and beautiful – some competition, I'd say.'

Rose's mouth fell open. She was speechless. She had never thought in those terms. More so than ever she wished she looked smarter. Surely she wasn't as bad as all that?

'All right, Mrs Trevelyan, let's move on to those screams you claimed to have heard. What were you doing out at the mine?'

'Painting.' Rose knew that whatever she said she would end up under suspicion.

'Inspector Pearce thinks there might be a connection between the death of Miss Manders and the body recovered from the mine. And, for whatever reason, you seem to have become involved with both of these women.'

'But I'm not. I had no idea there was a body there. How could I have done?'

'Perhaps the screams were in your imagination. Perhaps it was your way of telling us we ought to investigate.'

'That's a bloody stupid theory.' She was angry. How dare Jack have allowed this situation to have arisen. Hadn't he told her he would interview her himself?

WPC Sanderson raised her eyebrows sardonically. Rose thought her too smug for her own good. 'Maybe someone *did* know what was down there and the screams were meant to scare me away. Look, I can't explain why you didn't find anybody there at the scene but I definitely heard them. Could they have been recorded?' Rose asked doubtfully.

Her question was ignored. 'When did you move here?'

Rose was shaken. 'About twenty-eight years ago,' she said.

WPC Sanderson stood and gestured for her colleague to do the same. Her cat-like smile was explicit in its meaning. Rose had been around when the woman in the mine shaft had died. 'Thank you, Mrs Trevelyan, that'll be all for now.' DS Green nodded a farewell as his colleague followed him out into the hall. Rose let him open the front door himself.

'Right! Work,' she said with determination but before she could leave the house Nick telephoned.

'God, Rose, what a mess. It seems I'm a suspect.'

'Well, don't think you're so special. So am I.'

'You?' He started to laugh then realised just why she might be considered so.

'Older, jealous woman removes the obstacle to her happiness,' she said bitterly.

Nick was uncertain exactly what she meant by this. Did she feel more for him than her manner suggested? Did she want him that much? 'I'm sure they don't...'

'They do. Nick, when exactly did Jenny turn up at your place that night?' Rose suddenly realised she had, if not lied, then been economical with the truth. She did not know that Jenny had been there when Nick telephoned, she had, she realised, only guessed as much.

'After the preview. I told you.'

'Before or after you rang me?'

'Hey, what is this? As we were talking, actually. I wasn't expecting her. Why do you want to know?'

'No reason, really. Just curiosity.'

'Anyway, I know you're busy but is there any chance...?'

'No, Nick. Let's leave it until Saturday as arranged.'

'Okay. You're the boss. I'll see you then.'

His disappointment sounded genuine but Rose did have other things to do. Work, for a start, and she needed time to think about all that had occurred over the past few days.

She got into the car and found herself heading towards St Ives. She could not stop thinking that it was Nick who had had the perfect opportunity of following Jenny after she had left his place. Or Stella, she thought. But no, not Stella. Maybe she really had gone to bed. She had looked very tired.

It was another fine day, but chilly. Rose's hair, left loose, flew around her face when she got out of the car. In her uniform of jeans, shirt, sweatshirt and waxed jacket she made her way towards what was locally called the island although it was joined to the mainland. Her route took her past Stella's gallery.

Stella was behind the counter, some paperwork spread out in front of her. Daniel, dressed smartly in trousers, shirt, jacket and tie, was on the telephone. Both looked pale, as if they had not slept much.

'Rose. Nice to see you.' Stella looked up when the door opened. Her eyes shifted to the canvas bag over Rose's shoulder. 'Are you over here to work?'

'Yes.'

'I thought you'd be more adventurous. Absolutely everyone's had a bash at painting St Ives.'

Rose ignored the comment. 'Have the police been to see you?'

'Yes. Last night. We weren't able to be much help, I'm afraid. Do you get the feeling they think someone killed her? Perhaps it was a lover. She wasn't too fussy when it came to men.'

Shocked at such callousness so soon after Jenny's death, Rose was still aware of the odd look which was exchanged between husband and wife. The tell-tale flush spreading along Daniel's high cheekbones confirmed what Rose already suspected. Jenny had had an affair with Daniel Wright. Did Jack know? Well, it's up to him to find out, she thought, she was in enough trouble as it was. And did Jack know that Stella went walking after previews? No wonder the pair of them appeared anxious, she thought, if they weren't together it gives them both a motive: Stella's being jealousy, Daniel's the threat of being found out. It was crazy to be suspecting her friends, but perhaps no more crazy than the police suspecting her.

'Rose? I said, would you like a coffee?'

'Oh, no thanks, Stella, I've got a flask. I just called in as I was passing.' What's happening to me, she thought as she left the gallery. It's as if I don't trust anyone. She blamed it on the circumstances. Murder was ugly and its repercussions spread like ripples in widening circles of doubt and suspicion.

Once on the island Rose got to work, one eye on the sky as she waited for the weather to decide what to do. Grey clouds blew in from the sea then dispersed again and the threatened rain was held at bay because of the speed with which they scudded overhead. Despite the fingerless gloves in which she worked, Rose's hands were cold and stiff. She gave it up as a bad job, dissatisfied with what she had produced but not unduly upset as she had already seen ways in which it could be improved.

Gulls swirled in noisy flocks as she made her way down the grassy slope. On a high, jutting rock a black-back, neck stretched, sharp curved beak open, squawked noisily. Beneath her lay St Ives, peaceful on a winter's afternoon without the clutter of cars and tourists the season would bring. Herring-gulls lined the harbour wall, facing the wind, their feathers unruffled. They cocked their heads to watch her as she passed, each with one bright eye visible, assessing whether she was a danger to them, but they did no more than take a couple of sideways steps. These scavengers were used to people.

Rose had known all along what she intended doing but only now admitted it to herself. But was it the right thing to do? She was being presumptuous. She grinned. Barry Rowe would have certainly thought so. She pulled her hair from the confines of the collar of her jacket and walked on. But Barry Rowe isn't here to see me, she told herself.

She knew the street in which Alec Manders lived because Jenny had mentioned it, but not the number. It was Maddy who had filled her in on Jenny's childhood. Rose could not imagine what it must have been like to have a mother abandon you at an age when her presence was so necessary. Rose's own upbringing had been totally secure. Maybe that was why David's death had hit her so hard – she had taken security for granted. No, it wasn't that. It was because I loved him in a way I'll never be able to love any other human being, she decided. And with that thought she felt better about doubting Nick. She knew her feelings for him would never be as deep.

The street, like many others, was wide enough to allow only one car to pass because it had been built at a time when horses and carts dragged boxes of pilchards and other fish along the roads which wound steeply up from the harbour. The front doors opened directly on to the pavement.

Two women stood talking but paused in their conversation to eye her curiously as she approached them. 'Can you tell me where Alec Manders lives?' she asked with a smile.

'That's his place, there.' The one wearing a tightly knotted headscarf pointed diagonally across the road, avid inquisitiveness unconcealed in both her demeanour and her expression.

'The one with the plant pots?'

'Ess.' The woman nodded emphatically. 'What do 'ee want with 'en?'

'Thank you.' Rose smiled again, fully aware of their disappointed silence and their eyes on her back as she walked up the street.

The plant pots were stacked on the stone steps at the side of the building. They contained only dead things. Rose knocked and the door was answered by a woman younger than herself who smiled welcomingly and said, yes, Alec was at home.

Rose stepped over the threshold and smelled new wood and fresh paint.

Maddy Duke had a job to concentrate as she gave change to customers. In the run-up to Christmas the shop was doing well.

She felt unsettled. Stella was keeping something from her, she sensed it, and Nick was being evasive. It was beginning to get to all of them. Yet she could not bring herself to feel sorry that Jenny was dead. Watching her, distraught, running away from the direction in which Nick's house lay, Maddy knew what had happened. Jenny had tried to seduce him. Her remarks about Rose Trevelyan earlier that evening had not gone unheeded although Maddy could see that there wasn't much doing there. At least, not yet. Nor would there be if she had her way.

It was peculiar really because she had liked Jenny and she liked Rose. She hated herself for the ambiguity she felt towards her friends, liking but envying them. In Nick's case she wanted him badly but she also wanted her freedom, to have no ties if Annie should seek her out. She had invited Peter Dawson to accompany her in the hope of making Nick jealous. But now she was worried. What had Nick been doing that night? And, more to the point, had anyone seen her hurrying through the deserted streets? She wondered if she even cared.

Perhaps the way she was stemmed from the past, from the loss of her child, the one thing she really wanted and could not have. Even though her prayers would be answered if her daughter made contact when she reached her eighteenth birthday early next year, she would never be able to retrieve the years of her babyhood and childhood. There would be no compensation for that.

When she had closed the shop she went upstairs to study the script for the Christmas pantomine although she was almost word perfect. She had joined the drama group as a way of overcoming her lack of confidence as well as to make new friends. At first she had been rejected at every audition and had had to settle for helping with costumes and scenery but once she had begun to tape, in secret, the voices of her friends she had tried to copy them and had eventually become a good mimic. She had finally landed a decent part because she could now speak in voices other than her own accentless one.

On the stage she could become someone else but no one knew how far she carried this over into her real life. And certainly no one knew of her small collection of tapes on which were recorded the voices of her friends in conversation.

6

'It's not much to go on.' Inspector Jack Pearce hooked his thumbs in his trouser pockets and leaned his large frame against the windowsill in his office. The results, so far, of the examination of the bones of the female found in the shaft showed that she was white, of average height and build and aged somewhere between twenty-one and thirty-five. There was no jewellery, no remnants of a handbag, nothing at all to suggest who the woman was. This added to the likelihood that she had been murdered.

Jack walked to his desk and read upside down, as if to confirm what he already knew. He tapped the top sheet of paper. 'And that's all we needed to know.'

The only other occupant of the room was a grizzled sergeant, more astute than his amenable manner and gentle expression suggested. He knew Jack was referring to the dental report. All the woman's teeth were her own and there wasn't a trace of amalgam. Whoever it was had lain there for twenty-five to thirty-five years but the computer file which held the information regarding missing persons had not come up with anyone who fitted the flimsy description. The few who came closest had reappeared or had been found elsewhere somewhere along the line, either living or dead. He knew Jack had also gone to the trouble of checking an extra five years either side of the margins given them by Forensics.

Jack was baffled. A holiday-maker, even if alone, would have left some trace of herself. There would be unclaimed belongings in her accommodation, no matter how lowly or grand, and there would, presumably, be the matter of an unpaid bill. On the other hand, someone local would certainly have been missed. He hoped that the abruptly curtailed life had not belonged to some lonely individual with no one to care whether they had lived or died; someone who had come to the area with the sole purpose of ending it all. If that was the case her identity might remain a mystery for ever. But Jack had a feeling it was vitally important to know who she was.

For now there was the more pertinent case of Jennifer Manders. He needed to speak to the dead girl's father. She had been dead only a few days and therefore there was still a good chance of apprehending her killer. The other woman, whose death might yet turn out to be accidental, had waited twenty-odd years for someone to take an interest. A little while longer couldn't hurt.

Oh, Rose, he thought, as he went out to the car. Why on earth did you have to become involved? On the other hand, without her involvement they would not have found the anonymous female. He headed towards St Ives where Alec Manders had been told to expect him, praying that Rose would not get herself into deeper trouble.

Almost the same thought was going through her own mind as Rose chewed the ends of her hair, a childhood habit her mother thought she had cured but which recurred when she was deep in thought. She needed someone to talk to, someone to whom she could voice her suspicions aloud, but the most suitable listener was Jack, and he had too much else on his plate to spare her any time. Not that she had asked him to.

She glanced at her watch – six thirty – but rang his number anyway, surprised when he answered in person. 'I've just this minute got home,' he told her. He was tired and disappointed at the outcome of his interview with Manders.

It was some time since Rose had been to his flat in Morrab Road but she could picture it clearly. It was on the ground floor, one of two into which a solid-looking house had been converted. He had moved there after his wife had returned to Leeds, taking with her their two sons. They were men now and had always visited Jack regularly; the divorce was a thing of the past.

Jack, having yearned for experience away from the area, had been transferred and had met and married his wife in Yorkshire. When the boys were small he had moved back, drawn to his roots as were most Cornishmen if far from home for any length of time. His wife had been unable to settle. There was no chance of a compromise; Jack's wife refused to stay and Jack refused to leave again.

'I've decided to throw a party on New Year's Eve. Will you come, Jack?'

The way she said his name still gave him a strange sensation in his stomach. He thought about it then smiled wryly. 'Will I get a kiss at midnight?'

'If you're exceptionally well behaved you might.' But she had to warn him. 'The St Ives lot will be there, you know, Nick and everyone.'

'Ah.'

'And the Clarkes, Doreen and Cyril. Remember them? And Laura and her family, and Barry, of course.'

'I should hope so. The sycophantic Mr Rowe would cut his wrists if he didn't receive an invitation.'

Rose stiffened. Was he being sarcastic or gently mocking? If she could have seen his face she would have known it was the latter. It was true, though, Barry would have monopolised her if she had not been firm. However, if Rose ran him down silently now and then, that was one thing, but she was completely loyal to her friend and would not allow anyone else to do so. 'He's a kind, decent man, Jack, and a very good friend to have.'

'Sorry, Rose. I know that. And he succeeds in those things without trying.'

She had no idea what he meant but she was more intent on finding out if he was coming to the party. 'You still haven't said, will you be here?'

'Can you put me down as a maybe? It all depends, you see.'

'Of course.' Rose understood it might be awkward for all concerned as Jack would have already interviewed some of her guests, might even, she realised, have arrested one of them by then.

'Thanks for asking.'

Rose had wanted to talk to him but sensed that he was anxious to get off the phone. She said goodbye and hung up with a shrug. Her amateur detection work would have to wait. 'Really, Mrs Trevelyan, this won't do,' she told herself. 'Seven o'clock and no wine opened'

This remedied, she put a casserole in the oven to reheat then sat at the kitchen table doodling on a piece of paper. Rose stared at what she had written; the names Nick Pascoe, Stella Jackson, Daniel Wright and Maddy Duke, in that order. Maddy? Despite the animosity she had felt between Maddy and Jenny on that one occasion there was no reason to think she might have killed her. Then Rose remembered the pointed remarks concerning herself and Nick. What was going on there? And Maddy hadn't wasted any time in ringing Nick to confirm that Jenny had been with him after Stella's preview.

'Oh, no.' Suddenly Rose saw it clearly. Maddy wanted Nick for herself. How far would she have gone to get him? I was blind not to see it before, she thought. And Maddy was an actress. Had she been there at the mine and given those screams, throwing her voice in some way, or whatever it was called? But why? And what relevance did it have to the remains found there or Jenny's death?

Alec Manders, she wrote next, alongside the list. Not because she thought he was a suspect but because the written name helped to bring him closer. He had been touched rather than annoyed or upset at her visit and had recalled, without prompting, meeting her that day with Jenny and the fact that she was an artist. Rose had been flattered, and glad that she had called to offer her condolences. She knew from experience that it helped in the months to come, that comfort was taken from the kind words of friends and people whom you hardly knew. It had taken her a long time to realise how hard these words were to say, that the platitudes were meant despite being what they were – how else could anyone really express what they felt for the bereaved? And how much easier it was to ignore the one suffering.

At least he has Angela, Rose thought. And they did seem well suited, comfortable together, if an unlikely pair. From the little Rose knew of him via Jenny and Maddy she had gained the impression that Alec expected people living under his roof to obey him. Angela, however, appeared to have made him more biddable and had an air of being able to do more or less as she pleased.

Alec had been more open with Rose than she had anticipated. She was a virtual stranger, but that might have made it easier for him to talk, especially as she saw him as a man who did not waste words. But Rose was unaware that the brandy, which he was not used to, had loosened his tongue.

She ran a hand through her hair, tangled by the wind because she had left it loose. A faint smell of meat and vegetables escaped from the oven and made her mouth water but the casserole would not be hot enough yet.

With only the hum of the fridge and the low buzzing of the fluorescent tube for company, Rose sipped a second glass of wine.

Did Renata Trevaskis, or Manders, or whatever she might now be calling herself, know that the daughter she had abandoned was dead? Alec Manders had more or less told her the same thing as Maddy. Renata had taken to drink and running around with other men and had finally run off altogether with one of them. Alec had received one letter giving little more information than her address.

'I don't know why she bothered,' he said to Rose, 'she never wrote again, not even to the child. Still, it saved a lot of trouble when it came to the divorce. The solicitors needed to know where to write and to advise her to get her own lawyer.'

After a six-year separation there had been no need for either party to attend court. There were no objections on either side and Renata had made no claim upon his money. She had also admitted that she had not set foot in the marital home during that time and that she had been cohabiting with someone else. He had told her all this spontaneously, as if glad to have an opportunity to talk about the past. It was noticeable that he had chosen to do so whilst Angela was out of the room.

Alec's face had hardened when Rose asked if Jenny's mother would be attending the funeral. She got the impression that Renata didn't know. But perhaps after such a long time she had moved from the original address given and Alec had been unable to locate her.

The kitchen was becoming very warm. Rose turned off the gas, slipped on her oven gloves and, momentarily backing away from the blast of heat as she opened the oven door, bent her knees to reach for the smoked-glass dish with its bubbling contents.

She realised she was starving, which was a good sign, and looked forward to a slice of Doreen Clarke's home-made saffron cake afterwards. It was rich in colour and full of fruit, and she would spread it generously with butter.

Nick Pascoe was more worried than his friends knew. He had been on edge ever since Jenny had disappeared and he knew it didn't look good for him. He had lied to the police and he had lied to Rose. And although Maddy was the last known person to have seen Jenny alive as far as the police were concerned, he knew better. But he was in any case the last person known to have spoken to her. And he had made no secret of the fact that they had argued.

Rose seemed to have cooled towards him but whether this was because she was upset over Jenny's death or because she had heard what he had tried to keep from her, he didn't know. Maybe she was simply hurt because Jenny had been with him that night. At least she hadn't dropped him altogether. He knew little of Rose's past, only that she had been married, happily married, but the name Jack Pearce had cropped up often enough for Nick to have drawn the correct conclusion. If his assessment of her was accurate, Rose was a truthful, open and sensible woman, and certainly not prone to histrionics as Jenny had been. But he still couldn't bring himself to tell her the truth.

On Wednesday, unable to concentrate, Nick mooched about the bedroom he used as his studio for most of the long, wet day, assessing his work and finally choosing the last two paintings for the exhibition. The rain hammered on the corrugated iron roof of the bathroom extension below him. Less than thirty years ago these cottages had only had a stone sink with a cold tap in the kitchen. An outside lavatory had once stood at the end of each small back yard but since the modernisation of the row they now acted as storage sheds.

Normally Nick found the sound of rain soothing: today its constant staccato beat in time with his jumping nerves. The telephone receiver sat quietly on its cradle, although most of his friends knew he rarely answered it when he was working and left their calls until after six. Today he could have done with some company. His hands were shaking and did not feel as though they belonged to him. Angrily, he pulled on a leather jacket, closed the door of the cottage and walked down the hill to the harbour. The tide was out. A few small boats lay at an angle waiting to be righted by the incoming tide. The fine wet sand lay in hard rippled ridges in which herring-gulls left their footprints as they stalked aggressively across them. Far out to sea a beam-trawler cut through the swell, white spray sweeping over its bows. It would dip and roll a lot more once it was further out to sea. The smell of brine was mingled with that of wet tarpaulin and frying onions from one of the cafés. With his hands in his pockets Nick walked around as far as the lighthouse, breathing deeply as if he could clear the clutter in his mind. The rain was heavier than he had realised. His jeans clung to his legs stiffly and chafed. He ought to go home.

In dry clothes he stood by the telephone, hesitating before dialling Rose's number. She might be working and he would feel bad if he disturbed her. She had made it clear she was not prepared to see him before the weekend. Three times he lifted the receiver, three times he decided against calling her.

91

What the hell's wrong with me? Nick thought. It's more than Jenny and more than the weather and I'm acting like a petulant child. It struck him that he might be just that, albeit in an adult body. No attempt had ever been made to curb his selfish streak. He also had a deep-seated fear that he wasn't quite up to the mark and this caused him either to withdraw or to behave badly towards people whom he liked.

Although he was lucky enough to have been recognised during his lifetime he was far from sure his talent would outlive him. Which was worse? To die unknown then become famous when it was too late to matter, or to fear that your life's work would be forgotten once you were no longer around?

He did try to minimise the violent mood swings from which he suffered but perhaps other artists also underwent periods of self-doubt followed by bursts of euphoria. Could Rose Trevelyan cope with his moods? More to the point, could he cope with her? He was not used to her total independence and straightforward ways. Being the sort of man who, when he wanted something, had to have it immediately also meant the reverse applied. He was capable of rejecting whatever he had desired just as quickly. Jenny had not been malleable, far from it, but in retrospect Nick saw that he had been so busy double-guessing her that his own feelings had been put on hold.

Nick was an enigma to himself. He was unable to decide if his discontent came from getting too much or too little out of life. At the moment, as far as women were concerned, he seemed to be getting far too much. Maddy's visit that morning had disturbed him greatly and was too reminiscent of Jenny's last one. It was a mystery how he attracted such behaviour. Maddy Duke was obviously disturbed and had a deep-seated envy of Jenny. It was strange that he had never noticed this before. And now he had further cause for anxiety. Maddy had seen him on the night of Jenny's death. If he didn't go along with her wishes she might well go to the police.

Maddy had risen early, long before daylight. After a restless night she had come to a decision. She knew that Nick was an insomniac and guessed that he would also be up and about.

There was no point in opening the shop until ten, few people had fancy goods on their mind that early in the day. However, she rang the girl who helped out occasionally if Maddy wanted a few hours off and she agreed to open up. She had a spare set of keys. Maddy had had finally to trust someone and in Sally's case she had not been let down. Working a six-day week, seven in the height of the season, it was essential to have some assistance even if it did cut into her profits.

In the darkness she passed few people and no one she knew. She had not set eyes on Nick for several days but since Jenny's death none of them seemed to be communicating as much as usual. It was a shame, but nothing could compare to the loss of little Annie. No, not little, she reminded herself. A young woman now. The bitterness was always with her and she suspected it always would be. Stella had pointed out how well she had done for herself but had managed to make it more like an insult when she spoke of 'your little business'. But success wasn't enough. She wanted, not as most people seemed to, someone to love her, but someone whom she could love. At times she thought she could settle for simply being accepted as one of the crowd. Deep down she realised that this could not be. Not because she was neither Cornish nor an artist but because there was a barrier between herself and others, one of her own construction.

Layers of clothing disguising her reasonable body, Maddy set off up the hill. To see Nick, to hear his voice, would be balm to her miserable state. Hard as she tried to conquer these spells of depression there were some which were undefeatable.

As far as she could discern, he was not getting very far with Rose. This pleased her. And now that Jenny was no longer around Maddy was sure she could persuade Nick that she would be good for him. I can make him happy, I know I can, she told herself.

She slowed her pace to take the steep incline up to his house. Lights showed in the windows and the door was ajar. Nick always liked plenty of fresh air whatever the time of year. She rapped her knuckles on the weather-roughed wood of the door and called his name.

'Come in, Maddy. I'm in the kitchen.'

Already feeling more cheerful at his welcoming tone, she went through, picking her way amongst the general untidiness of the room where books and papers and picture frames were scattered. Nick was standing by the sink. She saw at once that lack of sleep was plaguing him again. The skin beneath his eyes looked bruised and the lines in his face more deeply etched. 'Are you all right, Nick?' she asked.

'Yes. Just can't sleep, dammit. It'll pass.'

'There's nothing worrying you, is there?' Maddy kept her voice light, hoping that Rose Trevelyan was not the cause of his sleeplessness.

'No, nothing apart from Jenny and that's hanging over all our heads.'

'Would you like me to make you some breakfast?' she had asked.

'What about the shop?'

'Sally's opening up for me. I just felt like an hour or two away from it all. It's been satisfyingly busy. Breakfast then?' She smiled widely, showing her neat white teeth.

'Food might be a good idea, actually. But only if you join me.'

It was a pleasure to be allowed the run of his kitchen although she had to open all the cupboards and drawers to find things. Nick ignored her, his mind elsewhere. How nice it would be if I could do this every day, she thought while she boiled the kettle and poached eggs as there was little else in the fridge. She fantasised that she was already living with Nick, that they would become an accepted couple. It was a shame he was so tired, his problems should be over now that Jenny wasn't hanging around his neck. Their relationship may have been over as far as Nick was concerned but Jenny had had other ideas. She had confided in Maddy that she was determined to get him back, hinting that it was never really over. Jenny had said something else, too, but for the moment Maddy couldn't recall the rest of the conversation. 'I can live with his moods,' Jenny had said, laughing. 'My God, I ought to be able to after all that time. He doesn't know what he wants, that's his problem. It takes a woman to show him. You'll see, I'll soon be moving back in.'

Maddy had doubted that very much. But now she realised that what Jenny had said may have held some truth. She *had* known him well. Perhaps it was time that she, Maddy, showed Nick what he wanted; namely, herself. The trouble was, she suspected, that they had met as friends and he was unable to see her as a desirable woman.

'It's ready.' Maddy carried the warm plates to the scarred wooden kitchen table and placed salt and pepper in the middle. Two eggs each, on thick slices of buttered toast. Steaming mugs of tea were at the sides of their plates.

Nick ate as if he was ravenous and she wondered if he was looking after himself.

'That's better. Food always tastes nicer when someone else cooks it.'

Maddy beamed. These were the sort of words she lived to hear. 'I love cooking,' she said. 'Come for dinner tonight, why don't you? I've got all morning to find us something special.'

'Thanks, Maddy, but I'll probably turn in early. I'm so damned tired.'

Her face fell but she was determined not to let her disappointment show. A tirelessly cheerful companion was what Nick needed. Then she thought of another way to help him relax. Slowly she cleared the table and washed the dishes in the old stone sink. 'Fancy another cup of tea?' she inquired artlessly, wanting to stay as long as possible.

'Yes, I do. Thanks.'

'Go and sit down, for goodness sake, Nick, before you fall down.' Jenny was right, Maddy thought, Nick only needs to be told what to do. She took the tea into the living-room, pleased to note that he was on the settee, and joined him there. They sipped it and Maddy asked him about his painting and what he was working on. When both mugs were empty she moved a little closer to him and reached for his hand, stroking the back of his roughened fingers gently. When he did not resist she brought her left hand around to his chest. Not until her hand was beneath his jumper and unbuttoning his shirt did Nick seem to realise her intentions.

'Maddy, don't.'

'Why not? Surely you like it.'

'Leave me alone, for God's sake.' He jumped up and stalked into the kitchen.

Maddy followed him. 'I just want to help, Nick, to make things right for you. I'll take care of you, I promise. Please believe me.' She was desperate. 'You have to believe me. I didn't tell the police I saw you, after all.'

'What?' Nick spun round. 'What're you talking about?'

'On the night Jenny died. I saw you. You were following her.'

'You're mistaken. How could I have been following her when I was on the phone to you?'

'Not immediately. But not all that long after she left.'

'It wasn't me,' Nick shouted. 'It wasn't me, you stupid bitch.' He left by the back door of the house, slamming it hard behind him.

Tears filled Maddy's eyes and her face was hot with shame and humiliation. She wanted to run and hide but she also wanted to stay, to ask him what was so wrong with her that he couldn't bear her to touch him. When he didn't return after a few minutes she left quietly and walked slowly down the hill. Reaching the bottom she turned left and began to run as suppressed rage boiled up within her. It's Rose's fault, she thought, Rose Trevelyan with her girlish figure and her bloody talent.

It was not yet nine thirty. Maddy knew the only release would be to return to the shop and work, to make an effort to be pleasant to the customers. As soon as she returned she rang Sally to say that her services weren't needed then she cried until she felt there were no more tears to be shed. By the time Rose walked into the shop around lunchtime she was more or less her normal self. The permanent ache she felt was still there but she realised her behaviour could hardly have endeared her to Nick. And she had had time to wonder just what he really had been doing that night.

Rose hated being under suspicion, hated the whole idea of Jenny's death and the way everyone had been affected, but at least she had worked out her next move. She was going to see Maddy, using the excuse of buying Barry's Christmas present for being in the shop. It was not even out of her way as she had arranged to meet Stella that afternoon. If it wasn't raining they would go for a walk. Stella hated the rain. Rose intended making the most of the opportunity by asking advice on holding her own exhibition and, if she was really lucky, persuading Stella to allow her to do so in her gallery.

The sky was dull but Rose decided to dress smartly in deference to her hostess. She put on an olive green skirt and a cream lambswool sweater then, after a leisurely breakfast, left the house, for once having read more than the front page of the newspaper.

St Ives was busy. Panic buying, she thought, and so much of it would go to waste. The narrow streets were crowded although Truro, Plymouth and Exeter were the places which benefited most at that time of year. As yet, apart from the awful superstores on the edge of Penzance, there were none of the big stores in the area. Rose preferred the small shops, run by individuals rather than by faceless men who sat around boardroom tables.

She walked down the hill, stepping off the narrow pavement every so often to pass slower, window-gazing pedestrians. Light spilled from the shops making the sky seem duller than it really was. The mouth-watering aroma of freshly cooked pasties wafted into the streets as she passed the various bakers'. Decorations glowed and even Rose began to feel festive.

A bell tinkled as she pushed open the door of Maddy's shop. There were already three other customers browsing. Maddy had stacked every surface with goods. Two women and one man handled objects as they decided whether or not to buy them. The whole gamut of Maddy's talents filled the shelves and the tables down the centre of the room. It was hard to know where to look first with so many brightly coloured articles to catch the eye. Mobiles swirled overhead, moved by the warm air of the fan-heater behind the counter, and silver bells tinkled. There were painted wooden toys, drawn-threadwork table linen, ceramics and papier mâché containers. Not wishing to draw attention to herself until they were alone, Rose kept her back to the counter where Maddy was writing a receipt for one of the women and had a good look around. Rose and her friends had given up sending one another cards many years ago. It seemed so pointless when they were in daily contact. Those few she did send had already been posted. Laura was often broke so she and Rose had made a pact years ago only to buy one another something inexpensive, a token. The only other gifts she bought now were for her parents and Barry, although she had made an exception last year and bought Jack a bottle of his favourite malt and framed a sketch of hers he had admired.

On a shelf, Rose spotted what she took to be a pen-holder, shaped and hollowed from a single piece of wood whose legend claimed it came from the wreck of a ship. The outside was rough, the wood grained and interesting, but inside it had been squared out smoothly. Six inches high and with a firm heavy base, it would act as one even if that was not what it was intended for. She peered at the sticky label which displayed the price. Five pounds. She would take it.

'Bye, and thanks,' she heard Maddy say as the shop door bell jangled again. 'Rose, I didn't see you come in. Need any help?'

'No, thanks. I'm going to have this, but I'm still looking.'

Maddy went back to serve an elderly woman with bow legs and an old-fashioned wicker basket which contained a Yorkshire terrier.

'It's good to be so busy,' Maddy commented when the shop was empty at last. 'Four fifty to you,' she added, tilting the wooden object to check the price. Her need to be liked was greater than her envy of Rose.

'Thank you. But I really didn't come expecting a discount.'

'What're friends for? Fancy a coffee and a sandwich? I'm closing for lunch. It's too long a day otherwise.'

Rose looked at her watch. There was plenty of time before she was due to meet Stella. 'Thanks, I'd love a coffee.'

There was nothing else she wanted to buy. For her parents, who claimed to have everything they needed at their time of life, Rose had ordered a hamper of food to be sent. It contained only Cornish produce: hog's pudding, clotted cream, pasties, fudge, saffron cake, ginger fairings and heavy cake. There was also a small box of salted pilchards. Enclosed with their card she had sent a recipe book in case her mother decided to try her hand at baking any of the cakes, and an explanation to go along with the heavy cake. 'Folklore says it goes back to biblical times,' she had written. 'It's also known as "fuggan" and was eaten by the "hewer" and somehow got its name from the cry of "hevva" which he'd shout from his look-out in the days when men were employed to watch for the shoals of fish, pilchards mostly, from a vantage point on the cliffs. Anyway, enjoy it, it's delicious, especially if you warm it up.'

Maddy locked the door and turned the sign to closed then led Rose out through the back and up a flight of uncarpeted stairs to her flat.

'Did you make everything in the shop?' Rose inquired.

'Yes. Well, most of it. I'm a real Jack-of-all-trades.'

'Amazing. Anyway, I'm really pleased with my find. It's for Barry Rowe, do you know him?'

'Does he run that greeting-card place in Penzance?'

'That's him. He produces all his own stuff too. All done by local artists.'

'Good for him. I don't actually know him, only the shop because his name's over the door.'

Rose had been about to comment that the pen-holder was an ideal present for a man who was so disorganised then realised Maddy might be offended if that was not its purpose. Although the desk in Barry's small office behind the shop was piled high with paperwork there was never a pen to be found.

'Have a seat.' Maddy indicated the over-stuffed chairs and a small sofa. The room was cluttered but not untidy. It made Rose a little claustrophobic.

'I won't be long. Ham okay?'

'Just coffee for me, Maddy, really.' She hesitated, then came straight to the point as Maddy turned in the kitchen doorway. 'I didn't come only to buy a present. Maddy, I wanted to tell you how sorry I am about Jenny. I know you were good friends.'

Maddy bowed her head but not before Rose had seen the sparkle of tears. Her outfit today was a little more subdued but still, Rose thought, bohemian, although for some reason she never quite succeeded in being more than a parody of herself. The thick black tights would be for warmth in the draughty shop but the deep purple skirt and the red sweater topped by a garish waistcoat were for effect. A large butterfly slide held back one side of her long, brittle blonde hair and what looked to Rose like fishing flies dangled from silver rods in her ears.

'I shall miss her more than anyone knows,' she said quietly then reached out a hand and pressed Rose's warm one. 'You're a very nice person, you know. Other people have hardly mentioned her to me.' Maddy was ashamed of her earlier antagonism towards Rose.

'Perhaps they didn't feel it was necessary. It's never easy in these situations.'

'Yes, perhaps you're right. I just wish I'd gone out after her that night like Nick...' She stopped abruptly and disappeared into the kitchen, leaving Rose wondering what she had been about to say. 'Like Nick said I should have?' 'Like Nick wished he had done?' Rose swallowed. 'Like Nick did?' It was beginning to seem as if everyone who had known Jenny was out in the streets that night.

She studied the room to the accompaniment of the clink of china and cutlery and the whine of the electric kettle as it came to the boil.

All the furniture was old-fashioned but not out of place with the building and although the windows were small the room was not as dark as it might have been because the curtains were hung well to the sides of the windows and did not cover the panes. On the floor was an old cord carpet, beige in colour. It was more practical than aesthetic but overlying it were a couple of bright rugs.

The ornaments and artefacts suggested no particular theme but were simply a random selection of pieces which Maddy liked. Rose had time to take this in before Maddy returned bearing a tray of coffee and a plate of cheese and biscuits. 'I couldn't be bothered to cut bread,' she admitted.

By the look of her face it seemed she had been crying. 'I'm seeing Stella this afternoon,' Rose said, trying to initiate some conversation. Something was seriously troubling Maddy. Guilt? Rose wondered, or guilty knowledge? Should she press her about Nick?

Maddy glanced towards the window, sticky with salt which had blown in with the wind and rain. 'You'll be lucky by the look of it. You know Stella won't get wet.' Her hands trembled as she picked up a cracker and a knife. 'Have you seen much of Nick lately?' She coloured, hating herself for asking the question.

'No. He's not ill, is he?' Rose frowned, unsure what Maddy was getting at.

'Oh, no, he's not ill.'

'Good. Anyway, I've been busy, I said I couldn't see him until Saturday.'

Maddy jumped to her feet, knocking her plate to the floor.

Rose was startled. Surely her harmless comment could not have caused such a reaction.

'So you're playing that little game, are you? Keeping him on a string, just like Jenny.'

Fighting the urge to get to her own feet and feel at less of a disadvantage, Rose tried to remain calm, tried to assess what turbulence was going on within the angry woman opposite her. 'No, I don't play games.'

'No, I don't play games.' Maddy mimicked her voice perfectly. 'Stringing him along, another bloody temperamental artist.'

'Maddy, I –'

'Oh, shut up. I know your sort. You've got a very high opinion of yourself. You use people, just like Jenny.'

So now we come to it, Rose thought. She equates Jenny with me because Nick was interested in us both. Rose was no longer sure if he *was* still interested in her, but this was irrelevant if Maddy believed otherwise. And Maddy was jealous, more than jealous. Was it the type of obsession which leads to insanity, even to murder?

Something was nagging at the back of her mind, some small action that Maddy had begun but not completed as they had entered the room. But something else struck her, too, her thoughts on Maddy having been at the mine. If she felt so strongly about Nick perhaps she had tried to entice Rose near the shaft hoping she would fall – or, worse, with the intention of pushing her.

Only seconds had passed. Maddy approached, shaking and white-faced. 'You deserve to die as well, you're just like that bitch.'

Rose tried to stand but it was too late. Strengthened by rage, Maddy grabbed at her throat, her strong potter's hands encircling it. Rose could not breathe. She knew that to panic would make matters worse. She had to fight back. Digging her heels into the base of the sofa she tried to force herself to her feet but only succeeded in sending the sofa backwards on its castors. She heard the sound of breaking porcelain. Maddy was on top of her, smothering her, but she had relinquished her grip. Her body was limp. 'Maddy,' Rose whispered. 'Oh, Maddy.'

'Oh, God, I'm so sorry,' she muttered before sobs shook her body and she started crying noisily into Rose's shoulder.

7

'That's odd.' Stella replaced the receiver. It was unlike Rose not to ring if she couldn't make it. Stella shrugged, her glossy black hair fell forward. Well, it wasn't the end of the world if something more important had cropped up.

Having already arranged to take the afternoon off she decided to go out anyway. The rain seemed to have stopped at last. Downstairs in the gallery her assistant was talking to a potential customer. Stella stopped to chat, hoping that the presence of the artist herself might help clinch the sale. With a smile she said goodbye and stepped out into the narrow, winding street. To err on the safe side she was wearing a shiny black raincoat and carried a folding umbrella in her bag. She made her way down towards the harbour, taking pleasure in window-shopping, stopping to stare into one of the bakers' as she tried to decide if she was hungry. Stella believed people ought only to eat when they felt like it, not at regulated times. The smell of hot pasties was tempting but she knew she would not manage a whole one, not even a small one. Her stomach had been in knots for days.

Like Rose, she appreciated the individuality of the shops, all of which were small. There was none of the impersonality of the chain stores which offered the same goods in every town.

Stella almost tripped on the cobbles as she passed Maddy's place. She was still trying to work out how the girl had managed to be at all successful. Surely there was a limited market for the goods she sold, even the ones she made herself. Seeing a figure behind the counter she was about to wave when she realised it wasn't Maddy. She carried on until she came to the lifeboat station where she stood staring at the sand and the sea, wondering how it would be possible to bear it if she was ever to be parted from such beauty. A few minutes later she turned left, having decided to visit the Tate Gallery where there was a new exhibition. According to the newspapers the gallery had attracted literally millions of people to the area and she had to admit that the design of the building was terrific. Inside, if you stood to one side of the concave semicircular glass frontage, the bay was reflected in the glass opposite, as had been the architect's intention. Visitors took pictures of this but Stella doubted if they would show the full effect of the architecture.

Engrossed in the paintings of an artist unknown to her, she remained in the gallery for an hour and a half. As she left, she glanced back at the white edifice of the gallery which many people had so wrongly predicted would fail.

Crossing the road she stepped down on to the fine, white sand. Her low heels sank into its softness and left tracks, the indentations of which were far larger than the size of her boots. Only when she reached the tide line were her footsteps reduced to normal dimensions as they stretched out behind her in the wet sand. A slight breeze ruffled the surface of the water but any surfers would have been disappointed that day. The frills of spray were only inches high. Despite the clarity of the air a vague headache lingered, the after-effects of last night, she thought. She and Daniel had sat down over a meal she had cooked with care and an expensive bottle of wine and talked out their differences. There was much that had needed to be said. Daniel had not previously understood the depth of the pain he had inflicted by his affair with Jenny. He had, he realised, been a fool to admit it, but it was over by then and he had wanted to tell Stella himself rather than have her hear it from another source. He and Jenny had been extremely careful, but that did not guarantee secrecy in a community where everyone knew each other.

Stella and Daniel had come to an agreement. They had sworn to try to put the affair behind them. But one thing was certain, it must not become known to the police. They would stick to the story that they had not been apart after the last guests had left the gallery. There was little chance that anyone could break their alibi. Stella had not passed a soul that night and there were certainly no people out on the cliffs. She smiled and dug the toe of her boot into the damp sand before turning and walking back up the beach.

We need to get away, she decided. Rarely did she and Daniel leave Cornwall and then usually not together. One or other of them made infrequent visits to a city if they were showing their work but they had not had a holiday for many years. The trouble is, she thought, this county of mine makes you that way. It weaves its spell, making you feel that you can't leave the place. She knew many outsiders who had to return time and time again, most of whom had ambitions to retire to the area. The trouble was, what was there to go away for? No scenery could be better, no beaches more beautiful, no coastline more spectacular. And where else could you be so at peace? But that was just what was lacking at the moment, and Stella needed peace badly.

She turned to look back at the white specks of gulls drifting on air currents high in the sky. Then she walked on, the incoming tide following slowly on her heels as it swept up over the sand.

There was still no answer from Rose when she telephoned again, only her cheerful voice on the answering machine, but Stella felt certain that she wouldn't have forgotten their arrangement. Did she suspect something and prefer to keep out of the way? Rose Trevelyan was too observant for her own good, Stella thought. Perhaps she ought to find out just how much she knew. Telling Daniel she was going out in the car and she wasn't sure how long she'd be, she had to repeat herself. Working away at his sculpture, he hardly acknowledged her existence but Stella was not annoyed. She reacted in much the same way if she was disturbed. They would be all right, their marriage was back on solid ground and she intended it to remain that way.

Jack and his team began to feel they were losing impetus. As the days passed they found that tongues were loosened, that people were not quite so reticent once they knew they were not the ones under suspicion. But instead of finding themselves nearer a solution, they merely discovered how many people had had cause to dislike Jennifer Manders. Not, they claimed, because she was unlikeable, far from it, it was agreed that she was good company, fun to be with, but her morals were a little questionable. And now it had been decided that Rose Trevelyan might hold the key. Her involvement appeared to be with not one, but both the corpses and, albeit inadvertently, she had led them to the first woman's burial place.

During that afternoon a detective sergeant tried Rose's number on six occasions but only got the answering machine. He did not leave a message. Inspector Pearce heard him grumbling to himself about people never being where you wanted them to be. Jack recognised the number on the display on the telephone. 'No luck?' he inquired, placing a file on the desk.

'Been at it since just before lunch.'

Jack frowned. 'Leave it with me.'

It was the sergeant's turn to frown. He had heard rumours that Jack and Mrs Trevelyan had once had a thing going; for all he knew they still did.

Jack glanced at the large round clock on the wall. Four thirty and daylight had long faded. Returning to his office he tried the number himself with no result. Then he left the building, shrugging his arms into his coat as he did so. His mind turned to the statement Alec Manders had made. What sort of a father was he to have virtually ignored Jenny in the years when it mattered, to have allowed his own mother, rather than the girl's, so much say? Jack had wondered about that. Renata Manders had disappeared, that much was common knowledge, and with another man. But Jack's suspicions had proved groundless when he had asked to see the marriage certificate and the divorce papers.

It had crossed his mind that the woman in the shaft might have been Renata. If she and Manders had not been married but had only lived as man and wife, there would have been no need for Manders to produce a decree absolute in order to marry Angela. If he had lied it might have been because Renata had never left the area and he had used the non-existent divorce which was supposed to have taken place six years later as an alibi. Jack was disappointed when he was shown the documentary evidence which proved his theory wrong.

Of Jennifer he had learned little. It was as if her father had hardly known her. Despite the fact that they lived so close to one another they rarely came into contact. Jenny's friends had borne this out. Why, Jack had wanted to know, had Jenny not gone to her father when her financial situation had reduced her to living in a squat? Alec said he did not know.

And as for the mystery woman, there seemed, for the moment, nowhere else to turn. It was time to concentrate on the weeks leading up to Jenny's death and probe a little more deeply into the alibis of those who had known her. It made Jack feel sick. Rose was without an alibi and she had now admitted that she had known Jenny was with Nick when he telephoned. There was no one to say she had not got back into the car and driven over to St Ives to wait for her to leave.

Traffic was building up. He cursed at the slow-moving queue at the roundabout by Tesco's. When he finally reached Rose's house he saw at once that she wasn't at home. There was no car in the drive and no lights shining from the windows. A sixth sense told him that she would not let matters rest, that she would end up in danger. He ought not to have ignored her for so long. If he had made more effort she would have confided in him or at least alerted him to her plans. Laura might know, he thought, and used his mobile phone to contact her rather than waste time by driving to her house.

'I'm sure she said she was taking a day off and going to St Ives. Jack, is she in trouble?'

'I don't know.' He didn't want to cause alarm. 'Do you know exactly where she was going?'

Jack's stomach muscles knotted. Knowing Rose she would start asking questions, would antagonise people and possibly place herself in danger. He had to find her. It was not like her to be out all day unless she was working, but as it was dark that was now an impossibility. 'Thanks, Laura.' He started the engine and headed towards St Ives. But which of them to approach first?

The interior lights of Stella's gallery were off and the sign on the door said 'Closed' but a spotlight illuminated a single large painting in the corner of the window. He rang the bell and waited. A man appeared in the dimness and unlocked the door. Ever observant, Jack did not miss the flinch as Daniel Wright's eyes registered instant recognition.

'Come in, please.'

Jack followed him up the spiral staircase. By the window, staring out into the darkness, was Stella, her tall willowy figure dressed in black, relieved only by a scarlet and gold scarf at her neck. Her hair gleamed and from behind she might have been oriental.

'Ms Jackson?' He hated the appellation but in this case could not think of a more appropriate one. 'I have to tell you that I'm here unofficially so you have every right to refuse to answer my questions. I'm trying to find Rose Trevelyan and I wondered if you had any idea where she might be.'

'How odd. I've been trying to get hold of her myself.' Stella walked across the polished boards of the floor and sat down, her posture as elegant as a model's. 'You see, she was supposed to come here this afternoon. We'd arranged to meet at two and go out somewhere.' She lifted her hands in a helpless gesture. 'I thought she'd changed her mind although I was very surprised she didn't ring me to say so. When she didn't arrive by three I tried ringing her and again twice since but I only get her answering machine. About tea-time I drove over to her house but there was no one there. Do you suppose something's happened to her?'

Does she mean anything by that? Jack asked himself. At least this confirmed what Laura had told him, Rose had been making for St Ives. Then where the hell is she? he thought. There had been no road traffic accidents that day, at least none that warranted police attention, so that ruled out one possibility. Besides, Rose had her mobile phone. He was sure he knew Rose better than Stella Jackson did and he would have sworn that she would have let Stella know if she had decided not to come. 'So you don't have any idea where she might have gone instead?'

'No. I suppose you could try Nick Pascoe. Other than that I can't help. I don't know her friends in Newlyn.'

Jack's jaw tightened at the mention of Nick's name. What if it was that simple, that Rose was there with him now, and he barged in to find them in a compromising situation? He did not think he could cope with that. But he must find Rose, he must know that she was safe. It was Daniel who showed him out, now smiling and chatting easily, his relief at not being questioned all too obvious. Jack decided to think about that later. Never again would he accuse Rose of meddling. Right now he was doing precisely that himself.

In order to regain his professional objectivity he drove around aimlessly for a few minutes, preparing himself for what he dreaded discovering at Pascoe's place. Seconds after he passed the car-park he stopped dangerously quickly, relieved that there was no car behind him. Had he seen right? Finding a place to turn he went back. Rose's car was parked neatly in an allocated space. The doors, when he got out to check them, were locked. Then she is with Nick, he thought. Controlling his anger at the idea of them together and her lack of consideration for Stella, he drove to Nick's small stone house. The curtains were open and as he approached the front door Jack saw a man in shirt-sleeves moving about the room. He knocked and waited. Pascoe opened the door. He was unshaven and looked a mess and he rubbed his eyes as he spoke. His breath smelled of alcohol, but not offensively so. A cigarette trailed smoke in an ashtray. 'Come in. Excuse the state of the place.'

'Are you all right, Mr Pascoe?' The man seemed exhausted, although it might be the physical effects of fear.

'Yes and no. Nothing serious. Insomnia, the bane of my life. I almost resorted to that –' he indicated a bottle of gin – 'but decided against it after two glasses. It won't solve anything and I'll only feel worse in the morning.'

'Mr Pascoe, I'm trying to locate Rose Trevelyan. Have you any idea where she might be?'

'No.' He sounded genuinely surprised. 'I haven't seen her all week. She said she couldn't see me until Saturday.'

Jack's face was expressionless. He was pleased to hear that but also disappointed that she intended seeing Nick again.

'Have you tried Stella? She goes there sometimes.'

'Yes.'

Nick shrugged. 'In that case I can't help you. I'm sorry, can I offer you something? Coffee or a drink if that's allowed?'

'No. I'm fine, thanks.' Jack turned to leave. 'If she does get in touch, will you let me know?' He handed Nick a card.

'Of course. Oh, God, you don't think anything's happened to *her* now, do you?'

'I hope not, Mr Pascoe. I sincerely hope not.' Twice in less than half an hour he had been asked that question. Did these people know something? Were they all in it together? Jack had been about to leave. He paused and turned. 'Do you often have trouble sleeping?'

'Yes. On and off over the years.'

'How do you overcome it?'

Nick shrugged. 'I don't. I refuse to resort to drugs, I tend to work or read or walk.'

'And on the night Jennifer Manders died?'

'I've already told you. She came here and we talked, then she left. I can't tell you any more than that.' Nick spoke too quickly and Jack could hear the rising panic in his voice. 'Oh, Christ!' He sank into a chair, knowing it was useless to dissemble further, his head in his hands. Jack waited. 'I should've told you before. I don't know why I didn't. I did go out that night. About twenty minutes after Jenny left. I spoke to Maddy and hearing how upset Jenny was I thought I ought to look for her. Once, I thought I saw her in the distance. I called out but whoever it was was too far away to hear. Then I lost sight of her. That was it.'

'Mr Pascoe, you do realise the seriousness of what you've told me? You can be charged with withholding evidence. May I use your telephone?'

Nick nodded, knowing what must happen next.

Jack requested a car to come and take Nick to Camborne where he would be asked to revise his statement. Pascoe had been drinking and Jack, who could have driven him, was more intent upon finding Rose. 'You'll be here when the car comes?'

'I won't be running away.' He laughed cynically. 'Where would I go?'

If her car's still here, Jack thought whilst at the same time hoping Pascoe could be trusted, she can't be far away, but where else was there to look? He left his own car parked near Pascoe's house and walked down towards West Pier then along The Wharf, stopping to gaze at the water which now filled the harbour and which was perfectly calm and still. Boats swayed imperceptibly on their moorings as the tide began to ebb. Almost opposite him, at the end of Smeaton's Pier, was the lighthouse.

I'll walk as far as that, he decided, and then I'll know what to do next. For the moment his next step was unclear.

A few minutes later he stopped, unable to believe what he was seeing. Walking towards him, her hair loose and blowing gently around her shoulders, was a small figure in a skirt and top, raincoat open and flapping in time with her footsteps. 'Rose?' he whispered. Then 'Rose!' he shouted.

Rose stood still and looked up, squinting into the darkness. Jack walked swiftly towards her. 'My God,' he said breathlessly. 'Are you all right?'

'Oh, I think so. A little shaken, but not hurt. And also extremely puzzled.'

'About what?'

She shook her head.

'Can I buy you a drink? Have you eaten?'

'No. No, I haven't.' She had difficulty in remembering,

Controlling an impulse to grab her hand Jack walked beside her, shortening his stride so as not to hurry her. They went into a small pub in Fore Street and joined the other customers. The beams were low and Jack had to duck beneath them. They stood at the curved bar in the over-warm room.

'You're pale,' he said when he had got their drinks. 'Why don't we sit down?'

Rose knew he preferred to stand but her legs felt weak so she complied.

'I think you'd better tell me what's going on, Rose.'

'I went to see Maddy Duke. I had arranged to see Stella but I was early so I thought I'd take the opportunity to buy Barry's present.' Jack flinched. Last year he had been given one. 'She invited me upstairs once the shop was closed for lunch. I wanted to talk to her, you see, because I remembered some remarks she made at Stella's that night. Remarks to Jenny about me and Nick. I had an inkling then that she fancied him herself. It made me wonder whether she was jealous and had somehow rigged those screams at the mine.'

'But what would she gain from that?'

Rose sniffed. 'No idea. Perhaps she thought I'd walk towards the sound and fall down the shaft or maybe she simply intended to scare me to put me off painting. Stella once said that Maddy was jealous of anyone with talent. I can't say I'd noticed, but Stella knows her better. Anyway, before we got a chance to talk she attacked me.'

'What?'

Rose nodded and ran a tired hand across her forehead. 'At one point I thought she was going to kill me.'

'My God.'

'I'd ruined her plans, you see. With Jenny out of the way she thought she had a chance with Nick.'

'I see.'

'I don't think you do, Jack. I managed to explain that there was nothing between us. At first I thought that there might be. I was attracted to him but it didn't take long to discover that apart from the fact that he isn't really looking for a relationship it wouldn't have worked.'

'Why not? If that's not too personal a question.'

Rose turned to look at him. There was a spot of colour on each of Jack's cheekbones and he appeared momentarily vulnerable. 'He would have been too demanding. He's talented but he's very moody and he would have expected me to pander to his moods. And that's not for me, Jack.'

'As I well know.'

'I intend telling him at the weekend, face to face.'

As you did with me, Jack thought, then grinned. Poor bastard, he didn't know what he was in for.

They were quiet for a few minutes, each thinking about what they had shared, Jack hoping it could be rekindled, Rose glad that she still had his friendship. 'That can't be all.' His tone was brisk now. 'There must have been more to make her behave in such a way.'

'There was. When she'd calmed down enough to speak coherently she burst into tears and couldn't stop apologising. I felt so sorry for her, she was so pathetic and forlorn. I can't understand how women can get that way about a man who has no interest in them. She'd been to see Nick this morning and he'd turned her away, just as he had Jenny.

'She'd closed for lunch but after that dramatic scene I thought it better if Sally, that's the girl who helps her out, came in and took over. She was surprised, for some reason. Anyway, Maddy

111

begged me to stay; she really was in an awful state. We went through the same thing all over again: the tears and apologies. I realised it wasn't safe to leave her on her own. By then I'd forgotten about Stella and when I did remember it didn't seem right ringing from there.

'When she was less emotional she was terribly embarrassed by what she had done and I could see that she wanted to talk. She admitted how lonely she was and how hard she'd tried to be one of the crowd. Oh, Jack, she really is a mess. She told me she had a child when she was young and her parents made her have it adopted.'

'Made her?'

'Yes. It's a complicated story, but they did. For that, she's never forgiven them or herself. What a way to live, wrapped up in a guilt you can't share or rid yourself of. Something else was interesting, too.' Rose rested her chin on her knuckles, her elbows on the table in front of her. 'I didn't believe her at first but when I thought about it I saw it was possible and that, without my noticing it, the same thing might have been happening to me. She said Stella's always putting her down.'

'How do you mean?'

'It's difficult to explain but it's as if the compliments Stella pays are deliberately back-handed. For instance, in my case she says my painting is good but I've still got a lot of hard work to do, and maybe one day I'll make it, that sort of thing. In Maddy's case she makes jibes about how surprising it is that so many people want to buy the sort of things she makes for "her little shop" as she puts it. And then she'll make a point of saying not everyone can be a great artist, as if this is supposed to cheer us both up.'

'Rose, she might have killed Jenny because she wanted Nick.'

'I'm sure she didn't. She admitted there were times she could've strangled her, especially when she told Maddy that she was going to try to get Nick back. And then she said...'

'Rose?'

Rose sighed with resignation. 'Then she said she'd seen Nick that night after she'd spoken to him on the phone.'

'I know.'

'What?'

'He told me. He's at Camborne now.' I hope, he added silently.

112

Rose was relieved. She knew it was her duty to inform Jack but it was better that Nick had done so himself. Here goes, she thought. 'There's something else.' She couldn't meet his eyes. These were her friends. 'Daniel Wright once told me that Stella always goes for a long walk after an opening night. Not that I'm saying she did,' Rose added hastily, glancing at his stern expression. 'It could've been an exception.'

The whole bloody lot of them seem to have been wandering around the streets of St Ives, Jack thought gloomily. So it's back to square one again. 'Is there anything else you feel I should know?'

Rose recognised the sarcasm but chose to ignore it. 'Well, yes, actually.' That'll teach you, she thought, gaining a brief satisfaction from the tightening of his jaw. 'Mind you, I don't know if it's relevant. Maddy has a collection of tapes. Ones she's made herself of her friends' voices.'

'What on earth for?'

Rose didn't answer for a few seconds. She was recalling the action which Maddy had curtailed, one which she now knew would have led to her own voice being recorded. The recorder was well hidden, Maddy only had to bend to flick a switch. Perhaps she sensed how the conversation would go and had thought better of it. 'She'll make a good actress, she got my voice off to perfection.'

'Rose, what're you talking about? What recordings?'

'To help her with her acting. Oh, don't you know?'

'No. Tell me.' Jack leaned back and folded his arms. Rose Trevelyan was a totally infuriating woman at times.

'Well, she joined the amateur dramatic company some months ago but she couldn't get parts because she, to use her own words, always came out sounding like Maddy Duke. She taped other voices and practised copying them.'

'And?'

'And she's got a part in the Christmas pantomime.'

Jack took a sip of his drink. His arm brushed against Rose's as he replaced his glass. He felt weak. 'Are you sure that's the only purpose of the tapes?' Jack could think of others, such as blackmail or using the recordings of her friends, edited, to cause who knew what mischief by way of a telephone.

'Mm. I think so. Except, and this is going to sound daft, it crossed my mind that she thinks she might feel more part of things if she had a touch of a Cornish accent.'

Jack shook his head in disbelief. Women's minds were often incomprehensible to him. He moved in his seat. Rose's flowery perfume was disturbing him now. However, Maddy Duke sounded like a suitable case for treatment: insanely jealous of everyone, making peculiar tapes, attacking a so-called friend and yearning for a long-lost baby. He sighed. Another suspect back on the list. 'What time did you leave her?'

'About an hour before I met you. Maddy went back down to the shop to relieve Sally. She was fine by then. I needed some air. It'd been a damn long afternoon. Jack, what's bothering you?'

'You are. Be careful, Rose. Think how much you know already. Whoever killed Jenny might not like it. And a couple of my colleagues are wondering why you're taking such an interest.'

'Oh, you mean they think I'm trying to cover my tracks?'

'There's no need for sarcasm, Rose. Most people prefer to distance themselves from crime of any sort.'

'But I'm not most people, am I, Jack, or you wouldn't be here now.'

Her comment hurt. 'Look, have you thought that someone may have been trying to implicate you rather than scare you?'

'How come?' This had not occurred to her.

'You've lived here long enough to have been a contemporary of the woman in the shaft. Guilt has strange ways of manifesting itself.'

'Including auditory hallucinations?'

'Yes. And returning to the scene of the crime. After that, you become involved with a man who's given his girlfriend, younger girlfriend, the boot and then you learn she wants him back. It wouldn't take a genius to set you up for both things.'

'But you don't even know who the first woman was.'

'No. But you might.'

Rose was very worried. Who would want to do that to her, and why? She looked down. Jack's hand was resting on her knee but it was a fraternal gesture.

'Jennifer Manders didn't lack for companions with whom to share pillow talk. There could be other men we don't know about, so don't think we've stopped looking.'

Rose knew she ought to voice her suspicions. Why hold back now? 'It's possible Jenny had an affair with Daniel Wright.'

'How do you know?' he asked quietly.

'I don't. It was just an impression I got. Oh, Jack, I really hate all this. These people are my friends.' She was near to tears.

'One other thing. I think Stella's jealous of your talent.'

'Stella? Don't be ridiculous.' But perhaps it was not as ridiculous as it sounded. There were the put-downs which Rose, who was unaware of the strength of her own self-possession, had not noticed until Maddy had pointed them out, and the advice not to go to a certain gallery owner because he charged an extortionate commission. Later Rose had found this to be untrue but assumed Stella had been mistaken. The idea of her friends being guilty was repugnant. She liked them, despite their various flaws, or maybe because of them. She recalled part of a conversation with Doreen Clarke who had telephoned for a chat recently. Penzance, Newlyn and Hayle were Doreen's known territories; she had, in her own words, no truck with St Ives people. 'Different breed, they,' she had remarked enigmatically. Rose smiled inwardly. To Doreen, anyone not from her own locality might as well have come from a different planet.

'How's Jenny's father taken it?'

Jack, too, had been deep in thought. He had a feeling that Rose's friends, no matter how stringently questioned, would all stick together. 'It's hard to say. I don't think he had much time for her.'

'I got that impression too.'

Jack closed his eyes. What now? he thought. What is she going to surprise me with this time? 'You've spoken to him?'

'I'd met him briefly a month or so ago. I was over in St Ives and he and Jenny had just bumped into each other. She introduced me. I thought, as I'd known her, the least I could now do was to tell her father how sorry I was. I couldn't have done that once, Jack. After David died so many people avoided me. They didn't know what to do or say, they were afraid they'd make things worse. It doesn't, though. However clumsy or lacking in tact

115

people are, it's still a comfort to know they care.' He looks exhausted, Rose realised. Jack's clothes were creased and the lines which gave his face character were amplified with tiredness and frustration.

'I'm sorry, Rose. I didn't think of it that way.'

'You thought, as Barry would say, I was interfering?' She took a sip of her wine. 'I suppose in a way I was. You see, I wondered whether the skeleton you found was Jenny's mother.'

Jack grinned. He immediately looked years younger. 'So did I.'

'And?'

He shook his head. 'I've discussed far too much with you already, Mrs Trevelyan. My major suspect, too. Hey, what're you thinking about now?'

Rose's brow had creased in a frown. 'Something Maddy said. I can't remember exactly what it was, but I'm sure she mentioned that Jenny said if Nick didn't take her back she'd go and live with her father again. But she didn't, did she? She ended up living rough. Still, I suppose if they didn't get on it wouldn't have worked. To be honest, the man gave me the creeps. I wonder if Renata'll go to the funeral.'

'There won't be any funeral, at least not for a while. The inquest hasn't even been opened yet. Anyway, what made you say that?'

'Well...' Rose began, feeling herself blushing because she hadn't asked Alec Manders whether his ex-wife would be coming down out of mere politeness. She had asked because she was as curious as everyone else was to know the identity of the first body and, like Jack, she had thought it might be Renata. 'He was evasive. I got the impression she might not even know her daughter was dead.'

'He told us he'd written to her.' Jack left it at that. He should not be discussing this with Rose but by giving her an answer he hoped to deter her from getting in deeper. Other officers were seeking the veracity of Manders' comment. 'Are you up to driving?'

'Yes, I'm fine, thanks.'

'Then I'll walk you to your car. And I want you to go straight home and stay there.'

Rose looked up at him and grinned. 'Yes, Inspector. Anything you say, sir.'

With a warm feeling of satisfaction Jack watched her drive away. They had parted on more amicable terms than on many recent occasions. But he knew Rose better than to read too much into that.

8

Because of the two consecutive inquiries, extra men had been drafted in from Charles Cross police station in Plymouth. Jack Pearce always felt a nagging resentment when this happened although he knew it was necessary.

He had come to some conclusions but was, for the moment, keeping them to himself. One thing he would like to do might or might not be approved. It would be costly and would take time but he thought it would probably be necessary in the end. For the moment the old method, the question and answer system, would suffice. And there was one question he really wanted an answer to.

Why, if the woman in the mine had fallen or been pushed, had she crawled further into the shaft instead of staying where she could see daylight above and where, if she called for help, she had the faintest chance of being heard? As in Jenny's case, it had to be that she had been killed first then her body taken down there and hidden. Colleagues agreed with him when they had discussed the similarities here. The method was the same in both cases. Forensics could not be certain and would only go as far as to say that it was possible, but they suspected the damage to the skull was in excess of what might be expected from such a fall. Both women hit over the head, then the bodies hidden in such a manner that if they were discovered their deaths might seem accidental. The same person? How neat that would be. Scene-of-crime officers had been of little use in Jenny's case. The evidence would be where she was killed, not on the edge of the sea. The laborious forensic task of examining cars and other forms of

117

transport was about to begin. Everyone who had known Jenny was being reinterviewed. Someone had moved the body, but how and from where? Boat owners of every description were being questioned. Information obtained from the coastguards regarding tides and currents suggested she had been taken some distance out to sea and thrown overboard. Had Jennifer Manders fallen from the cliffs anywhere along the stretch where she was found her body would have been washed up farther down the coast.

Jack sat at his desk, staring unseeingly at the work awaiting his attention. Not a fisherman or experienced seaman, he told himself. Whoever had tried to make it seem as if she had fallen and drowned had made a mistake.

The necessary paperwork to bring in the suspects' cars for examination, had they been unwilling to co-operate, had been issued. Jack was grateful that the advances in technology meant that, no matter how thoroughly a vehicle may have been cleaned, traces of blood and fibres would still be detectable. He realised he had been sitting there for over half an hour and hadn't achieved a thing.

Nick Pascoe had amended his statement the previous evening. He did not think anyone had seen him returning home after only fifteen minutes when he failed to catch up with the woman he believed was Jenny. Jack frowned. But Maddy Duke had said she had remained in her seat in the window until almost 1 a.m. It was where she always sat as she worked. Surely she would have noticed him? Any movement at that time of night in the quiet streets would have been noticeable even if his footsteps hadn't echoed in the night air. He would ask her about it when he questioned her again later that day.

By the time he left for home Jack's handsome face was drawn with fatigue. The problem here was not too many alibis but a complete lack of them. Rose, like everyone else, was still under suspicion.

By the weekend they had reached a hiatus. The frenzy of the initial inquiry was over, the repetitive slogging was to come. It would have been nice to talk to Rose, to discover her views, but for the moment he must avoid her. Maddy Duke had only repeated that she had not seen Pascoe return. It was beginning to look as if Jack's feelings about him were correct. However, for the moment, they did not have enough evidence to arrest him. Tests were being done on his car. Jack was banking on the results of these to back up his theory. As for the unknown woman, every division in the country now had the details and would be going back through their records of missing persons.

Dressing with care on Saturday morning Rose thought about what she had learned from her own solicitor whom she had telephoned the day before. Apart from the purchase of the house and David's probate she had had little need of Charles Kingsman's services over the years although, having known David long before he did Rose, he seemed to feel obliged to keep an eye on his widow and got in touch every couple of months or so. Not learned, Rose realised, I'd already worked it out. I needed it confirmed. She sprayed perfume on her neck and wrists and wondered how she could let Nick know, as tactfully as possible, that friendship was as much as she wanted from him. Flicking back her hair she grinned at herself in the mirror. My tact may be wasted if he's not interested anyway, she thought.

Nick was punctual and told her at once how lovely she looked, although she was not terribly flattered by the look of surprise on his face as he took in her appearance. She didn't always look a mess. 'Thanks,' she said, looking down at the plain pale blue dress she had bought when away on a business trip with Barry. It had been one of her better buys. She picked up her raincoat. It wasn't raining but it was the only outer garment which went with the dress.

'New car?' Rose asked, as he opened the door for her.

'No. Hired.' He paused. 'The police still have mine.'

'Oh.' There was little she could say. Nick was obviously still very much a suspect. She wished she hadn't asked and she tried to put from her mind the thought that she was possibly sitting next to Jenny's killer. They drove the rest of the way in way silence.

'Anywhere in particular you want to go?' Nick asked as they joined the throngs of shoppers.

'Not really. Shall we just stroll around and try not to get ourselves injured in the crush?' The pavements were overflowing.

They window-shopped for almost an hour, mooching around the alleyways and the markets, and stopping to admire the cathedral, which was built smack in the centre and towered overhead between the low-storey buildings. By twelve thirty they were still empty-handed and decided they might as well eat.

There was a wine bar nearby and they were early enough to get a decent table before the real rush began. It was typical of its kind: bare floorboards, tables with wrought-iron legs and marble tops and the cutlery presented in a rolled paper serviette. But the menu was interesting and the list of wines extensive. 'You choose,' Nick said, referring to the wine. 'You'll have to drink most of it.'

More people came in as they waited for their food. Rose ordered the Greek salad because she preferred to eat her main meal in the evening; Nick went for the more substantial pork and apricot stew with French bread.

'It's gone very quiet,' Nick commented when they had taken their first few mouthfuls.

Rose, a piece of pitta bread half-way to her mouth, looked around at the other chatting customers. 'What has?'

'The investigation.'

'I'd hardly say that. Jack said they're speaking to everyone again.'

'Yes.' He stared at something beyond Rose's shoulder because he was embarrassed to look at her. 'But we've all been to Camborne now and nothing's happened. No arrest, I mean.'

Rose wondered whether he was fishing, whether he believed because of her friendship with Inspector Pearce she would be privy to certain information. 'They're still testing the vehicles. I don't get mine back until tomorrow.' But Nick's, she realised, had been the first to be taken. Was that relevant? How she would have loved to know what went on in those interviews. Had Jack questioned Daniel about his relationship with Jenny? Had Maddy been more forthcoming after the catharsis of her outburst? And did the confirmation from Charles Kingsman mean what she thought it might mean? For the moment she must think about Nick and the appropriate words to explain how she felt about him.

'There's that other woman, too. I gather they still don't know who she is.'

The turn in the conversation had dampened Rose's mood and the carols playing in the background seemed to mock them. It was time to change the subject and talk of something more cheerful. Nick's work, she decided, would be a starting place.

'I haven't done much, lately, what with not sleeping and the miserable weather. No, to be honest, I just haven't felt like it. What about you?'

'Plodding along.' Rose speared an olive.

'I still find that business out at the mine baffling. Haven't the police come up with anything on that?'

'I think they've got more important problems on their mind.' This was not true. She knew that Jack believed there was a definite connection with what she had heard and what they had found. Rose was disappointed. As hard as she had tried to change the subject Nick kept reverting to it. The day was not turning out the way she had anticipated, and they finished the meal in another uncomfortable silence. Rose was annoyed because Nick could have made more of an effort. She wondered why she had bothered to come and why he had bothered to ask her, and, more to the point, why she had not told him how their relationship stood.

Deciding against coffee, Rose poured the last of the wine and lit a cigarette.

'I didn't know you smoked.'

Nick's tone was disapproving which infuriated Rose further. There were ashtrays on every table, it was not as if she was acting illegally. 'Well, I do. Not often, and not many, but I do enjoy one after a meal. I'll drink this then we'll go.' She indicated the inch or two of wine in her glass.

'I'm sorry, Rose, I really don't know what's got into me. Everything I say comes out wrong. I wasn't criticising.'

You were, Rose thought but did not say. Instead she smiled. 'It was a nice meal. Thank you.' He had insisted beforehand that he paid.

The streets seemed even busier as they left the wine bar. Between the buildings the sky was grey, not the greyness which promised rain but that of the half-light of an afternoon in late December. 'It's Stella's party tomorrow. Are you going?'

'She's invited me,' Nick replied.

My God, Rose thought, hastening her footsteps. What's wrong with a simple yes or no? He really is in a mood. 'Nick, is something bothering you?'

'No. Just the culmination of too many nights without proper sleep.'

'Shall we go back now? There's nothing I need to buy.'

'If you like.'

'I do like.' Several people stopped. Rose was unaware how loudly she had spoken but she found Nick's diffidence extremely infuriating.

The journey back was as silent as the one coming and Rose was angry. There was nothing wrong with not speaking if it was a companionable silence, as she often experienced with Barry and Laura and even Jack. This was downright moodiness. Rose was about to tell Nick to drop her in St Ives to save himself the extra miles when he rested a hand on her thigh and gave it a quick squeeze. 'I've behaved dreadfully. Forgive me. I just didn't realise how much Jenny's death had upset me. It's taken a while to sink in. I keep thinking I'll see her around the next corner.'

Now it was Rose who felt ashamed. How could she have not realised what he must be going through? They had lived together for over three years and it was less than a week since Jenny's body had been found. The man was grieving and she had expected him to entertain her. On top of that he probably felt guilty for having sent her away that night. 'It's hard, isn't it? Look, let's pretend today never happened and take it from there.'

'You're rather special, Rose Trevelyan. Don't let anyone ever tell you otherwise.'

With the change of mood Rose agreed to go back to Nick's house where, he said, she could listen to some decent music and drink more wine if she wanted because she wasn't driving. 'I'll abstain if you need a lift home. If you want to stay there's a spare room.'

Tactfully put, she thought. It leaves every option open. But in the end she drank only one glass of Chablis.

Nick opened the door and switched on the fire, knowing that most people felt the cold more than himself. Having settled Rose into the corner of the settee he went to get the wine from the fridge. Rose leaned back and listened to the swelling music of Beethoven. 'Thanks.' She took her glass which was misted with condensation and sipped the icy contents. 'Delicious, it's one of my favourites.' Cynically she wondered if this was the classic seduction scene; if so, Nick was about to be disappointed. And the flickering flames were from a coal-effect electric fire rather than a real one. She placed the wine on the small table beside her from which Nick had removed a pile of papers. As she moved back something firm nudged her hip. She reached down and pulled a hard-backed book from between the side of the settee and the cushion. It was a novel – a new one, only recently published. She had read the reviews. Nick had told her he didn't read novels. Always curious she opened it to read the blurb but before she could do so her eyes were drawn to the inscription. 'To Jenny, a gift to thank you for last weekend.' Rose's face felt hot and she closed the book quickly but not before Nick had seen her.

'I can explain,' he said.

'There's no need. It's none of my business.' But he looked so shifty that Rose wanted to hear that explanation.

Nick was on his feet. He slid one hand into the back pocket of his jeans and turned away, unable to look at her. His other hand raked through his hair.

I like the way his hair lies across his collar, Rose thought, surprised at her objectivity, because she now knew for certain that what little had existed between them before no longer did.

'She came here a few times. After she'd left, that is.'

'Nick, I'd rather not hear this.'

'There was nothing in it.' He smiled. 'She cooked me a meal. To make up for all those other times she didn't, I expect.'

'Nick, I'd like to go now. There's no need for you to drive me, I'll make my own way home.' He's lying, she thought. He's looking me straight in the eye and lying to me. It was never really over between them. Not for one moment could she imagine Jenny turning up just to cook a meal because she had been remiss in this regard before. And if he had still been seeing her did that make him more of a suspect or less?

'Please, don't go. I thought we were getting on so well.'

'I must. I have things to do.' She picked up her raincoat, put it on then grabbed her handbag decisively. 'Thanks again for the lunch.'

'Rose?'

'Bye, Nick.' She tried to smile but her face felt stiff.

Hurrying down the road she knew she was lucky it was still early, not much after three. There would be a choice of a train or a bus. No one stood at any of the stops she passed so she continued down into the main part of St Ives and up the hill towards the Malakof where the buses waited and which was adjacent to the railway station. The track was single-line, and the same train chugged back and forth. In the distance she saw it snake around the edge of the bay towards her. At least something was in her favour. She walked down the slope to the car-park and across it to the platform.

When the train arrived she got on and sat down, pressing her hot face against the window. It misted with her breath. Only a couple of other passengers joined her and soon they were rattling over the track. In less than twenty minutes she was back in Penzance.

They had walked a fair distance that morning but Rose needed air. She started making her way along by the harbour and on to the Promenade then decided to detour, to walk up into the town centre and see Barry. She longed for the honest solidity of him but recognised that she was using him. On the other hand, over the years he had tried to convince her that that was what friends were for, they were the people to whom you turned when you needed a sympathetic ear. Rose needed one then.

Barry was delighted to see her although he expressed concern for her appearance. 'You look a bit peaky, woman,' he said.

Rose smiled reassuringly. 'I'm fine. Anyway, I decided, as it's Saturday, I'm going to let you buy me a drink.'

'How very kind of you.' Barry thumbed his glasses back into place. There were red indentations on either side of his nose.

Rose waited the forty-odd minutes until he closed the shop and cashed up the till. Outside he locked the door, pushed it to check it was safe, then, after half a dozen paces, turned back to check again. Rose shook her head. He always did it and had once driven from her place in the middle of the evening to double-check because he couldn't remember having turned the key in the Chubb lock beneath the Yale.

Together they walked up to the London Inn in Causewayhead. Ensconced in the back bar, Rose downed a glass of wine quickly. Her face burned. It was dark outside but some shops were still open. Through the frosted glass window they saw shapes walking past. 'I think I'm beginning to feel quite festive,' Rose said.

Barry studied her face. 'I don't think festive's the right word, Rosie. Do you want me to get you a taxi?'

No.' Suddenly she was serious. 'I don't want to go home just yet.' Never in all the years she had lived in the house had she felt that way. It held nothing but happy memories.

Barry stroked her cheek. It was an avuncular gesture. 'What is it, Rose?'

'For one thing I'm a suspect. I had to go back and answer the same questions all over again. Jack thinks I killed Jenny and that other woman.'

'He thinks no such thing, and you know it. That's not what's really bothering you.'

'No. You're right. I don't know what's got into me. And it hurts to know my friends are under suspicion. I feel I ought to be able to tell if any one of them killed Jenny.'

'Why should you when the police can't?'

'I know. It's illogical. And there's Nick.'

'Ah. Yes. Nick.' Barry studied the contents of his glass and uncharitably wished he was the guilty party.

'It's over, you see. Well, not that much was going on anyway. I won't be seeing him again.'

Barry's spontaneous boyish grin left Rose in no doubt how he felt about that piece of news. 'Can I get you another drink?' She stood with her own glass in her hand.

Barry noticed the blue dress, the one she had bought to wear out to dinner in London with him. With her flushed face she looked lovely. 'One more then you're going home. Order a taxi while you're at the bar.'

The taxi turned up promptly twenty minutes later. Arriving home she heard the telephone ringing as she unlocked the kitchen door and reached it seconds before the answering machine cut in.

'It's me. Nick. I've tried several times but I didn't want to leave a message. I behaved disgracefully today. I hope you can forgive me. About Jenny, it was –'

'Please, Nick. I don't want to hear any more about Jenny.'

'Can I see you tomorrow?'

'No.'

'But you'll still come to Stella's?'

'There's no reason for me not to.' I can be as evasive as you, she thought.

'Good. Until then.'

'Nick, I'd rather you didn't ring me any more. I don't need complications in my life at the moment. Goodbye.' Rose replaced the receiver before he had a chance to argue.

In the morning Rose sat at the kitchen table sipping coffee and nibbling at a piece of toast. It was 23 December, the day of Stella's party. The coffee tasted strange and it hurt to swallow. By mid-morning her head was thumping and she felt sore all over. Her limbs felt heavy and it was an effort to stand as she dialled Stella's number to make her apologies. She was in no state to attend a party. Having swallowed two aspirins and filled a jug with fruit juice, Rose took herself to bed with a hot water bottle. For most of that day and long into the night she sweated out a dose of flu, not caring whether Nick thought it was an excuse to avoid him.

Too weak to do more than sit and read she spent a miserable Christmas Eve. Laura rang and offered to come over and cheer her up but Rose said she preferred to be on her own and the last thing Laura needed was to catch her germs when her whole family was there.

Luckily the bug was short-lived and she awoke on Christmas morning feeling better. After a leisurely breakfast, accompanied by a giant crossword she had saved for the occasion, she made a couple of telephone calls. Barry was delighted with his pen-holder and Laura with her ear-rings. 'It sounds like pandemonium,' Rose commented. In the background she could hear laughter and male voices and the high-pitched ones of excited children.

'It is. Must go, someone's calling me. Thanks, Rose. Happy Christmas,' Laura said.

At midday she uncorked a bottle of champagne and, an hour later, ate a lunch of smoked salmon and a ready-cooked chicken with salad. It was the sort of simple meal she most enjoyed and involved little effort or washing-up. She finished with ground coffee and a couple of the handmade chocolates Barry had given her. Having guessed what was in the inexpertly wrapped box, she had already opened it. The rest of her presents she saved until after lunch.

From her mother was a beautiful tan shawl threaded with gold, and the usual cheque from her father who was never sure what to buy his adult daughter. Her parents had always sent separate gifts.

'I don't believe it.' Rose shook her head. Laura had given her ear-rings almost identical to the ones she had bought for Laura; made of silver filigree with an amber stone, they were the work of a local craftsman. Still, their tastes had always been similar.

With one of her new novels and the last glass of champagne, Rose settled down on the settee. There had been no hardship in spending the day alone. In fact, she had thoroughly enjoyed it.

Maddy Duke spent Boxing Day morning in the few feet which served as her kitchen. She gave a brief thought to the police who would be working over the holidays and realised how other people's tragedies took second place at such times of the year. With her preparations well advanced and the afternoon to look forward to, it was as if Jenny Manders had never been.

When everything was ready she put on the green velvet dress she had found in a charity shop. It had a lace collar like a child's party frock but it suited her. She untied her hair and brushed it until it crackled with static then stepped into her lace-up ankle boots and waited nervously for her guests to arrive.

They all seemed to come at the same time but it pleased her to see them mingling and chatting amicably, all suspicions temporarily put on hold.

'I'm glad you could make it,' Maddy said to Rose, kissing her cheek. Her eyes glowed with gratitude. Rose Trevelyan had enabled her to express all that she had bottled up for so long. 'This is Peter Dawson,' she added with a touch of pride.

'I admire your work,' Rose said, which was true, although she preferred representational art over abstract.

'Thank you. From what I hear you're no slouch yourself.' Rose had not known what to expect, but certainly not this sophisticated, urbane man in his mid to late fifties. 'I have to admit I don't know your work,' he added.

You will, Rose thought, but did not say, hoping that Maddy's interest in Peter would divert her away from Nick who, she suspected, was not the stable person Maddy required.

'Jenny loved parties,' Maddy said, blushing because she wished she hadn't. Now was not the time to bring up her name.

Rose looked up and happened to see Nick across the room engaged in conversation with Stella. He nodded in her direction, his face grim, then, making one last comment, left Stella and approached her. 'Are you feeling better?'

'Yes, thanks. It was one of those twenty-four hour things.'

'I didn't see you there, Rose. You look lovely.' Stella had joined them.

'Thank you.' She had hoped she would not be over-dressed in a velvet skirt and a slinky blouse. Next to Stella, of course, no one would appear to be so. Today the ensemble was a black satin trouser suit enlivened by a chain belt which dipped over her narrow hips and lots of chunky costume jewellery.

'No wonder you got ill, with all that's been going on. You were probably run down. And the police. Are they leaving you alone now?'

'Yes. Why should they be doing otherwise?'

'Honestly, Rose, it stands to reason. You were the one who led them to that unfortunate girl. Ah, excuse me, I must have a word with someone.'

Rose watched her walk across the room to a couple she did not know. Too late Stella had seen her mistake and knew that Rose had seen it too. 'Nick, was it you who mentioned my idiotic panicking at the mine to Stella?' Rose had not doubted that everyone would know eventually but a thought had crossed her mind and she was interested to know exactly when Stella had heard.

'No. There was no reason to. Why?'

'I just wondered.'

Maddy had been watching this interaction with interest. Unable to paint herself, she still had a genuine interest in art and all its forms. And since that embarrassing encounter with Nick and what had followed with Rose, she had begun to see the man she thought she had been in love with in a different light. 'I hear you've finished the engine house. I'd love to see it.'

'Then you must come over one day.'

'Really? Thanks.'

Peter Dawson had not moved away. He was fascinated by the two women, who seemed to share some secret understanding.

'I wonder what it'd look like if you painted it again?' Maddy continued.

Rose frowned her lack of comprehension.

'I mean now. After what's happened. Would it affect your view of the place? I suppose what I'm trying to say is how much of what an artist sees is what's really there and how much depends on other stimuli?'

It was an interesting point. 'I think moods can affect the way you work. A scene might well come out differently if you painted it twice; once in a happy frame of mind and again when depressed. It would reflect more in the colours than anything else, I think.' How would that landscape look, Rose wondered, knowing what I know now? 'It's a good idea, Maddy. I just might try it again, although obviously from a different perspective. Perhaps even tomorrow.' Fully aware of the people who were listening and those who were not, she thought this might be one way to find out what was going on. But it was a good idea. Painted from the opposite side and with the hills in the background instead of the engine house outlined against the sky, it would be completely different. Jack's words unheeded, Rose did not stop to think that she might be putting herself in danger, that if someone who thought she knew too much was in the room then she would have given them the perfect opportunity to remove her from the scene.

The party was beginning to break up when Rose's taxi arrived at five. The food had been eaten and enough drink consumed and conversations were beginning to flag. Only the few, like Rose, who had spent a quiet Christmas Day had the stamina to continue. But Rose had had enough socialising and was ready to leave. She thanked Maddy and said her goodbyes.

Climbing into the front seat of the taxi, the better to gossip with the driver, she realised she had been a coward. She had intended to treat Nick normally but all she had done was to avoid him.

Having met the famous, or possibly infamous, Peter Dawson, Rose mentioned this to the driver, who was impressed. 'I thought he was virtually a hermit,' he commented.

'Reclusive, certainly, but he does come out and show his face now and again. In fact, he's coming to my New Year's Eve party.'

'We are moving up in the world. I take it you're going straight home?'

'Yes. Didn't I say?'

'No. And I'm not a mind reader. Here, did you know the girl who was killed?'

'Yes.'

'Ah. I'm sorry, Rose.'

After that there was no more conversation until they reached the bottom of her drive. Rose wished he hadn't mentioned Jenny.

The house was warm and welcoming and pleasantly quiet after the noise of the party. The light on the answering machine glowed steadily. There were no messages.

Rose kicked off her high-heeled shoes and switched on the television. An hour of viewing which required no thought would be welcome. She sat, her legs tucked beneath her, in the corner of the settee, her eyes on the screen. Later, she was unable to recall the programme that was on. All she could think about was Jenny and her friends.

Aware that Stella and Daniel, Nick, Maddy and Peter Dawson had all heard her say she intended going out to the mine again, she was not sure if she actually had the nerve to do so. And, more to the point, did she have the nerve to go back to St Ives and ask the questions that were worrying away at the back of her mind?

But where to start? She did not have a counterpart to Doreen Clarke there who knew everyone and all their business. Unless, she thought, she could rely on Maddy who saw all and said little.

9

There had been a meeting between Jack Pearce, his chief inspector and the superintendent and the conclusion drawn from it was that Jack's theory was more than worth a try. The forensic tests were still under way and the results not expected for several days. And now the Met was involved. Elimination, they said, was often as vital as hard evidence, and that was where the London lot could help them.

Over the holiday period only a skeleton forensic team were on duty in the lab they used. This would slow things down further but the results were useless unless they were accurate.

27 December. There were four days until Rose's party. Jack had optimistically told himself that at least one of the cases might be solved by then and he would be free to attend.

All Jack's hopes were now pinned on forensic evidence, but he knew how long he'd have to wait for it.

Several divisions had already come back with negative faxes regarding the identity of the first victim but there were still many to go. The reinterviewing of the suspects had provided little that was new except that it was now certain that Daniel Wright had had an affair with Jenny and his wife had known about it. Questioned individually, each had admitted it. The affair had been over for some time and although it gave them each a motive Jack thought it more likely that if Stella had been insanely jealous she would have acted immediately and if Daniel had been afraid of being found out he would not have confessed voluntarily. Still, sometimes emotions could simmer beneath the surface before they finally erupted.

Rose had been wrong, it seemed. Stella and Daniel swore they had been together after the preview. He did not want them to be guilty; he wanted Nick Pascoe to be the culprit because he was the most likely candidate and for a reason to which he did not care to admit. But that still leaves the problem of the first woman, he realised, then cursed for the lack of available evidence.

'I'll do it.' Rose stood in her sitting-room window, much as she did every morning of her life. Having decided to let the weather dictate her movements she had no option but to go ahead. But this time I'll be prepared, she told herself. She was almost certain she knew who was trying to frighten her and, if this assumption was correct, then it was not the same person who had killed Jennifer Manders, in which case she would not be in any real danger.

A flawless blue sky stretched into the distance and the water in the bay sparkled beneath it. Many fishermen were heading out to sea. Having landed just before Christmas they could not afford to waste good weather now.

Her resolve unwavering, Rose set off with her painting equipment.

In jeans, sweatshirt and a body warmer the chill in the air ought not to penetrate. And there was always her waxed jacket which lived on the back seat of the car. Her hair was tied back firmly to prevent it blowing forward on to her palette which she tended to hold high up and close to her body. As she drove she wondered if someone would be there ahead of her.

She parked and got out of the car. There was no one in sight and nothing different about the place yet Rose felt uneasy. She walked around the engine house, her hand shielding her eyes from the low winter sun as she planned from which angle to paint it. Glancing back, she checked how far away the car was if she needed to get to it in a hurry. It was unlocked. There would be no fumbling with the key.

The rocks cast strange shadows, but Rose was not afraid of shadows. She took out a sketchpad and soft pencil and drew a few lines. After forty minutes nothing had happened and only once had she been disturbed by a rustling in the undergrowth, which was too low to contain anything other than wildlife. Why then was she suddenly afraid? The hairs on the nape of her neck prickled. She turned her head slowly. There was nothing to see her but the rolling countryside, the boulders and the bracken and a crow wheeling in the sky. Had she heard someone approaching? People knew where she was, would know where to look if anything happened to her, but they were the wrong people and by that time it would be too late. How stupid she was to have come. Breathing deeply, she steadied herself. If she was in danger it was no good falling apart, she must be prepared. The winter sun was now lower still and made her squint. It was time to go home. She stood and stretched. More time had passed than she realised. Nothing was going to happen now.

'Rose?' The voice reverberated in the thin air.

'Jesus!' Instantly she froze. Her body was rigid, every muscle tense. Unable to move, she was close to hysteria. Then, just as quickly, her limbs took on a strange quality of fluidity as if they had turned from steel to blancmange. Adrenalin pumped through her veins and dictated movement. With a dry mouth and thudding heart she grabbed her belongings and ran towards the car, flinging everything in ahead of her haphazardly.

There was a rustling and someone grabbed her arm. She screamed. This time it was her own voice which echoed in the still air.

'My God, woman! I'm not that bad.'

It was seconds before she realised that Peter Dawson, who had jumped back in alarm, was standing a yard or so away, staring at her as if she was mad – which, indeed, she felt she was at that moment. What was he doing there? But he couldn't have been the one to frighten her previously because they had not met until Maddy's get-together. Until that day he had probably never heard of her. Rose saw the utter stupidity in having gone there alone. She took a deep breath. Her heart was pounding so loudly that she thought Peter must hear it too.

'Okay, so why so terrified?' He stood with his arms folded revealing the threadbare elbows of his mustard-coloured needle-cord jacket.

Rose shook her head. Fright had rendered her speechless.

'Do you want to walk for a minute to steady your nerves, or would you rather sit down?'

'Sit,' Rose managed to say.

'Let me take your arm.' This time he gave her warning. His touch was gentle as he led her to an outcrop of rock, smooth enough upon which to sit. 'What happened? The minute I called your name you took off as if the devil himself was after you.'

'It was your fault. I didn't see you. You scared the living daylights out of me.' She was trembling from head to foot.

'Look, I don't think you're up to talking yet. Why don't we find a pub and I'll buy you a drink, or coffee, or whatever you want.'

'Thank you.' It sounded like a good idea. And at least there would be other people around. Then it struck her. 'How did you get here? Where did you come from?'

'I drove, of course. How else? And there's another way in over there.' Peter pointed. Rose, peering into the distance, saw only deep shadows and realised why she had not seen him. 'I called at your place first hoping to change your mind about coming out here. I may not intermingle much but I still hear what goes on. It was a stupid risk to take. I wanted to dissuade you.'

Rose looked around and Peter interpreted her bewilderment. 'I'm parked out on the verge. I know you can see the engine house from the road but I had no idea there was access to it by car. I imagined it would've been fenced off for safety reasons. Anyway, you follow me. I'll go slowly. Okay?'

He escorted her back to the car and walked on ahead to his own, which was some way away – this explained why Rose had not been disturbed by the sound of its engine, But her instincts had been working overtime. She *had* known there was someone there. She drove automatically, letting Peter set the pace.

They came to the St Ives junction where Rose assumed Peter would indicate to turn off but he continued on past it. Who cares? She thought, the nearer home for me the better. The roads were quiet in that no man's land of post-Christmas and pre-New Year. A cattle truck lumbered towards them, the driver's visor down against the increasingly lowering sun. In the distance the purple clouds of evening were already building up. On they went, Rose keeping a respectable distance behind Peter although she could have driven faster now. They were in Penzance before he stopped, parking on the sea front where couples and family groups strolled and children rode their new bikes or sailed past on roller-blades. The tide was in and was slapping against the sea wall with a gentle suction. Droplets of spray flew over the railings. Rose locked the car and inhaled deeply, breathing away the last of her fear, calm enough now to appreciate the sharp, clean air in her lungs.

'The Navy's open,' Peter said, looking both ways for traffic before taking Rose's arm and guiding her across the road. 'I shall make do with a soft drink but you need something stronger. You can always leave your car where it is.'

The wind was stiffening. Rose shivered and wondered whether she was about to cry. Kindness sometimes did that to her. Turning the corner she saw the boards advertising all-day opening and bar food. She had eaten there with Jack; the portions were very generous.

They sat in a corner away from the bar because there were customers whom Rose knew and she was not up to making small talk. A tape was playing which meant their conversation could not be overheard. She accepted gratefully the rather large brandy Peter had ordered for her without consultation.

'Right. What was that all about back there?'

Rose told him, her embarrassment no less acute for having repeated the story several times before.

Peter stroked his chin thoughtfully. 'Mm. I had heard much the same thing, although not quite as concise an account of it. It puzzled me that you'd want to go back there after what they found. Good heavens, Rose, it couldn't have been whoever killed that unknown victim, could it? Maybe they didn't want anyone snooping around the area.'

'I was hardly snooping.'

'No. And it was a stupid idea. The last thing they'd do is to draw attention to it. Forget I said it. No one knew she was down there, you couldn't have done any harm just painting.' He rubbed his chin thoughtfully. 'Then that means there has to be another reason.'

'That's not what the police think.'

'They're not infallible, Rose. Tell me, what do you think?'

'I agree with you. Peter, tell me honestly, why were you there?'

'I have been honest. I heard what you said yesterday at Maddy's and the way you made a point of letting everyone know where you'd be. After you left I heard a lot more. Two unexplained murders and a middle-aged lady – who, if you don't mind me saying, looks nowhere near her age – hearing voices and intending to return to a place where she is likely to be in danger. Apart from that, an instinct told me this same lady and Maddy Duke are keeping some great secret. I was concerned for your safety, no more than that. And as far as I know there seems to be no one else to look out for you. I've also been informed that you have a knack of landing yourself in trouble. Does that explanation satisfy you?'

'It'll have to, but I didn't know you cared.' Rose bit her lip. 'I'm sorry. Forgive me, that was extremely rude.'

'It's shock. I wouldn't have put you down as rude. Outspoken, certainly, and with a excess of curiosity, but not rude.' He sipped his grapefruit juice and pulled a face. Sitting with one elbow on the table, his chin in his hand, he studied Rose's profile.

She was aware of his scrutiny and felt like a girl on her first date. 'Let me buy you another drink,' she said decisively, anxious to escape his gaze and what it was doing to her.

'No. Really. You have one if you like. I'll wait until I'm home and can have a taste of the real thing.'

'I'll leave it in that case. I'm already feeling a bit light-headed.'

'If you're not up to walking, I can give you a lift.'

'Thank you. I'd be very grateful.' Peter was the right age to have been involved with the girl down the mine and it wouldn't surprise her if he had known Jenny as more than a friend. It was only an impression, but Rose guessed that Peter Dawson was something of what her father would describe as a 'ladies' man'. He certainly had charisma and charm. He might not mix much but she sensed a warm personality behind the outward persona, and she found she was interested in what he had to say.

'Is it serious between you and Nick?' he asked as they made their way back to his car.

'A relationship that doesn't exist can hardly be described as serious,' she told him solemnly.

'Ah.'

'Ah, what?'

'Just interested. Rose, please don't think I'm an interfering old fool but be careful of Nick.'

'In what way?'

'It's hard to say. I've known him a good many years now. He's talented, extremely so, but he has a touch of the artistic temperament.'

'People use that as an excuse for bad behaviour.' They stood at the kerb. A line of cars approached from both directions.

'Do they? It hadn't occurred to me. Perhaps I had better look to some of my own bad habits. I don't mean he's a threat to you, it's just that he's never settled down. I think Jenny was the longest relationship he's ever had.'

'You're not married or living with anyone.'

'No. But I'm different.' He laughed when he saw Rose's cynical grimace. 'Of course, we all like to think that. But I know I have no staying power. The women I meet, and please don't take offence, bore me within a very short time. It's a lack in me, not them, you understand. I enjoy being solitary, I love not having to worry about anything other than my work. I walk or paint or read or eat or drink whenever the mood takes me. It would take a very unusual woman to put up with my selfishness. Yes,' he said, as if it had only just occurred to him, 'that's what it is. I won't allow myself to be changed or to fit in with anyone else's plans.'

There was a gap in the traffic and they were able to cross the road. Rose guessed he was saying it for her benefit, that he had known his faults for many years.

'I'm a little like that myself these days.'

'It must've been hard, losing your husband.'

'There are no words to describe what I felt. You see, we were lucky, our marriage worked. We sort of, I don't know, fitted each other.'

'Children?'

'None, but it didn't seem to matter. Anyway, since then I've pleased myself too.' She smiled and was rewarded with a conspiratorial grin. 'I have to admit I have the same problem with men. Not that there've been many, but the few I've met have tried to pin me down. They're possessive. David wasn't like that, we each had our own lives as well as each other.'

'Then I doubt you'll find a replacement.'

'I don't intend to.'

Peter bent to unlock the car and they got in. 'Nick isn't possessive, not in the usual way,' he continued. 'He'd allow you freedom, but he'd want to know how you used it. Does that make sense?'

'Peter?' Rose looked at him steadily. 'Could he have killed Jenny?'

'That idea has crossed my mind. However, the police haven't arrested him.'

'They suspect me, too.'

'So I had heard.'

'Do you think it's true?'

'My judgement is not always infallible, Rose, but if you killed Jenny Manders then I'm the Queen Mother.'

'Thank you,' she said with such warmth that she felt tears of relief behind her eyelids.

'Now we'd better make tracks. Do up your seat belt.'

'What do you mean about Nick? Apart from his being a little possessive?'

'He can be moody. He likes his own way. God, we're a selfish lot when you think about it. He doesn't believe women are equal and, apart from Jenny who was far stronger than most people gave her credit for, he'll bleed you dry emotionally if you let him.'

'Do you believe women are equal?' Rose was fascinated to learn that she was more interested in Peter Dawson's personality at that moment than Nick's.

'There's nothing to believe. All men are equal, and I use that term figuratively. It's not something I've come to a decision about, I've always known it. You only have to look around you. In some situations it's the female who keeps things going and in others the male. My own parents were a perfect example of the former.'

Rose would have liked to ask in what way but they had reached Newlyn and Peter was taking the sharp bend on the bridge and she did not wish to distract him. He dropped her at the bottom of her drive and made no attempt to get her to invite him in.

'Take care, Rose,' he said through the open window of the car.

'I will.'

I need something to eat, she decided, and began to arrange the ingredients for something quick and easy. Pasta with a bacon, tomato and garlic sauce. The onions were sweating and their mouthwatering smell made Rose aware just how hungry she was. As she slid them around the pan she thought of Nick. His moodiness had not gone unobserved. How much more pronounced would it have become if she had got to know him better? He had a temper, too, although he kept it hidden.

Lying in bed she listened to the wind and the familiar sounds of the house settling down: the creak of a stair, the ticking of the heating system as it cooled and the hum of the washing-machine as it reached the end of its cycle.

She had spoken to Maddy, who had been able to provide some of the information Rose wanted. It was certainly food for thought. But for now there was the party to think of and the less metaphorical sort of food to consider.

10

'Oh, to hell with it.' Inspector Jack Pearce scowled at the wall. Missing Rose was one thing, his personal decision not to contact her was another. There was nothing in the rule book to prevent him speaking to her, only his own sense of what was right. What he wanted, what he had hoped for was that Rose, in her distress, would contact him, use his shoulder to lean on. He had forgotten how perversely stubborn she could be.

Each of Jenny's friends had had the opportunity and possibly the motive to kill her but, as motives went, they were not strong. He was ashamed to admit that if Rose were not involved he would have taken it in his stride. It was, after all, what he was trained to do. If only there were some easy solution. Mostly there was, he thought, it was knowing where to look for it which was the hard part.

The forensic team was continuing its assiduous work and would not be hurried. Jack knew better than to pester them, it often provoked a slower response.

Against his better judgement he decided he would speak to Rose after all. Apart from an edge to the wind, it was a lovely day. He telephoned first because Rose might be taking advantage of it. He wanted to hear her theory – that she would have one he was in no doubt – but he had to be content to leave a message on her answering machine.

Towards the end of the day another piece of evidence was to hand. The Met had confirmed that the woman they had been asked to interview had not been seen for several days but they were continuing in their efforts to find her. Rather than disappointment, Jack felt only relief. This proved that he was on the right lines.

Feeling the need for a quiet evening in, Jack was about to leave for home when Rose returned his call. His spirits lifted until she spoke.

'I got your message. Is this business or pleasure?'

'A bit of both. Are you doing anything this evening?'

'Yes. Laura's coming over to help with the food.'

'The food? Oh, your party. Never mind, it wasn't important.'

'Will you be coming, Jack?'

'Is that a devious way of asking if an arrest is imminent?' Her light laugh cheered him; her initial words had sounded hostile.

'Well, is it?'

'No. But hopefully it won't be long.' Jack could almost feel her curiosity oozing down the line and pictured the furrow which dissected her forehead when she frowned with frustration.

'I wonder if you're thinking along the same lines as me?'

'Rose ... ?'

'Sorry, Jack. Must go. Laura's here.' Only when she put down the phone did she remember the book Nick had so recently given to Jennifer Manders. Did Jack know that the relationship had continued long after everyone thought it was over? If she told him, Nick would think that she had been acting like a woman scorned because she had been jealous. She decided to think about it. Nick may have volunteered the information already and Jack would start doubting her loyalty to her friends. Rose wondered why that should matter any more.

'Damn the woman.' Jack was listening to the dialling tone. He slammed down the phone with a further curse, wondering what Rose was up to.

Peter Dawson was sprawled on his sofa quite unconcerned that two men were searching his cottage and packing a few of his clothes into plastic bags. He reached out and poured himself a malt whisky although it was only ten thirty in the morning. He was quite unconcerned about that too.

'Do you always drink so early?' one of the men asked.

'If I choose to.' He smiled with a lift of an eyebrow as he read their minds.

Had Rose reported his having been at the mine or had they learned of Jenny's visits? It did not take long to establish it was the latter.

'Why didn't you come forward at the beginning?' one of the men asked. 'We know Miss Manders used to come here.'

'Your request was for information concerning her whereabouts from after the time she left Stella Jackson's gallery. I hadn't seen her for several weeks therefore I'd have been wasting your time.' He had no objection to them poking around, there was nothing for them to find, but he was fed up with their company and he needed a chance to think. It would have been nice to stride out across the cliffs and gaze at the sea, to smell the salt and the heady scent of grass as he crushed it beneath his feet. Instead he had to go to Camborne to make a statement. Peter couldn't understand why, with two of them present, he was unable to do so in the comfort of his own home.

One of the men stared suspiciously at Peter's cassette player.

'You won't find any traces of soil or anything. I wiped it clean when I got back from the mine.'

'What?' Both men spoke in unison.

Peter laughed mirthlessly. 'Just my little attempt at humour. Please, carry on.' He waved his hand to indicate the entire contents of the room. 'I'd be grateful if you'd leave the settee.'

He felt quite tired once they had left. Fingerprints had been taken, which he had explained was also a waste of time. They had come out with their trite phrase of 'for the purposes of elimination' but all the same he knew that there would probably be some of Jenny's around the place. He looked after himself and kept the cottage clean but not to such an extent that he went around wiping paintwork. He had already admitted that Jenny had been an occasional visitor but they had gone ahead with their dust anyway. He threw the receipt for the belongings they had taken on to the table.

Later that day, having abstained from drinking more whisky and substituted it with black coffee, he drove over to Camborne, arriving punctually for his appointment. The interview seemed interminably long. First there was the rigmarole of ensuring he understood what was going on then the tediousness of the questions themselves.

'How well do you know Mrs Trevelyan?' he was asked towards the end.

Because he realised that Rose was likely to be questioned he saw no reason not to tell them that he had encountered her at the mine. Peter said he had only followed her because he was worried about her safety. Two pairs of eyebrows were raised sceptically.

'In what way were you worried, Mr Dawson? You've just said you hardly know her.'

'I don't know,' he replied truthfully. 'I just had a feeling that she oughtn't to be out there on her own.'

'An odd thing to think without a reason?'

'I didn't think, I said it was just a feeling.'

'Are you having a relationship with Mrs Trevelyan?'

'Good heavens, no.' The question shook him. It was an honest answer but they seemed not to believe him.

'But Nicholas Pascoe is.' This came out as a statement.

'No, I don't think so. As far as I'm aware they're friends, no more than that. I think you should ask the lady herself if you really need to know.'

'Are you seeing anyone at the moment?'

'Seeing anyone?' His tone was mocking.

'A girlfriend? Mistress, whatever?'

'No. Not at the moment.'

'Not since Jennifer Manders.'

Peter's jaw tightened imperceptibly. 'She was not a girlfriend. It was a very casual thing.'

'Casual?'

'Look, I told you earlier, she came to the house on a few occasions. We enjoyed each other sexually, if that's what you're after, but it was no more than that. We had nothing else in common other than a desire for sex without emotional ties.'

'That may have been your wish, Mr Dawson, but most women think differently.'

'Do they? Perhaps in your experience, not in mine. I'm sure you'll find I was not alone in having a quick tumble with her.'

'Meaning what?'

'I suggest you ask around. My word is only hearsay and that, I believe, is not permissible evidence. Now, your men have ransacked my home, taken away certain of my possessions, and I've spent enough of the afternoon here. I would like to leave now.'

'You are perfectly free to do so, sir. Just one more question? If you're so keen to be emotionally free of women, maybe Miss Manders became more demanding than you cared for. Did you kill her?'

Peter sighed. 'No. I did not kill Jennifer Manders.'

'Thank you. Someone'll show you out.'

When he left he felt restless. A walk on the cliffs was out of the question now. It would be dark before he reached home and, as there was no moon, it would be foolhardy to risk the narrow path so close to the edge. Perhaps he would get blind drunk and wash the awfulness of the day from his system. On the other hand he could ring Rose Trevelyan to compare notes. This he did from a public telephone box before deciding whether it was worth going home. She answered on the second ring as if she had been waiting for a call. But not from him.

'Peter? Where are you?' Rose could hear background noises which she guessed were traffic.

'In a call box. I need some TLC. I have been grilled by the police. They tied me to a chair and shone a bright light in my eyes and whipped me with wet towels until I begged for mercy and confessed.' He was gratified to hear her laughing. 'So is there any chance of us meeting for a drink or dinner?' He was surprised to find himself holding his breath while she made up her mind.

'Not tonight, I'm getting ready for the 31st.' She hesitated briefly then added, 'But I'm free tomorrow.'

'Fine. What time shall I pick you up?'

'Oh, seven thirty?'

Turning the car around he realised how much he was looking forward to it. There was nothing run-of-the-mill about Mrs Trevelyan, he thought as he headed for home.

Rose's head was spinning. Another man wants to take me out? she thought, returning to the kitchen. Laura's suggestive smirk didn't help. 'You've got flour in your hair,' Rose told her acidly.

'Perhaps you'd better take a look in the mirror yourself, girl.'

They had been enjoying themselves, wrist deep in pastry dough as they prepared the cases for flans. Wineglasses stood near to hand, their bases dusted with flour, their stems smeared with greasy fingerprints. At least with Laura Rose could avoid the topic of Jenny Manders.

'For a woman who, not many days since, was crying into her beer over the inadequacies of men and who vowed to have nothing more to do with them, you're doing a fine impression of exactly the opposite. You're on the phone to Jack when I get here and less than an hour later someone called Peter rings up. That's two, without Nick.'

'Oh, honestly, Laura!' Rose made as if to slap her arm and knocked over the bag of flour. A small cloud of it settled on them both and they collapsed laughing.

'Rose?' Laura, who was facing the window, frowned over her shoulder.

Rose turned around. 'What is it?'

'God, I'm getting as bad as you. For a second I thought I saw someone out there. It was probably my own reflection.'

Rose went to the door and opened it. The sloping garden and drive were deserted. There was nothing but the bone-like rattle of the leafless trees as the wind lifted the boughs. Out in the bay the lights of three trawlers winked as they followed each other in procession. The chug, chug of their engines carried clearly across the expanse of water. 'There's no one there,' Rose said, closing the door again. She made them both supper while they waited for the flan bases to bake.

Spearing omelette on to her fork, Laura watched Rose surreptitiously. 'Okay, out with it, what's bothering you? Did you really think there was someone out there?'

'I don't know. I went over to St Ives today. They all seem to have hang-ups of some description.'

'By that you mean your arty friends?'

'Yes. But I can't believe one of them's a murderer.'

'Can't, or won't?'

'You're right. I won't. But I have been thinking about it and they all seem to have had something to gain by killing Jenny, even if it doesn't amount to much. But for the life of me I can't understand why there's so much mystery attached to the other body. I mean, surely someone knows who it is? I was convinced it was Renata Manders but it seems I was wrong.'

'It could be absolutely anyone. Not everyone's lucky enough to have people who'll miss them.'

'I know.'

'Rose, at the risk of sounding like Barry Rowe, leave it to Jack. I know there's something going through your pretty little head. If there is, tell him. Oh, God.' Laura jumped up, suddenly remembering the pastry which they could now smell.

Her hands encased in oven gloves, Rose lifted several fluted-sided dishes from the oven. She had borrowed some from Laura. 'Thank goodness you remembered. That was just in time.'

'On the other hand,' Laura continued, ignoring the results of their work, 'if you think you know something you really ought to tell Jack.'

'I know.' But Rose suspected Jack was ahead of her and that all he wanted was some conclusive evidence.

'But you want to solve it all yourself. I can tell by that grin that you're dying to show him what a clever girl you are.'

'Yes. Now are you going to help with the fillings or are you rushing off home now that I've fed and watered you?'

'That depends.'

'On what?' Rose followed the direction of Laura's gaze. 'I never was lucky in my choice of friends,' she said, reaching for the corkscrew.

After Laura had left Rose cleared up the kitchen and surveyed the food laid out on the worktops to cool. There was probably too much of it but some could be left in the freezer until the last minute.

Physically tired from her achievements in the kitchen but still on a high mentally from an idea that had crept into her mind, she was not quite ready for bed. She poured the last glass of wine, went through to the sitting-room and settled into the chair which faced the one where David had always sat and where she often pictured him.

Over the telephone she had asked Maddy if she knew of any of Renata's friends. Maddy had not been in the area very long but she seemed to soak up information like a sponge. And she had been close to Jenny who talked a lot.

'Jenny told me the name of one. She had a vague memory of her from when she was little but mainly because she was forbidden to go near her by her father. Alec said she was a bad influence on Renata. Anyway, Jenny always thought there had been something going on between her father and this woman.'

'What's her name?' Rose had asked impatiently.

'Josie Deveraux. At least, it was, she might have married.'

Rose had written it down, disappointed when Maddy went on to say, 'She moved away ages ago.'

Sitting quietly at the end of a long day Rose felt extremely sorry for Renata Manders. Her domineering mother-in-law had alienated her from her family and she had been more or less forbidden to see what may have been her only friend.

When Rose had gone to St Ives that morning she found the house where Josie Deveraux used to live was now inhabited by an elderly couple who had never heard of her. She realised now that even if they had done so they were hardly likely to have answered the questions of a complete stranger.

Why she wanted to know about the Deveraux woman, Rose wasn't sure, except it stemmed from her innate curiosity which would not be satisfied until she knew the whole story.

She had hoped the two women had kept in touch. Deep down she wanted to hear that, if it wasn't Renata they had found, things had worked out for her, that she was now happy.

Rose's head ached. A dull thudding behind her temples made her nauseous. It was time for bed.

By morning her headache was worse. Rose regretted acceding to Laura's wishes by opening the second bottle of wine. There was a heavy stillness in the air which did not help. As she watched, the grey canopy of the sky became sulphurous and then darkened. She realised that it was the weather rather than the wine which was responsible for how she felt. The bitter scent of the narcissi filled the room just as the first flash of lightning crackled over the bay. Seconds later thunder crashed and seemed to shake the house. The rain came suddenly, hammering down. Storms such as this had been known to roll around the bay for hours on end. Rose had intended going to Penzance to try to find something to wear for her party but for the moment it was impossible to go out.

The storm died down around eleven and the rain eased a little. She gave it half an hour then picked up her car keys and left the house.

The traffic was heavy and she joined the slow crawl up through Market Jew Street where buses were at the stops on both sides of the road causing further delays.

Her expedition was unsuccessful. Being a size eight and only five feet two inches tall, Rose was swamped by most modern fashions. She put it down to the after-effects of the headache which made her feel uneasy, but she had the impression that something was wrong.

As she turned into her drive she noticed a van parked across the road. The driver's face was turned away but she still recognised him. She quickly locked the car and went into the house, also locking the kitchen door, something she rarely did unless she was going out. Her heart was racing. Had she been right all along? She rang Jack immediately. Aware that she was gabbling she wondered if Jack had any idea what she was talking about.

'Stay there. Don't move,' he told her. 'I'm on my way.'

Minutes later there was a knock on the kitchen door. For a second Rose was filled with relief. It was too soon for Jack to have arrived but Laura had said she might call in with some paper plates and serviettes she had left over from her own Christmas preparations.

But on the other side of the glass stood Alec Manders, rain running down his face. 'Let me in,' he mouthed.

Rose froze, mentally urging Jack to drive faster. She backed out into the hall, terrified by the anger in the man's face. If she got to the front door she could reach the side of the house unseen and come out further down the drive below him. Then she would have a chance of making it to the road before he realised what was happening.

'Oh, God.' Her voice was hoarse. She had heard glass breaking. The key was on the inside of the kitchen door. If she had had the sense to remove it Alec Manders would have had to smash the wood which supported the four panes and she would have had more time.

In one movement she reached the front door and unlocked it. Grabbing the round, brass handle and the flat metal plate of the Yale, she heaved. The door didn't budge. So recently she had broken a nail doing this and promised to do something about it. More rain had swollen the wood further. It was too late now.

'Mrs Trevelyan.' His voice was low and controlled and therefore all the more terrifying. 'Why are you asking questions about me?'

He wanted to talk. Maybe that was all he wanted. 'I'm not.'

'You've been speaking to people in St Ives. You bothered an old couple who live near me. And you came to my house to offer your condolences which was just an excuse to poke your nose into my business. I know what you're thinking and it isn't true. And you're not the only one. I didn't kill my wife. She left me, you stupid bitch.'

Something about his words struck a chord. He had not denied killing Jenny. 'Why did you break in?' Rose knew she must keep him talking.

'So you'd know what it feels like to have your privacy invaded. You're in the phone book, it wasn't hard to find you. What were you doing out at the mine?'

She knew then that she was right. Alec Manders, most probably through Jenny, had learned that she was working there. 'Painting.'

'Painting.' His voice was scornful as he took a step nearer.

She had her back to the door. To her left was a small table which held a plant pot. Beside it was an old walking-stick stand. All it contained was an umbrella. Rose reached for it as Alec simultaneously reached for her. She felt the heat of his breath on her face and, as she tried to swing away and he grabbed at her hair, she thought how clean he smelled.

There was a jolt of pain in her back. Opening her eyes Rose realised that she was on the floor, that what she had felt was herself falling. Alec was on top of her, one knee pressed into her stomach, pinning her down. The pain made her want to vomit. 'I didn't want to have to do this,' she heard him say from a distance. 'But I didn't kill Renata.'

Weakly she raised her hand and brought the umbrella down on his head. It was the most ineffectual thing she had done in her life. It bounced off his thick hair causing him to jeer. 'I don't think so, Mrs Trevelyan.' He wrenched it from her and threw it down the hall, his knee still in place. Above Rose's head the ceiling began to swim as she struggled for breath. 'You're coming with me,' he said, pulling her to her feet. Rose tried to kick out at his shins but he twisted her arm behind her. She felt it might snap. There's still a chance, she thought, he hasn't killed me yet and I don't think he'll do it here. I've got to play for time, to give Jack a chance to get here. She was convinced that her destiny also lay in that mine shaft.

There was glass all over the kitchen floor from where Alec had stuck his elbow through the pane. It scrunched beneath the soles of Rose's boots. They had almost reached the door but Alec pushed her sharply against the edge of the sink, her arm still bent behind her. With his spare hand he rummaged in drawers, cursing when he couldn't find what he was looking for.

He has to tie me up, Rose realised. He has to do that before he can go and fetch the van. There was string upstairs, and whole rolls of strong cord with which she hung her pictures. Would he think of that? It would use up more time, he would have to take her up there with him, time in which Jack might arrive. Part of her mind was listening for cars but none had slowed. She sensed Alec was losing control of his temper. He yanked harder at her arm and she screamed in agony. 'There's string upstairs,' she told him, unable to help herself. She would do anything to make the pain stop.

Half-way up the stairs she stumbled. What if Jack wasn't coming? What if he was so fed up with her he couldn't be bothered or he had decided she was making a fuss about nothing again? Tears were rolling down her face and her nose began to run. If he did turn up she vowed she would never, ever be horrible to him again.

A car door slammed and was echoed by another. Downstairs there was a noise, quite a lot of noise, Rose thought.

'Let her go.' Jack took the stairs two at a time and twisted Alec around to face him. Rose fell awkwardly on the stair above but not before she had seen Jack raise his fist.

'Sir!' DS Green grabbed Alec's hands, one then the other, and encircled his wrists with the cuffs he had pulled from his pocket. He turned to Jack with a glare. 'It's just as well you didn't,' he said.

Jack nodded. He had nearly lost it there, had almost broken the rule about least possible restraint, and all because of Rose Trevelyan. 'Take him out to the car,' he said gruffly, reaching for Rose's arm.

Rose winced, staring at Jack uncomprehendingly as he got her upright with far more force than was necessary. Instead of gratitude she felt only disappointment. Hadn't she just provided the necessary evidence for them to arrest the murderer? Why did she always rub Jack up the wrong way?

There were two uniformed officers downstairs. One offered to make Rose a cup of tea. 'Thank you.' She sat at the kitchen table, trembling. Jack ignored her until the tea was in front of her. 'Tell us what happened,' he said. 'Not your assumptions or any wild guesswork, just the facts as they relate to today.'

Rose did so, wishing she had a chance to show him she had been right. It did not take long.

'Thank you. Now I suggest if Laura Penfold is busy you get your good friend Barry Rowe to come over.'

The way he spoke Barry's name made Rose cringe. Inspector Jack Pearce could be truly obnoxious when he chose. 'He'll be delighted,' she said spitefully, already having forgotten her earlier vow.

'Come on.' Jack nodded to the man who had made the tea, indicating that it was time to go. 'And ring someone to take care of this,' he added, pointing to the broken pane. 'We've got to go. Your other friend, Mr Pascoe, has just been arrested.'

'What?' She looked startled. 'You bastard,' she hissed loudly enough for Jack to hear as he walked away. As he closed the door firmly another shard of glass fell to the floor.

11

On the last morning of the year Rose began to lay out the food and drink for the party, which no longer seemed like a good idea. Since Alec Manders had broken into her house there had been no word from Jack, officers she did not know had taken her statement. Nor was there any further news of Nick.

With all that had happened she wondered how many people would turn up. Certainly not Jenny and Nick and, by his silence, not Jack either. That a man had been arrested for the murder of Jennifer Manders had been given out on the news, that his name had been withheld was irrelevant. Everybody locally knew it was Nick.

Alec's attack upon Rose convinced her that he had known of the presence of the woman in the mine shaft even if he hadn't put her there. Why else would he have been so angry and determined to stop Rose asking further questions?

I must forget it, she told herself. She had been way out in her calculations and was relieved now that she had not had a chance to mention them to Jack.

Tomorrow was the start of another year, one she would be entering with the loss of three friends. Jenny was dead, Nick in prison and Jack had finally abandoned her. The last, she thought, was no more than she deserved yet this loss hurt her most of all.

At lunchtime she walked down to Newlyn to buy the olives she had forgotten. What does Peter Dawson make of me? she thought as she stopped to count the fishing-boats in the harbour.

She had cancelled their dinner date after Alec's unwelcome visit but had offered no explanation.

It was a mild day and the smell of fish hung in the air. Rose returned with the olives, reassured by the sight of her car in the drive. It had been returned as promised a week ago with the cursory comment that it would not be required again. Nick's car had not been returned as far as she was aware so she could only assume the worst: it had contained incriminating evidence and that was why he had been arrested. To someone of Rose's temperament it was extremely frustrating not to know what was going on.

At six o'clock, satisfied that everything was ready, she ran a bath and tried to relax before spending some time on her hair and make-up. There was no new dress and the wardrobe didn't hold out too much promise. In the end she chose a plain black velvet dress she had had for a number of years. Around her neck was the single strand of pearls David had bought her for no other reason, he had said, than because he loved her.

By eight thirty everyone Rose had expected had arrived, including Doreen and Cyril Clarke. Doreen was even more matronly in a tight-fitting brocade dress. 'Leave it, do,' she said to Cyril as he fidgeted with his tie. 'I like a man to look smart,' she added. Despite her views on 'they people' Doreen made it her business to speak to everyone from St Ives. Knowing she would be grilling them about their backgrounds and who they were related to caused Rose some amusement. She would be interested in Doreen's opinion of them. That she would eventually hear it was certain.

Barry had turned up with a case of champagne which he suggested they put in the freezer half an hour before midnight as it would not all fit in the fridge. Rose was taken aback. He was thoughtful and kind but not renowned for such generous gestures. 'I thought it was time I spent something of what I earned,' he told her, kissing her cheek.

Drinks were flowing and Rose had turned up the music. When she turned around her mouth dropped open. Standing in the sitting-room doorway, a drink in his hand, was Nick Pascoe.

'I can see you weren't expecting me,' he said with a smile.

He looks awful, Rose thought, as if he's already served a prison sentence. It was also the first time she'd seen him dressed so smartly. He had not made the effort for Maddy's do and Rose was unsure what to make of it. Over well-cut trousers he wore a cream silk shirt and a black velvet jacket as if by way of telepathy they'd chosen matching outfits. 'They let you go? Well, obviously they did.'

'It was a mistake. In retrospect I don't blame them, there were things I should have said from the beginning.'

'What made them think it was you?' Rose blushed. Even at her own party, the first she had hosted for many years, she still could not help interrogating a guest.

'There was blood in my car. Jenny's blood. And to make it worse it was on the back seat. It was useless trying to explain that she'd stepped on some glass when we were out one day. She never did wear shoes if she could help it. Anyway, it was a bad cut. I put her in the back of the car and told her to keep her foot up then I drove her to Treliske hospital. It required several stitches. I'd forgotten about it until now.'

Rose realised that such an injury would have shown up during the post-mortem. However, the police would not have let Nick go for that reason alone. Rose had gone over all the possibilities then turned them on their heads. None of her friends came out well in her analysis but she still doubted their guilt. Could it be that Alec Manders, who had had no compunction about smashing his way into her house and becoming violent, had killed one or both women? But what possible reason could he have for harming his own daughter? 'Well, I'm really pleased you're here, Nick.'

'Are you, Rose?'

'Yes.' She was glad, but not in the way he might have imagined. He was extremely good-looking and quite sexy with that question still lingering in his eyes, but she saw all this objectively now. She was glad but only because she had not wanted one of her friends to be guilty and, more selfishly, she had not wanted to be wrong. 'I'd better circulate. And so had you. Just look at all the curious faces.' Rose moved away before he had a chance to say anything more.

As Rose crossed the hall on her way to the kitchen to pour more drinks she saw Stella, who was on her way up to the bathroom. Her face was flushed. Rose hoped she had not drunk too much. Several minutes later, when the food was uncovered and people had been told to help themselves, there was still no sign of Stella.

Rose went upstairs and knocked on the bathroom door. 'Stella? Are you okay?'

'Yes.'

'Open the door. Please?'

Seconds later Stella did so. 'Are you ill?' Rose was shocked at the misery in her face. It was covered in red and white blotches and there were smudges of mascara under her eyes. 'Come with me,' she said, leading her to her bedroom. 'Is it Daniel? Have you had a row?'

'No.' Stella's voice was low. She sat on the edge of the bed and laced her hands. The knuckles were white. 'I don't know what I've done.'

'What do you mean?' She sat beside her. If Stella needed to talk she would not do so with Rose looming over her judgementally.

'I can't understand what comes over me at times. Oh, Rose, why can't I be happy like you?'

Rose did not answer. There was none to give. Happy? Yes, with David she had been. Then had come the cancer which had destroyed them both in different ways. Since that time she had made the best of life and had come to accept that peace was the most that she could hope for. Happy? No. But there were still moments of pleasure and times of laughter. 'Was it you, Stella? Those screams at the mine?'

Stella still had not lifted her head. Now her lower lip was white as she bit it. 'I'm so sorry.'

'But why? Do you dislike me that much?'

'No. No, of course I don't. I just...I just couldn't bear it, watching you go through something I achieved years ago. I wanted it all back; the first hint of success, the first exhibition, the first large cheque and the knowledge that the future was ahead of me. Once you're successful you lose all that. You just end up treading water to stay where you are.'

'But that's not true, Stella, each painting is a new challenge.'

'It sounds so feeble now,' Stella continued, ignoring Rose's comment, 'but I just couldn't cope with the competition. It's hard enough with Daniel.'

'Is that how you see it?'

'He's always been more talented than me, yet he's far more relaxed about it.'

Poor Stella, Rose thought. With so many self-imposed obstacles life must be extremely difficult.

'I'm back on medication again but it doesn't seem to be working this time.'

Certain things fell into place. Stella's nervous habits and the occasional lapses where her expression was vacant and she lost concentration were not due to artistic temperament but to a genuine psychiatric disorder, the cause of her mild paranoia. 'But had I not returned to the mine, what would you have achieved? I'd have painted elsewhere, Stella, you wouldn't have stopped me.' But how far would she have taken it? Rose wondered with a shudder of fear.

'That painting was so good. I knew it immediately you showed it to me even though it wasn't finished then. I thought if I could stop you this time you might lose heart.'

She really is sick, Rose realised, and she probably ought not to be drinking on top of medication but perhaps the combination had prompted the admission. 'How did you do it?'

'I got the idea from Maddy. I knew she used tapes to practise accents. I recorded my own screams, right at the end of a blank tape, then I waited until I saw your car and set it going knowing there was at least forty minutes of silence until you heard the screams. I've lived here all my life, I knew exactly where to hide. Oh, Rose, what have I done?'

Rose handed her some tissues from the box on her dressing-table.

'I had no idea you'd ring for help, really I didn't.'

'But why do it again?'

'Nick told me you'd said you'd made a fool of yourself. I was certain you wouldn't call out the emergency services a second time.'

Oh, Nick, you lied to me more than once, Rose thought. He had denied telling Stella. 'Stella, tell me, did you leave the gallery that night after the preview?' She was unbalanced enough to have done anything, including killing Jenny. Being jealous of Rose's work was one thing, but being jealous of another woman in her husband's bed was another. When Stella did not answer Rose knew it was so. They had all, in their various ways, lied. She felt sick with disgust and near to tears herself. But what did any of it matter? She had done her duty by telling Jack all she knew – or, at least, most of it – and this evening was supposed to be a celebration. For a second she wished she could simply ask all of her guests, bar Barry Rowe, to leave. In Stella's case she did not have to.

'We'll go now, Rose. I think it's for the best. Will you tell the police?'

'I don't know, Stella, I honestly don't know.' And then Rose saw that not only had Stella lied about several things but she was also about the same age as the unknown female. Perhaps the whole story of wanting to damage Rose's career was a further fabrication. Had she been too trusting? Did Stella prefer to admit to a spiteful trick rather than more serious reasons for not wanting anyone in the vicinity of the mine? Rose hated the whole business.

Somehow she got through the rest of the evening. At least her guests were enjoying themselves. Laura's son had Barbara Phillips in fits of laughter and Nick Pascoe was dancing with Doreen Clarke who held herself stiffly, keeping a good three inches between her body and Nick's. Rose was tempted to go upstairs and get a camera. Laura, Maddy and Barry were in deep conversation in a corner and Peter Dawson, chatting to Mike Phillips, surveyed the room with an amused smile and winked at Rose as she carried out some paper plates. Daniel had made excuses for their early departure. No one, looking at Stella, could have doubted she felt unwell.

At midnight Barry poured the champagne and they toasted the New Year. The party finally broke up at two. Rose could hardly go back on her offer that those wishing to stay the night could do so.

Having settled Barbara and Mike Phillips in the spare bedroom and Peter Dawson on the settee with a sleeping bag and pillow, Rose stood in the kitchen surveying the detritus and wished Jack would get in touch soon. No one had heard what had happened to Alec Manders and there had been no further news bulletins regarding an arrest for either murder. But the more Rose thought about it the more confused she became. Nick had apparently been cleared but now Stella seemed a likely candidate. Yet deep down she had a feeling that it was Alec Manders who had put the woman down that shaft.

The first to wake, Rose recalled that she was still playing the role of hostess to three of her guests. Originally Nick had been intending to stay. Last night he been polite and friendly but had left around one. He had paid a lot of attention to Maddy but, to Rose's amazement, Maddy had treated his advances with a casual nonchalance even though she agreed to share the same taxi home. Surprisingly, considering he was supposed to be her guest, Maddy had been even more blasé about Peter Dawson staying the night.

Washing and dressing quickly to leave the bathroom free for her guests, Rose went down to make coffee and light the grill. She had never possessed a toaster. Above, floorboards creaked as someone else went to the bathroom. Ten minutes later Barbara appeared, closely followed by Mike. 'I hope you feel better than you look,' Barbara commented unkindly to her husband, holding his jaw between finger and thumb the better to scrutinise him. 'Ah, coffee. Wonderful.' They sat at the table and all three turned when Peter appeared in the doorway. He wore only his shirt and a pair of underpants. Rose felt herself blush when her eyes dropped to his long muscular legs. He seemed quite unabashed at his half-dressed state.

'I smelt the coffee,' he said, running a hand through his hair. There was reddish stubble on his chin, interspersed with silvery grey which glinted beneath the overhead light.

Rose handed them each a mug and placed the sugar bowl and milk on the table.

'Is the grill on for warmth or are we to be offered sustenance?'

Rose caught Barbara's eye. Her friend was trying not to laugh. 'Toast,' Rose snapped. 'I don't have any bacon.'

'Toast is fine.'

He had not mentioned their broken date. After the incident with Alec Manders she had only just remembered to ring him in time to prevent him setting off to meet her that evening; she had offered no excuse because she had not wished to tell a lie, but neither could she face talking about her ordeal. Barry had come over for an hour but had soon realised Rose wanted to be alone. As if the thought of him had made him materialise, he walked past the kitchen window. This time both Rose and Barbara could not suppress their grins as Barry adjusted his glasses and glared pointedly at Peter's bare legs. 'I came for the champagne glasses,' he said.

'I haven't washed them yet.'

'I'll do it.' Peter was on his feet and across the kitchen in three strides. 'While you make some toast,' he added over his shoulder in a proprietorial tone, unaware of the impression he was making. Barry's scowl deepened.

Within fifteen minutes the glasses were in the box in which they had come from the off-licence. Barry had borrowed them free of charge on the strength of the amount of his order. The toast had been eaten and Barbara and Mike said they were leaving.

'Can I give you a lift somewhere?' Barry asked Peter rather acidly.

'No, thanks. You carry on. I'm in no hurry.'

Rose turned away, unable to face Barry because she knew what must be going through his mind.

'I'll see you soon, Rose,' he said then he, too, had gone.

'I was sorry you changed your mind about dinner,' Peter said, scooping toast crumbs towards him.

'I didn't change my mind. Unforeseen circumstances.'

He stared hard. 'Another man? Nick, maybe?'

'Another man? Yes. You could say that.' Rose sighed then sat down to give him a shortened version of that day's events.

Peter whistled through his teeth. 'I have to admit, you can't better that as a way of getting out of dinner with a man. Dare I ask if our date is still on?'

'Yes. It is.'

'Good. I'll go and make myself respectable then you can tell me when.'

What have you done now? she wondered as she wiped the work surfaces, relieving them of sticky rings of alcohol and crumbs.

'Thanks for the bed,' Peter said when he returned fully dressed. 'Here's my number. Give me a ring when you fancy going out.'

Rose nodded and took the business card he handed her then closed the door behind him, glad to be alone at last.

It was another week before Rose saw Jack. He had decided to get away, to take some leave due to him and visit his sons. The younger boy was still living with his mother in Leeds where he was, Jack had once confided in Rose, turning into a perpetual student. The older son was in Sheffield, where he had gone into industry and lived with a woman three years his senior and equally a high-flier.

The weather had turned colder and although the winter solstice was weeks ago, the days seemed shorter than ever. Rose was taking a mid-morning break, drinking coffee in the bay window as she often did. The sky was leaden and the light was strange. She was wondering if there was that rare possibility of snow when the telephone rang. She walked across the room to answer it. The last person she was expecting to hear from was Jack.

'I've been away for a few days. How was the party?'

'It went really well.' She felt strangely tongue-tied.

'Would I be interrupting anything if I came over?'

'Don't you have work to catch up on?'

'No. I'm not due back until tomorrow.'

Because she had nothing better to do, Rose agreed. Jack said he would be there in ten minutes.

There was an awkwardness between them when she let him in and neither of them seemed to know what to say.

'I've been to see the boys. They're both well.' Jack was fully aware of the tense atmosphere but was unsure why it existed.

'I'm glad. Do you want some coffee?'

'No, thanks. Rose, this isn't public knowledge until the lunch-time news but Alec Manders has finally confessed he killed Jenny.'

'Oh, Jack. How could he?' She was filled with sadness that Jenny's own father had taken her life.

'Had you guessed?'

'No. Not exactly guessed, but I did wonder whether it was possible.'

'Why?'

Rose hooked her hair behind her ears in a businesslike manner which Jack knew meant she was going to put him right on a few things. But he was wrong. 'Because I couldn't really believe it was anyone I knew.' She blushed with mortification. In fact she had decided Stella may have done it. 'Well, to be honest, I didn't want to believe it. Did you really believe it was Nick?'

'Yes.' Rose saw the spots of colour on Jack's cheekbones and knew that he had his reasons, personal ones, for wanting the opposite from herself. 'But I always had it in mind that it was possible that Alec had killed Renata all those years ago, that she hadn't really gone away,' Jack continued, hoping he was misinterpreting the smug expression on Rose's face. If she's worked it out, I'll kill *her*, he thought. 'I think I will have that coffee after all.' Something stronger would have been preferable but it was too early in the day. Rose got up to pour it.

'Thanks. We knew that Jenny confided in Maddy Duke and Maddy, the second time we questioned her, suggested that Alec might have been having a fling with a friend of Renata's. This led us to think that he might have killed Renata either to be with this woman or on the spur of the moment during an argument over her, then put it around that she had left with another man. Everyone knew the situation, they wouldn't have questioned his explanation. Anyway, as we know, nothing came of the affair between Manders and Josie Deveraux.'

Rose turned away to hide a knowing grin but she was too late, Jack had spotted it. The look of astonishment on his face told her that he knew that she knew the name. But all she had had to do was ask one simple question to discover it.

'Our theory is that with Renata dead and safely in the shaft Alec simply sent all the relevant paperwork to Josie, who posed as his wife for the purposes of the divorce. There's no need for a court appearance in cases of mutual consent, especially after six years. A solicitor in London, where Josie had taken herself, would naturally assume the woman in possession of a marriage certificate, or a copy, and whatever other documents of Renata's Alec thought fit to send her, was who she said she was.'

'All right, but why would Josie Deveraux oblige?' Rose wanted to know.

'His wife was dead, Manders was free to marry again. But he couldn't tell anyone she was dead, not if he'd killed her. With an apparently legal divorce taking place six years later it gives him a perfect alibi. How could Renata be dead when she's agreed to divorce him? And now you're going to say why, then, didn't he marry Josie, and why did she help him in the first place, especially after all that time?'

'Exactly.'

'He didn't marry Josie because he didn't want to and had never intended doing so, even though she believed he did, but we think he was still able to use her because somehow or other she was involved, she knew what he had done or had even helped him do it. And this, we believe, is the reason we can't find the woman posing as Renata Manders. Before his arrest for attacking you, Manders had already warned her it was time she disappeared.'

'That's more or less how I saw it. I spoke to my solicitor and he confirmed what you just said, about not having to appear in court and that a divorce could be obtained that way. I gathered that Josie could have taken on Renata's identity from the time she moved away and would have been known by that name for years. Maddy told me about her. And, like you, I thought Josie Deveraux had held out hopes of getting together with Alec all that time but when he finally let her down she couldn't do anything about it without getting them both in trouble. Like you, I thought she must've known or been involved with the killing of Renata.'

'Rose, just stop there. You keep saying, "Like you, I thought". Are you trying to teach me my job? Are you trying to say I'm wrong?'

'Yes, Jack.'

'Dear God. I rue the day I met you.'

'Well, just think about it. Alec's admitted to killing Jenny, but what's his motive?'

161

'We'll come back to that.'

'Okay. So he's going to prison. He's not stupid, and I'm sure it's been made quite clear that if he holds up his hand to both murders things would go better for him. Then why is he so adamant he didn't kill his wife? I'll tell you. Because it's true.'

Jack groaned. It was impossible that with all the back-up and expertise they had at their fingertips they were wrong and Rose Trevelyan was right. But he had to listen.

'I think it's far simpler than that. I think Renata Manders is still alive.'

'What? Explain, Rose.'

'As I said before, because of Alec's denial that he killed his wife.'

'But there's only his word for it.'

'Have you found this Josie Deveraux?'

'No.'

'But have you been looking for her under that name or the name Manders?'

'Rose, give me some credit.'

'Okay, sorry. But shall I tell you how I see it? Think of the family history, the power that Alec's mother wielded over them all. She turned her daughter-in-law into a drunk and more or less wrote off her granddaughter because she couldn't bear to see her son happy with anyone other than herself. Imagine how she would have felt if, Renata having run off with someone else, another woman appeared on the scene.'

She has a point, Jack conceded. And a very good one at that.

'Let's say that Renata did go as everyone believed. Now the coast is clear Josie decides to make her move. Maybe she went to the house and created a scene or perhaps Mrs Manders found her with Alec. We know his mother had a violent temper and wasn't afraid to lash out. What if *she* killed Josie? Alec would have gone out of his way to protect his mother, even now, even after her death. If I'm right, he isn't lying, even if he hid the body.'

'That makes sense,' Jack said quietly. Rose was right, perhaps they had been making complications where there were none. But how would they get a man like Manders to own up to what his mother may have done? 'But a woman?'

'She used to hit Jenny, Jack, she was a strong woman. Maybe she picked up something to use as a weapon or it could have been accidental. Maybe Josie fell and struck her head. Anyway, at least you know who killed Jenny.' Rose frowned. 'You still haven't said why?'

'He won't tell us, although we now know that Jenny wanted to move back in with him and Angela.'

'He'd hardly murder her for that. All he had to do was to say no.'

'Yes. Unless Jenny had something over him and threatened to use it if he didn't agree.'

'What? You mean you think she knew the truth about Josie?'

'Possibly. Or maybe she'd come to the conclusion that her mother wasn't alive.'

Rose shrugged and stood to refill their mugs. 'But she wouldn't have had any proof and all Alec had to do was deny it. No, there has to be another reason. Hold on, didn't Jenny spend some time in London, after she came back from Paris?'

'She did. But what we don't know is if she visited her mother, or Josie, at the address Manders had been given.'

'I see what you mean.' Rose leaned against the edge of the sink. 'That means I'm wrong. If Jenny went to that address and discovered it wasn't her mother but her mother's friend then she'd have no difficulty guessing what may have happened.'

'Quite. Anyway, Manders has had experience of fishing and mining and he also has a van. He'd have had no trouble in disposing of either of the bodies, with or without help.' Jack lit a cigarette and looked around for the ashtray. Reaching behind him he grabbed it from the worktop. 'What I don't understand is why he thought you were such a danger to him.'

Rose thought about it. 'He'd met me, he knew I knew Jenny and liked her and Jenny probably told him about where I'd been painting. Then he spots I have ulterior motives for visiting him and begins to think I know far more than I actually do. Of course, he'd also have heard that I'd reported those screams and that the police et cetera had been out there to investigate. I can't imagine how he must've felt when you went back a second time and found the body. Naturally, he'd have blamed it all on me.

163

'Anyway, surely DNA testing would prove whether or not the two dead women are related?'

'It's in hand, Rose,' Jack said sternly, wondering if he ought to recommend her services to the Chief Constable. 'I must go, Rose, I've things to do at the flat before I start work again tomorrow. And I really am sorry about your party.' He stopped, his hand on the back door. 'Those screams. They're not connected to the murders even though they led us to the mine. One of your friends has it in for you. Please be careful, Rose.'

'I know who it was. Can we forget it? She's having treatment now.'

'I was right. It was Stella Jackson.'

Rose did not reply. Jack took her silence for agreement and nodded but he still made no move to leave. 'Did, uh, did Nick come to the party?'

'He did.'

'I see.'

'Jack, I already explained I'm not seeing him. It's definitely over. He lied to me on more than one occasion. Whatever your faults, and they're plentiful, believe me, you've never done that.'

And with that ambiguous praise Jack laughed and went on his way.

12

It was May before Rose was satisfied that she now had enough good paintings to make it worthwhile contacting Geoff Carter, the man whom Stella had once advised her against going to see.

Geoff turned out to be down-to-earth and shrewd, a business-man who happened to be interested in art. He scrutinised her work, made a few notes and said he would be in touch. Rose left his gallery bitterly disappointed that he had said so little but at least she had tried. That was two days ago and she had not heard from him since. The year was not, as she had hoped, turning out to be any better than the previous one.

There had been no word from Nick since her party, but Rose was not sorry. If their paths crossed she would not avoid him but she saw now that he was a child and in need of constant attention. Daniel had rung once, puzzled by the fact that she no longer visited. Rose had found it hard to give a reason but there was no way in which she would allow someone like Stella to undermine her confidence again. She made excuses about being busy and left it to Daniel to ask his wife for the real reason – if he hadn't guessed it already.

Peter Dawson had finally taken her to dinner. He was intelligent and entertaining company but her instincts told her to leave it at that. Apart from what he had told her about himself she guessed that he would find her fascinating as long as she remained unobtainable but if she allowed herself to feel anything for him she would end up hurt.

She was at a loose end. Laura and Trevor had gone away on holiday and would not be back for another week. Jack was in Plymouth on a course and Barry was tied up on various plans for the season which had started with the Easter weekend but would not be in full swing for another month or so.

Walking back along the Promenade after a trip to the library, Rose stopped to watch the sea, standing at a safe distance away from where it was sweeping up over the railings. It was a high tide, the water choppy but topped by a clear azure sky. Further down children screamed as they tried to dodge the spray but failed. A pair of herring-gulls perched on the railings, their heads into the wind. They flew off, drifting in an air current until the dog which had run towards them scampered past, then they returned to the same piece of rail. I'm as free as they are, Rose thought, watching the gulls. And with that cheerful thought she walked on home to find a postcard from Laura on the mat along with a letter from her mother.

It was another four days before Geoff Carter telephoned, by which time Rose had given up hope of hearing from him again. 'How about the last week of June?' he said. 'If you agree I'll contact the local papers right away. There isn't much time.'

'Yes, that's fine.' Rose wanted to shout with joy. Had he said June the following year she would still have agreed.

'Have you got any more I haven't seen?'

'A couple. They're smaller.'

'Well, let me have a look at them. I can come to you if you like, it'll save you packing them up and driving in.'

'Thank you, that'll be great. Whenever you like.'

There was a pause while he checked his diary. 'Tomorrow, some time between four thirty and five. Will that be convenient?'

'Yes. I'll see you then.' Rose hung up, unaware that Geoff had been about to say something else. 'Yes!' she cried punching the air. Tears of pure joy sparkled in her eyes. 'Hello?' She grabbed the phone which had started to ring again.

'Mrs Trevelyan,' Geoff Carter said, his voice deadpan, 'it would help if I had your address.'

Rose laughed and gave it to him, not caring if he thought she was scatty. It was one of the happiest moments of her life. I shall celebrate, she decided. But with whom? She could ring Peter but it might not mean much to him, having already established his own reputation many years previously. It had to be Barry, she realised. Barry who had supported her work all those years and had encouraged her to improve. He had always stood by her and he would be genuinely pleased for her.

He sounded harassed when he picked up the phone but mellowed when he knew who was calling. 'You're treating me? In that case there can only be one answer. Best bib and tucker?'

'Nothing less will do.'

'Why?'

'I'll tell you later. I'll pick you up in a taxi at seven thirty. Be ready.'

Too excited to think about work of any description, Rose rang her mother who could not stop telling her how proud she was. 'We'll come down, darling. We wouldn't miss it for the world.'

Rose said she would let her know the exact date as soon as she found it out herself. 'You have to be there on the opening night,' she insisted.

I can't stay indoors, Rose decided. Adrenalin surged through her. She threw on a jacket and almost ran down the path. She found herself nearly at the railway station before she realised how far she had come and stopped to draw breath. Checking her purse she saw that she had her credit card and rail card. Truro, with its shops, beckoned. A new outfit was required. She would wear it this evening then save it for her opening.

As if her luck had changed all at once, this mission was soon accomplished and Rose returned with three plastic bags. She had purchased a calf-length cream dress. It was sleeveless and hung simply from the shoulders. To go with it was a lace jacket in a darker shade of cream. The third bag contained strappy shoes with two-inch heels and a small matching evening bag and she had not even blinked at the prices.

Barry's eyes widened with surprise twice in quick succession. First at her outfit, which he said was stunning, especially with her auburn hair flowing over her shoulders, and secondly when she told him she was taking him to Harris's, a restaurant where media people ate when they were filming in the area. But when they arrived and Rose ordered champagne and told him her reasons he took both her hands in his and kissed her hard. 'I am so thrilled for you,' he said. 'I always knew you'd make it.'

'I haven't exactly made it, but it's a start.'

They were in the upstairs bar, picking at olives and crisps as they sipped their drinks. Having been shown down the curved stairs to their table they talked all evening in the way of old friends and Rose found herself feeling closer than ever to Barry.

'And now you must allow me to escort you home. I'll get the taxi to drop me back afterwards.'

Rose almost floated into the house. And tomorrow Geoff was coming to look at the rest of her work and finalise the details of her exhibition. She felt there was nothing more she could wish for.

'They're good,' he said simply and without exaggeration. 'We'll exhibit these as well. You'll need to get some invitations done for the preview. We can hold up to sixty guests.'

'I don't think I know sixty people.'

'Well, whatever. How do you want to play it? Wine and food or just coffee and biscuits? It depends on what you can afford.'

'Wine and food.' If it turned out to be her only exhibition at least she would have done the thing properly. 'Thanks for coming, Geoff.'

'My pleasure.' He hesitated, his hand on the kitchen door. Rose waited but he did not speak. Instead he glanced back over his shoulder and smiled.

It was after six but the evening felt more like summer than late spring. The change had occurred all of a sudden. One minute it was winter, the next there were days like this. Rose sat at the kitchen table and wrote down the names of everyone she could think of, even casual acquaintances. She would invite them all to her opening night. The shadow of a figure passing the window slid across the table. It was Jack Pearce. She beckoned for him to come in.

'Busy?' he asked, seeing her list.

'No.' She told him her news and said he would receive an invitation.

'I'm honoured. And well done, Rose. I really mean that.'

'You look better.'

'Better?'

'Mm. Less tired than last time I saw you.'

'You mean more handsome.'

'Honestly, Jack.'

Rose thought back to January and the day Jack rang to tell her that Renata Manders had been found. She had not received Alec's letter because he had not written. Renata had been in Scotland staying with friends for the whole of the Christmas period. Only upon her return did she learn of the death of the daughter she had never really known and the fact that her ex-husband had killed her. She had travelled down to Cornwall to visit the grave.

'And did Jenny visit her?' Rose had asked.

'Yes. Once. But they didn't hit it off at all. That's the odd thing, Renata claims she didn't say anything particularly derogatory about Manders, only that he treated her badly and was having an affair, but Alec has now admitted that when Jenny asked to be taken in by him and he refused, she said, "I know what you did. How can you live with it?" She meant driving her mother away, but he thought there was a more sinister meaning.'

'Why wasn't Josie missed at the time?'

'Only child of parents past the prime of youth. Father dead, mother senile and in a home for the elderly in Devon. Once we

168

had the DNA results we spoke to Manders again. We knew by then it wasn't Renata but it still could have been a stranger. This time he came up with the goods. His mother knew what Josie was up to and thought Alec might be keen to go along with it and move her in. There was a row, as we suspected, but Josie didn't fall, Agnes struck her with a poker.'

'My God. But wouldn't that have shown up on the post-mortem or whatever it is you do with bones?'

'Not necessarily. It depends upon where the blow connected with the skull, and there were many other post-mortem injuries.'

And Renata had gone to London with a man who had befriended her whilst on holiday in Cornwall. They were still together, although Renata refused to marry him. 'Never again,' she had told the police.

Rose had said to Jack at the time that if Renata had taken Jenny with her she'd still be alive.

'Probably, but even that's not certain,' he'd replied. 'Fate is a strange creature.'

Rose thought back to her years with David and knew it was true. Jack had gone on to explain that Manders had made a mistake, he had wanted Jenny unconscious when he put her in the water to make it look as though she'd drowned, but had not realised his own strength. There had been no love lost between father and daughter and, Jack had said, more murders were committed amongst families than otherwise.

It's in the past now, Rose told herself. And now it's time to celebrate. 'Would you like a drink? To my success?'

Jack's expression showed that he was astonished she had not got one in front of her already. 'Good idea. Thanks.'

'Cheers,' Rose said, handing him a glass of chilled white. 'Here's to us. Things seem to be working out well for us both.' Jack had had some good results workwise.

'Not as well as I'd hoped in some directions,' Jack said morosely. 'How's Peter?' He was not sure how she would take this but he could not stop himself from asking.

The cuffs of the baggy shirt Rose was wearing had slipped down over her hands. She took several seconds in which to fold them back. 'I don't know. It's ages since I've seen him. To be honest, Jack, I don't have the inclination to keep in touch with any of them. Only Maddy. She's a different person now. She's heard from the adoption people, you know. It's only an initial inquiry but it's a start and it's given her so much to hope for. I'm praying the girl won't change her mind about contacting her mother.'

'Yes, let's hope not.' Jack studied his fingers. 'Rose, would you let me take you out to celebrate? Just dinner. No strings attached.'

'Thank you, I'd like that.' She took in his handsome face, his large, well-formed body and his strong hands, recalling how they had felt on her own body, and was sad that, although for her it was over, Jack still wished it was otherwise. But they would probably end up killing each other if they lived under the same roof. 'Jack?'

'What is it?' He smiled kindly at the look of concern on her face.

'Thank you for being my friend.'

'I'll always be that, Rose. Always.'

She nodded. 'I know. And me yours.' There were a few beats of thoughtful silence before Rose looked up, excitement in her eyes. 'Anyway, did I tell you what Geoff said?'

Jack groaned and put his head in his hands. Without meeting Rose's eyes he asked, 'And who the hell is Geoff?'

Rose grinned. She wasn't quite ready to answer that yet, but she had had the impression that he had winked as well as smiled when he had paused at her kitchen door.